# MURDER
# TAKES A
# HOLIDAY

# MURDER TAKES A HOLIDAY

*Stories from*
*Ellery Queen's Mystery Magazine*
*and*
*Alfred Hitchcock's Mystery Magazine*

*Edited by*
## CYNTHIA MANSON

BARNES
&NOBLE
BOOKS
NEW YORK

Copyright © 1992 Bantam Doubleday Dell Publishing Group, Inc.
All rights reserved.

This edition published by Marboro Books Corp.,
a division of Barnes & Noble, Inc.,
by arrangement with Bantam Doubleday Dell Publishing Group, Inc.

1992 Barnes & Noble Books

ISBN 0-88029-821-9

Printed and bound in the United States of America

M  9  8  7  6  5  4  3  2  1

# ACKNOWLEDGMENTS

*Grateful acknowledgment is made to the following for permission to reprint their copyrighted material:*

*Blind Trust* by Gary Alexander, copyright © 1991 by Davis Publications, Inc., reprinted by permission of the author; *The Ching Lady* by Doug Allyn, copyright © 1988 by Davis Publications, Inc., reprinted by permission of James Allen, Literary Agent; *St. Anne Mystery* by Tonda Barrett, copyright © 1984 by Davis Publications, Inc., reprinted by permission of the author; *A Souvenir of Rumania* by Albert Bashover, copyright © 1991 by Davis Publications, Inc., reprinted by permission of the author; *By the Terrible Mountain* by Ron Butler, copyright © 1984 by Davis Publications, Inc., reprinted by permission of the author; *Oleander* by Dan Crawford, copyright © 1990 by Davis Publications, Inc., reprinted by permission of the author; *Whatever Happened to Crocodile Jarvis?* by Justin D'Ath, copyright © 1990 by Davis Publications, Inc., reprinted by permission of the author; *The Wellmaster's Daughter* by James S. Dorr, copyright © 1991 by Davis Publications, Inc., reprinted by permission of the author; *Incident in Bogota* by James M. Fox, copyright © 1988 by Davis Publications, Inc., reprinted by permission of the author; *Barbarossa and Company* by Kathryn Gottlieb, copyright © 1980 by Davis Publications, Inc., reprinted by permission of the author; *What's Afoot?* by Geoffrey Hitchcock, copyright © 1989 by Davis Publications, Inc., reprinted by permission of the author; *The Blackmarket Detail* by Martin Limon, copyright © 1990 by Davis Publications, Inc., reprinted by permission of the author; *Seven Nights, Six Days* by Janet O'Daniel, copyright © 1983 by Davis Publications, Inc., reprinted by permission of the author; *The Qatar Causeway* by Josh Pachter, copyright © 1985 by Davis Publications, Inc., reprinted by permission of the author; *Death in Egypt* by Henry T. Parry, copyright © 1979 by Davis Publications, Inc., reprinted by permission of the author; *The Curse of Istvan Kodaly* by Alec Ross, copyright © 1982 by Davis Publications, Inc., reprinted by permission of the author; *A Greek Game* by Walter Satterthwait, copyright © 1985 by Davis Publications, Inc., reprinted by permission of the author; *Ice Cave* by Emmy Lou Schenk, copyright © 1987 by Davis Publications, Inc., reprinted by permission of the author; *Aladdin's Curse* by Jeffry Scott, copyright © 1986 by Davis Publications, Inc., reprinted by permission of the author; *The Chinese Guilt Trip* by Wyc D. Toole, Jr., copyright © 1988 by Davis Publications, Inc., reprinted by permission of the author; all stories previously appeared in *Alfred Hitchcock's Mystery Magazine,* published by Davis Publications, Inc.

*The Black Cliffs* by Joan Aiken, copyright © 1982 by Joan Aiken Enterprises Ltd., reprinted by permission of Brandt & Brandt Literary Agents, Inc.; *The Alibi* by Isaac Asimov, copyright © 1989 by Davis Publications, Inc., reprinted by permission of the author; *A Hint of Danger* by William Bankier, copyright © 1978 by Davis Publications, Inc., reprinted by permission of Curtis Brown, Ltd.; *As Good as a Rest* by Lawrence Block, copyright © 1986 by Davis Publications, Inc., reprinted by permission of Knox Burger Associates, Ltd.; *Playing It Cool* by Simon Brett, copyright © 1980 by Davis Publications, Inc., reprinted by permission of the author; *Mr. Folsom Feels Fine* by Avram Davidson, copyright © 1986 by Avram Davidson, reprinted by permission of Richard D. Grant, Literary Agent; *In The Bag* by Robert L. Fish, copyright © 1975 by Robert L. Fish, reprinted by permission of Mamie K. Fish; *Little Fat Man* by Peter Godfrey, copyright © 1986 by Peter Godfrey, reprinted by permission of the author; *The Case of the Frozen Diplomat* by Tim Heald, copyright © 1978 by Tim Heald, reprinted by permission of Richard Simon, Agent; *When in Rome* by Patricia Highsmith, copyright © 1978 and 1981 by Patricia Highsmith (also appeared in *The Black House* published by William Heineman Ltd London and Penzler Books NY), used by permission of Diogenes Verlag AG, Switzerland, Agent; *The Gypsy Bear* by Edward D. Hoch, copyright © 1989 by Davis Publications, Inc., reprinted by permission of the author; *Grave Robber* by James Holding, copyright © 1984 by James Holding, reprinted by permission of Scott Meredith Literary Agency, Inc.; *While the Rain Forest Burned* by Clark Howard, copyright © 1991 by Davis Publications, Inc., reprinted by permission of Davis Publications, Inc.; *The Evidence I Shall Give* by H.R.F. Keating, copyright © 1989 by Davis Publications, Inc., reprinted by permission of Sterling Lord Literistic, Inc.; *Oracle of the Dead* by Peter Lovesey, copyright © 1988 by Peter Lovesey, reprinted by permission of John Farquharson, Ltd.; *Dover Without Perks* by Joyce Porter, copyright © 1978 by Davis Publications, Inc., reprinted by permission of John Cushman Associates, Inc.; *The Friends of Hector Jouvet* by James Powell, copyright © 1966 by James Powell, reprinted by permission of the author; *The Fever Tree* by Ruth Rendell, copyright © 1982 by Ruth Rendell, reprinted by permission of Georges Borchardt, Inc.; *Inspector Maigret Thinks* by Georges Simenon, copyright © 1967 by Georges Simenon, reprinted by permission of the author's Estate; *The Queen's Angel* by Janwillem van de Wetering, copyright © 1991 by Davis Publications, Inc., reprinted by permission of the author; all stories previously appeared in *Ellery Queen's Mystery Magazine* or in an Ellery Queen Anthology, published by Davis Publications, Inc.

I want to thank Cathleen Jordan for her invaluable assistance with this project and for her editorial acumen as reflected in *Alfred Hitchcock's Mystery Magazine,* where many of the stories in this book were first published. Thanks are also due to Charles Ardai for his editorial suggestions and to John Kelly and Cynthia Sternau for making this book happen.

# Contents

# INTRODUCTION

Some people say that a proper mystery story ought to be set in one of two places. If it is a classic whodunnit, it belongs in Agatha Christie country: the stately English manor house situated near a quaint rural village. If, on the other hand, the story deals with hardboiled crime, Raymond Chandler's milieu is a must: the mean streets of Los Angeles, New York City, or some other American urban jungle.

Both of these settings have a lot to offer, of course. They have tradition on their side, having provided a backdrop for some of the genre's best-known figures from Sherlock Holmes and Jane Marple to Philip Marlowe and Mike Hammer. But dedicated mystery readers know that there is a wider world out there, a world filled from hemisphere to hemisphere and from pole to pole with murder, mayhem, and mystery.

Take South America, with its steamy rain forests and remote mountain ranges, or the islands of the Bahamas with their sun-soaked beaches and exotic customs. Or look at Europe, with cosmopolitan cities in the West (Paris, Rome, Amsterdam) that provide a sophisticated setting for crime and detection, while rapidly changing countries in the East (Hungary, Yugoslavia, Rumania) offer strange and exciting new possibilities for mystery.

In addition, there is Russia, the classic locale for chilling intrigue; the Far East (China, Japan, and Korea), with ancient traditions and intricate history; and, while we're at it, is there anywhere in the world more steeped in mystery than Egypt? Even Agatha Christie sent her characters there, in one of her most popular novels, *Death on the Nile*.

Canny mystery writers from Edgar Allan Poe onward have seen the appeal of foreign vistas and have set stories in some of the world's most exotic locales. Seasoned mystery readers have gone along with them from the start, and joined in their travels to explore villainy and vice across the globe.

In the following stories you will be invited to share just such a homicidal holiday with some of your favorite authors: Ruth Rendell, Simon Brett, Isaac Asimov, Lawrence Block, Joan Aiken, Joyce Porter, Jeffry Scott, Georges Simenon, and many more. Along the way, you will stop at every continent in the world (even Antarctica!) and more than a few beautiful and deadly islands in-between.

Your trip will take you from the darkest depths of the Brazilian jungle to the banks of the Nile, from the back alleys of Colombia to the main avenues of Italy and France, and from the waterways of Greece to the endless desert of Saudi Arabia. As you wander from country to country you will meet other fellow travelers (some of them tourists, some just *pretending* to be tourists) as well as natives; and among the natives will be a general, a police chief, an arms dealer a TV star, spies, mercenaries, and quite a few thieves, con men, and killers. You'll visit the inside of a jail cell in Budapest, an ice cave at the South Pole, and a centuries-old tomb in Taiwan. You'll even get to see what goes on behind closed doors as a revolution begins in South America—what happens when the CIA tries to put a stop to it.

And, in the midst of all the murderous goings-on, you'll have a chance to sample some of the world's most tantalizing pleasure spots, fascinating cultures, and sites of historical interest.

As your tour guide, I offer a single piece of advice: keep your eyes open and watch your back. These are dangerous paths and a false step could mean . . . well, you know what it could mean.

Enjoy the sights, but remember: it's a nice place to visit—but you wouldn't want to die there.

Bon Voyage,
Cynthia Manson

# EUROPE

# IN THE BAG

*By Robert L. Fish*

*To go back to the Rue Cologne or not, that was the problem!*

CLAUDE BIESSY recognized that his appearance was a decided advantage, for he looked like a student at the Sorbonne and therefore dressed accordingly. With his student's satchel dangling indolently from one hand and his curly head obviously in some philosophical cloud, he always walked—strolled would be more accurate, though at times many miles were involved—from his small apartment in the Rue Collard near the university to and from his jobs.

His appearance may have been a bit of luck, but all else was thoroughly planned. No wheeled transportation to draw attention to the possible presence of an intruder in some untenanted-at-the-moment home or apartment; no curious taxi driver to recall a youthful fare following a safecracking in some office building or warehouse. No wallet with identification ever carried on a job, and never any accomplice. Nothing ever stolen except cash or objects easily transformed into cash without the services of a fence. No people, no chances. To date, it had worked fine.

He paused in his labors and listened. There was only the sound of the rising wind rattling the windows beyond the thick drapes of the old house; he had expected no other. With a brief nod he returned to work.

The chips were wiped from the hot drill bit, the bit dipped into oil. Claude tackled the safe door again. The beginning of the hole was clearly visible in the sharp beam of the adjustable flash. He had positioned it precisely at a certain point between the combination dial and the safe's handle —he knew this vulnerable spot very well. He turned the drill on and began again, putting as much weight against the drill handle as he could muster.

He was pleased with the near-silent humming of the small powerful motor, the eagerness with which the bit ate its way steadily through the thick metal. Easy did it; there was no rush. His careful scouting had made sure that the inhabitants of the house would not return until the following day.

The safe was a LeClair, an unusually large one for home use. Most home safes were simply meant to protect against fire and they presented no special problems. A LeClair was more complex—constructed in hopes of frustrating burglars—but Claude was familiar with it. He had spent four years under the tutelage of the famous Gil Lowendal himself and he had yet to find a small safe he couldn't enter.

The vibration of the drill changed; the bit slowed and then speeded up as it penetrated the last thickness of the steel shell. He had now drilled through to the locking linkage area. The rest was simple—even though it took a little more muscle.

From his bag, he extracted a punch made of the hardest steel and inserted it into the hole. Then, reaching into the bag once more, he produced an all-steel hammer. A few sufficiently strong blows against the punch would break the safe's lock bolt—and the job would be finished.

It was not the effort of the pounding that bothered him. It was just that, when he thought back afterward, he always had a nightmare scenario occur to him. Somehow the hammer would slip and there would be a loud clang. Or, even if it didn't, the noise of the blows might, by chance, reach the ears of a person in the vicinity. That person would rise up on one elbow in bed, perhaps, and say to himself, "Odd, I thought I heard something like hammering. Yes, there it is again. It would seem to be coming from the Duponts' house. Ah, well."

Then that person, sinking back in the bed again, would suddenly reflect, "But wait! Didn't I see the Duponts leaving for the weekend? There is something very curious here. Perhaps I should ask the police to have a look."

Claude snapped the flashlight off and went to the window to survey the street. Across the way the streetlight shone on an empty garden. There was no sign of life except for the very faint sound of music coming from some house a little farther along.

He moved back to the safe and grasped the hammer. This old house would have thick walls. Besides, he counted on the fact that the listener in his nightmare—if there ever were one in reality—would hesitate a minute, would take another minute to find his slippers, would spend a little more time getting to the telephone. There would be a further delay as the police-man at the other end of the line wrote everything down.

It took a few more blows than he'd expected—each one a cannon blast to his ears—but at last the lock was broken. It was only after he had disman-tled the drill and put each piece of his equipment carefully back into his satchel that he turned the handle of the safe. It moved easily.

He shone the beam of his flashlight inside. Silver plate; he pushed it aside without qualms. A jewel case; he whistled slightly as he opened it, and then closed it resolutely. A tin box! He dragged it out and tipped the cover up. Papers. He took one up. Papers? Securities! *Negotiable securities!*

He took one look at the face value of the top one and his eyes widened. A fortune! But this was no time to stand and count it. He dropped the bundle into the satchel, tossed the flashlight on top of it, buckled it hastily, and moved to the window.

He was three blocks away, his surgical gloves tucked into an inner pocket, his bag swinging negligently from his hand, when a police car passed him with flashing lights and keening siren. Claude began to look after it and then brought his head to the front. It was impossible that the sound of the hammer could have brought any investigation to the old house in that short a time.

Besides, a police car was certainly no unusual sight in Paris, even in the suburbs. Crime was certainly not limited to his small efforts, and automo-bile accidents were as common as the common cold. He put the police car from his mind and continued his stroll toward home. But subconsciously one ear listened for the return of the siren.

The streets through which Claude returned were not the same ones he had traversed in going to the job, but they were of the same general nature. Major arteries were avoided, as were streets that appeared completely de-serted. Avenues lined with spreading plane trees and strolling couples out for the evening air were the ones he preferred. Along several he saw other students—he always thought of them as *other* students—equally hampered by bags, walking alone or together, and he felt a certain kinship with them.

He crossed the Avenue Mozambique and turned down the Rue Co-logne, staying a reasonable distance behind a couple walking with their arms about each other. Here, well into the body of the city proper, traffic was still oddly light, but the night was pleasant and the breeze cooling.

Claude strolled along, enjoying the walk, when he heard the sharp clack of leather heels on the opposite pavement. His eyes came up, incurious. Marching along in the opposite direction was a uniformed policeman, vi-sored hat square on his brow, cape swinging in cadence to his almost mili-tary step.

Claude smiled faintly, a smile that faded as the footsteps suddenly stopped. There was the briefest pause, and then they resumed, but their owner had turned and was now moving in the same direction as Claude, just across the street.

Claude frowned slightly without breaking the evenness of his pace in the least. A coincidence? Quite obviously. But, still, here he was with a satchel full of negotiable securities, not to mention a lot of highly unusual implements it would be most difficult to explain. One should be allowed a touch of nervousness, should one not? Ah, well, he thought, taking heart, one could scarcely walk across half of Paris and not run into a policeman now and then, could one?

And if that policeman was walking in the direction he was, so what? They all had to walk in one direction or the other, did they not? Obviously, they did.

Still, this one had stopped dead and turned just after passing Claude, had he not?

He had.

On the other hand, look at it this way: If the *flic* had the slightest suspicion that he was following a much-wanted safecracker (*not* following, you idiot! Because he *isn't* following; he's merely walking in the same direction!), would he remain across the street, marching along so sedately? Not likely! He would be storming over, whistle blowing like mad, baton raised for action. So forget the man, for heaven's sake! Walk along like the student he thinks you are, and stop sweating!

Curbs came and went on the Rue Cologne. Step down, step up. The couple ahead had withdrawn into a shadowed alcove; giggles came from it as he passed. Would the *flic* cross over and investigate the giggles? He did not, but it had really been a lot to expect.

Ahead, the walk was now bare, the overhead streetlights throwing the shadows of the whispering trees in wavering patches on the walk. The two sets of footsteps echoed each other, one on each side of the pavement. Claude suddenly smiled to himself. Suppose he were to cross the street and plant himself in front of the policeman? Ask the *flic* for directions, say? Settle the matter once and for all—

His smile was wiped away immediately; he felt a sudden chill. You are an idiot, my friend, he said to himself grimly, soberly. You are beginning to show nerves. That idea was strictly from nerves. Don't. It is a bad habit to get into. Try not to get any more of those ridiculous notions.

Turn down one of the small side streets? And if the *flic* merely turns down the street with you, what then, my foolish friend? What did we just say about ridiculous ideas? Just keep walking. That's right. One foot ahead of the other.

The lights of the Place Duquesne appeared before him; a deserted sidewalk café beckoned hospitably from the broad sidewalk that flanked the empty flagstoned circle. Wait a minute! Approaching the *flic* was one thing, but pausing for a brief refreshment was quite another. One thing was certain; they couldn't keep up this silly charade all the way back to the university! Who was it who had said, if war must start, let it start here?

Claude smiled faintly, slowed his steps, and dropped into a chair well back from the curb. His satchel seemed to drape itself naturally across his thighs. And then he felt his heart lurch. The footsteps across the street had also stopped!

"M'sieu?"

Claude swung about, startled, staring up at a sleepy-eyed waiter. "What?"

The waiter stared at him. "Exactly, M'sieu. What?"

"Oh. A cognac."

The waiter nodded, yawned, wiped the table from force of habit, and wandered off inside. He returned with a glass of amber liquid and placed it down. Claude turned to the glass, refusing to recognize the existence of the uniformed figure hesitating across the small *place* from him; he raised the drink and downed it in one swallow. It was a cheap cognac, an embarrassment of the vine, but its warmth was welcome.

Claude forced himself to raise his eyes. The caped figure across from him had not moved.

"Waiter!"

"M'sieu?"

"Another cognac. A double!"

It was placed before him. He twisted the glass slowly and then raised it toward his lips. About to toss it down, his hand froze on the glass. The caped officer had ceased his vigil and was slowly crossing the stones of the *place*. His baton swung restlessly at his side.

Claude felt fear evaporate as quickly as it had come. He had always known the day might come. A plan formed, as plans always formed for him. He would not answer the questions; he would pretend he had not heard. When the *flic* bent lower, he would receive a double dose of cognac in the eyes!

The policeman was big, but he did not look very fast. Off and running! Take the securities from the satchel on the run and the rest jettisoned, maybe under the *flic*'s feet! Here he comes. Claude's fingers lowered the glass slowly.

The policeman shouldered his way through the scattered tables, passed Claude without a glance, and came to rap on the bar counter with his baton. The waiter looked up.

"M'sieu?"

"Your telephone—"

Claude frowned. Calling for the wagon? His muscles tensed, prepared.

The voice of the policeman came now, but it was surprisingly nervous, oddly cringing.

"Marie? Where have you been? I finished my tour nearly an hour ago . . . I've been up and down the Rue Cologne several times . . . No, no, my darling! Of course I'm not complaining . . . I'm merely . . . No, no, darling! Believe me, of course I still want . . . It's simply that . . ."

There was a pause as the uniformed man listened further. "I'm at the Place Duquesne, on the Rue Cologne . . . Ten minutes? . . . Of course, my sweet . . . No, no, I don't mind! . . . No, no, I'll wait . . ."

Claude bit back a grin, fighting hard not to burst out into nervous, almost hysterical laughter. A lesson here, he told himself, trying to sound stern, and took the cognac in his hand down in one huge swallow. He choked a bit on it but welcomed it. Never invent problems. Life furnishes us with sufficient. He swung an arm up to intercept the waiter.

"One last cognac, if you please. And the check, as well."

The policeman passed him, a foolish grin on his face, and took a stand at the curb, staring hungrily up the deserted avenue. Claude grinned in relief, gulped down the cognac and reached into his pocket. It was empty. He reached into another with equal results. What the—

His wallet! His wallet, of course, was home with all other identification. He looked up to see the waiter's eye on him, cold as only years of serving the public can chill an eye.

"I must have left my wallet at home . . ."

The waiter moved closer, preventing escape, managing a sneer without moving so much as a muscle of his face. The policeman had turned and was watching.

"Tomorrow I will come back . . ."

The waiter shrugged, caught the policeman's eye and jerked a thumb downward. The policeman stared and then shook his head in profound disgust as Claude sat frozen. The shoulders of the uniformed man slumped. Eight long, miserable, lonely hours on his feet, Marie about to meet him with almost assured results, and now this! Because of some idiot youngster who wandered off without money, he was going to have to waste hours at the office, fill out God-knows-how-many millions of papers—it was impossible! Would Marie wait for him to get back? What a dream!

No, damn it, no! Not tonight! He looked down at the pale face of the young man in the chair.

"I'll lend you the money for the cognac," he said, reaching for his billfold. "This is my regular beat; four in the afternoon to midnight. You can come by tomorrow and pay me back."

Claude felt his head whirling. He could not believe it. He came to his feet. "Oh, I will, I will!"

"I'm sure you will," the *flic* said confidently and picked the satchel from

Claude's fingers. "I'll hold your books for security." He was generous, but also cautious. "Don't worry. They'll be safe."

*To go back to the Rue Cologne or not, that was the problem!*

# WHEN IN ROME

*By Patricia Highsmith*

ISABELLA HAD soaped her face, her neck, and was beginning to relax in the spray of deliciously warm water on her body when suddenly—there he was again! An ugly grinning face peered at her not a meter from her own face, with one big fist gripping an iron bar, so he could raise himself to her level.

"Swine!" Isabella said between her teeth, ducking at the same time.

"Slut!" came his retort. "Ha, ha!"

This must have been the third intrusion by the same creep! Isabella, still stooped, got out of the shower and reached for the plastic bottle of yellow shampoo, shot some into a bowl which held a cake of soap (she removed the soap), let some hot shower water run into the bowl and agitated the water until the suds rose, thick and sweet-smelling. She set the bowl within easy reach on the rim of the tub, and climbed back under the shower, breathing harder with her fury.

Just let him try it again! Defiantly erect, she soaped her facecloth, washed her thighs. The square recessed window was just to the left of her head, and there was a square emptiness, stone-lined, between the blue-and-white tiled bathroom walls and the great iron bars, each as thick as her wrist, on the street side.

"Signora?" came the mocking voice again.

Isabella reached for the bowl. Now he had both hands on the bars, and his face was between them, unshaven, his black eyes intense, his loose mouth smiling. Isabella flung the suds, holding the bowl with fingers spread wide on its underside.

"Oof!" The head disappeared.

A direct hit! The suds had caught him between the eyes, and she thought she heard some of the suds hit the pavement. Isabella smiled and finished her shower.

She was not looking forward to the evening—dinner at home with the First Secretary of the Danish Embassy with his girl friend; but she had had worse evenings in the past, and there were worse to come in Vienna in the last week of this month, May, when her husband Filippo had to attend some kind of human-rights-and-pollution conference that was going to last five days. Isabella didn't care for the Viennese—she considered the women bores with nothing on their minds but clothes, who was wearing what, and how much did it cost.

"I think I prefer the green silk tonight," Isabella said to her maid Elisabetta, when she went into her bedroom, big bathtowel around her, and saw the new black dress laid out on her bed. "I changed my mind," Isabella added, because she remembered that she had chosen the black that afternoon. Hadn't she? Isabella felt a little vague.

"And which shoes, signora?"

Isabella told her.

A quarter to eight now. The guests—two men, Filippo had said, besides the Danish secretary who was called Osterberg or Ottenberg, were not due until eight, which meant eight thirty or later. Isabella wanted to go out on the street, to drink an espresso standing up at the bar, like any other ordinary Roman citizen, and she also wanted to see if the Peeping Tom was still hanging around. In fact, there were two of them, the second a weedy type of about 30 who wore a limp raincoat and dark glasses. He was a "feeler," the kind who pushed his hand against a woman's bottom. He had done it to Isabella once or twice while she was waiting for the porter to open the door. Isabella had to wait for the porter unless she chose to carry around a key as long as a man's foot for the big outside doors. The feeler looked a bit cleaner than her bathroom snoop, but he also seemed creepier and he never smiled.

"Going out for a caffè," Isabella said to Elisabetta.

"You prefer to go out?" Elisabetta said, meaning that she could make a caffè, if the signora wanted. Elisabetta was forty-odd, her hair in a neat bun. Her husband had died a year ago, and she was still in a state of semi-mourning.

Isabella flung a cape over her shoulders, barely nodded, and left. She crossed the cobbled court whose stones slanted gently toward a center drain, and was met at the door by one of the three porters who kept a round-the-clock guard on the palazzo which was occupied by six affluent tenants. This porter was Franco. He lifted the heavy crossbar and opened the big doors enough for her to pass through.

Isabella was out on the street. Freedom! She stood tall and breathed. An adolescent boy cycled past, whistling. An old woman in black waddled by slowly, burdened with a shopping bag that showed onions and spaghetti on top, carelessly wrapped in newspaper. Someone's radio blared jazz through an open window. The air promised a hot summer.

Isabella looked around, but didn't see either of her nuisances, and was aware of feeling slightly disappointed. However, there was the bar-caffé across the street and a bit to the right. Isabella entered, conscious that her fine clothes and well-groomed hair set her apart from the usual patrons here. She put on a warm smile for the young barman who knew her by now.

"Signora! Buon' giorno! A fine day, no? What is your wish?"

"Un espress', per piacere."

Isabella realized that she was known in the neighborhood as the wife of a government official who was reasonably important for his age which was still under 40, aware that she was considered rather rich, and pretty too. The latter, people could see. And what else, Isabella wondered as she sipped her espresso. She and Filippo had a fourteen-year-old daughter in school in Switzerland now. Susanna.

Isabella wrote to her faithfully once a week, as Susanna did to her. How was Susanna going to shape up? Would she even *like* her daughter by the time she was 18 or 22? Was Susanna going to lose her passion for horses and horseback riding (Isabella hoped so) and go for something more intellectual such as geology and anthropology, which she had shown an interest in last year? Or was she going to go the usual way—get married at 20 before she'd finished university, trade on her good looks and marry "the right kind of man" before she had found out what life was all about? What *was* life all about?

Isabella looked around her, as if to find out. Isabella had had two years of university in Milan, had come from a rather intellectual family, and didn't consider herself just another dumb wife. Filippo was good-looking and had a promising career ahead of him. But then Filippo's *father* was important in a government ministry, and had money. The only trouble was that the wife of a man in diplomatic service had to be a clothes-horse, had to keep her mouth shut when she would like to open it, had to be polite and gracious to people whom she detested or was bored by. There were times when Isabella wanted to kick it all, to go slumming, simply to laugh.

She tossed off the last of her coffee, left a five-hundred-lire piece, and turned around, not yet leaving the security of the bar's counter. She surveyed the scene. Two tables were occupied by couples who might be lovers. A blind beggar with a white cane was on his way in.

And here came her dark-eyed Peeping Tom! Isabella was aware that her eyes lit up as if she beheld her lover walking in.

He grinned. He sauntered, swaggered slightly as he headed for the bar to a place at a little distance from her. He looked her up and down, like a man sizing up a pick-up before deciding yes or no.

Isabella lifted her head and walked out of the bar-caffè.

He followed. "You are beautiful, signora," he said. "I should know, don't you think so?"

"You can keep your filthy ideas to yourself!" Isabella replied as she crossed the street.

"My beautiful lady-love—the wife of my dreams!"

Isabella noticed that his eyes looked pink. Good! She pressed the bell for the porter. An approaching figure on her left caught her eye. The bottom-pincher, the gooser, the real oddball! Raincoat again, no glasses today, a faint smile. Isabella turned to face him, with her back to the big doors.

"Oh, how I would like to. . . ." the feeler murmured as he passed her, so close she imagined she could feel the warmth of his breath against her cheek, and at the same time he slapped her hip with his left hand. He had a pockmark or two, and big cheekbones that stuck out gauntly. Disgusting type! And a disgusting phrase he had used!

From across the street, Peeping Tom was watching, Isabella saw; he was chuckling silently, rocking back on his heels.

Franco opened the doors. What if she told Filippo about those two? But of course she had, Isabella remembered, a month or so ago, yes. "How would *you* like it if a psychopath stared at you nearly every time you took a shower?" Isabella had said to Filippo, and he had broken out in one of his rare laughs. "If it were a *woman* maybe, yes, I might like it!" he said, then he had said that she shouldn't take it so seriously, that he would speak to the porters, or something like that.

Isabella had the feeling that she didn't really wake up until after the dinner party, when the coffee was served in the living room. The taste of the coffee reminded her of the bar that afternoon, of the dark-haired Peeping Tom with the pink eyes walking into the bar and having the nerve to speak to her *again!*

"We shall be in Vienna too, at the end of the month," said the girl friend of the Danish First Secretary.

Isabella rather liked her. Her name was Gudrun. She looked healthy, honest, unsnobbish. But Isabella had nothing to say except, "Good. We shall be looking forward," one of the phrases that came out of her automatically after 15 years of being the wife-of-a-government-employee. There were moments, hours, when she felt bored to the point of going insane. Like now. She felt on the brink of doing something shocking, such as standing up and screaming, or announcing that she wanted to go out for a walk (yes, and have another espresso in the same crummy bar), of shouting that she was bored with them *all,* even Filippo, slumped with legs crossed in an armchair now, wearing his neat, new dinner suit with a ruffled shirt, deep in conversation with the three other men. Filippo was long and lean like a fashion model, his black hair beginning to gray at the temples in a distinguished way. Women liked his looks, Isabella knew. His good looks, however, didn't make him a ball of fire as a lover. Did the women know that, Isabella wondered.

Before going to bed that night, Isabella had to check the shopping list with Luigi the cook for tomorrow's dinner party, because Luigi would be up early to buy fresh fish. Hadn't the signora suggested fish? And Luigi recommended young lamb instead of tournedos for the main course, if he dared say so.

Filippo paid her a compliment as he was undressing. "Osterberg thought you were charming."

They both slept in the same big bed, but it was so wide that Filippo could switch his reading light on and read his papers and briefings till all hours, as he often did, without disturbing Isabella.

A couple of evenings later Isabella was showering just before seven p.m. when the same dark-haired creep sprang up at her bathroom window, leering a "hello, beautiful! Getting ready for me?"

Isabella was not in a mood for repartée. She got out of the shower.

"Ah, signora, such beauty should not be hidden! Don't try—"

"I've told the *police* about you!" Isabella yelled back at him, and switched off the bathroom light.

Isabella spoke to Filippo that evening as soon as he came in. "Something's got to be done—opaque glass put in the window—"

"You said that would make the bathroom too humid."

"I don't care! It's revolting! I've told the porters—Giorgio, anyway. He doesn't do a damned thing, that's plain!—Filippo?"

"Yes, my dear. Come on, can't we talk about this later? I've got to change my shirt, at least, because we're due—already." He looked at his watch.

Isabella was dressed. "I want your tear-gas gun. You remember you showed it to me. Where is it?"

Filippo sighed. "Top drawer, left side of my desk."

Isabella went to the desk in Filippo's study. The tear-gas gun looked like a fountain pen, only a bit thicker. Isabella smiled as she placed her thumb on the firing end of it and imagined her counterattack.

"Be careful how you use that tear-gas," Filippo said as they were leaving the house. "I don't want you to get into trouble with the police just because of a——"

"*Me* in trouble with the police! Whose side are you on?" Isabella laughed, and felt much better now that she was armed.

The next afternoon around five, Isabella went out, paid a visit to the pharmacy where she bought tissues and a bottle of a new eau de Cologne which the chemist suggested, and whose packaging amused her. Then she strolled toward the bar-caffé, keeping an eye out for her snoops as she went. She was bareheaded, had a bit of rouge on her lips, and she wore a new summer frock. She looked pretty and was aware of it. And across the street, walking past her very door now, went the raincoated creep in dark glasses again—and he didn't notice her. Isabella felt slightly disappointed. She went into the bar and ordered an espresso, lit a rare cigarette.

The barman chatted. "Wasn't it a nice day? And the signora is looking especially well today."

Isabella barely heard him, but she replied politely. When she opened her handbag to pay for her espresso, she touched the tear-gas gun, picked it up, dropped it, before reaching for her purse.

"Grazie, signora!"

She had tipped generously as usual.

Just as she turned to the door, the bathroom peeper—her special persecutor—entered, and had the audacity to smile broadly and nod, as if they were dear friends. Isabella lifted her head higher as if with disdain, and at the same time gave him an appraising glance, which just might have been mistaken for an invitation, Isabella knew. She had meant it that way. The creep hadn't quite the boldness to say anything to her inside the caffé, but he did follow her out the door. Isabella avoided looking directly at him. Even his shoes were unshined. What could he do for a living, she wondered.

Isabella pretended, at her door, to be groping for her key. She picked up the tear-gas gun, pushed off its safety, and held it with her thumb against its top.

Then he said, with such mirth in his voice that he could hardly get the words out, "Bellissima signora, when are you going to let me—"

Isabella lifted the big fountain pen and pushed its firing button, maneuvering it so that its spray caught both his eyes at short range.

"Ow!—Ooh-h!" He coughed, then groaned, down on one knee now, with a hand across his eyes.

Even Isabella could smell the stuff, and blinked, her eyes watering. A man on the pavement had noticed the Peeping Tom struggling to get up, but was not running to help him, merely walking toward him. And now a porter opened the big wooden doors, and Isabella ducked into her own courtyard. "Thank you, Giorgio."

The next morning she and Filippo set out for Vienna. This excursion was one Isabella dreaded. Vienna would be dead after eleven thirty at night— not even an interesting coffee house would be open. Awful! But the fact that she had fired a shot in self-defense—in attack—buoyed Isabella's morale.

And to crown her satisfaction she had the pleasure of seeing Peeping Tom in dark glasses as she and Filippo were getting into the chauffeured government car to be driven to the airport. The figure in dark glasses had stopped on the pavement some ten meters away to gaze at the luggage being put into the limousine by the liveried driver.

Isabella hoped his eyes were killing him. She had noted there was a box of four cartridges for the tear-gas gun in the same drawer. She intended to keep her gadget well charged. Surely the fellow wasn't going to come back for more! She might try it also on the feeler in the dirty raincoat. Yes, there was one who didn't mind approaching damned close!

"Why're you dawdling, Isabella? Forget something?" Filippo asked, holding the car door for her.

Isabella hadn't realized that she had been standing on the pavement, relishing the fact that the creep could see her about to get into the protective armor of the shiny car, about to go hundreds of kilometers away from him. "I'm ready," she said, and got in. She was not going to say to Filippo, "There's my Peeping Tom." She liked the idea of her secret war with him. Maybe his eyes were permanently damaged. She hoped so.

This minor coup made Vienna seem better. Isabella missed Elisabetta—some women whose husbands were in government service traveled with their maids, but Filippo was against this, just now. "Wait a couple of years till I get a promotion," Filippo had said. Years. Isabella didn't care for the word year or years. Could she stand it? At the stuffy dinner parties where the Austrians spoke bad French or worse Italian, Isabella carried her tear-gas gun in her handbag, even in her small evening bag at the big gala at the Staatsoper. *The Flying Dutchman.* Isabella sat with legs crossed, feet crossed also with tension, and dreamed of resuming her attack when she got back to Rome.

Then on the last evening Filippo had an "all-night meeting" with four men of the human-rights committee, or whatever they called it. Isabella expected him back at the hotel about three in the morning at the latest, but he did not get back till seven thirty, looking exhausted and even a bit drunk. His arrival had awakened her, though he had tried to come in quietly with his own key.

"Nothing at all," he said unnecessarily and a little vaguely. "Got to take a shower—then a little sleep. No appointment till—eleven this morning and it won't matter if I'm late." He ran the shower.

Then Isabella remembered the girl he had been talking to that evening, as he smoked a fine cigar—at least, Isabella had heard Filippo call it "a fine cigar"—a smiling, blonde Austrian girl, smiling in the special way women had when they wanted to say, "Anything you do is all right with me. I'm yours, you understand? At least for tonight."

Isabella sighed, turned over in bed, tried to sleep again, but she felt tense with rage, and knew she would not sleep before it was time for breakfast, time to get up. Damn it! She knew Filippo had been at the girl's apartment or in her hotel room, knew that if she took the trouble to sniff his shirt, even the shoulders of his dinner jacket, she would smell the girl's perfume—and the idea of doing that revolted her. Well, she herself had had two, no three lovers during her married life with Filippo, but they had been so brief, those affairs! And so discreet! Not one servant had known.

Isabella also suspected Filippo of having a girl friend in Rome, Sibilla, a rather gypsy-like brunette, and if Filippo was "discreet," it was because he was only lukewarm about her. This blonde tonight was more Filippo's type, Isabella knew. She heard Filippo hit the twin bed that was pushed close to her bed. He would sleep like a log, then get up in three hours looking amazingly fresh.

When Isabella and Filippo got back to Rome, Signor Sore-Eyes was on hand the very first evening, when Isabella stood under the shower about seven thirty in the evening. Now that was fidelity for you! Isabella ducked, giggling. Her giggle was audible.

And Sore-Eyes' response came instantly: "Ah, the lady of my heart is pleased! She laughs!" He had dropped to his feet, out of sight, but his voice came clearly through the stone recess. "Come, let me see more. *More!*" Hands grasped the bars; the grinning face appeared, black eyes shining and looking not at all damaged.

"Get lost!" she shouted, and stepped out of the shower and began to dry herself, standing near the wall, out of his view.

But the other nut, the feeler, seemed to have left the neighborhood. At least Isabella did not see him during three or four days after her return from Vienna. Nearly every day she had an espresso at the bar-caffé across the street, and sometimes twice a day she took taxis to the Via Veneto area where a few of her friends lived, or to the Via Condotti for shopping. Shiny-Eyes remained faithful, however, not always in view when she came out of her big doors, but more often than not.

Isabella fancied—she liked to fancy—that he was in love with her, even though his silly remarks were intended either to make her laugh or, she had to admit it, to insult and shock her. It was this line of thinking, however, which caused Isabella to see the Peeping Tom as a rival, and which gave her an idea. What Filippo needed was a good jolt!

"Would you like to come for after-dinner coffee tonight?" Isabella murmured to Shiny-Eyes one day, interrupting his own stream of vulgarity, as she stood not yet pushing the bell of her house.

The man's mouth fell open, revealing more of his stained teeth.

"Ghiardini," she said, giving her last name. "Ten thirty." She had pushed the bell by now and the doors were opening. "Wear some better clothes," she whispered.

That evening Isabella dressed with a little more interest in her appearance. She and Filippo had to go out first to a "buffet cocktail" at the Hotel Eliseo. Isabella was not even interested in what country was host to the affair. Then she and Filippo departed at ten fifteen in their own government car, to be followed by two other groups of Americans, Italians, and a couple of Germans. Isabella and Filippo were earlier than the rest, and of course Luigi and Elisabetta already had the long bar-table well equipped with bottles, glasses, and ice, and platters of little sausages stuck with toothpicks. Why hadn't she told Shiny-Eyes eleven o'clock?

But Shiny-Eyes did the right thing, and arrived just after eleven. Isabella's heart gave a dip as he entered through the living-room door, which had been opened by Luigi. The room was already crowded with guests, most of them standing up with drinks, chattering away, quite occupied, and giving Shiny-Eyes not a glance. Luigi was seeing to his drink. At least he was wearing a dark suit, a limp but white shirt, and a tie.

Isabella chatted with a large American and his wife. Isabella hated speaking English, but she could hold her own in it. Filippo, Isabella saw, had left his quartet of diplomats and was now concentrating on two pretty women; he was standing before them while they sat on the sofa, as if mesmerizing them by his tall elegant presence, his stream of bilge. The women were German, secretaries or girl friends. Isabella almost sneered.

Shiny-Eyes was nursing his Scotch against the wall by the bar-table, and Isabella drifted over on the pretense of replenishing her champagne. She glanced at him, and he came closer. To Isabella he seemed the only vital person in the room. She had no intention of speaking to him, even of looking directly at him, and concentrated on pouring champagne from a small bottle.

"Good evening, signora," he said in English.

"Good evening. And what is your name?" she asked in Italian.

"Ugo."

Isabella turned gracefully on her heel and walked away. For the next minutes she was a dutiful hostess, circulating, chatting, making sure that everyone had what he or she wanted. People were relaxing, laughing more loudly. Even as she spoke to someone, Isabella looked in Ugo's direction and saw him in the act of pocketing a small Etruscan statue. Isabella drifted slowly but directly across the room toward Ugo.

"You put that back!" she said between her teeth, and left him.

Ugo put it back, flustered, but not seriously.

Filippo had caught the end of this, Isabella speaking to Ugo. Filippo rose to find a new drink, got it, and approached Isabella. "Who's the dark type over there? Do you know him?"

Isabella shrugged. "Someone's bodyguard, perhaps?"

The evening ended quietly, Ugo slipping out unnoticed even by Isabella. When Isabella turned back to the living room expecting to see Filippo, she found the room empty. "Filippo?" she called, thinking he might be in the bedroom.

Filippo had evidently gone out with some of the guests, and Isabella was sure he was going to see one of the blondes tonight. Isabella helped herself to a last champagne, something she rarely did. She was not satisfied with the evening after all.

When she awakened the next morning, at the knock of Elisabetta with the breakfast tray, Filippo was not beside her in bed. Elisabetta, of course, made no comment. While Isabella was still drinking caffè latte, Filippo arrived. All-night talk with the Americans, he explained, and now he had to change his clothes.

"Is the blonde in the blue dress American? I thought she and the other blonde were Germans," Isabella said.

Now the row was on. So what, was Filippo's attitude.

"What kind of life is it for *me?*" Isabella screamed. "Am I nothing but an *object?* Just some female figure in the house—always here, to say buona sera —and smile!"

"Where would I be without you? Every man in government service needs a wife," replied Filippo, using up the last of his patience. "And you're a very good hostess, Isabella, really!"

Isabella roared like a lioness. "Hostess! I detest the word! And your girl friends—*in* this house—"

"Never!" Filippo replied proudly.

"Two of them! How many have you now?"

"Am I the only man in Rome with a mistress or two?" He had recovered his cool and intended to stand up for his rights. After all, he was supporting Isabella and in fine style, and their daughter Susanna too. "If you don't like it—" But Filippo stopped.

More than ever, that day, Isabella wanted to see Ugo. She went out around noon, and stopped for an americano at the little bar-caffè. This time she sat at a table. Ugo came in when she had nearly finished her drink. Faithful, he was. Or psychic. Maybe both. Without looking at him, she knew that he had seen her.

She left some money on the table and walked out. Ugo followed. She walked in an opposite direction from the palazzo across the street, knowing that he knew she expected him to follow her.

When they were safely around another corner, Isabella turned. "You did quite well last night, except for the attempted—"

"Ah, sorry, signora!" he interrupted, grinning.

"What are you by profession—if I dare to ask?"

"Journalist, sometimes. Photographer. You know, a free-lance."

"Would you like to make some money?"

He wriggled, and grinned more widely. "To spend on you, signora, yes."

"Never mind the rubbish." He really was an untidy specimen, back in his old shoes again, dirty sweater under his jacket, and when had he last had a bath? Isabella looked around to see if anyone might be observing them. "Would you be interested in kidnaping a rich man?"

Ugo hesitated only two seconds. "Why not?" His black eyebrows had gone up. "Tell me. Who?"

"My husband. You will need a friend with a gun and a car."

Ugo indulged in another grin, but his attitude was attentive.

Isabella had thought out her plans that morning. She told Ugo that she and Filippo wanted to buy a house outside of Rome, and she had the names of a few real-estate agents. She could make an appointment with one for Friday morning, for instance, at nine o'clock. Isabella said she would make herself "indisposed" that morning, so Filippo would have to go alone. But Ugo must be at the palazzo with a car a little before nine.

"I must make the hour the same, otherwise Filippo will suspect me," Isabella explained. "These agents are always a little late. You should be ten minutes early. I'll see that Filippo is ready."

Isabella continued, and walked slowly, since she felt it made them less conspicuous than if they stood still. If Ugo and his friend could camp out somewhere overnight with Filippo, until she had time to get a message from them and get the money from the government? If Ugo could communicate by telephone or entrust someone to deliver a written message? Either way was easy, Ugo said. He might have to hit Filippo on the head, Isabella said, but Ugo was not to hurt him seriously. Ugo understood.

A few moments later, when they parted, everything was worked out for the kidnaping on Friday morning. Tomorrow was Thursday, and if Ugo had spoken to his friend and all was well, he was to give Isabella a nod, merely, tomorrow afternoon about five when she would go out for an espresso.

Isabella was so exhilarated she went that afternoon to see her friend Margherita who lived off the Via Veneto. Margherita asked her if she had found a new lover. Isabella laughed.

"No, but I think Filippo has," Isabella replied.

Filippo also noticed, by Thursday afternoon, that she was in a merry mood. Filippo was home Thursday evening after their dinner out at a restaurant where they had been two at a table of 20. Isabella took off her shoes and waltzed in the living room. Filippo was aware of his early date with the real-estate agents, and cursed it. It was already after midnight.

The next morning Elisabetta awakened them with the breakfast tray at eight thirty, and Isabella complained of a headache.

"No use in my going if you're not going," Filippo said.

"You can at least tell if the house is possible—or houses," she replied sleepily. "Don't let them down or they won't make a date with us again."

Filippo got dressed.

Isabella heard the faint ring of the street-door bell. Filippo went out. By this time he was in the living room or the kitchen in quest of more coffee. It was two minutes to nine. Isabella at once got up, flung on a blouse, slacks and sandals, ready to meet the real-estate agents who she supposed would be twenty minutes late, at least.

They were. Elisabetta announced them. Two gentlemen. The porter had let them into the court. All seemed to be going well, which was to say Filippo was not in view.

"But I thought my husband had already left with you!" She explained that her husband had left the house half an hour ago. "I'm afraid I must ask you to excuse me. I have a migraine today."

The agency men expressed disappointment, but left in good humor finally, because the Ghiardinis were potentially good clients, and Isabella promised to telephone them in the near future.

Isabella went out for a pre-lunch cinzano, and felt reassured by the absence of Ugo. She was about to answer a letter from Susanna which had come that morning when the telephone rang. It was Filippo's colleague Vicente, and where was Filippo? Filippo was supposed to have arrived at noon at Vicente's office for a talk before they went out to lunch with a man who Vicente said was "important."

"This morning was a little strange," Isabella said casually, with a smile in her voice, "because Filippo went off with some estate agents at nine, I thought, then—"

"Then?"

"Well, I don't know. I haven't heard from him since," Isabella replied, thinking she had said quite enough. "I don't know anything about his appointments today."

Isabella went out to mail her letter to Susanna around four. Susanna had fallen from her horse taking a low jump, in which the horse had fallen too. A miracle Susanna hadn't broken a bone! Susanna needed not only new riding breeches but a book of photographs of German cathedrals which the class was going to visit this summer, so Isabella had sent her a check on their Swiss bank. As soon as Isabella had got back home and closed her door, the telephone rang.

"Signora Ghiardini—" It sounded like Ugo speaking through a handkerchief. "We have your husband. Do not try to find out where he is. One hundred million lire we want. Do you understand?"

"*Where* is he?" Isabella demanded, putting on an act as if Elisabetta or someone else were listening; but no one was, unless Luigi had picked up the living-room extension phone. It was Elisabetta's afternoon off.

"Get the money by tomorrow noon. Do not inform the police. This evening at seven a messenger will tell you where to deliver the money." Ugo hung up.

That sounded all right! Just what Isabella had expected. Now she had to get busy, especially with Caccia-Lunghi, Filippo's boss, higher than Vicente in the Bureau of Public Welfare and Environment. But first she went into her bathroom, where she was sure Ugo would not be peering in, washed her face and made herself up again to give herself confidence. She would soon be putting a lot of money into Ugo's pocket and the pocket of his friend—whoever was helping him.

Isabella now envisaged Ugo her slave for a long time to come. She would have the power of betraying him if he got out of hand, and if Ugo chose to betray *her*, she would simply deny it, and between the two of them she had no doubt which one the police would choose to believe: her.

"Vicente!" Isabella said in a hectic voice into the telephone (she had decided after all to ring Vicente first). "Filippo has been kidnaped! That's why he didn't turn up this morning! I've just had a message from the kidnapers. They're asking for a hundred million lire by tomorrow noon!"

She and Filippo, of course, had not that much money in the bank, she went on, and wasn't it the responsibility of the government, since Filippo was a government employee, an official?

Vicente sighed audibly. "The government has had enough of such things. You'd better try Filippo's father, Isabella."

"But he's so stubborn!—The kidnaper said something about throwing Filippo in a *river!*"

"They all say that. Try the father, my dear."

So Isabella did. It was nearly six p.m. before she could reach him, because he had been "in conference." Isabella first asked, "Has Filippo spoken to you today?" He had not. Then she explained that Filippo had been kidnaped, and that his captors wanted 100,000,000 lire by tomorrow noon.

"What? Kidnaped—and they want it from me? Why *me?*" the old man spluttered. "The government—Filippo's in the government!"

"I've asked Vicente Carda." Isabella told him about her rejection in a tearful voice, prolonging her story so that Filippo's predicament would have time to sink in.

"Va bene, va bene." Pietro Ghiardini sounded defeated. "I can contrib-

ute seventy-five million, not more. What a business! You'd think Italy . . ." He went on, though he sounded on the brink of a heart attack.

Isabella expressed gratitude, but she was disappointed. She would have
to come up with the rest out of their bank account—unless of course she
could make a deal with Ugo. Old Pietro promised that the money would be
delivered by ten thirty the following morning.

If she and Filippo were due to go anywhere tonight, Isabella didn't give a
damn, and she told Luigi to turn away people who might arrive at the door
with the excuse that there was a crisis tonight—and they could interpret
that as they wished, Isabella thought. Luigi was understanding, and most
concerned, as was Elisabetta.

Ugo was prompt with another telephone call at seven, and though Isabella was alone in her bedroom, she played her part as though someone
were listening, though no one could have been unless Luigi had picked up
the living-room telephone. Isabella's voice betrayed anxiety, anger, and fear
of what might happen to her husband. Ugo spoke briefly. She was to meet
him in a tiny square which Isabella had never heard of—she scribbled the
name down—at noon tomorrow, with 100,000,000 lire in old bills in
20,000 and 50,000 denominations in a shopping bag or basket, and then
Filippo would be released at once on the edge of Rome. Ugo did not say
where.

"Come *alone*. Filippo is well," Ugo said. "Goodbye, signora."

Vicente telephoned just afterward. Isabella told Vicente what she had to
do, said that Filippo's father had come up with 75,000,000 and could the
government provide the rest? Vicente said no, and wished Isabella and Filippo the best of luck.

And that was that. So early the next morning Isabella went to their bank
and withdrew 25,000,000 lire from their savings, which left so little that she
had to sign a check on their Swiss bank for a transfer when she got home. At
half-past ten a chauffeur in uniform and puttees, with a bulge under his
tunic that must have been a gun, arrived with a briefcase under each arm.
Isabella took him into the bedroom for the transfer of money from the
briefcases into the shopping bag—a black plastic bag belonging to Elisabetta. Isabella didn't feel like counting through all the soiled banknotes.

"You're sure it's exact?" she asked.

The calm and polite chauffeur said it was. He loaded the shopping bag
for her, then took his leave with the briefcases.

Isabella ordered a taxi for eleven fifteen, because she had no idea how
long it might take her to get to the little square, especially if they ran into a
traffic jam somewhere. Elisabetta was worried, and asked for the tenth time,
"Can't I come with you—just sit in the taxi, signora?"

"They will think you are a man in disguise with a gun," Isabella replied, though she intended to get out of the taxi a couple of streets away from the square, and dismiss the taxi.

The taxi arrived. Isabella said she should be back before one o'clock. She had looked up the square on her map of Rome, and had the map with her in case the taxi driver was vague.

"What a place!" said the driver. "I don't know it at all. Evidently you don't either."

"The mother of an old servant of mine lives there. I'm taking her some clothing," Isabella said by way of explaining the bulging but not very heavy shopping bag.

The driver let her out. Isabella had said she was uncertain of the house number, but could find out by asking neighbors. Now she was on her own, with a fortune in her right hand.

There was the little square, and there was Ugo, five minutes early, like herself, reading a newspaper on a bench. Isabella entered the little square slowly. It had a few ill-tended trees, a ground of square stones laid like a pavement. One old woman sat knitting on the only sunlit bench. It was a working-class neighborhood, or one mainly of old people, it seemed. Ugo got up and walked toward her.

" 'Giorno, signora," he said casually, with a polite nod, as if greeting an old acquaintance, and by his own walking led her toward the street pavement. "You're all right?"

"Yes. And—"

"He's quite all right.—Thank you for this." He glanced at her shopping bag. "Soon as we see everything's in order, we'll let Filippo—loose." His smile was reassuring.

"Where are we—"

"Just here," Ugo interrupted, pushing her to the left, toward the street, and a parked car's door suddenly swung open beside her. The push had not been a hard one, only rude and sudden enough to fluster Isabella for a moment. The man in the driver's seat had turned half around and had a pistol pointed at her, held low on the back of the front seat.

"Just be quiet, Signora Isabella, and there will be no trouble at all— nobody hurt at all," the man with the gun said.

Ugo got in beside her in back and slammed the door shut. The car started off.

It had not even occurred to Isabella to scream, she realized. She had a glimpse of a man with a briefcase under his arm, walking only two meters away on the pavement, his eyes straight ahead. They were soon out in the country. There were a few houses, but mostly it was fields and trees. The man driving the car wore a hat.

"Isn't it necessary that I *join* Filippo, Ugo?" she asked.

Ugo laughed, then asked the man driving to pull in at a roadside bar-

restaurant. Here Ugo got out, saying he would be just a minute. He had
looked into the shopping bag long enough to see that it contained money
and was not partly stuffed with newspaper. The man driving turned around
in his seat.

"The signora will please be quiet," he said. "Everything is all right." He
had the horrible accent of a Milan tough, attempting to be soothing to an
unpredictable woman who might go off in a scream louder than a police
siren. In his nervousness he was chewing gum.

"Where are you taking me?"

Ugo was coming back.

Isabella soon found out. They pulled in at a farmhouse whose occupants
had evidently recently left—there were clothes on the line, dishes in the sink
—but the only people now in the house seemed to be Isabella, Ugo, and his
driver chum whom Ugo called Eddy. Isabella looked at an ashtray, recognizing Filippo's Turkish cigarette stubs, noticed also the pack empty and
uncrumpled on the floor.

"Filippo has been released, signora," Ugo said. "He has money for a taxi
and soon you should be able to phone him at home.—Sit down. Would you
like a coffee?"

"Take me back to Rome!" Isabella shouted. But she knew. They had
kidnaped *her*. "If you think there is any *more* money coming, you are quite
mistaken, Ugo—*and you!*" she added to the smiling driver, an old slob now
helping himself to whiskey.

"There is always more money," Ugo said calmly.

"Swine!" Isabella said. "I should have known from the time you first
stared into my bathroom! That's your real occupation, you creep!" A fear
of assault crossed her mind, but only swiftly. Her rage was stronger just
now. "After I tried to—to give you a break, turn a little money your way!
*Look* at all that money!"

Eddy was now sitting on the floor counting it, like a child with an ab-
sorbing new toy or game, except that a big cigar stuck out of his mouth.

"Sit down, signora. All will be well when we telephone your husband."

Isabella sat down on a sagging sofa. There was mud on the heels of her
shoes from the filthy courtyard she had just walked across. Ugo brought
some warmed-over coffee. Isabella learned that still another chum of Ugo's
had driven Filippo in another car and dropped him somewhere to make his
own way home.

"He is quite all right, signora," Ugo assured her, bringing a plate of
awful-looking sliced lamb and hunks of cheese. The other man was on his
feet, and brought a basket of bread and a bottle of inferior wine. The men
were hungry. Isabella took nothing, refusing even whiskey and wine. When
the men had finished eating, Ugo sent Eddy off in the car to telephone
Filippo from somewhere. The farmhouse had no telephone. How Isabella

wished she had brought her tear-gas gun! But she had thought she would be among friends today.

Ugo sipped coffee, smoked a cigarette, and tried to assuage Isabella's anger. "By tonight, by tomorrow morning you will be back home, signora. No harm done! A room to yourself here! Even though the bed may not be as comfortable as the one you're used to."

Isabella refused to answer him, and bit her lip, thinking that she had got herself into an awful mess, had cost herself and Filippo 25,000,000 lire, and might cost them another 50,000,000 (or whatever she was worth) because Filippo's father might decide not to come up with the money to ransom her.

Eddy came back with an air of disappointment and reported in his disgusting slang that signor Ghiardini had told him to go stuff himself.

"What?" Ugo jumped up from his chair. "We'll try again. We'll threaten —didn't you threaten—"

Eddy nodded. "He said . . ." Again the revolting phrase.

"We'll see how it goes tonight—around seven or so," said Ugo.

"How much are you asking?" Isabella was unable to repress the question any longer. Her voice had gone shrill.

"Fifty million, signora," replied Ugo.

"We simply haven't got it—not after *this!*" Isabella gestured toward the shopping bag, now in a corner of the room.

"Ha, ha," Ugo laughed softly. "The Ghiardinis haven't got another fifty million? Or the government? Or Papa Ghiardini?"

The other man announced that he was going to take a nap in the other room. Ugo turned on the radio to some pop music. Isabella remained seated on the uncomfortable sofa. She had declined to remove her coat. Ugo paced about, thinking, talking a little to himself, half drunk with the realization of all the money in the corner of the room. The gun lay on the center table near the radio. She looked at it with an idea of grabbing it and turning it on Ugo, but she knew she could probably not keep both men at bay if Eddy woke up.

When Eddy did wake up and returned to the room, Ugo announced that he was going to try to telephone Filippo, while Eddy kept watch on Isabella. "No funny business," said Ugo like an army officer, before going out. It was just after six.

Eddy tried to engage her in conversation about revolutionary tactics, about Ugo's having been a journalist once, a photographer also (Isabella could imagine what kind of photographer). Isabella was angry and bored, and hated herself for replying even slightly to Eddy's moronic ramblings. He was talking about making a down payment on a house with the money he had gained from Filippo's abduction. Ugo would also start leading a more decent life, which was what he deserved, said Eddy.

"He deserves to be behind bars for the protection of the *public!*" Isabella shot back.

The car had returned. Ugo entered with his slack mouth even slacker, a look of puzzlement on his brow. "Gotta let her go, he may have traced the call," Ugo said to Eddy, and snapped his fingers for action.

Eddy at once went for the shopping bag and carried it out to the car.

"Your husband says you can go to hell," said Ugo. "He will not pay one lire."

It suddenly sank into Isabella. She stood up, feeling scared, feeling naked somehow, even though she still wore her coat over her dress. "He is joking. He'll——" But somehow she knew Filippo wouldn't. "Where're you taking me now?"

Ugo laughed. He laughed heartily, rocking back as he always did, laughing at Isabella and also at himself. "So I have lost fifty million! A pity, eh? Big pity. But the joke is on *you!* Hah! Ha, ha, ha!—Come on, Signora Isabella, what've you got in your purse? Let's see." He took her purse rudely from her hands.

Isabella knew she had about twenty thousand in her billfold. This Ugo laid with a large gesture on the center table, then turned off the radio.

"Let's go," he said, indicating the door, smiling. Eddy had started the car. Ugo's happy mood seemed to be contagious. Eddy began laughing too at Ugo's comments. *The lady was worth nothing!* That was the idea. *La donna niente,* they sang.

"You won't get away with this for long, you piece of filth!" Isabella said to Ugo.

More laughter.

"Here! Fine!" yelled Ugo who was with Isabella in the back seat again, and Eddy pulled the car over to the edge of the road.

Where were they? Isabella had thought they were heading for Rome, but wasn't sure. Yes. She saw some high-rise apartment buildings. A truck went by, close, as she got out with Ugo, half pulled by him.

"Shoes, signora! Ha, ha!" He pushed her against the car and bent to take off her pumps. She kicked him, but he only laughed. She swung her handbag, catching him on the head with it, and nearly fell herself as he snatched off her second shoe. Ugo jumped, with the shoes in his hand, back into the car which roared off.

To be shoeless in silk stockings was a nasty shock. Isabella began walking —toward Rome. She could see lights coming on here and there in the twilight dimness. She'd hitch a ride to the next roadside bar and telephone for a taxi, she thought, pay the taxi when she got home. A large truck passed her by as if blind to her frantic waving. So did a car with a single man in it. Isabella was ready to hitch a lift with anyone!

She walked on, realizing that her stockings were now torn and open at the bottom, and when she stopped to pick something out of one foot, she saw blood. It was more than 15 minutes later when Isabella made her painful way to a restaurant on the opposite of the road where she begged the use of the telephone.

Isabella did not at all like the smile of the young waiter who looked her up and down and was plainly surmising what must have happened to her: a boy friend had chucked her out of his car. Isabella telephoned a taxi company's number which the waiter provided. There would be at least ten minutes to wait, she was told, so she stood by the coat rack at the front of the place, feeling miserable and ashamed with her dirty feet and torn stockings. Passing waiters glanced at her. She had to explain to the proprietor—a stuffy type—that she was waiting for a taxi.

The taxi arrived, Isabella give her address, and the driver looked dubious, so Isabella had to explain that her husband would pay the fare at the other end. She was almost in tears.

Isabella fell against the porter's bell, as if it were home itself. Giorgio opened the doors. Filippo came across the court, scowling.

"The taxi—" Isabella said.

Filippo was reaching into a pocket. "As if I had anything left!"

Isabella took the last excruciating steps across the courtyard to the door out of which Elisabetta was now running to help her.

Elisabetta made tea for her. Isabella sat in the tub, soaking her feet, washing off the filth of Ugo and his ugly chum. She applied surgical spirits to the soles of her feet, then put on clean white woolen booties and a dressing gown. She cast one furious glance at the bathroom window, sure Ugo would never come back.

As soon as she came out of her bathroom, Filippo said, "I suppose you remember—tonight we have the Greek consul coming to dinner with his wife. And two other men. Six in all. I was going to receive them alone— make some excuse." His tone was icy.

Isabella did remember, but had somehow thought all that would be canceled. Nothing was canceled. She could see it now: life would go on as usual, not a single date would be canceled. They were poorer. That was all. Isabella rested in her bed, with some newspapers and magazines, then got up and began to dress. Filippo came in, not even knocking first.

"Wear the peach-colored dress tonight—not that one," he said. "The Greeks need cheering up."

Isabella began removing the dark blue dress she had put on.

"I know you arranged all this," Filippo continued. "They were ready to kill me, those hoodlums—or at least they acted like it. My father is furious! What stupid arrangements!—I can also make some arrangements. Wait and see!"

Isabella said nothing. And *her* future arrangements? Well, she might make some too. She gave Filippo a look. Then she gritted her teeth as she squeezed her swollen feet into "the right shoes" for the evening. When she got up, she had to walk with a limp.

# THE QUEEN'S ANGEL

*By Janwillem van de Wetering*

S HE WALKED over to the gentleman sitting on a weathered bench on Prince Island, an ancient suburb on the south side of the river—part of the city of Amsterdam, Holland's capital. The lady in red sat down next to the little old gentleman.

She said, "You're a nice man, sir."

"I am?" Amsterdam's Chief of Detectives asked.

A cold finger touched his hand. "Yes."

He had been watching a pair of mallard ducks courting on the waterway ahead. They'd been circling each other, the female in charge and bobbing about; now they were nodding and bowing. He wondered whether he was expected to nod and bow, too.

He thought she was attractive: long-legged, firm-bodied, the red dress demurely expensive. The face might be operated on and she might be in her forties. Her scanty makeup was effective, outlining large, alluring, gleaming eyes, full moist lips, high cheekbones. She had elf's ears, small and pointed, set off against short black hair. She was slim.

"You're neat," she said.

He was. His shantung-cotton suit, somewhat worn, was tailored to fit a slight body elegantly. The new straw hat shaded intelligent pale-blue eyes. He had a straight nose under large gold-framed glasses. His narrow hands rested on the gold knob of a thin bamboo cane.

"Make your point, dear," the Chief of Detectives said firmly.

"You think I'm a whore?" the lady asked.

"Are you?" he asked.

She shook her head. "You think I'm panhandling? For drug money maybe?"

He checked her pupils. "I don't think so, dear."

"Am I bothering you?" the lady in red asked. "I can go away."

An overcultured voice, the Chief of Detectives thought. A university accent? Her manner reminded him of female relatives who had studied at the exclusive University of Leyden. And she seemed self-assured. A successful professional? A lawyer? No, he dealt with lawyers all the time. Lady lawyers are sharp-snooted. She seemed quiet and introverted in spite of her momentarily forward manner.

"M.D.?" he asked.

She laughed. "Correct."

He noticed a diamond ring, a gold watch, the smartly cut red dress again —matching shoes, scarf, pocketbook. The getup seemed suggestive of professionally beautiful models as shown in the magazines his wife kept scattered on coffee tables. "You practice medicine?" he asked.

"Not for some years now," the lady said.

He noted the consistently coldly defensive voice contrasting with her direct pushy manner. His manner of observation was the police manner, of course—always focused on contradictions. The punk in the Rolls Royce, the quietly well dressed gent staggering about drunk in the worst alley in town, the shy pushy lady. The punk stole the car. The gent is about to shoot a male prostitute for blackmail. What did the shy, pushy lady do?

He got up, lifted his hat, said his name, that he was pleased to meet her, put out his hand.

"Marion," she said, shaking his hand.

He sat next to her again. "Marion who?"

"Can I be a little anonymous for now?" Marion asked. "Would you mind, commissaris? Until I know you a little better?"

She would have seen his face in the papers, he thought. He'd been in the news again: a tricky case, he hadn't even solved it. Sergeant de Gier did the work but the journalists liked to have the commissaris' picture in the paper —the wise old man, as the morning paper had it.

"What can I do for you, Dr. Marion?" he heard himself say kindly. Does a wise old man allow his meditations on the weathered bench on Prince Island to be disturbed? He liked to come here to ruminate on the relativity of things. Stare at the rippling river. "Reflections on the sea of illusion." He had read that somewhere.

It was true—the older he got, the less things seemed real.

"I need to ask you something," the lady said.

The guru syndrome, the commissaris thought. The lady wanted free information from above. Why come to me? he thought. What did she think he knew? He was just another ignoramus, bumping about on the miracle, manipulating the riddles, but tell that to the morning paper. Wise old man.

"I live with death," Marion said.

We all do, the commissaris thought, but he didn't say that.

"Everything I live with dies," Marion was saying.

He noticed her voice was hoarsely dead itself, as if a dry wind blew through a delicate mask—her face. The fingers that touched his wrist were cold. Her smile was cold.

He shivered. She withdrew her hand: "Low body temperature, commissaris, it's been with me ever since. I'm used to it now."

He saw that her tight skin wasn't due to a face lift. Marion's face was a live skull. The eyes seemed no longer mysteriously attractive but hollow, quite empty.

"I'm sorry," she said when he shivered again.

"What died?" he asked. "What did you live with that died?"

The process started slowly, she explained. First her house plants started dying. She always liked growing greenery. She cultivated mini palms and large ferns in a solarium on the back porch. Prize geraniums in the windows. Then all the plants died on her.

"Disease?" the commissaris asked.

Yes, Marion explained, but plant disease can be treated. She washed the palms, dusted the ferns, cut the geraniums down. They withered anyway.

Peabody died, too. Peabody was the dog, a cute little mutt. He got a cancer.

"Was he old?"

"Only five."

Albertine, the Siamese cat, was next.

Marion got a puppy and a kitten from the pound—an undefined virus interfered, they never grew up. She took up horseriding in Amsterdam Forest. Any horse she rode sickened. The stable canceled her membership card. She bought her own horse. Kaiser died, too.

"Of what?"

"Of a shot in the head. His leg was broken."

The commissaris sat quietly.

"Bad luck?" Marion asked.

He told her that that interpretation was her own. He told her about his wife's uncle and the bombing of Rotterdam during World War II. German three-engined Juncker airplanes bombed the open city when it refused to surrender to SS commandos smuggled in on river barges. When Dutch marines pushed the enemy back, the Junckers set the city on fire.

Uncle drove to town to try to save expensive merchandise in his store.

The warehouse burned. While Uncle watched his uninsured fortune blaze, fleeing folks stole his car. Uncle walked home, and found it flattened—no wife left, no kids. Uncle had always been irritated by breaking shoelaces. At that moment, one broke. Uncle laughed, laughed, laughed.

"The broken shoelace was good luck?" Marion asked.

The commissaris couldn't define the event, but Uncle, having nothing more to lose, became a much decorated freedom fighter. He married again, started a business again, never cared much again.

"Free forever?" Marion asked.

The commissaris pursed thin lips. "Mustn't exaggerate, my dear."

"My story is different, perhaps." Icy lips touched the commissaris' cheek, and he was alone again, watching ducks.

"This isn't over yet," his wife said when he told her that evening, feeling guilty a bit while touching feet under the eiderdown—an intimacy he enjoyed.

"You want to see the lady in red again?" his wife asked.

"Not really, Katrien."

"Then stay away from Prince Island."

The commissaris did that, to please Katrien. He didn't think that at age sixty-four, crippled on bad days by a rheumatic hip condition, plastic-toothed, coughing painfully at times—he no longer smoked but carbonized lung tissue takes a while to grow back—he presented much of a challenge.

He still wanted, on days off, to reflect on the sea of illusion, so he rented a dory on the Amstel River.

Marion showed up on the dock.

"Mind if I join you?"

"Be my guest."

She had elegant legs. The short red skirt wasn't designed for boating.

"You should play a guitar," Marion said.

"I could sing."

The commissaris sang "My Funny Valentine."

"The Chet Baker version," Marion said. "I used to have the record, but it got scratched at parties." She caressed his knee. "You're very courageous, aren't you? I thought that long note had to break until you folded it round." She smiled. "Just barely, but that's all it needs."

"Miles Davis sometimes plays like that," he said.

She smiled. "You must really know jazz."

"Two of my associates play the genre. Adjutant Grijpstra on drums and Sergeant de Gier on flute. They encourage me to join them." He looked at wavelets, set up by a fresh breeze.

"You've been singing long?"

"I sang as a boy," the commissaris said. "Then, for a hundred years, I was too shy. I'm glad my associates got me into it again." He was rowing with long strokes, feeling vigorous for a change. "Jazz singing can reach far."

"How far?"

"All the way?" he asked.

She laughed.

He rowed the dory into a cove. The sun was still warm. Pink-striped carps did their ritual mating dance between waving cattails. A marsh heron, its squat brown-and-yellow body hidden perfectly in shadows of waving reed rushes, startled them by bursting out in booming warning calls like sudden drumbeats.

"Grijpstra sometimes explodes like that," the commissaris said, "and then he's back on the edge of his snaredrum, doing dry ticking: the crackle of understatement that drives the listener wild." He grinned. "It's the understatement that makes jazz truthful."

He had brought a thermos filled with strong coffee and a bag of ginger cookies. She shared his silver mug.

He began to feel cold and blamed his old bones.

"Dear old bones." Marion smiled. "Maybe we shouldn't be meeting like this. Next time we'll have lunch." She told him about a divorced father she hardly knew but ran into in Paris. He had asked her to lunch and they ate fried sole in a little restaurant with a view of the Seine. "The only time we were close."

"I'm a father figure to you?"

"What else?" She laughed her chilly laugh again. "But you're not my father."

"I'd like fatherly advice," Marion said when the dory entered the rental marina.

"All an old man is good for," the commissaris joked.

She didn't pick that up. He noticed again that her mask didn't move. "Even the weeds in my garden are dying," she said. "Do you think it's something I did?"

"What did you do?" the commissaris asked.

She waited until the dory was tied to the dock and he helped her out. "You know I'm a doctor," Marion said, hand on his shoulder, stepping up on the dock. "Doctors heal. But I killed my husband."

The breeze blew his boater into the Amstel. By the time he retrieved the hat, Marion's car drove off.

"A wrong diagnosis, perhaps," the commissaris told his wife. "Doctors can't help making tragic mistakes sometimes. Remember Cousin Jasper?"

"Jasper," Katrien said, "was an apprentice, and the professor in charge was unwell when they brought in the little girl."

"The little girl died," the commissaris said, "because of Jasper's tragic mistake."

"Jasper lives in the country now," Katrien said, "growing tomatoes as a hobby. He also keeps healthy goats. You stay away from that killing woman."

"But, Katrien . . ."

The commissaris and Marion ate fried sole in a restaurant next to the Concertgebouw, at his invitation by phone. "How did you locate me?" Marion asked.

He didn't tell her, but it was simple enough. Sergeant de Gier found her. The leads were few but clear: a forty-plus lady called Marion with a Leyden medical degree driving a red Ferrari.

"How did you find me renting the dory?" the commissaris asked.

Chance. She happened to see him there. The meeting at Prince Island was chance, too. She knew what he looked like from published photographs and approached him by instinct.

"Would you have contacted me again?" he asked.

She said yes, even the huge tree in front of her house had died. "Am I killing the city?"

The sole *a la meuniere,* served whole, larger than the large silver dish it came on, was just excellent, crisp on the bone, tender inside. The little potatoes were good and crumbly. The Belgian endive salad was fresh and chewy. Marion wore a red dress again, not the same as the second time, not the same as the first time. She looked very good in red.

"So you killed your husband?" he asked conversationally. "How did you do that?"

"I aggravated a psychosomatic condition," Marion said. "Paul thought his heart was bad. His worrying brought on palpitations. I prescribed drugs that made the palpitations kill him."

"Why did you want him dead?"

"I wanted his money," she said, "and I wanted his brilliant friend, Bad Bart."

"Define 'bad,' " the commissaris said.

"Do you," Marion asked, "believe that nothing matters?"

"Did Bart?"

"Do *you?*" she asked coldly.

"I believe the experiment of creation is unplanned," the commissaris said, "but I find random evolution fascinating, anyway, perhaps because of its chaotic essence."

She sighed. "Bart talked like that. He found everything senselessly fascinating, including me. I thought I agreed. I wanted to prove my insight, to astonish him. We were reading Sartre then. Bart told me we were free."

"You *are* free," the commissaris said.

"I wish I wasn't," Marion said.

"And nothing matters," the commissaris said. "But maybe there's more to that." He poked about in his sole. "Was it Bart's idea that you would kill your rich husband?"

"No," she said. "He said he couldn't, because of some conditioned hangup, sleep with a friend's wife, so I removed his friend." She massaged her tight cheeks. "Doesn't that sound stupid now?"

"This is like the meeting with your father in Paris?" the commissaris asked.

"No." She put down her fork. "I didn't want anything from him then. We just happened to meet and then we had that nice lunch."

"What do you want from me?" the commissaris asked.

"I want things to stop dying around me." Her voice had become brittle.

"When did this murder happen?"

"It *happened*," she said, "that's my point. Everything happens. We happen. Nothing is planned. Life happened to start up four billion years ago and eventually we happened along with it, and I happened to kill Paul. That's what I thought then—I don't know what I think now."

He had wanted to order the peche melba or a chocolate mousse perhaps, delicacies that replaced nicotine—this was the day he could grant himself a dessert. She wanted only coffee. He sipped his own, watching her smoke.

"You smoke a lot?"

"Rarely." She laughed. "I don't have bad habits. I just killed my husband." She rummaged in her bag and brought out an enlarged snapshot. It showed a smiling male corpse, lying on an oriental rug. It wore a tuxedo. The dead right hand held a note. Penciled handwriting said, "Farewell my love," signed by a red print of lips. A female foot in a red high-heeled shoe rested on the corpse's chest. A long leg. The hem of a red skirt.

"Ah," the commissaris said. "Paul? After the heart attack? He looks pleasant enough to me."

"Boring," she said. "Repetitive. Paul drank a lot."

"*Your* leg?"

"Yes," she said.

"Your note, your handwriting, lipstick imprint of your mouth?"

"Yes, yes," she said impatiently. "Yes!"

"Who took the photograph?"

"I had my camera set up for delay," she said, "with the button on automatic."

"I'm a policeman," the commissaris said. "You sought me out twice.

Deliberately. You made an effort. You've managed to make me curious. I may be after you now. You know what you're doing?"

"You think I'm giving myself up? The photograph is proof."

"When did this happen?" the commissaris asked.

She smiled sadly. "Fifteen years ago. Deadline for arrest is after sixteen years. You can still arrest me. I took that photograph to impress bad Bart. It aggravates my crime. Isn't this a good case?"

He played with his napkin. "You've done some research—but have you considered what you're presenting here? A weird confession hardly supported by circumstantial evidence. There was no autopsy?"

She shook her head. "I called in a colleague. She diagnosed heart trouble. A natural death."

"Any witnesses?" the commissaris asked, holding up the snapshot. "Bad Bart saw this happen?"

"No."

"You and Paul were going out?" the commissaris asked.

"To a concert."

The commissaris looked thoughtful. "Oh, dear."

"The evidence might be good," she said. "My handwriting, my leg—"

"No," the commissaris said. "I wouldn't handle the case." He gave her the photo. "The prosecutor wouldn't, either. Neither would a judge. That photo might be a joke, made long before your husband's death, as your lawyer would point out. Your confession could be hysterical." He waved his napkin. "This country's roots are Calvinistic, we're all obsessed with guilt."

"I am now," she said. "I was then. Bart wasn't even bad."

"What happened to the man?"

"Weak Bart didn't like everything dying around me, either, and then he died, too, due to a heroin addiction. He fell off a streetcar."

"You didn't arrange that?"

"No." The cold smile was back. "I was paying for treatment. He slipped out of the clinic."

The commissaris helped Marion into her coat.

"I know what I'm doing," she said while he walked her to the Ferrari. "You're a top-ranking policeman, serving both the citizens and the Queen. The Queen is the crown. The crown is the magic intermediary through which citizens reach divinity. The symbolism is clear. If I apply for grace, I have to see the Queen's angel . . ."

On Sunday morning, the commissaris walked to Marion's house. His hips were hurting again, he couldn't sleep. It was five A.M. The birds were singing, the summer sun filtered pale-orange light through narrow streets. Marion Janssen, M.D., lived, Sergeant de Gier reported, in a silver-grey slender-gable house at Gentlemen's Canal—a most superior address in the old city's very core. She was a widow. Paul Janssen was heir to a brand of good cookies. His death made her rich. And crazed, perhaps, the commissaris thought.

The commissaris was sorry now that something like this had happened to him again. He should have refused. Why would he accept a crazed citizen's bother?

Was he like the German university professor who striptease artist Marlene Dietrich made a despicable fool of in the movie *Blue Angel* that he owned on video—a self-destructive drama he watched sometimes, sipping hot cocoa, when Katrien was out?

Had he wished for a witch?

Was he caught up in some nonsense again?

Then, on the empty quay, in the thin early-summer-Sunday-morning's glow, as the only citizen about in a still-dehumanized city, he saw the dead tree.

There were lots of trees on the Gentlemen's Canal, spaced evenly—majestic elms branching out widely, each loaded with a million leaves—but only Marion's tree was dead. Its imposing skeleton gestured bleakly in front of an ailing house. The commissaris checked cracked basement windowsills and doors, painted recently, the paint already flaking off. The massive brass doorknob was dull. The granite steps were cracked. The house, seven stories high, seemed to be leaning far forward. He painfully climbed the steps to the front door, leaning on his cane, peering into the first-story windows.

No plants anywhere. No dog yapping. No slinky cat movements. No twittering sparrows, not even a crow in the dead tree, no pigeons fluttering around tiles or gutters. But this is Amsterdam, the commissaris thought, bird city. He did see waterfowl farther up and down the canal. On the water nearby there was only a duck, upside down.

The door opened. Marion, in a red kimono, attempted a smile of welcome. "See the dead duck? You think I shot it because I felt you were coming?"

So he believed her now.

"Explain it to me," Marion said, serving instant coffee.

He shrugged.

She pointed at his chest. "No, you're a chief of detectives, you hold a law degree. The papers say you're a genius. You're a public servant. Am I not the public?"

She slid out of her chair, knelt on the bare floor, touched his foot. "I know I'm doing this to myself. I'm sorry I killed Paul. There is no end to this misery. Please save me."

He just sat there, drinking the instant coffee that he didn't like. A neat little old gentleman who couldn't sleep and went for a walk and landed up in a demon's lair, a dying house in the midst of Old Amsterdam's splendor of graceful Golden Age architecture and ever-alive waterways. He saw the dead duck outside, orange webbed feet upward, mini-sails that caught the wind. He grimaced. The coffee was awful. Why didn't she serve filtered Sumatra, store-roasted at one of the city's deli-outlets? She drove a Ferrari.

"How's the Ferrari, Marion?"

"Carburetor trouble," she said, still kneeling. "The fuel injection gets clogged, too. They keep fixing it wrong. I'm walking everywhere now." She tugged the seam of his crisply ironed trouser leg. "My machines sicken, too."

He almost smiled. The coffee was bad, but having this exotic creature humiliating herself was pleasurable in a way. He sighed. One demon creates another?

"Please," Marion said.

"I'll see what my wife says," he said. "Let me go now and I'll ask her."


"So simple," Katrien said. "Look, I don't like your new woman, but surely she has suffered enough. Just do as I said."

"But Katrien—"

"Just do it."

So the black Cadillac, the Mayor's car—but the Mayor was a friend—drove up, escorted by two white BMW twin-cylinder motorcycles, ridden by extra-tall extra-wide Military Police sergeants—the MP colonel was another friend. The Mayor's driver wore his lackey uniform, with a triangle papier-maché hat. The sergeants rode in bearskins, white-leather crossbelts and pistol holders, black-baize uniforms, silver buttons, white braid. The commissaris wore a similar tunic and tight pants, but his buttons and braid were gold. His hat was flat, with more braid on the visor. Crowns shone on his shoulders. His boots were spit-polish. He wore his short sword.

("Oh, dear—" Katrien had laughed when she dressed him "—oh, dear.")

Marion opened the door. The commissaris, flanked by the sergeants, limped up the stone steps. The sergeants stopped at attention, the commissaris limped on.

Her large sitting room contained nothing but two straight chairs and a small rug. She sat on one chair, he on the other.

"Marion Janssen," the commissaris said, "you sinned, by your own rules, against another lifeform of your species. Since then you have punished yourself. You cannot undo your crime and neither can the crown, but the crown now forgives you. Kneel down on that rug."

He got up and unsheathed his sword. He touched her shoulder with the shiny steel. He sheathed the weapon, stood up straight, made his voice sing: "Rejoice and do better!"

* * *

"Did she feel better?" Katrien asked when she helped him take the stiff uniform off.

"She did," he said.

She yanked his boot. "Did she kiss you passionately afterward?"

"Please, Katrien," he said, rubbing a painful hip. "She cried, she trembled, she was awed. The poor thing wouldn't dare. I was the Queen's angel."

"Sure," Katrien said.

"But I do believe that horseplay you came up with broke the spell. She says she's off to Florida, to work in a clinic that breeds healthy offspring from damaged waterfowl—pelicans mostly, an endangered species."

"Good!" Katrien kissed his bald spot. "Good. I'm glad."

# BARBAROSSA AND COMPANY

*By Kathryn Gottlieb*

ON THE last Monday in hot and gritty August, I found myself marooned, to all intents and purposes, on the island of Manhattan. In my pockets were my flight ticket back to Geneva, an ancient address book, and not much else. I hadn't expected to stay more than a day. When I finally did get away, my pockets were bulging, my heart subverted, and my mind reeling.

Had she? Hadn't she? Had I aided and abetted? As to what happened, some will consider me an opportunist and some something worse, but—outside of the White House, or should I say Washington?—where are the moralists? The moral, of course, are everywhere.

The deal that had me hanging involved, as usual, surplus electronic equipment of the kind used by the military all over the world. Three years ago I opened an office in Geneva, for those reasons correctly associated in the public mind with conducting a business from there rather than, say, Cleveland, Ohio. I signed my first contract there on my twenty-ninth birthday, and it is my recollection that I fully expected to be a millionaire at thirty. That didn't happen—but one never knows, of course, about the future. Contrary to what Max told Anna, I am not a gun runner, and when I denied it, I told the truth: I do, however, sell equipment to governments you and I wouldn't vote for. But then, so does the U.S. government, so I make no apologies.

I had flown into New York that morning to wind up a business deal, but nothing was right and nothing was ready. Contracts and equipment were promised again, this time for the thirtieth, and I was left with a week to kill. Cash was low and nothing urgent called me back so I decided to wait it out. There was one stroke of luck—my old friend Hal Pierce handed me the key to his apartment. Hal's quarters occupy the front half of a reamed-out brownstone. You know the kind of place—bare brick walls, dying house plants, chrome, glass, last week's bread crumbs. The usual. Why do they do it? Why can't they at least leave the plaster on the walls?

Hal was on vacation, headed for Cape Cod. As soon as he took off I got busy with the telephone.

Two years can make a difference. Hedi Blume now had an unlisted phone, and so did Mary Bell. John Fischer, whose gallery handles paintings for me, was in Canada. George Becker's British secretary informed me in cutting tones that Mr. Becker was at the Vineyard. Toni Warren (female) didn't answer. Tony Marano (male) didn't answer. The whole world was out of town. Aggrieved, I walked out into the afternoon glare and into a place called Volstead's Retreat—it's a *cute* neighborhood—and picked up a bottle.

I was putting my change away when my eyes hit on a display of fine Holland gin—Bols Genever, in its brown earthen crocks—and I remembered Max Klinck.

There *was* someone to talk to after all.

Max is an incunabulist—for those of you not in the trade, a dealer in rare books and manuscripts. He is a towering, red-bearded Dutchman with blazing blue eyes and a wooden leg of the best bird's-eye maple—which is, he assures me, much handsomer than the other. Max was a war casualty after the war ended. One day while playing with other children on the sandy beach of Oostmahom on the North Sea, he had the misfortune to trigger off a buried land mine. He was eight or nine at the time.

I find Max a genial man with no illusions about the world—it's a bad place, he says, and he's lucky to be in it. I was first introduced to him a couple of years ago in John Fischer's gallery on one of his rare ventures away from East 74th Street, where, in the ordinary course of work, he handles some of the rarest and most beautiful books in the world. I can imagine, perhaps foolishly, no more satisfying life.

Max is clumsy on his crutches, and attracts every eye. It is no pleasure for him to go out in the world and he rarely leaves his desk. And that, at the end of a fast hot walk up Lexington Avenue, is where I found him—but only after a brief and curious episode which barely caught my attention at the time.

Reaching 74th Street, I paused in front of Max's establishment to mop my forehead and collect myself for a moment before going in. The place is, like Hal's, an old brownstone, but its antique and rotting splendor has so far escaped improvement. Max calls himself, for business purposes, "Barbarossa"—the name had been fixed beside the doorway in small bronze letters. I was taken aback a little to see that the letters had gone and in their place was a sign that said "Barbarossa and Company." I shook my head. Was Max about to vanish too?

I was frowning at the words when the heavy door at the top of the steps flew open and a small man hurried down to the sidewalk. I'd have paid no attention to him if he hadn't paid attention to me, attempting, as he brushed past, to conceal his face with a sudden, awkward lift of his hand.

I looked after him, curious. A little past middle age, heavy-featured, expensively tailored, vaguely familiar: not someone known to me, but someone well known. The name escaped me. No matter. What mattered was if Max was in.

I climbed the stairs, rang, and was admitted. The first floor is devoted to the sale of fine and rare books, and is presided over by staff. Max's private domain, where treasures change hands, is up a flight of stairs. One of the first floor flunkeys rang ahead to announce my name and unlocked an iron gate toward the rear of the place. I mounted the mahogany-railed flight into Max's worm-eaten paradise and there he was, behind his desk, beaming, bellowing a welcome, his eyes sparkling, the same old Max.

"Sit! Sit!" he commanded, and I did, first gazing all around with remembered pleasure. A fine place to work, of handsome proportions, dark paneled, shelved all around, smelling of leather and ancient paper and noble dust.

"Max, I envy you."

He grinned at me. "Don't be a damn fool. You're fine?"

"I'm fine. You?"

He nodded, reached behind his chair, took from a shelf a crock of Holland gin and two ruby tumblers, and filled them. I took my glass and he took his. "Now," he said, "tell me everything."

What was he—friend? acquaintance?—I was never sure. In any category, good company. But, for all the surface sparkle, the wit and gratifying curiosity, Max runs deep, and I have never known what Max was thinking.

We talked through several refills: about my business, some gossip—what else can I call it?—about mutual friends. He described to me, in a tone of cordial condescension, some of the peculiar treasures that had lately come into his hands. Max says that I am illiterate, and by his standards that's so. And then I remembered.

"Barbarossa and Company," I said. "What's that all about?"

"Ah! I have a partner. Wait, wait till you meet her. You will say I am the luckiest fellow in the world."

Directly behind Max's desk is a wall of the controlled-atmosphere room that serves as vault and workroom, where his earliest and most fragile wares are stored. Max swung around in his chair and directed a shout at the wall. "Anna!" And again, a good bellow, "Anna!" There was silence for a moment, then the door to the strongroom swung open and Max's new partner stepped into the room.

She smiled at me. Yes, a beautiful woman. "Anneke. This is Peter Hessberg, whom I have not seen for two years. Anna Eykert." She took a step forward and extended her hand to me, a good square hand. I grasped it.

Another tumbler appeared. Anna sat and we had gin all around. There was chitchat, and then Max said, "Peter has a most interesting profession."

"Oh?"

"He is a gun runner."

Anna's eyes looked into mine. "Listen to him! Is that true?" Her voice was round and clear, with an undertone of amusement. The cadences were foreign.

"No."

She shook her head. "I thought not. Max is a terrible liar. A terrible liar." She looked at him fondly. A little unwarranted pang of jealousy pinched off my smile. Why was I jealous—what was Anna to me? Is there such a thing as jealousy at first sight?

Max was speaking. "Indeed a small world. Anna grew up in my own little village by the North Sea."

"It is called Oostmahom," said Anna. "Have you heard of it?"

"He has heard of it from me," said Max. "Peter is the only man in America who has heard of Oostmahom."

We talked on, of inconsequential things, while I stared at the woman from Oostmahom. She conformed to no conception of beauty that I consciously carried around with me, but she was beautiful just the same: a good body of the sturdy kind; a broad and well modeled face; long, heavy-lidded blue eyes under straight brows; and a marvelously shaped mouth. When she spoke, I couldn't look away. Her hair was very fair, very thick, cut short— very Dutch. I told myself that she was stocky, square-jawed, and too old for me. My age, at least. And, of course, she belonged to Max, who said, "You're looking thoughtful."

I shrugged.

Anna asked me if I made my home in New York.

"Geneva."

She raised her eyebrows. "Such an elderly city! Are you happy there? It is so cold. So grey! And the people—nobody speaks!"

"Money speaks," said Max.

"Ah, that's dreadful," said Anna. "It is rude. Don't pay any attention to

him, Mr. Hessberg. He has no humor. No funniness. He lacks good quali-
ties."

"Peter sometimes deals in paintings," said Max. She shot him a look—
startled, I thought—which he did not return. "Tell Anna about your business. It is interesting."

The units I purchase from the U.S. military I ship to Amsterdam to my
friend Piet Bonta at P. Bonta Electrische, N.V., where they are tested,
rebuilt, and shipped out to my clients—in most cases, the so-called third-
world governments, who pay me a long time after with first-world money.
All this I described, briefly, for Anna's benefit, omitting the problems.

When I finished, she said, "I think Max is right. You are a gun runner. I
see no difference. One of those terrible people who keep the world in a
ferment."

"You might not approve of my customers, but they're legitimate governments, all of them. I don't deal with terrorist organizations."

Max raised his coppery eyebrows. "All governments are terrorist organizations."

"Don't be childish," said Anna, laughing.

"It's true," said Max. "Someday you will agree with me. Now, Peter, tell
Anna about the paintings."

From time to time business takes me to Africa; the new nations—uncomfortable places, but they fascinate me. In the last couple of years paintings,
along with other heirlooms, have begun to surface; pathetic, abandoned
collections, once the property of families established for generations in colonial Africa. Those families are gone; most left empty-handed, the victims
of upheaval. Some of the paintings belonged to the dead. Most are the sort
of thing you couldn't give away just a few years back: landscapes, genre—
nineteenth century, most of them, modest, agreeable works. Today there's
a market for them. What comes my way I ship to New York, to John
Fischer's gallery.

Anna listened to me, frowning. "I think it is sad," she said.

Max, on the other hand, looked pleased. "I think Providence has sent
our friend here today."

"No. No, Max. I know what you are thinking."

"He has a whole week to waste. Surely he doesn't want to spend it in this
grimy city!"

"Then let him spend it in Timbuktu. Oh, Max—" she clasped her hands
"—I am not happy about this!"

"What are you talking about?" I asked them.

Max leaned forward, his powerful arms resting on the polished surface of
his admirable desk. "I have promised to pick up a painting in Amsterdam
and bring it back here this week. Nothing out of the ordinary—a little

nineteenth century landscape, the kind of thing you have just been describing.

"I am doing this as a favor for a client who is important to me. He has formed a sentimental attachment to this painting—and he must have it at once." Max laughed shortly. "I can tell you, he is a man who is accustomed to getting what he wants. So, I have very foolishly undertaken to pick it up for him myself. Peter, I don't want to go. I don't know when I was last out of the city. Or *in* the city." He nodded in the direction of the crutches propped against the wall behind his desk. "I totter through the streets like a falling building. Heads turn."

"Can't Anna—"

"I need her here. Listen to me, Peter. New York in August is an abomination. You don't want to stay here. I will pay you a nice fee—let's say ten percent of the selling price—and all expenses, of course. You'll pick up the painting from the dealer, a man named Gerrit Till. He is ten, twelve miles outside the city, that's all. And you'll bring it here."

"What kind of money are we talking about?"

He grimaced. "I am almost ashamed to tell you. My selling price is twenty thousand dollars. As you will see, too much money for this little painting. For your share? Two thousand."

"Do you mind telling me how much you're paying for it?"

"Not at all. After all, you will pay the dealer for us. Two thousand dollars, that's all. In cash. It's worth a little more to him that way."

"Is the buyer that fellow who was leaving when I got here?"

Anna's eyes widened. "What?"

Max shook his head. "No, no. You would not know this man, you have not seen him here. Who it is doesn't matter. What do you say?"

"What's the catch?"

"None." His gaze was a model of candor. "This is not a painting that the Netherlands Historical Commission is interested in. There are no restrictions against its sale or export. I promise you there is nothing to worry about. If I could move around more easily I'd go myself. And I'll tell you the truth—Anna had a little run-in with the commission a few years ago. So I prefer not to send her. Why stir up old complications?"

A plausible tale. Did I believe it?

Again Anna glanced at him and for some moments their eyes carried on a mutual discussion. Then she said, almost whispering, "I have a bad feeling about this."

"Anneke, my love. This is nonsense!"

Anneke-my-love shook her head, and the fine fair hair flew back and forth. "No."

"You'll do it?" Max asked me.

Anna's blue eyes held mine, willing me to refuse.

"I'll do it."

It was agreed I would go on Wednesday, as the painting wouldn't be ready before then. Max said there had been a little damage to a corner of the landscape—no more than a square inch was involved—and Gerrit Till, the dealer, who was fortunately an expert in restoration, was doing the necessary patch-up. I was not to be concerned—the buyer was aware of the state of the canvas.

"Gerrit's a fine fellow," Max told me. "Interesting, too. An Indonesian background. A good contact for you. Maybe someday you'll do business with him yourself—who knows?"

Anna left with me. It had begun to rain, bringing up a strong smell of wet stone and city dust from the sidewalks.

The afternoon had grown prematurely dark. Here and there the lights of store windows were reflected on the pavement; the city looked cosy and glistening. I walked beside Anna for a block or two toward the East River. She seemed distracted and had nothing to say. She disliked me, I thought, or distrusted me. I stopped under a street lamp at the corner of Third Avenue and put a hand on her arm. "Why don't you want me to go?"

She shrugged. "Max knows that I would be glad to do it, but he says I mustn't. He is stubborn, something terrible. It's a waste of money to send you, that's all."

"That's not the only reason. I think I ought to know."

"I've told you, there's nothing else. Now if you don't mind, I'll go along without you."

"Why should I mind?" In the harsh light of the street lamp she looked a little older than she had in Max's softly-lit domain, but only by an hour or two. Max's property.

I bent my head and kissed her forehead. I said, "I'll bet you were a beautiful woman."

"I *am* a beautiful woman," said Anna serenely. She patted my arm and walked off down the street.

Forty-eight hours later I turned the key in the door of my apartment in Amsterdam and threw open the windows to the familiar maritime air. For the past two years I've rented the ground floor of a skinny old house on Verimus Straat that belongs to a youngish widow who lives on the upper floors. We maintain a pleasant, if formal, relationship. Our paths cross occasionally in the little entrance hall we share, and when they do we talk about the weather. My part of the house consists of a sunny, bow-windowed front room that serves me as office and sitting room and a small bedroom opening off it. At the very back there's a tiny kitchen, and at the back of that a window looks out over a walled garden. A narrow road, little used, runs past the end of the garden, and beyond lies a stretch of low, open land—whence the sea-tasting breezes. I have no staff working for me there, but I keep duplicates of the files on current contracts. It's a useful, peaceful place, and quite handy to Piet Bonta's factory.

I slept until mid-afternoon, then I drove out in the direction of the coast along the road that took me to Ihmuiden, turning off to the north, as instructed, just past the ISOL Works on a potholed road through land that appeared unstable and was surely empty. Over my head a pewter sky hung heavy, wide, and unsupported—there appeared to be nothing to keep it from moving downward in a swift, enveloping motion. I told myself not to be fanciful. I had been under a lot of grey Dutch skies and none had ever fallen on my head.

Still, land and weather were oppressive, and my worries returned. I asked myself why they had sent me here and why I'd been fool enough to come. Besides the cash, of course. It must be very nice to be rich and not have to do foolish things for money.

Five miles beyond the turnoff I came to a cluster of little houses, then emptiness again, and then, alone in the fields, Gerrit Till's house, a small, ill-proportioned place too tall for its base, standing in a stretch of empty fenland. I pulled to the side of the road and got out of the car. The place was dead quiet except for the whine of the wind in the wires over my head. What a place to live! I crossed the road, climbed the steps, and rang the bell.

Gerrit Till opened the door and I recalled Max's reference to an Indonesian background. Dark Oriental eyes, sparkling with welcome, looked out at me from a round Dutch face, surmounted by a thatch of fair and greying hair.

"I'm Peter Hessberg."

"Of course! I am expecting you. Come in!" His voice was deep, his English, like Anna's, without accent but European in its cadences. He showed me into a room jammed with books and papers and heavy Dutch furniture. There was a smell of turpentine in the air. Business, said Gerrit Till, could wait a moment. First we must have a drink together—and he poured the inevitable portions of Genever. I accepted mine, smiling, very much at my ease—I found him charming, likeable.

He was talkative. How were Max and Anna? What did I think of the art market? Did I know there was quite a market suddenly in the paintings of Albert Boertson? Very odd. What did I think, was there any merit in them? It was so very good of me to come. He hoped I had had a pleasant journey. We talked, we drank. "Now," he said, "if you will excuse me for a moment."

He went out through a door toward the rear of the room, shutting it behind him. There would be a kitchen back there, I supposed—the usual layout. I realized with surprise that we were not alone in the house. I heard his voice, at least I supposed it to be his—just a murmur through the heavy door—and then a woman laughed, and I thought I heard her say *es niet stom, es niet stom!*—don't be silly!—and then a man's voice, his, no doubt, the words indistinguishable.

A moment later he came back into the room. The painting was under his arm. He placed it across the arms of a chair and stooped to look at it, grunting.

"I'm getting to be an old man, with old complaints," he said with a laugh. "Would you believe it? I had a letter today from my mother, who is in Soerabaya. She worries and she scolds me—she thinks I am a boy still, a boy who does not take care of himself. She is very old now. I suppose I will always seem like a child to her. Well, come, let us examine this painting."

I moved to his side.

"It's nice, isn't it?"

I nodded. It was very nice. An ordinary, pleasant landscape, sentimental in the way of the past century, and somehow very attractive. A quiet scene —blue sky, broken clouds above a broad valley, and in the foreground a wide-branched oak and a cow placidly cropping grass.

"Behold the cow," said Gerrit Till. "I cannot look at her without wanting to sleep. All summer afternoon is in that cow."

I agreed, laughing. "It's very well done."

"You realize that there is a little patch in the corner. Max knows about this, of course."

"He told me you had had to do some work on it."

"Can you smell it? Poof!" He wrinkled his nose. "You do not mind the smell of turpentine?"

"No, I don't mind it."

"It should vanish soon enough."

He then disappeared himself through the door at the rear, returning with paper and string, and proceeded to wrap the painting neatly. "Voilà!" he said. "She is ready to travel."

I was leaving when I remembered the money. He hadn't mentioned it. I dug it out of my pocket—a packet of American bills of mixed denominations—and handed it to him.

He took it, smiling.

I said, "It doesn't seem enough."

"That's true. It's worth a little more. Max, of course, will get more. But I owe Max some favors. This is fine. I am satisfied."

I drove back to Amsterdam. The weather hadn't improved, but my spirits were considerably higher. Why not, I thought, have dinner with Piet Bonta?

There was no reason to conceal the fact that I was in Amsterdam. Everything was on the up-and-up.

Piet, as I mentioned earlier, is head of the plant that reprocesses most of the equipment I buy and sell. We met at seven at a place run by Pauli BenBroek on the Reguliergraat—nothing fancy, but you get good food there, and plenty of it. We talked for a while about this and that. Maia and the kids were fine, the problems were almost solved with the last shipment of battery chargers I had shipped over—an ordinary conversation. And then Piet, shaking the sauce bottle over his rice, said that he didn't know what the world was coming to. "You would think," he said, "that at least outside the city you would be safe in your own home. But now I don't know. Did you hear the radio?"

"I haven't had it on. What happened?"

"Some fellow was shot to death this afternoon right in his own home. A harmless old man, it sounds like. Perhaps not old—I don't remember."

"It's terrible, all right. Sounds like New York. Was it a robbery? You know," I said, waving a fork at him, pontificating my way through—had I known it—my last carefree moment, "the way to cut down on this sort of thing is to get rid of the fences. As I understand it, you can place your order for your favorite brand of TV or a yellow Toyota and they'll pick it up for you in twenty-four hours."

"This wasn't a TV," said Piet. "They think a picture was stolen."

I put my fork down. "A painting?"

"Yes. I think they said it was an oil painting. This fellow's body was found by a woman who comes late in the afternoon to cook his dinner and tidy up. It seems he was an art dealer. She had seen him working on a painting—touching up the frame, she thinks, or putting varnish on. Is that possible?"

"Yes."

"Well, whatever it was, she noticed him working on it yesterday afternoon. Nothing of great value, she says—a picture with a cow in it, ordinary stuff. But this woman says that today it's not there."

"Maybe he sold it."

"That could be. Or maybe some hoodlums who broke in looking for a color TV took the painting instead. God knows! In any case, the fellow was shot and he's dead. It's a terrible world when you're not safe in your own house."

"Where did this happen?"

"It was out along one of those roads in the direction of Ihmuiden. I'll tell you the truth, I never cared for the area myself. It's desolate. But people live there. There's no accounting for tastes."

I pushed my plate away.

"You're not hungry?"

I shook my head. "I had a late lunch."

"Oh."

"Did the radio say anything else?"

"About the killing? Oh yes, it was full of it. Let's see. An old lady who lives down the road, closer in to the city, told the police she saw a little blue car going down the road in the afternoon. She thinks it must have come from the dead man's house since no one lives beyond. A blue station wagon. Don't ask me how she saw it. Maybe she has a telescope. Wonderful witnesses, old men and women. They sit all day in their parlor windows and witness." He made a wry face; the clear blue eyes caught mine for a moment with a look of amusement. "That's how we'll end our days, old friend. Witnesses."

"I wonder—"

"Yes?"

"Nothing. As you say, hoodlums out for a lark. Or a killing. Well. Have you finished?"

"Oh, yes." Piet patted his stomach. "No dessert. I promised Maia to take off five pounds. It's the only birthday present she wants. I'd rather give her a diamond necklace." He pushed back his chair. "Will I see you at the plant tomorrow morning?"

"I doubt it. Not this trip. I have business to do at the bank and then I'm due back in New York."

He looked at me thoughtfully. "All right. Let's go." He walked out with me to the cobbled road beside the canal and stood talking odds and ends of business, leaning with one arm braced against the hood of the car. Suddenly he paused, smiled, and said, "Aha! Here's a little blue station wagon right under my elbow! You didn't drive to Ihmuiden today, yourself?"

I smiled too. "Damned if I can remember. You'd better watch your fingerprints."

When he had covered a dozen yards in the direction of his own car he looked back and called to me, "Gerrit something. Do you know the name?"

I shook my head.

The painting seemed to be what it seemed to be. I examined it, my door locked, blinds drawn, for a quarter of an hour, tilting it this way and that, running my fingers over the surface. I remembered Gerrit Till's wiry body crouched down in front of the painting, his voice saying something about the cow and summer afternoons. Dead. I frowned at the painting. No one would have killed for it. I reminded myself that no one had. The proof of that was here in my hands. I had the painting, and I had paid for it fair and square. And yet, an odd-chance break-in? I didn't believe it. The police didn't believe it, either. They were looking for a blue station wagon.

I covered the picture with a blanket, stepped out into the hallway, and shouted up the unlit staircase. After a moment a light went on and Mevrouw Hendrix appeared on the landing above. She was clutching an old bathrobe, a man's robe, about her. She looked apprehensive, a little absurd, and very pretty. "What's wrong?" she asked me.

"Nothing's wrong. I'm sorry to disturb you. Do you have a flashlight?"

"Has your electric gone off?"

"Nothing like that. I just want to look at something."

"I'll get it for you." She came down the stairs, crowded past me in the narrow hallway. I allowed myself to observe all those attributes to which in her case I normally closed my eyes—the fine-grained skin, the silky hair now falling over her shoulders, the desirable figure. I reminded myself that this was no time to abrogate, as they say at The Hague, my nonintervention policy. I heard her rattling things in the little pantry behind the stairs and then she was back with a square plastic flashlight which she put into my hands. After a considering glance which met my eyes, she climbed the stairs.

I waved the flashlight at her. "I'll bring this up to you later."

"No, thank you. When you are finished using it, put it on the stairs. I'll pick it up in the morning.

"But—"

"We have a perfect relationship," she said firmly. "Let's not tinker with it. We meet, we talk about the weather, we will go on that way."

"Tina—"

She closed the door.

The flashlight revealed what ordinary lamplight had failed to disclose, minute elevations and depressions in the clear blue patches of sky. It was the only anomaly I could find. The brushwork in the area should have been smooth, and it was, but something lay underneath. Gerrit would have been wiser to fill the sky with storm clouds—the busy brushwork would have concealed the brushstrokes underneath. But then, of course, the cow's afternoon would have been spoiled.

I spent a restless night, pacing through the little rooms, gazing alternately across the dark salt meadows at the back and out into the street, where foot traffic, none of it sober, went on through the night. I kept my windows locked, carried the steel-tipped roller of a window shade for a weapon, and knew myself for a fool. There was no longer any doubt in my mind that Gerrit Till's death was connected with the painting, that Max and Anna had sent me there to avoid danger to themselves, and that the painting now resting under my mattress was a national treasure. I felt a strong urge to get rid of it—to dump it in the nearest canal—and the nearest canal wasn't far. But I can't drown a kitten and I can't drown a painting. Art lives.

Near dawn I dozed off in the armchair in the bay window, and when I awoke—don't ask me how the mind works—I knew the name of the man who had walked quickly and furtively out of Max's doorway. We have all seen his picture in the papers. Ambrose Voyt—multimillionaire, art collector, a man of unknown origins and manifest destiny.

Ambrose Voyt, it is said, buys nothing worth less than half a million. I looked at the time. It was half past five, and the housefronts opposite were pink in the early light. I got to my feet, made myself a cup of coffee, drank it, tore the paper backing off the picture, studied it, killed time till the stores opened, went out, returned the car, wasn't arrested, came back on foot with packages, and said goodbye to the cow.

"Thank God you're back," said Max. "You are back, aren't you? Where are you calling from?"

"I'm back."

"I expected to see you two days ago. What happened?"

I told him I'd had a number of things to take care of.

"Do you have the painting with you?"

"Yes."

There was a sigh of relief. "It is charming, is it not?"

"Charming."

"You'll bring it right around?"

I said I was afraid I couldn't do that.

There was a throbbing silence, and then Max said, in a voice I hardly recognized, "What's wrong?"

I told him I thought perhaps there'd been a little misunderstanding and that I'd be there shortly to talk things over.

I let an hour go by and then walked uptown. Max nodded when I came into his presence and motioned me to a chair. He was pale, and—it may have been my imagination—his hair seemed to have lost its coppery gleam. Anna was there, composed and unsmiling. No one could be beautiful, I thought, who didn't look like Anna. Moments passed in a heavy silence and then Max spoke. "I hope you're not going to tell me something has happened to that painting. It's not damaged?"

"No. Nothing like that."

"And you brought it back with you?" I nodded. "Good, then!" He forced a smile. "It's the money, is it? I'll give you your money and *then* you'll bring it here. How's that?"

I said nothing.

"Or perhaps you'd like us to pick it up. Anna will go back with you to wherever you are staying, and perhaps you would not mind to see her safely back here."

"It's not that simple."

Max stiffened and looked away—not at Anna, just away, then back. "Perhaps you will tell us what it is that is not simple."

"Our arrangement, Max. Ten percent—"

"Ah!" He smiled. "Perhaps I have been ungenerous. And of course we are very grateful. Shall we say fifteen? Although I must say I would not have expected this of you. After all, we made our bargain."

"Ten percent's fine. Ten percent of the selling price."

"Yes. As we agreed. Two thousand dollars."

"Forty."

"Oh!" said Anna.

"Explain yourself," said Max, in a voice of ice.

I settled back in my chair. "Let's have some schnapps, Max—then we can talk like civilized people. And you don't have to worry—I'm not going to tell you anything you don't already know."

Max reached for the bottle on the shelf behind him, not taking his eyes off me. Anna handed me a tumbler, staring at me from an immeasurable distance.

I waited until she was back in her chair. "Gerrit Till is dead."

Anna's hand flew to cover her mouth. Max looked wary.

"Murdered."

"No," said Anna. "Oh, please, no!" Her hand dropped to her lap. The dismay in her voice and in her eyes was real.

I felt a rush of anger. "Do you know that his mother is living? An old, old woman living out in the Indies somewhere? Her heart will be broken." I looked from one to the other of them. "It was a wicked thing to kill that man."

"Yes, it was," said Max. "Tell us what happened."

I described what the broadcast had said, in particular the statement of the housekeeper, who had found the body at about five o'clock when she turned up to fix the murdered man's dinner. The morning newspaper had described her as grief-stricken.

"Oh, it's so sad," said Anna. "It's so sad."

I said, "You set me up, you two."

"What?" said Max. "What?"

"I've had plenty of time to think things out. You bought that painting for Ambrose Voyt—" Max's jaw tightened "—and I figure that makes it worth half a million. But I can't be sure, so let's say, at a conservative guess, four hundred thousand. All right? At a hundred percent markup you would have had to pay Gerrit Till two hundred thousand—a quarter of a million, maybe. The two thousand you gave me to hand him was to pacify me, not to pay him. He laughed when I gave it to him. Now I understand why."

"This is fascinating," said Max. "Here—let me fill your glass."

"No, thank you. You gave him his quarter million, waited for me to pick up the painting—which I so obligingly did for you—shot him, and took back your money. Ambrose Voyt's money."

"But why send you?" said Max. "Why didn't I do it all myself?" He smiled at me. "You're my good friend, Peter, but you're a crazy fellow, too."

"You sent me—" I groped for a reason "—to get the merchandise through customs. To be seen. I am known to be a dealer, after all, in a small way. To take the heat off, Max! Why do I have to tell you this? You know it better than I do. If they had picked me up, who would have believed I didn't kill him? I was there. My car was seen."

"This is nonsense." He poured himself a gin, drank it, and set the tumbler down with a sigh. "That's better. Look, this has all been a great shock, you know? Gerrit was a fine man. What has happened is terrible. And you—I am afraid you are suffering from an overwrought imagination. The painting is what it is, no more—a pretty little landscape—and it reminds Ambrose Voyt of the farming country where he was born—somewhere in Eastern Europe, I think. He's a sentimental man. The picture is worth twenty thousand to him, and half that to anyone else. Less. Everything else is fantasy."

I got to my feet.

Anna spoke. "Max and I have been here in the city the whole time you were gone. *The whole time.*" Her voice was earnest, and her eyes shining with the will to be believed.

I walked to the door at the head of the stairs.

"Where do I reach you?" Max's voice was calm, but I heard the turbulence underneath. It reminded me of the blue sky Gerrit Till had painted over the unknown work.

"I'll call you tomorrow after the banks are open," I said.

Max came thumping into Hal's apartment a little after half past ten in the morning. Anna was with him. I indicated the sofa. He handed Anna his crutches and they both sat down.

He gazed around the room as though he hadn't a thing on his mind. "This is your friend's apartment?"

I nodded. "It's hideous, isn't it?"

He looked at me for confirmation. "Who would do this to such a handsome old house?"

He turned to Anna.

"Oh, Max," she said faintly, "I don't want to talk about this."

But Max was himself again. His hair had regained its fire. "That painting over your chair, Peter. Behind your chair, should I say? Dreadful!"

I turned my head and squinted up at the painting: broad black slashes crossing a dead-white ground. Up and down, left and right. Zip-zap.

"A poor man's Kline," said Max. "And if I am not mistaken, a left-handed painter." He narrowed his eyes. "Who is it, Peter? Can you tell me?"

I obligingly swiveled around again. " 'P.H.,' 'P.L.,' something like that."

"Peyell?" He shrugged. "It's not familiar."

"Please, Max," said Anna. "Can't we do what we came to do and get out of here?"

"Of course," said Max. "Peter, the painting."

"The money."

He brought out a sheaf of bills and placed them on the table beside the sofa. "Two thousand," he said. "We'll forget yesterday's nonsense."

"Forty."

"No," said Max. "I'm sorry Gerrit was killed. May I remind you, I have known him longer than you. And I'm sorry for his mother as well. She is a fine woman—no one should have to suffer so. But what happened has nothing to do with Anna or with me, nothing whatsoever. My dear friend, I must insist that you hand over the painting."

I shook my head.

"Oh, for God's sake!" Anna jumped to her feet. "Max will give you the money, the forty thousand. All you are asking. We deceived you about the value of the painting, that's true—but you wouldn't have brought it out if we hadn't, would you? You know you wouldn't! We had no intention to place you in jeopardy and we didn't! We didn't! The customs people didn't make any trouble, did they? What happened was a coincidence, a terrible coincidence! Unless—" a look of the remotest amusement crossed her face "—*you* didn't do something foolish, did you?"

That wasn't worth an answer and it didn't get one.

"Max—pay him. You promised me—you promised me."

"No," Max said. "He has not a shred of evidence. Of course—" he looked at me "—the blackmailer is in a position of power. Accusation is a powerful weapon, a bludgeon. I assure you I understand that. But I repeat —you have no evidence."

"Evidence can be gathered," I told him. "Let's say I start with the passenger lists of airlines flying into Schiphol on Tuesday."

"I doubt if they will be made available to you."

"The police will have no trouble getting hold of them."

"Max, I beg you. He is crazy. He will make endless trouble." Anna was staring at the floor, all color gone from her face.

Max looked at her for a long moment, a peculiar slanting look under half-lowered lids. "All right, Peter," he said in a toneless voice. "I agree to your terms. Let's have it."

"The money, if you don't mind."

He reached into a pocket, and this time the roll of bills was considerably thicker. He threw them onto the little table with a gesture of contempt, then put out a hand and fanned the money across the surface. He didn't remove his hand. "Don't touch it." There was no emotion in his voice, but a nerve jumped spasmodically under his eye. "I'll have the painting first. You are to understand that this is your commission at ten percent of approximate value. That is all it is. It is neither an admission nor a coverup. It is an adjustment of price and an abatement of a nuisance."

"Fine."

"Let's have it then." He placed himself between me and the table, unsteady on his feet but managing without the crutches, which Anna was holding with a white-knuckled grasp.

I turned away from them and lifted the poor man's Kline down from the wall.

"Oh," said Anna.

"That's it?"

"It's there. Under your landscape, where you buried it."

"If you have damaged it!" His eyes were bulging. "It is priceless!"

"If your landscape didn't do it any harm, then my small effort didn't hurt it either," I told him. He opened his mouth and shut it again. "Tell me," I went on, "how did you protect the painting when Gerrit painted over it? That is—was—his landscape?" I smiled at them. "Gone now, I'm afraid."

Anna's voice was vibrant with relief. "It's overpainted on a styrene wrap. Three-millimeter. It's a trick to get it to take the paint, of course. Gerrit knew what to do." At the mention of his name, she burst into tears.

I looked at Max. "What's under it?"

"You don't want to know," said Max. He took his crutches and they left without another word. Anna carried the painting.

I picked up the money from the table and went to the door to close it. Max and Anna were standing just inside the old fashioned vestibule. I saw Max shift his crutches, then reach out and brush the tears from Anna's cheeks with his strong, ruddy fingers. Then he leaned down and murmured something very low. Anna smiled. The heavy glass door muffled her words, but I heard the familiar rise and fall of her voice. "I'm all right," I think I heard her say. "Really, I'm all right."

They left.

I told myself I wasn't stealing, only demanding a fair return on a business deal. Nor was I concealing a crime. I had no shred of evidence in my possession, only a moral certainty; some words not clearly overheard and a theory that could indeed have fit the case and was quite possibly wrong. And Max, of course, had given me the money. I closed the door and turned back, a sour old man of thirty-two, wondering what the use of money was anyway.

I finished up my business in New York and flew back to Geneva.

I keep thinking of Anna, standing in the vestibule, crying. What if I'm wrong? Is it possible for a woman with such a broad, calm brow, such eyes, such lips, to murder a decent man—or any man—in cold blood, even for a substantial sum of money? I tell myself it isn't. And yet, there is Anna's trick of repeating her words, and the recollection of a voice, a murmur, behind a heavy door—someone saying to Gerrit Till, in the last hour of his life, *es niet stom*—don't be silly—and saying it again.

I'll be back in New York in October. I'll ask her to have dinner with me, just the two of us. We'll talk all evening, quite possibly all night, and Anna will tell me all I want to know.

But how much do I really want to know?

Maybe we'll just talk about the weather.

But I should know the truth, shouldn't I? The truth is an absolute good.

*Es niet stom*. I'd rather have Anna.

# THE GYPSY BEAR

*By Edward D. Hoch*

I T WAS on one of Michael Vlado's periodic journeys into the city to buy supplies for his horses that he encountered the dancing bear named Vladimir. He was a big brown beast, a bit shaggy, but friendly in appearance, and about five feet tall when he stood on his hind legs.

Michael liked the bear at once but couldn't say as much for its owners, a Gypsy couple with two small children and a horse-drawn wagon. In the Romany world, bear tamers were only one step above beggars and looked down upon by most other Gypsies. As he petted the animal, Michael was aware of the owners' eyes on him. Finally the man came over and warned, "Be careful, Vladimir's been known to bite strangers."

"Never one offering money, though," the woman said, trying out her smile on Michael. She was young—barely out of her teens despite the two children—and looked like a dirty-haired child herself. She wore a plain grey sweater, a multicolored skirt that hung unevenly below her knees, and a scarf that seemed to match the skirt.

Her husband's name was Zoran Nikoli and her name was Cashmere. They had come up from Turkey earlier in the year, working their way through Bulgaria and into Romania, living on what the bear earned and what they could beg. "Do you have a Gypsy village nearby?" the man asked Michael.

"Up in the mountains," Michael answered, purposely vague. "I've come down to buy supplies."

"We have been traveling long and are looking for a place to stay. The police have told us to move from this park."

"Romania isn't a friendly place for Gypsies," Michael told them. "In fact, the government's official position is that there are no Gypsies at all in the country—despite the fact that our nineteen seventy-seven census showed nearly a quarter of a million."

Zoran Nikoli was unimpressed. "We are travelers, unconcerned with governments and boundary lines."

The bear had begun to lick Michael's hand in a gesture of friendship and as Michael patted the furry head, he relented a bit. "You could stay in our village for a short time if you wish. It's about two hours from here."

"Who is the king of your tribe?" Cashmere asked.

"Our king died last year. I have assumed his powers."

"Such a young man to be a Gypsy king!" she marveled.

"Not as young as all that. I was born during the war and named for King Michael, the Romanian leader at the time."

A small crowd had begun to gather around the wagon, attracted by Vladimir. Performing bears were a rare sight in the city—a rare sight even for local Gypsies—and among the spectators Michael recognized Rajko, a gold-toothed Rom from a nearby village. Zoran and Cashmere were quick to react to this sudden display of interest. Zoran produced a drum and a long pole and the bear went into his act. While Zoran beat out a crude rhythm on the drum, he guided Vladimir through its dance routine with the pole and a chain around its neck.

Rajko spotted Michael and came over to stand by him. "Who are these beggars with their bear?" he asked.

"They come from Turkey."

"Then better they go back there. The girl has the evil eye."

When Vladimir had completed his performance, the two children ran among the spectators with wicker baskets held out for donations. Michael noticed only a few lei were thrown in and he added a ten-leu coin himself.

Zoran watched as Cashmere counted up the coins. "We will never get rich in this country!" he said with disgust, snatching the coins from her hand as she finished the count.

"Then begone from us!" Rajko told him, leaning close as he spat out the words.

Zoran merely smiled and asked, "Why do so many Rom in this area cover their teeth with gold? You must be rich, to carry your money in your mouth."

Michael could see that the two men were fast becoming enemies. It was true that Romanian Gypsies liked to cap their teeth with gold, but he'd

never heard it remarked on before. It was a custom he took for granted.
"They will have their knives out in another minute," Cashmere remarked,
coming to sit by Michael in the shadow of the wagon.

"Can't you calm your husband down?"

"I lost a tooth the last time I tried it. Now I let him fight if he has a mind
to. If he dies, he dies."

"We live very differently in my village," he told her. "We respect human
life."

As he spoke, Rajko made an insulting remark to Zoran and the Turkish
Gypsy drew his knife before Michael could move: "Bite on this with your
gold teeth!" he snarled, lunging forward. Rajko went over backward trying
to ward off the blade and the two rolled in the dust, locked in combat.
Cashmere leaped to her feet, but only to secure Vladimir's chain before the
suddenly freed bear decided to wander off on its own.

Michael cursed softly and reluctantly entered the fray, first trying unsuccessfully to pull the men apart and then placing a few well directed kicks
with his heavy boots. Finally Rajko broke free and crawled away. Michael's
boot came down on Zoran's hand before it could reach the knife again and
the brief battle was over.

"Get out of here," Michael told the local Gypsy. "We've had enough
fighting for one day." Rajko grumbled but moved away, his passion cooling.

Cashmere bent over her husband and wiped the streak of blood from his
lips. "Are you all right?"

"I'll live," he muttered, rubbing his hip where Michael's final kick had
landed.

"It's best you move on," Michael told them. "A visit to my village could
bring you into further contact with Rajko. He lives not far from there."

"With larger crowds we might get more money for Vladimir's performance," Cashmere speculated. "The place for us is in the cities, Zoran."

But Zoran was undecided and they agreed to spend the night camped in
the city—in the morning they would press on, possibly to Bucharest, or
follow Michael to his mountain village for a few days. While Zoran went off
to buy food with their meager supply of coins, Michael remained with
Cashmere in the event Rajko returned to cause trouble. The bear dance and
the fight over, the crowd had drifted away. It was late afternoon, and growing chilly.

"Do you have a wife back in your village?" Cashmere asked.

"Yes, I do."

"Of course. The king of a Gypsy tribe would have the most beautiful
wife in the village."

"I think she's beautiful."

The bear was growing restless, fretting at its chain. Cashmere tried to soothe him, speaking in a soft, almost musical tone. "He is a big baby," she told Michael after she had succeeded in settling him down.

"You're very good with him. Did you train him?"

"I raised him from a cub. But Zoran taught him to dance."

"Have you ever trained other animals?"

She ran a finger through her tangled hair. "Last year in Turkey I tried a goat. They're supposed to be easy to train, but I had no luck."

Michael nodded. "The Gypsy Esmeralda had a goat in *The Hunchback of Notre Dame.*"

"What's that?"

"A famous book by Victor Hugo."

"Ah," she said with a touch of sadness. "I cannot read."

At that moment Michael felt a great pity for this woman with her children and her bear. There were so many others like her. He wanted to tell her to flee from her brutal husband, who had once knocked out her tooth, who drew a knife at the least provocation. But it was not his affair.

Soon Zoran returned with some food and Michael departed, promising to return early in the morning to learn their decision. He petted the bear as he left and was rewarded by a rough lick of his hand.

Michael spent the night at a small inn where he'd stayed before when business or a sudden storm kept him from driving back up the mountain road to Gravita. He knew his wife Rosanna wouldn't worry unless he was absent a second night.

In the morning he slept later than planned and was rudely awakened by a pounding on the door of his room. He opened the door and was surprised to see his friend Captain Segar of the government militia, the law-enforcement body of the region. "Michael," Segar greeted him, "get dressed—it's time you were up and about!"

"It's barely seven o'clock."

"A Gypsy has been killed."

"In a knife fight?" Michael asked without thinking.

Segar looked at him oddly. "That seems to have been the case. His wife mentioned you and told me where to find you."

"His wife—It was Zoran Nikoli?"

"That's his name. A Turk who came here with his family and a dancing bear."

Michael nodded, starting to dress. "I met them for the first time yesterday."

"What's this about a knife fight?"

"Zoran pulled a knife on another Gypsy yesterday. I managed to break it up."

"Who did he fight with?"

"Rajko, from the village of Siblu. It's near Gravita."

"I know the place, and I know Rajko. A troublemaker."

Michael finished dressing and picked up his leather jacket. "I'm ready. Let's go."

Zoran Nikoli had met his end less than a hundred yards from his camp site in the park. Captain Segar lifted the plastic sheet to show Michael the body, but one glance was enough. The knife wound had been to the throat and the weapon was still in the wound. It appeared to be Zoran's own knife, the one he'd drawn against Rajko the previous afternoon.

"Corporal Havers found the body," Segar said, motioning toward a pale young man in the uniform of the auxiliary militia. In some cities with a limited police force, the militia used auxiliary members for street patrol, especially at night. "Tell him what you know, Corporal."

Havers offered the beginning of a salute to Michael, which brought a smile from Segar. "No, no—it's not necessary to salute a Gypsy, even if he is a king."

The Corporal blushed and recovered himself. "I was on my usual patrol around four o'clock this morning when I heard voices down here in the park area," he told Michael. "It sounded like an argument, but I couldn't be sure. I started down the footpath and then I saw the body, lying right here."

"Was there anyone nearby?" Michael asked.

"It was still dark, but I thought I heard someone running away. The park is poorly lit at night. I could see no one."

"Was Zoran already dead?"

"He died within a minute or two. I blew my whistle to summon help."

"How did you know who he was?"

"He carried a Turkish passport in his pocket, and I remembered seeing him earlier with the dancing bear. When I told the Captain, he went to their wagon."

Michael turned to Segar. "What did his wife say?"

"It was a shock, I suppose. She didn't even know he was gone from the wagon. The children were with her and the bear was chained up nearby."

"She's seen the body?"

He nodded. "Someone had to identify him."

"I'd better go see her."

Michael found Cashmere sitting in the wagon with the children, looking tired and drained. She blinked her eyes as he lifted the flap and for an instant he thought she'd forgotten who he was. Then she said very quietly, "We won't be going."

"I know. What happened?"

"It was the bear. I knew he'd bring us bad luck."

"You mean Vladimir? How could—?"

"Zoran came here to deliver the bear to someone. I don't know what it was all about. He must have gone off to meet the person during the night, after the children and I were asleep."

"He didn't take the bear with him."

"I know nothing else!" she insisted. "I only want to be away from here! And now this Captain says we must stay until his investigation is complete!"

Michael placed a reassuring hand on hers. "I'll speak to him," he promised.

He went over to Vladimir and ran his hands through the bear's thick brown fur. "What is it, boy?" he said, almost to himself. "Is there something valuable about you?" In response, the bear tried to lick his face.

Michael had visited Captain Segar at his office only once before, and the drab grey building still depressed him. He'd heard once that it had formerly been a convent for Orthodox nuns before the war and the coming of the Socialist government had forced it to close. Perhaps it was better suited to religious matters than secular ones, Michael thought as he climbed the wide wooden stairway to Segar's office on the second floor.

"Welcome, old friend!" the Captain greeted him. "Have a chair while I finish with this report."

"Is that about Zoran Nikoli?"

"Yes. We're still searching for Rajko, but so far my people have been unable to locate him. He may have returned to his village. I suppose I'll have to drive up there later today."

"Is Zoran's wife free to leave the city?"

Captain Segar looked up. "Why do you ask?"

"Before her husband's death I had offered them the hospitality of my village for a few days. It might be a good place for her to go now. I could even arrange for her husband's burial there."

"I need to find Rajko first."

"Suppose I trade you some information for her release."

Segar eyed him suspiciously. "What sort of information?"

"Zoran came here to sell or give his bear to someone. The implication is that the bear has some value other than as a bear."

Captain Segar picked up the dead man's passport. "He came from Turkey. I wonder if the poppy fields still flourish there."

"Drugs?"

"Has it ever occurred to you, Michael, that the routes of the modern drug trade in the Middle East and Europe are quite similar to the routes of Gypsy migration over the centuries?"

"There has never been any unusually large involvement of Gypsies with the drug trade, Captain, as you well know. The route you mention, across

Turkey, has been the traditional land link between the Middle East and Europe for centuries. It's the *only* link, except through Russia."

"Still, a bear could carry a valuable amount of drugs inside him, in some sort of plastic or metal capsules. Isn't that an old Gypsy trick, to take a child into a jewelry store and divert the owner's attention while he or she swallows a diamond ring?"

"Vladimir wouldn't be nearly as good-natured if he'd been forced to swallow a dozen or so capsules of narcotics," Michael assured him, his anger showing.

"You have to understand, Michael. My superiors know I'm friendly with you and other Gypsies, partly because I speak your language. In the past I've been accused of favoritism toward Gypsies. I can't show it in this case."

"Why are you so intent on pinning the crime on a Gypsy?"

Captain Segar sighed. "I hadn't wanted to get into this with you, Michael. I do it only because of our long friendship. We have three pieces of evidence pointing toward a Gypsy killer. First, he was killed with a Gypsy dagger."

"It was his own knife! I saw him use it earlier yesterday in the fight with Rajko."

"Second, Zoran Nikoli lived long enough to say one word before he died. The word was 'Gypsy.'"

"Does that mean I'm a suspect, too?"

"Come, Michael."

"Perhaps you should round up all the Gypsies in the city for questioning. What's your third piece of evidence?"

Segar opened his desk drawer and took out a plastic evidence bag that contained a bright, multicolored piece of cloth. "A Gypsy scarf. We found it under the body."

Michael tried to remember why the scarf seemed familiar. "Anyone can buy a Gypsy scarf," he argued. "There are probably shops selling them right here in the city."

"The three clues go together, Michael. They establish the likelihood that the killer is a Gypsy."

Michael Vlado got to his feet. "I'll see you later," he said, his anger undiminished.

He found a telephone book for the city and looked in the alphabetical listing under Gypsy. Perhaps the dying man hadn't meant that a Gypsy had killed him—he might have died before he could finish a phrase. Michael found several place listings beginning with Gypsy, but only one seemed likely to have been open anywhere near the time of Zoran's murder. It was a cafe called the Gypsy Pavilion and was located about a mile from the scene of the stabbing—not too far for Zoran to have walked, even in the middle of the night.

The Gypsy Pavilion was a big barn of a place, virtually empty when Michael reached it around noon. Except for a small lunch counter, most of the room was roped off, still being swept and mopped from the previous night's business. He imagined dancing, and much drinking of what passed for beer and wine in this sort of place. The manager was a bald man named Kammet who took in Michael's single gold earring with his first glance. "You've come to the right place, Gypsy, but you've come too early. The bar doesn't open until five o'clock."

"I want information, not a drink."

"What information?" The man wore a sheepskin vest, a favorite with Gypsies in the region, but Michael could see he wasn't one of them.

"Some Gypsies may have been here last night, after midnight."

"Not here. We close at midnight."

"A man named Zoran Nikoli?"

"I don't know the name. Actually, we get few Gypsies here. With the government's policy of not recognizing them, they stay clear of a place called the Gypsy Pavilion. Sometimes I think I should change the name to something else."

Unfamiliar with the city's night life, Michael had no way of verifying the man's words. Perhaps he told the truth. "Thank you, anyway," he said.

As he turned to leave, he saw a familiar figure coming through the door. It was the missing Rajko, his gold teeth glistening as they caught the light. But then Rajko saw Michael and in an instant he was out the door, running. Michael took off after him, cutting across the cobblestoned street in an attempt to head him off. "Rajko!" he shouted. "Come back—I only want to talk!"

But the man kept going, leaping a low fence with an agility that surprised Michael, who was growing short of breath. Then, with a stroke of luck, a youth on a motor scooter shot out of a side street directly in Rajko's path. The running Gypsy swerved to avoid a collision and slipped on a muddy spot. He went down hard, and before he could gain his feet again Michael was on top of him.

"Why do you run from a fellow Rom?" Michael demanded. "Have you done something that shames you even before Gypsies?"

Rajko struggled to his feet while Michael held a firm grip on his neck. "I've done nothing!" he panted. "I thought you came after me because of the other one, Zoran. The man deserves to *die*."

"Then he has already gained what he deserves. Someone killed him in the early hours this morning."

Rajko seemed startled. "Where was this? In the city?"

"Near where they camped in the park. Tell me about the bear, Rajko. Why were you so interested in it?"

"I?"

"You stopped to watch it perform."

"Only as the rest of the crowd did."

"You didn't know Zoran before? You didn't arrange to meet him in the park?"

"No—why would I?"

"And yet you ran from me just now."

"I told you—I feared you were in league with him. He nearly killed me with his knife!"

"If you are so innocent, come along with me."

"Where?" he asked, his eyes darting like a frightened animal.

"To see the dead man's widow. And the bear."

Rajko's lips twisted into a golden grin and he said, "You think the bear will betray me, or the widow with her evil eye?"

"Come along and we'll see."

Michael kept a firm grip on his captive all the way. He wasn't about to lose him again.

As they came in sight of the Gypsy wagon with its sad-looking horse, Michael saw Captain Segar talking with Cashmere. Segar glanced at Michael's prisoner and said, "This looks like the elusive Rajko."

"That's who it is."

"Why bother me with this business?" Rajko whined. "I know nothing about it."

"We'll see," Segar told him. "Come with me."

As he led Rajko to his car, Cashmere looked moodily after them. "What does he expect is at the bottom of this?"

"Drugs, perhaps. You told me Zoran came here to deliver the bear to someone."

"Zoran was never involved in drugs."

"What was it, then?"

"I don't know. He didn't tell me everything."

Half an hour later, Michael went back to Segar's vehicle, where the Captain was finishing his interrogation of Rajko. Segar got out and delivered his verdict. "I don't see anything we can hold him for unless we can actually place him at the scene."

Rajko climbed gratefully out of the car. Segar didn't have to tell him twice that he was free to go.

"Now what?" Michael asked.

"You go home to your family. Cashmere and her children go wherever they want. Not every murder gets solved, you know. In the city, people are killed almost every day."

"Can we gamble one more night on this case?"

"On what?"

"If Zoran Nikoli came here to deliver the bear to someone, as Cashmere claims, he didn't succeed. He was killed first. If the person who wanted the bear still wants him, we can assume he might try to take Vladimir tonight, before Cashmere moves on."

Captain Segar nodded. "You want my men to stake out the place."

"No. I think the fewer people know about this, the better it will be. Suppose just you and I do it?"

Segar thought about it. "I've trusted you before, Michael, and you've always come through. I suppose I could take another chance."

Michael ventured a smile. "Then I'll get word to my wife that I'm staying one more night."

The children were asleep in the wagon, and Michael again mentioned the possibility of Cashmere's spending a few days in his village of Gravita and of burying Zoran there. She seemed something of a new person since the death of her husband and, far from mourning, she'd actually washed her hair and made some attempt to improve her appearance.

"I know I must no longer rely on him," she told Michael. "The children depend on *me* now."

"And the bear?"

"Ah, Vladimir. I fear I must sell him."

"Bring him along to Gravita. You might find a buyer there."

She smiled. "How can I ever repay you for your kindness?"

"A kindness to one person is often repaid by someone else."

"I have never really been kind to anyone except Katrina and Fando," she said, looking fondly at her sleeping children.

"I don't know if bears count, but you've surely been kind to Vladimir."

She laughed quietly. "Only kinder than Zoran was. I think sometimes he would torture that bear. He often whipped him when he was training him to dance, and once before we left Turkey he shaved off a portion of his fur. Another man had come to the camp and they tormented poor Vladimir for hours. The bear howled all night, and when I told them to stop they laughed at me. In the morning Zoran had bandaged the bear's side, and he kept the bandage on until the fur had grown back."

Michael nodded through her story and said nothing. Then he stretched casually and told her he thought he'd take a look around outside.

"What are you waiting for?" she wanted to know. "Do you think someone will try to kill me, too?"

"I don't know," he answered honestly, lifting the canvas flap and dropping off the back of the wagon to the ground.

There was a full moon and he was thankful for that. Vladimir was awake, prowling restlessly at the limit of his chain, and Michael wondered if he sensed the tension in the air. He went immediately to the bear and started stroking its fur, using the light from the moon to see as best he could.

Finding what he sought was easier than he'd expected. Once he'd known about the hair growing back, the location was obvious. Now all he needed to do was—

Suddenly a shadow passed across the face of the moon. Michael started to turn, but not fast enough. The blow caught him on the side of the head.

When he opened his eyes, he was on his back and Captain Segar was bending over him. "Michael, are you all right?"

"I—what happened to me?"

"Someone knocked you out. I came running as soon as I saw it, but whoever it was got away in the darkness."

"They were after the bear," Michael said. "And now I know why."

Cashmere had appeared from the wagon. "What happened?" she asked.

"Bring a lantern over here by Vladimir," Michael told her. He went to the bear and examined the fur more closely, then asked her, "Do you have a razor in your wagon?"

"Yes."

"Bring it, please."

Within five minutes he'd completed his task, carefully shaving away a patch of Vladimir's fur. Segar examined the lines and markings that had come into view and asked, "What is it?"

"A map. Zoran had it tattooed onto the bear's hide, and when the fur grew back it was hidden."

"What's it a map of?"

Michael held the lantern more closely. "It appears to be an area of the Black Sea off the coast of Turkey, just north of Istanbul."

"The boat!" Cashmere said with a sudden gasp.

"What boat?"

"Last year Zoran bought a little boat. It was full of leaks and I couldn't imagine why he wanted it. Gradually he started bringing things to our wagon—gold candlesticks and chalices, things like that. I accused him of robbing a church, but he only laughed. He carefully wrapped each item and stowed it on this boat. Then one day he took the boat a little way offshore and sank it. He would never tell me why."

"This was before he shaved the hair from Vladimir?"

"Yes, shortly before."

Michael turned to Captain Segar. "If you'll check with the Istanbul police or with Interpol, I think you'll learn of some sort of robbery in the city at that time—possibly a church, but more likely a museum of some sort. Sinking the loot in shallow water means that it could easily have been recovered by skindivers off a yacht from any country without the danger of someone having to cross the border with it."

"He could have carried a map across," Segar pointed out.

"It might have been stolen from him, or seized for some reason at Customs. The person who'd agreed to buy the map might have killed him instead of paying him—which in fact is exactly what did happen. But now the killer has the problem of getting the map off the skin of a full-grown bear."

"You believe it's someone here in the city?"

"Of course. Zoran told Cashmere he came here to dispose of the bear. He met someone in the park at four in the morning and that person killed him. The killer probably didn't believe the story of the bear at first. He was convinced Zoran had a copy of the map on him, but he didn't."

"The killer got away," Segar pointed out. "We missed our chance."

"We'll have another one. The next time we won't miss."

"When will that be?"

"At four in the morning, if you can stay up that late . . ."

Cashmere and the children were asleep when they left shortly before four. Segar had called in a militia patrol car to make certain the killer didn't use the opportunity to have another try at the bear. Then the Captain and Michael set off across the park, walking the short distance to the spot where Zoran had died.

The moon was obscured by clouds now, and the night had turned suddenly dark.

"How do you know the killer will be here at four o'clock?" Segar wanted to know.

"Because that's the time he arranged to meet Zoran. The Gypsy, after all, would have been available at any time of the night. Four in the morning must have been the most convenient time for the murderer."

As they crossed the park in the darkness, Segar advanced another theory.

"Cashmere was wearing a skirt that matched the scarf we found under the body. How did it get there, unless perhaps she killed him herself?"

Michael shook his head. "It's the most natural thing in the world for two strangers meeting for the first time—even at four in the morning—to arrange to wear some special article of clothing as identification. Zoran wore his wife's scarf. It came off in the struggle."

"Who says there was a struggle?"

"He was stabbed with his own knife, Captain. There must have been some sort of struggle."

Ahead, in the darkness, there suddenly appeared a figure, dimly illuminated by the lights from the street. "Someone's coming—" Segar was impressed. "And it's exactly four o'clock." His voice dropped to a whisper as they stepped off the path and waited in the shadows. "But why should the killer return at the same time two nights in a row?"

"Because he has to come," Michael said.

"An obsession to return to the scene of the crime?"

"No."

The man was closer now, walking quickly, and Captain Segar stepped out suddenly to confront him. Then he laughed. "For once you are wrong, Michael. This is merely Corporal Havers of the auxiliary militia, the man who found the body."

"I am right, Captain. He is the murderer."

At first Havers appeared frightened and confused. He argued, and struggled, and finally wept. "He pulled his knife," he confessed finally. "I feared for my life."

"But you arranged to meet him because you wanted the map," Michael said.

Havers turned his startled eyes on him. "You know that, Gypsy?"

"Loot from a robbery, worth a small fortune, sunk in the shallow waters on the coast. He was selling you the secret."

"He was selling me the map. I didn't know it was tattooed onto the skin of a bear!"

"Is that what you fought about?"

"Yes. I told him to put the map on paper, I did not want a bear! He knew I had the money with me and he drew his knife. I got it away from him and in the struggle I killed him."

Later, when they were telling Cashmere that she had nothing more to fear and she was free to go, Captain Segar asked Michael how he had come to suspect Havers.

"Two things," Michael explained. "If Zoran went to meet the man at four in the morning, that had to be a convenient time for the killer. We knew Havers reached the park on his nightly patrol at that time, but there was no reason to consider him at first. Then there was the matter of the dying message, invented by Havers to shift the blame to a Gypsy. Zoran was killed by a single stab wound to the throat, and the knife was still in the wound. He may have lived a minute or so, but it's impossible that he could have spoken in that condition. You never told me it was Havers who reported the dying message, but since he was alone with the victim when he died, it could have been no one else."

"It was stupid of me not to think of that," Segar said.

Cashmere, silent until then, said, "Michael has said I may bury Zoran in his village. What about Vladimir? May he go with us?"

Segar examined the bear's skin by daylight. "Michael did a skillful job of shaving off the hair. I think we can get a good photograph of the map and send it on to the authorities in Istanbul. Vladimir will be free to go."

She turned to Michael. "You said I could bring Vladimir to your village. Did you mean it?"

"Certainly," Michael said. "So long as he doesn't dance. We are not ready for dancing bears in Gravita, but Vladimir himself will be very welcome."

# INSPECTOR MAIGRET THINKS

### By Georges Simenon

THE LOCK-KEEPER at Coudray was a thin sad-looking chap, dressed in corduroys, with a drooping moustache and a suspicious eye—a type one often meets among bailiffs.

He made no distinction between Maigret and the fifty people—detectives from Corbeil, officials from the public prosecutor's office, and reporters—to whom, for the last two days, he had been telling his story; and while he did so he kept watching, up and down river, the greenish-blue surface of the Seine.

It was November. It was cold, and a white sky—garishly white—was reflected in the water.

"I had got up at six in the morning to look after my wife," he said, and Maigret thought to himself how it was always these decent sad-looking men who have sick wives to take care of.

"Even as I was lighting the fire, it seemed to me that I heard something. But it was later, while I was upstairs preparing the poultice, that I finally realized that someone was shouting. I went downstairs again. From the lock itself I made out a dark shape against the weir.

" 'What is it?' I shouted. A hoarse voice replied with 'Help!'

" 'What are you doing there?' I asked him.

"He went on shouting, 'Help! Help!' So I got out my dinghy to go over. I saw it was the *Astrolabe*. As it was getting brighter, I was finally able to make out old Claessens on the deck. I'd swear he was still drunk, and knew no more than I did what the barge was doing on the weir. The dog was loose, even though I had asked him to keep it tied up. That's all—that's all I know."

What mattered for him was that a barge should have come and run aground on his weir, at the risk, if the current had been stronger, of smashing it. The fact that the only thing found on board—other than the drunken old stableman and a big sheepdog—was two hanging corpses, a man and a woman—that didn't concern him at all.

The *Astrolabe,* afloat again, was still there, about a hundred and fifty meters off, guarded by a policeman who kept himself warm by marching up and down on the towpath. She was an old motorless barge—an *écurie,* or stable, as they call the boats that ply mainly on the canals and keep their horses on board. Passing cyclists looked round at this greyish hull that all the newspapers had been full of for the last two days.

As usual when everyone else had failed to uncover anything new, Chief Inspector Maigret was called in. Everyone concerned had been engaged on the inquiry, and the witnesses had already been interrogated fifty times, first by the police, then by the Corbeil detectives, the magistrates, and the reporters.

"You'll find Emile Gradut did it," everybody kept telling him.

And Maigret, who had just questioned Gradut for two hours, had come back to the scene of the crime and stood there, hands in the pockets of his thick overcoat, looking surly, smoking his pipe in little short puffs, staring at the sullen landscape as if he wanted to buy a plot there.

The interest lay not in the Coudray lock where the barge had been stranded, but at the other end of the reach, eight kilometers upstream at the Citanguette lock.

The same setting as down here, in short. The villages of Morsang and Seineport were on the opposite bank some distance away so that one saw only the quiet water fringed with trees and, here and there, the hollow of a disused sandpit.

But at Citanguette there was a bistro. The barges went to any lengths to lie there overnight. A real waterman's inn where they sold bread, tinned food, sausage, ropes, and oats for the horses.

It was there that Maigret really conducted his investigation, without seeming to, having a drink now and then, sitting by the stove, going for little strolls outside while the owner—a woman so fair she might almost have been an albino—watched him with respect tinged with irony.

This is what was known about the Wednesday evening.

Just as it was beginning to get dark, the *Eaglet,* a small tug from the upper Seine, had brought her six barges like chicks up to the Citanguette lock. At that time a fine rain was falling. When the boats had been moored, the men as usual had gathered at the bistro for a drink while the lock-keeper was putting away his gear.

The *Astrolabe* appeared at the bend only half an hour later when darkness had already fallen. Old Arthur Aerts, the skipper, was at the helm, while on the path Claessens walked ahead of his horses, his whip on his shoulder.

Then the *Astrolabe* moored at the end of the line and Claessens had taken his horses aboard. At the time nobody was paying any attention to them.

It was after seven o'clock, and everybody had already finished eating, when Aerts and Claessens entered the bistro and sat down beside the stove. The skipper of the *Eaglet* was holding forth and the two had no need to say anything. The flaxen-headed innkeeper, a baby in her arms, served them four or five cheap brandies without paying much attention.

This, Maigret now understood, was the way of things here. They all knew one another, more or less. One entered with a casual greeting. One went and sat down without saying anything. Sometimes a woman came in, but it was to do her shopping for the next day, after which she would say to her husband, busy drinking, "Don't be too late coming back."

It had been that way with Aerts's wife, Emma, who had bought bread, eggs, a rabbit.

And from this moment onward every detail became of the utmost importance, every piece of evidence was tremendously valuable. So Maigret was insistent. "You're sure that when he left, about ten o'clock, Arthur Aerts was drunk?"

"Blind drunk, as usual," the patronne answered. "He was a Belgian, after all. A good chap, really, who sat quietly in his corner and drank until he had only just enough strength to get back on board."

"And Claessens, the stableman?"

"It took more than that to make him drunk. He stayed about another quarter of an hour, then he left, after coming back to look for his whip, which he had forgotten."

So far everything was going well. It was easy to picture the bank of the Seine at night below the lock, the tug at the head, the six lighters behind her, then the Aerts barge—on each boat a stable lantern and, falling over it all, a fine steady drizzle.

About half past nine, Emma arrived back on board with her shopping. At ten, Aerts got back in his turn—blind drunk, as the woman in the bistro had said. And at a quarter past ten the stableman finally made for the *Astrolabe*.

"I was only waiting for him to go to close up, for the watermen go to bed early, and there was no one else left."

So much for what was tangible and reliable.

From then on, there was not a scrap of exact information. At six in the morning, the skipper of the tug was amazed that the *Astrolabe* was no longer to be seen behind his lighters, and a few moments later he noticed that the mooring lines had been cut.

Just then the Coudray lock-keeper, tending his wife, heard the shouts of the old stableman and shortly afterward found the barge grounded against his weir.

The dog on the deck was loose. The stableman, who had just been wakened by the impact, knew nothing and claimed that he had been asleep all night with the horses as usual.

But, aft in the cabin, Aerts had been found hanged, not with a rope but with the dog's chain. Then, behind a curtain that screened off the washbasin, his wife Emma was found hanged—in her case, with a sheet pulled off the bed.

And this was not all: when he was on the point of sailing, the skipper of the tug *Eaglet* called in vain for his engineer, Emile Gradut, and found he had disappeared.

"It was Gradut who did it," everyone was agreed, and that evening the newspapers had headings like:

GRADUT SEEN PROWLING NEAR SEINEPORT
MANHUNT IN THE FOREST OF ROUGEAU
AERTS SAVINGS STILL MISSING

All the statements confirmed that old Aerts had a nest egg, and everyone even agreed on the amount—one hundred thousand francs. Why? It was quite a story—or, rather, it was very simple. Aerts, who was sixty and had two grownup sons, married, had taken Emma as his second wife—and Emma, from Strasbourg, was only forty.

Now things weren't going at all well with them. At every lock, Emma complained about the meanness of the old man, who barely gave her enough to eat on.

"I don't even know where he keeps his money," she used to say. "He wants it to go to his sons if he should die. And *I* have to kill myself looking after him, steering the boat, to say nothing of—" She would go into cynical detail, to Aerts's face if need be, while Aerts stubbornly confined himself to shaking his head.

Only after she had gone he would murmur, "She only married me for my hundred thousand francs. But she'll be diddled."

Or Emma would say, "As if his sons needed it to live."

In fact, the elder, Joseph, was skipper of a tug in Antwerp, and Theodore, assisted by his father, had bought a fine motor launch, the *Marie-France,* which had just been reached on its way to Maastricht in Holland.

"But I'll find them, his hundred thousand francs—" She would tell you this without thinking, even if she had known you for only five minutes; she would give you the most intimate details about her old husband and would then conclude cynically, "All the same, he doesn't imagine it was for love that a young woman like me—"

And she was deceiving him. The evidence was indisputable. Even the skipper of the *Eaglet* knew all about it.

"I am only telling you what I know. But without a doubt, during the fortnight we were lying idle at Alfortville, and while the *Astrolabe* was loading, Emile Gradut often used to go and see her, even in broad daylight."

So?

Emile Gradut, who was twenty-three, was a rat, that was clear. Actually, he had been arrested twenty-four hours later, starving in the forest of Rougeau less than five kilometers from Citanguette.

"I haven't done anything!" he screamed at the policemen as he tried to ward off the blows.

An unhealthy little lecher, repellent, whom Maigret questioned for two hours in his office and who had repeated obstinately, "I haven't done anything."

"Then why did you clear off?"

"That's my business!"

As for the examining magistrate, who was sure that Gradut had hidden the money in the forest, he had the place combed again—without result.

There was something infinitely dreary about all this, like the river which reflected the same sky from morning to night, like the string of boats that announced their presence with hooters—one blast for each barge under tow —and which were endlessly edging their way in and out of the lock. Then, while the women on the deck, busying themselves with the kids, kept an eye on the barges, the men went up to the bistro, had a quick drink, and came back with heavy tread.

All crystal clear, one of his colleagues had said to Maigret. And yet Maigret, surly as the Seine itself, as a canal in the rain, had come back to his lock and couldn't tear himself away again.

It's always the same thing: when an affair appears to be clear, nobody thinks of going deeper into the details. For everyone it was Gradut who had done it, and he looked so much the type who might that this in itself was taken as evidence.

Notwithstanding, there were now the results of two post-mortems, which produced some strange conclusions. Thus, for Arthur Aerts, Dr. Paul said, "Slight contusion under chin. From the degree of rigor mortis and the contents of the stomach can state that death by strangulation took place between ten and ten-thirty."

Now, Aerts had come back on board at ten. According to the blonde patronne, Claessens had followed him a quarter of an hour later, and Claessens had stated that he had gone straight to bed.

Was the light on in the Aertses' cabin?

"I don't know."

Was the dog loose?

The poor old man had thought for a long time, only to end with a helpless gesture. No, he didn't know—he hadn't noticed. Could he possibly have foreseen that his doings on that particular evening would become of prime importance after the event? He was half-seas-over. He was sleeping fully dressed on the straw, in the pungent odor of the horses.

"Didn't hear anything? Anything at all?"

He didn't know, he couldn't have known! He was asleep, and when he woke up he found himself in midstream, up against the weir.

There was another piece of evidence, but could it be relied on? It was by Madame Couturier, the wife of the skipper of *Eaglet*. The chief inspector at Corbeil had questioned her as well as the others before letting the convoy proceed on its way toward the Loing Canal. Maigret had the transcript in his pocket.

Question: You heard nothing during the night?

Answer: I wouldn't like to swear that.

Q: Tell me what you heard.

A: It's so hazy. At one time I woke up and I looked at the time on the alarm clock. It was a quarter to eleven. It seemed to me that someone was talking near the boat.

Q: You didn't recognize the voices?

A: No. But I thought it was Gradut having a rendezvous with Emma. I must have gone back to sleep straight away.

Could one rely on this? And even if it were true, what did it prove?

Below the dam, a tug, its six barges, and the *Astrolabe* had been moored for the night, and—

The report on Aerts was clear: he had died by strangulation between ten and ten-thirty. But the story grew complicated with the second of Dr. Paul's reports, the one that referred to Emma.

"The right cheekbone bore traces of bruising caused either by a blunt instrument or by a violent blow from a fist. As to the time of death—caused by hanging—it must have been about one A.M."

And here was Maigret, sinking deeper and deeper into the slow, heavy way of life of Citanguette, as if it was only there that he could think. A motor launch flying Belgian colors made him think of Aerts's son, who must by now have arrived in Paris.

The Belgian colors made him think, too, of the gin. For on the table in the cabin, a gin bottle had been found, more than half empty. The cabin itself had been ransacked from top to bottom: even the mattress had been ripped open, and the stuffing was spread all round.

All this, of course, in a search for the savings. Those who had been first on the scene were saying, "It's all very simple. Emile Gradut killed Aerts and Emma. Then he got drunk and hunted for the money, and now he's got it hidden in the forest."

But there was one difficulty: Dr. Paul's post-mortem on Emma revealed that *she* had drunk all the gin.

Well, so what? Then it was Emma who drank the gin, and not Gradut.

Perfectly clear, was the answer. Gradut, having killed Aerts, got his wife drunk so as to have the upper hand more easily—for you remember she was a strong woman.

If you believed that story, Gradut and his mistress had both stayed aboard from ten or half past, when Arthur Aerts died, until midnight or one in the morning, when Emma died.

It was possible, of course. Anything was possible. But Maigret wanted— it was hard to put into words—he wanted to come round to "thinking bargee"—that's to say, to thinking as the barge folk did.

He had been quite as hard as the others on Gradut. For two hours he had kept grilling him. To begin with, he had used the same old velvet-glove line, as they call it at Headquarters. "Now, listen to me, my boy, you're mixed up in this, that's obvious. But, frankly, I don't believe you killed them both."

"I didn't do anything!"

"All right, you didn't kill them. But own up, you pushed the old man round a bit. It was his own fault, after all—he disturbed you, so in self-defense you—"

"I didn't do anything!"

"As for Emma, of course you wouldn't have touched her, seeing she was your mistress."

"You're wasting your time—I didn't do anything!"

Then Maigret got tougher, even threatening. "Ah, so that's the way it is. Well, we'll see once you're on the boat with the corpses."

But Gradut had not flinched at the prospect of a reconstruction of the crime. "Whenever you like. I didn't do anything."

"Wait till they find the money you've got stowed away."

At that Emile Gradut had smiled, and it was such a pitying, superior smile.

That evening there were only two boats lying at Citanguette, a motor launch and an *écurie*. Below, at the weir, a policeman stood sentry on the deck of the *Astrolabe*. He was very surprised when Maigret climbed aboard, saying, "I haven't time to go back to Paris. I'll sleep here."

You could hear the soft lapping of the water against the hull; then the policeman, who was afraid of falling asleep, started marching up and down the deck. He, poor man, soon began to wonder if Maigret had gone mad, for he was making as much noise down there all by himself as if the horses had been let loose in the hold.

"Tell me, young man—" It was Maigret emerging from the hatchway. "You couldn't find me a pickax?"

Find a pickax, at ten at night, in a place like this? However, the policeman woke the lock-keeper with the mournful look. And the lock-keeper had a pickax that he used in his garden.

"What's that Inspector of yours going to do with it?"

"I haven't the faintest."

As for Maigret, he went back to the cabin with his pickax and for the next hour the policeman heard muffled blows.

"Look, young man—"

It was Maigret again, sweating and puffing, who stuck his head through the hatch. "Go and make a phone call for me. I want the examining magistrate to come over first thing tomorrow morning, and he is to have Emile Gradut brought along."

Never had the lock-keeper looked so lugubrious as when he piloted the magistrate toward the barge, while Gradut followed between two policemen. "No, I swear to you, I don't know anything—"

There was Maigret, fast asleep on Aerts's bed. He didn't even make any excuse; he gave the impression of not noticing the magistrate's amazement at the state of the cabin. The floor had, in fact, been torn up. Under this floor there was a layer of cement, but this had been shattered by great blows from a pickax—it was complete chaos.

"Come in, sir. I went to bed very late, and I haven't yet had time to tidy myself up." Maigret lit his pipe. Somewhere he had found some bottles of beer and he poured himself a glass.

"Come in, Gradut. And now—"

"Yes," the magistrate said, "and now—?"

"It's very simple," Maigret said, sucking at his pipe. "I'm going to explain what happened the other night. You see, there's one thing that struck me from the start: old Aerts was hanged with a chain and his wife was hanged with a sheet."

"I don't see—"

"You will. Look through all the police records and I swear you won't find one case—not one single one—of a man who hanged himself using a wire or a chain. It's strange, perhaps, but it's true. Suicides tend to be soft, more or less, and the idea of the links biting into their necks and pinching the skin—"

"So Arthur Aerts was murdered?"

"That's my conclusion, yes. Especially as the bruise on his chin seems to prove that the chain—which was thrown over his head from behind while he was drunk—first struck his face."

"I don't see—"

"Wait! Next you should note that his wife, for her part, was found hanged with a twisted sheet from the bed. Not even a rope, though on board a boat there are plenty of them. No—a sheet from the bed, which is about the nicest way of hanging oneself, if I may put it like that."

"Which means what?"

"That she hanged herself. Obviously she did, because to give herself courage she had to swallow half a liter of gin—she who never drank at all. Remember the doctor's report."

"I remember."

"So, one murder and one suicide—the murder committed at about a quarter past ten, the suicide at midnight or one o'clock in the morning. From then on, everything begins to get simple."

The magistrate was looking at him with some distrust, Emile Gradut with ironic curiosity.

"For a long time now," Maigret continued, "Emma, who didn't get what she wanted by her marriage to old Aerts, and who was in love with Emile Gradut, had been haunted by one idea: to get hold of the old man's savings and go off with her lover.

"Suddenly she has the chance. Aerts comes home in a very drunken state. Gradut is only a few steps away, aboard the tug. She has seen, on going to make her purchases at the bistro, that her husband is already well on the way to being drunk. So she unchains the dog and waits with the chain all ready to slip round the old man's neck."

"But—" the magistrate objected.

"All in good time. Let me finish. Now Aerts is dead. Emma, drunk with triumph, runs to get Gradut, and here don't forget that the tug skipper's wife hears voices at a quarter to eleven. Is that right, Gradut?"

"That's right!"

"The two of them come back on board to look for the savings, search everywhere, even in the mattress, and don't find the hundred thousand francs. Is *that* right, Gradut?"

"That's right!"

"Time passes, and Gradut grows impatient. I bet he even starts wondering if he hasn't been hoaxed, wondering if the hundred thousand francs really exists. Emma swears it does. But what's the use of that, if it isn't discovered? They start searching again. Gradut has had enough. He knows he will be accused—he wants to be off. Emma wants to go with him."

"Excuse me, but—" the magistrate murmured.

"Later! As I was saying, she wants to be off with him, and, as he has no wish to be encumbered with a woman who hasn't even any money, he gets out of it by punching her on the jaw. Then, once he's on shore, he cuts the mooring ropes of the barge. Is that right, Gradut?"

This time Gradut was slow to reply.

"That's almost all there is," Maigret concluded. "If they had discovered the money, they would have gone off together, or they would have tried to make the old man's death look like suicide. As they didn't find it, Gradut, scared out of his wits, roams around the countryside trying to hide.

"As for Emma, she comes to to find the boat drifting on the current and the corpse swinging beside her. No hope left. Not even a chance of getting away. Claessens would have to be wakened to pole the boat along. Everything's gone wrong. And she, in turn, decides to kill herself. Only she hasn't enough courage, so she takes a drink, chooses a soft sheet from the bed—"

"Is that right, Gradut?" the magistrate asked, watching the wretch.

"Since the Inspector says so."

"But wait a moment," the magistrate retorted. "What is there to prove that he didn't find the savings, and that just to keep the money—?"

At that, Maigret merely stretched out a foot and pushed away some pieces of cement, revealing a neat hiding place containing Belgian and French gold coins. "Now you understand?"

"Almost," the magistrate murmured, without conviction.

And Maigret, refilling his pipe, grumbled, "One ought to have known in the first place that the bottoms of old barges are repaired with cement. Nobody told me that."

Then, with a sudden change of tone, "The best of it is that I've counted it, and it does in fact amount to one hundred thousand francs. Queer kind of couple, don't you think?"

# LITTLE FAT MAN

## By Peter Godfrey

NORMALLY, THE case would never have been deemed important enough to bring to Inspector Joubert's attention, but the young man with the American accent was so flustered and so determined to have his problem dealt with by nobody but "the chief" that eventually Sergeant Coetzee, having failed to draw any other information out of him, took him up to the room in Caledon Square where Joubert was enjoying a cup of tea with his uncle, Rolf le Roux, and Detective-Sergeant Johnson.

The young man declined the offer of tea, but sprawled himself in the proffered easy chair. He introduced himself as Jefferson Carlisle. He was obviously anxious to come to the crux of his business and his how-do's to the others were completely perfunctory.

Joubert, half amused and half irritated at his manner, said, "Well, Mr. Carlisle?"

The other spoke, almost with relief. "Listen, Chief, I'm being haunted."

Joubert had visions of the psychopathic ward. "Really?" he said. "And what does the ghost look like?"

Carlisle grinned. "Pretty substantial," he said. "He's a little fat man with heavy hornrimmed glasses. He's been haunting me for over three months. And he's not dead—far from it."

Joubert said, "Oh."

"It wasn't so bad," said Carlisle, "while I was on the move, but somehow I don't fancy it now I've got to spend a month in this burg. If it hadn't been for those letters, I'd think he was a con man following me and waiting for a break—"

"Just a minute," interrupted Joubert. "What letters are you talking about? How about telling us the story from the beginning?"

"Sorry," said Carlisle. "I guess I was running away with myself. I've got a downtown house in New York, in a fairly quiet spot—as quiet as anywhere in New York can be. Because my father cleaned up on some Texas oil wells, I don't have to work unless I want to. On the morning this began, I was upstairs typing a letter on my portable when a stone was thrown through the open window. It landed on the floor next to my desk, startling me some. There was a piece of paper tied around it. Here it is."

He handed Joubert a wrinkled sheet of cheap notepaper he had fished out of his wallet. By means of complete words and individual letters cut from newspapers, a message had been pasted on it. There was no signature or sender's address and the date was conveyed by the dateline of *The New York Times* of August 21.

The message read, "Forget what you saw in the lane yesterday. Memory will be fatal. I will be watching."

Joubert passed it around to the others. "What's this reference to the thing you saw in the lane?" asked Rolf.

"Search me! It made no sense to me then and it makes no sense to me now. At first I thought it was some kid's prank.

"Well, I went to the window and leaned out. There were only four people in sight. Almost below me there was a blonde woman talking to a fair-haired guy, a few yards beyond them a policeman was moving slowly on his beat, and some distance farther there was a little fat guy with hornrims and a walking stick.

"I don't know why I took such particular notice of the fat guy, except that he was the only one of the four who didn't seem to be doing anything. He was standing and staring at something across the street, but when I followed his gaze I couldn't see anything worth looking at. Whatever the reason, I took him in pretty thoroughly and I had quite a clear picture of him in my mind after I'd turned back into the room.

"Maybe some sixth sense warned me then that there was more to this than a kid's joke, but all of a sudden I got an urge to get out of the States and travel for a couple of months. I believe in playing my hunches, so I went uptown and booked a seat on a plane to London leaving next morning.

"I've developed the habit of sleeping on long plane trips, so I hardly noticed the other passengers during the journey. But as we disembarked at Heathrow, I saw a passenger who chilled me to the bone. It was the little fat man."

Carlisle paused long enough to hand out cigarettes and light one up himself.

"I made myself believe it was a coincidence," he went on, "until the next morning, when I found this note pushed under the door of my hotel room." He handed over another slip of cheap paper, on which had been pasted the dateline of an English journal and the message, "Silence pays, speech slays."

Carlisle immediately changed hotels, keeping a vigilant eye open for the fat man. "I booked in at the Carlsford, just off Bloomsbury Square," he said, "and after I'd been there a week without seeing him, I began to think I'd shaken him off. Then this letter came to me through the post."

The third missive followed the by now familiar pattern. It bore the dateline of the *Daily Telegraph* and the wording was, "Remember to forget."

"That shook me enough," said Carlisle. "Then I saw the man at breakfast. I'd just sat down, and he was leaving, but he passed within ten yards of me. I asked the waiter who he was. He told me he signed as Rufus K. Heiderberg, room number 304. After breakfast, I went and looked him up in the register. He was listed as Rufus K. Heiderberg of New York and he'd checked out ten minutes previously."

Joubert asked, "Didn't you take the letters to the police?"

"No," said Carlisle.

"Why not?"

"Search me. Of course I should have. It was just that I looked on the letters not as criminal, but as a nuisance. I suppose there was an element of competition about it. I was wondering how far this man would follow me, and whether it wouldn't be possible for me to shake him off. At any rate, I decided to move on."

He went, he told them, to Paris. After he had been there three days, a taxi passed him in the street, and the little fat man was peering at him through the window. He hired a car the next day and struck out for a little junction where he caught a train to the south. Two nights after he arrived at Marseilles, another of the pasted notes was waiting for him at the hotel. There was no message this time, just the dateline of a local newspaper, but that was quite enough. Four hours later Carlisle was an unexpected passenger on a little Greek tramp bound for Suez.

At the American Express in Cairo he found a letter addressed to him. He slit it open and withdrew another of the notes, bearing the dateline of the previous day's newspaper. He managed to obtain lists of ship and airline passengers who had arrived during the last three days. It didn't take him long to find the name of Rufus K. Heiderberg.

"I should have found out where he was staying and faced up to him," said Carlisle, "but if he denied writing the notes and played innocent, what could I do? So I cooked up a scheme to shake him off.

"I took a plane to Zurich, then to Frankfurt, down to Rome, then back to Tripoli, where I changed to a Dutch line going south. I got off at Kano, stayed two nights there, then went hopping across Africa by Central African Airways to Nairobi. After a week's rest, I caught a British jet to Johannesburg.

"In almost two weeks there had been no letters and no little fat man. I took a taxi at Jan Smuts Airport to the Hotel Crayle. The desk clerk there handed me the register to sign, and as I was taking my fountain pen out of my pocket my eye wandered over the other signatures. The third one from the bottom was Rufus K. Heiderberg of New York.

"I didn't say a word. I walked out of the hotel and lost myself in the streets as quickly as I could. I spent the night with some hobos on a bench at Park Station and the next day jumped a Durban train without a reservation. At Durban, under a different name, I got passage on a coaster to Port Elizabeth, traveled by air to Cape Town under another name, and booked at the Hilldene Hotel under a third name—Jackson.

"That was three days ago. This morning I found this letter at the desk."

He handed Joubert an envelope with the typewritten address "Mr. J. Jackson, Hilldene Hotel, Cape Town." Inside there was a sheet of cheap paper with a pasted message reading, "Lethe waters are safest." The dateline was that of the *Cape Mail* of the previous day.

"And Heiderberg," asked Joubert, "have you seen him?"

Carlisle shook his head. "I haven't seen him yet, but he's staying at my hotel. His signature is on the register."

Rolf asked, "After not going to the police all this time, Mr. Carlisle, what made you change your mind now?"

Carlisle shrugged. "Up to now it was a game, but all games come to an end. I don't mind telling you, this last letter shook me. It's uncanny. If I knew what he was after, I could take it—I can look after myself—but it's getting me down. It's no good my facing him with it, either—it seems to me it's time to enlist the police."

"We'll see what we can do," said Joubert.

Excusing himself from the group, he telephoned the Hilldene Hotel. After a short conversation with the manager, he returned and passed a set of keys to Johnson. "Take Mr. Carlisle back to the hotel," he said. "Use my car. According to the manager, Heiderberg is in the lounge. Bring him back with you." He added, "I'm keeping these letters in the meantime, Mr. Carlisle."

"That's fine by me," said Carlisle, and touched his hat in a salute as he followed Johnson out of the room . . .

Within twenty minutes Johnson was back with a fat little man.

Heiderberg was a strange contradiction. His clothes were well cut and of good cloth, typical of the unconventional American businessman who buys the best—but for comfort, not for show. But his voice, his face, his actions and mannerisms, and his watery eyes peering through spectacles were those of a Prussian gentleman of the old school.

He acknowledged Joubert's introductions with a little bow and sat down carefully and precisely, hitching up his trousers to preserve the crease. But the dignified gesture was overdone—the trousers were hitched up too far for the short socks, showing two ludicrous pink patches of shin.

"Why have you brought me here?" he asked. "My passport—there is nothing wrong there, no?"

"Not exactly," said Joubert, who had spent the previous twenty minutes preparing a list of places and dates from the letters Carlisle had left with him. "We simply want to ask you a few questions."

He read out details from his list. "Were you in those places at those times?" he asked.

"Yes, but—"

"Can you tell me why?"

Heiderberg, his hands one on top of the other on his belly, seemed to beam good humoredly, but there was a worried undertone in his voice.

"I am traveling. My firm, Heiderberg and Company in New York, doesn't need me there any more. I feel I would like to see the world. I am not married, I have money, and I want to travel. Is there anything wrong in that?"

"Not in that, no. But, Mr. Heiderberg, we've received complaints that you have been following a certain person."

"Following? I am not following anybody."

"There is no room for doubt," said Joubert abruptly. "If you were in these places at these times, you must have been following the person who has complained."

Heiderberg drew himself up. "This person you talk about, has he given reasons why I should follow him?" He waited for a reply. "No? Well, I do not follow anybody. Why should I, Rufus Heiderberg, follow anybody? Yes, once upon a time, a customer for an order—but not today."

Joubert looked down to swallow his impatience and then thrust one of the pasted-up letters in Heiderberg's face. "Why did you send this?"

The little fat man peered myopically through his glasses. "I did not send that," he said, and rose to his feet. "You wish to make charges?" He waited a moment, but Joubert did not answer. "Then I will say good afternoon," he said and bowed stiffly and slightly before going out the door.

Joubert turned to Rolf. "Well, old-timer, what do you think?"

The full lips behind the black beard pursed to puff meditatively at a battered pipe. "I do not like it. Coincidence cannot explain this list of yours. One man does not follow another all these thousands of miles without a purpose."

Detective-Sergeant Johnson said melodramatically, "The old vulture smells blood."

Rolf nodded. "Blood? Perhaps. After all, murder is threatened in those letters."

Joubert said, "I don't like it, either. I'm sending a cable to New York. They may have information about Heiderberg or Carlisle that will shed new light on the matter."

"At the same time," said Rolf, sorting through the pile of letters Carlisle had received, "ask if they know of anything that happened in a lane in New York on August twentieth that might account for one man threatening to kill another."

The reply came toward midday the following day.

It read, "Heiderberg head of Heiderberg and Co., drapers, this city. Small man, German-American, fat, age 53, wears glasses. Semi-retired. Informed by firm traveling your country. No police record. Carlisle only son late J. M. Carlisle, oil tycoon. Also traveling. Tall, brown hair, age 27, no permanent occupation. No police record. Very much interested your other query. Unsolved crime in Makin's Lane, this city, 2:30 P.M. August 20. Chorus girl Frances Vezman, alias Donovan, strangled to death in broad daylight. No witnesses or clues. Can trace no connections between Heiderberg or Carlisle and deceased but victim promiscuous and might have known either. Please cable further information."

Joubert had just handed the cable to Rolf when the telephone rang. It was Carlisle. "I've just had another letter," he said.

"Yes? How does it read?"

"Just three words. *So you talked.*"

"All right. Carlisle, tell me this—have you ever heard of Makin's Lane?"

"Sure—it's a dead end just behind the garage where I park my car in New York. I pass it every day."

"Did you pass it on August twentieth?"

"I must have."

"About what time? Think carefully."

"Well, let me see. August twentieth—that was the day before I got the first letter. I remember now. I must have passed it somewhere around half past two."

"Right. Now, listen. I think I know why Heiderberg has been following you, and I don't want you to take any chances. Stay where you are—"

*   *   *

It was apparent even as their car turned into the driveway of the hotel that something was amiss. Someone was shouting at the top of his voice from inside and a mixed group of waiters and guests were milling in the hotel entrance. The manager said, "Thank God," when Joubert introduced himself and told him a man had been shot in room 77.

They went there, pushing past sightseers in the passage.

As Carlisle stood up to greet them, there were lines of strain on his face. Heiderberg lay face-down on the carpet, strips of pink flesh showing between the tops of his socks and the cuffs of his trousers.

"He knocked at the door," Carlisle explained, "and when I called to him to come in, he rushed at me with a knife. Luckily, I'd taken your advice to watch out and had my pistol handy."

Rolf's voice came then, as though he were reading an epitaph. "Poor little fat man."

Carlisle echoed him. "Poor? What do you mean?"

"I mean we came too late to save him," said Rolf, "but his murderer will not go free."

"Murderer?" said Carlisle. "I've told you I killed the man. He came at me with a knife and I shot him. That's not murder."

Joubert was uneasy. "Listen, Oom—" he said to his uncle.

"No, Dirk, you listen. You remember the timetable you drew up? You were right when you thought that if two people were in all those places at the same time, coincidence was out of the question. One must have been following the other, you thought, and Heiderberg must have been following Carlisle. But couldn't it quite easily be the other way around? After we interviewed Heiderberg, I saw the second alternative was by far the more likely."

Carlisle's face was tense and angry, but he made an effort to retain the nonchalance in his voice. "At the risk of waking you from your pipedream," he said, "I want to remind you of a few things. First, there are those letters."

Rolf said, "Yes. Of course, it's possible Heiderberg sent them to you, just as it's possible he was following you. But it is just as likely that you sent them to yourself and that you were following him."

"Likely, unlikely!" Carlisle's voice was full of venom. "What about some proof? Why should I send such letters to myself? And if I did, why should I take them to the police?"

"I'll tell you why. On August twentieth you strangled a girl in Makin's Lane. As you were doing it, or as you were coming out of the lane, a fat little man passed and looked in your direction. It was very casual, and he probably didn't even notice you, but you couldn't be sure, could you? And so you followed him. After the evening papers came out, you realized that he didn't associate the casual meeting with the crime, but the cold hand of doubt still gripped you. Someday another little thing might happen and Heiderberg would remember and understand. While he lived, he was the only person who could link you with the crime. The man must die.

"Your plan probably came to you when, in first tracking him, you learned he was catching a plane overseas—the plan to send yourself fake letters, building up a circumstantial case against this poor soul so that when you finally did kill him you could bolster your plea of self-defense."

"That's some story," said Carlisle. "Go on, let's have the rest of it. If I did kill the girl and had the brains to think up a scheme like this, how come I'd let you get your hooks on Heiderberg and give him a chance to spill the beans about what he was supposed to have seen back in New York?"

"There was so little chance of that," said Rolf, "that the risk was well worth it. If the newspaper reports of the murder hadn't stimulated Heiderberg's memory, what chance was there of the oblique reference to a happening in a lane in the original pasted-up letter doing it? No, your only danger lay in Heiderberg's recognizing you personally. You must have kept well out of his way while you were following him, and you were determined to kill him before there was the slightest chance of him pointing you out to the police. And even there," he added, "the danger was only in your mind. He was shortsighted, remember. It's doubtful he even saw you that day."

"Theories, suppositions!" Carlisle shouted. "You haven't a single shred of evidence! I've given you the facts. Heiderberg knocked on the door just now, rushed me with a knife, and I shot him. There he is, knife and all. Theorize your way around that."

Rolf asked, "Did you touch the body at all?"

"No."

"Then you've convicted yourself, Carlisle. I'll tell you what *actually* happened. You somehow got Heiderberg into this room, and then, because you're not as confident of your aim as you try to imply, you got him to sit in a chair before you took aim and fired. Then you pulled the chair away so that he slumped on the floor, put the knife in his hand—"

The muscles in Carlisle's face were moving. "More theories."

Rolf turned to Joubert. "Do you remember, Dirk, when Heiderberg sat down in your office, how he hitched up his trousers over the tops of his socks—the way they're pulled up now? There are only two ways that could have happened here—either he sat down on a chair or he was lifted and dragged by the ankles. In either eventuality, the story Carlisle is telling is a lie. And if his story is a lie—"

He reached forward and clamped his fingers over the wrist of the hand Carlisle was stretching forward to his pistol on the table. "I'm not a violent man," said Rolf, "but I can understand a violent crime, done on the spur of the moment and with passion. I cannot condone a murder such as you have just committed. If I let you get that gun, Dirk here will shoot you, and you will die suddenly and quickly. I don't think that would be fair to Heiderberg. You must die, yes, but only after all the evidence against you has been so carefully gathered that the little fat man will be avenged."

# A HINT OF DANGER

*By William Bankier*

C ARTER VARLEY was accustomed to writing mystery stories, having them published, and then hearing no more about them. His friends seldom read one or, if they did, they kept silent about it. Varley considered this to be a kind of passive hostility motivated by envy. As for strangers—the anonymous public who were exposed to his work in various magazines—he supposed they turned the pages, were amused or not, and then went about the business of their lives.

But now, on this drafty November morning with a gray rain sweeping across Wimbledon Common and spattering against the window beside Varley's desk, here was an astonishing letter from America. It had been forwarded to him by the editor of a magazine published in New York, but the postmark was Chattanooga, Tennessee.

"Imagine my surprise," the letter began, "when I read your story entitled 'Forgotten, Not Gone' and discovered it was about me!" The writer went on to identify himself as William Stoke (indeed the name Varley had invented for the villain in his story) and to say that, furthermore, he was a practicing lawyer. This compounded the coincidence almost beyond belief because Varley's fictional Stoke had been a lawyer, too.

With an ethereal feeling Varley cranked paper into his machine and typed an answer. He apologized for any embarrassment and expressed his amazement at the sort of coincidence that happens in real life, too bizarre ever to be written into a story. Varley thanked Stoke for his letter and then, uncharacteristically, invited the American to call if ever he should be in London.

The rain stopped in early afternoon. Varley went out for a walk in the High Street, paid an outrageous price at the grocer's for some salad ingredients, posted his letter to America, and then went to The Dog and Fox for a pint.

Tucked away in a corner, his portly torso wedged into a leather armchair, the mug of brown ale glowing on polished oak easily within reach, Varley stared at the hissing glow of the gas fire and worried about what he had done. He did not want people dropping in on him, not friends, not strangers, certainly not an aggressive American who would think he had a claim on Varley simply because his name had fallen into the author's mind by sheer happenstance.

Varley drank the ale, making up his mind to have another. And perhaps a couple of those Scotch Eggs. The crusty, breaded eggs improved his mood and so did the second pint. He was fretting for nothing. Stoke had written because he was surprised and pleased to see his name in print. Varley's reply was no more than proper, and the invitation was the sort of formality that nobody takes seriously. Chattanooga was a long way from London—nothing more would ever come of it.

Christmas arrived and Varley was forced to recognize that he had not got over the death of his wife two years ago. By burrowing like a mole into mountains of work, he could deceive himself for months at a time into thinking he was self-sufficient and secure. But when he lifted his head at the end of the year he encountered all kinds of ferocious reminders—the scent of oranges, frost in his nostrils on night walks, lights on trees seen through curtained windows, and at his doorway three children singing a carol.

Varley gave them fifty pence and sent them away, then turned out all his lights and sat shivering in the dark, drinking Scotch whisky and facing the past like a martyr submitting to the fire. He saw the old chapel with himself in his twenties, dressed in cassock and surplice on the tenor side of the chancel, holding his hymnbook high and looking across it at Beatrice in the front row of the altos. Midnight service on Christmas Eve.

Those had been the good years, the early days of his life with Beatrice. Time eroded the relationship until it became something no longer worth preserving. But now that he was going it alone, Varley's mind would only deliver up memories of sweet events.

The year finally turned and delivered a cold January followed by a gray wet February, both of which were improvements on the festive season as far as Carter Varley was concerned. Then came a surprisingly sunny March, milder than the month had been in a decade. These were ideal working days and he got his head down and tunneled busily into the material of his experience.

Then the telephone rang.

Varley jumped, barking his knee on the desk and spilling milky coffee on the cherrywood surface. Leaving a paper napkin to absorb the overflow, he limped out of the study and into the bedroom, balancing the clamor of the bell with short angry responses.

"Yes. All right. Hang on."

The voice on the line was, to Varley's ear, almost stage-American. "Hello, this is Mr. Billy Stoke speaking. Is that Mr. Carter Varley?"

"Yes, it is." Said with heart beginning to pound.

"I hope I'm not interrupting your work but we got into London last night and I figured that after the very kind invitation in your letter I had to call and say hello."

"Yes, rather. Very glad you did."

Stoke laughed in a boyish way. "I don't suppose you get telephoned very often by a character in one of your stories."

A few generalities were exchanged during which Stoke mentioned the name Irene. He was not traveling alone and, for some reason, this eased Varley's anxiety. Then the American said, "I know you writers have a schedule to stick to, but I was hoping Irene and I might persuade you to come to London and have a meal with us."

Varley had not ventured beyond the High Street in months. London meant the train to Waterloo, crowds, taxis, a strange hotel lobby. "Yes, very nice. It's a question of time. Perhaps a day next week."

"Afraid we're only in London for a couple of days. We've rented a car and we plan to drive along the south coast."

A momentary silence. Then Varley was astonished to hear himself saying, "Then come out here for dinner. Yes, by all means, come this evening."

The American's pleasure at the invitation was so gratifying that Varley found himself going further. It was as if some hospitable impulse buried long ago had been uncovered. "Look here," he said, "why don't you check out of the hotel? I have a perfectly good guest room here."

That was the end of writing for the day. Varley set aside his current manuscript, took a fresh sheet of paper, and drafted a menu for dinner. Under it he listed the items he would have to buy at the shops, including wine and beer and a bottle of cognac.

By six o'clock the roast of beef, surrounded by potatoes, carrots, and onions, was in the oven, filling the house with its appetizing aroma. A litre of Italian red wine was uncorked and resting on the Jacobean sideboard. Varley admired the table setting—gleaming silver, polished plates, folded linen, four tall candles in antique brass sticks. A long time since he had drawn the oak table away from the wall and raised the drop leaves.

He was placing a few additional lumps of smokeless coal on the open fire when he heard the swing of the iron gate followed by the scrape of footsteps outside the front door. Varley paused at the hall mirror to adjust the knot in his tie and smooth the edges of his graying hair. There was color in his face for the first time in a year and his eyes were clear and alert.

William and Irene Stoke from Chattanooga, Tennessee turned out to be everything Varley could have hoped for and nothing he might have feared. For one thing, they were not dressed in what he considered to be the style of children—no turtleneck sweaters, no peaked caps, no blazers with crests on them. Stoke, tall and heavyset, deeply tanned and handsome, ten years younger than Varley's half century, was wearing a dark suit, white shirt, and modest tie. His shoes had laces and were polished black. Too good to be true.

Irene Stoke could not have been older than thirty. She had a stage beauty, regular features made up immaculately, hair like burnished copper worn in one thick braid over her shoulder, and classic eyes of penetrating green.

They sat with drinks in upholstered chairs drawn close to the fire while rain came out of the darkness and rattled on the windows. Billy Stoke said, "Always wanted to see England but kept putting it off. It was that nice letter of yours that did it."

"What a charming room you've given us," Irene said. She smiled and then raised her eyes to gaze at the rough beams set in the ceiling over two hundred years ago. "I love this house."

The dinner table was small and brought the three of them close together in an intimate circle. Stoke's massive shoulders leaned in and overshadowed the other two and as they turned their heads during conversation they looked into each other's eyes at close range, saw reflected candlelight, and something else they could not identify.

"These people are strangers," Varley said to himself in amazement, wondering how they could be so simpatico.

A possible explanation sprang into his mind over coffee when the huge wine bottle was empty and he was pouring cognac. What if they were professionals? It was a preposterous premise and had he not been half drunk he would have buried it away. But he *was* nicely drunk, happily drunk for the first time in years, so he said, "I've just had a fascinating idea. You're going to laugh."

"What is it?"

"It's more than likely that you aren't really the William Stokes at all. You are American adventurers, a team of con artists if you like, and you wrote that letter simply to gain access to my house, my life, my confidence." Varley spread his arms to encompass the scene. "Done it rather well, too, I should say."

Was he mistaken or did a frown pass between Stoke and his wife? It might have been a trick of the candlelight. The American said, "But what about my letterhead? It identifies me as William Stoke, Attorney at Law, of Chattanooga, Tennessee. And that happens to be who I am."

"Easiest job in the world to have a fake letterhead printed up. First thing you'd do on a scheme like this." Why was he pressing the idea? It might be taken as uncommonly rude unless his guests accepted it as banter. And how could they do that when Varley himself was not sure whether he was serious or not?

But Stoke did laugh. "The author's mind at work," he said. "I guess you've got to see a twist in everything. But why would we go to all this trouble? What's our motive?"

"That's obvious," Varley said. "Financial gain. You get me on good terms, find out where I keep my assets, perhaps persuade me to draw out some money or write a large check. Then you vanish, discarding the false identity as you go."

Had anyone spoken at that moment, Varley might not have felt the hint of danger. But there was silence and he did feel it, a deep thrum like the clong when a tuning fork is struck. It caught him in the chest and buzzed there for seconds, gradually fading away and leaving him feeling cold. He glanced at Stoke, looking for confirmation of the threat, but the big man was tipping back his cognac, lowering the glass and shaking his head, his mouth pursed with amusement.

They sat up till midnight, talking by the fire. The Americans shared the telling of stories about motor trips to New Orleans, to Atlanta, even as far away as California. These distances seemed interstellar to the Englishman who considered the fifty miles to Brighton a long haul.

The visitors acted like a drug on Varley and he found himself opening up about his life, a thing he seldom did. Perhaps the lawyer's subtle questioning led him—he only realized this later; but at the time he rambled on about his solitary state in the world now that he was a widower. No children, no relatives living anywhere; he was a man who could fall off the edge of the earth and never be missed.

"How did you wife . . . ?" Irene began.

Stoke cleared his throat but Varley said, "No, it's all right. An accident. She struck her head while bathing and drowned."

Hours later, waking in darkness, Varley sensed movement on the stairs outside his bedroom door. He got up, stepped into slippers, pulled on a robe, and went out quietly onto the landing. He had left the bathroom light burning for his guests' convenience. It illuminated the stairs to the angle where they turned five steps below. Silence. But a fragrance in the air —a woman's scent. It was some time since Varley had experienced this sensation in his house late at night.

He crept down the stairs into a chilly hallway, found the front door standing open, and passed through it onto the flagstone entrance to the narrow garden running along that side of the cottage. Irene Stoke was standing halfway down the path dressed in a long robe. Her braid was undone, the hair brushed out to shoulder width and halfway down her back. He approached her and they stood together in silence. Then she said, "I couldn't sleep. I'm sorry."

"It's all right."

The moon was full. Its pale illumination flooded the brick wall beside them almost like stage lighting. Not yet in leaf, the dormant vine creeping over the wall seemed a dead thing. Varley could smell moist earth and a flood of ozone from the nearby forest. It occurred to him that he ought to spend a couple of hours outside on every night as fine as this one.

Now the woman put a hand on his shoulder in the sort of companionable contact practiced by old friends. She leaned forward and kissed him, a touch as cool and fragrant as if she had brushed his cheek with a rose.

"Oughtn't to do that," Varley said.

She turned her head and looked up at the silhouette of tiled roof and chimneypots with the white, pocked globe of the moon suspended over it. He saw her mouth form a self-deprecating smile as she said with a note of finality, "I love this house."

After breakfast Varley found himself alone with William Stoke. Irene had insisted on going around to the shops to bring back some food. Stoke toyed with his third cup of coffee. "I guess Irene made a nuisance of herself last night," he said. "Sorry about that."

Having done nothing, Varley felt guilty. "No trouble at all. Difficult to sleep in strange surroundings."

But the American was intent on saying more. "I never expected to tell you this bit of background. But then, I never thought I'd be spending the night in your home." He went on to explain that this was not a holiday trip. The Stokes were preparing to move to England—under some duress. It seemed Irene had been stealing from department stores for years. She had been in police hands more than once and it had reached the point where Stoke's legal influence was wearing thin. They were talking about putting her away.

"Kleptomania," Varley said. "Surely she ought to be seeing a psychiatrist."

"We've tried that. Some people don't respond very well to analysis. Irene is one of them." The American gave his host a troubled smile. "No, I think the only answer is a complete change of scene. Perhaps a small town, a village even, where there's less opportunity for her."

"But how will you practice law?"

"Fortunately we've done well enough. Money is no problem."

The front door closed and Irene came through into the kitchen depositing a laden shopping basket on the counter. She sensed the atmosphere in the room. "My husband has been talking, has he?" Her voice was ultracheerful. "That's Billy's big problem. He never knows when to shut up." Briskly she began unloading the basket.

It was William Stoke's suggestion that they get into the rented sedan and drive down to the south coast. The weather was pleasant enough, the warmest March day on record. As they set out, Stoke said, "We may even see a village we might like to settle in." The truth was now in the open, though nothing more was said.

They took the Brighton road, then bore east through Sussex, touching the coast at Hastings where they got out of the car and walked along the beach for half a mile. Then on past Winchelsea, New Romney, Dymchurch, and Hythe, and thence along the cliffs toward Folkestone and Dover.

"Not too keen on these areas ahead," Stoke said. "Too metropolitan."

"Sandgate is a nice little place," Varley suggested.

Then Irene Stoke said in a bitter tone, "Or we could pitch a tent in a field. Or how about a small cabin, of clay and wattles made."

Varley realized how serious Stoke was when the man stopped by a real-estate office and went in to find out what was for sale and for how much. Irene refused to accompany him, so Varley waited with her in the car. They were silent for a few minutes. From his place in the back seat he had a view of her shoulders and the shiny back of her head, the dark hair tightly braided. The interior of the car smelled of leather and paint. Finally Irene turned around and said brightly, "He's taken you in completely."

"How do you mean?"

"You believe he's what he says he is."

"I'm still not with you."

She closed her eyes while she said, "You were perceptive last night. Don't be dull now." She opened her eyes and stared at him. "Don't you see? Your writer's instinct was correct. He is *not* William Stoke. I am not his wife. This *is* a confidence trick to relieve you of a lot of money."

"But last night I was only joking." As he said this, he remembered his uncertainty at the time as to whether he was joking or not. And he recalled the hint of danger that came to him from somewhere across the table.

"Joke or not, you had it right. Ted—that's his real name—got this idea and he's been crafty enough to follow it through. It was all as you said, even to having the letterhead printed."

Carter Varley felt the sting behind his eyes, called it pure anger, but was not ready to admit he could weep with disappointment at this betrayal. "Then I'll just have a word with your Ted when he comes back. What's this house hunt, then? Part of the window dressing?"

"Yes. He lives a part one hundred percent."

"But why the story about your kleptomania? Is that true?"

"Of course not. It's all designed to lull you, to make you feel sorry for us." She reached across the seatback and took Varley's hand. "But be careful. Don't say anything to let him know I've told you. He's a psychopath and you'd be in real danger. Just watch him and say nothing."

"Why are you telling me this? It can't be in your interest."

"No. But I think you're a good man." She squeezed his hand and let it go. "Protect yourself and I'll take Ted away tomorrow."

The man who said he was William Stoke came back from the real-estate agent's office with a handful of data sheets on homes for sale. These were passed around and discussed while he drove on. After half an hour the road climbed to a headland with a vast ocean horizon spread out below a high chalk cliff.

"Now there's a view," Stoke said, pulling the car onto a grassy verge. "How'd you like to live with that outside your bedroom window?"

Irene was the first one out of the car, running to the very lip of the cliff where she stood with fists on hips, owning everything the eye could see.

"Not too close," Stoke called. "It's a lovely fall, but the last couple of feet are murder."

They studied the view from every direction and began to feel the spank of sun and wind on their cheeks. Then Irene noticed a coffee wagon parked far down the slope by the edge of the highway where a cluster of construction huts bordered a building site.

"That's what we need," she said. "Hot coffee."

Varley insisted on going to get three cups. As he walked down the hill, he wondered what he ought to do about the dangerous situation he was in. Morally, he should call the police. If the pseudo-Stoke character was as bad as Irene said he was, then he deserved to be locked up. But it would be a tricky procedure to approach a policeman. No crime had been committed. There would be no reason to hold him. But once the American knew Varley had become suspicious, he might be capable of anything.

Trudging back up the slope with three coffee cartons in a perforated tray, Varley decided to keep silent and ease the strangers out of his house tomorrow. Once alone, he could consider putting the police on their track.

He was crossing the low mound that prevented a person farther down the hill from seeing anyone on the promontory when he heard Irene calling and saw the struggle taking place near the edge of the cliff. Stoke had Irene by the arms but she was fighting hard, out of her shoes, tearing one arm loose and swinging the free hand in a wide arc against the side of his head. It looked like a slap but it was more; she was holding a rock in that hand. Stoke's knees buckled and he sank to the grass.

"He knows that you know," she gasped as Varley ran up and set the coffee aside.

"You told him?"

"He suspected. He hurt me." She showed crimson marks on a pale arm. "I had to tell him."

Carter Varley knelt to look at the ugly wound on the man's head. He was moaning, barely conscious. "You could have killed him."

"I had to act. He was going to throw you over the cliff as soon as you got back." Irene reached out to turn Varley's head so that his eyes met hers. They were wide with shock. "I told you, he's mad."

When Stoke tried to raise his head, Varley whispered, "What do we do?"

"We've got to finish him. No, don't think about it. If he comes round, he'll go crazy. We'll never be able to handle him. If we run away, he'll come back to the house. If you call the police, he'll stay out of sight, but you'll never be safe. Believe me, I know him."

"But what—?"

"Over the edge. Quickly. We'll both say he fell. The head wound will be part of the fall."

"I can't do that."

But Irene had Stoke by the arm, his torso half off the ground. She was surprisingly strong. "Take my word," she gasped. "He deserves to die. The things he's done to so many people. You'll be serving justice."

Stoke's bloodied head was coming up, the whites of his eyes showing, his mouth hanging open. It was a terrifying sight and suddenly Varley wanted an end to it. His heart pounding, he seized the other arm and, together, he and Irene walked the man to the cliff edge. Two steps away they let him go and he tottered forward, stepped crazily into space, and was gone.

The first thing was to wipe away a few traces of blood from the grass, the next to drive to the nearest town for the police. It took some time but by sundown the accident was confirmed, William Stoke was well and truly dead, and Carter Varley was at the wheel of the car driving home.

Irene turned on the radio to a commercial music station. This seemed wrong, so he snapped it off.

"Well!" she said petulantly.

Something else was wrong. "His papers all tallied with the identification of William Stoke from Chattanooga," Varley said. "Driver's license, social security card, and so on. If he wasn't Stoke, and this was a temporary con game, why had he gone to all that trouble?"

"That's easy. Because he *was* William Stoke. Everything he told you was true. I'm the one who has been lying."

Varley's creative imagination prevented him from being too surprised. He remembered the hint of danger at the dinner table last night and understood why Stoke had appeared oblivious. The hint of danger had come from Irene.

"Why have you done this?" he asked.

"Because he made my life a hell. He kept sending me to psychiatrists and now he was trying to bury me in some remote village. Away from temptation." She said this last word contemptuously. "That's a laugh."

"Then you've just murdered your husband."

*"We've* murdered him," she said. "Never forget that. I could tell a story to the authorities that would put us both away for a long time. I hope there'll never be a need."

Varley drove on in outraged, frightened silence. The next time Irene spoke was when he parked the car outside the cottage and went to unlock the front door. She took the key from his hand and turned it in the lock. "I love this house," she said.

That night and the next one had their compensations. Varley had almost forgotten what it was to have a woman in his bed. But still he was shocked by the recent events and deeply angry at the way she had manipulated him. He felt she could not be allowed to get away with it. His mind was made up for him when he went into the market a couple of days later and was approached by the manager holding a slip of paper.

"Sorry to trouble you, Mr. Varley, but the American lady, staying with you I understand, took a few items and forgot to check them through. Only a small amount, but I thought you'd want me to mention it."

Varley paid and walked home, his chest rising and falling. He went upstairs and sat at his desk, looking out of the window, thinking. The fine weather had changed and a more seasonal cold wind was blowing across the common.

Yes, he would have to take care of her. A simple household accident was the best way. But not the fall in the bath and the drowning that had done for poor Beatrice. This would have to be something else, perhaps a broken neck at the bottom of those twisting stairs. They were dangerous till you got used to them.

The office door opened and Irene came in without knocking. She was carrying a glass of whiskey—he frowned at his watch—at eleven in the morning. "What are you up to all alone in here?" she asked, sounding bright and self-satisfied.

Carter Varley picked up a pen and added a few words to a paragraph of recent scrawl. "Oh, just busy with my plotting," he said.

It was her second drink, so Irene did not catch the hint of danger in his voice.

# SEVEN NIGHTS, SIX DAYS

### By Janet O'Daniel

T HE SMALL mixup at the hotel desk when they arrived was certainly
annoying, but had not seemed—at first—in any way sinister. In
fact, Harriet Pryce was inclined to put it down to nothing more
than the laxness of Italian management. Not that the Stella wasn't a perfectly comfortable hotel, and preferable, in her opinion, to the newer, more
vulgar ones farther down the Via Veneto. This one, at the top of the street
near the Borghese Gardens, had a well-used look of quality that Mrs. Pryce
approved of. Marble steps slightly worn down in the centers, good red
carpeting in the lobby, twelve-foot ceilings. Still, management was another
matter. And that contretemps at the desk *had* disturbed her.

"I do not intend to share a bath with anyone," Mrs. Pryce had snapped
at the apologetic room clerk.

"It would be for one night only, Signora Pryce," the young man had
coaxed in his attractively accented English. "And only a few of your party
will be inconvenienced. It is because of the convention of scientists here.
They will be gone by noon tomorrow, and I can then give all of you your
choice of rooms and assure you of completely private baths." It was a
source of some satisfaction to Mrs. Pryce, even in her frustration, that the
clerk had elected to address her rather than the young woman who was the
official tour guide, and who now stood beside her in wavering dismay.
Against her better judgment then, Mrs. Pryce had acquiesced. Rome was

warm in mid-May. She was weary. She was longing to sink into a tub. Still, she summoned up a sharp parting salvo. "I shall take it up with the tour company the moment I return home. You people should not be allowed to bully us simply because we're good-natured Americans." The little guide looked concerned, then relieved, as the matter appeared to be settling.

Mrs. Pryce glanced around at the straggle of tour members standing behind her at the desk, all of them warm and spent after the ride in the bus from the airport. " 'Hobson's choice—take that or none,' " she quoted darkly, and led the way to the elevators. She had felt compelled to make a show of resistance since she had, from the outset, sensed herself to be the unofficial but tacitly acknowledged leader of the tour. The guide had met them at Fiumicino, of course—this thin young woman with blonde hair and brown eyes. Scarcely more than a child, to Mrs. Pryce's mind. But by that time Mrs. Pryce, an old hand at tours, had already whipped the fourteen wavering and bemused travelers into a unit as cohesive as a well-run army platoon.

"There will be someone to meet us," she had reassured them as they left the plane. "Watch for a sign—someone will be holding up a sign saying Prestige Tours." "No, no. Don't be concerned about your luggage, they'll take care of it." "The ladies' room? Just over there, as I recall. And don't worry about missing the bus. I shall make sure it's held for you." She had, in sum, been a tower of strength to the fourteen, none of whom had been in Italy before, and none veteran tourists like herself.

It was this matter of trust that she felt had been violated in the matter of the room assignments: her powerlessness to alter the situation made her feel in some way diminished as a leader. She was somewhat consoled when Mrs. Benning, pale and tired-looking, touched her elbow and thanked her as they parted before the doors of their adjoining rooms. "I can't think what we'd have done without you, Mrs. Pryce. You've been so helpful."

Her husband echoed her. "Yes, indeed. Very helpful." He was small and quiet like his wife. An inoffensive pair—good people, Mrs. Pryce decided, slipping them into a slot so labeled in her mind. And it was fortunate, actually, that they were to be her neighbors. Sharing the bath with them would not be too distasteful.

Once in her room, however, she discovered that the bathroom door was, unhappily, to the right, not to the left where the Bennings were. She was to be thrown in with strangers after all, then. Mrs. Pryce's forehead gathered in a frown. She glanced around the room, noting the heavy wooden bed, the numerous chairs—there were always too many chairs—the worn, defeated-looking rug. Then she crossed to the bathroom door and pushed it open quietly. White-tiled, unremarkable. Overlarge, as bathrooms were apt to be in these older places—a not displeasing feature. A second door was opposite her: obviously it led to the next room and her unknown neighbors.

As she stood there she heard voices from beyond it and moved closer to listen. They were women's voices, two of them, and decidedly British— both raised in what sounded like agitation. Mrs. Pryce sensed an argument and tilted her head forward, its angle alert and attentive.

"Really, Grace—you've said the same thing twenty times over. I wish you'd let it rest."

"Sorry if I've been tedious. I'm sure I never meant to burden you."

"I didn't say you were tedious, dear. It's simply that it's no good saying it over and over. And who's going to listen—except me? He's a very important man in the field."

"Oh, of course. No mystery how he came to be so. Anyone could build up quite a shelf of publications if he stole regularly from his colleagues."

"Darling, what a word to use. You mustn't, you know. Dr. Brand's terribly well thought of in the field."

"Oh, for God's sake—I hate it when you talk about the *field*. And certainly he's well thought of—by all those devoted associates of his!" Venom overflowed the room, seeped under the bathroom door. "It makes me absolutely livid, Violet, when I see you running to fetch his tea and then standing there panting like a dog as you wait for a smile from the great man. And I'm sure if he suggested that you hop into bed with him you'd do that, too—if you haven't already—"

"Grace Harwood!"

"You, with your background in scholarship and research, toadying to someone like that—"

"You're absolutely round the bend over this, Grace. Overlooking those beastly things you're saying about me, it's most irresponsible of you to malign Dr. Brand this way. All scholars borrow from one another's finds, surely—build upon them, at any rate."

"They don't steal papers from staff members and pass them off as their own! That Macedonian research was mine, word for word!"

"Really, Grace, you're being a most awful bore about all this. After a time you'll come to see how you've overstated everything and you'll feel a really prize fool. I myself consider us both lucky to be working with such a big man in the f—in our profession."

The voice belonging to the one called Grace replied with a short pithy word that brought color to Mrs. Pryce's cheeks. Much as she would have liked to go on listening, she feared one of the two might come bursting into the bathroom and discover her, so she hastily turned on a loud gush of water in the tub. When she turned it off after a moment, the voices were still. Mrs. Pryce went to the closed door and knocked.

The woman who answered was in her early thirties, tall, with straight brown hair cut shoulder length. She wore oversized eyeglasses. Yet, strangely, neither the straight hair nor the glasses made her look plain.

Different, rather, and striking. Behind her Mrs. Pryce could see the other woman lighting a cigarette. She was darker and her thick, tightly curled hair lay close to her head. Her features were drawn into a scowl which indicated quite clearly that she was Grace.

"I do beg your pardon," Mrs. Pryce said crisply, "but I've been assigned this adjoining room—for tonight only—so I'm afraid we'll be sharing the bath."

The brown-haired woman managed a stab at looking cordial. "Oh, fine. No one's had that room all week. But it's quite all right. We'll be leaving tomorrow anyway."

Mrs. Pryce essayed a random shot. "Are you by chance with the convention of scientists?"

"Oh—well, archaeologists, actually."

"Archaeologists! How fascinating!" Mrs. Pryce paused, straightening out archaeology in her mind. Not primitive tribes—that was the other one. It was ruins, digging for artifacts. "I'm Harriet Pryce, by the way."

"How do you do," the young woman answered. Then, without enthusiasm, "I'm Violet and this is Grace."

Mrs. Pryce, nodding cordially, did not say that she knew this already. In the background, dark-haired Grace was glaring at her with a malice that seemed to Mrs. Pryce quite uncalled for. Nevertheless, she herself stayed calm and dignified. Dignity, she felt, could usually carry the day.

"I wonder if I might have a quick bath now—without putting you out?"

"Help yourself," tall Violet said.

"Thank you. I've just arrived in Rome—from the U.S.?—and the dust of travel, you know."

Grace's eyes moved toward the ceiling. "Yes, of course," Violet said. "Do carry on."

"Suppose I—tap on the door when I'm done?" Mrs. Pryce suggested, raising a knuckled hand to illustrate.

"Jesus," Grace murmured, and Violet said hastily, "That would be fine—most considerate." Mrs. Pryce gave Grace a withering look as she withdrew.

After she had bathed and rested, she felt quite restored and, for the first time since taking off from Kennedy airport, allowed herself to put into words a guilty thought that had been lurking in one of the dustier corners of her mind. She found herself actually glad that Bernard had decided against taking the tour with her. Here she had—quite innocently—stumbled upon this splendid bit of intrigue. Tonight in the dining room or lobby she might catch sight of the controversial Dr. Brand—no doubt he would be easy to recognize—and there would be a whole ready-made plot which she could watch unfolding. If Bernard were with her he would frown and be disapproving. None of our business, Harriet. For heaven's sake, Harriet. And he was so quick to criticize things like foreign cooking—always making remarks that mortified her, like, just bring me a soft-boiled egg if you can't manage anything else. Mrs. Pryce considered herself both worldly-tolerant and adventurous, and while she did bring along her own soap and teabags, she was willing to try anything recognizable—at least once.

Still when he had said that, about not coming along on the tour, she had put up an automatic argument.

"Not coming! But Bernard, we've been planning it all winter."

"I know, Harriet. But I've seen Rome."

"Well, yes, of course. But seeing Rome once hardly means we've tasted all its treasures. And I don't mind saying I'm terribly disappointed. Well, all right, if that's the way you feel, we'll go somewhere else. We've never done Scandinavia—"

"No no, that's not what I mean—you go ahead. I want you to have the trip. It's just that I think I'll go to the international convention in Boston instead."

"You've always said you hated those conventions!"

"I know. But orthodontics are like anything else. If you don't keep up with the new things, you're left in the backwash. Some big men will be there. I should go, Harriet."

"Well, I'm sure I don't see why. You're five years away from retiring. You said yourself you could coast the rest of the way."

"Good God, you're ready to wheel me into a retirement home! I won't even be sixty till August, you know. I *want* to keep up, Harriet. I'm not ready to pack it in yet. Besides, you don't need me to enjoy the tour—you've always managed well by yourself."

Had there been a twist of bitterness there, or had she only imagined it? Odd behavior—not like Bernard, Mrs. Pryce thought. Yet perhaps men of that age—she paused, thinking about it. And quite possibly both of them needed to define their personal spaces a bit more clearly. She repeated the phrase to herself, deciding that it reflected a good grasp of current thinking. She slipped into her two-piece blue, surveyed her greying brown hair critically in the mirror, and contemplated the evening ahead. An adventure, Mrs. Pryce thought, leaving the room and turning her key in the lock.

The tour had divided itself early in the trip into segments. Ten of the fifteen were couples. Two of these—in their mid-forties—had come together, and they remained a unit. Two younger couples had introduced themselves to each other on the plane and found common interests. Mrs. Pryce guessed they would go dining and sightseeing together. That left the Bennings, who had from the first clung to each other, bewildered and frightened, and Mrs. Pryce had thus been prompted to look out for them

and reassure them, after which they had clung to *her,* two limpets out of
their depth. There was one man by himself, a sober, decent-looking fellow
named Prescott, who Mrs. Pryce guessed might be a recent widower. He
had a reflective, inward look about him that she read as bereavement. That
left three odd ones, all in their early twenties, who had come together, two
men and a girl. They carried no luggage except canvas shoulder bags and
they had been assigned one room. Mrs. Pryce speculated with pinched
nostrils what *that* arrangement might be.

She dined that night in the hotel dining room with the Bennings. Most
of the tour people had gone scattering about, rushing off to stare at other
tourists on the Via Veneto, to seek out a trattoria, to reassure themselves
that they really were in Rome. Mrs. Pryce explained her views on this to the
Bennings.

"I always feel the first night should be for light dining and early retiring.
It fits one up for the rest of the tour," she explained, and the Bennings were
quick to agree.

"Perhaps you could suggest something from the menu," Mrs. Benning
said worriedly as she saw the waiter approaching, and Mrs. Pryce graciously
agreed to do so after giving the menu careful study.

*"Vorrei de sogliola,"* she told the waiter, speaking slowly and distinctly.
*"E insalata—"*

"Sole for all three?" he said briskly, writing it down. "What salad dressing?"

Mrs. Pryce, a little hurt, nevertheless went on to order the house wine
and *aqua minerale.* "So convenient that English is spoken quite univer-
sally," she said. But the Bennings were open-mouthed with admiration
nonetheless. Across the dining room at a table against the wall Mrs. Pryce
saw Mr. Prescott, the lone man, eating by himself. She had tried to approach him as they entered and to invite him to dine with them, but he had
only bobbed his head and pushed on to his solitary table. Pity, she thought,
for she could see that he had ordered a quite unsuitable meal that might
give him trouble later. She was quite sure she spotted both clams and sausage, and what looked to her like stuffed artichokes. Mrs. Pryce shuddered
and shook her head.

"The guide will be taking us out tomorrow morning, won't she?" Mr.
Benning inquired, and took out his tour schedule to examine it.

"Oh yes. I believe the bus tour of Rome is in the morning, and then in
the afternoon isn't it the Vatican Museum?"

Mr. Benning's finger ran down the paper. "Yes, that seems to be it. Do
we get to see the pope?"

Mrs. Pryce's eyes closed briefly and she managed a tolerant smile. "Not
in the museum," she said. "On Sunday, I believe there will be a trip to St.
Peter's Square, when he will no doubt appear on his balcony."

"Oh—" Mrs. Benning's breath was a trembling sigh and Mrs. Pryce could see the television shots of this scene flashing through her memory. She suggested, "Perhaps after we've eaten we might take just a small stroll out on the Via Veneto before turning in. Would you like that?"

"Oh, how exciting—yes, let's—" The rest of Mrs. Benning's effusion was lost on Harriet Pryce as she noticed a threesome just entering the dining room. The two Englishwomen from the room adjoining hers, and with them a tall good-looking man of forty or so—a younger Burt Lancaster type, Mrs. Pryce decided, rather on the rugged side. But of course an archaeologist—all that digging and outdoor work—for it had to be Dr. Brand, if for no other reason than the shining look of Violet's eyes behind their large spectacles when she looked at him. Yes, Grace had probably figured it right, even though she *had* been quite spiteful about it. Violet was in love with him: any fool could see it.

They took a table nearby, where Mrs. Pryce could observe them only obliquely, but there was little to observe anyway, for they ordered quietly and chatted inaudibly as they ate. Only when the Bennings and Mrs. Pryce were about to get up and leave was there a small flurry from that table. Mrs. Pryce saw that Grace had stood up, her dark eyes passionate with anger, her hand making a quick gesture that upset her half-full wine glass. She said something sharp and angry which Mrs. Pryce could not quite make out and then turned and left the dining room, almost running. The other two had risen as well and Mrs. Pryce saw Violet put a restraining hand on Dr. Brand's sleeve and heard her say, "Wait, Nigel, I'll go after her . . . I'm sure she'd never . . . she didn't mean . . ."

Violet hurried after her friend, and Mrs. Pryce turned abruptly to the Bennings. "Do excuse me for just a second, won't you? I've forgotten my sweater, and the evening air may be cool. Wait for me in the lobby."

She did not bother with the elevator, but hurried up the marble stairs to the second floor, fumbling for her key as she went. She could hear angry voices the moment she was in her room, and she made her way in the dark to the bathroom and crept inside. However, she found the conversation disappointingly less audible than it had been earlier. The speakers were at the far end of the bedroom, away from the bath, she guessed. Grace, by the look of her as she left the dining room, might have flung herself on the bed. Mrs. Pryce could hear no more than snatches and phrases. "Absolute madness, Grace . . . do yourself no good at all . . . can't possibly get away with . . ."

There were sounds of sobbing, then silence. Mrs. Pryce returned to her own room, closing the door behind her. She heard someone enter the bathroom and use it, heard water running as a faucet was turned on. Then presently there was the sound of a door opening and closing. Mrs. Pryce hurried to her own door and looked out into the corridor, in time to see

Violet disappearing at the end of it. Mrs. Pryce snatched her sweater from the bed and hurried back down to the lobby, once again using the wide marble staircase, which she thought infinitely more trustworthy than the quivering elevator.

In the lobby she saw the Bennings waiting by the front door and watching anxiously for her. She gave a reassuring wave, then looked around for Violet. The young woman stood near a large ficus tree on one side of the lobby. She, too, was looking around for someone—Dr. Brand, of course. Mrs. Pryce fancied a look of distress in her face. He appeared presently from the opposite side of the lobby, the side where the phone booths, restrooms, and elevators were situated. He and Violet spoke in low tones for a moment, then went out through the front door, their arms about each other's waists, their heads close together. Mrs. Pryce joined the Bennings, who were obviously so titillated by their surroundings that they had actually missed the whole thing. Just as well, Mrs. Pryce told herself. "Now then," she said expansively, "shall we start?" But television news clips were flashing in her own head now, and headlines from the *Times*. PROMINENT SCHOLAR CHARGED IN FRAUD . . . NOBEL COMMITTEE SAYS IT WILL ENTER PROBE . . . AMERICAN TOURIST'S TESTIMONY SOUGHT . . .

They walked down one side of the street and up the other, stopping at an open air cafe to have a cool drink and rest for a few moments, watching other tourists doing the same thing, then returned to the hotel.

"Well, I think I'm quite ready to turn in now," Mrs. Pryce announced as they entered the lobby, and the limpets were quick to agree. "Do be sure to wear comfortable shoes tomorrow morning," she counseled, and then, looking across the lobby, stopped short.

At the main desk where several guests were standing, some selecting newspapers, some receiving room keys, Mrs. Pryce saw the solitary traveler, Mr. Prescott, half-turned toward the door and obviously ill. He had sagged at the knees suddenly, and was supporting himself on the desk. Two men, a porter and a guest, at once seized him by the elbows to assist him, and Mrs. Pryce, quick in an emergency, started across the lobby herself. Sausage, she was thinking angrily. Really. Inexperienced travelers are their own worst enemies. But by the time she reached him he was shrugging off the hands that held him. "No, no. I'm all right," she heard. Nevertheless, she approached him. "How do you do, Mr. Prescott. I'm Harriet Pryce—from your tour group? If I can be of any help—"

He looked so self-conscious, so vastly uncomfortable, that she thought he was ashamed of having given way—men are overly sensitive in these circumstances, she reminded herself. She said tactfully, "If I might suggest —the simpler the food one eats on these tours, the better. It's a great temptation, of course, to try the more exotic things, but one is infinitely safer with the ordinary. But I'm sure you'll be better by morning."

He agreed, mumbling his thanks, and hurried off to the elevator. Mrs. Pryce and the Bennings took the stairs.

There was a moment, as she turned the key in the lock to enter her room, that Mrs. Pryce experienced a brief, heightened awareness of something— not wrong, perhaps, but slightly out of alignment, not jibing with the normal. She could not define it more accurately to herself. Yet as she entered the dark room and reached for the lamp whose location she had noted earlier—just to the left of the door, near the bed—she felt some unaccountable reason for haste, as if she must reach the small dangling chain quickly lest another colder hand reach it ahead of hers.

Then, at once, the inadequate bulb came on, dimly lighting the room, and furniture, drapes, tired rug all settled back to their proper aspect, and all was as she had left it. Mrs. Pryce let her breath out in a little relieved puff and dropped her purse and sweater on the bed. Tiptoeing, she went to the bathroom door and pushed it open. Darkness and silence, except for a persistent taxi horn in the street outside, and a sudden strident laugh from the cafe tables across the street—but distant, muted through the closed windows. I must open them, Mrs. Pryce thought. The place is quite stuffy. She reached for the bathroom's wall switch.

She was back at the bedside table in seconds, seizing the telephone, but it was seconds more before she could adjust her breathing, summon up a voice that would be audible. And at last she raised the instrument and said as clearly as she could, "This is Harriet Pryce. Signora Pryce, Room 22— *ventidue*. There is a dead woman in the bathroom here. Her name is Grace something, I believe."

The next twenty-four hours were for Mrs. Pryce an unreality so bewildering that she seemed to be moving through an alien landscape, wading through ground mists and swamp water that clutched and sucked at her with every step. She forgot where she was, lost track of time, and felt, most of all, a vast smothering sense of make-believe swaddling her. She was no longer Harriet Pryce of Mamaroneck, New York. She was a performer in some absurd Italian opera—*The Daughter of the Regiment,* perhaps—surrounded by the fancy-dress uniforms of the *carabinieri,* bombarded by voices. And all those vowels! So ill-suited to the grim mechanics of the law, it seemed to her. The very language was all wrong for law enforcement. Still, she had to admit that the steps they were going through—the photographing, the taking of fingerprints, the questioning—all seemed to be according to standard practices everywhere, as much as she knew of them from films and television. And one man, a plainclothes inspector, or the Roman equivalent, named Marillo, was quite calm and civil and was able to question her in English, which was a relief. Talking through an interpreter made Mrs. Pryce feel that perhaps her answers were not being accurately passed along.

Not that there was much to tell, although she was obliged to tell it over and over. She had dined with two other tour members, she had fetched a sweater from her room, she had gone walking on the Via Veneto with her friends, she had returned to her room, she had found the body.

Yes, he had the picture, Marillo said, not unkindly. And at what hour had she fetched her sweater?

"I really don't think I noticed the time."

Marillo turned to the police doctor, a tall, stooping man, and asked something. Mrs. Pryce saw the doctor's hands turn up and out, heard the low answer, *"Nove—nove e quindici."* Nine or nine fifteen. She understood that—the time of death, no doubt.

"You wear a wristwatch, signora," Marillo suggested.

"Yes, but really, I never even thought to look at it."

He studied her, nodded, changed the subject.

"The dead woman's friend, Miss Violet Shallcross. She left the hotel dining room ahead of you. The headwaiter has mentioned this."

"I did see her leave, yes." Mrs. Pryce had already decided that she would not mention the argument in the dining room unless someone else brought it up. In a crowded, noisy room it had not been noticeable, unless one was paying close attention, which of course she had been. Others might have missed it. It was not up to her to blow it out of proportion. It would look bad for Violet Shallcross, and surely, Mrs. Pryce told herself, Violet could not be the guilty one.

"And you followed her upstairs."

"No, indeed. I did not follow her. I simply went upstairs. To fetch a sweater."

"Ah, forgive me, Mrs. Pryce. My English is so inadequate. I did not mean to imply—let us say then that you left the dining room after Miss Shallcross did. You went to fetch your sweater."

"Yes."

"Was she in the adjoining room with Miss Harwood when you were in your room finding your sweater?"

"I believe she was."

"You heard their voices?"

"I heard—voices."

"But not what was said?"

"Just snatches—very indistinct. I could not repeat a thing, no."

"Did you think they were arguing?"

"Not arguing, exactly—"

"What, exactly?"

"Just talking—really, you should discuss it with Miss Shallcross."

"I shall do so, of course, when she returns to the hotel. We have not been able to locate her. Now. You followed Miss Shallcross—excuse me, you returned to the lobby after Miss Shallcross did."

"Yes."

"What did she do there?"

"She joined Dr. Brand—no, he joined her, actually. He was not in the lobby when she got there, but he arrived shortly."

"How shortly?"

"Oh, two or three minutes. Almost right away."

"Where did he come from?"

"From across the lobby where the elevators are," Mrs. Pryce answered. After all, she thought, she had no desire to protect *him*.

The detective paused for a moment, then asked, "You have met Dr. Brand?"

"No."

"How did you know, then, that it was he?"

Mrs. Pryce temporized. "I knew about the convention here. And he's quite well known—in his field. I merely assumed."

Dark eyes studied her briefly. Then he backtracked. "How long did you stay in your room before leaving with your sweater? A guess."

"Perhaps three minutes. And I should like to say, inspector—Signor Marillo—that I feel absolutely certain it could not have been Violet Shallcross who did it. There couldn't possibly have been time."

He studied her again, liquid brown eyes deepset and tired-looking. "You know how Miss Harwood was killed?"

"I heard the officer say—a knife." *Coltello,* he had said.

"A very sharp, slender knife, almost a stiletto. How long do you think it would take to kill someone with such a weapon, Signora Pryce?"

When Mrs. Pryce hesitated, her hand at her throat, he made a lightning-quick thrust in air. "Ten seconds—no more."

And Violet Shallcross had a strong, sturdy look despite her slenderness, Mrs. Pryce thought. Archaeologists spent a great deal of their time outdoors, did they not? With picks and mallets and such things—Mrs. Pryce shuddered, and looked around the room they had cleared for her across the hall. She had no idea who had been put out nor did she care. The hotel had had her suitcase moved and *carabinieri* were milling about in the room that had formerly been hers.

"You have been most helpful, Mrs. Pryce," Marillo said, and just then there was a knock at the door. An officer stuck his head in and said something to Marillo, who answered, *"Bene."*

He turned back to her and said, "I will leave you now, signora. Thank you for your help. It seems Miss Shallcross has returned."

Mrs. Pryce remained where she was, seated in an uncomfortable chair with a harsh overhead light above her. She was no longer curious, no longer excited. She felt let down, heavily depressed. Suddenly Grace Harwood was becoming a real person to her, a person who might be forgiven for her bristling anger and rudeness, for who could say? She might have had her reasons.

She heard a long high scream from out in the hall. It propelled her out of her chair and to the door, which she opened enough to hear Violet crying out wildly, "It can't be! I don't believe it! It has to be a mistake!"

Mrs. Pryce closed the door and went to the bed, lying down on top of the spread with her knees drawn up, not even turning off the ceiling light.

Tomorrow, she thought, she would telephone Bernard.

She did not put the call through until midafternoon. Astonishingly, she slept until noon, after which the management sent up a lavish breakfast, and by the time she had bathed and dressed and started dealing with the hotel switchboard, the day was well along. She felt a need to discuss the whole matter with Bernard. She could not have said why; perhaps it was no more than a need to restore a sense of stability to her inner self—to reaffirm that she was who she was—to rid herself of this strange theatricality she felt herself wearing like a costume.

It would be early morning there; she decided to try the house first. No answer. Then he had already left for the office. She dealt with the operator again, giving her the office number. A woman's voice answered. Dr. Pryce was not there, not expected. He had gone out of town.

"Out of town? To the convention? But that doesn't start until Monday!"

"I couldn't say where's he's gone."

Mrs. Pryce identified herself and asked, "Who is this? Is it Karen?" Karen would be able to give her the facts and she would be reassuring to talk to. A remarkably sensible girl. When Bernard had hired her as a technician and assistant six months ago, Mrs. Pryce had sworn she'd be absolutely useless. Too young, too delicate, too lovely, with her pale hair and blue eyes and slender hands that looked incapable of work. But her efficiency had surprised both of them. Irreplaceable, Bernard said of her now.

"Karen's not here either. It's Mrs. Kemp, the bookkeeper. I'm just doing some catching up, Mrs. Pryce. Are you really calling from Rome?"

"Thank you," Mrs. Pryce said hastily, and hung up.

Late in the day the Bennings knocked at her door timidly to see how she was. "We didn't want to disturb you earlier, Mrs. Pryce. We heard all about it—we were so shocked. And what you must have gone through! I simply can't believe we slept through it all!"

Mrs. Pryce, who could believe it, thanked them for their concern and asked about the tour.

"Everything cancelled for today, of course. The hotel is simply upside down. Policemen all over the lobby and in the corridors, all over the place. But Miss Florio, our guide, says we'll be able to pick up our activities tomorrow. A bus tour of the city in the morning, and then the Tivoli gardens in the afternoon. Perhaps you'll feel like joining us."

"Yes. Well, perhaps."

"The police say now that it was a sneak thief, you know."

"They do?" Mrs. Pryce was at once alert.

"Yes. I daresay it's something they've seen before—"

"We reconstruct it somewhat this way," Marillo said, sitting opposite her. "The thief used the back service stairs. No doubt he was on his way up when Miss Shallcross left her room and when you yourself went out moments later with your sweater. Both of you ladies took the front stairs. He thought the rooms were empty. He entered one of them—yours or your neighbors'—"

"Mine was locked," Mrs. Pryce said quickly.

"Ah. Well, a locked door poses no problem for this type of thief. It's a common worry to hotels—all too common. Only it is unusual—" Marillo broke off.

"What is?"

"For such a person to commit a crime more serious than robbery. Murder is most rare in these circumstances. Yet we feel it's the only possible answer. We found that money was missing, and there are other indications as well, so—" Marillo raised expressive eyebrows and shrugged.

Mrs. Pryce did not go on the bus tour of the city the next morning, but she appeared in the lobby early in the afternoon, in time for the trip to the Tivoli gardens, and was gratified to note that the other tour members regarded her with some awe. The Bennings hovered over her solicitously, looking after *her* now. Certainly a new spirit of enterprise and courage there, Mrs. Pryce noted. An ill wind that had blown some grains of courage in their direction. Briefly she wondered whether any of the archaeologists remained in the hotel: there was no sign of them.

Even the reserved Mr. Prescott spoke to her as the tour group assembled around Miss Florio preparatory to boarding the bus. "Back with us again, Mrs. Pryce?" he said with a diffident smile.

Mrs. Pryce was touched at his remembering her name. But then, of course, she must have been discussed extensively after the part she had played in the investigation. She answered, "Mr. and Mrs. Benning have coaxed me out. And it may do us good." Generously she included them all in the crisis even though her importance had been so much greater than theirs. "A change of scene."

He nodded, and she, remembering, added hastily, "I do hope you're feeling fit again, Mr. Prescott. That little spell you had the other night—"

"Nothing at all," he said. "I took your advice about the food."

"I'm so glad."

The bus pulled up in front of the hotel and they filed on, young Miss Florio reminding them about sweaters. "You'll need them, even on such a warm day—the gardens are very cool." Mrs. Pryce saw the Bennings seat themselves with quite independent aplomb in the front of the bus and decided she had done a good job of stiffening their spines. Mr. Prescott went to the rear and sat by himself. Even though he seemed disposed to be pleasant now, she was relieved that he had not sat with her. Now she could have a seat to herself. Her head was aching, and she needed solitude to consider the moral problem confronting her. The police seemed quite convinced that a hotel sneak thief was responsible for the murder. Marillo had said money was missing. They were spreading a dragnet over the city, alerting other hotels, he had told her. Was it right, then, that she not report the rest of what she knew? The argument she had overheard in the dining room? Of course, others might have heard it, too—but she alone, with her greater knowledge, was able to attach significance to it.

The bus began climbing. Long sweeps of twisted gray olive trees covered the slopes. Mrs. Pryce turned blind eyes to them. She could still hear Violet's agitated voice. "Really, Nigel . . . I'm sure she'd never . . . she didn't mean . . ." Mrs. Pryce weighed the words. She'd never what? Didn't mean—what? A threat was certainly implied. Had Grace threatened to make public what she considered to be Nigel Brand's plagiarism? To destroy his reputation? And how far might a man thus threatened go to protect his professional standing? How far might a woman like Violet Shallcross go, for that matter, to protect a man she was in love with?

Mrs. Pryce felt the throbbing in her head grow until it was a steady, painful pounding. No, it could not have been Violet. There was something too fine, too gentle about her. Mrs. Pryce was quite unable to fit her into the role of murderer. And besides, there had been an absolutely genuine horror in her reaction when the police told her what had happened. Even Dr. Brand—she was finding it almost as difficult to believe him capable of such a crime. A scholar, a historian-scientist, a man of libraries and museums and learned societies. Perhaps the police had been right and perhaps she should let it go. If only she could rid herself of this feeling that lingered, shivering, far back in her mind where the rarefied atmosphere was too thin for logic. This feeling of something wrong that kept nudging at her.

They drove into the parking area and the bus stopped. Still dull and unfocused, Mrs. Pryce took passing note of the souvenir shop with its trashy plates and vases and its garish postcards. She made a point of never patronizing such places. She watched as another bus drew up—this one full of school children. A nun herded them out and clapped for their attention. The breeze caught her short veil and sent it snapping behind her. The doors of their own bus opened, and Mrs. Pryce realized the young woman, Miss Florio, was speaking to them.

"—created in the sixteenth century by a prince of the church, Cardinal Ippolito d'Este, the villa is a superb Renaissance residence set in an extraordinary garden—"

Something moved, lightning-like, in Mrs. Pryce's aching head and began clawing for her attention. Violet's voice again, this time overlaying the voice of the little tour guide:

*"It can't be! It has to be a mistake!"*

"—which features five hundred fountains, reflecting pools and artistic plantings—"

A mistake.

Mistakes could happen, in a dim-lit room in the soft Roman evening. A woman of about my size, Grace Harwood was, Mrs. Pryce thought, and felt hysteria creeping up behind her on soft feet. Could it have been someone after me? Someone hired, perhaps, by a man longing to dispose of an unwanted wife? Karen's pale hair and soft hands swam before her, an underwater dream. Then another picture supplanted it. Herself entering the hotel with the Bennings. And across the lobby a man at the desk sagging and stricken. But perhaps not with indigestion. Perhaps with shock, at the sight of her alive and well.

Because he had made a mistake.

Frantically she sought for a glimpse of the Bennings, but they had been far ahead of her, striding forward in their Hush Puppies, full of their new confidence. But I must not be alone! Mrs. Pryce thought with desperate fear. I must be with someone—I must stay with the group! The married couples, laughing and chattering, had gone. She had lingered too long. The three young shoulderbag people had also dashed forward and disappeared into the villa.

Miss Florio cast a last caveat over her shoulder.

"Do step carefully when you get into the gardens, all of you. Once we're out of the villa, many of the walkways will be wet and mossy, and there are some steep drops—"

Mrs. Pryce glanced over her shoulder and saw Mr. Prescott approaching, walking with a steady stride that covered the distance between them rapidly. He remembered my name, Mrs. Pryce thought. Perhaps he knew it always, right from the start of the trip.

He caught up with her. She noticed how cold and gray and narrow his eyes were.

"Shall we walk along together, Mrs. Pryce?" he said. "The others seem to have left us."

# THE SUICIDE OF KIAROS

### By L. Frank Baum

MR. FELIX Marston, cashier for the great mercantile firm of Van Alsteyne & Traynor, sat in his little private office with a balance sheet before him and a frown upon his handsome face. At times he nervously ran his slim fingers through the mass of dark hair that clustered over his forehead, and the growing expression of annoyance upon his features fully revealed his disquietude.

The world knew and admired Mr. Marston, and a casual onlooker would certainly have decided that something had gone wrong with the firm's financial transactions; but Mr. Marston knew himself better than the world did, and grimly realized that although something had gone very wrong indeed, it affected himself in an unpleasantly personal way.

The world's knowledge of the popular young cashier included the following items: He had entered the firm's employ years before in an inferior position, and by energy, intelligence, and business ability, had worked his way up until he reached the post he now occupied, and became his employers' most trusted servant. His manner was grave, earnest, and dignified; his judgment, in business matters, clear and discerning. He had no intimate friends, but was courteous and affable to all he met, and his private life, so far as it was known, was beyond reproach. Mr. Van Alsteyne, the head of the firm, conceived a warm liking for Mr. Marston, and finally invited him to dine at his house. It was there the young man first met Gertrude Van

Alsteyne, his employer's only child, a beautiful girl and an acknowledged leader in society. Attracted by the man's handsome face and gentlemanly bearing the heiress encouraged him to repeat his visit, and Marston followed up his advantage so skillfully that within a year she had consented to become his wife. Mr. Van Alsteyne did not object to the match. His admiration for the young man deepened, and he vowed that upon the wedding day he would transfer one-half his interest in the firm to his son-in-law.

Therefore the world, knowing all this, looked upon Mr. Marston as one of fortune's favorites, and predicted a great future for him. But Mr. Marston, as I said, knew himself more intimately than did the world, and now, as he sat looking upon that fatal trial balance, he muttered in an undertone: "Oh, you fool—you fool!"

Clear-headed, intelligent man of the world though he was, one vice had mastered him. A few of the most secret, but most dangerous gambling dens knew his face well. His ambition was unbounded, and before he had even dreamed of being able to win Miss Van Alsteyne as his bride, he had figured out several ingenious methods of winning a fortune at the green table. Two years ago he had found it necessary to "borrow" a sum of money from the firm to enable him to carry out these clever methods. Having, through some unforeseen calamity, lost the money, another sum had to be abstracted to allow him to win back enough to even the accounts. Other men have attempted this before; their experiences are usually the same. By a neat juggling of figures, the books of the firm had so far been made to conceal his thefts, but now it seemed as if fortune, in pushing him forward, was about to hurl him down a precipice.

His marriage to Gertrude Van Alsteyne was to take place in two weeks, and as Mr. Van Alsteyne insisted upon keeping his promise to give Marston an interest in the business, the change in the firm would necessitate a thorough overhauling of the accounts, which meant discovery and ruin to the man who was about to grasp a fortune and a high social position—all that his highest ambition had ever dreamed of attaining.

It is no wonder that Mr. Marston, brought face to face with his critical position, denounced himself for his past folly, and realized his helplessness to avoid the catastrophe that was about to crush him.

A voice outside interrupted his musings.

"It is Mr. Marston I wish to see."

The cashier thrust the sheet of figures into a drawer of the desk, hastily composed his features, and opened the glass door beside him.

"Show Mr. Kiaros this way," he called, after a glance at his visitor. He had frequently met the person who now entered his office, but he could not resist a curious glance as the man sat down on a chair and spread his hands over his knees. He was short and thick-set in form, and both oddly and carelessly dressed, but his head and face were most venerable in appearance.

Flowing locks of pure white graced a forehead whose height and symmetry denoted unusual intelligence, and a full beard of the same purity reached almost to his waist. The eyes were large and dark, but not piercing in character, rather conveying in their frank glance kindness and benevolence. A round cap of some dark material was worn upon his head, and this he deferentially removed as he seated himself, and said:

"For me a package of value was consigned to you, I believe?"

Marston nodded gravely. "Mr. Williamson left it with me."

"I will take it," announced the Greek, calmly. "Twelve thousand dollars it contains."

Marston started. "I knew it was money," he said, "but was not aware of the amount. This is it, I think."

He took from the huge safe a packet, corded and sealed, and handed it to his visitor. Kiaros took a penknife from his pocket, cut the cords and removed the wrapper, after which he proceeded to count the contents.

Marston listlessly watched him. Twelve thousand dollars. That would be more than enough to save him from ruin, if only it belonged to him instead of this Greek money-lender.

"The amount, it is right," declared the old man, rewrapping the parcel of notes. "You have my thanks, sir. Good afternoon," and he rose to go.

"Pardon me, sir," said Marston, with a sudden thought. "It is after banking hours. Will it be safe to carry this money with you until morning?"

"Perfectly," replied Kiaros. "I am never molested, for I am old, and few know my business. My safe at home large sums often contains. The money I like to have near me, to accommodate my clients."

He buttoned his coat tightly over the packet, and then in turn paused to look at the cashier.

"Lately you have not come to me for favors," he said.

"No," answered Marston, arousing from a slight reverie. "I have not needed to. Still, I may be obliged to visit you again soon."

"Your servant I am pleased to be," said Kiaros with a smile, and turning abruptly he left the office.

Marston glanced at his watch. He was engaged to dine with his betrothed that evening, and it was nearly time to return to his lodgings to dress. He attended to one or two matters in his usual methodical way, and then left the office for the night, relinquishing any further duties to his assistant. As he passed through the various business offices on his way out, he was greeted respectfully by his fellow-employees, who already regarded him a member of the firm.

Almost for the first time during their courtship, Miss Van Alsteyne was tender and demonstrative that evening, and seemed loath to allow him to leave the house when he pleaded a business engagement and arose to go.

She was a stately beauty, and little given to emotional ways, therefore her new mood affected him greatly, and as he walked away he realized, with a sigh, how much it would cost him to lose so dainty and charming a bride.

At the first corner he paused and examined his watch by the light of the street lamp. It was 9 o'clock. Hailing the first passing cab, he directed the man to drive him to the lower end of the city, and leaning back upon the cushions, he became occupied in earnest thought.

The jolting of the cab over a rough pavement finally aroused him, and looking out he signaled the driver to stop.

"Shall I wait, sir?" asked the man, as Marston alighted and paid his fare.

"No."

The cab rattled away, and the cashier retraced his way a few blocks and then walked down a side street that seemed nearly deserted, so far as he could see in the dim light. Keeping track of the house numbers, which were infrequent and often nearly obliterated, he finally paused before a tall, brick building, the lower floors of which seemed occupied as a warehouse.

"Two eighty-six," he murmured. "If I remember right there should be a stairway at the left—ah, here it is."

There was no light at the entrance, but having visited the place before, under similar circumstances, Marston did not hesitate, but began mounting the stairs, guiding himself in the darkness by keeping one hand upon the narrow rail. One flight—two—three—four—

"His room should be straight before me," he thought, pausing to regain his breath. "Yes, I think there is a light shining under the door."

He advanced softly, knocked, and then listened. There was a faint sound from within, and then a slide in the upper panel of the door was pushed aside, permitting a strong ray of lamp-light to strike Marston full in the face.

"Oho!" said a calm voice, "Mr. Marston has honored me. To enter I entreat you."

The door was thrown open and Kiaros stood before him, with a smile upon his face, gracefully motioning him to advance. Marston returned the old man's courteous bow, and entering the room, took a seat near the table, at the same time glancing at his surroundings.

The room was plainly but substantially furnished. A small safe stood in a corner at his right, and near it was the long table, used by Kiaros as a desk. It was littered with papers and writing material, and behind it was a high-backed, padded easy-chair, evidently the favorite seat of the Greek, for after closing the door he walked around the table and sat in the big chair, facing his visitor.

The other end of the room boasted a fireplace, with an old-fashioned mantel bearing an array of curiosities. Above it was a large clock, and at one side stood a small bookcase containing a number of volumes printed in the Greek language. A small alcove, containing a couch, occupied the remaining side of the small apartment, and it was evident these cramped quarters constituted Kiaros's combined office and living rooms.

"So soon as this I did not expect you," said the old man, in his grave voice.

"I am in need of money," replied Marston, abruptly, "and my interview with you this afternoon reminded me that you have sometimes granted me an occasional loan. Therefore, I have come to negotiate with you."

Kiaros nodded, and studied with his dark eyes the composed features of the cashier.

"A satisfactory debtor you have ever proved," said he, "and to pay me with promptness never failed. How much do you require?"

"Twelve thousand dollars."

In spite of his self-control, Kiaros started as the young man coolly stated this sum.

"Impossible!" he ejaculated.

"Why is it impossible?" demanded Marston. "I know you have the money."

"True; I deny it not," returned Kiaros. "Also to lend money is my business. But see—I will be frank with you Mr. Marston—I cannot take the risk. You are cashier for hire; you have no property; security for so large a sum you cannot give. Twelve thousand dollars! It is impossible!"

"You loaned Williamson twelve thousand," persisted Marston.

"Mr. Williamson secured me."

Marston rose from his chair and began slowly pacing up and down before the table, his hands clasped tightly behind him and an impatient frown contracting his features. The Greek watched him calmly.

"Perhaps you have not heard, Mr. Kiaros," he said, at length, "that within two weeks I am to be married to Mr. Van Alsteyne's only daughter."

"I had not heard."

"And at the same time I am to receive a large interest in the business as a wedding gift from my father-in-law."

"To my congratulations you are surely entitled."

"Therefore my need is only temporary. I shall be able to return the money within thirty days, and I am willing to pay you well for the accommodation."

"So great a chance I cannot undertake," returned Kiaros, with a slight shrug. "You are not yet married, a partner in the firm not yet. To die, to quarrel with the lady, to lose Mr. Van Alsteyne's confidence, would leave me to collect the sum wholly unable. I might a small amount risk—the large amount is impossible."

Marston suddenly became calm, and resumed his chair with a quiet air, to Kiaros's evident satisfaction.

"You have gambled?" asked the Greek, after a pause.

"Not lately. I shall never gamble again. I owe no gambling debts—this money is required for another purpose."

"Can you not do with less?" asked Kiaros. "An advance I will make of one thousand dollars; not more. That sum is also a risk, but you are a man of discretion; in your ability I have confidence."

Marston did not reply at once. He leaned back in his chair, and seemed to be considering the money-lender's offer. In reality there passed before his mind the fate that confronted him, the scene in which he posed as a convicted felon; he saw the collapse of his great ambitions, the ruin of those schemes he had almost brought to fruition. Already he felt the reproaches of the man he had robbed, the scorn of the proud woman who had been ready to give him her hand, the cold sneers of those who gloated over his downfall. And then he bethought himself, and thought of other things.

Kiaros rested his elbow upon the table and toyed with a curious-looking paper-cutter. It was made of pure silver, in the shape of a dagger; the blade was exquisitely chased and bore a Greek motto. After a time Kiaros looked up and saw his guest regarding the paper-cutter.

"It is a relic most curious," said he, "from the ruins of Missolonghi rescued, and by a friend sent to me. All that is Greek I love. Soon to my country I shall return, and that is why I cannot risk the money I have in a lifetime earned."

Still Marston did not reply, but sat looking thoughtfully at the table. Kiaros was not impatient. He continued to play with the silver dagger, and poised it upon his finger while he awaited the young man's decision.

"I think I shall be able to get along with the thousand dollars," said Marston at last, his tone showing no trace of the disappointment Kiaros had expected. "Can you let me have it now?"

"Yes. As you know, the money is in my safe. I will make out the note."

He quietly laid down the paper-cutter and drew a notebook from a drawer of the table. Dipping a pen in the inkwell, he rapidly filled out the note and pushed it across the table to Marston.

"Will you sign?" he asked, with his customary smile.

Marston picked up the pen, dashed off his name, and tossed the paper towards Kiaros. The Greek inspected it carefully, and rising from his chair, walked to the safe and drew open the heavy door. He placed the note in one drawer, and from another removed an oblong tin box which he brought to the table. Reseating himself, he opened this box and drew out a large packet of banknotes.

Marston watched him listlessly as he carefully counted out $1000.

"The amount is, I believe, correct," said Kiaros, after a second count. "If you will kindly verify it I shall be pleased."

Marston half arose and reached out his hand. But he did not take the money. Instead, his fingers closed over the handle of the silver dagger, and with a swift, well-directed blow he plunged it to the hilt in the breast of the Greek. The old man lay back in his chair with a low moan, his form quivered once or twice and then became still, while a silence that suddenly seemed oppressive pervaded the little room.

Felix Marston sat down in his chair and stared at the form of Kiaros. The usually benevolent features of the Greek were horribly convulsed, and the dark eyes had caught and held a sudden look of terror. His right hand, resting upon the table, still grasped the bundle of banknotes. The handle of the silver dagger glistened in the lamplight just above the heart, and a dark-colored fluid was slowly oozing outward and discoloring the old man's clothing and the point of his snowy beard.

Marston drew out his handkerchief and wiped the moisture from his forehead. Then he arose, and going to his victim, carefully opened the dead hand and removed the money. In the tin box was the remainder of the $12,000 the Greek had that day received. Marston wrapped it all in a paper and placed it in his breast pocket. Then he went to the safe, replaced the box in its drawer, and found the note he had just signed. This he folded and placed carefully in his pocketbook. Returning to the table, he stood looking down upon the dead man.

"He was a very good fellow, old Kiaros," he murmured. "I am sorry I had to kill him. But this is no time for regrets; I must try to cover all traces of my crime. The reason most murderers are discovered is because they become terrified, are anxious to get away, and so leave clues behind them. I have plenty of time. Probably no one knows of my visit here tonight, and as the old man lives alone, no one is likely to come here before morning."

He looked at his watch. It was a few minutes after 10 o'clock.

"This ought to be a case of suicide," he continued, "and I shall try to make it look that way."

The expression of Kiaros's face first attracted his attention. That look of terror was incompatible with suicide. He drew a chair beside the old man and began to pass his hands over the dead face to smooth out the contracted lines. The body was still warm, and with a little perseverance, Marston succeeded in relaxing the drawn muscles until the face gradually resumed its calm and benevolent look.

The eyes, however, were more difficult to deal with, and it was only after repeated efforts that Marston was able to draw the lids over them and hide their startled and horrified gaze. When this was accomplished, Kiaros looked as peaceful as if asleep, and the cashier was satisfied with his progress. He now lifted the Greek's right hand and attempted to clasp the fingers over the handle of the dagger, but they fell away limply.

"Rigor mortis has not yet set in," reflected Marston, "and I must fasten the hand in position until it does. Had the man himself dealt the blow, the tension of the nerves of the arm would probably have forced the fingers to retain their grip upon the weapon." He took his handkerchief and bound the fingers over the hilt of the dagger, at the same time altering the position of the head and body to better suit the assumption of suicide.

"I shall have to wait some time for the body to cool," he told himself, and then he considered what might be done in the meantime.

A box of cigars stood upon the mantel. Marston selected one and lit it. Then he returned to the table, turned up the lamp a trifle, and began searching in the drawers for specimens of the Greek's handwriting. Having secured several of these he sat down and studied them for a few minutes, smoking collectedly the while, and taking care to drop the ashes in a little tray that Kiaros had used for that purpose. Finally, he drew a sheet of paper towards him, and carefully imitating the Greek's sprawling chirography, wrote as follows:

*My money I have lost. To live longer I cannot. To die I am therefore resolved.*

KIAROS

"I think that will pass inspection," he muttered, looking at the paper approvingly, and comparing it again with the dead man's writing. He placed the paper upon the table before the body of the Greek, and then rearranged the papers as he had found them.

Slowly the hours passed. Marston rose from his chair at intervals and examined the body. At 1 o'clock rigor mortis began to set in, and a half hour later Marston removed the handkerchief, and was pleased to find that the hand retained its grasp upon the dagger. The position of the dead body was now very natural indeed, and the cashier congratulated himself upon his success.

There was but one task remaining for him to accomplish. The door must be found locked upon the inside. Marston searched until he found a piece of twine, one end of which he pinned lightly to the top of the table, a little to the left of the inkwell. The other end of the twine he carried to the door, and passed it through the slide in the panel. Withdrawing the key from the lock of the door, he now approached the table for the last time, taking a final look at the body, and laying the end of his cigar upon the tray. The theory of suicide had been excellently carried out; if only the key could be arranged for, he would be satisfied. He blew out the light.

It was very dark, but he had carefully considered the distance before-hand, and in a moment he had reached the hallway and softly closed and locked the door behind him. Then he withdrew the key, found the end of the twine which projected through the open slide in the panel, and running this through the ring of the key, he passed the key inside the panel, and allowed it to slide down the cord until a sharp click told him it rested on the table within. A sudden jerk of the twine now unfastened the end which had been lightly pinned to the table, and he drew it out and carefully placed it in his pocket. Before closing the slide of the panel, Marston lighted a match, peered through the slide, and satisfied himself the key was lying in the position he had wished. He breathed more freely then and closed the slide.

A few minutes later he had reached the street, and after a glance up and down stepped boldly from the doorway and walked away.

To his surprise, he now felt himself trembling with nervousness, and despite his endeavors to control himself, it required all of his four-mile walk home to enable him to regain his normal composure.

He let himself in with his latch-key, and made his way noiselessly to his room. As he was a gentleman of regular habits, the landlady never bothered to keep awake for his return.

Mr. Marston appeared at the office the next morning in an unusually good humor, and at once busied himself with the regular routine of his bank duties.

As soon as he was able, he retired to his private office and began to revise the books and make out a new trial balance. The exact amount he had stolen from the firm was put into the safe, the false figures were replaced with correct ones, and by noon the new balance sheet proved that Mr. Marston's accounts were in perfect order.

Just before he started for luncheon a clerk brought him the afternoon paper.

"What do you think, Mr. Marston?" he said. "Old Kiaros has committed suicide."

"Indeed! Do you mean the Kiaros who was here yesterday?" inquired Marston, as he put on his coat.

"The very same. It seems the old man lost his money in some unfortunate speculation, and so took his own life. The police found him in his room this morning, stabbed to the heart. Here is the paper, sir, if you wish to see it."

"Thank you," returned the cashier, in his usual quiet way. "I will buy one when I go out," and without further comment he went to luncheon.

He purchased a paper, and while eating read carefully the account of Kiaros's suicide. The report was reassuring; no one seemed to dream the Greek was the victim of foul play.

The verdict of the coroner's jury completed his satisfaction. They found that Kiaros had committed suicide in a fit of despondency. The Greek was buried and forgotten, and soon the papers teemed with sensational accounts of the brilliant wedding of that estimable gentleman, Mr. Felix Marston, to the popular society belle, Miss Gertrude Van Alsteyne. The happy pair made a bridal trip to Europe, and upon their return Mr. Marston was installed as an active partner in the great firm of Van Alsteyne, Traynor & Marston.

This was twenty years ago. Mr. Marston today has an enviable record as an honorable and highly respected man of business, although some consider him a trifle too calculating.

His wife, although she early discovered the fact that he had married her to further his ambition, has found him reserved and undemonstrative, but always courteous and indulgent to both herself and the children.

He holds his head high and looks every man squarely in the eye, and he is very generally envied, since everything seems to prosper in his capable hands.

Kiaros and his suicide are long since forgotten by the police and the public. Perhaps Marston recalls the Greek at times. He told me this story when he lay upon what he supposed was his death-bed. . . .

# DOVER WITHOUT PERKS

*Joyce Porter*

AND THIS is where the body was found, sir."
Detective Chief Inspector Dover, having with difficulty been in-
duced to leave the shelter of the police car, stood shivering inside
his overcoat. He tossed an indifferent glance at the site before transferring
his disgruntled gaze to his surroundings.

'Strewth, what a dump! Like the back of the bloody moon!

He was standing on a short stretch of access road which led from the
busy dual carriageway on his left to a new housing development, just beginning to spread its unloveliness over the hillside on his right. From this
distance the development was a jumble of unmade roads, scaffolding,
patches of raw earth, and a few demoralized houses poking up like sore
thumbs into the cold sky. Beyond, as far as the eye could see, lay acres of
deserted, frost-bitten fields with only the occasional windswept hedge to
break the monotony.

Such desolation made it all the more surprising that the access road
proudly sported a brand-new pedestrian crossing, complete with black and
white stripes and flashing orange beacons. It was here, some fifty yards
before the access road swung round to glide into the dual carriageway, that
the dead man had been found at 5:25 that morning.

"Funnily enough, sir, it was his son-in-law who found him. He's a milk
roundsman and he was cycling down to his depot. It was still dark then, of

course, but he spotted the old chap in the light of the beacon." Even Inspector York, the local man who was doing the honors, was stamping his feet to warm them.

But Dover, who had been transported from London to the scene of the crime with what he considered unseemly haste, still hadn't got his bearings. "Where the hell are we?" he demanded crossly while his young, handsome, and long-suffering assistant, Detective Sergeant MacGregor, turned aside to hide his blushing.

Inspector York was a little disconcerted, too. It was his first encounter with Scotland Yard's famous Murder Squad and he didn't know quite what to make of it. Surely they couldn't all be like this?

"Well, this is Willow Hill Farm Housing Estate, actually, sir," he said, indicating the miserable clutch of dwellings on the hillside. "Part of Bridchurch's slum-clearance scheme. Bridchurch is where you got off the train, sir. It's three miles away." He pointed down the dual carriageway. "Someday, sir"—this time he made a generous, encircling gesture—"all this will be covered with houses. Meantime, it's all a bit isolated. Still, that should make our job a bit easier, shouldn't it, sir?"

Dover's response might have been a belch or it might have been an encouraging grunt.

Naively, Inspector York plumped for the encouraging grunt. "There are not likely to be many people knocking about round here on a dark November night," he explained earnestly. "We've been working on the hypothesis that the murderer has some connection with the housing estate. In fact, he probably lives there. We found a lump of dried mud not far from the body and it probably came off the car that hit him. Now, we're pretty certain that the mud came from the housing estate—it's a proper quagmire when it rains, as you can imagine. It hasn't, however, rained for a fortnight. Well, if our chappie was on the estate a fortnight ago, the odds are that he lives there. Or, at the very worst, he's a frequent visitor."

Dover's habitual scowl deepened appreciably. "If it's a local case, why the hell fetch us into it?"

Inspector York quailed before such naked fury. "Our Chief Constable thought the Yard would want to handle it themselves, sir, since the dead man was one of yours."

"One of ours?"

"Malcolm Bailey, sir. He was an ex-Metropolitan policeman. We thought there might be—well—ramifications."

"Ramifications? Was he Special Branch or what?"

"No, sir." Inspector York wished the Chief Constable was there to do his own dirty work. "His last job before retirement was court usher at Ealing actually. Since then he's had fifteen years with the Corps of Commission-aires in the West End. He was a Londoner, you see. Nothing to do with Bridchurch at all."

But Dover's butterfly mind had already moved on to weightier problems. The murder of obscure superannuated coppers could wait. "Here," he said, trying to disappear into the depths of his overcoat, "where've you set up the Murder Headquarters? I'm getting bloody frozen out here. Got us a nice cosy pub, have you?"

To date, unfortunately, there were no pubs on the Willow Hill Farm Estate. Nor were there any shops, cinemas, or other amenities.

"We were going to use a caravan, sir, but it hasn't arrived yet. I've been trying to chase it up but—"

But Dover was already stumping back to the comparative warmth and shelter of the police car. After a moment's hesitation MacGregor and Inspector York followed him.

Once they were all in the car, MacGregor took charge of things since Dover appeared to have lost all interest and was sitting slumped in a corner with his bowler hat pulled well down over his eyes. If it hadn't been completely unthinkable, Inspector York might have been tempted to conclude that old Mastermind was having a bit of a snooze.

"If Bailey was a Londoner," said MacGregor, resting his notebook awkwardly on his knees, "what was he doing down here?"

"He'd come for a few days' holiday with his daughter. He arrived only yesterday."

"That's the daughter who's married to the milkman who found the body?"

"Yes. They're named Muldoon. Apparently, last night, the dead man decided to go out for a drink. Like I said, there aren't any pubs on the Estate, so he had to catch a bus out there on the main road and go into Bridchurch."

"The Muldoons didn't go with him?"

"No. They don't go out much at night in the middle of the week because of him having to be up so early in the morning."

MacGregor pondered. "The Muldoons didn't raise the alarm when Bailey failed to return home at a reasonable hour?"

"They didn't know. It's this milk business again. Both Muldoon and his wife go to bed early—about half past nine, they say. Last night they simply gave Bailey a key and told him to let himself in when he got back. They'd no idea, they claim, that he wasn't fast asleep in the spare room until Muldoon himself practically fell over the dead body on the pedestrian crossing."

Dover, roused by a crick in the back of his neck, joined in the conversation. "Damned fool place to stick a zebra crossing," he grumbled, massaging the offending spot. "Right out here in the back of beyond."

Inspector York risked a placatory smile. "It's supposed to be a mistake on the part of the Highways Department, sir. It should have been erected on another housing development on the other side of town."

" 'Strewth!" said Dover and surrendered himself once more to torpidity.

Inspector York, a novice at Dover-watching, waited to see if any more pearls of wisdom were going to drop from beneath that moth-eaten little black mustache, but luckily MacGregor knew a snore when he heard one. "What about the medical evidence? Have we got a time of death yet?"

Inspector York dragged his eyes away. "Er—oh, yes, sorry, Sergeant! Time of death? About eleven last night. That fits with the supposition that Bailey would be on the last bus from Bridchurch which would drop him out there on the main road just before eleven. He wouldn't hang about on such a cold night and I reckon he simply walked from the bus stop to where he was found and was killed there. He wasn't robbed, by the way."

"And the cause of death?"

"Head bashed in with a blunt instrument. However"—Inspector York leaned forward so as to deliver his *bonne bouche* with maximum effect— "before that he'd been knocked down by a car. The doctor's absolutely sure about it. Bailey was severely bruised all down the left side, though it's unlikely the car was damaged. Still, you see what it means, Sergeant?"

"Oh, I think so," said MacGregor with a patronizing smile, the local bobby not having yet been born who could catch him napping. "It means that Bailey was probably knocked down by a car which was coming *from* the housing estate." He flapped a languid hand. "If Bailey got off the bus at that stop, he'd walk down there and cross this road here at the crossing with his left-hand side towards the housing estate. Interesting."

Inspector York suppressed an unworthy longing to sink his fist up to the wrist in a certain smug young face, then reminded himself that it was his job to be helpful. He got a couple of sheets of paper out of his pocket. "Luckily," he said, "there aren't many people on the estate who can afford to run a car these days. It takes some of 'em all they can manage to pay the bus fares. Anyhow"—he passed one sheet of paper over—"there's a list of those who have got cars. And here"—he held out the second sheet—"is a real bonus!"

"You don't say!"

Inspector York gritted his teeth. Much more of this and he'd leave the pair of 'em to stew in their own juice! "It's the name and address of an old lady who may narrow the field down even further. My lads had a chat with her earlier on and she seems bright enough. However, she's no chicken, so you'll have to use your own judgment."

"Your lads seem to have been very busy," said MacGregor as he accepted the second sheet.

Inspector York let some of the bitterness show through. "My lads," he muttered angrily, "could have had this case tied up a couple of hours ago if they hadn't been told to hang back and wait for you lot."

Mrs. Alice Golightly was 84 years old and still fighting back in spite of the fact that she had been sentenced to virtual solitary confinement by a caring community. The sheltered housing, into which she had been moved, was miles away from all her friends and relations and consisted of a drab row of two-roomed units built halfway up a steepish hill and fronting onto a block of communal garages.

"Bloody motor cars!" quavered Mrs. Golightly. "I'd ban 'em if I was prime minister, straight I would." She leaned across and gave Dover a poke in the paunch to gain his attention. "Nasty stinking things! They're more bloomin' bother than they're worth."

MacGregor smiled a kindly smile.

Mrs. Golightly leered back. It had been a long time since she'd had two fine chaps like this hanging on her every word. "There's that young punk up at the back," she went on. "You know—What's-his-name." She rummaged around in her memory. "Miller—that's him! Woke me up at ten past seven this morning trying to start his car—grind, grind, grind! Well, that meant I had to go to the toilet, didn't it? I'd hardly got sat down when— damn me!—he finally gets it going and all these stinking, smelly petrol fumes come pouring in through the bathroom window where there's gaps you could drive a corporation bus through. It's a public scandal! There isn't a bloody window in this whole bloody row that fits proper."

Dover roused himself to recall his hostess to a sense of what was fitting and proper. "Don't you," he bellowed at her, "usually have a cup of coffee about this time, missus? And a butt and a few biscuits?"

Mrs. Golightly was not amused and MacGregor rushed in before she could start expressing her opinion of those who attempted to sponge on old-age pensioners. "Er—does this Mr. Miller often wake you up starting his car?"

"He'd better not! Next time I'll have the law on him. Bloody motor cars!" She looked up. "I remember when it was all horses," she boasted. "Not but what they hadn't got some disgusting habits, but at least they didn't go messing your telly up!"

"Ah," said MacGregor with heaven-sent inspiration, "your television, Mrs. Golightly! Is that how you know when the cars use the garages opposite?"

Mrs. Golightly nodded grimly. "They break my picture up something cruel," she grumbled. "Every last one of 'em! And don't talk to me about suppressors! They've all had 'em fitted and it doesn't make a ha'porth of difference. I've had them Post Office engineers round here," she went on savagely. "Endless. Nothing but kids, most of 'em, and about as much use

as my old boot. I have to keep a bloody record for 'em now, you know."
She snatched a small writing pad off the table and waved it contemptuously.
"Like I told her from the Welfare—it's coming to something when a lady's
word isn't good enough!"

MacGregor tried to unravel things, just in case Dover was still listening.
"You keep a note of every time there's interference with your television
picture," he said, "and that means every time a car enters or leaves those
garages opposite."

Mrs. Golightly's sniff acknowledged that this was so.

"And you watch television all evening?"

"I watch it all day," came the forthright answer. "And so will you when
you're my age, sonny! I'd have it on now if you lot weren't here putting me
through the third degree."

"And last night?"

"None of them went in or out after six o'clock. Well, they never do on a
Thursday, do they?"

"Don't they?"

"Everybody's skint on a Thursday." Mrs. Golightly appreciated a bit of
company but you could have too much of a good thing. "Friday's payday.
Nobody's got any money left to go gallivanting on a Thursday. I should
have thought even you'd know that."

Dover heaved himself to his feet. Although, to the untutored eye, his
role in the interview may have appeared completely passive, some information had evidently filtered through. "I'll just go and have a look at that
toilet," he said.

MacGregor tried to pass the time in small talk, but Mrs. Golightly's aged
ears didn't miss a thing. Eventually she raised her voice over the sound of
rushing water. "That fellow who's been killed—"

"Malcolm Bailey?" asked MacGregor.

"I saw him when he arrived," said Mrs. Golightly. "A fine figure of a
man." She paused spitefully to underline her point. "What I call a *real*
policeman!"

So, if old Mrs. Golightly's evidence was to be believed, none of the cars
habitually kept in the block of garages could have been involved in the
murder.

"And that, actually, sir, leaves us with only three suspects." MacGregor
gazed unhappily around at the wilderness of builders' rubbish and half
finished houses. "The people who own cars but who leave them parked out
on the road. Always assuming, of course, that Bailey was killed by whoever
knocked him down. I wonder what the motive was. It can't be anything to
do with his past life, surely. He's been retired for ages and he doesn't seem
to have been exactly a ball of fire when he was in the Force. On the other

hand, he's hardly been down here long enough to make enemies. Less then twenty-four hours and this was his first visit." MacGregor sighed. "I think we'll have to have a good long look at this daughter and her husband."

Dover was not the man for idle speculation. "For God's sake, let's get out of the bloody wind!" he growled. "It's enough to freeze a brass monkey!"

MacGregor, being MacGregor, knew where he was going. "Azalea Crescent, sir," he said as he led the way into a slightly curving, potholed stretch of road. "Mr. Jarrow lives here. And that, I imagine, is his car." Ever mindful that Dover's eyesight was something less than keen, MacGregor indicated an enormous black Humber parked by the curb and sparkling magnificently in the pale sunlight.

Sparkling?

*"Stop that!"* MacGregor leaped forward and screamed like a banshee.

The man with the soft duster jumped back as though stung. "Eh?"

"You're destroying evidence!"

"What?"

"Didn't the police tell you we might want to examine that car?"

The unfortunate perfectionist shook his head. "A couple of 'em had a good look at it earlier on," he said lamely.

"Didn't they tell you not to touch it?"

Bill Jarrow gesticulated feebly with his duster. "I was just passing the time, like."

It was Dover—he of the aching feet and the rumbling stomach—who moved the proceedings indoors. Bill Jarrow put his duster away and called to his wife to put the coffee on. He thus insured that, unless the evidence was *very* strong to the contrary, he'd be able to get away with murder where Dover was concerned. He further endeared himself by keeping his answers short and to the point, seemingly knowing by instinct that Dover valued brevity well above truthfulness.

Mr. Jarrow proved to be a taxi driver and the car he had been polishing belonged to the company for whom he worked. Most weekday evenings, when business was slack, he was allowed to bring the car home with him and answer any calls from his house. "It saves 'em keeping the office open," he explained.

"Did you get called out last night?"

"No. Me and the missus sat watching telly till it was time for bed."

"So your wife is the only witness?"

Bill Jarrow didn't seem unduly perturbed that his alibi was being questioned. "You can check the mileage if you like. They'll have a note at the office of what it was yesterday evening when I left. You can soon see if it doesn't tally."

Since Dover had got his National Health Service dentures inextricably

sunk in Mrs. Jarrow's homemade treacle cake, MacGregor carried on with
the questioning. "There's no meter on the taxi?"

"Not this one. We use this one for funerals, you see," said Mr. Jarrow,
passing Dover's cup through the kitchen hatch for a refill. "Folk don't like
to see a meter clicking away when they're following their loved ones to the
crematorium."

MacGregor examined Bill Jarrow thoughtfully. "Anything to stop you
getting a call, doing the job, altering the mileage reading, and pocketing the
fare?" he asked pleasantly.

For the first time, Mr. Jarrow's occupational antipathy to the police
showed through. "Trust you bloody cops!" he said disgustedly. "Look,
mate, I've been a taxi driver for twenty years. I wouldn't last five minutes if
I started pulling tricks like that. What do you think my boss is, stupid or
something? Petrol consumption alone'd be a dead giveaway. And suppose I
had a smashup? Or somebody saw me?"

Bill Jarrow continued to wax indignant for some time, but eventually he
recovered his equilibrium sufficiently to direct MacGregor to Japonica
Mount, their next port of call. It was so close at hand that even Dover
didn't think it was worth demanding a police car. . . .

"That chap might have run us there in his taxi," Dover observed sourly
as he and MacGregor proceeded slowly on their way back past Mrs. Golightly's humble abode, "if you hadn't been so bloody rude to him. What
got into you? Any fool could see he's too thick to be anything but honest."

MacGregor didn't agree. "You don't need much intelligence, sir, to alter
a mileage reading. And he was giving that car a thorough cleaning. He
could have been removing traces of incriminating evidence."

"Stuff!" puffed Dover, already finding the going hard. "Besides, where's
the motive? He'd never even met What's-his-name."

"Bailey, sir." MacGregor was well used to Dover's inability to remember
any name (including probably his own) for more than five minutes. "Besides, I don't think we're looking for that kind of motive."

"Oh, don't you?" sneered Dover in a poor imitation of MacGregor's
refined accent. "Well, what kind of motive are we looking for, Smartie-
boots?"

"I think the murder is tied up with the car accident, sir."

Dover paused to contemplate the young mountain which had suddenly
loomed up in front of them. 'Strewth, if he'd realized that the "couple of
hundred yards" was going to be straight up . . . "Of course it's tied up
with the car accident," he growled, once he'd got his breath back. "The
killer runs Whatd'yecall'im down and immobilizes him, and then gets out
to finish him off with a tire lever or something. Gangsters in America are
doing it all the time."

"It'll be just by that small red car, sir," said MacGregor, cringing as Dover grabbed his arm and hung on. As a 240-pound weakling, the Chief Inspector wasn't fussy about who shared the burden. "I was thinking of a slight variation, actually," MacGregor went on, failing to appreciate that aching feet were now looming larger in Dover's mind than violent death. "I was wondering if the murder had to be committed *because* of the accident. That would fit Jarrow, you see.

"Suppose he had been doing a job without his employer's knowledge, and during the course of it accidentally knocked Mr. Bailey down. Well, to report the accident in the normal way would expose what he'd been doing and he'd get the sack. So"—even MacGregor was beginning to sound unconvinced—"he finished Bailey off. I admit it sounds a bit thin, sir, but"—MacGregor cheered up—"plenty of murders have been done for less."

"This it?"

They had climbed almost to the top of the steep incline that was Japonica Mount and were now level with the small red car. According to its number plate it was fourteen years old and it was obvious why its owner wasn't paying out good money to rent a garage for it.

Dover turned thankfully through the little wrought-iron gate and waddled up the path. The curtains in the front room had twitched but he stuck his finger in the bell-push and rested his weight on it.

A woman opened the door and Dover was halfway inside before he discovered, to his undisguised chagrin, that it was the wrong house.

"No," said the woman, "I'm Mrs. Jedryschowski. The Millers live the next house down." She moved forward fractionally and pointed.

Dover's fury mounted as he realized that the Miller house was one they had already passed.

"You'll not find her there, of course," said Mrs. Jedryschowski, "but he's in. The police turned him back when he was going to work."

Dover wasn't prepared to let the matter rest there. It was MacGregor's fault for dragging him to the wrong address, of course, but this Mrs. Whatever-her-name-was must take some of the blame. "That his car?" he demanded, with menace.

"Mr. Miller's?" Mrs. Jedryschowski eyed Dover with some suspicion. "Yes, it's his car."

"Then why is it parked outside your house?"

Not for the first time MacGregor marveled at Dover's unerring ability to grasp at the inessential.

It was all one to Mrs. Jedryschowski, of course. "You might well ask," she said, leaning forward to stare at the vehicle in question. "He always leaves it there. We have spoken to him about it but it makes no difference. He says it's something to do with saving his battery."

MacGregor, of course, understood perfectly. "Oh, you mean he starts it by letting it run down the hill."

Mrs. Jedryschowski, something of an ignoramus where the internal combustion engine was concerned, nodded. "Something like that. If he leaves it outside his own front door, he doesn't get a long enough run or something." She watched her visitors go back halfway down the path before closing the door on them.

Henry Miller was a livelier character than his next-door neighbor, though not by much. He welcomed Dover and MacGregor into a house that was clearly lacking a woman's touch. Dover realized there was a fat chance of being offered any decent light refreshments here. He shoved a bundle of old socks out of the most comfortable-looking armchair and flopped down. This was going to be a bloody short interview.

Mr. Miller cleared a couple of dirty plates off another chair for MacGregor. "Bit of a mess," he mumbled in apology. "What with the wife being away—"

"Not ill, I hope?" asked MacGregor politely as he got his notebook out.

"Not exactly." Mr. Miller perched himself on the arm of the settee and looked hunted. Like everybody else on the housing estate, he knew all about the murder. He didn't, however, know Mr. Bailey or his daughter and her husband. "People keep themselves to themselves round here," he explained. "We don't want to impose. And this time of year you don't want to leave your own fireside, do you?"

Mr. Miller paused in the hope that somebody else might like to say something, but they didn't. "I work as a groundsman," he volunteered. "At Bridchurch Central Junior School. The police stopped me when I was driving off to work this morning and said I was to stay at home till somebody came and took a statement off me or something. They had a look at my car, too."

There was another pause. Mr. Miller mopped his brow. This time, however, MacGregor took pity on him and tossed a question.

Mr. Miller was grateful but unhelpful. "No, I didn't. I got back from work about four o'clock and I didn't leave the house again till this morning."

Even MacGregor was obliged to swallow a yawn. Dover, of course, wasn't even pretending to listen and was now resting his eyes against the light.

"You're alone in the house?"

Mr. Miller blinked. "Yes. With the wife being away like."

MacGregor looked at the layer of burnt crumbs which covered one corner of the table. "Has she been away long, sir?"

Mr. Miller sighed. "Only three days. I'm afraid I've been letting the housework slip a bit."

Having been given MacGregor's solemn word that the home of the last car owner could be reached in three minutes and that it was downhill all the way, Dover reluctantly consented to walk.

Since it really was downhill, the Great Detective had breath to spare for an in-depth discussion of the case so far. "That milksop?" he questioned incredulously. "You must have lost your marbles! He couldn't say boo to a goose!"

"He hasn't got an alibi, sir."

"Innocent people never have alibis," retorted Dover, generously imparting the fruits of his many years of experience. "Besides, where's his motive? What's-his-name could hardly get *him* into trouble for driving his own blooming car."

"Miller might have come up against Bailey in a professional capacity, sir. Bailey might have nabbed him for something and this is a revenge killing."

"A revenge killing?" Dover's uninhibited hoot of mirth sent the sea gulls winging up from a nearby field. " 'Strewth, you've been at those detective-story books again! Revenge—on a clapped-out copper from Ealing who's been retired for twenty years?" Dover, seeing that MacGregor was about to correct his figures, rushed raucously on. "That Miller pouf would still have been in his cradle when Who's-your-father was pounding the beat."

MacGregor quietly resolved to check whether Miller had a police record and if there was any possible earlier connection between him and the deceased. "Ah, here we are, sir."

They had just turned into Viburnum Avenue and the car this time was a huge and very ancient Ford, liberally decorated with anarchistic slogans, Mickey Mouse stickers, pictures of nude ladies, and rust. Inside the appropriate house they found the owner of this vehicle—Lionel Hutchinson. He was a moronic-looking, slack-mouthed teenager, the epitome of a petty, unsuccessful crook. Lionel's mother, having let Dover and MacGregor into the house while her ewe-lamb remained lolling full-length on the sofa, returned wearily to her ironing.

Young Lionel was uncooperative. "You must be joking!" He removed neither his eyes from his comic book nor the cigarette from his mouth. "Drive that jalopy out there? Watcher trying to do—trap me?"

"I was merely asking if you went out in it last night," said MacGregor.

"Not last night and not for months!" said Lionel. "Because why? Because it hasn't passed its M.O.T. test, it isn't licensed, and it's not insured. Damn, I should have thought even you punks knew it was a criminal offense to take a car like that on the bleeding road. Besides"—he chucked his cigarette stub vaguely in the direction of the fireplace and reached for the packet on the floor at his side—"I can't afford the petrol."

Mrs. Hutchinson spoke up. "He doesn't get hardly anything from Social Security."

Dover looked hopefully at the packet of cigarettes, but it was not handed round. That was the trouble with these working-class crimes—no bloody perks! Dover vented his disappointment on Lionel. "You took that car out last night, didn't you?"

Lionel turned over the page. "Negative, Fatso."

"Just because it wasn't taxed and insured?" sneered Dover. "Try pulling the other one!"

Mrs. Hutchinson came galloping to the rescue again. "He's got to watch his step," she explained. "It's prison next time they catch him."

Lionel raised himself up and glared at his mother with less than filial affection.

Dover had another spot. "You took that car out last night and—"

"Stuff yourself!"

"—ran Bailey down because he was a copper and then—"

"Aw, get knotted!"

"—got out and finished him off as he lay there helpless."

Lionel Hutchinson struggled into a sitting position. "Without nicking his wallet?" Almost as exhausted by the effort as Dover would have been, he sank back. "I was home all evening. Ask my mum!"

Once they were safely outside, Dover waxed bolder. "I'll get that little bleeder!" he promised, looking fierce.

MacGregor took a more moderate line. "I doubt if he'd have the guts to kill a grown man, sir. Mugging old ladies for their pension books is about his limit."

"There's probably a gang of 'em," grunted Dover. He was bored, hungry, thirsty, and suffering from nicotine starvation.

"Perhaps forensic will turn up something on the murder weapon," said MacGregor hopefully. "And I think we must examine these cars again, too. I can't really believe that the car that knocked Bailey down would be completely unmarked."

They were walking slowly back up the hill and Dover was in no condition to contradict everything MacGregor said just for the hell of it.

"Oh, look, sir!" MacGregor pointed. "There's the caravan at last. Good! Now at least we'll have somewhere we can settle down to work in."

Dover shied like a nervous horse at the mere mention of work. "I want my lunch! I'm starving."

"Oh, there'll be coffee and sandwiches in the caravan for sure, sir."

By some miracle Dover found the puff to tell MacGregor what he could do with his coffee and sandwiches, interrupting his tirade only to stick his tongue out at old Mrs. Golightly who was peeping out from behind her curtains.

MacGregor hastened to make amends by giving her a cheery smile and raising his hat. "Poor old thing," he said when he could get a word in. "You'd think they could do something better for them than this, wouldn't you, sir? Sticking them out here miles away from anywhere and right on top of those noisy garages, to say nothing of having petrol fumes seeping in through your bathroom window. Good God!"

Afterward, both MacGregor and Dover claimed to have spotted it first but, since Dover had fewer inhibitions about bawling his head off on the public highway, he tended to hog the glory at the time.

He stopped dead in his tracks. "But there shouldn't have been any petrol fumes!"

By great good fortune there they were, standing right on the spot. Branching off on the left as they went up the hill was the row of houses for the old-age pensioners. And running up even higher behind them was Japonica Mount. Miller's small red car was clearly visible, not more than a couple of hundred feet away, still outside Mrs. Jedryschowski's house and still with its nose pointing down the hill.

Dover's brain nearly blew a gasket as he struggled to work it out. "How far," he panted, "on a cold morning would you have to let that car roll down the hill before you could start it?"

MacGregor was amazed at Dover's grasp of the technical problem involved. "Oh, right to the bottom, I imagine, sir. Certainly well past Mrs. Golightly's bathroom window."

"We've got him!" said Dover, and rested his case.

MacGregor felt they needed a little more than that. "Miller could have started his car on the starter this morning for some reason or other, sir."

"Why the hell should he? And even if he did, the fumes still wouldn't get into that old biddie's bog, would they?"

"Not if the car was parked outside Mrs. Jedryschowski's house where it is now, sir," agreed MacGregor. "On the other hand"—his eyes narrowed as he took in the topography of the area—"if he started the car on the starter outside his own house, old Mrs. Golightly would certainly have got the full benefit of both the noise and the smoke. He'd be hardly any distance away as the crow flies."

Dover had had his fill of the Willow Hill Farm Housing Estate. "Come on," he said with unwonted enthusiasm, "let's go get him!"

MacGregor was appalled. "But there could be dozens of perfectly innocent explanations, sir," he bleated anxiously. "I think it would be a big mistake for us to go off half cocked like this before we've—"

"You speak for yourself, laddie!" snorted Dover, already charging up the hill like a two-year-old tortoise. "Me, I've never gone off half cocked at anything in my whole bloody life!"

It was fortunate for the Cause of Justice that Henry Miller was one of Nature's losers.

"I knew I'd never get away with it," he said dejectedly as Dover lay panting like a stranded whale in one of the armchairs and MacGregor, getting his notebook out, issued the formal caution. "Oh, I don't mind making a statement. Why not?"

"Keep it short," advised Dover, cursing himself for not having had his lunch first. He accepted a cigarette from MacGregor, unaware that it was offered with the sole aim of stopping his mouth up.

But Miller had never been much of a talker in any case. "My wife left me a couple of days ago," he mumbled. "Just went. Late last night I got to wondering if she'd gone to stay with her sister. I thought I'd drive over and see."

"What time did you leave?"

Miller shrugged. "Latish."

"How did you start your car?"

"Like I always do—I let it roll down the hill."

"And you headed for the main road?"

"That's right. I wasn't going fast or anything. Then, just by the zebra crossing, he stepped out right in front of me and—bang!—I hit him. Not hard. I wasn't doing more than twenty. I stopped and got out. Well, he just lay there in the road, cursing me up hill and down dale. A right mouthful. Said I knocked him down deliberate on a pedestrian crossing and he'd have the Law on me.

"Said he'd charge me with dangerous driving and God knows what. I tried to calm him down a bit and ask if he was hurt, but he just kept on shouting. Said he was an ex-policeman and that he'd see me behind bars if it was the last thing he did. Well, he would have, wouldn't he? My word against his? I wouldn't have stood a chance. So I killed him."

"Just like that?" Dover didn't like to hear of policemen being disposed of so casually.

"I couldn't afford to be found guilty, you see," said Miller drearily. "Not on any charge. I've been in trouble before, you see."

"I'm not surprised," sniffed Dover. "Was it Bailey who nabbed you?"

"Oh, no, nothing like that. I didn't know Mr. Bailey from Adam."

"Then why kill him, for God's sake?"

Miller sighed heavily. "It was when I was still up north. I"—he cleared his throat and avoided looking at either of his two inquisitors—"well, it was sort of to do with sex."

"Oh, yes?" said Dover, on whom the mouth-stopping cigarette was not working too well.

Miller moistened his lips. "Children, actually," he muttered. "I got six months. But"—he raised his head with a faint show of defiance—"that was four years ago and I haven't been in trouble since. I pulled myself together, see? I moved down here and got myself a good job and got married and everything."

MacGregor understood. "You were afraid that if you were convicted on this motoring charge, your previous record would come out in open court?"

"They say they don't punish you twice for the same offense, but they do. I'd have lost my job straight off. I work at a school, you see. Kids everywhere. And then there's the wife. She'd have never come back if she knew I'd been in the nick for molesting kids. And then there's the neighbors." He appealed to the more sympathetic face confronting him. "You can see how I was fixed, can't you? I couldn't just do nothing and let him ruin my life. I didn't want to kill him, but he gave me no choice. I hit him with the wheel brace."

But Dover's heart was not made of stone. He saw how distressed Miller was and was ready with solace. He addressed MacGregor. "Why don't you go and make us all a nice cup of tea, laddie?"

Miller raised his head. "There's a bottle of whiskey in the sideboard," he said shyly.

Dover beamed. "Even better! Where do you keep your glasses?"

Miller's statement was completed in an increasingly convivial atmosphere and he had to be asked several times about the parking of his car after the murder.

"Oh, that," he said. "Well, I forgot all about going after the missus and I come rushing back here. All I wanted was to get out of sight as quick as possible. That's why I left the car right outside instead of driving it to the top of the hill and turning it around ready for the morning like I usually do."

"So when you left for work today you had to start the car on the starter?" MacGregor, of course, didn't drink on duty and was as sober as a judge.

"That's right. I had the devil of a job with it. It really needs a new battery but what with one thing and another . . . Anyhow, I won't have to bother about that now, will I?"

"What did you do with the murder weapon?"

"It's under the coal in the shed. I was going to chuck it in the canal when things quietened down. Here"—for the first time Miller showed a flicker of curiosity—"how did you get on to me?"

"It was the break in the pattern, laddie!" said Dover, feeling he owed his host something for the whiskey. "If you'd turned your car and parked it like you always did outside the Jedryschowskis, you'd have got away with it."

MacGregor gawped. How on earth had the old fool managed to hang onto a name like Jedryschowski, for heaven's sake?

"You got cloth ears or something, laddie?"

MacGregor abandoned his disloyal speculations. "Sir?"

"I said, go and get somebody to take him away."

MacGregor hesitated. Leave Dover alone with a self-confessed murderer? "Will you be all right, sir?"

Dover winked wickedly and reached for the whiskey bottle. "Oh, I'll be fine, Sergeant!" he said: "Just fine now!"

# THE CURSE OF ISTVAN KODALY

*By Alec Ross*

Déjà vu is the name given to the feeling that you have experienced something before. I never really believed in it. I guess I'm just a down-to-earth kind of person who doesn't hold with any of the so-called psychic phenomena that lots of people seem to want to believe in.

The reason I'm telling you this is that something happened to me that makes me stop and wonder if I've been too hasty about my lack of belief in things out of the ordinary.

My name is Stefan Balint, and I'm Hungarian. Or at least I'm of Hungarian descent. My father was given the same name and so was his father before him. I was the first of my line to be born in this country. My father was the first to come here, and when he was settled in, he sent for his mother and father. Before you could shake the paprika, as they say in Budapest, the Balints were Americans.

Well, most of the Balints were Americans. Grandpa never quite made it. Oh, he was glad to be living here, all right, but he didn't want to cope with the problems of a new world. He wouldn't learn English because if he had he would have had to use it. "Hungarian has been good enough for me all these years. I'm not going to desert it now," he would say, or at least that's a pretty fair English approximation of what he really said.

Listening to Grandpa was one of my delights. I was never conscious of being bilingual. I just somehow managed to follow what he said and to respond to him in Hungarian. When you're young, learning a language is no big deal. You don't know any better so it just happens naturally.

I would always ask Grandpa to tell me about the curse that was put on him back in Budapest in the old days. And Grandpa would sigh and shiver, and with intense drama in his voice he would tell me the story. I couldn't get enough of it, and I would enlarge upon it with my friends, and we would all play out the curse instead of cowboys and Indians.

The curse was hurled down upon Grandpa's head by his old friend Istvan Kodaly. (Grandpa had grown up with him.) The center of the situation was, of course, a woman, the woman who later became my grandmother. Istvan had wanted her for his wife, and when she chose Grandpa instead, Istvan was very upset. He called down the curse upon the Balints "unto the tenth generation." Nobody paid much attention to it, curses being out of style at the time, but it was remembered years later when my father sent word for his parents to join him in America. Somehow or other, Grandpa's passport disappeared just before the journey was to begin. Then in quick order his visa was lost and his plane ticket. "It's the curse come round at last," cried all the relatives, but then that's what one expects assorted cousins and uncles and aunts to say, so Grandpa didn't pay any attention to their voices of doom. Even though his departure was delayed for a long time, Grandpa just blamed the missing documents on his own carelessness or nervousness. He had learned to ignore Istvan Kodaly long, long ago.

Throughout the years in his new home, any time something went wrong, which was at least daily in the early days of adjusting to a new world, Grandpa would laughingly blame all disasters on the curse. When my father lost his job, when my younger brother was in an accident in his car, when I flunked geometry, when any of us got sick, it was always the curse that was blamed. That was good. Things were never our fault. Always it was the Kodaly curse that was at the root of the trouble. As a result, I never had to take the burden of blame for anything I did or didn't do. It was a delightful way to live. And so I grew up with a touch of drama in my life. After all, ours was the only curse on the block and it was worth taking pride in.

When I graduated from college, my present from my family was a long dreamed of trip to Europe with, of course, special emphasis on Hungary. I admit I was curious about seeing the sights and meeting the remaining relatives, and so, loaded with greetings and messages from Grandpa and Papa, I set off to conquer the old world that neither parents nor grandparents had ever gone back to visit.

I had a marvelous time. The relatives were much nicer than I had expected, the countryside was more beautiful than I had dreamed, and the cost was deliciously less than I had feared. My Hungarian came back in practically no time, and I knew I was going to miss everything and everyone when I left. Well, I haven't left yet, and I may never go home. But that's not through choice, you understand. I blame it all on Istvan Kodaly.

The loss of my passport the day before I was to leave Budapest didn't really bother me too much. It was an inconvenience, of course, but, after all, we have an embassy in Budapest, and all I had to do was apply to the U.S. Consul for a temporary passport to get me home. Losing the replacement, however, was more of a burden, and I began to think that I was simply about to enter a period of bad luck. I've had those before, but I was calm because they eventually sort themselves out and everything gets back to normal.

I didn't really do any worrying until my airplane ticket disappeared, and while I was searching high and low for that, my wallet also vanished from its usual place. Something about this whole sequence of events began to seem very familiar to me, but as I hadn't ever been in a similar situation, I put it all down to nervousness. I didn't know whether to blame my troubles on my own stupidity (always easy) or some outside agency (the relatives recommended that).

The real panic began setting in when the consular office indicated that I would need some proof of my U.S. citizenship. With all my papers missing, I wasn't able to provide that documentation. To add insult to injury, on my way back to my hotel from the consulate, I was stopped by the Budapest police, who demanded to see my papers. Their excuse was that a dangerous criminal was loose in the area.

Now, one of the great things about being an American at home is that you can go everywhere and do anything within reason without having any papers. But in Hungary, without a passport I was obviously a criminal type, and so I ended up in the local police station where I was given a chance to explain my situation.

I couldn't have asked for nicer treatment. The people I talked to were as polite as could be, and when I was thrown into the pokey they were relatively gentle about it. I can't blame them, really. I was probably the only person in all of Budapest without any identification at all. Everything I owned in the way of significant paper was missing.

The consulate refused to accept my calls, the jailer didn't believe my story, my relatives were keeping as low a profile as they could by refusing to recognize my existence, and no one would allow me to write a letter or make an overseas telephone call.

I lost track of time after a while, but I estimate that after a week or so, I was finally sent for and put face to face with the top man.

"You say you are Stefan Balint?"

"I am."

"Can you prove it?"

"I've lost all my papers—passport, plane ticket, wallet with identification."

"Then how do I know that you are who you say you are?" While I had not allowed myself to panic before, I now was ready to scream the place down.

"Can't you take my word for it?"

"Why should I?"

Now, you have to admit that his question was reasonable. I accepted that, but it didn't help my situation any.

"We will have to hold you in protective custody until your identity is established."

"How can that be done?"

"You will have to regain your papers—all of them." His voice was positive, allowing for no argument.

"I wish to speak with the U.S. Consul and call my home in Chicago."

"Nonsense," he asserted. "This is not the crime capital of the world. We do not indulge prisoners here. If your papers are turned in, we will notify you. Until that time, you will remain here."

*Here* was a rather moldy jail cell, and I was not looking forward to spending any more time in it. He started to leave, and I interrupted his departure. "Who are you?"

"I am the Head of the Security Police. My name is Istvan Kodaly."

Istvan Kodaly. The name of the man who had put the curse on Grandpa. Evidently, the closer to Budapest a Balint was, the stronger the curse. At that point I knew beyond any doubt that I would never regain my papers. Grandpa had overcome the curse by sneaking over the border, but I couldn't do that while I was locked up in a jail cell. It may not have been *dejà vu*, but it was close enough.

Three days of banging steadily on the bars of my cage finally resulted in my gaining another interview with the Head of Security Police.

"Was it your father or grandfather who put the curse on my family?" I asked without pausing for any polite generalities.

"My grandfather," he replied. "But surely you don't believe in that kind of old woman's nonsense?"

"It seems to work, so it can't be nonsense."

"It only works on Hungarians. You claim to be an American. If you really were an American, you wouldn't be cursed." He was apparently convinced of the logic of his position.

As he went over the same ground about my identity, I was busy planning a way out.

"If you don't believe in the curse," I said, "then you should be willing to help me remove it."

He agreed to indulge me, largely, I felt, because he was embarrassed over what could prove to be an international incident.

"You have an idea for negating the curse?" he asked.

"Yes," I answered quickly. "Write it down, and I'll try to reverse it."

He gave an indulgent smile, yet he took out a notebook and wrote for a minute. He handed me the paper, but before I could read what he had written, the paper disappeared. One minute it was there, but as I put out my hand to take it, it was gone.

"Interesting," Kodaly admitted.

"Yes." My voice was emotionless. I was determined not to allow myself to shiver.

"Do you know anything about removing curses?" He might almost have been asking if I knew how to stop the rain.

"No," I admitted, "but a talent for curses is supposed to run in our blood." I didn't know if that was really true, but as my grandmother used to say when she urged us to do or not to do something, "How could it hurt?"

I could see that Kodaly really was interested in what was happening, or not happening as the case may be, and we smoked two of his dreadful Hungarian cigarettes quietly for a few minutes.

"Just what does the curse involve?" he finally asked.

"It seems to deal only with paper," I said. "Is there such a thing as a paper curse?"

"If there wasn't before, there is now," he said. "Let's try something." He reached into a folder on his desk and removed a sheet of paper which he slid over to me. "Here is your confession about your career as a spy. Sign it and let's see what happens."

Now of all the things I have never been in my life, a spy is right up there at the top along with Hollywood sex symbol and Olympic decathlon winner. I certainly wasn't going to risk signing a confession because if the curse really wasn't centered on paper I would be doomed forever. I tried to stall for time: "Surely you wouldn't mind if I read it first?"

A flash of victory appeared in his eyes. "Certainly read it. The details of your treachery to the state are all included."

I pulled the sheet of paper toward me. Just as I lifted it to reading level, it disappeared. There's no other way to say it. One minute it was there and the next minute it was gone and I was trying to pick up empty air.

We both looked at the space the paper had occupied, and then, foolishly, we looked up, down, around—all over the office for a clue to what had become of the confession. There was a long silence and we smoked some more. I was beginning to get used to the Hungarian cigarettes.

"It is a paper curse," Kodaly said softly. "This bears out the stories your grandfather used to tell before he sneaked over the border. Not that any-body ever believed him," he added quickly.

"It must only work within the borders of Hungary." I was thinking aloud. "Maybe I'll get back all my papers if I leave Hungarian soil."

Kodaly nodded his head sagely. "Possibly. However, you cannot leave Hungarian soil without your papers. That is the law." We both thought for a long time.

"I don't suppose," I began, and he shook his head. "I didn't really think so," I said, and we smoked some more.

Back in my cell I was still sufficiently interested in the other-worldliness of the whole affair that I didn't allow myself to fall into what I once read is called the slough of despond. Surely there was a way out. Surely superior American know-how could solve this whole mess. I thought about Hungarians I had known. I thought about my family. I thought about Grandpa. And then I had an idea. I stopped speaking Hungarian. If the curse only worked on Hungarians, then I would be American all the way.

I refused to understand what the guards said to me when they brought me my meals. And when I was led off to another interview with Kodaly, I refused to understand his greetings and his questions.

His English was rudimentary, and in desperation he had to bring in an interpreter to whom I announced that I was an all-American victim of an eastern bloc bureaucracy. "I do not understand why I am being detained here. If this matter is not settled at once, there will be serious international repercussions."

Kodaly's eyes registered admiration at the cleverness of my ploy. "Maybe it will work," he murmured. The interpreter looked puzzled, and Kodaly gestured for him to leave the room. Kodaly took a small notebook out of his pocket and wrote for a minute or two. "Yes, maybe it will work," he repeated. He handed me the slip of paper, and I started to read aloud what it said. "Istvan Kodaly called down a curse upon the name of Stefan Ba-lint . . ." And just then the sheet of paper disappeared.

Kodaly roared with laughter. "Ah, you're too smart for your own good. You were reading Hungarian. Pretending not to understand is not going to counter an authentic curse."

I was furious with myself. I had almost had it. The curse was almost on the run, and then I had to spoil things by being too anxious.

It's been three months now, and I'm still trying to think of some other approach. Istvan is thinking, too, and strangely enough we have come to be quite good friends. We spend a lot of time together, whenever he's not busy chasing down spies or something like that. I've taught him to play gin rummy while we wait for inspiration. Unfortunately, the score sheet keeps disappearing, and at times the cards themselves seem to be very pale and thin. It's the plastic coating that saves them from total destruction or whatever, I guess.

Yesterday I overheard two of the guards talking in the corridor outside my cell. They revealed two interesting bits of information. First, there is a rumor that Budapest is running out of paper. And second, the jail will probably soon be quite full. There is to be a gypsy encampment just outside the city, and the arrest rate is always higher when gypsies are around.

Gypsies. Now there's a possible solution for me. If anybody knows anything about hurling and removing curses it's gypsies. Just as soon as I get a Magyar cellmate I intend to request a professional consultation with him. If he will remove the curse, I will pay him with all my missing Hungarian paper money. How could it hurt?

# A SOUVENIR OF RUMANIA

### By *Albert Bashover*

THE CALEA Victoria in Bucharest is a gorgeous, ultra-wide boulevard lined on both sides with impressive, fat marble government buildings. It appears to have been designed for a grand opera stage setting, meant for choreographed parades of brass bands, brightly colored flags, and equestrian soldiers riding twenty abreast towards the Piata Victoria at its end. Unfortunately, in the Rumania of 1982, it was a dull gray expanse of nearly empty pavement, marked only by an occasional antique truck spewing oily gas fumes, an overcrowded public transport, and a government car or two.

Maxim turned into the driveway of a small building off the Piata Victoria. He was old enough to have memories of a brighter past, and the route up the grand old boulevard to his office always made him feel a little sad. Maxim's little known department was responsible for the gathering, evaluation, and dissemination of information dropped by tourists as they passed through Bucharest. The insignia on his little Fiat indicated that he worked for the Ministry of Tourism, but his office was separate from the ministry's. His work was done better in a less conspicuous location than the big Ministry of Tourism building on Boulevard General Magheru.

He entered the faded marble-faced building that still held a hint of pre-socialist grandeur. His small office was at the end of a corridor dimly lit with naked bulbs burning at reduced voltage. There was no information on the door, just the number 124. This was less for secrecy than because the Ministry of Justice and the Ministry of Tourism were constantly fighting for control of his little bailiwick. At the moment, he was under the jurisdiction of the Ministry of Tourism, but in this Rumania of Ceausescu, who knew where he would be next week?

Nistor, his secretary, looked up as Maxim entered.

"Marin Buganou, the manager of the Continental Hotel, called. He would like you to get in touch with him when you have a chance—no emergency."

Maxim's face betrayed an expression of displeasure. He had to deal with many unsavory characters in his job of information gathering and evaluation, but he particularly disliked Buganou. His was a job that had to be done and he was a dependable government worker who was doing it, but Buganou seemed to enjoy the destructiveness of his work. He often questioned Maxim about the results of information that he or his hotel employees had supplied. He seemed to gloat over any particularly painful outcome. Maxim sometimes thought that Buganou was a plant by the secret police to check up on him. It would be standard operating procedure for them. The Continental Hotel was where the government housed the tourists from America, and sometimes tourist groups from Israel. This combination often produced some very interesting bits of information that should filter through Maxim's department and end up at the Ministry of Justice. Maxim didn't like it, but he knew that very often his reports found their way directly to the offices of the hated secret police. The manager of the Continental Hotel would be in a good position to shortcircuit Maxim's department and supply information directly to the police. For this reason Buganou had to be watched.

Another reason Maxim disliked Buganou was Ana Enashu.

Stephan stretched to try to relieve the stiffness of his back muscles from the long flight. The trip from the United States to Constanza on the Black Sea would have been tiring enough in any plane, but on Tarom Air, the official airline of the Rumanian government, it was a form of torture. His seat was broken so it could not assume a reclining position, the "stewardesses" had obviously received their training at the official Rumanian school of brusqueness, and the food was as bad as he remembered it. It was a strain for Stephan to remember that he was now "Steve Ender," an American schoolteacher on summer vacation, who could not understand Rumanian. There were many times when he would have liked to respond to the remarks made among the Tarom employees, but it was more important that he keep a very low profile.

"Steve" tried to look unconcerned as his luggage was loaded on the big

Mercedes buses that would transport them from the airport to the "luxurious beach hotels on the Black Sea," as the brochures described them. His single large brown piece of luggage had been chosen so it would not stand out among the others in the teacher tourist group from America. It would take a very close inspection to detect the false bottom he had constructed.

From a distance, on the road south of Constanza, the high white hotels of Jupiter City did indeed look like a piece of Miami Beach transplanted to the Black Sea. The Ceausescu regime had built a string of resort "cities" south of Constanza on the Black Sea. Each city was an exact duplicate of the other. Each had a romantic name from Roman mythology: "Neptune," "Jupiter," "Apollo." The only difference between them was that each "city" housed tourists from a different country. In that way the government was more easily able to "supervise" the movements of the visitors. Though the government was fearful of the taint to their pure Communist regime by outside influences, they needed the tourist dollar, mark, or lira. The Rumanian "lei" and "bani" were worthless outside the country. Tourists, and their currency, had to be lured into the country. It was only after a tourist had been there for a time that he discovered the elevators did not work, the food was poor, the beach was stony, and boats for fishing (or escaping) were unattainable.

Even though Stephan knew all this, he had to go through the process of being a tourist. He would have preferred to go directly to Bucharest, but that might have aroused suspicion. It was necessary to spend the week in Jupiter with the American teachers and retirees. Then, the brochure promised them, they would have a "restful drive through the country to the beautiful capital of Bucharest."

Stephan was not interested in the beautiful city of Bucharest. He was only interested in seeing Ana Enashu.

The lobby of the Continental Hotel was as dimly lit as the rest of the buildings in the city. The shortage of electricity was just another shortage the government was struggling with. Maxim did not go directly to Buganou's office. He went instead to the Comturist shop off the lobby, where the tourists were asked to buy souvenirs with their own country's currency at the official rate of exchange. Even in the dim light from the bulbs operating at reduced wattage, the shop appeared almost colorful with dolls, glassware, and woodcarvings, but the brightest thing in the shop in Maxim's eyes was Ana Enashu.

She might have been simply pretty were it not for her glittering green eyes and her jet black hair. Maxim was in his late fifties. When his wife died so many years ago, he had been sure that the capacity to feel the way he did about Ana died with her. He was amazed that this woman, this girl twenty-five years his junior, could awaken the feelings in him that she did.

"Good afternoon, Mr. Unger." She flashed a blinding smile at him. Though her address was formal, the proper one for a place of business, her tone told Maxim of her affection for him. It was affection, Maxim knew, nothing deeper. Ana was not the kind of woman who could disguise her feelings. Maxim was her friend, her big brother, her protector. When she first came to work as salesgirl for Comturist from her little town near the Black Sea, it was Maxim who found her a decent lodging in the over-crowded city. It was Maxim who, with his connections in government, was able to get an occasional pound of beef without standing in the long lines in front of the butcher shops. And most important, it was Maxim and his position in the Ministry of Tourism that kept her boss Buganou from coming on to her as he did with anything that wore a dress and was under his jurisdiction.

Maxim was surprised at himself. He was not a naive youth. In his job especially, he knew that nothing came free and that debts had to be paid, yet with Ana he felt he could give and give without expecting repayment—except perhaps an occasional view of that flashing smile and those amazing green eyes.

"Hello, Ana. Has Mr. Buganou been keeping his proper distance lately?"

"As long as you are around he is no problem. He's in his office. I think he is expecting you."

Buganou's office was bigger than Maxim's. It was set up to impress. Buganou's smallness made the large desk he sat behind look even larger. In deference to Maxim's position, he rose when Maxim entered.

"Good afternoon, sir. I'm so happy you could find the time to see me."

Buganou was an expert at groveling.

"I don't have much time, Buganou. What is it you wanted to tell me?"

"Oh, I won't keep you long, Mr. Unger. It's just a matter of giving you some information that I think you should know about, that perhaps has not yet come to your attention.

"You see, I could not help noticing that you have, shall I say, been showing some, ah, interest in one of my girls—one of my workers, Ana Enashu."

Buganou paused and looked out of the corner of his eye for some reaction.

"Yes, yes. Out with it, Buganou."

"Well, as you know, we make a check on all our workers when they come to us, and I have learned that Ana Enashu, though she is living alone and claims to be single, is a married woman. I thought you should know."

It was difficult for Buganou to suppress a gloating smile.

"Is that it? Is *that* what you called me down here to tell me? I have better things to do with my time. For your information, I have always known that Ana—Miss—Mrs. Enashu was married. Since our relationship has always been one of friendship only, it has never made a difference. Goodbye, Mr. Buganou."

Maxim tried not to slam the door behind him. His anger was beginning to redden his face. He was angry at Buganou for thinking that his motives might require Ana to be single. He was angry at Ana for not letting him know she was married, that he had to learn of it from Buganou.

Maxim forced himself to calm down before he entered the Comturist store across the hall. The store was empty except for Ana, who was dusting some glassware.

"Ana, could I see you this evening?"

"Of course, Maxim—Mr. Unger. I will make dinner for you after work. Is everything all right? You look—disturbed."

"I can't talk right now. I'll see you this evening."

That evening, the flowers that Maxim always brought did not seem to brighten Ana's little kitchen as they usually did. Ana moved silently around the room, serving dinner, waiting for the pensive Maxim to unburden his mind.

"Ana, why did you never tell me that you are married?"

Maxim was sorry as soon as he said it. It had come out explosively, as an accusation, and he knew he had no right to accuse.

Ana's face first showed shocked fear; then it relaxed to sadness and resignation. She sat down at the table.

"Maxim, you have been a good friend. I want you always to be. But we will never be more. I thought you knew that." She paused. "Stephan and I were married when we both were quite young. He was an engineering student. Before we were married, he had become involved with an anti-Ceausescu group at the university. He left the group when we married so that our lives could be more secure.

"One night we were told that the security police had arrested many members of his old group, and that they had confiscated lists of old members that included his name. We put together all the *lei* and *bani* we owned and all we could borrow, and we blackmarketed it into foreign currency. It was just enough to smuggle Stephan out of Rumania.

"We are still married, Maxim. Not just by the civil authorities, but forever, by the church. We both wanted it that way.

"I would have told you in time, Maxim. Please forgive me for not telling you sooner. It should have been I who told you, not Buganou."

Maxim found that he could not be angry with Ana. He was beginning to realize that he saw her not so much as a woman to be wooed but as a daughter to be protected. Perhaps it was because he did not have a family of his own once his wife died. Whatever the reason, he found that his heart had adopted Ana, and his dislike for Buganou had grown to hatred.

* * *

Stephan, along with the other tourists in the busload, followed the guide into the lobby of the Continental Hotel. He pretended to listen while the guide explained the room location procedure and points of interest to be seen in Bucharest. Stephan's eyes were swiftly scanning everything in the lobby. The latest information he had before leaving the States was that Ana had taken a job of some sort at this hotel. He looked at the group of Israeli tourists jabbering away in a group near the drab-colored lobby sofas, the three clerks behind the reception desk, the chambermaid and the waiter walking through the lobby to their work stations.

Ana was here somewhere.

"And you will find the souvenirs in our Comturist shop right here in the hotel lobby to be as good as you can get anywhere. They are priced in American dollars so you can pay for them without converting any of your dollars into Rumanian *lei*. You can also buy American cigarettes here."

Stephan noted that the guide did not mention that they could get many times the official conversion rate from any one of the blackmarket money hustlers in the street, or even from the waiters in the hotel. Gold, jewels, or foreign currency was the key to freedom for any Rumanian willing to take the chance of getting arrested for possessing foreign money, and almost any young Rumanian was willing.

Then he saw her. She was coming out of the Comturist store. Even in the colorless, shapeless clothes available to the locals, Ana stood out.

She did not see him till she was halfway across the lobby. A look of joyous surprise started to form on her face. Then she saw Stephan glare at her, and turn away quickly as if to hear the guide's recitation better. Ana missed only half a step as she continued on her way to the lobby door and out to the street. She knew she would see him soon again, but this was obviously not the time or the place.

The next morning, Stephan tried to be the first tourist to visit the Comturist shop, but he was beaten by a husband and wife team of teachers from Boston who had many questions to ask Ana about the sources of the wood-carved dolls. Stephan noticed how much Ana's English had improved. It was almost as good as his own.

It seemed like years, but at last the American couple left without buying anything. There was a glass wall between the Comturist shop and the lobby. Stephan tried to make his approach to Ana look as casual as possible. They could be seen from the lobby, but not heard.

Ana spoke swiftly but softly. "Stephan, darling, you are crazy to come here. You are still a fugitive. If they catch you, you will never get out of prison."

Neither Ana nor Stephan realized that they were both speaking in Rumanian.

"Don't worry, dear. I couldn't trust this mission to anyone else.

"Listen carefully. We will not have much time to talk, and we can't afford to be seen together much. I have smuggled in five thousand dollars in American money. When I leave, I will forget my camera bag. The money is in there. My address in New York is also there. Contact Ion Dorsky in the village of Krasnit. He is the one who helped me to get out. Give me a week to get out of the country before you do so. Remember—Ion Dorsky in Krasnit."

Stephan had rehearsed this speech a hundred times. It had to be said quickly, correctly, and only once. He could not afford to be seen with Ana more than that.

"I'll see you soon," he said in English. He turned and left the shop to go to the bus that was waiting to take him on a sightseeing tour of "beautiful Bucharest."

Maxim was one of the few people allowed to have an automobile and a telephone. Because of his job, he sometimes had to be contacted at odd hours. He felt lucky that the phone was out of order as much as it was in service. At least he was able to sleep through some nights. He was surprised when it rang as he entered his apartment after work. People usually didn't call at six o'clock.

The tone was strained and gasping, as if the caller could not catch her breath, but Maxim recognized Ana's voice.

"Maxim, I'm sorry to bother you, but I didn't know who else to call."

"Ana, what's wrong? Where are you calling from?"

"I'm sorry—I'm sorry, Maxim. Please help me."

"Ana. Calm down. Tell me where you are."

The firmness of his voice must have helped.

"I'm at the hotel. In Buganou's office. Please come!"

"What is the trouble?"

"I've killed him. I've killed Buganou."

It took Maxim only ten minutes to reach the Continental Hotel. Maxim did not enter through the large glass front doors. A glance through the glass indicated that no one in the lobby seemed to be aware of any problem. The clerk behind the desk was sound asleep behind a copy of *Romania Libera*. Maxim went around the side of the building, through an alley that led to the parking plaza in the rear. Buganou's office had a door to the plaza. He knocked twice, then twice more. After a moment there was the sound of a key turning, and the door opened. Maxim entered quickly, then closed and locked the door after him.

"Did anyone else try to come in?"

Ana's face was a pale ivory. "No. I waited for your knock as you told me."

Maxim looked beyond Ana, to the end of the office. On the floor along-side his desk was the body of Buganou lying on his back. From his chest protruded the copper-colored handle of a letter opener that Maxim had often seen on Buganou's desk. The letter opener had been commandeered by Buganou from the Comturist shop. It was a cheap white metal casting that had been painted to look bronze. Maxim remembered seeing *A Souvenir of Rumania* stamped in gold letters on the blade. Next to the body was a camera bag, partially opened, with green currency in view.

Ana was beginning to tremble in shock. Maxim made her sit down in one of the office chairs.

"Tell me what happened."

Ana's voice started out weakly but grew in strength as she spoke.

"I saw him today. Stephan, my husband. He just walked into the Comturist shop. He had come with a group of American tourists. He was traveling with an American passport. I don't know how he did it, but he gave me a great many American dollars so I might join him in New York. We would be together again. Away from this terrible place.

"Oh, Maxim, you are a wonderful man, but to be with Stephan and to be in America! These are dreams that I thought never could come true.

"Then Buganou called me into his office. I can't figure out how he knew, but he knew all about Stephan and our plans."

Maxim frowned. "Ana, I thought you did know. The Comturist shop is bugged. Buganou gets much of his information from there."

"I didn't. But it's too late now. He threatened to turn Stephan over to the secret police unless I gave him the money that Stephan gave me."

"I understand, Ana."

"No, you don't, Maxim. I was willing to give him the money, even if I had to stay here the rest of my life, as long as he let Stephan go, but he wanted—wanted more! More than money. I realized there would be no end, so I—I—"

She was beginning to shudder again. Maxim put his arms around her. It was the first time he had ever done that. She fell against him and started to cry softly.

In a few moments she had cried herself out. Maxim spoke to her firmly, kindly, in a fatherly way.

"Don't worry, Ana. I'll take care of you.

"You were seen coming in here, so you will have to be seen leaving. I will wait for a while after you leave, then I will take Buganou's body and put it in the alley. It won't be found until tomorrow. The police will probably think he was mistaken for a tourist and was done in by one of the blackmarket money changers. They have been known to get violent occasionally."

Maxim grasped the handle of the knife to remove it, but there was a snap and the porous casting cracked, leaving the blade still deep in the body.

"Damn!" hissed Maxim.

"What's the matter?" whispered a wide-eyed Ana.

"I'm afraid my idea won't work now, at least not for long. There will probably be an autopsy, and when they find that blade in the body, they will know it was not done by a chance thug in the street. They will trace the action back to this hotel. Possibly back to you." He paused, then looked at Ana sadly.

"Ana, you are going to have to leave the country immediately."

"But Stephan said—"

"Immediately. Take the money. Go home and pack a few things—not in a suitcase—in a shopping bag. Meet me in my office at seven tomorrow morning. I will finish up here."

When Ana left, Maxim turned to his work. Luckily Buganou was small and Maxim was strong. It was long past business hours, so the alley and the street were deserted. Maxim was able to place his burden near the street entrance of the alley without being noticed.

Tomorrow the body would be discovered and the police would be called. He and Ana would have a day, perhaps two, before an investigation would lead back to the hotel. That was all the time he had to get Ana out of the country.

Maxim had never thought of himself as privileged, but now he realized the power he had in his ability to use an automobile, to get gasoline, to travel outside Bucharest, at least to some extent, without special travel papers.

As soon as Ana appeared at his office the next morning, Maxim packed her shopping bag in the trunk of his car and left a hurriedly-invented note for his secretary, Nistor. They drove west, out of the city, toward the highway to Constanza. On the way, Ana told Maxim about Stephan's instruction to contact Ion Dorsky in the village of Krasnit. Krasnit was a tiny village on the Black Sea near the Bulgarian border. Ana and Stephan knew it because Ana had some relatives living there.

Maxim thought about this information for awhile. His original idea had been to take Ana to a cousin he had in Constanza so she could hide until he found a way for her to leave the country, but he knew that his cousin, like himself, was a conservative old-liner who probably had no contacts in the underground world that served the illegal emigres. Making contact with Ion Dorsky was a danger. Men had been known to become informers even after years of working in the underground; still, Dorsky represented the fastest way to get Ana out of Rumania.

They drove for four hours in nervous near-silence. About fifteen miles out of Constanza, Maxim made his decision. He turned south on a badly paved two lane highway that paralleled the coastline of the Black Sea. Up until then his official license plates had gotten them past the occasional army roadchecks on the main highway. The heavier traffic on the main highway had made the army personnel that manned these roadblocks perfunctory in the performance of their duties, but any soldiers on the less used byway might be more inquisitive about an official car with a young woman in it heading towards either the Bulgarian border or the coast of the Black Sea. Anyone between the ages of fifteen and thirty going in that direction was suspect.

For a while the only traffic on the road was an occasional farmer riding in his rubber-tired open wagon, pulled by a well-scrubbed but underfed horse. The farmers looked straight ahead and did not even acknowledge the passing of the dusty little Fiat.

Ana pulled from her memory the landmarks they needed to guide them to Krasnit. The village was too small to earn its own mention on road signs. "We're almost there," Ana said as Maxim rounded a curve in the road.

That was when Maxim saw the khaki-colored army truck straddling the narrow road. The thick forest trees came close to the road on both sides so that there was no chance of skirting the truck. Maxim knew it would be foolish to try it in any case. He braked to a slow stop and waited for the armed young soldier sitting on the hood of the truck to approach him.

But he didn't move. Instead, the door of the truck cab opened and an erect soldier climbed out and approached. A cold steel case enveloped Maxim's chest as he saw the sunlight sparkle off the gold colored insignia. An officer! Not just a farm boy waiting out his tour of duty, but an officer for whom the army was life. How could he explain being so far from his office in Bucharest with no travel papers, and with a young woman—

"Maxim?—Maxim Unger? What are you doing way out here?"

The coldness in Maxim's chest slowly melted as the features of the officer's face coalesced to fit a pattern in Maxim's memory.

"Jan Novotny! Why, I haven't seen you since—since—"

"Since your wife's funeral, Maxim. It's been a long time. I'm sorry I haven't kept in touch, but the army has kept me moving around, and, oh, hello . . ."

For the first time the officer's eyes went past Maxim to focus on Ana huddled in the passenger seat of the car.

"Jan, this is, uh, a friend of mine. She has a very sick relative in the village of Krasnit. I promised to take her there."

Ana picked up on Maxim's cue quickly. She brushed her hair away from her beryl-green eyes and smiled wanly at the soldier. "I hope you don't mind, officer, but she is awfully ill and I must get to her soon." She projected just the right amount of childlike helplessness and womanly allure.

The soldier gave Maxim a knowing smile. "You always had good taste, Maxim. You had better get there quickly. It will be dark soon, and we double the patrols after seven P.M. Security is pretty tight around here."

Jan waved at the truck, and the vehicle with the soldier still sitting on the hood backed off into one lane, leaving the other open for Maxim and Ana to pass.

Twenty minutes later Ana signaled Maxim to turn off onto a dirt road between two rows of wood and stone houses. The only thing that indicated that this was a village was the open well in the middle of the road. Even in the eighties, piped water was a rarity in many of the outlying villages.

The sky was beginning to darken, not only because of the setting sun but also because of the gathering of thick black clouds coming in from the east over the sea. In a little while a rainstorm could turn the hard-packed dirt road to a river of brown mucilaginous soup that could make it impossible for the auto to return to the highway.

A very tall woman wearing pants and heavy work boots was hurrying up the road toward a house near the highway. Ana leaned out the window of the car and called to her.

"Can you help me? I am looking for the house of Ion Dorsky."

The woman appraised the car with its official insignia and the older man behind the steering wheel. The young, pretty girl talking to her didn't seem to fit.

"I don't know any—"

"Please, I am Ana Enashu. My aunt lives here. You might remember me. I have to see Ion Dorsky."

The woman made a quick decision.

"The third house past the well on the right." She hurried on without looking back.

Maxim pulled the car between two houses so it would not be too obvious from the road. He let Ana knock at the door while he waited in the car. She would arouse less fear or suspicion in anyone who answered the door. He would keep the money in the car until he felt it was safe to turn it over to Dorsky.

The door opened a crack. The dim light from inside painted a yellow line down Ana's body. For about two minutes Maxim watched as there was earnest conversation between Ana and the person behind the door. Finally the door opened just wide enough for Ana to slip in; then it closed, completing the darkness that had fallen.

Maxim took a nearly empty pack of American cigarettes from his pocket. He counted them. Four. They would have to last till the end of the week. Even for government officials they were expensive to get. He leaned back in the car seat and lit one. It was the first time in a long while that he had been able to relax his body, but his mind was still racing.

If it was he who had all those American dollars, he knew he could get out of the country and find his way to New York. But an innocent like Ana? That money would attract danger like a magnet. There were so many miles and so many pitfalls between Krasnit and New York. But what more could he do? He had already put his job—his very life—in danger to help this girl. He would have enough of a problem to get back to Bucharest without being arrested. How much of a knight in shining armor could he be?

His cigarette was finished and he was longing for another one when the door opened and let a flood of yellow light out into the now deep darkness. Two figures emerged and hurried to the car.

"Maxim, this is Ion. I have explained everything to him, and he said he could get me to Turkey and get me a passport and it would only cost one thousand American dollars."

Ana's face was flushed with excitement. She looked happy for the first time in many hours. But Maxim's heart froze. Why had the child said "only?" That was advertising that she had more money. That was asking for trouble. Maxim looked closely at Ana's companion. It was a strong face. A farmer's face, deeply weathered and dark. It had strength, but not obvious compassion. He could possibly do what he promised, but he would have to be watched—and once she got to Turkey?

There was a split second of silence while a million thoughts raced through Maxim's mind.

"Dorsky, I will give you twelve hundred American dollars if you get two passports and passage for two to Turkey."

Dorsky thought for a second. "It's a deal. We will leave by boat tonight. You will not have time to return your auto, so that will be part of my payment. Get your things and come into the house when you are ready." He turned and walked back to the house.

Ana stared wide-eyed at Maxim. "What are you doing, Maxim?" she whispered. "You can't—"

"Quickly, Ana. We'll talk later. Take your things from the trunk. I will take out the money we need for now. The rest we will divide and hide under our clothing. Whatever you do, don't give anyone a hint that we have any more money. We may need every dollar we have left to get out of Turkey." As he talked, Maxim had loosened his belt and was lining the flat packs of greenbacks under his shirt at his beltline. Ana watched, then put some packets of dollars through the neck of her blouse where they fell against her leather belt. She distributed them so that at a casual glance she would not look too fat.

"I should have brought some extra clothing," said Maxim with a half smile to Ana. Ana returned the half smile. A small tear was forming in her eye. A tear made up of equal parts of affection for Maxim and fear of the future.

"Don't worry, Ana. We will make it to New York and your Stephan. I probably could not have made it back to Bucharest without being stopped and arrested anyway. When I think about it, there was nothing much there for me to return to."

He closed the car door and they started toward the house.

I may be a little old for this sort of adventure, thought Maxim, but change is what life is all about, and by God, I may be old, but I'm still alive! Maxim quickened his step so that Ana had to hurry to keep up with him. From a distance one might think that the tall man was the younger of the two figures going toward the house.

# OLEANDER

*By Dan Crawford*

THE MUCH-PUBLICIZED ending of the Cold War warmed many people. But there were some left out in the cold.

Jacob had served as a border guard for seven years without promotion, largely because nothing much ever happened along his border. His gun had been fired only at passing wildlife, though he never had any venison to show for this. Being a true soldier, he knew this kind of easy, lazy life could not last forever.

So he was not totally surprised when summoned to his commandant to be told that the State would henceforth try to do without him.

"There are these budget cuts," said the big, sweating major. "I am sure Comrade Jacob understands."

Jacob had been reading the newspapers, and he did understand. The ship of state had been rocking in the storm and was now jettisoning excess weight. He hung up his rifle, turned in his uniform, and hunted up his suit of civilian clothes, which did not fit nearly as well as it had seven years before. After bidding farewell to Bruno, the fattest, laziest German shepherd ever to infest a striped sentry box, he started walking to the capital.

His was not a large country and, with the help of an occasional farmer with a wagon, he reached the city in two days. Jacob intended to look up Rose, his girlfriend. She would do for a new commandant, telling him where to look for work, where to live, and how to go about making a new life in this new country.

But there was a man in Rose's apartment, a man who seemed to know the apartment very well.

"This is my fiancé, Josef Franks," Rose told Jacob. "He is a travel agent. Now that the borders are open, he thinks there should be money in that."

Certainly there would be more money in travel than in a pension that might or might not be paid next month. Jacob wished Rose well and set off to find a life of his own.

At first, it was not much of a life. All of Jacob's friends were in the army or in the same fix he was. Rents and prices were steep; his little pension was soon exhausted. There was certainly no surplus for new clothes. Half the managers he asked for work looked at his suit and said, "How long were you in the army, comrade?" The other half did not say "comrade."

Things were not improved by the fact that, after seven years as a border guard, Jacob was best suited for standing around or leaning against a wall. He was leaning on the wall of the Citizens' Savings Center, wondering where he could get a new gun, and whether he would turn it on others or on himself, when someone called, "Pssst! Comrade!"

Jacob looked down the street, away from the Citizens' Savings Center. A hand beckoned from an alley. Jacob thought about it, realized he had not so very much to lose, and strolled to the alley.

Towering above him was a massive fat man in a long black coat. Jacob's major had been a tall man; this man was inches taller and yards wider, with white hair and pink eyes.

"You look as if you need help, comrade," said the fat man.

Jacob spread his hands out, palms up. "That is no secret," he said.

"Hee hee," the fat man replied. "No secret. Yes. You were in the army, comrade?"

Jacob shrugged. "That seems to be even less of a secret."

The fat man shook his head as his features settled into a mournful pattern. "A very great pity," he said, "that after your years of protecting the State, the State cannot reward you. Still, that is no doubt an oversight, and the reward will be coming one day. Until then, comrade, you need help."

"I suppose you know where such help can be purchased?" said Jacob, a little sharply. He did not like the way the fat man kept jiggling, as if enjoying private laughter.

"Yes, yes, I do, comrade," the fat man replied. "And purchased at so slight a price you might never know you had paid it. Do you know the bank?"

Jacob blinked. "The Citizens' Savings Center?"

"Yes, yes," said the fat man. He reached into a pocket of his vast overcoat. "Take this."

For a moment, Jacob feared it would be a gun. A tiny key glittered between the fat man's thick white fingers.

"The director of the ba . . . Citizens' Savings Center and I do not speak to each other," said the fat man. "It was a woman: you soldiers may understand such things. I would like you to go into the bank and transact some business for me. Take this and ask for the safe deposit box with the number matching that on the key."

Jacob plucked the key from the man's hand and looked at the number on the side. "What will I find there, comrade?"

"On top," said the fat man, "there is a layer of rubles. You may take these or leave them, as you wish."

On the whole, Jacob thought he would leave them, but one never knew. "And?"

"Under those, a layer of assorted marks. You may take them or leave them, as you will."

This sounded more promising. "Yes?"

"Then a layer of dollars. You may take these or leave them, as you will, just as you may do with the layer of yen beneath those."

Jacob was wishing he had a suit with larger pockets; perhaps he could borrow the fat man's overcoat. "But what . . ."

"Beneath all these," said the fat man, leaning forward, "you will find gold, in coins and in bars, a few pieces of jewelry, and some unset diamonds."

"Ah!" said Jacob.

"Ah!" answered the fat man. "Of course, you may take these or leave them, as you will. What do you think, comrade?"

"I think my heart will break if you ever ask to have this key back," Jacob said.

The fat man laughed. "Keep the key, comrade! It is small enough reward for you, after your years of service. I want only one thing."

He lowered his voice. "Behind the bag of diamonds, you will find a brown envelope, just so long. It would fit in a wallet. There will be a notebook inside. Bring me the envelope, comrade, and you shall do as you like with the rest."

Jacob frowned. "A notebook?"

"A memento of my misspent youth," said the fat man. "The director would be upset to see it, so tuck it into a pocket before you come out. Go now, comrade. It is nearly closing time, and one would weep to see your just reward postponed until tomorrow."

Jacob had by now decided this was all either a prank of some kind or the product of a madman's dream. Yet, as he had told himself before, he had nothing he would regret losing. So he walked into the Citizens' Savings Center.

The manager stared at him, obviously feeling Jacob was a man who had never saved anything. But there was a box that matched the key. The manager took this, and Jacob, to a small room and locked them in.

Jacob licked his lips. Then he unlocked the box.

And everything was quite as the man had said: diamonds, dollars, gold, and all. There were even a few loose emeralds and rubies the fat man had not mentioned. At first Jacob began to cram things into his pockets. Then he swallowed hard, and put everything back.

"If this is to be my box," he said to himself, "there is no need to burden myself with everything at once. If this is a trick, and I will have only one chance to fill my pockets, I must do this in a disciplined manner."

So he took only several of the nicest-looking pieces of jewelry, and a few gold coins. People might look askance at a border guard who tried to sell such things, so he took enough paper money to support himself until the valuables could be disposed of.

He was about to close the box when he remembered that he had to save room in his pockets for one more thing. Nudging aside the bag of diamonds as if it were a bag of marbles, he found the brown envelope. He took it up and hefted it.

A peek inside showed him a little notebook, worn, with a creased brown cover. Jacob shrugged, and thrust it in among his paper money.

But he did not immediately close the box and call for the manager.

"This man values this notebook above diamonds," he said to himself. "What can fit into a notebook and be so valuable? Nothing the likes of me could fool with; that's for certain. This man may well be a criminal, a spy; he has that look about him. Why should such a person have anything at all?"

Once outside the Citizens' Savings Center, Jacob walked right to the alley. The fat man looked bigger and less trustworthy than ever.

"Well, comrade?" demanded the fat man. "Do your pockets feel better now?"

Jacob pulled a long face. "A fine joke, my friend. This is what I found." He pulled out the three little coins which had been his entire fortune earlier that afternoon.

The fat man's eyes bulged. "What? Is that all? He must have taken it with him! The dog!"

"Some fine friends you have," growled Jacob. He took out the key to the box and made as if to throw it on the ground. "The joke is on both of us."

The fat man stepped up and clapped a hand on Jacob's wrist. "The joke is on one of us at least, comrade," he said, his eyes running up and down Jacob's suit. "Come, let us forget it and drown our sorrows. There is a nice tavern down this way."

"I don't think so," said Jacob. "I . . ."

"I insist," said the fat man, reaching into one pocket with a free hand.

Jacob was bracing himself for what he knew would be a bitter fight when a whistle shrieked. With a cry, the fat man released Jacob and ran. Jacob flattened himself against the wall as nine topcoated men dashed past him in pursuit of a fugitive who was moving very quickly for a man of that bulk.

Once they had passed, Jacob turned to go, only to find himself confronted by a tall man wearing the insignia of a colonel. "Was that man a friend of yours?" demanded that official, his eyes cold.

"Why, no, comrade!" Jacob replied, at attention automatically. "He was offering me a drink. I don't even know his name."

"Well, see that you don't learn it," snapped the officer, and charged after his men.

Jacob waited all night for a knock on the door that never came. In the morning, he tucked the coins and jewelry away and bought new clothes with his money. The rest of that day and night he spent studying the Citizens' Savings Center. At last, around noon on the second day, he went in.

The manager did not summon police. The key had not melted like a dream in daylight. And the box was not empty.

After days of want, and seven years in the army, Jacob was ready to party. And because the capital was in much the same mood, he did not find this difficult. He threw away the new suit he had bought; it was far too shoddy for a young man of such fortune. He found himself a new apartment and fine new friends: men and women who, like Jacob, were willing to play in the new sort of capital created by the changing government. Thanks to his days along the border, Jacob spoke more than one language and found himself hailed as a cosmopolitan wit by the men and women willing to drink wine that he bought.

The yen were quickly spent. After them went the dollars and the assortment of marks. Gold, jewelry, and gemstones presented no problems. A man of such obvious standing could dispose of such trifles without being asked embarrassing questions, and his new friends were always happy to help Jacob out with transactions outside his previous experience.

When one's money is used so openly, it quickly evaporates. Jacob could not be expected to know this, never having had much of it. But ignorance of the law excuses no man, and soon all Jacob had left were some very nice suits and, in the pocket of each suit, a few rubles. His friends found other wines to drink.

Jacob sat alone in increasingly smaller apartments, finding markets for his suits more easily than for the rubles. Finally he sat alone in one room, with his oldest clothes and no rubles at all. He had just one thing he had not had before he met the fat stranger. Now he had a gun.

"What a fool," he said to himself, sitting on the lumpy mattress. "I had enough wealth to last a lifetime." He looked at the gun and laughed. "It did."

But before he raised the gun to his head, he felt he ought to set down a few straightforward remarks about his old friends as a warning to any other soldiers who came to the capital and found themselves wealthy. Since he could hardly afford to buy a piece of paper, he rummaged through the room for a scrap of newsprint or wallpaper that would do.

He found his old wallet, but there was nothing in it besides his identification papers. And he couldn't write on those. There'd be trouble.

Next to the wallet, though, he found an old brown envelope. Inside it was the brown notebook so earnestly desired by the fat man. "Let's just see what this was all about," said Jacob. "Like as not it's something I couldn't understand."

He was correct. The book held nothing but telephone numbers: some forty on pages that were headed "Buttercup," twenty or so on pages headed "Cyclamen," ten on a page titled "Mimosa," and just one on the page marked "Oleander."

"That's that," he sighed. And he turned to a blank page.

But he paused, partly because he had no pen and partly because he had an idea. He thrust the notebook into his pocket and hurried off to his landlord.

"Please, comrade," he said, when the old man came to the door. "May I use the phone?"

"When you pay your rent," said the landlord, frowning.

Jacob clasped his hands. "I think I might be able to pay if I could use your phone just once."

"Young fool!" said the man, drawing back into the apartment. "Don't you know the horse always finishes last when you need the rent?"

"Let me try," Jacob pleaded.

The landlord stood aside and let Jacob walk past him. "Very well, I will wait outside. But don't try to take that lamp and pawn it. They know all my lamps, new and old, down at the shop."

Jacob paid no attention and quickly called the first number in the book. The phone rang twice.

"How did you get this number?" demanded the voice on the other end. "Who is this?"

"Buttercup," whispered Jacob.

There was a gasp, followed by two clicks. A new voice said, "Buttercup? What do you want?"

Jacob shrugged. "Money is always nice."

"Where are you?"

Jacob gave him the address. Whoever was at the other end hung up.

"Well?" demanded the landlord as Jacob stepped into the hall. "When do I get my money?"

"I don't know," Jacob answered. "Soon, perhaps."

He walked down to the street. Not much later, a long black car pulled up in front of the building. A tinted window rolled down just a crack.

"Buttercup?" a voice demanded.

"You brought money?" answered Jacob.

A hand came up through the opening. Clenched in it was enough money to pay Jacob's rent for two years. But Jacob said only, "Rubles?"

The hand jerked back inside the car and then came out, trembling, holding West German marks. Jacob decided not to press his luck. He took the money and the car sped away.

Jacob paid his rent and moved out that same day. A young man of his resources needed a better address.

He was a bit more choosy about his friends now, but the capital was still a place to enjoy life and spend money. He tried out his phone numbers carefully, just one at a time. There were differences that he learned quickly. Buttercup numbers brought him money, but Cyclamen numbers brought more, and Mimosa numbers more than that. And money was not all there was to life, even in a city succumbing to capitalism.

Was a soccer game sold out, with no tickets available? Buttercup numbers brought tickets. Did Jacob need his phone hooked up? Buttercup pleaded for mercy, but Cyclamen numbers resulted in quick service. Was there a champagne shortage, with all the better years going to government officials? A Cyclamen number or a Mimosa number. Had some friend of Jacob's gotten a bit too much of the champagne and started to shout very funny but very treasonable things about the Premier? Definitely a matter for a Mimosa number, though a Cyclamen number might do if Western journalists were visiting the capital.

Jacob kept the notebook in an old tobacco pouch, and never explained to his friends how he did so many wonderful things. "Oh, I just sit and have a smoke," he would say, "and the answer comes to me."

No matter what the problem, Buttercup, Cyclamen, or Mimosa could handle it. Jacob never had occasion to call the last number in the book, even when his current sweetheart, the daughter of the Vice-Premier, became the daughter of the Premier. (There had been a little accident counting the votes, but the results could not be changed because the West had sent reporters.) Lulu (her name was Louisa, a far too antiquated name for a young party animal in a swinging city) was told by her father that, for the good of the government's image, she must stop associating with these decadent playboys. Lulu missed a few parties, but Jacob missed her. He called a Mimosa number. Soon Lulu was among her friends again.

But this was the one call too many. Anyone with any political knowledge might have warned him that the Premier's family was beyond the reach of an ex-guard, even one with such a talented telephone. But Jacob had never bothered much about the politics of his little country. He knew some people made money that way, but it looked too much like work to him.

One night, just as the party was starting, but before Lulu arrived, four dozen uniformed men rushed into the hotel, thrusting aside waiters and guests alike.

"Where's Mimosa?" they shouted. "We've come for Mimosa!"

No one there knew what they meant except for Jacob, and he said nothing. So all the guests were arrested. Jacob and two other men could not explain how they had made their money. They were charged with treason and sentenced to death. Jacob learned all this later, for he had been left in his cell while his trial took place. They asked him again and again about Mimosa, but he said only, "Mimosa is some kind of Oriental plant. I'm no florist."

The government could not decide which of the men was Mimosa, and finally decided none of them was. But they would die anyway, just to show Mimosa what was what.

The night before he was to die, Jacob was asked if he had any last request.

"Well, I would like to have a last smoke of my own tobacco, from my own pouch," he said. "Alone, perhaps in the warden's office, so that I could pretend I was in my own study at home."

The warden frowned. "I oughtn't to allow it," he said. "You know that's bad for your health."

"It is my last request," said Jacob.

So the warden sent to Jacob's house for the tobacco. "There are no guns in this room and the windows are barred," he said, locking Jacob in. "And I have guards outside the doors."

"I won't try to escape," said Jacob. And the warden went away.

Jacob took up his pipe, but waited a long time before he opened the pouch. Surely his house had been searched; at the least, the warden would have checked through the pouch for weapons. Well, at least he would have a smoke.

He opened the pouch and there sat the notebook among the pungent leaf fragments. With trembling hands, Jacob reached for the warden's phone and dialed the last number in the book. The phone at the other end rang once, rang twice . . .

"Who's this?"

"O-oleander," said Jacob.

"You are in trouble?"

"Oh, yes."

"Well, then." And the person at the other end hung up.

Jacob dialed the number again. The phone rang and rang, but there was now no answer. Finally he sat back and lit his pipe. He didn't enjoy it much.

"That was foolish, comrade," said the warden later, leading him back to his cell. "We listened to your phone call."

Jacob shrugged. "I've been a fool before," he said. "Why change things now?"

He tried to sleep, but it wasn't easy, knowing he was to die at dawn. He had neither watch nor window, and no idea when dawn was coming. Getting out of bed, he started to pace around the little room. He felt hungry.

"I should have asked for a last meal," he muttered. "I'd have had more pleasure from that."

Pacing and pacing, he grew hungrier and hungrier. "It must be breakfast time," he thought. "At least for those of us who have a full day ahead of us."

He thumped his fist on the cell door. "Hey, comrade!" he bellowed. "What time is it? Are you going to starve me to death to save the price of the firing squad?"

No one answered. He waited, banged again, and then went back to pacing. When he passed the cell door, he gave it a thump, just for something to do.

His hand was sore, and his legs so tired he thought he might go back to bed, when a faint voice cried, "Coming, brother!"

Someone banged at the other side of the door. Jacob turned toward it as he heard a click. He took a deep breath and prepared to die.

Instead, he found himself being hugged. "You are free, brother!" shouted a man Jacob had never seen before. "All political prisoners are to be freed!"

"Political . . ." Jacob began, but the man was too excited to listen.

"The Premier has fled the country, and all his government with him. Someone last night delivered boxes and boxes of such stuff to all the journalists that hardly a man or woman above the rank of dogcatcher has not been implicated in some scandal or another."

Jacob understood. "Oleander!" he whispered.

The man heard that. "What did you say, brother?"

"Er, I said, I said . . . Lulu? And her? Did Lulu go?"

"Who's Lulu, brother?"

"The Premier's daughter," Jacob replied.

The man took a step back. "You knew her, brother?"

"Er, well," Jacob replied, shuffling his feet and wondering how best to answer, "that's one reason I'm here."

The little man turned toward the door of the cell. "Hail, brothers!" he shouted. "Here's the man we want!"

Jacob's cell was filled in moments, and moments after that, Jacob found himself being deplorably bounced along on the shoulders of the mob. His identity was verified, and all were impressed to learn he had been sentenced to die at dawn. At dusk, he had been hailed as the new Premier. Lulu, who had given the mob her father's keys, and pointed out the key to the wine cellar, gave him her full endorsement.

Jacob never saw his tobacco pouch or his notebook again. In the confusion, they had probably been snatched up by some member of the crowd. He doubted that they would be much good to him any more. There was no time to be making phone calls anyway, with all these journalists pushing microphones at him.

"And what will be your first act as head of state, Mr. Premier?" one of them demanded.

Jacob thought about it. "There will be a decent pension plan for former border guards," he said. He saw no point in tempting fate.

# THE BLACK CLIFFS

*Joan Aiken*

IT WAS cold on the crossing, but calm; a sea nip in the air. Dark had fallen already by the time the two Americans boarded the ferry, but in spite of this they stayed on deck most of the way over to Rosslare, watching while the sky merged with the sea and then, by degrees, became pounced at irregular intervals by large brilliant white stars. Irving murmured this phrase aloud.

"*Pounced?*" Charley said. "What sort of crazy word's that, Irv? *Pounced* with stars? How can the sky be pounced with stars?"

"It comes from Latin," Irving answered absently, "Meaning to punch, or pierce with claws—from which you get pounce-work, decoration by perforations; it's the same word as puncture—which used to mean a sudden swoop with intent to seize."

"Hey, Irv, what a hell of a lot you know," Charley exclaimed admiringly. "A sudden swoop with intent to seize—like this, hey?"

And he grabbed his friend with rough, jocular affection.

"Watch out—you'll have us over the rail!" Irving cast a quick glance towards the open lounge door, where half a dozen other passengers were standing with their drinks, admiring the luminosity of the sky. If those people had not been there . . . The rail was not very high. But they *were* there; and Irving said to Charley, hardly troubling to keep the acid from his voice, "You'll have to remember not to be too demonstrative on the other side. The Irish may not like it."

"Oh, rats, Irv. Why ever not?"

"And *don't* call me *Irv.*"

Irving Christopher St. John his full and distinguished name was, lately dignified by the addition of Professor. He had discovered, also, that on this side of the Atlantic the surname became even more aristocratic by being pronounced Sinjun; he had determined to adopt this usage forthwith. He did not think he would be able to bear it if Charley persisted in referring to him as "My friend Irv Saint John."

"Sorry, Bimbo," Charley said humbly. "I'll try to remember."

A flitting shaft of light from the swinging door briefly outlined Charley's hopelessly plebeian, undistinguished face, the shiny balding brow, with a straw-colored wavy cowlick hopefully and thinly spread over it, the doglike pleading eyes fixed on those of his friend, who made so little attempt, these days, to conceal irritation and boredom.

"Oh, let's go and eat before those louts mop up every crumb of food on the boat."

Two coachloads of Irish sports fans were returning homewards from an international match at Wembley. They wore colored paper caps, sang and laughed uproariously, and had queued up ten deep for Guinness the moment the bar showed signs of opening. Now some of them were singing "In Dublin's Fair City," strewn like wreckage from a storm all over the lounge, while clumps of others moved purposefully in the direction of the cafeteria, clutching two glasses of drink apiece. Nothing but fish and chips remained by the time Irving and Charley joined the line at the counter.

It was like that all the way over—vomit in the lavatories, empty beer cans rolling about the floor. When the ferry berthed and passengers went down to the enclosed car-deck to drive off, there ensued an endless, claustrophobic wait, because some drunken sportsman was lost in oblivion, curled up sleeping off the chagrin of his team's defeat, and could not be found to shift his car from the foot of the ramp. Irving, at the wheel of their rented automobile in the stuffy, clanging cave, which vibrated furiously with the sound of motors being irritably revved and was humid with exhaust fumes, could have screamed with exasperation at the delay; one more interruption to his plan, he felt, and he might lose all control, go berserk, do something crazy and irremediable.

Just let us get to the west coast, he thought.

At last they were off, proceeding fast but cautiously through the misty Irish night.

"It's so late now, what's the point of stopping at a hotel?" Irving said. "We'd only get half the night we'd paid for, it would be a waste of money. Why don't we just travel straight on, across to the other side? The middle of

Ireland's a bore, anyway, might as well get through it in the dark. I don't mind driving if you want to sleep."

Charley, of course, was perfectly agreeable to this plan, but insisted that he must do a stint as well.

"Anything you say, Irv. I'll take the first spell if you like."

"No, I'll do first spell. I'm wide awake now, don't feel as if I could ever sleep again. You take a nap."

"Sure? Certain sure? Okay—if you say so, Bimbo," Charley replied biddably, wound his seat back, and wrapped himself in the blanket they had brought with them. They planned to camp if the weather proved suitable; otherwise stay at farms, hotels, bed-and-breakfast places, whatever offered. The project was to see the sights of the west coast, make leisurely search for Irving's ancestors (supposed to have originated from a small town called Lismaley in County Clare), and then return at a relaxed pace towards Dublin, where Irving was shortly to commence on a year's exchange from Chicago University, teaching American literature at Trinity College. A pleasant, peaceful program; they had two weeks of leisure.

In the first place, Irving had not intended Charley to come to Dublin.

"I really think it would be better, Charley, if you didn't. A year's not so long. And it would be good for you to be on your own. Give you time to get down to some course of study."

Charley had simply not taken him seriously.

"Oh, come on, Bimbo, you've got to be kidding! Not come to Dublin? Are you crazy? Why, I'm living for the day. Want to see the Ould Country." (Charley's ancestors had come from Sweden.) "I won't be in your hair, though, pal. Don't you worry about little old Charley."

"But what will you do with yourself?"

"Don't you fret about old Chas. I'll find myself some job—soda jerk in a drugstore or sump'n."

*"Chemist,"* Irving said irritably.

"Chemist, okay, or a laundromat, or any old thing. I can always find a job," Charley said with simple pride, and it was true, he could; prepared to turn his hand to anything, with a nonexistent threshold to boredom, he could work on a lathe, a production belt, mind babies, deliver groceries. Tolerant, good-tempered, dull, he was happy performing any task, however menial.

At one time this had seemed an asset; he was endlessly hardworking and useful, had painted Irving's apartment, spent hours sanding down furniture or pasting up wallpaper. Now all this dumb docility and refusal to take offense merely added to the aggravation.

A misty hunter's moon rose behind them. Irving drove on and on, his lips compressed. The road held no other traffic. For miles they passed no dwelling; untidy hedges, garlanded with late hay brushed from farm wagons, reeled by endlessly on either side.

Charley slept the sleep of the innocent. Mouth open, gently snoring, he lay childishly curled under the blanket, his heavy-boned frame utterly relaxed in the security of knowing that his friend was driving.

And Irving, brows knit, drove on through Wexford and County Cork and Limerick. Long obsessive analysis of his problem had not made its solution any plainer beyond a certain vague urge; he simply told himself over and over that he had to get rid of Charley. This stultification, this prison life, could not continue. He was not going to have his new colleagues in Dublin form their first impressions of him as Charley's friend, Charley's patron. In the hugeness of Chicago, okay; the chaos of such a city made all lives anonymous and therefore free. But he had sensed instantly on his preliminary visit to Dublin that here was a small, observant, bright-eyed, talkative community, ready to pounce on anybody's foibles, discuss them at length, and pronounce on them either with prudish disapproval or ribald indulgence. Irving could not stomach the prospect of either attitude. No, there had to be a clean break, and Charley must be brought to accept this.

Morning found them well across to the west. They breakfasted in Limerick, a grey, lively town, set about with spires of churches. Charley grumbled that he could not understand a word the Irish said, but Irving was delighted by their conversation and asked frequent questions in order to elicit the absurd, poetic torrent of speech that flowed so readily on any and every topic.

"Yerrah, sir! And is it the back end of Erin ye would be visiting? And how do ye ever hope to get to a little ramscramble place like Lismaley—and that from here, might I ask? I'd say it couldn't be done! Ye'd do better to remain in Limerick—faith, for all know 'tis the finest town in the west, and let ye enjoy yourselves while ye may!"

Despite this advice, by mid-morning they were off again, skirting the northern shores of the Shannon estuary. Beneath his preoccupations, Irving found himself enjoying this peaceful small country—the hazel and fuchsia hedges, the lonely silences, the weed-wrapped rocks by the shore, swans and gulls amiably competing on the tidal waters. But Charley's presence became more than ever an irritant.

How could I have borne his conversation for so long? Irving demanded of himself, listening in disgust to the sophomoric jokes, the inane comments on roadside objects, the pointless questions.

"Why are the Irish villages so poor-looking? Why don't they ever fix up their ruined churches—that must be the sixth we passed since lunch. Why aren't there any factories in Ireland?"

Charley was a hopeless map-reader, and signposts confused him; he could never be brought to understand the principle whereby a sign coupling two places that lay in diametrically opposite directions must indicate a fork in the road ahead. "But, Irv, how can it lead to *both* Dublin and Kilkee? Dublin's way over on the east, and Kilkee ought to be ahead of us."

In consequence they were continually lost and had to keep pulling up to study the map. Oh, for a companion who would understand this journey, Irving thought ragingly, and then asked himself what kind of a companion that would be? Some quiet, undemonstrative intelligence, somebody who knew the land and could expound it, not this vacuum of ignorance and ill-considered pawky humor.

"Gee, I'm hungry, I could eat a horse, Bimbo," Charley suddenly burst out in the late afternoon. "Aren't *you* hungry, Bimbo? What say we start looking for somewhere to stay the night?"

"Why didn't you suggest that in Killane?" Irving demanded coldly.

"Oh, no, Irv. That was a dismal hole. Not a decent-looking joint in the whole dump."

Irving had been rather taken by Killane, a mysterious little port, silent as death, not a human to be seen in the whole length of its immensely wide main street leading down to a couple of apparently disused warehouses. If he had not been so anxious to press on, he would have liked to investigate it further. But, like some migrating bird, he was feverishly anxious to continue, to keep moving, not to rest for a moment on the road, to reach the point where the land came to an abrupt stop.

"Well, there's plainly not much chance of finding a bed round *here*," he said.

Charley was driving and they were in the process of traversing an immense tract of brown peat-bog, from which the top layer had been cut out at intervals in black strips and piled up in black heaps—a desolate, gloomy stretch of country.

"What do they *want* with all that peat?" Charley wondered.

Another hour's driving brought them at length to a melancholy, strung-out, scattered village called Ballybaha: slate-roofed, one-storey houses behind fuchsia hedges, at long distances apart, with an occasional view of the ocean behind tufted sand-dunes in the distance.

"Who'd want to live here?" demanded Charley in disgust. "Why aren't there any pretty villages like we saw in England? Thatch? Tudor cottages?"

"The Irish were too poor," Irving pointed out. "They were living in mud huts when the English were building those Tudor cottages—and the Irish were paying them taxes. The only peasant artifacts left over from those times—the only things that didn't get worn out with constant use—are the things that fell into bogs."

*Bogs!* he suddenly thought. Why didn't they occur to me? But the summer had been a cold, unusually dry one; the bogs they crossed seemed baked into a substance like dark fruitcake. Besides, a bog is too indefinite, its embrace is incomplete; what it takes it may give back again. Whereas ahead, on ahead . . .

"There's a bed-and-breakfast place!" said Charley in triumph.

"Well? Will it do for you?" Irving coldly inquired.

"Oh, sure. Anything will do for *me*, you know that, Irv." Charley's placid humor was unimpaired. He ran the car off the road onto an earth patch in front of the largish bungalow whose sign announced *Inishkeen Guesthouse. Select bed and breakfast. Holiday accommodation.*

"*Select*—whatever can they mean by that, Bimbo?"

"Suitable for distinguished strangers such as ourselves. Give us the key and I'll get out the bags."

But Charley insisted on doing that—as he always did. Watching him, stooped, red-faced, with his head under the boot lid, Irving had a wild wish to leap back into the car and drive off, leaving him stranded in Ballybaha.

The quiet, genteel, sad lady who ran the Inishkeen Guesthouse received them without comment, and promised a meal at seven. "Till then, if ye should wish for a drink, they'll be glad to accommodate ye at the Anglers' Arms."

Accordingly, since the guesthouse bedroom was tiny and the lounge dismal, the two travelers later strolled along the usual wide, empty, dusty street to a dour-looking establishment by the crossroads in the middle of the village. On their way they were startled to observe, not far from the customary grey fragment of ecclesiastical ruin, a shatteringly avant-garde contemporary structure, apparently the modern church replacing the ruin. It was hexagonal in shape, low, presumably to hug the windswept ground, but with a curiously peaked and angled roof made of pink slate. It had narrow slit windows, like those of a frontier-post, and a short prong in the middle of the roof.

Like an aerial, Irving thought, to get in touch with the upper regions.

Charley said predictably, "Hey, man, what a crazy building! Is that a *church*? Looks like those folded paper boats we used to make as kids—know what I mean?"

Irving did know, but said, "I never played with paper boats."

"Want to go have a look-see?"

"I'd sooner have a drink. It would be too dark to see much, anyway."

"Okay, Bimbo—you're right, as usual."

At such an early hour, they were the only drinkers in the bar and had all the white-haired landlord's friendly attention. Thomas Roche, his name was, he told them, and happy he was indeed to meet travelers from the other side of the Atlantic. To be sure, his own brother was in Boston and his cousin in Cleveland but he himself hadn't crossed the water, and what could he be bringing them? Charley, only an occasional drinker—he usually stuck to Coke—chose sherry, which looked appalling. Irving had whisky. Its fine dryness put heart into him, and he politely congratulated the landlord on the remarkable modern church, so unusual for such a small community. To their surprise, Mr. Roche's face darkened.

"Well ye may say it is a remarkable building, and the heart's blood of the whole village draining away into it, year after year!"

He was evidently bursting to talk about it, and a few questions brought out the whole story: how when the old church finally collapsed in a winter gale five years ago the priest, Father Hegarty, fetched down an architect all the way of the road from Dublin to give them an estimate—the architect was a friend of his, d'ye see?—and how this fine fellow, with a tongue as long as his yard-measure, managed to throw a spell over the whole congregation so that they believed him when he said that for twenty thousand he could build them the finest church in the west of Ireland. "Twenty thousand! Long will his soul weep in purgatory for that lie! Faith, you'd think they were all bewitched that believed him!"

"How many inhabitants in the village?"

"Three hundred, if that."

"So what happened?"

"So his lordship the Bishop accepted the plan and the work went forward. A grand job they were doing! Only it took three years longer than was estimated, and cost five times as much. And the troubles that ensued in the course of the building ye'd never credit! Twice the steeple fell down, till they were under the necessity of settling for the thing you see. Three times the foundations sank under them. Glory be, and them wondering if the church would ever be finished before Judgment Day! And when at last finished it was, what do you think? They found Father Hegarty's fine friend had forgotten to install any heating, so it all had to be pulled apart again."

"Is it really finished now?" asked Irving.

" 'Tis, 'tis, for what it's worth. And it barely sufficient in size now for all the summer visitors, and in wintertime the tremendous noise of clangs and rumblings made by the costly heating-system will often be drowning out Father Hegarty's voice—and yet for all of that, more often than not you can freeze half out of your skin before Mass is finished. And as for paying off the great debt that it has incurred on the village, we shall be waiting to do that until our children's children are bringing home their wages, and isn't that an iniquitous thing? What a burden to lay on the poor people!"

Mr. Roche's eyes flashed angrily. The two Americans began to understand that if Father Hegarty constituted the chief spiritual power in the village, Mr. Roche the innkeeper was his main temporal opponent. He went on, talking faster and faster, to tell them how the money was dragged out of the villagers in dribs and drabs for the church fund, how if this one sold a load of hay, or that one got a good price for a few fish, Father Hegarty would be round in a flash to demand an extra contribution. " 'Tis an imposition, so it is, are ye not in agreement with me?"

Irving, who had begun to be bored by the topic some time back, said smoothly that indeed it did seem a great waste, but he believed they must be going back to the guesthouse now, for Mrs. Kelleher would have their supper waiting.

"Come back after, and I'll be telling ye more."

God forbid, Irving thought. He explained that they had to make up for a sleepless night, and they escaped. Charley, surprisingly, looked a little mulish.

"You didn't *want* to stay and hear him ranting on about the wrongs of the parishioners?" Irving asked when they were out in the wide, empty road.

"It was interesting. Those conniving monsters of priests really screw the people," Charley grumbled. "They have it all their own way—"

He pursued this theme all the way back to the guesthouse. Irving, with his chin on his chest and hands thrust into his pockets, paid little heed. Soon, now, he was thinking. And his mind expanded to embrace the image of the cliffs ahead, the Cliffs of Scath, where the land comes to a sudden stop, as if sheared off by a guillotine. Nine hundred feet of vertical black rock. The Great Wall of Thomond. That is the place. Tomorrow. Enough of this.

That night he slept uneasily, tossing from side to side in the narrow chilly bed; Charley, across the room, snored peacefully on his back, clenched fists flung above his head like a baby. Such rest as Irving had was broken by dreams: he was struggling to build a great stone tower, but lumps of rock kept coming loose in the gale that was blowing and thundered down menacingly around him. Then the whole tower began to sway from side to side overhead. He managed to wake himself just in time before the unstable structure fell and crushed him. Awake, he found that a real gale had blown up. How would that affect his intentions? All to the good, he decided vaguely—nobody goes sightseeing in a gale. And he fell at last into a heavy sleep.

When he woke he found Charley already up, shaving and whistling to himself. This habit of tuneless whistling, half under his breath, usually flung Irving into a frenzy of irritation, but today he was able to bear it, thinking: the last time.

After they had breakfasted and paid their bill, Charley insisted on walking along to inspect the new church.

"What's the point of that? You *know* all about it already." Irving was in a fever of impatience to be off.

"After all he said, I'd like to *see* it, Irv. Hell, you're always saying why don't I take an interest in things?"

"Interest in things that *matter*, for pete's sake!"

"Well, this matters to me," Charley said doggedly. Reluctantly, Irving accompanied him. By now the gale had blown out. Wet leaves, fuchsia twigs, and wisps of hay littered the ground; a heavy damp mist lay in the air. We shan't be able to see the Aran Isles, Irving thought regretfully.

In front of the church, they discovered a tall, black-robed figure, sweeping up the storm's debris from the cobbled approach path. This must be the wicked Father Hegarty, Irving thought, the despoiler of the people. It will be interesting to see how Charley deals with him.

Straightening from his task, the priest gave them an assessing glance and a polite smile. He was a strongly built man—in his forties perhaps—with a bland unreadable face and a pair of shrewd grey eyes, rather small, set close to his nose. He seemed very much at ease with himself, and who'd wonder, Irving thought. Look what he has achieved. It would be interesting to know, though, what official process brought him here; he looks such a capable man, wasted in this tiny parish. Don't they send priests to such remote spots for disciplinary reasons?

"Good morning, Father," he said. "We were impressed by your church last night and thought we'd like to take a closer look in daylight."

"You are welcome, the both of you." His eye swept over them.

What did he make of two such ill-assorted friends? Fidgety under the priest's intent scrutiny, Irving was glad to move inside the church and observe its expected banalities: the mock-Byzantine mosaics, angular Stations of the Cross, gaudy abstract window-glass, the jazzy geometric chandeliers, the concrete crucifix with its caricature of a Christ. There was a shrill, self-conscious air about the whole interior, he thought, like a girl with her first lipstick and cigarette, hoping to shock her mother.

And there was something else, too. Something out of proportion. Something strange, mocking, *wrong* . . .

Charley, needless to say, seemed highly impressed by it. Prowling about, looking at everything.

"Wow!" he muttered. "They sure got their money's worth, even if they did have to pay through the nose for it."

"It's a dreary, phony mess. And worse. There's something the matter with it. Let's get out of here."

Irving strode toward the door without attempting to conceal the disgust the place aroused in him. Regrettably, at this moment, the priest came in and, after saluting the altar, asked what they thought of the building.

"Very striking," Irving said. Father Hegarty gave him a quick glance.

Charley burst out, "It's a great building, sir—I'll say that for it! Only, be honest now—was it really worth squeezing all the dough out of those poor people for? Wouldn't a plain wooden drill-hall have done just as well, and then the kids could use it on wet days for volleyball or something?"

Irving wished he had been close enough to give Charley a kick. But the priest was not in the least offended. Evidently quite accustomed to this criticism, he remained perfectly amiable and bland in the discussion that followed, while Charley became more and more impassioned. Irving, refusing to become involved, stood aside, smiling faintly with his brows raised, while Charley, as might have been expected, soon found himself driven into a corner by Father Hegarty's trained powers of disputation.

"After all, what else would the people be spending their money on? Is it not best to devote your wealth to the glory of God?"

There was something ironic about his smile.

"A few comforts—diversions—in this back-of-beyond spot," Charley muttered.

"And fifty years from now, what would remain of those same comforts and pleasures? Who will remember that Mrs. O'Brien once had a TV set? But this church will endure from generation to generation."

Will it? Irving wondered skeptically.

"Do you not think the builders of Chartres, of Burgos, of St. Peter's, gave up a few comforts and pleasures in their day—and were justified by the result?"

"Oh, come on, Father, you can hardly compare—" Irving unwisely put in, and received such a razor-keen sideways glance from the small grey eyes that he fell silent. *And what in heaven's name was that little thing on the priest's watchchain?*

Father Hegarty said smoothly, "We can only do our best and hope it will meet the approval of future generations. And of our Lord. But now, tell me about yourselves. I can see at once what you are—" He allowed a fractionary pause and added, "You have the air of academics, am I not right?"

"Oh, sure, my pal's a professor," Charley said, again eager as a friendly dog. "He's going to teach for a year at Dublin College—"

"Is that so now? From Chicago University? And ye'll be spending a year in Dublin? Aren't you the lucky pair? And Professor St. John—" Father Hegarty pronounced it Sinjun "—will be searching for records of his forebears. That's very interesting. So we may hope to see more of you in these parts?"

"Possibly," said Irving, forming a private resolve that he personally would never again set foot in the village of Ballybaha. Something in Father Hegarty's questions made him profoundly uncomfortable: a touch of slightly patronizing amusement, as if the priest were saying, "Don't think for a moment you can fool me—I have you taped."

But I have you taped, too, Irving thought.

"And now you must sign our visitors' book."

Charley immediately wrote his name and tucked a pound into the offertory box. Irving managed to avoid doing so, as Charley remarked naïvely, "You weren't offended by the argument, sir?"

"Indeed, no! It's always a pleasure to talk to visitors—though little enough time I have for it. And where are you off to now, may I ask?"

"Oh, we're going to Lismaley," Charley said. "But first Irv here wants to take in the Cliffs of Scath. Not me! I've no head for heights."

"Is that so? Well, I hope the visibility improves for you. The cliffs can be a grand sight. Now I must be off with myself—I've twenty or more calls to make. I cover as much as fifty miles in a day—"

He had walked them to the gate and nodded a courteous goodbye as he mounted his bicycle, which had been leaning against the churchyard wall, and rode away.

"Quite an okay guy, really, wasn't he?" Charley remarked.

Irving said coldly, "It's my opinion that he's a warlock."

"Always kidding, Irv." Charley guffawed and slapped his friend's shoulder.

Driving north along the coast, as the sea-mist came and went, they began from time to time to get glimpses of their objective. From the height of a headland, the panoramic vista of the curved coast ahead was interrupted by a thick black bar across the horizon abruptly cut off in the middle, like an arm ending in a clenched fist. A black arm.

"Good grief," Charley muttered, peering ahead. "And that's a *cliff*? How far is it now?"

"Oh, twenty miles maybe."

"Do we really have to go there, Irv? I never was too keen on the Empire State Building—"

"Certainly we have to go. Those cliffs are one of the outstanding features of the whole country."

"Well, okay. Hey," Charley said, reverting to a more cheerful topic, "that priest really wasn't a bad guy, was he? He didn't get mad because I disagreed with him."

"It's his job not to. Besides, he wanted your money. It wasn't in his interest to antagonize you."

"Yeah, I guess," Charley said slowly. "To him we were rich Yanks. He seemed to know all about professors' salaries in American universities, didn't he? D'you think he really has a cousin at Chicago University?"

"Oh, very likely. Irish families are huge."

"You should have given him a donation, Irv."

"Why? I'm not obliged to subscribe to his meretricious church."

"If you think it's got merit, why not subscribe?"

"*Meretricious,* Charley, means phony."

"Oh, really?"

Irving did not trouble to voice his real feelings about the building and its use.

Road signs in Gothic now began directing them to the Cliffs of Scath.

"I wonder what Scath means?" said Charley idly.

"She was the Queen of Darkness," Irving briefly replied.

Another half hour's driving brought them to the official car-park for the cliffs. It was, as Irving had hoped, empty; the weather had turned wet, and in any case the holiday season was over. The seaward end of the car park lay quite close to the edge of the cliff. An arrow indicated the gift-shop but Irving was pleased to see a sign had been pasted over it which said, "Closed for the winter."

"What say we have lunch before we look at the cliff?" Charley said. He was sweating slightly.

He ran a hand up over his smooth shiny forehead. "You know how I feel about high drops, Bimbo—I guess I could take it better on a hard-boiled egg."

"Hell, Charley! We wasted such a lot of time already cashing checks in that wretched little bank—"

"Please, Irv."

"All right."

At least, Irving thought, it would be for the last time.

The mist was too thick, damp, and cold for lunching on the grass. They sat uncomfortably in the car, munching the hard-boiled eggs and sodabread Mrs. Kelleher had put up for them. Irving's raging impatience nearly choked him. At any minute somebody might arrive and spoil his chance. Though in this weather it was not too probable.

For dessert Charley produced a couple of chocolate bars he had bought in the village—he had a childlike fondness for sweet things.

"Want a bite, Irv? No? Sure?"

He had bought a Madeira cake, too, and hacked at it with a plastic knife purloined from the ferry cafeteria, grumbling, as he had all the way across Ireland, "Why in God's name, Irv, didn't you remind me to bring my Swiss army knife? That's what we need. This thing's no damn good."

That's another thing I shan't have to hear again, Irving thought detachedly.

He glanced down at the zigzags of the empty road leading up to the car park and said, "Come on, Charley—I think the mist's lifting a bit. We'll be able to see the Aran Islands in a minute. Put that stuff in the trunk and let's go."

Charley, rather slowly, rather reluctantly, packed the remains of the meal together into the plastic bag, walked round to the rear of the car, and raised the lid of the luggage compartment.

"Stick it well in between the bags," Irving said. "I can't stand loose milk bottles rolling around in the back while I'm driving."

He judged his moment carefully, as Charley began to withdraw his head and shoulders after obeying this order, and brought the trunk lid crashing down with all his force, so that the sharp edge took Charley exactly on the dome of his head, splitting it as if it had been one of the hard-boiled eggs they had just eaten.

Irving had ready a large polythene bag. With a quick glance round—still no car in view or audible—he slipped the bag over Charley's head and then, hoisting the body with difficulty—not far to take it, thank goodness—staggered to where the cliff-edge was barricaded off by a rampart of earth, reinforced all along by massive rock paving-slabs, set upright against it. Rolling Charley over this parapet was not too hard. In one spot it was only about three feet high—he had marked the best point while they were eating lunch. From there to the real brink was only the width of a narrow sheep track.

He thrust the body over and saw it recede to what seemed an infinite depth before it passed the curve of the cliff to vanish completely. The black, silky sea, visible from moment to moment in the mist, lay so far below that no sound, no splash, came back to him—even the sound of the waves was audible up here only as the faintest sigh.

Briskly, Irving dusted his hands on a clump of sea-thrift, stepped back over the earth-and-rock rampart, and walked across to the rented car. A wipe with a tissue and the boot lid—beaded over already with raindrops—showed no trace. The tissue could be burned later. What about Charley's bag? Should that follow its owner over the cliff? No, he decided; he would think of some other way to dispose of it.

He shut down the lid and, turning, was badly discomposed to see the black-robed figure of Father Hegarty walking slowly up the last section of the hill, wheeling his bicycle.

"Quite a stiff climb, that," the priest remarked, nodding backward toward the road behind him.

"Surely your pastoral visits don't bring you up here, Father?" Irving said, unsticking his tongue from the roof of his mouth. Where the *devil* had the man sprung from, so suddenly? Had he been concealed by one of the bends in the road? And what—if anything—could he have seen?

"No. But I have a couple of parishioners living not far inland from here. Once in a way I take a notion to come by and wonder at God's handiwork in this mighty place. Your visit put it in my mind to do so. Did it ever occur to you, I wonder now, to ask yourself where the rest of the cliff went?"

Irving echoed stupidly, "The rest of the cliff?"

"We see this great broken edge—like a sliced loaf. What did God do with the other half?"

"Could the Aran Islands be the bit that fell off?" Irving suggested vaguely, glancing out to sea. But the mist had thickened again—no islands were visible.

"And—speaking of the other half—where is your young friend? Not over the cliff, I trust?" Father Hegarty said playfully.

"Oh—" Irving had had time to take breath now, and felt calmer. "We decided to go different ways. He caught a bus."

"Is that so, now?" Father Hegarty's slow words and cold glance were like a bowlful of icy sea mist between the shoulderblades. The priest added with seeming irrelevance, "Since I am so lucky as to meet you again, might I mention that, back there in the church, you perhaps forgot to give us a donation for our church fund? Your young friend was so generous that I am sure it was nothing more than forgetfulness on your part—"

"Oh, right—I believe I did forget. Sure—a couple of pounds. Naturally I'd be glad—"

Irving dug with wet, shaking hands in his back pocket.

"*Well*, now—I was thinking of something more in the nature of a regular subscription," Father Hegarty said gravely. "We won't trouble about the details at present—I'll be in touch with you later. You need not give me your Dublin address—I've a cousin in the English department at Trinity. I'll tell him to look you up. A fine young fellow he is—you'll take to him, I'm sure. Bless me! look at the time—I must be getting on with my visits."

And, throwing a leg over his bicycle, the priest rode off downhill, disappearing into the mist as silently as if he had flown away on black wings.

# THE FRIENDS OF HECTOR JOUVET

*By James Powell*

THE OLD man came up the path that sloped between the benches and flowerbeds, but he stopped short of the edge of the cliff where Brown stood waiting. Instead, he sat down on a bench a few yards away, drew a folded newspaper from his coat pocket, and began to read.

Brown hesitated. His French wasn't really that good and for a moment he couldn't think of the verb "to follow." When he remembered, his chin started to tremble, and throwing his cigarette over the edge he went up to the old man.

"Why are you following me? Is it good to follow people? I do not like being followed. Do you like being followed?" These were all the forms of the verb Brown could muster and rather than start over again, he stopped.

The old man, who had been listening attentively, slipped the newspaper back in his pocket and smiled. "I am afraid you are mistaken, young man. I am not following you." His English was meticulous and the quiet conviction of his words told Brown it was the truth.

"Oh," said Brown, and stepped back in confusion.

"Actually," said the old man, as if to cover the other's embarrassment, "I come here quite often. The sea is blue; the rocks are white. I have always thought that this would be the ideal place for a visitor like yourself to see our gay, carefree little principality for the first time. Regrettably, that is impossible, for to come upon this prospect first, one would have to scale the cliff."

"Maybe a good place to see San Sebastiano for the last time, then," said Brown with a half smile.

"Ah, you are leaving us?" asked the old man sadly. "Well, I hope you have seen more of our happy, light-hearted city than the inside of the Casino."

"I guess that was about as far as I got," admitted Brown.

"But that is terrible, terrible," said the old man, throwing up his hands in mock horror. "But all is not lost and if you will permit me I can still point out a few highlights from here."

He led Brown back to the edge of the cliff. "Below us, of course, is the harbor and over there, the romantic old quarter. Its reputation is exaggerated, I assure you. Our women are not promiscuous; songs have been written about that. On the left you have our celebrated Reptile Museum founded by Prince Adalbert, an ardent herpetologist and the grandfather of our present prince. My father had many stories of the misadventures of the good Prince Adalbert who prowled the streets of San Sebastiano at all hours hunting snakes with his forked stick, returning the salutes of the policemen and chatting quietly to himself.

"And there, behind the Cathedral, you can see the roof of the Casino into which, you are perhaps aware, the citizens of the principality are not allowed to enter. That is quite appropriate. A good host does not laugh at his own jokes."

Brown took a wristwatch out of his pocket, looked at it, and put it back.

"Am I keeping you? I hope not," said the old man. "Actually I cannot stay much longer myself. I must see a friend off on the train—the 4:45."

"You don't have much time," warned Brown.

"Enough for a bit more of our history," said the old man, leading Brown back to the bench. "Were you aware, for example, that our mineral waters were held in high esteem as early as the days of the Romans? One might wonder why, since it is quite sulphurous and abominable. Perhaps they had more horrible diseases in classical times than we do today.

"Within the memory of my grandfather, the elderly and infirm flocked to San Sebastiano to take our waters. They sat on park benches and scowled at our pigeons; they let themselves be pushed along our promenades in wicker chairs; they pulled wry faces and sucked at our mineral waters. But we were more than a spa. We were renowned for personal sobriety and dignified compassion toward those who frequented our life-giving waters.

"Yes, believe it or not, the gay, carefree people of today's San Sebastiano were all that. In the generation preceding the Franco-Prussian War acute depression of the liver was fashionable and our waters were highly recommended.

"Those were the fat years for us, years of building and, as it later turned out, of overbuilding. For with the close of the war an epidemic of disorders of the spleen swept across France and non-Germanic Europe. Less carbonated waters came into style and almost overnight our little city was as deserted and forlorn as an overgrown cemetery. Today one is at the top, tomorrow at the bottom."

Brown's mouth worked soundlessly. Then he said, "Life is a real double-crosser."

"Why, that is quite philosophical for someone so young, and an American at that," smiled the old man.

"Canadian," said Brown.

"A Canadian, how delightful," said the old man, still smiling.

"You're going to miss your train," said Brown.

"I still have a bit more time," said the old man. "Now let me see, where were we? Ah, yes. Now, as it happened, a modest, unassuming little Casino had been established on an out-of-the-way street to accommodate the younger, faster set which frequented our little principality at the height of its popularity. A mere accommodation—"

Suddenly the old man clapped a hand to his forehead. "I have just thought of something I should have thought of before," he said. "Perhaps you can help me. The Canadian and the American dollar are worth the same, are they not?"

Brown stared at him for a moment. "No," he said finally.

"Then the Canadian dollar is worth more?" said the old man.

"Less," said Brown.

"Ah, I am sorry," said the old man. "Forgive me for dwelling on it but would you happen to know the exact—"

"The Canadian dollar is worth between ninety-two and ninety-three cents," said the young man.

"Let us say ninety-three," insisted the old man graciously. He pursed his lips and calculated. "Fine. Fine," he said. "I have just had what you would call a false alarm. But let us get back to what we were talking about. Imagine the city fathers' surprise when at the very time the attraction of our waters declined, the revenue from the Casino showed a healthy increase, due, in part, to our abundance of economical hotels and hungry waiters.

"It soon became obvious that San Sebastiano was at a crossroads. Should we wait, sober, compassionate, with tightened belts for the prodigal elderly and infirm to return? Or should we cut a new path through the history of San Sebastiano, expand the Casino, become gay, hurdy-gurdy, and carefree?

"It was decided to have a referendum. Feelings ran high. A man walking down the street laughed with pure delight at some enchanting thing his daughter, a child of five, had said. He was jumped upon and severely beaten by a group of mineral-water supporters who believed him to be demonstrating in favor of the Casino. A crowd of Casino supporters, returning in an ugly mood from a mass rally, came upon a funeral procession in the street and interpreted it as a counter-demonstration by the mineral-water faction. The ensuing clash provoked three solid days of rioting. Et cetera. Et cetera. The outcome of the referendum you know, for it is as you see us now."

"You know, you've missed your friend's train," said Brown.

"Why, then I'll see him off on the next," said the old man. "As I was about to say, San Sebastiano, with its expanded gambling facilities, entered what has been described as its 'laughing years.' In 1909 an entirely new Casino, constructed in the style of the Ottoman Turk, was opened amid fireworks, balloon ascents, and a magnificent sailboat regatta.

"On the opening day Casimir Vaugirard in his tri-wing Prentis-Jenkins Hedgehog flew from Perpignan to San Sebastiano in a matter of hours. He circled the dome and minaret of the Casino, dropping projectiles trailing the colors of the Vaugirards and San Sebastiano, then dipped his wings in a majestic salute to the cheering crowd and crashed into the side of this very hill.

"What might have spelled disaster for us—since tragedy was hardly the mood we hoped to associate with our little principality—became instead a supreme gesture of love when, in the cockpit, his body was found locked in the embrace of his mistress, the celebrated beauty known as Lola.

"Well, missing one train is no excuse for missing the next," said the old man, "and a few formalities still remain. I trust what I have said will enable you to appreciate what is about to happen."

"Formalities?" said Brown.

"May I see your passport?" said the old man. Brown stared at the out-stretched hand. Nodding toward it, the old man said, "I am the police, you see. Your passport, please."

Brown handed it over.

The old man skimmed down the vital statistics, shook his head sympathetically over the photograph, then thumbed through the pages, turning the passport this way and that to read the frontier stamps.

"But I haven't done anything wrong," said Brown.

The old man shrugged genially and without pausing in his examination of the passport, drew an envelope from his pocket and passed it to the young man.

"Mr. Brown, here you will find one second-class railway ticket, San Sebastiano to Paris, and banknotes to the sum of fifty new francs—ten of your dollars, more or less. I would appreciate your checking to see that this is exactly as I say, for I am required to ask you to sign a receipt."

In the midst of counting the bills, Brown stopped. "But this is crazy. I haven't done anything."

The old man closed the passport and handed it back. "Mr. Brown, let me say directly what both you and I know: your coming here this afternoon was for the purpose of doing away with yourself."

"A lie—an out-and-out lie," said Brown indignantly.

"No, it is not," said the old man calmly. "You are not being honest with me."

"Honest?" shouted Brown. "You're a fine one to talk about honesty. Didn't I ask you if you were following me and didn't you say"—he switched into a falsetto—" 'I am afraid you are mistaken, young man'?"

"You are not being quite fair, Mr. Brown. Granted I did walk behind you from the Casino. But I was not following you. Except for my superiors' primitive attitude regarding expenses, I could have come by taxi and arrived here well ahead of you."

The old man shrugged at Brown's look of disbelief. "Mr. Brown," he said, "have you ever considered the possibilities of suicide open to a tourist? He does not have a gun—his intention in coming abroad is rarely to shoot himself. Our pharmacies confuse him and he does not know the name in our language for the poison he might have used with every confidence at home. He distrusts our hotel furniture, and rightly so. Will a chair that looks as though Louis XIV sat in it hold his weight as he ties a rope to the chandelier? And in what store would he buy the rope?

"No, if you think about it, Mr. Brown, there is only one way—to throw oneself from a high place. Here in San Sebastiano there is really only one spot high enough to do the job without risking half measures. And here we are."

"Look," said Brown with a facsimile of laughter, "you've really made a mistake. I came here to try my luck at the Casino and now I'm off to Florence or someplace. I'm making a kind of grand tour."

The old man smiled patiently.

"Look," said Brown, "the whole trip is a reward for my graduating in dentistry from McGill University—that's in Montreal. When the trip's over I go back home to Drumheller, Alberta, and go into practice with my father. A guy with his future all cut out for him would be the last person to commit suicide. What I mean is, you don't have any motive."

The old man sighed and took a notebook from his pocket. " 'On August 15 last,' " he read, " 'the Eighth Bureau of the Judiciary Police' "—he half rose and tipped his hat—" 'was alerted by the local American Express office that one Brown, Norman, had that day cashed in the return portion of a first-class airplane ticket, Paris-Montreal-Calgary. Subsequent routine investigation revealed that on the preceding day the subject had checked into the Hotel de l'Avenir and the same afternoon at the Casino had lost chips amounting to $520.

" 'The afternoon following the subject's visit to American Express he lost chips amounting to $450. That evening he sent the following cablegram to a Miss Annabella Brown, Drumheller, Alberta: DEAR AUNT BELLA, MONEY AND RETURN TICKET LOST IN FIRE THAT DESTROYED MY HOTEL. BEST NOT TO WORRY NORMAN SENIOR. $1000 SHOULD COVER IT NICELY. NORMY.

" 'August 16, subject loses chips amounting to $1000.' Miss Brown is very prompt. 'Subject leaves Casino and walks to the Parc de la Grande Armée'—which is where we are now—'and stands in contemplation at edge of cliff, then leaves park and sends following cablegram: DEAR AUNT BELLA, HOTEL FIRE NO ACCIDENT. HAVE STUMBLED ON VAST INTERNATIONAL PLOT LINKING JAPANESE BEETLES, DISAPPEARANCE OF AMELIA EARHART, AND RADICAL CHANGES IN WEATHER THESE LAST FEW YEARS. CONFIRMS YOUR SUSPICION, WAS NOT SUNSPOTS. HAVE CONTACTED DISILLUSIONED FOREIGN AGENT. NEED $5000 AS PROOF OF MY GOOD FAITH. LET'S KEEP THIS TO OURSELVES. NORMY.

" 'August 17, subject's losses: $5,000. That evening sends following cablegram: DEAR AUNT BELLA, WE ARE REALLY ONTO SOMETHING. AGENT AGREES TO BE ON OUR SIDE AND SAP THEM FROM WITHIN. HE SAYS DOUBLE AGENTS GET DOUBLE PAY. SOUNDS FAIR ENOUGH. NEEDS ANOTHER $5000. MUM, DON'T FORGET, IS THE WORD. NORMY.

" 'August 18, subject's losses: $5,000. Sends following cablegram: DEAR AUNT BELLA, THINGS COMING TO A HEAD. NEED $5000 FOR INCIDENTAL EXPENSES— MICROFILM, INVISIBLE INK, SECRETARIAL HELP, ETC., ETC. ITEMIZED LIST TO FOLLOW. KEEP THIS UNDER YOUR HAT. NORMY.' "

The old man looked up from his notebook. "Might I ask you about this Miss Brown?"

"She doesn't happen to be any of your darn business," said Brown through clenched teeth. The old man waited. At last Brown said, "You might say that I'm her favorite nephew. You might say that the money was her life savings."

"I meant is she a bit—potty? Do you still say 'potty'?"

" 'Peculiar' might be better," said Brown.

"I must jot that down," said the old man, scribbling in his notebook. "And now where were we?

" 'August 19, by 5 P.M. subject's *winnings* total $38,000; by midnight, $88,000; by closing time, $123,000. Subject returns to hotel where, in answer to inquiry, is informed that next train for Paris is at 1:47 P.M.

" 'August 20, subject checks out of hotel at 10:37 A.M., leaves bags at station, wanders through streets looking in store windows. Noon finds subject in front of Casino. Subject smiles as if pleasantly surprised, and with glance at wristwatch, enters Casino.' "

The old man closed his notebook and looked up. "By 2:30 you had lost $56,000, and by 3:30, $123,000. And here we are. I must add in conclusion that San Sebastiano for several years now has requested in the most vigorous terms that the railway provide us with a morning service to Paris. Now perhaps we had better go," he said, preparing to rise.

"Hold on a minute," said Brown, and he began to slap the palm of one hand with the back of the other. "I have certain rights. You can't just put me on a train and run me out of town. Nothing you've said would hold up in a court of law."

The old man settled back on the bench. "Ah, now I can understand your hostility," he said. "Believe me, there was never a question of a law having been broken. Consider for yourself how odd it would look if gay, carefree, light-hearted San Sebastiano had a law making it a crime to attempt suicide. What would people say? Why would anyone even dream of committing suicide here?"

"You mean that technically speaking," said Brown, "I could jump off this cliff this very moment and you could do nothing?"

The old man nodded. "It would be perfectly legal. But law is a funny thing, Mr. Brown. If some future historian, for example, were to try to understand the people of the Twentieth Century from a study of their books of law alone, would he, do you think, see them as they were, or as they feared they were, or as they hoped they might be?

"A particular case: what would this future historian of ours think of a certain law in force in San Sebastiano which says that our police must clean their revolvers daily—nothing unusual in that—but, the law continues, in a secluded yet public place in the open air? Legend has it that one Sub-Inspector, Auguste Petitjean, discharged his revolver as he was cleaning it while seated in his bath. The tub and walls, as it happened, were marble, and Sub-Inspector Petitjean was shot seventeen times in as many places by that single ricocheting bullet.

"By some miracle he recovered and returned to the force only to be subsequently discharged when it was discovered that he had developed a psychological block against firing his revolver—or, as another version of the story has it, against taking a bath. Whichever version is correct, the law is there nevertheless. Were you to try to jump, I would be obliged to clean my revolver in public and it might accidentally discharge, the bullet striking you in the left calf. Conveniently enough, the hospital is located right next to the railway station.

"I had intended, by the way, to say before that I am sorry your train ticket is second-class. By all rights it should be first-class, but the authorities view the situation otherwise. You see, our Eighth Bureau, dealing exclusively in cases such as yours, is organized into three divisions based on the amount of money lost by the subject—not winnings that happen to be lost again, you understand, but his own personal investment.

"The first division, headed by Inspector Guizot, deals with amounts of $5,000 or less: the butcher, the baker, and the candlestick maker. Traditionally his subjects travel third-class.

"My own division, the second, deals with amounts of $5,000 to

$50,000. By the way, we use American dollars as a standard out of simple convenience. That was why I received quite a start a while back when I realized that in your case we were dealing in Canadian dollars. For a moment I was afraid, forgive me, that you might be in Guizot's division. In any event, traditionally my subjects go second-class.

"The third division, under Baron de Mirabelle, deals with sums in excess of $50,000. His subjects, of course, go first-class.

"However, a few years ago the railways did away with third-class. It was decided that Guizot's would go second-class. What else could they do? Fine, I said, but then I humbly submit that mine should go first-class. But the authorities were blind to the justice of it, and de Mirabelle, though sympathetic, kept smiling in that cultured way of his.

"A very distinguished person, the Baron: always in evening dress and with a black patch, sometimes over one eye, sometimes over the other. I often tell the story of how the Baron acquired his eye patch. I like to think it makes my own subjects' losses appear less significant.

"One day around the end of the last war a large burly soldier arrived in San Sebastiano. He had a system for roulette, as we all do, and $200,000— the accumulated combat pay and savings of his entire regiment, which he had promised to increase a hundredfold.

"This he promptly proceeded to do. His system was based on what he called his 'lucky lower-left bicuspid.' He would survey the roulette table, from number to number, until his bicuspid throbbed. That number he would bet. And he would win astronomical sums—millions—night after night.

"Finally the day arrived when the Casino, short of a miracle, would open its doors for the last time. The soldier dined alone beforehand at Chez Tintin. At the end of the meal there was an altercation. The waiter accused him of overtipping. The soldier threatened to ram a wad of banknotes down the waiter's throat and moved toward him with a bobbing and weaving motion, the result, we were later to learn, of considerable experience in the ring, where he was known as—"

The old man thought for a moment. "Breaker Baker, or something like that," he said. "Politely but firmly, the waiter struck him on the head with a bottle, Chateau Pommefrit, 1938.

"The soldier regained consciousness to find his celebrated tooth on the floor in front of him. He rushed to the Casino and, with the tooth clenched in his fist, surveyed the table. Nothing happened.

"But then, as his eye passed number 14, something in his jaw throbbed faintly—his lower-*right* bicuspid! He bet and lost. Again the bicuspid throbbed, more insistently. He bet again and lost. And so on into the night. By closing time he was penniless and the right side of his jaw was swollen, throbbing as indiscriminately as any common toothache.

"The next day, when the soldier tried to take his life, Baron de Mirabelle, of course, was waiting. But at the railway station the soldier grew belligerent and came at the Baron, bobbing and weaving, catching the Baron with a right cross to the eye. Finally two Travelers' Aid people had to force the soldier onto the train. Not a moment too soon either, for at the news of his losses his regiment had mobilized and units had already reached the outskirts of San Sebastiano, thirsting for his blood. The Baron's eye had a fine bruise for a week. He fancied himself in the eye patch and has worn it to this day."

"Let's get back to me," said Brown. "What if your bullet didn't stop me? What if I crawled to the edge and with my last breath threw myself to my death?"

"Believe me," said the old man, "that is just not the way it is done. The suicide, above all others, wants to leave life erect, not on his hands and knees. He wants to savor that last moment. He stops to smoke a final cigarette, to gather his thoughts together into an epigram of one sort or the other, to—and this happens more frequently than you might imagine—to remove his wristwatch. Placing it where? Of course, in his pocket.

"How 'peculiar' we are and how lovable, eh, Mr. Brown? And here is something equally convenient for me in my work: how many turn to say, 'Why are you following me?' As if it should make any difference to them if I were to leap over the cliff right behind them. No, Mr. Brown, man always wants to pause a bit before spitting in life's eye, before jumping, before becoming both the spitter and the spittle."

Brown rested his head in his hands and without looking up, said, "I guess you win." Then his chin began to tremble again. "I just want you to know that I can see right through you people," he said. "You don't give a darn if I kill myself or not as long as I don't do it here. I can lose my aunt's life savings in your Casino, oh, sure. But I can't jump off your gay carefree little cliff." He rubbed his eyes. "Well, I say the hell with you all."

The old man moved to put his hand on the young man's shoulder, then thought better of it. He leaned forward. "Mr. Brown, we must all set a boundary on our compassion or we would turn our faces to the wall and not get out of bed in the morning. San Sebastiano's humble frontiers are the limits of mine. You must forgive me if I find that quite enough. Before, when I told you something of our history, I hoped to prepare you to understand why we cannot allow you and the others to carry out your little plans. For what would be the result? A suicide rate, a per capita statistic so misleading and grotesque that it would reflect on the whole tenor of life in light-hearted, hurdy-gurdy San Sebastiano.

"Besides, aren't you being a bit severe? The railway ticket and the money will take you to Paris where your Embassy will arrange modest transportation home. Confess your little indiscretion. Give Aunt Bella the pleasure of forgiving her favorite nephew."

"And what about my father?" said Brown. "Did I tell you he's got fists like hams? Like hams!" Brown stared down at his shoes and shook his head back and forth.

After watching him for a few moments, the old man looked down at his own shoes and said in a quiet voice, "You know, Mr. Brown, soon I will be retiring and I have often thought these last few years of all the people I have taken to the train. What are they doing? How are they getting on? How many children do they have? Do they, I wonder, ever remember the day Hector Jouvet—that is to say, myself—put them on the train? I am not being sentimental. I tell you this because I want to describe for you a silly daydream of mine, solely because it might amuse you.

"In my daydream it is the day of my retirement. I enter my favorite café. Georges, the owner, stands behind the bar reading a newspaper. 'Good day, Monsieur Jouvet,' he says. 'Would you step out back with me for a moment?'

"Puzzled, I follow him out to the back where they have the large room they rent out for banquets. Everything is dark. Suddenly the lights blaze on. I am taken aback. I am surprised. The room is filled with half remembered faces—stockbrokers, bank tellers, church wardens, trustees of estates of widows and orphans. Across the front wall is a large banner: THE FRIENDS OF HECTOR JOUVET. FIRST ANNUAL CONVENTION.

"Amid applause and well wishes I take my place at the head table beside those special people, whoever they might be, who had gone on from their visit to San Sebastiano to positions of eminence in their own countries—a statesman, a bishop, a magnate or two, and—who knows, Mr. Brown?—perhaps even a famous dentist.

"We eat and at the end of the meal I am presented with a gold cigarette lighter. I could show you the very one in a shop window not far from where I live. It is inscribed: *To our friend Hector Jouvet from The Friends of Hector Jouvet.* Then in six different languages they sing 'For He's a Jolly Good Fellow,' and end by pounding on the tables.

"I stand up. I am deeply moved. I always feel this particular moment most vividly and how deeply I am moved. Then I speak. In my mind's eye, I see all this very clearly. But though my mouth is moving I cannot hear what I am saying. I only feel my own astonishment at the wisdom and simplicity of my words. They are saying everything I had wanted to say to each person in the room on his particular day. But I cannot hear the words. I can only see their faces smiling and nodding."

The old man stopped abruptly and cleared his throat. "But of course all this nonsense takes place only in my imagination. The people I have taken to the train do not know each other. Oh, one or two might meet by chance.

Perhaps in his cups, while talking of youthful indiscretions, one might mention Hector Jouvet. 'What?' the other might say, 'you knew Jouvet too?' And they might talk of afternoons at the cliffside in San Sebastiano or even of forming a club. But it would come to nothing because they were only one or two.

"How regrettable, Mr. Brown, because I have all their names and they wouldn't be so hard to locate—except, you understand, it would be out of place for me to take the initiative. As a matter of fact, I carry the list with me should the same idea occur to someone or other as I take him to the train. You might be interested in seeing the list, Mr. Brown. I think I have it here somewhere."

As the old man fumbled through his pockets, he laughed nervously and said, "I don't imagine, Mr. Brown, that you would care to be the first president of The Friends of Hector Jouvet?"

Brown looked up from his shoes. "Did I tell you my father was heavyweight champion of the Canadian Army? Did I tell you what they called him because of those big fists of his?" said the young man with a shudder. "They called him The Buster."

The old man looked puzzled. "Buster Brown. Buster Brown," he said thoughtfully. "But of course, of course—it was Buster Brown, not Breaker Baker. How stupid of me and how delightful! Buster Brown was the name of the soldier who gave the Baron his eye patch."

"You mean the one who lost all those millions was my father? The one with the lucky lower-left bicuspid?" said Brown with an astonished and broadening grin.

The old man nodded. "How appropriate he should have turned to dentistry. Your father was the man who almost broke the bank at San Sebastiano. A popular song was written about him at the time. As we walk to the station I will teach it to you, if you like."

Brown jumped to his feet. "I'll say I would!" he said. "Even just enough to hum the tune every once in a while!"

"I'm sure that would be very useful, Mr. Brown," smiled the old man. "Ah, it is a great day for the Eighth Bureau. First the father and now the son. And after that who knows, eh, Mr. Brown? A fine-looking young man like yourself. Well, come along or we will miss our train."

He took Brown by the elbow and they started down the path. "Mr. Brown," said the old man as they went, "do you recall my mentioning The Friends of Hector Jouvet? It occurs to me that if such a club were ever formed it might offer your father an honorary membership. I don't imagine he's being invited to many regimental reunions."

# As Good as a Rest

### By Lawrence Block

ANDREW SAYS the whole point of a vacation is to change your perspective of the world. A change is as good as a rest, he says, and vacations are about change, not rest. If we just wanted a rest, he says, we could stop the mail and disconnect the phone and stay home: that would add up to more of a traditional rest than traipsing all over Europe. Sitting in front of the television set with your feet up, he says, is generally considered to be more restful than climbing the forty-two thousand steps to the top of Notre Dame.

Of course, there aren't forty-two thousand steps, but it did seem like it at the time. We were with the Dattners—by the time we got to Paris the four of us had already buddied up—and Harry kept wondering aloud why the genius who'd built the cathedral hadn't thought to put in an elevator. And Sue, who'd struck me earlier as unlikely to be afraid of anything, turned out to be petrified of heights. There are two staircases at Notre Dame, one going up and one coming down, and to get from one to the other you have to walk along this high ledge. It's really quite wide, even at its narrowest, and the view of the rooftops of Paris is magnificent, but all of this was wasted on Sue, who clung to the rear wall with her eyes clenched shut.

Andrew took her arm and walked her through it, while Harry and I looked out at the City of Light. "It's high open spaces that does it to her," he told me. "Yesterday, the Eiffel Tower, no problem, because the space was enclosed. But when it's open she starts getting afraid that she'll get sucked over the side or that she'll get this sudden impulse to jump, and, well, you see what it does to her."

While neither Andrew nor I is troubled by heights, whether open or enclosed, the climb to the top of the cathedral wasn't the sort of thing we'd have done at home, especially since we'd already had a spectacular view of the city the day before from the Eiffel Tower. I'm not mad about walking stairs, but it didn't occur to me to pass up the climb. For that matter, I'm not that mad about walking generally—Andrew says I won't go anywhere without a guaranteed parking space—but it seems to me that I walked from one end of Europe to the other, and didn't mind a bit.

When we weren't walking through streets or up staircases, we were parading through museums. That's hardly a departure for me, but for Andrew it is uncharacteristic behavior in the extreme. Boston's Museum of Fine Arts is one of the best in the country, and it's not twenty minutes from our house. We have a membership, and I go all the time, but it's almost impossible to get Andrew to go.

But in Paris he went to the Louvre, and the Rodin Museum, and that little museum in the 16th arrondissement with the most wonderful collection of Monets. And in London he led the way to the National Gallery and the National Portrait Gallery and the Victoria and Albert—and in Amsterdam he spent three hours in the Rijksmuseum and hurried us to the Van Gogh Museum first thing the next morning. By the time we got to Madrid, I was museumed out. I knew it was a sin to miss the Prado but I just couldn't face it, and I wound up walking around the city with Harry while my husband dragged Sue through galleries of El Grecos and Goyas and Velasquezes.

"Now that you've discovered museums," I told Andrew, "you may take a different view of the Museum of Fine Arts. There's a show of American landscape painters that'll still be running when we get back—I think you'll like it."

He assured me he was looking forward to it. But you know he never went. Museums are strictly a vacation pleasure for him. He doesn't even want to hear about them when he's at home.

For my part, you'd think I'd have learned by now not to buy clothes when we travel. Of course, it's impossible not to—there are some genuine bargains and some things you couldn't find at home—but I almost always wind up buying something that remains unworn in my closet forever after. It seems so right in some foreign capital, but once I get it home I realize it's not me at all, and so it lives out its days on a hanger, a source in turn of fond memories and faint guilt. It's not that I lose judgment when I travel, or become wildly impulsive. It's more that I become a slightly different person in the course of the trip and the clothes I buy for that person aren't always right for the person I am in Boston.

Oh, why am I nattering on like this? You don't have to look in my closet to see how travel changes a person. For heaven's sake, just look at the Dattners.

If we hadn't all been on vacation together, we would never have come to know Harry and Sue, let alone spend so much time with them. We would never have encountered them in the first place—day-to-day living would not have brought them to Boston, or us to Enid, Oklahoma. But even if they'd lived down the street from us, we would never have become close friends at home. To put it as simply as possible, they were not our kind of people.

The package tour we'd booked wasn't one of those escorted ventures in which your every minute is accounted for. It included our charter flights over and back, all our hotel accommodations, and our transportation from one city to the next. We "did" six countries in twenty-two days, but what we did in each, and where and with whom, was strictly up to us. We could have kept to ourselves altogether, and have often done so when traveling, but by the time we checked into our hotel in London the first day we'd made arrangements to join the Dattners that night for dinner, and before we knocked off our after-dinner brandies that night it had been tacitly agreed that we would be a foursome throughout the trip—unless, of course, it turned out that we tired of each other.

"They're a pair," Andrew said that first night, unknotting his tie and giving it a shake before hanging it over the doorknob. "That y'all-come-back accent of hers sounds like syrup flowing over corn cakes."

"She's a little flashy, too," I said. "But that sport jacket of his—"

"I know," Andrew said. "Somewhere, even as we speak, a horse is shivering, his blanket having been transformed into a jacket for Harry."

"And yet there's something about them, isn't there?"

"They're nice people," Andrew said. "Not our kind at all, but what does that matter? We're on a trip. We're ripe for a change. . . ."

In Paris, after a night watching a floorshow at what I'm sure was a rather disreputable little nightclub in Les Halles, I lay in bed while Andrew sat up smoking a last cigarette. "I'm glad we met the Dattners," he said. "This trip would be fun anyway, but they add to it. That joint tonight was a treat, and I'm sure we wouldn't have gone if it hadn't been for them. And do you know something? I don't think *they'd* have gone if it hadn't been for *us.*"

"Where would we be without them?" I rolled onto my side. "I know where Sue would be without your helping hand. Up on top of Notre Dame, frozen with fear. Do you suppose that's how the gargoyles got there? Are they nothing but tourists turned to stone?"

"Then you'll never be a gargoyle. You were a long way from petrification whirling around the dance floor tonight."

"Harry's a good dancer. I didn't think he would be, but he's very light on his feet."

"The gun doesn't weigh him down, eh?"

I sat up. "I *thought* he was wearing a gun," I said. "How on earth does he get it past the airport scanners?"

"Undoubtedly by packing it in his luggage and checking it through. He wouldn't need it on the plane—not unless he was planning to divert the flight to Havana."

"I don't think they go to Havana any more. Why would he need it *off* the plane? I suppose tonight he'd feel safer armed. That place was a bit on the rough side."

"He was carrying it at the Tower of London, and in and out of a slew of museums. In fact, I think he carries it all the time except on planes. Most likely he feels naked without it."

"I wonder if he sleeps with it."

"I think he sleeps with her."

"Well, I know *that.*"

"To their mutual pleasure, I shouldn't wonder. Even as you and I."

"Ah," I said.

And, a bit later, he said, "You like them, don't you?"

"Well, of course I do. I don't want to pack them up and take them home to Boston with us, but—"

"You like *him.*"

"Harry? Oh, *I* see what you're getting at."

"Quite."

"And she's attractive, isn't she? You're attracted to her."

"At home I wouldn't look at her twice, but here—"

"Say no more. That's how I feel about him. That's exactly how I feel about him."

"Do you suppose we'll do anything about it?"

"I don't know. Do you suppose they're having this very conversation two floors below?"

"I wouldn't be surprised. If they *are* having this conversation, and if they had the same silent prelude to this conversation, they're probably feeling very good indeed."

"Mmmmm," I said dreamily. "Even as you and I."

I don't know if the Dattners had that conversation that particular evening, but they certainly had it somewhere along the way. The little tensions and energy currents between the four of us began to build until it seemed almost as though the air were crackling with electricity. More often than

not we'd find ourselves pairing off on our walks, Andrew with Sue, Harry
with me. I remember one moment when he took my hand crossing the
street—I remember the instant but not the street, or even the city—and a
little shiver went right through me.

By the time we were in Madrid, with Andrew and Sue trekking through
the Prado while Harry and I ate garlicky shrimp and sipped a sweetish white
wine in a little cafe on the Plaza Mayor, it was clear what was going to
happen. We were almost ready to talk about it.

"I hope they're having a good time," I told Harry. "I just couldn't
manage another museum."

"I'm glad we're out here instead," he said, with a wave at the plaza.
"But I would have gone to the Prado if you went." And he reached out and
covered my hand with his.

"Sue and Andy seem to be getting along pretty good," he said.

Andy! Had anyone else ever called my husband Andy?

"And you and me, we get along all right, don't we?"

"Yes," I said, giving his hand a little squeeze. "Yes, we do."

Andrew and I were up late that night, talking and talking. The next day
we flew to Rome. We were all tired our first night there and ate at the
restaurant in our hotel rather than venture forth. The food was good, but I
wonder if any of us really tasted it?

Andrew insisted that we all drink *grappa* with our coffee. It turned out to
be a rather nasty brandy, clear in color and quite powerful. The men had a
second round of it. Sue and I had enough work finishing our first.

Harry held his glass aloft and proposed a toast. "To good friends," he
said. "To close friendship with good people." And after everyone had taken
a sip he said, "You know, in a couple of days we all go back to the lives we
used to lead. Sue and I go back to Oklahoma, you two go back to Boston,
Mass. Andy, you go back to your investments business and I'll be doin'
what I do. And we got each other's addresses and phone, and we say we'll
keep in touch, and maybe we will. But if we do or we don't, either way one
thing's sure. The minute we get off that plane at J.F.K., that's when the
carriage turns into a pumpkin and the horses go back to bein' mice. You
know what I mean?"

Everyone did.

"Anyway," he said, "what me an' Sue were thinkin', we thought there's
a whole lot of Rome, a mess of good restaurants, and things to see and
places to go. We thought it's silly to have four people all do the same things
and go the same places and miss out on all the rest. We thought, you know,
after breakfast tomorrow, we'd split up and spend the day separate." He
took a breath. "Like Sue and Andy'd team up for the day and, Elaine, you
an' me'd be together."

"The way we did in Madrid," somebody said.

"Except I mean for the whole day," Harry said. A light film of perspiration gleamed on his forehead. I looked at his jacket and tried to decide if he was wearing his gun. I'd seen it on our afternoon in Madrid. His jacket had come open and I'd seen the gun, snug in his shoulder holster. "The whole day and then the evening, too. Dinner—and after."

There was a silence which I don't suppose could have lasted nearly as long as it seemed to. Then Andrew said he thought it was a good idea, and Sue agreed, and so did I.

Later, in our hotel room, Andrew assured me that we could back out. "I don't think they have any more experience with this than we do. You saw how nervous Harry was during his little speech. He'd probably be relieved to a certain degree if we did back out."

"Is that what you want to do?"

He thought for a moment. "For my part," he said, "I'd as soon go through with it."

"So would I. My only concern is if it made some difference between us afterward."

"I don't think it will. This is fantasy, you know. It's not the real world. We're not in Boston *or* Oklahoma. We're in Rome, and you know what they say. When in Rome, do as the Romans do."

"And is this what the Romans do?"

"It's probably what they do when they go to Stockholm," Andrew said.

In the morning, we joined the Dattners for breakfast. Afterward, without anything being said, we paired off as Harry had suggested the night before. He and I walked through a sun-drenched morning to the Spanish Steps, where I bought a bag of crumbs and fed the pigeons. After that—

Oh, what does it matter what came next, what particular tourist things we found to do that day? Suffice it to say that we went interesting places and saw rapturous sights, and everything we did and saw was heightened by anticipation of the evening ahead.

We ate lightly that night, and drank freely but not to excess. The trattoria where we dined wasn't far from our hotel and the night was clear and mild, so we walked back. Harry slipped an arm around my waist. I leaned a little against his shoulder. After we'd walked a way in silence, he said very softly, "Elaine, only if you want to."

"But I do," I heard myself say.

Then he took me in his arms and kissed me.

I ought to recall the night better than I do. We felt love and lust for each other, and sated both appetites. He was gentler than I might have guessed he'd be, and I more abandoned. I could probably remember precisely what happened if I put my mind to it, but I don't think I could make the memory seem real. Because it's as if it happened to someone else. It was vivid at the time, because at the time I truly was the person sharing her bed with Harry. But that person had no existence before or after that European vacation.

There was a moment when I looked up and saw one of Andrew's neckties hanging on the knob of the closet door. It struck me that I should have put the tie away, that it was out of place there. Then I told myself that the tie was where it ought to be, that it was Harry who didn't belong here. And finally I decided that both belonged, my husband's tie and my inappropriate Oklahoma lover. Now both belonged, but in the morning the necktie would remain and Harry would be gone.

As indeed he was. I awakened a little before dawn and was alone in the room. I went back to sleep, and when I next opened my eyes Andrew was in bed beside me. Had they met in the hallway, I wondered? Had they worked out the logistics of this passage in advance? I never asked. I still don't know.

Our last day in Rome, the Dattners went their way and we went ours. Andrew and I got to the Vatican, saw the Colisseum, and wandered here and there, stopping at sidewalk cafes for espresso. We hardly talked about the previous evening, beyond assuring each other that we had enjoyed it, that we were glad it had happened, and that our feelings for one another remained unchanged—deepened, if anything, by virtue of having shared this experience, if it could be said to have been shared.

We joined Harry and Sue for dinner. And in the morning we all rode out to the airport and boarded our flight to New York. I remember looking at the other passengers on the plane, few of whom I'd exchanged more than a couple of sentences with in the course of the past three weeks. There were almost certainly couples among them with whom we had more in common than we had with the Dattners. Had any of them had comparable flings in the course of the trip?

At J.F.K. we all collected our luggage and went through customs and passport control. Then we were off to catch our connecting flight to Boston while Harry and Sue had a four-hour wait for their T.W.A. flight to Tulsa. We said goodbye. The men shook hands while Sue and I embraced. Then Harry and I kissed, and Sue and Andrew kissed. That woman slept with my husband, I thought. And that man—I slept with him. I had the thought that, were I to continue thinking about it, I would start laughing.

Two hours later we were on the ground at Logan, and less than an hour after that we were in our own house.

That weekend Paul and Marilyn Welles came over for dinner and heard a play-by-play account of our three-week vacation—with the exception, of course, of that second-last night in Rome. Paul is a business associate of

Andrew's and Marilyn is a woman not unlike me, and I wondered to myself what would happen if we four traded partners for an evening.

But it wouldn't happen and I certainly didn't want it to happen. I found Paul attractive and I know Andrew had always found Marilyn attractive. But such an incident among us wouldn't be appropriate, as it had somehow been appropriate with the Dattners.

I know Andrew was having much the same thoughts. We didn't discuss it afterward, but one knows. . . .

I thought of all of this just last week. Andrew was in a bank in Skokie, Illinois, along with Paul Welles and two other men. One of the tellers managed to hit the silent alarm and the police arrived as they were on their way out. There was some shooting. Paul Welles was wounded superficially, as was one of the policemen. Another of the policemen was killed.

Andrew is quite certain he didn't hit anybody. He fired his gun a couple of times, but he's sure he didn't kill the police officer.

But when he got home we both kept thinking the same thing. It could have been Harry Dattner.

Not literally, because what would an Oklahoma state trooper be doing in Skokie, Illinois? But it might as easily have been the Skokie cop in Europe with us. And it might have been Andrew who shot him—or been shot *by* him, for that matter.

I don't know that I'm explaining this properly. It's all so incredible. That I should have slept with a policeman while my husband was with a policeman's wife. That we had ever become friendly with them in the first place. I have to remind myself, and keep reminding myself, that it all happened overseas. It happened in Europe, and it happened to four other people. We were not ourselves, and Sue and Harry were not themselves. It happened, you see, in another universe altogether, and so, really, it's as if it never happened at all.

# THE
# MEDITERRANEAN

# PLAYING IT COOL

*By Simon Brett*

THERE WAS only one girl worth looking at in that planeload. I'd been doing the job for two months, since May, and I'd got quicker at spotting them.

She was tall, but then I'm tall, so no problem there. Thin, but round in the right places. Dress: expensive casual. Good jeans, white cotton shirt, artless but pricey. Brown eyes, biscuit-colored hair pulled back into a rubber-band knot, skin which had already seen a bit of sun and just needed Corfu to polish up the color. (Have to watch that. With a lot of the girls—particularly from England—they're so pale you daren't go near them for the first week. Physical approaches get nothing but a little scream and a nasty smell of Nivea on your hands.)

The girl's presence moved me forward more keenly than usual with my little spiel. "Hello, Corforamic Tours, Corforamic Tours. I am your Corforamic representative, Rick Lawton. Could you gather up your baggage, please, and proceed outside the arrivals hall to your transport."

I ignored the puffing English matrons and homed in on the girl's luggage.

It was then that I saw the other one. She looked younger, shorter, dumpier; paler brown hair, paler eyes, a sort of diluted version, as if someone had got the proportions wrong when trying to clone from the dishy one.

They were obviously together, so I had to take one bag for each. They thanked me in American accents. That in itself was unusual. Most of the girls who come on these package tours are spotty typists from Liverpool.

But then their destination was unusual, too. The majority of the Corforamic properties are tiny, twin-bedded apartments in Paleokastritsa and Ipsos. But there's one Rolls-Royce job near Aghios Spiridion—a converted windmill, sleeps eight, swimming pool, private beach, live-in maid, telephone. And that was where they were going. They'd booked for a month.

I read it on their labels. *Miss S. Stratton* (the dishy one). *Miss C. Stratton* (the other one). And underneath each name, the destination—Villa Costas.

By six I'd seen all the ordinary ones installed, answered the questions about whether it was safe to drink the water, given assurances that the plumbing worked, given the names of doctors to those with small children, told them which supermarkets sold Rice Krispies, quoted the minimal statistics for death by scorpion sting, and tried to convince them that the mere fact of their having paid for a fortnight's holiday was not automatically going to rid the island of mosquitoes.

Villa Costas was a long way to the north side of the island. I'd pay a call there the next day.

I drove to Niko's on the assumption that none of my charges would venture as far as his disco on their first evening. You get to value your privacy in this job. I sat under the vine-laden shelter of the bar and had an ouzo.

As I clouded the drink with water and looked out over the glittering sea, I felt low. Seeing a really beautiful woman always has that effect on me. Seems to accentuate the divide between the sort of man who gets that sort of girl, and me. I always seem to end up with the ugly ones.

It wasn't just that. There was money, too, always money. Sure I got paid as the Corforamic rep, but not much. Winter in England loomed, winter doing some other demeaning selling job, earning peanuts. Not the sort of money that could coolly rent the Villa Costas for a month. Again there was the big divide. Rich and poor. And I knew to which side I really belonged. Poor, I was cramped and frustrated. Rich, I could really be myself.

Niko's voice cut into my gloom. "Telephone, Rick."

She identified herself as Samantha Stratton. The dishy one. Her sister had seen a rat in the kitchen at Villa Costas. Could I do something about it?

I said I'd be right out there. Rats may not be dragons, but they can still make you feel knight-errantish. And as any self-respecting knight errant knows, there is no damsel so susceptible as one in distress.

Old Manthos keeps a kind of general store just outside Kassiope. It's an unbelievable mess—slabs of soap mixed up with dried fish, oil lamps, saucepans, tins of powdered milk, brooms, faded postcards, coils of rope, tubes of liniment, deflated beach balls, dusty Turkish Delight, and novelty brandy bottles shaped like Ionic columns. Most of the stock appears to have been there since the days of his long-dead father, whose garlanded photograph earnestly surveys the chaos around him.

But, in spite of the mess, Manthos usually has what you want. May take a bit of time and considerable disturbance of dust, but he'll find it.

So it proved on this occasion. With my limping Greek it took a few minutes for him to understand the problem, but once he did, he knew exactly where to go. A crate of disinfectant was upturned, a bunch of children's fishing nets knocked over, a pile of scouring pads scattered, and the old man triumphantly produced a rusty tin, whose label was stained into illegibility.

"Very good," he said, "very good. Kill rats, kill anything." He drew his hand across his throat evocatively.

I paid him, and as I walked out of the shop he called out, "And if that doesn't work—"

"Yes?"

"Ask the priest. The Papas is sure to have a prayer for getting rid of rats."

It was nearly eight o'clock when I got to Villa Costas, but that's still hot in Corfu in July. Hot enough for Samantha to be on the balcony in a white bikini. The body fulfilled, or possibly exceeded, the promise I had noted at the airport.

"Candy's in bed," she said. "Shock of seeing the rat on top of all that traveling brought on a migraine."

"Ah. Well, let's see if we can put paid to this rat's little exploits," I said, in a businesslike and, to my mind, rather masculine manner.

"Sure."

I filled some little paper dishes with poison and laid them round the kitchen floor. Then I closed the tin and washed my hands. "Shall I leave the poison with you, so you can put down more if you want to?"

She was standing in the kitchen doorway. The glow of the dying sun burned away her bikini. Among other things I saw her head shake. "No, thanks. Dangerous stuff to have around. You take it."

"Okay."

"Like a drink?"

She was nice. Seemed very forthcoming with me, too. But I didn't want to queer anything up by moving too fast.

Still, when she asked where one went for fun on the island, I mentioned Niko's disco. And by the time I left—discreetly, playing it cool—we'd agreed to meet there the next evening.

And as I drove back to my flat in Corfu Town, I was beginning to wonder whether maybe after all I was about to become the sort of man who gets that sort of girl.

When I arrived at nine, there were quite a lot of people at the disco. But no tall beautiful American girl. Come to that, no less tall, less beautiful American girl.

I could wait. Niko signaled me over to where he was sitting, and I ordered an ouzo.

The group drinking at the table was predictable. Niko's two brothers (the one who drove a beer lorry and the one who rented out motor-scooters) were there, along with his cousin the electrician, and Police Inspector Kantalakis, whose relaxed interpretation of government regulations about overcrowding, noise, and hygiene always insured him a generous welcome at the bar.

There was also a new face. Wiry black hair thinning on top, thick black mustache draped over the mouth, healthy growth of chest hair escaping from carefully faded denims. Solid, mid-thirties maybe, ten years older than me. "Rick, this is Brad," said Niko.

He stretched out a hairy hand. "Hi." Another American. "We were just talking about Niko's wife," he said with a grin.

They all laughed, Niko slightly ruefully. Whereas some people have bad backs or business worries to be tenderly asked after, Niko always had a wife problem. It was a running joke, and from the way Brad raised it he seemed to know the group well. "How are things at home, Niko?" Brad continued.

The proprietor of the bar shrugged that round-shouldered gesture that encompasses the whole world of marital misery.

Brad chuckled. "Sure beats me why people get married at all."

Inspector Kantalakis and the others gave man-of-the-world laughs, siding with him and conveniently forgetting their own tenacious little wives. The American turned to me. "You married?"

I shook my head. "Never felt the necessity."

"Too right. There is no necessity."

The married men laughed again, slightly less easily. Brad called their bluff. "Now come on, all you lot got wives. Give me one good reason *why,* one argument in favor of marriage."

Inspector Kantalakis guffawed. "Well, there's the bedroom—"

"You don't have to get married for that," I said.

The Inspector looked at me with distaste. For some reason he never seemed to like me much.

"Come on, just one argument for marriage," insisted Brad.

They looked sheepish. Faced by this transatlantic sophisticate, none of them was going to show himself up by mentioning love, children, or religion. They wanted to appear modern, and were silent.

"You think of any reason, Rick?"

"Money," I said, partly for the laugh I knew the word would get, but also because the idea had been going through my mind for some years. Marriage remains one of the few legal ways that someone without exceptional talents can make a quick and significant change in his material circumstances. I reinforced the point, playing for another laugh. "Yes, I reckon that's the only thing that would get me to the altar. I'm prepared to marry for money."

As the laugh died, Brad looked at me shrewdly. "If that's so, then you ought to set your cap for what's just arriving."

I turned to see the girls from Villa Costas getting out of a rented car. "Those two," Brad continued, "are the daughters of L. K. Stratton of Stratton Oil & Gas. When the old man goes, the older one gets the lot."

I was feeling my usual frustration. The two girls had joined us at the table and had a couple of drinks. Seeing them together again had only reinforced my previous impression. Miss S. (Samantha) Stratton was not only beautiful she was also poised and entertaining. Miss C. (Candice, to give her full name) Stratton was not only drab in appearance she was mouselike and tentative in conversation. I waited for a lull in the chat so that I could ask Samantha to dance. If she had needed any recommendation other than that body, Brad's words had just supplied it.

But the minute I was about to suggest a dance, damn me if Brad, who seemed to know the girls quite well, didn't say, "C'mon, Sam, let's bop," and lead her off into the flashing interior of the disco. The way they started dancing suggested that they knew each other very well.

Within minutes Niko and his relations and Inspector Kantalakis had melted away, leaving me in a role I had suffered too often in double dates from schooltime onward—stuck with the ugly one.

And what made it worse was that I gathered in this case she was also the poor one.

I stole a look across at her. The sun had already started its work on her pale flesh. The nose glowed; in a couple of days the skin would be coming off like old wallpaper.

She caught my eye and gave a gauche little smile, then looked wistfully to the thundering interior.

No, no, I wasn't going to be caught that way. That terrible old feeling that you *ought* to ask a girl to dance. Hell, I was twenty-six, not some creepy little adolescent.

Still, I had to say something, or just leave. "Your big sister seems to be enjoying herself," I commented sourly.

"Half-sister, actually. And only big in the sense that she's taller than I am."

"You mean you're older than she is?"

"Two years and four months older."

"Would you like to dance?"

Candice was very shy and I treated her with exemplary tact. Met her every evening for most of the next week. Picked her up at the Villa Costas and took her down to Niko's. She was too shy to go there on her own, and Sam and Brad (who turned out to be engaged, for God's sake!) seemed anxious to be off on their own most of the time.

So I courted Candice like a dutiful boy-next-door. Looked at her soulfully, danced close, kissed her sedately goodbye. I was the kind of young man every mother would like her daughter to meet—serious, respectful, with intentions honorable even to the point of matrimony.

And once I'd written off any chance with Samantha, Candice really didn't seem too bad. Not unattractive at all. Any personal lustre she lacked I could readily supply by thinking of her father's millions.

The fourth night, as I kissed her goodbye with a kind of boyish earnestness, I explained that a new planeload of tourists was arriving the next day and I wouldn't have time to pick her up. She looked disappointed, which showed I was getting somewhere. Rather than not see me, she agreed to go under her own steam to Niko's and meet me there at nine. That was a big step for her. I promised I wouldn't be late.

By the middle of the following afternoon it was clear I was going to be. The flight from London was delayed by an hour and a half.

Never mind. Still the dutiful, solicitous boy-next-door, I rang the Villa Costas. Brad answered. Sorry, would he mind telling Candice I couldn't get to Niko's till half-past ten? Either I'd see her there or pick her up usual time the next evening.

Sure, Brad would see she got the message.

When I saw her face at 10:20 that night at Niko's, it was clear she hadn't got the message. She was sitting at the same table as, but somehow not with, Niko's relations and Inspector Kantalakis. And she looked furious.

It didn't surprise me. Greek men don't really approve of women, even tourists, going to bars alone, and that lot wouldn't have made any secret of their feelings. I moved forward with smiling apologies on my lips.

But I didn't get a chance to make them. Candice rose to her feet. "I only stayed," she spat out, "to tell you that I think you're contemptible, and that we will not meet again."

"Look, I left a message with Brad. I said I'd be late and—"

"It is not just your lateness I'm talking about. Goodbye." And she swept off to the rented car.

I sat down, shaken. Inspector Kantalakis was looking at me with a rather unpleasant smile. "What the hell did you say to her?" I asked.

He shrugged. "I may have mentioned your views on marriage."

"What? Oh, damn—you mean about marrying for money?"

"I may have mentioned that, yes."

"But when I said it, it was only a joke."

"You sounded pretty serious to me," said the Inspector, confirming my impression that he didn't like me one bit.

But that evening wasn't over. I started hitting the local paint-stripper brandy. I was fit to be tied. The Inspector and the others sauntered off, as if satisfied by their evening's destruction. I gazed bitterly across the black sea to the few mysterious lights of Albania.

"Rick." I don't know how long a time had passed before the sound broke into my gloom. I looked up.

It was Samantha. And she was crying.

"What's the matter?"

"It's that swine, Brad."

"Oh, I've got a bone to pick with him, too. What's he done?"

"Oh, he's just—it's always the same. He treats me badly and he goes off with some other girl and always reckons he can just pick up again as if nothing has happened and—well, this is the last time, the last time." She was crying now.

"Can I get you a drink or—?"

"No, I just want to go back to the villa. I was looking for Candy. I wanted a lift. Brad's driven off in his car and—"

"Candy's gone, I'm afraid."

"Oh."

"I'll give you a lift."

When we were in the car park, she was seized by another burst of crying and turned toward me. Instinctively my arms were round her slender, soft body and I held her tight as the spasms subsided.

"Doesn't take you long," said a voice in Greek.

I saw Inspector Kantalakis' sardonic face in the gloom.

"Mind your own business," I said. At least, that would be a paraphrase. The expression on the Inspector's face showed that I was making great strides with my colloquial Greek.

"She's upset," I continued virtuously. "I'm just comforting her, as a friend."

But I wasn't, I wasn't.

Amazing how quickly things can change. Actually, since by "things" I mean women, I suppose it's not so amazing.

I got to know a lot more about Samantha on that drive back, and I discovered that appearances can be distinctly deceptive. For a start, the engagement with Brad was not, as it had appeared, the marriage of true minds, but a kind of professional blackmail exerted on an unwilling girl by a selfish and violent man. She had been trying to break it off for years.

Also—and this was the bit I enjoyed hearing—the reason for the quarrel of that night had been her admitting she fancied someone else. Me.

"But if you're so keen to get rid of him, why did you mind his going off with another girl?"

"Only because I know he'll be back. He never stays away for long. And then he thinks he can just pick up where he left off."

"Hmm. But he couldn't do that if he found you'd got someone else."

"That's true."

The car stopped outside Villa Costas. We were suddenly in each other's arms. Her body spoke its clear message to mine, while our tongues mumbled meaningless nothings. Yes, I was the only man who she'd ever felt like that about.

But no, I'd better not come into the villa now. Because of Candy. And she didn't really fancy the beach. Tomorrow. Tomorrow afternoon at three. She'd see that Candy was out. And then. . . .

I arrived sharp at three the following afternoon in a state of—well, let's say in a predictable state of excitement.

But things weren't initially as private as I had hoped. Theodosia, the live-in maid, was sitting on the veranda under the shade of an olive tree. (Corfiots, unlike the tourists, regard sun as a necessary evil, and avoid it when possible.) She grinned at me in a way that I found presumptuous.

And then as if that wasn't enough, Candice Stratton appeared from the villa and stood for a moment blinded by the sun. She wore a bikini in multi-colored stripes that accentuated her dumpiness; she carried a box of Turkish Delight that would no doubt, in time, accentuate it further. The other hand held a striped towel and a thriller.

When her eyes were accommodated to the brightness, they saw me, and an expression of loathing took over her face. "You creep! I said I never wanted to see you again. So don't think you can come crawling back."

Any intentions I might have had to be nice to her vanished. "I didn't come to see *you*," I said, and walked past her into the villa. I felt Theodosia's inquisitive eyes follow me.

Samantha was on the balcony in the white bikini. Momentarily I played the aggrieved lover. "I thought you were going to see Candy was out."

"Sorry, we got delayed. Brad came round."

I hadn't reckoned on that.

"Don't worry, Rick. I sent him off with a flea in his ear." She looked at me levelly. "I haven't changed my mind."

I relaxed. "How'd he take it?"

"Usual arrogance. Said he'd be back. Even tried his old trick of making up to Candy to make me jealous. Brought her a big box of Turkish Delight and all that. He ought to know by now it doesn't work."

"On you or on her?"

"On me, you fool." She rose and put an arm round my waist. Together we watched Candy across the little private bay, settling on her towel for further ritual peeling.

I looked into Samantha's brown eyes, squinting against the glare of the sun. I was aware of the tracery of fine lines around them as her body touched mine.

"Candy be out there for some time?" I murmured.

"You betcha. She'll eat her way right through that box of Turkish Delight. Always eats when she's unhappy."

My hand glided up the curve of her back. "Shall we go inside?"

There was a double bed (a rarity in the world of Corforamic, another luxury feature of the Villa Costas). I reached more purposefully for Samantha.

"Oh, damn," she said.

"What?"

"Candy didn't take her drink."

"So?"

"There's a large Coca-Cola in the fridge. She was going to take it with her."

"So?" I shrugged.

"So . . . if she hasn't got it she'll be back here as soon as she's thirsty. And the Turkish Delight's going to make her very thirsty."

"Ah."

"You take it over to her."

"But she doesn't want to see me."

"Then we won't be disturbed." There was a kind of logic in that. "Go on, Rick. And while you're away I'll get more comfortable."

When I got back, Samantha was waiting with a bottle of Remy Martin and two glasses.

Candy had been predictably annoyed to see me, but had accepted the bottle of Coke wordlessly. And Theodosia's beady little eyes had followed me all the way across the beach and back.

But I soon forgot both of them. Samantha's charms would have cleaned out the memory bank of a computer.

Time telescoped and distorted. . . . Darkness came and we didn't notice it. I didn't hear whether Candice came in or not, and eventually sleep claimed us. . . .

It was therefore an unpleasant shock to be awakened by the sight of Inspector Kantalakis at the foot of the bed, and by the sound of his voice saying, in English, "Still furthering your marriage plans, Mr. Lawton?"

We both sat up. Samantha was still half asleep. "Marriage?" she echoed. "You did mean it, Rick, what you said last night, about wanting to marry me?"

"Uh?" I was still half asleep myself.

"I have bad news," said Inspector Kantalakis.

We looked at him blearily.

"Miss Stratton, your sister was found this morning on the beach. Dead."

"What?"

"She appears to have been poisoned."

I don't know if you've ever been involved in a murder inquiry in Greece, but let me tell you, it is something to be avoided. Questions, questions, questions, endlessly repeated in a hot concrete police cell. And expressions on the cops' faces that show they don't subscribe to the old British tradition of people being innocent until proved guilty.

I was with them for about twenty-four hours, I suppose, and the first thing I did when I got out was to go up to the Villa Costas. Samantha looked shaken. She'd had quite a grilling too, though some connection of her father's had pulled strings through the American Embassy in Athens and it hadn't taken as long as mine.

"And now the swine has disappeared," were her first words.

"Who?" My mind wasn't working very well.

"Brad."

"What do you mean?"

"Brad must have poisoned her."

"Why?" I couldn't catch up with all this.

"Because of the money."

"Uh?"

"He wanted me *and* Daddy's money. With Candy dead, I inherit."

"Good lord, that never occurred to me."

"Well, it's true."

"But how did he do it?"

"Obvious. The Turkish Delight."

"Are you sure?"

"The Inspector says he hasn't received the forensic analysis yet—everything takes that much longer on an island—but I'd put money on the results."

"Brad'll never get away with it."

"Oh, he'll have managed some sort of alibi. He's devious. He *will* get away with it, unless we can find some proof of his guilt."

"But it will all have been for nothing if he doesn't get you."

"Yes." She sounded listless.

"And he hasn't got you, has he?"

She pulled herself together and looked at me with a little smile. "No, he hasn't. You have."

"So that's all right."

She nodded, but still seemed troubled. "The only thing that worries me—"

"Yes?"

"—is that he still has power over me when I see him."

"Then we must make sure you don't see him. If he's disappeared, that doesn't sound too difficult. Anyway, as soon as the analysis of the Turkish Delight comes through, the police'll be after him."

"But suppose they're not. Suppose he's arranged some kind of alibi—"

"Don't worry." Suddenly I was full of crusading spirit. "If the police won't do it, I'll prove myself that he poisoned Candy."

"Oh, thank you, Rick. Thank God I've got you."

I tried all the contacts I had on the island, but none of them had seen Brad. I didn't give up, though. I wanted to do it for Samantha, to prove Brad's crime and see to it that he was put behind bars where he belonged.

It was the next day she told me she was going to have to fly back to the States. Her father, L. K. Stratton, had had a mild stroke when he heard the news of his older daughter's death, and the younger one had to fly back to be by his side. Inspector Kantalakis had cleared her from his inquiries, and she was free to go. Apparently, he was near an arrest—just needed the results of the forensic analysis to clinch it.

Though I was depressed about her going, the news on the investigation front was promising. The police were obviously close to nailing Brad, merely needing proof of the poison in the Turkish Delight.

All they had to do then was find him.

Unless I could find him first.

I promised to see Samantha off at the airport.

It was less than two weeks since I'd first seen her when I kissed her goodbye. A lot had happened in less than two weeks. When I first saw that splendid body I hadn't dared hope that it would ever be pressed to mine with such trust and hope.

"I'll come back as soon as I can, Rick. Really."

"I know. Let's hope you're back to give evidence at a murder trial."

"I will be. Don't worry."

Her baggage was checked through to Kennedy via London. There didn't seem much more to say. Our togetherness didn't need words.

Not many, anyway. "And then, Sam, we'll get married, huh?"

She nodded gently and gave me another kiss. Then she turned and went off toward the Departure Lounge. Tall, beautiful—and mine.

Not only mine, it occurred to me, but also very rich. Suddenly I had got it all, suddenly I was the sort of man who got that sort of girl.

I watched her into the Departure Lounge. She didn't turn round. We didn't need that sort of clinging farewell.

Suddenly I got a shock. A dark, denim-clad figure had appeared beside her in the Lounge. Brad.

I couldn't go through the ticket control to save her. I had to find the police. And fast.

I was in luck. As I rushed into the dazzle of sunlight, I saw Inspector Kantalakis leaning against my car.

"The man who murdered Candy—I know who it is," I panted.

"So do I," said the Inspector.

"He intended to marry Samantha, but he wanted the money too, so he poisoned Candy."

"Exactly."

"Well, why don't you arrest him?"

"I've been waiting for a forensic report for final proof. Now I have it. Now there will be an arrest."

"Good. He's in the airport building. The plane leaves in half an hour."

"Yes." The Inspector made no move.

Fine, he must have the place staked out. We could relax; there was plenty of time. I grinned. "So the poison *was* in the Turkish Delight."

He shook his head. "No."

"No?"

"It is really a very straightforward case. Our murderer, who made no secret of his intention to marry for money, tried first with the older sister, the heiress. Unfortunately they quarreled, so he took up with the younger one. But she would only inherit if her older sister died. So. . . ." He shrugged.

"I didn't realize Brad had ever made a play for Candy."

"He hadn't. Nor did he kill her. After he saw the girls in the Villa Costas, he spent the rest of the day of the murder with me."

"Then who are we talking about?" I asked blankly.

Inspector Kantalakis drew one hand from behind his back. It held a rusty tin, a tin which had been bought from Manthos' shop. "I found this in the trunk of your car."

"Yes, I bought it to deal with the rats at the Villa Costas."

"Really? It was this poison that killed Candice Stratton. It was put in the bottle of Coca-Cola."

"The Coca-Cola!"

"Yes. The Coca-Cola you gave to the murder victim. Do you deny you gave it to her? The maid Theodosia saw you."

"No, I gave it all right. I see! Brad must have dosed it, knowing Candy would drink it sooner or later. He must have fixed it when he came round that morning with the Turkish Delight. Samantha may have seen him go to the fridge. Ask her."

"I have asked her, Mr. Lawton. According to Miss Samantha Stratton, there never was any Coca-Cola in the Villa Costas. Nor, incidentally, were there any rats," Inspector Kantalakis added portentously.

Then he arrested me.

And I realized that, after all, I wasn't the sort of man who got that sort of girl.

# ORACLE OF THE DEAD

*By Peter Lovesey*

THE ORACLE of the Dead is not to be missed," said the tour representative. "It doesn't sound like a bunch of laughs, I know, but it makes a fascinating sea trip. I see the honeymooners shaking their heads. Other things on your mind, eh? Personally, if I'd come all this way I'd want to visit at least one historical site, and that's the one I recommend."

He started taking names.

Outside, the warmth and color of Corfu waited to be experienced. Helen felt David's hand tighten around hers. "Let's slip away," he murmured.

She was only too happy to go. She'd put up with as many easy laughs about newlyweds as she could take, particularly after David and she had made no secret that this was their second time around. They were both past thirty-five.

"Everything he told us is in the brochures, anyway," said David as they jigged into Corfu Town in a victoria drawn by a horse wearing a straw hat.

The scents of jasmine and orange blossom were on the air. Helen leaned back and felt the sun on her face and sighed happily.

"Incredible!" said David.

Helen was staring at the sky. "What?"

"A cricket pitch."

"Cricket?" She sat forward and saw that he was right. "Give me strength! Not here!"

"Is true," Georgios, their driver, turned and informed them. "Crickets this afternoon. Esplanade Square. Famous crickets field more than hundred years, since British rule Corfu."

"That's this afternoon taken care of," said David.

"You'd better be joking," said Helen, without much confidence that he was. Cricket took up every Saturday and Sunday in summer. If he wasn't playing for the local team, he was off to a one-day match at the Oval. She'd been hoping that marriage would wean him away from the silly game.

"Got to give it a try," he said, trying to sound reasonable. "See what the standard's like out here."

"It's our honeymoon."

"I know, love. If it's poor stuff, we'll find something better to do."

Stung by his remark, Helen turned and found herself looking at the bronze statue of a former high commissioner who had probably started it all.

"You play crickets, sir?" she heard Georgios ask David. "Maybe you get a game. You like me to find out?"

So Helen found herself that afternoon seated behind the boundary line, bored, hurt, and humiliated. It made no difference that David waved to her between overs. It made no difference that other women had been persuaded to watch. This was the first day of her honeymoon.

She wasn't certain how long she endured it. She took no interest in the cricket even when there was clapping. She sat with her eyes closed.

"You don't like see your husband bat?"

She looked up into the bearded face of Georgios.

"You like to do something else?"

She shook her head.

"Come on," he coaxed her. "I take you nice ride."

She was about to say no, imagining David looking across the field and seeing the empty chair, when the idea suddenly had some attraction. He'd just assumed she would dutifully sit watching all afternoon as she did at home. But she hadn't promised to remain there—a small shock to his complacency might not come amiss.

She got up. . . .

Georgios drove her up one of the main streets giving glimpses of flag-stoned lanes, tall houses linked by bridges, and ornate balconies festooned with washing. Presently she saw the blue-green strip of the sea again.

"This the harbor," explained Georgios. "Now you meet my cousin Spyros."

"I don't want to meet anybody."

"Spyros has beautiful speedboat."

She had evidently been brought here for a sea trip. To protest was futile. Cousin Spyros, dark-skinned and athletic in build, wearing black jeans and white T-shirt, was waiting on the quay beside a sleek white boat.

"I must get back to the cricket," Helen said.

"Plenty time," said Georgios. "Crickets go on many hours."

"I don't have enough money with me."

"No need moneys," he said in a shocked tone.

She'd heard of the tradition of hospitality in Corfu. You could give grave offense if you tried to pay for something that was freely given.

Spyros apparently spoke no English. He helped her into the boat and started the engine. Georgios shouted that he would wait for her and then the boat careered toward the open sea. Helen's long black hair lifted from her back. The boat bucked and bounced at incredible speed. She would have adored sharing the experience with David.

They headed toward the purple land-mass of mainland Greece and saw it turn steadily green and brown as they approached. For a few minutes they followed the shoreline, then Spyros steered into a river estuary and cut the engine. They glided to a landing-stage under a willow.

Spyros gestured to her to climb out. Helen shook her head. He was insistent. He said something angry in Greek and flapped his hands at her. She obeyed, realizing that she relied on his good will to get back to Corfu.

Some people were walking up a barren, rocky hill toward what looked like a church. She glanced back at Spyros. He nodded and pointed, so she started the climb. At the top was a man selling admission tickets, but the church wasn't the attraction. A set of steps led down into a massive pillared structure built into a natural cave.

Ahead of Helen a voice said in English, "So this is where Odysseus came to visit the underworld, the kingdom of Hades. Brave men came here to consult the oracle."

The Oracle of the Dead. Helen shivered. She hadn't wanted to visit this place. A hand pressed against her back, pushing her forward, into a corridor that became a labyrinth.

The voice said something about rituals and sacrifices. Helen found herself being ushered through an arched entrance into a dimly lit vault. Chill air prickled her flesh. "So we come to the inner chamber, once guarded by the priests," the voice announced with an eerie echo. "Here, if you got so far, you might put a question to the oracle, and you might see the shades of the dead rise up. But you were sworn to keep secret whatever you saw and heard. The punishment for breaking this oath was death. Some say the power of the oracle remains. You are welcome to try if you wish."

All I wish, thought Helen, is to get out of this dreadful place. Immediately a horrid image flashed into her mind of David wrapped in a shroud and lying in a coffin, deathly white except for the mark of a bruise on his forehead. With a sob she turned and pushed her way frantically toward the exit.

From the jetty, Spyros grinned and waved. Helen ran down the steep slope. "Take me away. Something dreadful has happened."

Although he didn't understand, he appreciated that she was in a state of shock. He produced a blanket for her, then he cast off and set the speedboat racing toward Corfu. All the way, Helen couldn't shift that terrible image from her brain.

Georgios met them at the harbor, grim-faced. Something was said in Greek. He reached out to help Helen ashore. As she settled into the victoria, she started to slip the blanket off her shoulders. "No, no," said Georgios. "You keep."

"What's happened?" Helen asked. "Take me to the cricket field!"

"Crickets is finished today," said Georgios tersely as he whipped up the horse. They drove in another direction, skirting the hill dominated by the fortress that overlooks the town. Some way up a main road, they wheeled sharp right into the Corfu Hospital grounds.

"No," moaned Helen. "No, please, no."

Georgios stopped at the casualty department and they went inside together. They were met by a sister who spoke in a subdued voice to Georgios, their eyes on Helen. She felt the blood draining from her head. She swayed and pitched forward. Someone must have caught her, because she wasn't conscious of hitting the floor.

She came round by degrees, sensing first that she was lying in bed. Her eyes struggled to focus. She could see venetian blinds. People were nearby, speaking English—if only she could catch more than a few words at a time.

"Full force of the bat—sheer bad luck."

She found her voice and said, "He's dead, isn't he?"

Someone said, "She's coming round."

"David," she said. "My husband. He was hit in the face. I know it."

"No, dear."

To her amazement, David spoke. "You're a bit muddled, darling, and no wonder. You were sitting with your eyes closed and someone made a big hit. The ball struck you on the forehead. You were brought straight here from the cricket field. You've got a nasty bruise and some concussion, but they promise me you'll be all right."

She could focus better now. It was certainly David, and he wasn't marked.

She was profoundly relieved to see him, even if she couldn't quite believe it. She squeezed his hand.

He said, "You must have imagined things while you were concussed."

"It was very real. I was taken there in a speedboat."

"Where?" David asked. "Tell me about it."

She hesitated. "No. I'm not at liberty to say. But one thing I will tell you: you've played your last game of cricket."

# A Greek Game

*By Walter Satterthwait*

Today, as he climbed up the steep sun-splashed dirt road to the house hidden in the grove of fig trees, the wind was so strong that he could almost lean against it, like a wall. Grey clumps of thyme shuddered in the fields; ripples of silver raced through the green of the gnarled wild olive on the ridge. With his canvas duffel bag slung over his left shoulder, his speargun in his right hand, he pressed himself against the swell of air, thrust himself through it, digging his sandals, muscles clenching, into the dusty white gravel skittering beneath.

Today's spearfishing had hardly been worth this effort. Or any other effort, for that matter.

He was, he realized, still annoyed. For the first time in two weeks he had been offered a shot at a fish, and he had blown it. He had flippered out to the big rock that stood alone seventy yards from the shingle beach, sucked a deep breath in through the snorkle, and dived, planning to circle its broad base at bottom level, forty feet from the surface.

He was running out of air, ribs beginning to clutch at his lungs, when, skimming above the sand, he rounded a spur of rock and saw the fish. A plump mullet, suspended a foot above the bottom, nuzzling and poking at the dull grey weeds that furred the rock. Excited and yet completely sure of himself—so sure that he tendered the usual silent apology—he raised the speargun and pulled the trigger. The gun bucked against his hand; ahead, a metallic muscular flurry, a billow of smoky sea-dust. And then nothing: only the irrevocable spear lying on the sand. Mocking.

Now, trudging up the hill, he smiled. Not the fish's fault, after all. His alone: overeager, he had fired too soon. And so now, my friend, he told himself, you pay the price. No fried fresh mullet for lunch today.

He looked up at the massive shoulder of white rock, jagged, speckled with thyme and sage, that rose behind the fig trees, soaring a hundred feet toward the bright blue cloudless sky. Perched halfway up it he saw (how the *hell* did they do it?) two goats, a beige and a black, tiny at this distance, and indistinct.

And then he saw, below them, parked alongside his Land Rover just this side of the fig trees, the police car.

Any car would have surprised him. His infrequent guests never arrived unannounced; and the road had been graded, intentionally, in such a way that only a four-wheel-drive vehicle was likely to make it to the top. But a police car?

He glanced quickly around. Police cars invariably made him uneasy. No one was in sight.

The car, he learned when he reached it, was empty. The gate to the fence was open, its padlock hanging on one of the wooden struts of the frame. When he left, the gate had been shut, the padlock locked on the hasp. He entered, closed the gate, walked along the flagstones to the front of the white-washed house. No one beneath the portico. He circled round to the back.

A man, immensely fat, wearing a policeman's uniform, was sitting in one of the chairs under the almond tree on the patio. It was a cheap wooden director's chair, and it looked very frail now as it supported the man's bulk: at least two hundred and fifty pounds of it, probably closer to three.

The man's head was tipped forward, the brim of his cap covering his eyes. His thick arms were folded together above the broad swell of belly. Asleep?

No. Abruptly the man raised his head and, beneath dark black sunglasses, grinned with what was, apparently, huge delight. "Ah," he said, and in Greek: *"O kýrios Fallon, then eísteh?"* Mr. Fallon, are you not?

Fallon nodded. Once; warily. In polite Greek he said, "Yes. How may I help you?"

The man uncrossed his arms and pushed himself from the chair. It squealed, protesting. Grinning, he stepped around the coffee table and offered his hand.

Fallon shifted the speargun, took the hand.

"I am Nikos Mikalis," the fat man announced cheerfully, "the new chief of police for the town. Forgive me for intruding, but I presumed upon your hospitality and waited for you here. Your gate was open."

Fallon smiled pleasantly. "I must have forgotten to lock it." He knew he hadn't. A chief of police who picks locks and then brazenly lies about it: what have we here? "But you are, of course, welcome. I didn't know that Chief Daskalos was no longer with us."

The fat man frowned sadly. "Oh yes, it was very sudden. Four days ago. A family tragedy. His aunt, I believe. Or his cousin." He moved his hand in small vague circles in the air. "Who can say? We have so many relatives here in Greece."

"Welcome to the island, then," said Fallon. "And, as I said, to my house. And is your visit today professional, or social?"

Mikalis grinned again. "Ah wonderful! You Americans. So direct, so forthright. It is a quality I very much admire."

Fallon nodded, waiting, wishing he could see the man's eyes behind the dark glasses.

"Well," said Mikalis, "to match your admirable directness with my own, it has occurred to me that it is my obligation, now that I am here, to make the acquaintance of the residents of the town."

Fallon, who noted that the man had not, in fact, answered his question, said, "Very conscientious of you."

"Yes," agreed Mikalis happily, "I believe it is."

"And I'm very flattered that you chose to make mine so soon after you arrived."

"Oh, but Mr. Fallon, you are one of the earliest foreign residents of the island. You are *famous,* of course."

Fallon smiled. "I doubt that. Look, would you mind if I put these things away? It won't take long. And could I get you something? An ouzo? A coffee? Both?"

"Splendid!" said Mikalis. Two enthusiastic bushy eyebrows jumped up from behind the sunglasses. "Both, yes, absolutely."

Fallon nodded. Then, as he turned to leave, Mikalis said, "Are you a lucky man, Mr. Fallon?"

Fallon turned back. The very blandness of the question had itself been suggestive. "Pardon me?"

"With the fish," said Mikalis, grinning again, ingenuous, as he pointed at the speargun. "Did you have good luck today?"

"No," Fallon said. "Not today."

"Ah well, it doesn't matter." He waved a hand. "They slip away from time to time, but sooner or later we nab them, eh?" He grinned.

Fallon looked at him for a moment, and then said, "If we're lucky." He smiled.

*    *    *

As he busied himself in the kitchen, Fallon wondered what it was the fat man wanted. A bribe? But Fallon's papers were in order, his record on the island spotless.

So why the games? The picking of the padlock, those generalissimo sunglasses, that deliberately ambiguous remark about nabbing fish? Fallon, who had a certain unhappy familiarity with police procedure, and knew that it was, in some respects, similar throughout the world, had the uncomfortable feeling that he was being Mutt-and-Jeffed. With the fat man playing both roles, trying to get him off balance and keep him there.

Well. We shall see.

Onto a large silver tray Fallon loaded everything—the ouzo bottle and two empty glasses, the two tiny cups of Greek coffee, two glasses of water, two forks, some paper napkins, a plate holding sardines, black olives, slices of tomato and cheese—then carried the tray out to the patio.

Chief Mikalis, sitting once again, raised both hands in a gesture of surprised pleasure. "And *mezedes* as well! *Wonderful!*" He leaned slightly forward, confiding: "But I really shouldn't eat anything, you know. I've already had lunch." He patted his round stomach. "Someone told me, just yesterday, that I begin to resemble Orson Welles in the movie *A Touch of Evil.*"

In English, Fallon said, "You arrested him, of course." He placed the tray on the table, sat down opposite Mikalis.

Mikalis was looking at him, puzzled. "I'm sorry. I speak no English."

Fallon thought that unlikely, but repeated himself in Greek.

"No, no," said Mikalis. "It was my wife."

Fallon smiled. He opened the bottle of ouzo, poured some into each empty glass, handed one to Mikalis, took one himself. He raised his glass and Mikalis clinked his own against it. *"Styn yeia mas,"* Mikalis said. To our health.

*"Yeia mas,"* said Fallon.

Mikalis downed his ouzo in one gulp, gave a blissful sigh, and sat back. The chair, once again, squealed beneath him; he ignored it. He looked around him. *"Beautiful* grounds," he said expansively. "And such a house! I understand you built it yourself."

Fallon refilled Mikalis's glass. "With quite a lot of help."

Mikalis took a fork, stabbed at a sardine, and popped it between his teeth. He chewed, swallowed.

"You did a *splendid* job." He lifted the ouzo, tossed it off, sighed again. "Truly quite splendid. But tell me, isn't it true that foreigners are not permitted to own land here in Greece?"

"Of course," said Fallon, and sipped at his ouzo. "I'm only leasing."

"Ah yes," said Mikalis. "Yes, I believe I heard something of this. You lease the land from Dimitri Kostakis, who is also your partner in the night-club, eh?" With his fork, he impaled a slice of tomato.

Fallon nodded. "You're well informed."

Chewing the tomato, Mikalis shrugged. "Part of the job, merely. Nothing." He leaned forward, aiming the prongs of the fork thoughtfully at Fallon. "Help me, however, to become more well informed. There is a story that one day, out on your boat, you saved the life of this Dimitri Kostakis. Is this true?"

"An exaggeration," Fallon told him, pouring more ouzo into Mikalis's glass.

"Oh no," said Mikalis, frowning. "Surely not. A sudden storm, was it not? Very violent. And Kostakis's caïque had capsized, and the poor man couldn't swim. But you came along and plucked him, yes, *plucked* him—" he speared a sardine and held it up, grinning merrily, "—from a fierce and hungry sea."

"I happened to be nearby," Fallon said. "Luck."

Mikalis ate the sardine, nodding, smiling. He swallowed. "Luck, yes. Very good luck. Excellent luck." He frowned. "As a matter of fact, the luck of Kostakis has been excellent since that day, eh? Soon after this lucky accident at sea he begins to buy land—this piece of property first, and then the piece by the beach, where the two of you built the nightclub." The dark sunglasses peered at Fallon. "Curious, is it not? Where do you suppose a poor fisherman like this could find so much money?"

"The fishing was good that year."

Mikalis smiled. "Without a boat?"

"I sold him mine. Later, when he resold it, he made a profit."

Mikalis smacked his forehead. "This foolish memory of mine, it betrays me every time. Yes, I had forgotten. He made a *splendid* profit, if I've been properly informed. He sold it to that drunken Englishman, did he not? Another friend of yours, as it happens, eh?"

"I know him."

"Of course, yes, now I recall." He lifted his ouzo, swallowed it all. Sighing, he put his elbows on the table and leaned toward Fallon. "Tell me, Mr. Fallon, merely to satisfy my curiosity, how much are you paying for the lease on this property?"

Fallon was certain the man already knew; the information was on public record. "Thirty drachmas a year." He refilled the fat man's glass once again.

Mikalis nodded. "And how much is that, approximately, in your currency?"

"Approximately twenty-five cents."

Mikalis nodded. "Quite a bargain, it would seem."

"You underestimate Dimitri's cunning," said Fallon. "The lease is for ninety years, and he knows I'll be dead before then."

Mikalis looked at him for a moment, then sat back and grinned. "And so here you are, Mr. Fallon, living on a picturesque Greek island, running a popular and lucrative nightclub. What a life you lead. I envy you. Like Humphrey Bogart, eh, in the movie *Casablanca?*"

"Exactly," Fallon smiled. "Exactly like Humphrey Bogart."

Mikalis smiled, speared a piece of cheese. "Tell me," he said, "are you familiar with Kostakis's sister?"

"Anna? Yes, of course." Anna? Where was all this leading?

Mikalis chewed on the cheese, swallowed it. "And with her husband? The Turk?"

"Ali once worked for us, at the bar."

"Once?" Spearing another sardine. "No longer?"

"We had a disagreement." The boy had broken one of Fallon's, and Dimitri's, cardinal rules, had been selling drugs to tourists. Hashish, in small amounts only, and discreetly. But to the Greek government, there was no such thing as a small amount of hashish; the prison sentences handed down for drug possession were always long ones.

What had Ali done now?

Mikalis swallowed the sardine. "He was found this morning. Stabbed to death. We discovered, in his pocket, a piece of paper with your telephone number on it."

Far off, up the mountainside, the faint tinkle of a goat bell; nearby, the intoxicated humming of a bee. The wind had died when Fallon came over the ridge, rounded a huge upthrust fist of rock, and padded down a narrow path between yellow thistles. The path ran for a while now along the rim of a ravine choked with ragged boulders and thickets of oleander, the flowers small explosions of pink against the polished green of the leaves. Across the gully, a magpie shrieked and launched itself from a wild olive tree, its white wingtips flickering like flames as it wheeled and banked.

Not Mutt-and-Jeffed, Fallon thought. *Sandbagged.*

For a moment, after Mikalis had told him about Ali, Fallon had very nearly let his anger overwhelm him. He wanted it, perhaps needed it: a cleansing cathartic rage, at Ali's death, at the fat man's stupid games. He realized, immediately, that it would be a mistake.

He took a sip of ouzo, set down his glass, and said, "I'm surprised you didn't bring someone along with you, to take down my confession."

After swallowing a mouthful of cheese, Mikalis smiled. "Why? Did you kill him, Mr. Fallon?"

Fallon kept his voice steady and even. "No."

"Did you see him last night, or speak to him?"

"No."

"When was the last time you did see him?"

"Two weeks ago, maybe three. We passed on the street. We said hello."

"The two of you got along?"

"Well enough."

"He harbored no resentment toward you for this . . . disagreement at the nightclub?"

"No." Fallon remembered Ali's face when he had told him. No resentment there, only puzzlement and hurt. Fallon had explained that the drugs endangered not only Ali himself, but his wife, his brother-in-law, the business. And Ali had nodded sadly, eyes averted, and said in his broken English, "Yes, boss, understand. Sorry, boss."

"And he did not telephone you last night?" Mikalis asked.

"I told you. No."

"Where were you, Mr. Fallon, between three and six o'clock this morning?"

"Here. Asleep. The bar closes at two. I got home a little before three."

"Can anyone corroborate this?"

"Would you like a note from my mother?"

"Mr. Fallon—"

"He was killed sometime between three and six?"

Mikalis frowned, as though it were not his role to answer questions. Then, at last, he shrugged. "There is no proper pathologist on the island. The doctor who examined him is guessing, merely, but I suspect he is correct. All the bars, like yours, close at two o'clock. By six o'clock, there are people up and about. His body was lying not far from main street. If he had been killed before three, or after six; I believe someone would have seen it happen."

Fallon nodded. "Has the weapon been found?"

"No," Mikalis said. He considered Fallon for a moment. "You were a policeman once yourself, is that not true, Mr. Fallon?"

Fallon said nothing, wondering how Mikalis had known.

"For eight years, I believe, in New York City. Then, some difficulties. Testimony before an investigating committee, innocent yourself but the star witness. Corruption in the police department, bribes, payoffs. Your fellow officers never quite forgave you, eh? Like Al Pacino, yes, in the movie *Serpico?*"

"Daskalos," Fallon said, suddenly realizing. "Daskalos had a file on me." It surprised him.

Mikalis shrugged. "Of course. This is a frontier island, only thirty miles from Turkey. You are a foreigner. He felt he needed to know. He had an associate in the American government. It took only a letter to him."

Mikalis lifted the ouzo bottle, poured some into his glass, some into Fallon's. He set down the bottle, clicked his glass against Fallon's, and tossed back the ouzo. He put the glass on the table and leaned forward, elbows on the arms of the chair. "As a former policeman, perhaps you can understand something. Whoever killed that boy was someone who knew how to use a knife. He stabbed him once, just below the rib cage and up into the heart. And he did this in what is now *my* town, on *my* island. Whoever he is, wherever he is, I am going to find him."

He poured more ouzo into his glass, returned the bottle to the table. "Now," he said. "Can you tell me why he would have your phone number?"

"No," Fallon said. "Have you talked with Anna or Dimitri?"

Mikalis nodded. "The boy telephoned Kostakis at one o'clock last night, asking for your number. He wouldn't explain why he wanted it."

"He could have come to the bar. Or called me there. He knew I stayed there until three."

"Presumably, what he wished to discuss was private."

Fallon frowned. "Have you talked to the people he worked with? I heard that he got a job on one of the boats."

Mikalis nodded. "A Turkish boat, yes, the *Yesmin*. I spoke with the other hands. Ali left the boat, they said, at twelve o'clock last night. He never returned."

"You've searched the boat?"

Mikalis smiled blandly. "For what?"

"The obvious," Fallon said. "Drugs."

"Ah," said Mikalis. "Drugs." He nodded. "I know, you see, about the cause of your 'disagreement' with the boy. And here is a boat registered in Turkey, from where hashish comes, and opium. Drugs were the first thing I considered. I telephoned to Rhodes, and had the harbor police there send up, on this morning's hydrofoil, one of their trained dogs. We searched the boat, the dog searched the boat. No drugs.

"Besides," he said, "the *Yesmin* has been out of the harbor only once in the past few weeks, yesterday, and for only two hours. They are getting her ready to sail to Amsterdam, where the owner is waiting for her. A Mr. Hadji."

"Amsterdam," Fallon said. It was the point, he knew, at which most hard drugs entered Europe by ship.

Mikalis smiled. "There are no drugs on the boat."

"Perhaps they plan to load the boat after they leave, on their way to Holland. Perhaps Ali learned about it."

"The boat," said Mikalis, "will of course be watched after it leaves port."

"And when will that be?"

"A day or two." He shrugged. "I have neither the authority nor the desire to hold her. I can establish no connection between the boat and the boy's death."

"This Hadji," Fallon said, "who is he?"

"A financier. Whatever that is. All I know is that he is rich, and that he is influential. Why all these questions about the boat?"

"You said that the boat went out into the harbor yesterday. Ali was killed last night. You don't find that suggestive?"

"Mr. Fallon," Mikalis said, "I can, if I wish, find *anything* suggestive. But in terms of actual facts, I have only a dead Turkish boy and a slip of paper with a telephone number on it. *Your* telephone number." He raised the ouzo, drank it off. He stood, reached into his shirt pocket, took out a pen and a piece of paper, scribbled something. He handed the paper to Fallon. "*My* telephone number, at home. Call me if you remember anything else."

And, without offering his hand, he had turned and waddled off through the shade, toward the gate and his car.

A nice exit, Fallon had thought.

And now, an hour later, gravel crunched beneath Fallon's sandals as he approached the ruined Doric temple. Small, no more than twenty feet long, it stood in the midst of a grove of cypresses, overlooking the sea on a rise of land jutting out from the mountainside. Two of its columns had been reassembled atop its uneven marble floor; segments of others lay nearby among the weeds and grasses and brown pine needles.

The Italian archaeologists who had begun excavating it in the early 1920's had never finished their work, probably because larger and more important sites had been unearthed on the other, more easily accessible, side of the island. It was still mentioned by one of the tourist books (in a nicely-phrased aside: "small temple of undetermined god"), but the only road approaching it was rutted dirt, poorly maintained. Fallon had never seen anyone else there. It was his favorite place on the island.

He sat down at midpoint on the marble floor in the full lotus position, spine erect, his back to the deep, distracting blue of the sea, and began *zazen*. After his wife's death, he had slowly become involved in Zen Buddhism, trying, he realized later, to fill up the emptiness that the loss of Megan had left within him.

Years ago, that had been, before he sold the restaurant he and Megan had opened and once run together. Before the boat, before the island.

He sat now in the center of a stillness, attending only to his breath. Time passed. Twenty minutes. Forty. At last, taking in a final deep lungful of air, he stood. He knew, without having thought about it consciously, exactly what he was going to do.

No blame, the I Ching would say. In one sense, no one is responsible for the life of another. But guilts, nevertheless, sometimes still remain.

*"Yes, boss, understand. Sorry, boss . . ."*

When he returned to the house, he called Anna, offered condolences and any help she might need. He called Dimitri, and from him learned that the

*Yesmin* had been moored in the harbor for a year, having left it only for an occasional day trip.

Then, in the storeroom, he checked his scuba tanks. The air pressure was down slightly, so he topped them off with the compressor. He carried them, and the duffel bag containing his mask, flippers, and weight belt, out to the Rover and stashed them in the back. He drove into town.

The *Yesmin* was moored in a slip not far from his own former boat, the *Meltemi*. He had seen her before, over the past year, without really noticing her. As he drove past, he looked her over.

A ketch, standard configuration, maybe forty-five feet long, white fiberglass hull, teak decking. Good lines, probably Swedish built. No one was topside.

He parked before the *Meltemi*, went aboard, asked Brian Leonard, the Englishman who eight years ago had bought her from him, via Dimitri, if he could have the use of the boat later that night. Brian, who preferred to sleep at the house of his mistress, a widow who owned a local taverna and kept him supplied with free Greek brandy, agreed.

Fallon drove to Le Cirque. It was a long night, tourists crowding the room until closing time, and he couldn't get away until two thirty.

A full moon hung overhead. On the deserted street fronting the harbor, the cafes and tavernas were locked; all the sidewalk tables and chairs, arranged in neat geometrical rows, were empty. From the bowline of the *Meltemi*, Fallon lowered himself into the water.

It was dark and not particularly clean. Diesel fuel filmed the surface, bits of refuse—an orange peel, a limp scrap of paper—bobbed and drifted. Still holding onto the line, he tested the regulator with two quick breaths. Then, letting go of the line, he dived.

Slowly, blindly, he went to the bottom, twenty-five feet down; his fingers jerked back instinctively as they sank into the ooze. He righted himself, then waited there, blinking behind the mask, letting his eyes adjust to the faint moonlight sifting down through the darkness. At last he could make out, directly overhead, the black silhouette of the *Meltemi's* hull against the silvered surface. Twelve hulls down lay the *Yesmin*.

He paddled off toward her, into the murk, his regulator hissing and gurgling as he inhaled and exhaled. Although it sounded preternaturally loud in the blackness, he knew it was inaudible above the water. More dangerous was the trail of bubbles in his wake. Anyone up there, awake and watching, could spot it.

He had paused beneath the fourth dark hull when, in the cloudy water off to his left, something moved. Something large, a ponderous, predatory shadow. He froze, and suddenly his heart was thumping against his ears.

Not a shark, he told himself. How many sharks have you seen in eight years? No, a grouper, or maybe a big mullet, magnified by the water, by the mask.

He waited, suspended in the water. He saw nothing. Whatever it had been, it was gone now.

He let out his breath and began swimming again.

Not a shark, he told himself. But the water seemed colder, more alien, than it had before.

Ten hulls . . . eleven . . . twelve.

He rose very slowly, keeping his breathing shallow to minimize the bubbles. Flippering up along the keel, he reached out and let his fingers trail against the cool, slick fiberglass. Now, in the filtered moonlight, he could see the white glow of the underhull.

And then a powerful hand clamped around his left ankle.

Without thinking, without even looking back, Fallon made a great twisting lunge, thrusting out with his right foot. He wrenched free, his left flipper gone.

Later he realized what had happened. One of the Turks, on guard topside, had seen the water roiling where Fallon's bubbles emerged, had at once known what they meant. Had quietly slipped into the water and come after him. Even without tanks, without a mask, he would have had no fear of the sea: Fallon knew of Turks and Greeks alike who could freedive to a hundred feet, and stay there for a full minute.

Fallon raced headlong into the gloom, still not looking back. He thought he had made it, that he was clear, when suddenly the hand clutched at him again.

He whirled, bubbles boiling around him. *Knife*, he thought. *There has to be a knife.*

The Turk was only a vague dark shape against the grey, an impossible sea creature. Fallon kicked his left foot out toward the shadowy face. The Turk jerked back. Fallon ripped free the weight belt at his waist and, holding one end in his right hand, let it swing before him. Watching the Turk, he backed away.

The advantage was still Fallon's. His mask provided visibility, his tanks provided mobility. The other man couldn't stay under much longer.

When the Turk darted forward, right arm swinging toward him, Fallon saw the moonlit gleam of the knife blade as it slashed for his stomach. He whipped the weight belt at the knife hand, furious at how slowly he moved against the resistance of the water.

The Turk's move had been a feint; the blade slipped away from the belt, tore up toward Fallon's face, sliced past it. And sheared his air hose.

All at once Fallon's mouth was filled with water.

The Turk shot toward the surface to snatch another breath before he returned and finished Fallon off.

Quickly, knowing he had little time, Fallon unbuckled the scuba harness, shrugged out of it, then, holding the tanks above him like a weapon, kicked himself upward.

The Turk was still at the surface, and Fallon's tanks caught him just below the sternum. He doubled up around them, as though trying to fold them in an embrace. And then Fallon was up himself, face free of the water, lungs lurching for air as his left hand went for the knife and his right arm coiled around the Turk's neck, going for the chokehold. . . .

"Neh?" Yes? The voice of Chief Mikalis.

"This is Fallon."

"Ah, Mr. Fallon! What a pleasure! I was just thinking of you."

"You sound very cheerful for five o'clock in the morning."

"Thank you. But you, I am afraid, do not."

"I'm using the public phone here in the square, and I can't stop this stupid shaking."

"Shaking? Whatever for?"

"Never mind. Listen, I have a gift for you."

"Indeed?"

"A Turkish deck hand."

"Yes?"

"Yes. Tied up, unconscious, on the *Meltemi*."

"Ah."

"And I have a knife. It may be the same knife that killed Ali."

"Ah."

"He tried to use it on me. I swam out to the *Yesmin* tonight, to see if I could find something you people missed."

"Ah."

"*Ah?* Is that all you can say?"

"Well, to be perfectly frank, Mr. Fallon, I already knew about the Turk."

"You—wait a minute. You had someone watching the boat."

"Yes. I just finished speaking with him. He is stationed in a room above one of the cafes."

". . . So he saw everything."

"Oh yes. Everything. Saw you arrive at the Englishman's boat with your underwater equipment, saw you enter the water. He was quite concerned there, for a moment, when the Turk went into the water after you, with the knife."

"Concerned."

"Quite, yes. But by the time he got down to the water, you were towing the man to the other boat."

In English, Fallon said, "You suckered me. You set me up."

"*Signómeh?*" Excuse me?

"You used me," Fallon said in Greek.

"Yes. Yes, I am afraid I did. The relationship between Greece and Turkey is, as you know, at the moment rather delicate. I could afford to bring only so much pressure to bear on the crew of that boat—we need no diplomatic incidents here. But it occurred to me that you, as an American, would have no such restraints. From what I had learned of you, you appeared the sort of person who would seek things out for himself. Yes, my friend, I confess that I did use you as a sort of, what is the word?, yes, *catalyst.*"

"The word is *pawn.* You realize that I nearly got myself killed?"

"Ah, yes, that is most regrettable. I am truly sorry. And truly surprised. I had not expected them to react with so much . . . enthusiasm. They must be very frightened. I thought that if you . . . ah . . . *prodded* them in some way, they would merely make an attempt to frighten you off."

"They frightened me, all right."

"But even that, you see, would have been enough pretext for me to hold the boat while I continued the investigation. Now, of course, things have worked out splendidly. I have already dispatched a car to pick up the Turk. If you are willing to testify against him, we can bring a charge of attempted murder. The knife will be sent to Athens for examination. I have learned from the doctor that the blood of the boy, Ali, is of an unusual type. Perhaps we can establish that the knife was the murder weapon. Perhaps not. The important thing is that I can keep the boat here until I learn more."

"Keeping the boat is a very good idea."

"*Signómeh?*"

"That boat isn't the *Yesmin.*"

"I do not understand."

"The *Yesmin* has been here, in the water, for over a year. She would be ready for cleaning, in drydock. That boat in the harbor has been in the water no longer than a week. Her hull is brand new. No fouling, no barnacles, nothing. It's a duplicate. A copy. They switched boats when they took the *Yesmin* out the other day."

". . . So you are telling me—"

"The keel. The drugs are built into the keel. That's why the dog couldn't smell them. And there are probably a lot of them, judging by all the time and effort required."

"Ah. Good. *Good.* Excellent, Mr. Fallon."

"I doubt that you'll be able to prove anything against the owner, Hadji. He can always claim he knew nothing about it. But you should be able to send the crewmen away for quite a while. And they're the ones responsible for Ali's death. Ali must have had second thoughts about being involved in something like this. The others suspected, and they killed him." Killed him before he could call Fallon and ask for his advice.

"Mr. Fallon," said Mikalis, "I am most grateful."

"Fine," said Fallon. "I'm going home."

Then, in a demonstration not only of fluent English, but also of considerable skill as a mimic, Mikalis said, "You know, Louis, this could be the beginning of a beautiful friendship." Bogart, to Claude Rains.

Despite himself, Fallon laughed. He said, "That's supposed to be *my* line." But Mikalis, with a mimic's sense of timing, had already hung up.

# THE MIDDLE EAST

# THE QATAR CAUSEWAY

*By Josh Pachter*

*Sinterklaas, kapoentje,*
*Gooi wat in m'n schoentje!*
*Gooi wat in m'n laarsje!*
*Dank je, Sinterklaasje!*

THE TALL, thin man in the long red robe and cotton beard was circled by a ring of gaily-dressed children who sang and giggled as they skipped around him hand in hand. His merry eyes sparkled behind the small round lenses of his wire-rimmed spectacles, his bishop's mitre sat snugly on his head, his golden staff glittered cheerfully in the bright fluorescent lighting of the messroom. Outside the ring of children stood half a dozen gangly youths in gaudy pantaloons and floppy felt hats, their faces glistening with coal-black greasepaint, their lips daubed a rich crimson. Each of them held a bulky burlap sack in his ebony hands.

The bearded figure in the robe was not the only adult present. The parents of the dancers were there, too, clustered in groups of three and four around the walls of the room, sipping strong coffee and watching their sons and daughters enjoying the party. And off in a corner stood a small-framed Pakistani in the olive green uniform of Bahrain's Public Security Force, listening earnestly to the explanations of the stocky business-suited man at his side.

The stocky man in the business suit was not a businessman. He was Roelof Smit, a detective lieutenant with the Amsterdam police, and he was visiting Bahrain to observe the workings of the emirate's law enforcement machinery. Since the abortive coup attempt in 1978, fully two-thirds of the island's security troops were Pakistanis, fiercely loyal to the Arab government that employed them; Mahboob Chaudri, originally from Karachi, was the *mahsool* who had been assigned to work with the Dutchman during the two weeks of his stay.

Today was December fifth, Sinterklaas, and Smit had brought his host out to al-Qalat—the housing compound of the Dutch construction company Nederbild—for the festivities.

"What are they singing?" asked Chaudri, his English careful and lightly accented.

Smit's walrus mustache shivered with pleasure. "It's a simple little song," he chuckled, "and typical of the spirit of the holiday. Let's see if I can translate it for you: 'Sinterklaas, you little elf'—because, you see, the 'tje' or 'je' at the end of every line is our way of saying 'little' or 'cute'—'Sinterklaas, you little elf, leave some goodies on my shelf! Leave some candy in my shoe—thank you, Sinterklaas, thank *you!*' That's not a literal translation, you understand, but it gives you the general idea of the thing—and at least it rhymes."

"And, lieutenant, is it typical of the spirit of the holiday?"

The Dutchman laughed again. "In most Western countries, Christmas has become so commercialized that it's hard to remember its original religious significance. Well, we Hollanders have our spiritual side, like everyone else, and the spiritualist in us wants to keep Christmas a holy day. But we're a practical people, too, and our practical side tells us that we can't just ignore the commercial aspects of the Christmas season. So we invented Sinterklaas. This way, we can stay quietly religious on Kerstmis—in fact, we've even added on a second Christmas Day, December 26th—because we've gotten all the shopping and gift-giving out of our systems three weeks earlier, on the fifth, on Sinterklaas.

"Like the American Santa Claus, our Christmas Man—the Kerstman—is fat and jolly. Sinterklaas is also jolly, but he's much more, ah, *netjes*. 'Distinguished,' that's the word. After all, he *is* a saint, you know—Saint Nicolaas, which is where the names Sinterklaas and Santa Claus both come from. Every year he travels all the way to Holland from Spain, by steamboat, with his band of helpers—the Zwarte Piets, or Black Peters. Foreigners sometimes misunderstand, and object to the Piets. But they're helpers, not slaves, and there's really nothing racist about them. Besides, the children love them, and I don't know *what* would happen if we ever tried to get rid of them!"

The children finished their song to loud applause, with Chaudri and Smit joining in wholeheartedly, then whirled away from Saint Nicholas to face the crowd of Black Peters. Burlap sacks were flung wide, black hands dug deep, and the boys and girls exploded with cries of "Piet! Piet!" as the saint's assistants showered them with fistfuls of candy and tiny ginger cookies.

"*Strooigoed* and *pepernoten*," Roelof Smit informed his companion—and then a real explosion sounded from somewhere outside, and every window in the messhall shattered inward in a horror of screams and flying glass.

Sobbing children, panic-stricken adults, the floor littered with a mosaic of candy and glass, the dull reverberation of the blast shaking the walls and deafening the ears.

When at last the first shock faded, Sinterklaas ripped off his beard and mitre and flung away his staff and raced out the back door of the building. Chaudri and Smit were close behind him, their feet slipping on the shards of glass and sticking on the gooey candy.

At the door, Chaudri grabbed a bewildered father by the front of his shirt. "Sir!" he shouted into the vacant face. "Is there a hospital here on the compound?"

There was no reaction.

"A hospital! A doctor! Some of these children have been hurt! Is there anyone here to help them?" Chaudri shook the man violently until at last he blinked his eyes and nodded.

"A hospital," he repeated softly. "Yes." A thin line of blood trickled from the corner of his mouth, and he licked it away absently.

"Get someone here to look after these people!" Chaudri cried, releasing him. "Hurry!"

Suddenly awakening, the man muttered, "*Ja, natuurlijk!*" and jumped for a telephone.

With a last look back at the confusion in the room, Chaudri and Smit went out the door. Sinterklaas was standing on the narrow strip of rocky beach that lay between the messhall and the blue-green iridescence of the gulf. A half-mile to the north, the skeleton of a bridge under construction reached across the water to a small islet not far offshore. A dense cloud of grey smoke billowed up from the point where the bridge met the islet, staining the pale blue of the sky and spreading evilly.

"*Mijn God,*" Sinterklaas whispered, and when Chaudri looked at him, he saw tears in the man's tired eyes. "*Oh, mijn hemel.*"

"What is it?" he asked. "What's happened?"

"My bridge," Sinterklaas replied. "They've blown it up."

"*They?* Who are *they?*"

The man shook his head. "I don't know. He. She. They. Someone. It doesn't matter who. They've destroyed my bridge."

"What do you mean, *your* bridge?"

At last the man turned towards him. "Come with me," he said, recognizing Chaudri's uniform, "and I'll tell you."

"Where are you going?"

The man in the red robe pointed a trembling finger towards the offshore islet, where the heavy grey smoke was draped across the sky like a shroud. "Out there," he said, and his voice was dull and dead.

"My name, if you can believe it," the man introduced himself, "is Nicolaas. Nicolaas Sjollema. When I was a boy, the other children used to call me Sinterklaas. I always wanted to play the part for real, and today—today was my first chance."

They were in Sjollema's car, a Japanese import with right-hand drive, barreling along a rough dirt track toward the company harbor. Chaudri, in the passenger seat on the left, found himself automatically trying to brake and steer; in the back, Roelof Smit clenched his teeth on the stem of an ornate meerschaum pipe and jounced.

"I'm the foreman on this phase of the construction project," Sjollema went on. He had taken off his robe, revealing faded denims and a chambray workshirt. "I didn't design it and I'm not paying for it, but I'm in charge of building it. That's why I call it *my* bridge. I've been with the project for three years, now—well, almost three years—and I feel as if it's become my child, my son."

"An expensive son to raise," remarked Smit from the rear.

Sjollema smiled grimly. "The second most expensive stretch of highway in the world," he agreed. "Concrete piles sunk into the sea floor, with four-lane slabs of roadbed the length of football fields laid on top of them. About thirty-two kilometers long from here to Qatar, at a total construction cost of more than half a *billion* dollars: that's over fifteen thousand dollars a meter. An expensive child, *inderdaad.*"

Chaudri's right foot pumped the spot where the brake pedal should have been as the car squealed to a stop inches away from a modern pier lined with launches and a long, flat-bedded barge. The only craft showing any signs of life was an old wooden fishing dhow, its mast horizontal, its canvas sail spread out as a sunscreen. A powerfully-built Arab in a grimy, once-white *thobe,* his *ghutra* wrapped carelessly about his head, was standing in the stern, shaded by the sail overhead and cutting a squid into bait-sized pieces. In the prow a young boy—naked except for worn cutoff shorts, his skin charred black by the sun—sat hunched over a spool of nylon, his fingers moving swiftly as he tied a heavy barbed hook to the free end of the line. Neither of them paid the slightest attention to the dark smoke that still rose from the offshore islet. To see them at work—stolid, emotionless, completely absorbed in their tasks—it was hard to remember that, not fifteen minutes earlier, not a thousand meters away, the world had been rocked by a devastating blast. They were living in their own dimension, in another century, where all that mattered was the frantic pull of a ten pound *hamour* as it strained to loosen the killing barb from its cheek.

"We need to go out there, to Umm as Hawwak," Sjollema told the fisherman, who raised his head slowly and regarded them without interest.

*"La, la,"* the Arab said tonelessly, not singing but refusing. "No, no."

"Police business." Chaudri's Arabic was crisp. "Let's go."

The fisherman shrugged his shoulders and, as Chaudri and the two Dutchmen climbed aboard, put his knife aside and moved to his vessel's primitive controls. Moments later the engine was growling; the weathered deckboards trembled beneath their feet as the boat pulled ponderously away from the dock.

"At least there's no one working out there today," Sjollema sighed. "I don't want to *think* about what would have happened if . . ." He left the sentence unfinished.

"You shut down construction for Sinterklaas?" asked Smit.

"Oh, no, not that. But this is Friday, the Muslim day of rest. We employ very few Arabs, but we observe their work week—like all foreign companies in Bahrain. Takes a while for our people to get used to, but it seems the simplest way to schedule in the long run."

The water was made of emeralds, frosted with the pearly turbulence of the dhow's wake and the reflected glitter of the late afternoon sun. Halfway across to Umm as Hawwak, the fisherman's son stabbed a finger off to port and cried, *"Uthor!* Look!"* Chaudri spun around in time to see a gunmetal grey tailfin wave a greeting at them and disappear beneath the surface of the sea.

"Dolphin," he said. "Do you have them in your country, too?"

Roelof Smit shook his head. "Not like that. Only in the seaquarium, trained to jump through hoops and balance beach balls on their noses."

The dhow's engine stuttered and stopped. For a moment, as they glided the last few meters to the islet's wooden mooring, silence engulfed them. Then they could hear the lapping of waves on the shore and the sad crackle of brush fires dying.

Chaudri ordered the fisherman to wait, and they left the boat for the desolate islet. There was rubble everywhere, blackened clumps of shattered concrete, the ruins of what must have been supply sheds and temporary office space, machinery twisted beyond recognition. What little vegetation Umm as Hawwak had supported was cinders now; scattered tongues of flame licked hungrily at the last remaining morsels of green. Here and there were geckos—the small, scurrying lizards which the Arabs claimed brought luck to the home. Many of them were missing their tails or heads or limbs; all of them were dead.

"Who could have had a motive for doing this?" Roelof Smit was numb with the horror of the scene.

His countryman shook his head despondently. "I don't know," he said. "It doesn't make any sense. If it had been the Saudi causeway, which another company is building on the other side of the country, I could understand it. That's a controversial project and there's been a lot of opposition to it. But if there's anything at all the people of Bahrain are in agreement on, it's that this bridge across to Qatar is a good thing. Trade will be easier in both directions, and the security of both countries will be strengthened. I—"

Sjollema turned away from them and walked off. Roelof Smit hesitated for a moment, then went after him, leaving Chaudri alone in the rubble.

He watched them go, watched Smit catch up to the other man and put a hand to his elbow, watched them reboard the dhow and sit side by side in its stern, Sjollema with his head in his hands and Smit with an arm around the foreman's shoulder.

The sea birds were beginning to return to the islet, squawking angrily at the invasion of their privacy. The hum of a motor launch's powerful engine grew louder; by now, several craft were setting out towards Umm as Hawwak from the dock on the mainland.

Mahboob Chaudri hunkered down on the ground, selected a small chunk of scorched concrete from the debris at his feet, and passed it slowly from hand to hand. This morning a bridge stood here, he thought, and now I sit here with its ruined remnants in my hand. Tomorrow the Dutchmen will go back to work, and they will build the bridge again.

It is a wheel, he decided. An ever-spinning wheel of life and death.

He rose, slipped the fragment of concrete into his pocket as a reminder of the day's events, and stepped carefully through the rubble towards the waiting dhow.

The Bahraini headquarters of Nederbild BV occupied the fifth and sixth floors of a concrete and glass tower in the al-Khalifa Road, in the center of Manama's business district. When Mahboob Chaudri and Roelof Smit stepped off the elevator into the sixth floor reception area at eight o'clock the next morning, the atmosphere of tension that washed over them was even more noticeable than the chill of the air conditioning.

The blonde receptionist was pretty, Chaudri supposed, if you liked European women, but he found her neckline and the tightness of her sweater immodest. She looked shocked when he asked for the firm's managing director, and assured them that Mr. Hofstra was much too busy to see them. When Smit explained the purpose of their visit to her in rapid Dutch, though—the only words Chaudri could make out were *"bom"* and *"explosie"*—she frowned nervously and ushered them along a carpeted corridor to the executive suite. Her tailored tan skirt ended an inch above her knees, and she wore spiked high heels that accented the firmness of her calves.

Shameful, Mahboob Chaudri thought as they followed her. His own dear wife Shazia would be ashamed to be seen in such garments. He would never understand these Western women, he knew, never.

Hendrik Hofstra's office was a large, plush room with a picture window running the length of one wall and looking out over the *suq*. A second wall was covered with an artist's rendering of the causeway, sketched in bold, confident strokes that contrasted starkly with the smoldering reality of the scene at Umm as Hawwak. A scale model of the bridge stood on a table in the center of the room, complete with tiny vehicles frozen in mid-transit. Hofstra's oversized desk was in a corner by the window, cluttered with papers and books and rolls of blueprints; on the wall behind it were half a dozen framed photographs of a towheaded child of six or seven, sometimes alone and sometimes with a rather plain, large-boned woman who could only be the boy's mother.

Hofstra himself was a middle-aged bantam rooster in a badly-cut grey suit, his tie pulled loose and his collar button undone. What he lacked in stature, though, he made up for in temper. "Hofstra," he introduced himself abruptly. He offered them neither a handshake nor a seat. "I've got almost two hundred meters of downed roadway to rebuild, gentlemen, and I need to get that done in about one week and without spending a *stuiver* if I want to keep this project on schedule and under budget. What do *you* want?"

"Information, sir," Chaudri began. "About the bombing. I am Mahboob Chaudri, and this is Lieutenant Smit of the Amsterdam police."

"The *Amsterdam* police!" Hofstra roared. "Listen here, Mr. Tawdry, or whatever your name is: I've got a twenty-five man security team out there on Umm as Hawwak right now, turning that little islet upside down. They don't need any help from you, and they *potverdorie* don't need any help from the Amsterdam police!"

"Lieutenant Smit is here only as an observer, sir," said Chaudri implacably, "and as for me, when the crime of industrial sabotage is committed on Bahraini soil, our Public Security Force is charged with conducting a complete investigation of its own. As I was on the scene at the time of the explosion, my superiors have assigned me to the case."

"The case," Hofstra fumed. It was clear that he realized he was in the wrong, and equally clear that he was unhappy about it. "All right, then. Ask your questions."

"Our explosives experts were on the islet within an hour of the blast yesterday afternoon. They report having found traces of at least nine separate charges and possibly more, spaced ten to twenty meters apart and simultaneously detonated by a single timing mechanism which was put in place beneath the roadway no more than twenty-four hours before the explosion. Several indications lead to the conclusion that the charges and timer were set by a single individual."

"I got that information from my own people last night, Mr. Tawdry, now—"

"The name is Chaudri, sir. Excuse me."

"Mr. Chaudri, then. Now, what do you *want?*"

Chaudri pulled a notebook and a pen from the pocket of his uniform shirt. "I would like to know who had access to Umm as Hawwak during the twenty-four hours that preceded the blast, Mr. Hofstra. I would like to know who had the opportunity to set those charges."

*"Getverdemme."* Hofstra ran a hand through his close-cropped, greying hair. "The islet was not guarded, Mr. Chaudri. Night before last, any *uil-skuiken* with a boat could have gone out there completely unobserved."

"A half-billion dollar project and you leave it *unguarded?*" Smit was incredulous.

*"Left* it unguarded. We won't make that mistake again."

"But you made it once?" the Dutch policeman insisted.

Hofstra answered through clenched teeth. "Yes, Lieutenant Smit, we made that mistake once. This is Bahrain, lieutenant, not the Zeedijk in Amsterdam. We were led to believe that the local police"—he glared angrily at Chaudri—"had created a climate of order here where we wouldn't need to worry about theft or sabotage. Do you have any further questions?"

"You suggested that the charges could have been set on the evening of the fourth of December," said Mahboob Chaudri, "or in the early morning hours of the fifth. What about the afternoon of the fourth, a full day ahead of the explosion?"

"We had a crew working out there from eight A.M. until six P.M. Anybody crawling around setting explosives would have been seen."

"But what about the crew themselves? Could one of them have done it?"

"How would *I* know? I wasn't out there, I was here. Ask Nick Sjollema that kind of question. It's his job to know who's where at all times. Anything else?"

Chaudri looked up from his notebook. "One possibility, Mr. Hofstra, is that the bridge was blown up by a former employee, someone nursing a grudge against Nederbild. Have any of your people been let go recently?"

The director glanced impatiently at his watch. "Mr. Chaudri," he said slowly. "Nederbild BV has over twelve hundred employees in Bahrain, from cleaning ladies through senior executives here in this building, from gate guards and maintenance men to a twenty-four-hour child-care center at the al-Qarat housing compound, and from construction workers all the way up to Nicolaas Sjollema on site. I direct the entire operation from this office, yes, but I do *not* keep my fingers on the names and work histories of all twelve hundred of those employees. You can take that question down to the fifth floor, where you will find our personnel department. Do you have anything else you would like to ask *me*, Mr. Chaudri?"

"Yes, sir," the Pakistani said promptly, "I do. I didn't notice you at the Sinterklaas party yesterday. Why weren't you there?"

For the first time, the fight drained out of Hofstra's face, leaving him looking tired and old. "I have no children, Mr. Chaudri. There was no reason for me to be there."

Chaudri glanced quickly at the framed pictures on the wall. "No children?" he mused. "Then—"

"My son," said Hofstra, his voice hoarse. "Three weeks ago—twenty days ago—my son Pieter was playing on the beach, behind our house at al-Qarat. His mother was in a deck chair, knitting, and Pieter strayed away from her while she was absorbed in her work. When she noticed he had gone, she went to look for him. She found him in—in the water. He was dead, Mr. Chaudri. He had drowned."

Down on the fifth floor, as they were heading for the personnel office, Chaudri and Smit met Nicolaas Sjollema coming out of Purchasing. He looked haggard and harried, but his drawn face lit up when he saw them. "I've been wondering how to reach you," he greeted them. "I thought you'd like to know about the people at the party. I checked with the compound hospital after I dropped you yesterday, and then again later on last night, and there were no serious injuries at all. Minor cuts from the flying glass, several of the adults who were closest to the windows required some stitches, a few of the children were pretty badly shaken up—but that was the worst of it. Everyone was home in time for dinner, *Godzijdank.*"

"Indeed, that *is* good news," Chaudri grinned. "And you've saved us a trip out to Umm as Hawwak. We need to ask you a question about your crew, if you can spare us another minute."

"Yes, of course. They're sweating this morning, I can tell you that: I've got every laborer on the payroll out there cleaning up the islet today, loading rubble onto company barges and dumping it out in the gulf. If they can finish up by tonight, we'll be able to start right in on the reconstruction. That's why I'm in town now, trying to rush-order enough supplies and tools to get us rolling again." Sjollema seemed about to go on, but changed his mind. "You don't need to hear about *my* problems," he said. "What was it you wanted to ask me?"

"Your crew," said Chaudri. "Could one of your men have placed the explosives that blew up the causeway during the afternoon of December fourth, during working hours, without being observed? He would have needed an hour or more for the job."

"No." Sjollema's answer was immediate and definite. "Impossible. I was

on site all day, running our standard weekly inspection. I would have seen
him."

"*U bent er absoluutzeker van?*" Roelof Smit put in.

The foreman answered in English for Chaudri's benefit: "Yes, lieutenant,
I'm positive. Those charges were not set during working hours on Thursday. It had to have been done after we'd all left for the day, after six. I'd
swear to that in court."

Nederbild's personnel manager was a severe woman in her mid-forties,
dressed simply in a long black skirt and plain white blouse. She wore her
hair frizzed in that strange style that never lasted more than a few months
but was called—for some reason which was not clear to Mahboob Chaudri
—"permanent." A pair of eyeglasses was suspended around her neck by a
thin silver chain; when the two policemen approached her, she put them on
and eyed them carefully. There was a clipboard in her left hand.

"Gentlemen," she said. "I am Annemieke Stutje. I manage this office.
You are the police. You want to know the names of Nederbild employees
who have recently been fired." It was a statement, not a question, and it
took them by surprise.

"You've just spoken with Mr. Hofstra?" Chaudri guessed.

"I have not."

"Then how did you—"

"How did I know what you want?" She put a forefinger to the bridge of
her spectacles and pushed them a millimeter higher. "I am not a fool,
gentlemen. Someone blew up the Qatar causeway yesterday afternoon. Perhaps it was a disgruntled former employee. I expected a representative of
the police to call on me this morning, and here you are. I have already gone
through my files for the information you need." She riffled through the
pages on her clipboard and selected one of them, a half sheet of yellow
flimsy. "Yes, I have it here. Within the last thirty days, only two of our
employees have been dismissed. On November 26th, a Korean laborer
named Kim Lee Kwan was fired for attempting to steal sweet water from the
Umm as Hawwak site."

"He was fired for stealing *water?*" Smit looked amazed.

Mevrouw Stutje adjusted her glasses again and peered at him. "You are
new to Bahrain," she decided. "As I said, Mr. Kim was fired for stealing
*sweet* water, which is pure spring water and the only water in this country
that is fit to drink. It is used on site for mixing concrete, and Mr. Kim was
caught trying to sneak a large jug of it back to his barracks. Sweet water is
rather expensive here, and neither Nederbild BV nor the Bahraini government is prone to tolerate thievery: Mr. Kim's visa was immediately revoked,
and he was on a plane to Seoul that same evening. I checked with the

authorities at the Immigration and Passports Directorate earlier this morning, and he has not returned to Bahrain."

"And the second former employee?" Chaudri asked, scribbling furiously
in his notebook.

"Ebezer Kwaja," the woman read, "Indian, employed as a clerk in our
purchasing office until his dismissal four days ago, on December second. He
is still in the emirate, working at the Central Market. He has a cousin who
sells fruits and vegetables there, and who took over sponsorship of Kwaja
when we let the man go."

Chaudri looked up. Annemieke Stutje had omitted something, which
seemed out of line with her usual brisk efficiency. "Why was Kwaja fired?"
he asked.

She hugged her clipboard to her chest. "I don't know," she admitted,
plainly troubled. "I *should* know, but I don't. No explanation was given.
That is unusual for Nederbild BV."

"Whose decision was it to get rid of him?"

She pulled her spectacles down to the tip of her nose and appraised him
silently over the rims. At last she spoke. "The order came down from the
sixth floor," she said. "From Mr. Hofstra personally."

Manama's Central Market is a huge grey barn that sits just outside the
western edge of the *suq* between the Naim Hospital and the Budaiya round-
about, within sight of the gulf. It is an ugly, windowless, characterless structure, whose metal walls trap the stifling heat all summer and the odors of
meat and fish the year round. Shopping in the tangled maze of the old
produce *suq* had been an adventure, but shopping at the new Central Market was a chore.

When they entered the vast fruit and vegetable hall, Roelof Smit was
overwhelmed by the enormity of it. It was as if a half dozen copies of
Amsterdam's outdoor Albert Cuypmarkt had been laid side by side, with
four drab walls and a high ceiling thrown up around them.

They were instantly surrounded by a gaggle of grinning Indian and Pakistani boys with wheelbarrows, who followed closely behind them, eager to
carry their purchases for a few hundred fils.

But Smit and Chaudri walked down the seemingly endless rows of merchants—all males, from young boys in bluejeans to toothless old men in
threadbare *thobes,* each sitting patiently on a tall stool, surrounded by his
mountain of goods—without buying. They were not looking for tomatoes
or eggplants or cabbages from Jordan, for cucumbers or lettuce or sweet
peppers from Cyprus, for hot peppers or okra from India, for onions from
Pakistan or cauliflowers from Australia or potatoes from Egypt or garlic
from Thailand, for bananas, pears, oranges, mangoes, guavas, kiwis, or African lemons the size of grapefruit. They were not looking for local produce,

either, or for an infinity of burlap sacks overflowing with peas, rice, raisins, flour, lentils, fava beans, pumpkin seeds, peanuts, pistachios, walnuts, almonds, chickpeas, red peppers, kidney beans, popcorn, or shredded coconut.

They were looking for Ebezer Kwaja, and at last they found him. His cousin had allowed him a brief rest period, and he was sitting on a pale blue wooden bench along the north wall of the cavernous building, holding a small glass of steaming tea in both hands, and watching the tide of buyers and sellers and wheelbarrow boys flow by.

"Mr. Ebezer Kwaja?" Chaudri approached him.

The man eyed them curiously. He wore a satiny longsleeved shirt in a loud floral pattern and navy blue slacks with grey pinstripes, tightly cut but flaring widely at the ankles. His deep brown forehead glistened with perspiration; his dark hair was styled but greasy.

"Most certainly," he said. "If you are looking for Mr. Ebezer Kwaja, then I am most certainly the Mr. Ebezer Kwaja you are looking for." He raised his glass of tea to his lips and blew on it, then lowered it untasted. "But why, I am asking myself, are you looking for Mr. Ebezer Kwaja at all?"

Mahboob Chaudri was not a tall man, but standing over the seated Kwaja in his immaculate uniform, with his gun on his hip and his black-peaked cap and the military braid on his shoulder, he was an impressive figure. "Until recently," he said, "you were employed as a purchasing clerk at the Nederbild headquarters in the al-Khalifa Road. Four days ago, on December second, you were fired. Why?"

The Indian's jet black eyes gleamed. "Ah," he said, nodding his head sagely, "I am waiting for this very question to be asked. I am waiting every day to be asked why big man from the distant Netherlands is dismissing humble Mr. Ebezer Kwaja from his trivial post. And now, at last, you have come." He paused for a sip of his tea, then looked up at them with a broad smile on his face. "Big man is dismissing Mr. Kwaja," he continued, "because Mr. Kwaja is knowing the truth. Yes, indeed, Mr. Kwaja is knowing *too much* truth."

"Too much truth about what?" Chaudri asked patiently, amused by the man's air of self-importance.

"Too much truth about his baby," Kwaja announced. "Too much truth about the—"

A muffled report sounded from somewhere behind them, and the look of pride on the Indian's face warped into a mask of shock and pain. The glass of tea dropped from his hands and shattered on the concrete floor. He slumped back against the pale blue bench and clawed weakly at his chest, where a crimson blossom grew quickly among the flowers of his shirt.

"Water!" he gasped, and his clear black eyes were glassy now, and filled with tears. "Water!"

A minute later, someone came forward with a paper cup of water for him, but by then it was too late.

"*Jeetje mina!*" Roelof Smit wheezed huskily. "This is *hot!*"

They were sitting in a curtained-off booth at the Star of Paradise, a small Pakistani restaurant not far from the police barracks in Juffair. Mahboob Chaudri was enjoying a large order of brains masala, but the Dutchman was having trouble with his bowl of beef rogan josh.

Smit filled a tumbler from the metal pitcher in the center of the table, and drained it in one noisy swallow. "I don't understand how you can eat this *spul*," he complained. "*'S Niet te geloven!*"

"I am glad you took my advice and ordered your dinner mildly seasoned," Chaudri chuckled. "If you had gone ahead and asked for it spicy, I'm afraid I would have had to carry you back to your hotel. Here, let me pour you some more sweet water."

Smit took another long swallow and wiped the back of his hand across his bushy mustache. "Why *sweet* water?" he wanted to know. "It tastes like ordinary drinking water to me."

"The word 'Bahrain' is Arabic for 'two seas,'" Chaudri explained, "which is a reference to the gulf on the one hand, and the fresh-water springs that lie beneath the island on the other. Compared to the brackish salt water of the gulf, the spring water is sweet indeed."

"And expensive, like the Stutje woman said?"

"Oh, dearie me, yes. In fact, until the last round of increases in the price of oil, the service stations here in the emirate would wash the windows of your car with gasoline because that was cheaper than using sweet water." He ripped a large piece of bread from his bubbly round chapati and sopped up curried gravy from his plate. "You're not eating, lieutenant."

"I've had enough," Smit sighed, pushing his plate away and shaking his head sadly. "Anyway, I don't want to eat, I want to talk."

"You talk," mumbled Chaudri around a mouthful of brains, "and I will eat for both of us."

The Dutchman settled back in his chair. "All right," he said, "I'll talk." He leaned forward, elbows on the table and chin cupped in his hands. "We're dealing here with four separate incidents: the drowning of Hendrik Hofstra's son, the dismissal of Ebezer Kwaja, the explosion at Umm as Hawwak, and Kwaja's murder. Each of these incidents gives rise to one or more questions. Was the death of Hofstra's child an accident, for example, as Hofstra himself told us—or was it something else? Was Kwaja really fired because of what he knew about the drowning—as *he* told us—or, if the boy's death was accidental, was there some other reason? Who blew up the

Qatar causeway, and why? And, again, why and by whom was Ebezer Kwaja killed?"

Mahboob Chaudri nodded attentively, but his eyes never left his plate.

"Finally," Smit pressed on, "what relationships exist between these various events, if any? *Was* Kwaja fired because of what he knew about the drowning—and, more important, was he killed to keep him from passing that knowledge on to us? Did Kwaja take revenge for his dismissal by blowing up the bridge, or was the explosion nothing at all to do with him? Were the blast and the drowning connected, or the blast and the murder—and, if so, how?"

Chaudri set down his knife and fork and poured himself a glass of water.

"We need to talk with Hofstra again," Smit suggested. "We need to know his explanation of the firing of Ebezer Kwaja, and why he sent us down to personnel instead of telling us about it himself, and where he was this afternoon when the Indian was shot. We need to know more about young Pieter's death, too—perhaps a conversation with Mrs. Hofstra would be worthwhile. And we need to find out who might have had a motive for setting those explosives. What do you think our next move should be, *mahsool?*"

Chaudri said nothing. He was staring, transfixed, at the glass of water in his hands.

*"Mahsool?"* said Smit, more loudly. *"Mahsool?"*

Startled, Chaudri looked up. "Oh, lieutenant," he said. "I'm sorry. I was just thinking."

"About what?"

" 'About what?' " he repeated slowly. "How strange, lieutenant. That is exactly what I asked Ebezer Kwaja a moment before he was shot." He shook his head and took a small sip of water. "I was thinking about a book I have been reading to practice my English, a book of the many adventures of your great European detective, Mr. Sherlock Holmes. 'You *see,* my dear Watson,' Mr. Holmes chastised his friend in one of the stories, 'but you do not *observe.'* And now I am chastising myself. Sometimes, my dear lieutenant, it seems that I *hear*—but I do not *listen."* A dazzling smile suddenly illuminated the nutbrown face. "But what was it you were asking me while my thoughts were far away in Victorian England?"

"Our next move," the Dutchman supplied. "What do you think our next move should be?"

"Aha!" said Mahboob Chaudri. "Our next move, I think, should be to order some khulfi for dessert. It is a combination of vanilla ice cream and spaghetti and you will almost certainly hate it, but it is very typical of my country and I would like for you to try it."

"You're avoiding my question. I mean, what's our next move about the case?"

Chaudri beckoned to a white-jacketed waiter. "Ah, yes," he said indulgently, "the case. Well, my friend, there's nothing more we can do tonight. Tomorrow morning, when the university opens, we have a delivery to make, and then we shall see what develops."

"We haven't got a forensics laboratory of our own yet," Chaudri explained as he steered the dusty blue Public Security jeep into the main parking lot of Gulf Polytechnic's Isa Town campus. "So when we need some lab work done, we bring it out here to one of the professors. Usually they are able to help us. *Insh'Allah*," he added automatically.

"That's not the first time I've heard that word," said Smit, swinging out of the vehicle and following Chaudri up a covered walkway towards the science department's modern building. "What does it mean?"

"*Insh'Allah?*" Chaudri smiled. "It is the Arab's constant prayer. 'Tomorrow it will be cooler, *insh'Allah*.' 'Your car will be fixed by this afternoon, *insh'Allah*.' 'Their marriage will be a happy one, *insh'Allah*.' It means: if Allah is willing. If Allah is willing, anything can happen."

"We might even solve this case," the Dutchman grimaced.

"*Insh'Allah*," laughed Mahboob Chaudri.

They found Professor Emad Rezk in his classroom, going over his notes for the day's first lecture. Rezk, an Egyptian, had been with Gulf Polytechnic since the establishment of the school several years earlier. He was a talented chemist and had held a tenured position at the University of Cairo, but the offer of a substantially higher salary, a house, a car, and complete academic freedom had lured him—along with a large number of his colleagues—to the gulf. Though his thoughts were always perfectly organized, Rezk's exterior was usually dishevelled. His white lab coat showed acid burns in various places, his fingers were permanently yellowed from exposure to caustic chemicals.

"Mahboob Chaudri!" he exclaimed with delight as they edged between two rows of students' desks. "And a friend! How charming it is to see you both!"

Chaudri introduced Roelof Smit to the Egyptian, then pulled a small package wrapped in brown paper from his pocket. He unwrapped it carefully, to reveal the chunk of rubble he had taken away from Umm as Hawwak two days before. "How soon can you analyze this for me, professor? It is, I believe, quite important."

Rezk took the rock from Chaudri's hand and squinted at it. "Concrete," he said simply. "Is that soon enough for you, my impatient friend?"

Chaudri rolled his eyes comically.

The professor pushed back the right sleeve of his lab coat and checked his watch. "I have a class in fifteen minutes," he said. "Second-year students. Hopeless cases, most of them, but they are trying. *Very* trying, much of the

time, I'm afraid. They visit with me for one hour. When they leave, I will
have time to apply myself to your intriguingly important mixture of cement,
mineral aggregate, and dihydrogen oxide. What, if I may ask, am I to analyze it *for?*"

"If I'm right," said Mahboob Chaudri cryptically, "you will know it
when you see it. May I phone you in, say, two hours?"

"Back to personnel?" Roelof Smit ventured, as they stepped off the elevator at the fifth floor of the tower in the al-Khalifa Road.

"Not this time," said Chaudri. "This time we are here to pay a call on
the purchasing department, where the late Mr. Ebezer Kwaja was employed
as a clerk."

The director of purchasing, Egbert Merkelijn, received them in the cub-
byhole that had been partitioned off in a corner of the large workroom to
provide him with a private office. The space was barely big enough for his
desk, two filing cabinets and the man himself: Merkelijn was no taller than
Mahboob Chaudri, but he weighed at least two hundred fifty pounds. His
tiny eyes were sunk deep in layers of fat; in spite of the air conditioning, his
puffy face was flushed and damp. He seemed broader than the entrance to
his cubicle, and Chaudri wondered if he was able to leave it at day's end, or
if the partitions had been erected around him and had trapped him there.

There was nowhere for Chaudri and Smit to sit, so they stood in front of
the desk and spoke down at him.

"Did you know Ebezer Kwaja?" Chaudri began.

"Yes, of course," the fat man rasped. "He worked here in my department."

"What can you tell us about him?"

"About Kwaja? He was quiet, he was respectful, he did his work efficiently."

"Then why was he fired?"

Merkelijn jutted out his lower lip and exhaled noisily through his nose.
"I don't know. I had no complaints. But the order came down from the
sixth floor: get rid of him."

"How long had he worked for you?" The question, this time, came from
Roelof Smit.

"*Ach, ja*—a year, perhaps a bit longer. I'd have to look it up."

"What was his job?" asked Chaudri.

"He processed purchase orders. When an order was submitted from any
of the other departments, it went to Kwaja. He countersigned it, and made
out an authorization for disbursal of the necessary funds."

"Would it be possible to see some samples of his work?"

Merkelijn grunted and swung ponderously around to the file cabinet
nearest him. He slid open a drawer, drew out a thick file folder, and laid it

on his desk. "That contains all the purchase orders we have handled so far this quarter," he said, "in chronological order with the most recent on top. You'll need to go back a few days before you reach the last of the ones that went through Kwaja."

Chaudri leafed quickly through a dozen or more sheets, most of which had been filed that morning by Nicolaas Sjollema, then slowed down and began to examine each page individually. "There are three signature lines," he commented. "The first signature is apparently that of the person requesting a purchase, then underneath that is Kwaja, and then comes the first signature again."

The fat man nodded. "That's right, verifying that the monies requested have been paid out—either directly to the supplier or, in some cases, to the person submitting the request for transfer to the supplier—and that the merchandise ordered has been delivered."

Chaudri turned farther, then found a sheet that interested him and paused to make a note. He continued in this way through the entire pile, glancing at most of the order forms cursorily, stopping occasionally to jot down a line on his pad. When he finished, he straightened up the papers and handed the file back to Merkelijn. "Yes," he said, "this seems to be in order. May I use your telephone?"

Egbert Merkelijn waved a bloated hand at the instrument, and Chaudri picked up the receiver and dialed the number of Gulf Polytechnic. He asked the operator for Emad Rezk, and waited patiently as the call was switched through. "Professor Rezk?" he said at last. "This is Mahboob Chaudri speaking. Have you had a chance to examine that specimen I brought you? . . . Yes? . . . Yes? . . . Yes, that's exactly what I expected. And what would the consequences of that be? . . . Can you estimate how long that process would take? . . . About five years, you think, or perhaps a bit more or less. . . . Yes, I see. Very well then, professor, I thank you for your time. . . . No, no, thank *you*." He cradled the phone.

"Well?" said Smit, recognizing the grim satisfaction etched across Chaudri's face. "What did he tell you?"

"He told me why the causeway had to be destroyed, and why Ebezer Kwaja had to be silenced," Mahboob Chaudri replied. "And he told me who it was who committed both of those crimes."

Hendrik Hofstra and Nicolaas Sjollema were huddled over Hofstra's model of the causeway when Chaudri and Smit walked into the office without knocking.

The director was furious. "What's the meaning of this?" he demanded. "This is a private office, Mr. Chaudri. You can't just barge in here unannounced like that!"

"*Rustig aan,* Dirck," Sjollema soothed him. "They wouldn't have done it if it weren't urgent. Would you like me to leave, officer?"

"I'd rather you stayed," said Chaudri. "What I have to say concerns you, too. Sit down, gentlemen—this may take some time."

Hofstra growled under his breath, but he did not argue. The four men settled themselves into comfortable armchairs, and the Dutchmen turned expectantly to Chaudri.

"First," he began, "a question. Mr. Hofstra, you personally ordered the dismissal of Ebezer Kwaja from your purchasing department on December second, just under a week ago. Why did you issue that order?"

"I—" The director glanced quickly at Nicolaas Sjollema, then turned back to Chaudri. "My reasons have no bearing on your investigation," he said gruffly.

"Your reasons, if you will excuse my saying so, do not *exist,*" Chaudri corrected him. "You gave the order to get rid of Kwaja, true, but I suggest that you did so at the instigation of someone else. Kwaja knew who was truly responsible for his dismissal: the 'big man,' he told us, 'from the distant Netherlands.' He said that the big man had fired him because he—Kwaja—knew too much about the big man's baby. We assumed that he was speaking figuratively when he said the words 'big man,' and that he was speaking literally when he referred to the big man's baby: the big man, we thought, was the big boss—you, Mr. Hofstra—and the baby was your son Pieter."

"My son was not a baby," Hofstra objected. "He was six years old, almost seven."

"Exactly. Ebezer Kwaja was speaking *figuratively* when he used the word 'baby.' He was not referring to the death of your child. But he spoke *literally* when he said that a 'big man' had fired him. And you, Mr. Hofstra, are hardly big.

"Who, then, was the big man who convinced you to dismiss Ebezer Kwaja, for reasons that were clear to the Indian if not to you? Who was the big man whose 'baby' Kwaja knew too much about? Who was the big man who killed him in order to keep him from telling us what he knew?" Chaudri paused for a moment, observing Hofstra closely. Then he went on: "You do not look surprised, Mr. Hofstra, to hear that Ebezer Kwaja is dead."

The director's aggressiveness seemed to have melted away from him, leaving him tentative, confused. "No," he said, "I—I'm not surprised. Nick told me, shortly before you burst in here."

"Ah," Chaudri nodded, "now that is very curious. Because Kwaja's murder has not been mentioned on the radio news, or on television, or in this morning's paper. Which leads me to wonder, Mr. Sjollema, how you could possibly have known about the killing? Unless, of course, you were there at the Central Market when it happened. Unless, in fact, you murdered Ebezer Kwaja yourself."

Nicolaas Sjollema eyed him narrowly. "You're crazy," he said. "I barely knew the man. What possible reason could I have had for shooting him?"

"*Shooting* him, Mr. Sjollema? Oh, dearie me, and I am *quite* certain I never mentioned that Mr. Kwaja had been shot. 'Killed,' I said, and 'murdered,' but never 'shot.' "

"Nick," Hendrik Hofstra said angrily, "what is all this? What's he trying to say?"

"I am not *trying* to say anything, sir," Chaudri told him. "I am *saying* that your foreman, Nicolaas Sjollema, shot and killed Ebezer Kwaja at the Central Market early yesterday afternoon."

"But why, dammit? *Why?*"

Chaudri sighed. "Kwaja told us that as well, though I am afraid we didn't understand him at first. He said that he had been fired because he knew too much. 'About what?' I asked him. 'About his baby,' he replied, speaking figuratively. 'About the—' And then the shot was fired, and he gasped the word 'water' twice, and died. We thought that, in his final moments, he was asking for something to drink. He was not. He was finishing his sentence. 'About the water,' he was saying. He was fired because he knew too much about the water."

"I still don't understand," said Roelof Smit. "What *about* the water?"

Chaudri ticked the points off on his fingers. "The Qatar causeway is made of concrete. Concrete is mixed with water, pure water—in Bahrain, with *sweet* water. Nicolaas Sjollema needed money—or wanted money—and he saw a way to amass quite a bit of it. He ordered sweet water for the project, ordered it frequently and in large quantities—I have the dates and amounts right here." He patted the pocket of his uniform shirt. "But he built the Umm as Hawwak section of the bridge with ordinary tap water, and kept the money he was to have paid out for the sweet water for himself."

Sjollema sat there, impassive, motionless, silent.

"Then things began to go wrong. A few weeks ago, a Korean laborer named Kim Lee Kwan stole a jug of Mr. Sjollema's tap water from the site, but Mr. Sjollema caught him in the act. Perhaps Kim tasted the water, and realized that there was a swindle going on. Perhaps he never had the chance: Mr. Sjollema had him on a flight out of Bahrain that very same day. For a while, he must have felt safe again. Then Ebezer Kwaja became suspicious. The Indian was not under Mr. Sjollema's supervision, so Mr. Sjollema could not get rid of him directly, but he went to you, Mr. Hofstra, with some vague, trumped-up story—"

"He said he'd heard the man was working out a method of siphoning money away from the company." Hofstra filled in the details dully. "He had no evidence, so I couldn't come out and make a direct accusation. But since it was Nick, I—I believed him. And I had personnel let him—Kwaja—go."

Chaudri drew a breath and went on. "Mr. Sjollema expected that the Indian would be deported, as was Kim Lee Kwan. He hadn't counted on Kwaja's having a cousin here who would take over sponsorship of his visa. And, meanwhile, he realized that the Umm as Hawwak section of the bridge would have to be destroyed. Made of concrete mixed with brackish tap water, he knew that it would last only a few years, perhaps half a decade. Then it would collapse—there would probably be loss of life, there would *certainly* be an investigation, and the truth would be discovered. No, it was better to sneak back out to the islet late at night on the fourth of December, after work, and to set the charges that would rip the structure apart on Sinterklaas, while Sjollema himself was in full view of dozens of impeccable witnesses."

At last the accused man stirred.

"You have no proof," he said. His voice was flat, emotionless.

"I have your signatures on the purchase orders," Chaudri replied, "requesting the purchase of thousands of liters of sweet water. And I have Ebezer Kwaja's signatures, authorizing the monies to be paid to you, rather than directly to a supplier. Which, of course, is why you finally decided that you had to kill him: so he would never reveal what he suspected about your bridge—your 'baby'—and about your phony purchase of sweet water. Then I have your signatures again, confirming that the sweet water Nederbild paid for was in fact delivered."

"It *was* delivered," Sjollema snarled. "I ordered sweet water, I paid for sweet water, I *got* sweet water, and I built that roadbed with nothing but pure sweet water. And you can't prove otherwise, Mr. Chaudri: after the explosion, I had my crew dump every last bit of rubble so far out to sea that you'll *never* be able to find it."

"A clever move," Chaudri admitted. "But what you do not know, my clever Mr. Sjollema, is that I happened to pick up a small piece of concrete debris when I was out at Umm as Hawwak that day, after you and Lieutenant Smit went back to the fishing dhow. I had it analyzed this morning. And according to that analysis—"

But there was no need for Chaudri to continue. Nicolaas Sjollema put his head in his hands and began to sob.

At Roelof Smit's insistence, they had dinner that night at Mansouri Mansions, where it was possible to eat a Western meal and drink large mugs of foaming Dutch beer.

"So the analysis showed that the concrete *had* been mixed with tap water," Smit said, wiping suds from his bushy walrus mustache contentedly, "which was enough to prove Sjollema a crook even without his confession. But there's one thing I still don't understand. Right after the explosion, when we rushed out of the messhall to the beach, Nicolaas Sjollema was standing there crying, and he was crying real tears. Was he so upset about the destruction of his bridge, even though he'd blown it up himself?"

Chaudri shook his head. "Mr. Sjollema stopped caring about the causeway the day he began building it with worthless concrete. It was not his baby when he killed it, not any more."

"Then why the tears?" Smit frowned.

Chaudri picked up his hamburger and bit into it hungrily. "You know quite a lot about police work, lieutenant," he said, "but you must learn to pay more attention to human beings. Mr. Sjollema planned the blast for a day when no one would be working out at Umm as Hawwak, a day when he could devastate the bridge without hurting any people. Yet he needed to ensure that the contaminated section of the structure would be completely destroyed, so he used a very large amount of explosive. Much more, as it turned out, than was needed."

"You mean—?" Smit's face cleared.

"The children," Mahboob Chaudri nodded. "Sinterklaas cried because he hadn't meant to hurt the children."

# THE WELLMASTER'S DAUGHTER

*By James S. Dorr*

Touila . . . toufourine . . . Oum el Asel. From there, six days'
journey to Bir Ounane. And who am I, who camp in this wadi,
surrounded by the stinking corpses of camels? I am the master of
Bir Ounane.

From there, five parched days more to El Mraiti. These are the links that
hold the caravan routes together—the wells in the desert within the Great
Desert. These are the pearls that Allah has cast in the midst of the furnace,
lest men should come to forget His mercy.

I am but a man—a just man, I think. Yet a man who has lived his whole
life in the desert.

I have no mercy.

I had a daughter whose name was Zumur'rad, the Jewel of the Desert. I
named her myself and, after my wife died, I raised her alone at Bir Ounane.
I taught her the values of the oasis and of the desert: about the camel trains
that came to us and why, when spring's briefness gave way to summer, most
ceased their travel. About Allah's grace that made me a wellmaster, serving
at the Caid's pleasure, and made her my daughter.

And always she would have me say more.

"Tell me, Ab'sahib"—Lord and Father—"about the sands of the Erg
Sekkane," she would ask as we sat in the evening, washed in the final light

of the sun. "Tell me about the crescent sands, and how they strive to mount even the rock cliffs until all is covered. Tell me as well of the great star dunes, and how they rise to reach the height of two hundred men." We would listen awhile to the faroff wind, and I would then tell her about the djinn of the trackless desert, away from even the caravan routings, and how they pleased Allah as I in turn pleased my earthly master, I by doling out water to travelers and they by proclaiming the Lord of All's might.

"And tell me," she would ask yet again, "about the wadis. Tell me about the phantom rain." And again we would listen and I would explain why the desert grows hot—so hot in summer that when storm clouds come, such rain as they carry boils back to the sky before reaching its surface. And how the wadis—the burnt remains of what once had been rivers—thus stay bone dry until a second cloud follows the first, discharging *its* water onto a ground that, even if thirstier now than before, at least has been cooled enough to receive it.

And so we would often continue to sit the entire night through, I speaking, she learning, beneath patterned stars so bright one could touch them.

We spent our time that way until her twelfth spring.

I have met the Caid. He has a palace near the ocean which he departs from only twice every fourteen years. On one of these journeys he visits his cities along the rivers and by the sea, making sure they are garrisoned strongly, while on the other he enters the desert.

On this second journey, seven years after the first is completed, he visits the wells. He checks to be sure that his commerce is flowing—to see with his own eyes that what his soldiers, who visit the wells every two or three seasons, have told him is true. It is on this journey that he makes sure that tools and seed, and fresh, healthy camels, and such other things the wellmasters need to tend their oases are being supplied. It was on this journey that he met me.

My daughter had scarcely known five springs when the Caid arrived at Bir Ounane. She does not remember the way he greeted me like a friend. The way he confirmed me as his wellmaster and later, as we drank tea together, told me that when he arrived again, in fourteen more years, he would see that Zumur'rad had a husband.

She does not remember the way we spoke of many things in the perfumed shade of the Caid's pavilion. And so she would ask me, when she became twelve:

"Sahib," she would say, "tell me about the Caid's palace beyond the desert. Tell me about the cities he visits, and what the ocean is like that he lives by."

And I would tell her what he told me, about the djinn of the ground and the water. I would explain how, in parts of the world, the water lies beneath rock and sand—as it does in our desert—but yet, in other parts, through Allah's mercy, these djinn change position.

"And this is what the Caid called the ocean?" she would ask further. "This changing position. How can such things be?"

"For Allah," I would say, "it is as easy as blinking one's eye." I would have her be silent and we would listen to the earth's murmur beneath the sand, and then I would tell her how rivers of water flowed under the ground, to feed wells such as ours. But elsewhere, such rivers flowed on the surface, and fed not wells, but vast basins of water that stretched as far as man could see.

I would repeat what the Caid had told me, about dunelike waves that moved through the water, about dustlike ripples that washed on the shore. I would tell of the storms, when the djinn of the air fought those of the water, and how they were feared more than even the storms we knew in the desert—the storms where sand would sweep up to the sky and the sun's face would blacken. And she would weep then.

"Tell me not about storms on the desert," she would say, "nor about an ocean that frightens me more. Tell me instead about the gardens. The cities where the caravans come from and where they go. Tell me about the things of beauty."

At those times I would wipe Zumur'rad's tears away on the hem of my own sleeve. I would then describe, in a gentle voice, how the caravan routes came out of the desert into a land filled with trees and flowers, no matter what season. How birds would sing when the camel drivers arrived at a river, and how that river would flow to the ocean, its waters sweeter than even the honey the caravans' merchants sometimes gave to her when they passed by us. I would describe to her how, where the water was at its sweetest, men built vast cities of emeralds and gold; and how they built palaces out of marble as white as milk, with roofs and domes and turrets so thick the sun couldn't reach through; and how the air within these great halls was at all times as cool as the water of Bir Ounane in the first days of springtime.

Zumur'rad would smile then.

By Allah's grace, the world lies in layers. Layers of sand over layers of water. Layers of heat. Even the phantom rain is a layer—a layer of promise above the dry desert. A promise fulfilled with the second rain.

And so, in this wadi, I bury my camels beneath the sand. I have little strength—my leg has been wounded and even now festers—but I do not have to bury them deeply. A hand's-breadth or two beneath the surface, the ground is cool enough for insects and worms to burrow. A hand's-breadth of sand sprinkled over the corpses protects from the sun.

I work on my knees. When my work is completed, I dig a trench, also, to fit my own body. A place I can lie in relative coolness, conserving the moisture that keeps me alive.

By Allah's grace, thus might I endure forever.

I think about layers—how even a child's growth is patterned in layers. How even trade changes. When Zumur'rad reached her fifteenth spring, the nature of the goods that came by us was different from what it had been in past years.

Where once the caravans had carried iron tools from the north, and brought back ivory and spices, many now carried weapons for trading and brought back slaves. And these were larger than most camel trains. As well as the camel and caravan-masters, the boys—apprentices—who swept dung for the evening fires, the cargomaster when one was needed, the slavers' caravans also had guards.

In part for this reason, the slavers were shunned by those who knew more of the ways of the desert. In part they were shunned because slaving is evil—because Allah punishes those who would deal in their fellow men. And yet they continued.

So worried was I about these changes I did not realize that the nature of Zumur'rad's questions had changed as well.

This time she asked: "Why is slaving evil? Why, if the slavers gain riches from it, do others insist that Allah disdains it?" And I tried to tell her about men's suffering, and death in the desert. About the maltreatment of human cargo by men who sought too great and too fast a profit.

I tried to explain this by telling her stories—unpleasant stories—of Allah's wrath. Of one caravan, in ancient times when they carried slaves, too, that was led by inexperienced masters into a sandstorm, cargo and all; and how, unlike the storms of the Caid's ocean, this storm sucked it dry. How it stands to this day in the Erg Iguidi, beyond the well of Oum el Asel, as a silent warning, its camels and slaves and guards and drivers all turned into statues. Their flesh hard as stone.

And I told her that these were the fortunate ones—in Allah's mercy, their deaths were at least swift. That there were other caravans whose masters allowed their camels to sicken until, still days from the nearest well, they could go no farther . . .

And she interrupted. "Tell me not about death," she said, "but about those who live to enjoy the riches they gain from such cargo. Tell me about the things they buy, the places they live, when they have enough wealth, far away from the desert."

I looked at her when she asked these questions, and saw, for the first time, how much she had grown. I tried to explain how Allah punishes, in the long run, *all* who traffic in evil. She would not listen.

"Tell me," she demanded instead, "why the Caid wishes to stop the slave trade." I had no answer—I had not known.

I asked her how she had heard such things and she answered with yet another question.

"Tell me about men."

Spring had ended. Summer was on us and, because of the heat of the season, all caravans had ceased their travel. And so I told Zumur'rad about men.

I told her of the Caid's promise and how, if she would be patient for only a few years more, a man would be found who would be worthy of her. She would have a husband, and I a partner to help in my old age. And yet she defied me.

"I will not wait for your Caid's man," she said when I had finished speaking. "I have gotten a lover already. His name is Bes'fariq and he is the leader of one of the largest slave caravans—it was he who told me about the Caid. And when we are married, unlike the man *you* would choose for my husband, he will not force me to stay in the desert."

Spring had ended. The wind had shifted, the burning wind from the south combating the final remnants of air from the north—from the Caid's ocean. This was the time when such clouds that were seen—high, mist-like wraiths above the Hamada, the rock-crowned plateau that separates the Erg Sekkane from Oum el Asel—produced sudden downpours but no lasting rain. When the true water that comes to the desert, through layered rock underneath the dry courses of ancient rivers, had slowed to a trickle.

This was the time when even the sparse green jewels of Allah—the wells that break through the desert's surface—have seen the grass that surrounds them turn yellow, the flowers die, and the trees fold their leaves, and so there was little that I could do but pray that one of the Caid's supply trains would come in the fall. I would then send Zumur'rad north to his palace in hopes he could find her a husband right then—even a husband who would not wish to apprentice himself to me at Bir Ounane. But there were no caravans that fall, nor during the winter or early spring of the following year.

Until, finally, Zumur'rad was sixteen.

Again, spring was ending. Again the winds battled when, out of the north, from Oum el Asel, a caravan came. Zumur'rad ran out with a dipper of water to the lead camel, offering it to the rider who swung down. The water consumed, the rider took Zumur'rad into his arms and kissed her as if they had been long married, then brought her back to me.

"Old man," he said, "my name is Bes'fariq. You may as well know that I deal in slaves."

"I have seen you before," I answered. "In past years I have given you water—that is my job. But it is not too late in the season for seeking slaves? Or do you intend to spend the whole summer south of the desert, and bring your cargo back in the fall?"

The rider turned and conversed with Zumur'rad, speaking in whispers, then motioned to his fellows to dismount. "It is late in the evening, old man," he finally said when he turned back to me. "My men are thirsty and need to be fed. We will leave in the morning."

"To spend the whole summer south of the desert?" I asked again. I looked at my daughter, pressed close to his side, and purposely spoke in mocking tones. "Slavers spend weeks to gather their cargoes—even such prosperous slavers as you—and by then it would be too hot to cross back with such a burden . . ."

"Not to spend the summer, old man," Bes'fariq said, his voice rising in anger. "Nor to seek slaves—at least not for this journey." He paused and twisted again for a moment, to ask a question of one of his men, and Zumur'rad continued.

"There has been a war," she said—she did not call me Lord and Father. "Your Caid attempted to put down the slavers, and they have revolted. Bes'fariq goes south to join an army that's already gathered at El Mraiti, to bring it back north . . ."

"To bring it back north, with the first heat of summer, and push the Caid into the ocean," Bes'fariq added, again at her side. "We will ride on the edge of the wind, old man. At the very end of the caravan season, stopping only to refill our waterskins, in order to strike when we're least expected." He lowered his gaze and looked at Zumur'rad, then back to me.

"And she will ride with us."

"No!" I shouted. I pushed myself between him and my daughter. Grappled with him. Saw—from the corner of an eye—the hot flash of metal.

I twisted and lunged—felt pain sear my thigh.

And looked at my daughter. Saw how she had stabbed me.

*I had no daughter.*

I looked at the knife. Looked up at Zumur'rad from where I had fallen.

Watched as the blood—the water and flesh that had bound us together—dripped from her hand.

I wake in the desert, stiff in my trench, my nostrils filled with the odor of half-rotted camels—the three already sickened camels Bes'fariq gave me. I heard him talking when I woke *that* morning at Bir Ounane, discussing the camels with the man he had questioned before. I woke in the hut where I keep summer fodder for my own beasts and heard Zumur'rad join their conversation. It was she who suggested the camels be given to me.

"He fears the desert," she told Bes'fariq. "He fears the slow dying.

Therefore, let him ride one of these as far as it takes him. Let him have the others as well. You have no need for them."

"That is true," her lover replied. "The ones we have gotten at Oum el Asel, plus the ones we have here, will be more than sufficient. But what if he does not go into the desert? What if he stays here, where there is at least water?"

It was Zumur'rad who kicked the door open and looked down at me where I lay on the ground. She inspected the wound she had given me the night before, looked approvingly at the signs that it had already begun to fester.

She nodded and turned back to Bes'fariq. "Give him a shovel before he sets off—he has several here that he uses to clear the well after sandstorms. Give him a choice. He may go into the desert and dig his own grave, or, if he stays here . . ."

Bes'fariq cut her off with a laugh. "Or, if he stays here," he finished for her, "I will kill him when we return, more slowly than even the desert might kill him, and cut his body into pieces. I will then strew them across the desert, so widely that not even Allah will find them to bring them to heaven. If that is your meaning, then you *are* worthy of me, Zumur'rad."

I raised my head. "You would desecrate my corpse?" I asked. "What kind of man are you?"

"Then you have heard what we said, old man—you know what is expected. As for me, I am a strong man. A man who takes from wellmasters like you. Do you understand me?"

"You have taken from *other* wellmasters?" I whispered my horror. *"You would blaspheme Allah by raiding His gardens . . ."*

"You do understand me. We leave as soon as our camels are saddled. In five days' time we will reach El Mraiti and join with my army. We will rest one day, then make our return, arriving back here on the eleventh day after this morning. Do you see those clouds?"

I looked out the hut's door to where he pointed and saw wisps of cloud high above to the north. Empty clouds, but when one sees the first whiteness, he always hopes that others may follow. I did not speak but only nodded.

"Good," he said. "Those clouds will have long disappeared when eleven days have passed. You will be like those clouds—do you understand me?"

I nodded again. "You will leave water bags and food—my knife and my clothing—along with a shovel and three dying camels. Enough to allow me to get as far, perhaps, as the Hamada before the beasts perish."

"You do understand me," he said as before. He smiled and put his arm around Zumur'rad's waist, and led her outside to where his men waited.

\* \* \*

Ten mornings ago I left Bir Ounane. In two days' time I reached this wadi and slaughtered my camels, then made my camp. I buried my camels, the better to let their flesh grow putrescent. Away from the drying rays of the sun.

I dug my own grave.

I lie in it this morning, the stench of my camels assailing my nostrils. It vies with the rot of my own wounded leg, a rot that has long since spread itself into the rest of my body. I lie and wait, gazing north toward the Hamada, where new wisps are forming.

I think about layers. And second rains.

The phantom rain already fell this morning, boiling the stench and the rot into steam. The morning before Bes'fariq's army is due to return, weak with thirst from its own desert journey.

I think about layers—I dreamed of my daughter last night while I slept.

Except I have no daughter.

I look at the sky.

And the second rain hisses above the Hamada—it ends in moments, but this time the ground has been cooled to receive it. To let it puddle and gather and swirl on the rocky plateau. To spill into the wadi . . .

I hear a humming, still far in the distance—the sound that water makes moving on sand. A trickle, a flood, that will take my life's spirit—the rot of my body, the stench of my camels, the poison and death that Zumur'rad left to me.

And give it all unto the thirsty djinn who, by Allah's grace, lie under the wadi, jealously guarding the ancient course that feeds the well of Bir Ounane.

# RUSSIA

# A Dacha To Die In

### By *Anthony Olcott*

L ook, i just told you, Anatolii Markovich categorically forbids *any-body* to see him before a broadcast, and besides, you shouldn't even be in here, this area is just for camera crews and electricians."

I didn't have to ask him how he'd gotten to the sound stage; the packet of fifties he was slapping gently against his left palm pretty much answered the question. Still wrapped with the bands from the savings bank, that neat little bundle would have twenty bills in it. A thousand rubles. About what my invalid's pension will come to between now and November seventh, assuming, of course, that the bills in the middle aren't just cut newspaper. The gamblers call these bundles "bricks," but they might as well call them keys because there aren't many doors that one of them won't open.

Especially for a man like this, who had the shearling coat, tanned and polished skin, Turkish coffee eyes, and sculpted mustache of a Central Asian boss visiting Moscow. Nobody ever knows who the devil these types are, but they have that air about them, like they haven't heard the word *no* since maybe they were four. Whether they are Mafia or Party, you can never tell, so people just do what they ask and stuff the rubles in their pockets. "Please, it's terribly important," he said, not raising his voice but swiftly adding a second "brick" to the first. "Anatolii Markovich phoned that I should meet him here, it is very urgent, please, put yourself in my place, it's . . ."

His Russian was good. Too good, with that slight precision of enuncia-
tion and absolute grammatical correctness that tells you he got his tongue
behind the school desk, not at his mama's knee. More important, I was
pretty sure I had him tagged; the accent suggested he was Tadzhik.

"A thousand pardons, learned friend, but you have erred, in the best of
intentions I am sure. Anatolii Markovich never speaks on the telephone. It
interferes with his magnometry." I made an exaggerated eastern bow, hoping that would distract his attention from any grammar mistakes I might
have made.

"You know Persian?" He looked surprised and focused on me; I was
suddenly a person, not just another Russian between him and what he
wanted. Which is why I had done it, of course.

"Three years in Afghanistan was a good teacher." I smiled sparely, then
grabbed my left stump with my right hand, which is the closest I can come
to crossing my arms.

The man studied me, his eyes like two puddles of motor oil. After a
moment he said softly, still in Persian, "Many were there, but not many
learned the language."

I shrugged, smiled. Further questions were not welcome. I grew up in a
military household, listening to fat old men refight the Great Fatherland
War, so I'm damned if I'll explain about the Blue Berets to anybody, and as
for the bearded old wormwood root of an *aksakal* that I was trying to bring
back from forward recon even though there were orders not to take any
more *dushmen* prisoners . . . well, him I can't explain even to myself. I felt
sorry for him, I suppose, until he pulled his rusty, dung-smeared blade out
of his turban. Dima Bychok, who was in front, got one in the lungs that
took three weeks to send him home sewn up in a "black tulip," and I got
one in the arm when the old man swung around. I was lucky; it only cost
me my left arm. And my commission because I had disobeyed orders.
Which meant the best they would give me was a Category II invalid pension, a hundred and twenty-seven rubles a month.

The newspapers, the television, and all the experts are saying the problem
with our economy is that there are too many rubles and nothing to buy
with them. None of those people live on a hundred twenty-seven rubles a
month; if they did, they'd know there are lots of things to buy that a
hundred and twenty-seven rubles won't cover. Food, clothes, those sorts of
things.

Which is why I guess I'm glad that the cosmic vibrations or whatever it is
he listens to told Anatolii Markovich that he should be nice to us vets from
the 'Stan.

God knows where Anatolii Markovich sprang from. Eighteen months
ago, the great A. M. was running fat clinics in the basement of a workers'

club in Kiev, making Ukrainian whales think they were getting thinner. There are a lot of fat people in this country, and I suppose word got out, because now here we are. A. M. doesn't do fat any more, or at least not just fat; maybe Gorbachev is better known than A. M., but it would be a close count, and I know for sure that while A. M. never quotes Gorbachev, the opposite is not true. Especially since A. M. got his regular television show. An hour on the Moscow First Program, every Sunday evening.

The first half is testimonials, people famous and unknown thanking the great A. M. for what his hypnosis has done for them. A. M. makes hair grow back, he unparalyzes legs, he cuts blood pressure in half. The reason A. M. gets two hundred million viewers every Sunday, though, is the second half of the program, when he upcues the background music, the camera tight-focuses on his unblinking head, and then A. M. hypnotizes you, right over the TV set.

A few learned types complain that A. M. is dangerous, that his trances have set off epileptic fits and that people get so carried away that they thrash around. Nobody's even figured out the main danger, though, which is that some Sunday night when A. M. is feeling more herring than vinegar he's going to tell all his hypnotized listeners to wake up and hail their new tsar.

And why not? Grisha Rasputin only cured hemophilia. Anatolii Markovich cures everything from bad breath to cancer.

Which is why, unless he forgets, A. M. gives me two hundred rubles every Sunday, cash, to be the last guard dog between him and his slavering public. Two hundred rubles is about what A. M. is paying for a pair of socks nowadays, but if A. M. paid me more, I might have to believe in him; as it is, all he wants is that I keep those who do believe out of his dressing room, and that I don't call him A. M. to his face.

So what I mean is, this Tadzhik wasn't the first one I'd ever thrown off the sound stage. One thing Russia isn't short of is important people, used to throwing their weight around. I've been threatened and bribed and even . . . well, one time this girl . . . she was a little taller than me, with long straight blonde hair, blue eyes, cheekbones . . . what I mean is, the sort of body and face that guys like me never even get to *see* close up because girls that beautiful never have to ride a bus. . . . Anyway, she asked to go in, I said no, and she just unzipped her skirt and started peeling off her sweater, right there, in the middle of the mike booms and camera dollies and cables and stagehands.

The Tadzhik was the first one who ever fainted, though.

Four cups of tea and half a pack of his cigarettes later, most of which I smoked, I had a little better idea why Rakhman had collapsed and still looked like what's left after somebody had used him to make juice. What I didn't understand was why he had thought A. M. could help.

So far, anyway, A. M. just heals people, not resurrects them from the dead.

"I understand that now," Rakhman said wearily, cupping his tea like some catastrophe survivor, "but I am desperate, and when people spoke of the miracles this Anatolii Markovich works . . ." he shrugged. "You understand, my sister Shakhira would *never* have done what the militia say, *never*. She is not some Turkomen peasant woman, to set herself on fire. She was educated, a modern woman. She was in Moscow to address the Committee on Women, and people were speaking of her as a candidate for People's Deputy in the republic legislature, in the elections next spring. It would be an *unthinkable* scandal. . . . Our family," Rakhman looked up, his gaze searching my face to be certain that I fully understood the significance of his words, "is quite prominent."

I nodded, even though "prominent" is a pretty pale description for any offspring of Sharif Sadriddin, Hero of the Revolution and Founder of Modern Soviet Tadzhik Literature; "co-owners of the republic" would give you more of the flavor of the status of Rakhman's family. So why couldn't Rakhman get anyone in Moscow to share his conviction that Shakhira's death couldn't have been suicide?

In the first place . . . "Ever since that damned article in that damned *Ogonyok*, any Central Asian woman who dies in a fire anywhere, everybody in Moscow tsk-tsks about barbaric Central Asian traditions and says we should improve our social conditions so women won't immolate themselves any more," Rakhman repeated, his face ashen with fury.

And in the second place, he hadn't told everyone in Moscow. In fact, he'd told almost no one because, as nearly as I could make out between what he was telling me and what he wasn't, Rakhman was almost as afraid of the scandal if Shakhira hadn't committed suicide as he was if she had.

Whichever it was, though, Rakhman's hands trembled as we talked, scattering cigarette ash onto the already filthy floor; he had to know soon, before the affair rose high enough to get sucked into the Ministry of Justice. Shakhira had died on Thursday, today was Sunday; even Soviet justice would start functioning soon. Rakhman was a desperate man, so desperate he asked for my help. So desperate even I agreed to give it.

By the time I finally located what was left of the dacha Shakhira had died in, I was wondering when I would learn to keep my mouth shut, because I could see that getting what Rakhman wanted was not going to be like Saturday morning in the steam bath. Her grandfather's status gave Shakhira access to the writers' colony at Peredelkino, but not to any of the dachas that look like *December* in some calendar that they sell to tourists, for dollars; what Shakhira had gotten the use of was one of five identical two room cabins just off the access road from the nearby village, where the groceries came in and the garbage out.

Now they were four houses, with char between numbers one and three and crumbly black spars jutting through the fresh white snow. The new snow covered but didn't conceal the well-stomped paths that the firemen and militia men had trod around the burning house, which only made more obvious that the snow around the surviving houses was completely undisturbed. So much for what the neighbors would tell me.

And I'd been two hours on the suburban train, and forty-five minutes floundering through wet snow. . . .

So I figured I might as well poke through the debris with a long birch twig I found. Not that there was anything else to find. How much can a two room cabin hold? The bedspring, charred stuffing hanging through the mesh; the skeleton of an armchair; the kitchen pump, still dangling a drip bucket. All of it covered in about three centimeters of fluffy white snow, which only made the charred bits of wood, the candle stubs and twisted lumps of metal, the jagged green bits of a broken jar that my stick churned up, seem even more dismal.

"You're too late," someone said behind me. "The only thing worth taking was the television, and that's gone."

A big solid militia man, the sort you'd expect to be guarding an important place like the writers' colony, if I'd had the good sense to expect anyone.

I floundered back out of the mucky debris, formulating lies, but then the militia man surprised me by offering his grey-sleeved, leather-gloved hand, which, after a moment's hesitation, I took.

"There was a television?" I asked coolly when I was standing next to him, my nose even with his epaulets.

"And a video player, too." He pointed his big chin towards the remnants of the chair. "Wouldn't do you any good, though, even if they were still here. Melted, you might say. When were you there?"

"There?"

"In the 'Stan." He clapped me on the shoulder. "That's where you donated your wing, wasn't it? I was a dirt-eater outside of Herat, myself."

As nearly as I can figure it, this fraternity of Afghan vets is sort of like how you never notice how many one-armed guys there are until you become one yourself. Then you notice each other, just the way us vets always seem to recognize each other, even those that managed to come home with all the parts they came out of mama with. I suppose it's because you couldn't sleep too many nights under those big, dusty Afghan stars before one of your pals took in more lead than was good for him, or you happened to catch the look in some kid's eyes as you set fire to his house, or your political officer gave you one too many lectures about Socialist Fraternity and Internationalist Duty. After that, just like maple leaves in a hard early frost, your soul curls up into a delicate brown tissue. Each of us senses that in the other, that fragile remnant, quivering on its stem in the chilly wind.

Which meant at least that my new pal didn't need much convincing to drive me back to the train station instead of to the militia holding pen.

We rumbled back through the yellow trunks of the enormous pines, Sasha all red-apple cheeks and splayed horsey teeth as he twiddled the gears of the four-wheel drive Niva in and out, bitching loudly about the pig's breakfast his boss usually made of his job. "Supposedly Pustyshkin got his job through Churbanov," Sasha confided, downshifting violently to slew us sideways through a wallow of ice and mud. Churbanov was Brezhnev's son-in-law, once number two at the Ministry of Justice, now doing eight years for pocketing better than a million in bribes. "That's why, most times, digging through one of his crime sites wouldn't be such a bad bet."

"This time was different?"

No fool, Sasha sensed my excitement but didn't know what to make of it. "The husband is Somebody, I guess. Yesterday there was a man brought an order, crate everything, and on the hop!" Unexpectedly, Sasha smiled, a dimple deep enough to eat kasha from suddenly blossoming on his cheek. "You should have seen the inspector when he got to the signature at the bottom. No less than Comrade Bakatin's first secretary." Taking both hands off the wheel, Sasha showed me how the inspector had begun to tremble on reading an order from someone so close to the Minister of Justice. He grabbed the wheel just before we hit an oak. "Whoever he is, the husband, he wanted supervision while the debris was boxed, so the inspector went up himself. Even helped hammer the lid down, or so he says."

"Where did they sent it?"

Instead of answering, Sasha jerked his thumb over his shoulder, meaning south, Vnukovo Airport, or even Dushanbe.

"Any idea why the hurry?"

"The jewelry, most likely . . . after all, that's what you're out here looking for, isn't it?"

"Jewelry? There was jewelry?" I was stunned at my own stupidity. Central Asians don't trust banks; they prefer gold. And if anyone knew that Shakhira was out here, an isolated cabin, a woman alone. . . . "Wait a minute, what do you mean that's why I'm here?"

Sasha made a clicking noise with the side of his mouth and jerked his head in the direction of my missing arm. "It's not like they ever gave you value for that, is it? So if you want to undertake a bit of individual economic initiative, can't say it's my business, really, as long as it's not my eggs they'll be boiling." A superstitious grab at his crotch clarified the eggs he meant. "The jewelry, though, that was on a list."

"The husband sent a *list?*"

"And I'd say our local Poirot found everything on it," Sasha pulled the Niva to an abrupt halt at the platform of the Peredelkino *elektrichka* stop, "or else he'd never have gone back to his tea and blintzes as cheerfully as he did."

The tracks were empty, but enough people were standing around the northbound side that I knew my wait couldn't be long; I decided to take advantage of this Sasha's good humor. "This fire, who reported it?"

I tried to let my voice tell Sasha that I had a right to ask the question and he had no right to inquire what that right was. After a glance up and down the line, he said, "The widow Voolfson . . . you ever read Voolfson's stories when you were a kid? He wrote under the name Volkov . . . *Red Kerchieves, White Birch, and Black Shirts,* that's one I remember, about the war and these Komsomol partisans. Absolute nonsense, but it seemed exciting when I was seven. . . ." As he talked, he was studying me, sizing me up. "Anyway, she lives on the other side of that little ridge that runs along the road there, year-round. Almost crippled now, depends on some friends from the city. But she's lived here so long that she notices things, like that there was more light than there should have been, over the trees. She watched for a while . . . thought it was the moon coming up, she said . . . but then she called us. All it really required was the fire truck, but we came along, too, Pustyshkin and me . . . not a lot happens out here, bit quieter than pacifying *dushmen,* you know?" He smiled that complicated grin of a man who has chosen a soft and quiet post, which every now and then he regrets. I brushed it aside.

"And . . ."

"Those new huts, so much material got stolen from the construction sites it's like they ended up made mostly out of sprats tins or something. Should have been, in fact, they'd have burned a bit slower. By the time we got up there, there was nothing but some sparks and a little smoke, and her. . . ." Sasha for a second got that faraway look soldiers get when they think about dead people. He sniffed wryly. "Of course, hard to tell it was a her, sitting on what was left of an armchair, staring at this lump of melted plastic. She was so dried out you'd have thought it was some sort of sculpture at first, like out of wire or something. Maybe that sounds weird, but you don't know these writers. They're rich, they've got all kinds of strange art. Maybe of interest . . . to someone in your line." He sniffed, staring straight ahead, though a smile tugged at the corners of his mouth.

I could see the Moscow return spraying snow farther up the tracks, so I didn't bother explaining that my line isn't what he thought. I thanked him, made empty promises about having a glass together sometime, and left, thoughtful. Most of the seats in the *elektrichka* had had their guts ripped out, but I managed to find one that was still intact, and far enough away from the broken windows up front that it wasn't actually freezing. True, at Meshcherskii two punks with a guitar got on and tried to take the seat, but a thumb in the throat of the taller one convinced them I really *did* prefer to sit where I was because I had a lot to think about.

One thing war teaches you is how *wet* people are; it takes a *hot* fire to make charcoal out of somebody. I wondered about that all the way back to Moscow, how hot could a wooden hut get? Sasha said there'd been no lab work, so there was no way of knowing whether there had been an accelerant. Even if there had been, though, it would have been inconclusive; the kerosene a suicide pours over herself, that's an accelerant, too.

*Could* it have been suicide, in spite of what Rakhman believed? Most women in Central Asia live a little worse than a donkey; a wife you can pay for with cash, but a donkey, that requires you pay with something real, gold or livestock. Forced into your mother-in-law's house at age maybe thirteen or fourteen, and your parents would kill you if you went back to them because of the shame you had brought onto them, so you slaved away from before dawn until long after dark, toddler on the floor, baby on the knee, and a third swelling the belly, all gifts of some man you had never seen before the wedding day, and didn't see too often afterwards. For a lot of girls, the only way out of that fix was a big glass of vinegar concentrate, or the bright clean flame.

Shakhira Sadriddin, however, was definitely not most women. Rakhman had described her education at Moscow State University, an undergraduate degree in journalism, then a master's. Her job, second editor at a publishing house in Dushanbe, with responsibility for most of the poetry. The dacha on the Vacha River, with the bedroom window that framed Mt. Victory of Communism, where it caught the first flare of sunrise. The container shipments from Moscow filled with French shoes. Italian coats. Polish furniture.

To a one-armed guy with fourteen rubles in his pocket and a half bottle of sour milk in the refrigerator, Shakhira's life didn't sound like the stuff that bonfires are made of. If four months in a Kabul hospital ward trying to twiddle a thumb you no longer have teaches you anything, however, it's that misery's got nothing to do with reality. If you think you're miserable, then you are, miserable enough even to put a match to yourself.

What I kept wondering, though, from Sasha's description of the body, was even if you were that miserable, why would you put on your Finnish shearling, your mink hat, and your English walking boots, then sit in an armchair, in front of the television, just to set yourself on fire?

When I was a boy, you had to get almost out of Moscow before people figured the Kremlin was far enough away that they didn't have to shovel the snow. Now, even in Manezh Square, just spitting distance from Red Square, the sidewalks might as well be up in Vorkuta, for all the snow removal people worry about them. With a million Muscovites and visitors a day shuffling back and forth from GUM, any snow that falls is immediately packed down into ice, thick as tank armor and slippery as a greased devil. You two-armed types wouldn't know it, but one of the things an arm is for is to help you regain your balance when you're falling, and cushion you when you fail. But the Committee on Women, and the rest of the People's Deputies, were headquartered in the Moskva Hotel, so I had to slither along from the Sverdlov metrov stop, holding onto walls with my right hand. Even the stooped old ladies in their zippered felt footies moved faster, but still, I eventually got to the hotel without falling, being offered help, or having somebody take me for drunk.

Among the things we don't have in Russia is what to do and where to turn to when your boss or the judge or the local Party chief does you wrong, so life becomes the survival of whoever can complain the highest. You write letters, you telephone, and when everything else fails, you come to Moscow, to clasp the knees of the most exalted official you can snag and hope he will hear out your misery. Gorbachev has tried to improve this system, but only by providing more people to petition for redress; maybe he would have done the country more good by outlawing that foreign word "petition" instead, and get us all to think about why our homegrown Russian word for the same thing means "beat-your-head," like on the floor.

Still, the new People's Deputies are good to complain to. Their powers are so vague that everybody, even the deputies themselves, believes they can put right the old wrongs. Also, they are on TV all the time, which makes them appear important. Access is easy, too; all of the deputies that don't live in Moscow are put up in the Moskva Hotel. Which is why, when I finally got inside the huge double parade doors, I felt as if I had entered the registration hall for hell. The gloomy lobby was dense with weeping old women in woolen head scarves and cheap overcoats, lumps as thick as they were tall, wailing and rattling papers; old men with hands like cowhorn and cheap medals tinkling on their imitation-tweed lapels, worriedly smoking cheap gaspers and trying to look brave; dark women with mustaches, gold teeth, and floral headscarves, shrieking in some language that could loosen phlegm. Here and there a deputy murmured with someone, eyes blinking seriously behind square-framed East German glasses, jotting notes on a deputy's leatherlike embossed pad with a deputy's Hungarian ballpoint, but mostly the delegates hurried through the lobby, talking intently to each other, in self-defense. It was useless to ask anyone questions, so I just jumped into the elevator after one such scuttling pair, then said, as if it had slipped my mind, "And what's her name, that runs the Committee on Women? She's on eleven still?"

It was the ninth floor, actually, and her name was Liudmila Ivanovna. A cool grey-eyed number with tightly-bunned ash-blonde hair and a faint whiff of a German accent about her that only made her seem more efficient. She glanced at my lapel, which didn't have a deputy's insignia, but she must have also noticed the arm I didn't have because she didn't throw me right out. I explained what I wanted to know.

"Sadriddin?" she asked indifferently, still undecided about chasing me off.

"Shakhira Sadriddin. She was supposed to be addressing the committee, that's what she came to Moscow for."

"We are reading draft variants of the proposed law on the family, young man," she said sparely, letting that "young man" tell me how much she figured separated us, even if we were about the same age. "Our committee meets three days a week, from ten in the morning until eight at night, with breaks for dinner and supper. We hear testimony, accept petitions, take complaints, and listen to arguments that entire time, from women from all over the country. How am I supposed to recall. . . ."

"She hadn't spoken yet," I reminded her. "She was to speak later, this week, I guess."

Liudmila Ivanovna shrugged impatiently, but then went to look in some sort of book. "Where's she from?" she asked, not looking up.

"Tadzhikistan, Dushanbe. . . ."

She ran her finger down a page, letting me admire her three centimeter long blood-red fingernails and the slender curve of her well-cut jersey dress. When she looked up, her eyes had changed, so at least she wasn't going to shut the door on me.

"There is a Shakhira Rutaki who is to address us on Friday. . . ."

"Rutaki?" I asked, surprised again.

"That's what the book says," she waved vaguely, the questioning gaze not flickering as she studied me.

What she was seeing was an ass; why had it never occurred to me to ask just who Shakhira was married to? If anyone outranked Sharif Sadriddin on Red Parnassus it was Rutaki, People's Poet; Stalin's favorite, Rutaki had not even had to bother to have two names, like normal people. If Shakhira had married into *the* Rutaki family—and into what other Rutaki family would a Sadriddin marry?—then it made more sense than ever that Rakhman had looked like an overwound Vietnamese wristwatch.

"Was to address you," was all I gave Liudmila Ivanovna in explanation. "What I was wondering, can you tell me anything about her, what she was going to speak to you about, or what brought her to Moscow?"

"Why was?"

"She's dead."

"Dead, you say?" The woman shook her head, then shrugged. "My god, what have we come to. . . . You say she was murdered?"

I hadn't said, but it's a good question; what *have* we come to, that when you hear nowadays that somebody is dead, your first assumption is murder? "The militia is calling it a suicide." I knew I was compounding the mystery, but didn't care. "Look, can't you at least tell me what her topic was?"

There was a knock at the door, which swung immediately open, admitting a plump woman with hennaed hair and a mole the size of a two kopek coin on her second chin. "Liudochka, time for supper, ducks. . . . Oy! If I'd known you had a *cavalier* here," she appraised me expertly while curtseying elaborately, her gaze flicking to my stump, then politely away. She straightened and said in a more businesslike way, "You be long, Liudochka? Because the girls in the buffet said that probably the Hungarian hams would be in tonight, and they can't save them forever."

"Just a second," Liudmila Ivanovna hissed, then straightened as though she were at the microphone in parliament. "The social dimension of the cotton mafia."

"Ekh, you were a sly one," I winked at Rakhman as I broke a *bublik* in my teeth; I tried to chew it, but the little doughy ring was too stale, so I took a mouthful of the bitter beer, swished the mixture together, and swallowed. "You might have told me your sister was a Rutaki, and an activist besides."

Rakhman moved his otherwise untouched beer glass, brushed the stand-up table, saw that it would take more than that to clean away the decades of spilled beer, so just stood, hands in the pockets of his camel-colored woolen coat. "What activist?"

"What?" I tilted my head, indicating I couldn't hear.

Rakhman looked around unhappily, then repeated, a little louder, "What activist? She was a journalist, you know how it is. Everybody has to have sensational stories now, so . . ." he shrugged.

I don't know what had made me tell Rakhman to meet me in the basement beer hall on the corner of Stoleshnikov and Pushkin, but I was glad I had. Rakhman clearly didn't like the stench, the blue-gray undulating curtain of smoke, the gravelly bawl of Muscovites relaxing. Hell, he didn't even like the bread-black beer or the rosy flesh of the slightly stale pickled herring and dry bagels it came with. Meaning not only did I pay back some of the irritation I had been nursing, at having been told so little, but he also had whispered something effective to the guys at the head of the line, so I got to drink some decent beer for a change, without having to stand through the two hour wait. Besides, now that the Great Friendship of Peoples has begun to wear a bit thin, Russian is the only language you want to be talking in a Moscow basement beer hall full of half-sloshed patrons. Even if my Tadzhik is good, I was glad of the home-tongue advantage.

"Journalists make enemies now," I said lightly. "It's hard to make much of a sensation about honest guys who are doing their jobs right."

Rakhman acknowledged the point with a nod, but said nothing. He twisted up his face, as though he were chewing thoughtfully on the inside of his cheek.

"Cotton, that's a touchy subject in Central Asia." I kept probing, like a toothpick searching for the rotten bit stuck between the back molars. "Biggest cash crop, so you keep your kids out of school to pick it and plant it, and you spray them with defoliants and insecticides while they're working, so they get so poisoned that babies can't drink their own mothers' milk, it's so full of chemicals, and most of the babies anyway come out looking like something an anatomy professor would keep pickled in a big jar, and . . ."

"*Enough!*" Rakhman hissed, banging his smooth leather glove into the sticky ash and beer of the tabletop. "I know what the cotton industry is, you don't have to lecture me. It's a terrible thing, but it has *nothing* to do with my sister's death. Believe me."

I didn't, so far. "That's what she was going to testify on this week. It could be, you know, somebody didn't want . . ."

Rakhman was scornful. "How many secrets do you think there can be about cotton? The whole country knows by now that we are killing ourselves to keep you ivans in shirts. And besides, she was to address a committee, not the whole parliament."

"Yes," I persisted, curious as to how mad I could get him and, I confess, more than a little piqued by that "ivans," "but you never know what the evening news is going to pick up, it could have been her testimony. . . ."

Here Rakhman shook his head, smiling a little as you might at a hopelessly defective child who persists in soiling his trousers. "Listen, my friend, you fail to understand one simple truth . . . *there are no secrets!*" He said it so close, so vehemently, that I couldn't decide whether the saliva was spray, or my face had just been spat in. "Everybody knows everything is terrible! We know the government lies, the administrators steal, the militia are corrupt, and the people are lazy! All of this has been said, all of this has been written, and *so what?* So Shakhira gets up on television and tells everyone that cotton is choking us to death. *So what?* You watch television? So you tell me, all the terrible new truths they talk about, what have you done about any of it? Honestly, can you even remember *one specific horror?*" I hate to admit this, but he was right. I couldn't. Might as well ask someone caught out in an icy cloudburst whether he remembers a particular drop.

I shrugged, drained my second mug, then asked with an eyebrow about Rakhman's untouched beer; he shoved his mugs across to me, and I lifted one, shivering pleasantly at the burnt sugar taste. "Well, so that couldn't be it, then. How about Shakhira's husband, what does he say about . . ."

"I don't know, we haven't spoken," Rakhman tried to sound indifferent, but the sudden tension was obvious, and too much for him to contain. "The uncircumcised dog," he spat, in Persian.

Here, here! I grinned; my toothpick had apparently missed the food, but found a nerve.

"You haven't spoken with your brother-in-law about your sister's death?"

"I haven't spoken to him in four years!" Rakhman shouted, this time loud enough to make heads turn.

I got two more beers out of his story, and a growing sense of excitement. Abutalib Rutaki, Shakhira's husband, was not only the youngest son of *the* Rutaki's youngest son (the son to whom Muslim law gives precedence in inheritance, in other words), but he was also the head of all the fruit and vegetable warehouses for Dushanbe. Our newspapers and television have been clamoring recently about the narco-mafia of Colombia, and how rich they live, but there's no comparison between what those guys make by growing cocaine and what guys like Abutalib make just by storing tomatoes. Narco-mafia is pocket change compared to the veggie-mafia.

Meaning that Abutalib was most probably not the sort of person that you'd want to be quarreling with, as Rakhman was apparently doing, and *definitely* not the sort of person you'd want to divorce, as Shakhira was doing. *Had* been doing.

"Of course, some may say it was a disgrace for my family." Embarrassment forced Rakhman into Persian again, even though it was a good bet that any of the men within earshot of our table who weren't divorced were that way only because they had never married. "But doesn't the Koran say clearly that it is the duty of the man to support the family, and to respect the wife? The disgrace is on the dog Abutalib. . . ."

"Hold it," I patted his arm, enjoying the way the beer seemed to tingle in the fingers I no longer had. "This Rutaki runs a fruit and vegetable warehouse, and he can't support a family?"

"Won't. Wouldn't," Rakhman confessed after a pursed-lip pause. "Not my sister's family."

Perhaps the din, the smoke, and the beer had finally addled me because I felt as though I understood nothing. "This Abutalib has abandoned your sister, has abandoned his own children?"

The mottled look that crept across Rakhman's tightly-clenched jaw reassured me that I had understood.

"There were no children . . . from this wife. And then when his new wife had a son . . ."

Anatolii Markovich had agreed to do a special show at the Central Army Club on Tuesday for brass that were a lot more used to giving orders than to following them, meaning I had to let Shakhira rest for a day. Which was as well, since Rakhman's admission had brought me full circle in a way. Unable to have children by her, Shakhira's husband had brought in a sec-

ond wife, who had recently presented him with a son, prompting Shakhira
to sue for divorce.

So what's the problem, you're wondering? Any Soviet judge would have
granted Shakhira a civil divorce, but what she really needed was a religious
one. Or a Muslim one, anyway. Without that, the *makhallia* would have
made her life miserable, no matter where in Central Asia she settled. The
*makhallia,* meaning the neighborhood organizations of elders, guards the
Islamic morality of every square centimeter of Central Asia with all the vigor
and cunning of a starving mongrel on a fat soup bone. They would see to it
that Shakhira was shunned, hounded, spat upon, unless she got a religious
divorce.

The problem is, for women there is almost no such thing.

Shakhira had no children, and she had no future, so why not take the
"honorable" way out?

A. M. was in good form that night. My job before the show wasn't as
difficult as I had feared; the junior officers I kept away from the dressing
room just by having the senior officers order them gone, and as for the
senior ones, well. . . .

You'll probably have been wondering why Rakhman's offer of two
"bricks" to find out what happened to his sister was so attractive if I could
have made that much just by letting him into A. M.'s dressing room. The
easy answer is that I could only profit from that sort of bribe once because
after that A. M. would toss me out on my ear. The *real* answer, though, is
that the crowd that tries to bribe or bully its way past me long ago became
convinced that anyone who gets in the way can be cowed, bought, or
ignored. Given the sums those people throw around, it's a damned expensive pleasure, but I get a lot of fun out of showing them they're wrong,
saying no and meaning it. Even that pleasure pales, however, compared to
telling generals what you think of them.

Meaning my mood was about as good as it ever gets by the time A. M.
finally began his routine—the unblinking stare and the low voice, the quick
flick of tongue on dry lips, the assurance that all is well, all is well, all is
well. . . .

Those pudding-necked generals with their chests full of ribbons lolled
their heads and waved their arms as happily as any granny in from the farm,
leaping into A. M.'s trance like it was a tub of warm sour cream. I watched
from the coulisses, wishing that just this once A. M. would tell his drooling,
head-rolling crowd of military geniuses to hop like bunnies and quack like
ducks.

Why was I so angry with the brass? Well, on top of the normal reasons,
such as the mess they made of our Afghan adventure, and the good lads
who came home in the "black tulips" because of it, I had more personal
reasons, like the way the examiners insinuated that my wound was, if not

precisely self-inflicted, then at least encouraged so I could go home. As if anyone would wish four months in that hospital on himself, lying in your own dung because the only nurse on the whole wing is in a stupor, drunk on the bottle she bought with the bribe you gave her to bring the bedpan in the first place. And that was after almost dying of blood poisoning because no one cleaned the wound properly. They put that right by lopping off the arm, which made the two molars I lost to vitamin deficiencies in the hospital food seem almost incidental. Did I ever wish I had just followed orders and shot that old Afghan who knifed me? Probably. The man I used to put myself to sleep by imagining what I would do to him someday, however, was the corpulent little colonel who had written me up in such a way that I was lucky to get away with just second-class invalid status, and not a charge of treason.

Which got me thinking about Shakhira again. . . . No arm, no children; second-class invalid, second-class wife. . . .

I suppose I could have taken an easy way out, too, like drinking myself into an early grave, but I hadn't, had I? You know why I hadn't? Because I had finally gotten mad, that's why. Mad that I had been taught to sit around like a baby bird, waiting for *them* to drop a few worms into my wide-open mouth. Waiting for *them* to give me permission, *them* to put things right, *them* to provide.

So, what if this Shakhira had gotten mad, too?

Looking out over the theater seats stuffed with arm-waving officers, I had to acknowledge that the pride I took in no longer accepting anything from *them*, in making my life by my own efforts, was all very well, but what was *really* fun was getting even. Causing the bastards as much trouble as they had caused me.

I don't know how you'd figure out who had been caused more trouble, Shakhira or me, but I know for a fact which of us could *cause* more trouble.

And if Shakhira was anything like me, even a little, she not only wouldn't commit suicide, she would make her husband wish she had.

Which led into a line of thinking which in fairness I should have left, until I could learn more about Abutalib Rutaki. The problem with fairness was that Rutaki was rich, powerful, and in Dushanbe, while I was here in Moscow, with one arm and fourteen rubles.

Besides, if you were going to imagine anybody with good reason to fake his wife's suicide, Abutalib didn't make a bad candidate. The veggie-mafia tend towards the greasy-lipped bazaar type, unctuous and wheedling, with lots of money to give to illegal mosques, plenty of favors to dispense, and no problems in finding "assistants." What really recommended Abutalib to me, though, was that, search my brains as I might, I could remember only one reason why a Muslim woman would ever be granted a divorce. If her husband was infertile.

Even soggy sausages like Swedes and Americans don't exactly boast about being sterile, but a Moslem man would rather have it torn off him than admit it didn't work.

Which is why Shakhira would have to force him, by threatening to write up in the newspapers the people to whom her husband had given gifts, and from whom he had received them, the people for whom he had done favors, and those who had done them for him, the vegetables he had let rot to drive up the price, and the money he had made with the good vegetables that he had written off as rotten, then sold.

Even an idiot of a wife, which it didn't look like Shakhira was, would have had more than enough scandal to blackmail Abutalib into a choice between confessing to sterility or getting the entire Party and government of Tadzhikistan arrested. Which would you do? Lose the bosses' respect but keep their patronage, or lose their patronage and gain their hate?

Or look for a third alternative? A permanent one.

"How are the dachas at Peredelkino heated? Who are you to be asking?" He was younger than me, this fourteenth under-third secretary of the Writers' Union they had finally let me see at the headquarters on Herzen Street after a lot of bullying and waving my stump, but his soft desk job and dinners in the Writers' Union cafeteria had given him an old man's belly, and a deep conviction that he was farther up the evolutionary ladder than any one-armed life form in off the street.

"Someone who was sleeping in Afghan mud while you sucked down chicken soup here." I gave him the crazy-eyed combat-fatigue stare that especially unsettles guys who should have served and didn't. I had been so excited last night that I had left the Army Club without getting paid—again —but no matter how much I tossed and turned, I couldn't dream up a quick and discreet way of getting more certain whether Abutalib would have wanted to kill Shakhira and so had decided to pursue the only goose I had, which was how the killing could have been done.

"I stood for the call-up," this bureaucrat fidgeted, "but I have asthma. . . ."

"If you have breath enough for questions, you've got breath enough for answers."

Less self-assured, he still insisted. "But who are you?"

"Someone who wants to know, which is why you should tell me, tubgut."

Curses always unsettle bureaucrats because no one in his right mind would abuse someone who controls your fate; therefore, if you curse them, either you're crazy, or worse, you actually control *theirs*. Either way, you're dangerous, and it's safer to do what you're asking.

"Coal stoves, the older ones," he capitulated, but kept his voice low, "and some woodburners. And the newer ones, those are on a central plant, steam piped in from the village . . . but those houses aren't as . . . some of them are a bit too far from the boilers. We use them more in the summer. . . ."

Or give them to Tadzhiks, I thought, with a better idea why Shakhira might still have been in her coat. "These newer ones," I asked, "are they like guest houses? What sort of amenities do they have?"

"Drainage, and water, and . . . electricity. . . ." He could see I wanted something, but he didn't know what.

"People sit on the floor?"

"Furniture, you mean?" he looked relieved to have his mystery cleared up, even if my interest made no sense. "Depends. The older ones, people have their own furniture, of course, but the temporary ones, for people on assignment . . . well, it's state furniture, what can you say? Not the Metropole Hotel, but then people are usually only there for a week or two. . . ."

"Electronics?"

"Beg pardon?" he leaned forward, his tie describing three arcs over the mounds of his belly. The office we sat in was no more than a closet, and I knew that this fellow, for all his air of superiority, was in a building full of people who made him as miserable as he was trying to make me. Compared to me he was well paid, of course, and got the food and the trips and the books I couldn't, but nobody ever counts what he has; we only count what we don't have, and you could bet this guy's daughter was in the wrong kindergarten, or his wife was torturing him because he couldn't get her French pantyhose, or maybe it was something as simple as he had forgotten to take his windshield wipers off the car last night and they'd been stolen again. What I mean is, he had his problems, just like I had mine. Even so, the sight of that round little belly did make me want to put my good fist into it, as deep as my arm could make it go.

"Electronics, I said, what kind of electronics do you put in the transient houses? Televisions, that sort of thing."

Again he looked relieved, which made me realize he thought I was asking whether the huts were bugged. "A radio receiver, of course . . . and televisions in some of them. . . ."

"Videotape recorders?"

"When even I can't get one?" the secretary's astonishment was so great that for a moment he was frank with me.

"How about the cabin occupied last week by Shakhira Sadriddin? Did it have a television?" I decided I could show my cards at last.

"Look," the secretary had gotten over his discomfort, "I have no idea who you are, and I've already told you more than I should. You can't very well expect that I discuss who is . . ."

People are often surprised by how strong one arm can become when you don't have the other to help; certainly this secretary didn't expect to have his face pulled so close to mine that I could smell his soap, and he the fact that I don't have the patience for standing in lines to buy any.

"A woman died there," I growled, tightening my grip on his necktie as he winced. "I want to know why. Was there a television in that cabin?"

Maybe my hold on the tie was a little too tight. His face was turning the color of a pickled pepper, and his watery blue eyes were starting to pop out. As much as my grip permitted, he shook his head.

I said goodbye and got the devil out of the Writers' Union before my secretary friend recovered enough to call the militia. Fortunately Herzen Street is in an old part of Moscow where it's easy to get lost. I cut through a couple of courtyards and down an alley and eventually wound my way out onto Kalinin Prospekt, reasonably secure there was nobody behind me. Then I laughed, as excited as a kid stealing apples. I had an idea how Abutalib could have murdered his wife. Not did. Could have.

No televisions in those cabins, yet Sasha had plainly seen one in Shakhira's place. He had told me so, hadn't he? What he hadn't told me, and what I now had to go all the way back to Peredelkino to find out, was what make of television it was. That meant a bus to Kiev Station, the *elektrichka* to Peredelkino, and, because I hadn't had anything to eat yet today, two sausages with a slice of stale bread and half a sour tomato, as hard and green as a young walnut, that I bought at a co-op stand across from Kiev station. When I finally got down at Peredelkino I had three rubles left, not counting change. It was going to be a cold walk back to town if I couldn't find Sasha.

Luckily, he found me. Again.

"Hey, hey! The one-armed devil!" Sasha clubbed me around the shoulders, coming up behind me on the village's perfunctory street, no more than a half-score of shops. A shipment of something—the size of a baby's fist and covered with mud, so either potatoes or swedes—was being shovelled from the back of a truck into a vegetable kiosk, and women were already jostling into queues, elbowing each other for position. "You come back for that glass?"

"Pick some of those up and we'll have hors d'oeuvres." I pointed at the potatoes rolling on the ground; from every shovelful the man tossed into the hoppers that a plump blonde wearing a white lab coat over her overcoat was indifferently holding up, a handful of potatoes rolled down to the ground, where they lay, ignored, in the muck and puddles. Actually, considering my financial position at the moment, I could have done worse than pick them up.

"Ehh," Sasha waved his hand dismissively, pushed his fur cap back on his tow-blond head, then checked carefully that the microphone clipped to his Sam Browne belt was turned off. "So what, you got bored without me?" he stopped playing the clown.

"In a manner of speaking . . . there was something I wanted to ask you . . . about that fire. . . ."

Sasha took my good arm and strolled toward the corner with me, wading through the crowd of squat, squabbling potato buyers, ignoring their muttering and dark looks. When we were farther on, past a paper goods store containing nothing but some dusty red children's flags and an extraordinarily bored salesgirl, Sasha said out of the corner of his mouth, "You don't get juicy answers out of a dry conversation."

We stopped under a sign that said "Wines," though a glance through the windows revealed only ranks of five-liter jars filled with some liquid the color of urine and stacks of wire crates filled with bottles of Essentuki water, which no one ever buys because it's so salty that drinking it makes you thirstier. Sasha made a jolly whistle through his front teeth, then rapped on the window; the girl, who had been slouching nearly comatose with boredom, didn't exactly brighten, but she stood up, peered at Sasha, then made a circling motion with her hand.

Sasha grinned at me, "Come round back, I'll introduce you to Galochka."

She was an eighteen year old girl with eyes like a poodle and the sort of figure that right now is sweet and springy like fresh-baked meringue but in ten years will become vats of clabbered milk. As she led us into the back of the wine store, it was plain that Sasha's relations with this Galochka weren't entirely commercial. She slouched around in that sullen cow way that shopgirls will, shuffling her slippers and cursing us absentmindedly, but the half-liter she pulled from behind a stack of wire crates filled with five-liter bottles of birch water was made from Polish rye, and the two pickles she put on the newspaper-spread upturned crate between us were fresh, crisp as a February frost. Sasha put his hat on a stack of crates full of more Essentuki, concentrated as he poured precisely equal amounts of the vodka into the two teacups this Galochka brought, then, beaming, held one out to me.

"To the ones who didn't come back," he said solemnly, clicking the rim of his cup against mine.

Two more glasses, one to brothers-in-arms and one to beautiful women (which got a grin, and another bottle, out of Galochka), and at last I was able to ask my question. With only the pickles and sausages to soak up the vodka, though, the question came through rubbery lips.

"The TV? It got sent in the box." Sasha looked faintly put out at my bad manners. Mixing work and pleasure.

"I know, but you wouldn't happen to know . . . the TV and the video recorder, were they on the list?"

Sasha shrugged, then shook his head. "Don't think so because the inspector didn't know what to do with them." Then, unexpectedly, the militia man giggled. "That order from Minjustice scared Pustyshkin so bad, he'd have thrown last year's leaves in the box. I told him that stuff was junk now, but. . . ." He rubbed his nose, sniffed. "Don't know how it could have been on the list, actually," he added thoughtfully. "She only got it last week."

That jolted me, but I did my best not to shout. "You know when she got the TV?"

The squeak in my question put Sasha on guard. "Yes," he said but didn't elaborate, instead toying with the lead seal from the first bottle.

"You don't happen to know . . . you didn't notice. . . ."

"What?" he threw the rolled-up ball of lead seal into the corner.

"What kind of television it was?"

The question was sufficiently unexpected to make Sasha push back from the crate and stare at me, head cocked to one side; this made him look more than ever like some kind of big work dog, an Armenian wolf-crusher, say, or a Bernard, that had been taken into apartment life and gotten fat. "Color," he said slowly, "a big color one."

I waved my hands, meaning no. "The make. Was it an *import,* or was it ours?"

Sasha's eyes had the clouded look of someone in thought, but whether he was trying to recall the insignia on that melted pile of plastic or calculating whether to lock me up I couldn't be sure, so I added, "At least, what do you think, was it a Rubin?"

Comprehension dawned like a morning in early June, and Sasha slammed his hand onto the crate, making our two bottles tinkle against each other. "You clever son of a bitch!" he shook his head admiringly. "You think it could have been?"

I pointed at the bottle that still wasn't empty, then at our cups, which were. Sasha's approval was nice, but an answer to the question would be even nicer. "That's what I was hoping you could tell me."

Sasha was excited enough at the thought even to stand and begin pacing about the store room. "The television, sure. I mean, I figured it was just, you know, she'd been on a shopping expedition or something."

Pleased with the way Sasha was heading, I still thought he could do with a little more herding. "Did she buy the set herself? Or was it delivered? Did someone bring it out here?"

Sasha stopped pacing, put his hands on his hips; with his service greatcoat spread wide and a thoughtful glower growing on his face, he seemed to fill the whole room, like a July thunderhead boiling across the sky. "You know," he said, nodding, "it's a chancy way to do somebody in, but it's got class, no question. Assuming you've got the thousand *babki* to waste on the set, of course," he added, more businesslike.

I let myself look grim. "I don't think there was any problem with *babki,* and anyway, what's chancy about it? There's enough guys who came back from the 'Stan knowing something about wires, and if you were to help a Rubin 750 along with some extra wiring, who's ever going to ask, after the fire?"

I didn't have to cross the T's for Sasha; by now everybody knows that you're safer around the house with an open five-liter tin of petrol than with a Rubin 750. A big expensive color console, which not every *muzhik* can afford, that model is a particular marvel of our engineering, with an internal transformer so poorly designed that it overheats even when the set is turned off. Sometimes the sets just ignite spontaneously and burn out the proud owner's apartment, but there've been almost a thousand instances over the years when the consoles actually blew up, killing the people watching. What better gift for the wife you didn't want but couldn't afford to discard than a Rubin 750?

I could tell from Sasha's face, however, that he was still pondering until he sat down across from me again and gave me a blue-eyed, searching look. "Just who are you?"

"Or in translation, why do I care?"

"For a start," Sasha nodded but kept his eyes fixed on mine.

He was twice as big as me, with twice as many arms, and a cop besides, but I let my voice tell him that none of that would matter if he answered the next question wrong.

"Are you saying that maybe I didn't serve in the 'Stan? That I'm maybe faking *this?*" I held up what remained of my left arm.

"Mother of god, no." Sasha paled and sat up, the shadow of doubt burned away by shame. "I mean, no, no, it's just strange, you're not CID or anything, but here you are, doing all this . . . was she something to you?"

I was going to say something clever, but a note in Sasha's voice caught me.

"Why? Was she something to you?"

"To me?" he looked thoughtful, then shrugged and grinned. "I don't know about that, but *something?* Yes, she was something for sure."

"I never could figure why she was so excited about the TV because there's some problem with reception in those cabins, mostly you get just snow. You wouldn't believe the complaints about it." He snorted, amused in a self-pitying way. "Like the militia is supposed to take care of the air-waves now, too, or it's a crime that you can't watch Dinamo play Central Army. . . ."

Conserving future pleasures, Sasha wisely wouldn't tell me any more about Shakhira within earshot of Galya, so we filled the teacups, tossed them down without bothering to toast, and pushed off, Sasha giving Galochka a parting pat on the rear end that was just the company-manners side of a fondle. Outside it was a real sunset, like we never get in Moscow any more, gold and crimson swabs through the ragged patches in the clouds, long slanting shafts of ruddy sunlight skewering the world like God's shish kebab. The bare treetops were inked against the dying light, and infrequent snowflakes twinkled as we squeaked along, the frost making the nose hairs stiff when you breathed in.

"There's my TV, of course," Sasha said when we were in the street, "but whenever she came over, we . . ." He laughed, then shook his head, jingling and steaming in the cold like some healthy draft horse. "You know, I've never seen a woman be so single-minded about getting it!"

Normally, listening to people talk about sex is like watching people fish; the only way to make either subject interesting is to be doing it yourself. Sasha's description, however, of the grim intent with which Shakhira ingested him on three successive afternoons—"like a nurse in a goddamned polyclinic!" as he put it—told me what I should have understood earlier.

That Shakhira had a one hundred percent guaranteed way to prove it was Abutalib who was infertile, and not she.

She could get pregnant.

As an argument-winner, that would have been as effective, and as final, as a hydrogen bomb, especially if she managed to come up with a blond, blue-eyed baby Sasha. Abutalib would have been a laughing stock three times over, a eunuch cuckolded by two different wives.

I could feel the distant tickling of an idea beginning to knit together. I stopped Sasha by grabbing his arm. "You say the reception is terrible out at the dachas, and she had just gotten the TV?"

He nodded, still thinking about sex.

"But she had it out, right? It was working? She was watching it when you found her?"

"When we found her, she was fried like an overdone omelette." Sasha pulled his arm free, then looked around the street, to see whether anyone had noticed us.

"Yeah, but the television and the video recorder were hooked up?" Trying to pull my thoughts together was like trying to catch bats in a pike net; there was *something* whooshing around my head in the dark, but so far my frantic swoops were coming up empty.

"So?" Sasha started walking.

"So why? Why would she go to all that trouble? She was supposed to go back to Dushanbe in a few days. . . ."

"She said she wanted to watch something," Sasha grunted, then impatient, said, "Look, I'm supposed to be patroling here. . . ."

I stepped squarely in front of him. "You know what she wanted to watch, don't you?"

"How should I know what she wanted to watch? A movie, or I don't know, maybe *Domestic Academy,* learn how to make a sailboat out of a hard-boiled egg and a slice of cheese."

"Sasha, Sasha," I took his Sam Browne in my hand, tugging him toward me. "Where is she going to get movies? She hardly knows anybody here in Moscow."

"How should I know where she got them? Maybe she did like everybody else and rented those films from a video salon," Sasha said, but we both knew he was lying. *Nobody* rents from video salons because nobody wants to see the movies they have. All Soviet movies, and not even new ones. No matter how rich you are, nobody's going to pull all the strings and spend all the money it takes to buy a big color television and a video recorder in order to watch Soviet movies.

"Sasha," I reached up and gently took his chin in my hand so he would look at me, "you were taping television shows for her, weren't you?"

He snatched his head away angrily, glared at me hotly, then shrugged, readjusting the Tokarev's holster that had come awry. He smiled in a way that said any more questions would put my teeth down my throat. "You buy me a video recorder and bring your own blank tapes like she did, and I'll record anything you want."

"You are saying there was no murder and no suicide? How can you be sure?" Rakhman's voice sounded close to cracking.

I sighed, weary and flat after so much labor to get so little. "I told you, she had bought all this stuff for recording Anatolii Markovich and Aleksandr Chumak."

"Who's this Chumak? Another shaman like your Anatolii Markovich?" Rakhman wrenched himself sideways in the driver's seat, doing his best to be witheringly sarcastic.

I let the "your" pass. "Chumak is a healer, like Anatolii Markovich, except he uses something he calls 'energy pulsations.' You take a liquid in a clear container and you put it in front of the television set while Chumak does his mumbo-jumbo, beams his energy pulses or whatever at you."

"My sister burned to death, not drowned," Rakhman reminded me condescendingly. I ignored him.

"According to Chumak, the liquid concentrates the pulses and stores them so you can absorb them later, if you drink it, or you can rub the fluid on the part that hurts. Then the pulses make you healthy or heal your wounds or grow your hair back. The same things that A. M. claims to do."

We were in Rakhman's Zhiguli, parked in a side street off the Garden Ring. He began jingling the keys, meaning he was impatient and skeptical. "Most people use water because it's cheap and easy to drink. But Chumak says that other liquids work better, that they concentrate the pulses even more. Vodka, for example."

Rakhman's face was furious in the sodium-yellow of the street light. "My sister was a Muslim! She never drank!"

"Not even to overcome infertility?" I asked, so tired that my ghost arm ached. "Anyway, I never said she drank it, I said she put it in front of the television. Maybe she was going to rub it on herself, or give it to her husband to drink." Actually, my best guess was that she was giving it to Sasha to drink, but so far I'd spared Rakhman the trickier details of how Sasha came into the story.

"It?"

"Your sister was desperate. I think most likely she used a five-liter jar, probably of spirit alcohol."

Rakhman thought for a moment, then shrugged. "Perhaps, perhaps not. Either way, it wouldn't kill her."

I agreed. "It could, if the next tape was Anatolii Markovich."

Rakhman wiped both hands down his face, then shook vigorously, as if trying to wash himself clean. "Vibrations, hypnosis, videotapes!" he waved his hands wildly, banging the rear view mirror hard enough that the glue gave way and the mirror dangled from its stem for a second, then dropped onto the gearshift, where it shattered.

*"Damn!"* Rakhman hissed.

"I've seen people flap worse than that, once Anatolii Markovich gets them in a trance," I said quietly. "Even enough to knock a five-liter jar off a table by a television, for example."

Rakhman was cursing steadily, fastidiously picking slivers of silvered glass from the carpeted hump. He looked up, his eyes now wide in understanding.

Spirit alcohol isn't the most volatile accelerant you can find; compared to aviation fuel, for example, it burns slowly and is quite cool. For a poorly-made cabin slapped together mostly out of cheap pine and furnished with low-grade furniture, however, five liters of pure alcohol would make a nice funeral pyre in no time.

"But the flame," Rakhman said after a long silence. "You still need a flame. . . ."

"Where would you get a flame, in a *mazar?*"

"That dacha is no *mazar.* . . ." Rakhman growled, but he got the point. Shakhira was a Muslim woman who wanted desperately to get pregnant; long before she got to Moscow she would already have tried all the illegal shrines and cult sites, the *mazars,* where unhappy women lit candles and prayed to Allah.

All the way in from Peredelkino I had been haunted by the scene as I imagined it now. The flickering candles laid out on the floor in some ritual pattern. The blue light of Anatolii Markovich's tape-recorded face, looking unblinking but unseeing at his unintended victim. Head filling the screen, tilted slightly down so his eyes seem to be peering from a deep cave. Relax, he drones, all is well, all is well. . . . Shakhira goes into her trance, flails her arms, and crash goes Chumak's jar of spirit, onto the candles. *Boom* . . . Afghanistan, in your own living room.

"I'm sorry," I said softly when Rakhman's silence had grown to what seemed minutes. Through the window I could see ten or fifteen apartment windows, most of them glowing with that chill blue of television screens. I wondered how many of *them* were watching Chumak or tapes of A. M. or rock videos or overdubbed Bruce Lee movies or . . .

"An accident, then?" Rakhman asked at last, the odd note in his voice making me look at him. He was smiling. "Not suicide, not murder? An accident?"

Why did he sound so pleased now, the spotted devil? I nodded, decided I wouldn't think about it because I'd had enough mystery. "That's how I read it, anyway. . . ."

"So my dear brother-in-law has not been dishonored by suicide and need not fear the prosecutor?" The question was soft, not intended for me. "He will be very glad to hear that . . . very *grateful,*" Rakhman corrected himself, reaching across me to open the Zhiguli's door. "I must hurry to tell him."

The gust of chill wet night air and Rakhman's words hit me together.

"That's why you were so worried!" I pointed at him, startled. "You were living off Shakhira, and the money was drying up, since the new wife. Divorce or suicide, either way you'd lose Abutalib's money, unless maybe you could prove it was murder, and even that . . ."

Actually, I got to finish my clever remarks in the gutter because Rakhman suddenly put an arm in my chest and shoved, tumbling me out into the muck. *"God damn you!"* I shouted after him, to make myself feel better, *"What about my money?"*

I don't suppose he would have driven by again if not for the new steam pipes they started putting into the neighborhood two summers ago, so most of the streets were still gutted and closed. I just had time to pick myself out of the slush before the Zhiguli roared back. I stepped aside to let Rakhman pass, but he stopped for a second, the window rolled down.

"Your money?" he snarled. "In general, ivan, it's money that makes facts, not the other way around. But here . . . I'm going to be getting more." He dropped my four bricks out the window, then accelerated, splashing me again. This time Rakhman's Zhiguli disappeared for good, the taillights slipping into the ruby stream of the Garden Ring.

Those "bricks" turned out to be false, of course. Newspapers, cut to the size of fifty-ruble notes. Words instead of money. . . .

But the outer bills were real, at least. Four bricks, eight sides. Four hundred rubles.

Well, that's something, isn't it?

# THE SAFETY MATCH

*By Anton Chekhov*

O N THE morning of October 6, 1885, in the office of the Inspector
of Police of the second division of S— District, there appeared a
respectably dressed young man, who announced that his master,
Marcus Ivanovitch Klausoff, a retired officer of the Horse Guards, separated
from his wife, had been murdered. While making this announcement the
young man was white and terribly agitated. His hands trembled and his eyes
were full of terror.

"Whom have I the honor of addressing?" asked the Inspector.

"Psyekoff, Lieutenant Klausoff's agent and director; agriculturist and
mechanician."

The Inspector and his deputy, on visiting the scene of the occurrence in
company with Psyekoff, found the following: near the wing in which
Klausoff had lived was gathered a dense crowd—the news of the murder
had sped swift as lightning through the neighborhood and the peasantry,
thanks to the fact that the day was a holiday, had hurried together from all
the neighboring villages. There was much commotion and talk. Here and
there, pale, tear-stained faces were seen. The door of Klausoff's bedroom
was found locked. The key was inside.

"It is quite clear that the scoundrels got in by the window!" said Psyekoff as they examined the door.

They went to the garden, into which the bedroom window opened. The window looked dark and ominous. It was covered by a faded green curtain. One corner of the curtain was slightly turned up, which made it possible to look into the bedroom.

"Did any of you look into the window?" asked the Inspector.

"Certainly not, your worship!" answered Ephraim, the gardener, a little gray-haired old man, who looked like a retired sergeant. "Who's going to look in, if all their bones are shaking?"

"Ah, Marcus Ivanovitch!" sighed the Inspector, looking at the window, "I told you you would come to a bad end. I told the dear man, but he wouldn't listen. Dissipation doesn't bring any good."

"Thanks to Ephraim," said Psyekoff; "but for him, we would never have guessed. He was the first to guess that something was wrong. He comes to me this morning, and says, 'Why is the master so long getting up? He hasn't left his bedroom for a whole week!' The moment he said that, it was just as if someone had hit me with an ax. The thought flashed through my mind, 'We haven't had a sight of him since last Saturday, and today is Sunday.' Seven whole days—not a doubt of it!"

"Ay, poor fellow!" again sighed the Inspector. "He was a clever fellow, finely educated, and kind-hearted at that. And in society, nobody could touch him. But he was a waster, God rest his soul! I was prepared for anything since he refused to live with Olga Petrovna. Poor thing, a good wife, but a sharp tongue. Stephen!" the Inspector called to one of his deputies, "go over to my house this minute, and send Andrew to the Captain of Police with this information. Tell him that Marcus Ivanovitch has been murdered. And run over to the orderly—why should he sit there kicking his heels? Let him come here! And go as fast as you can to the Examining Magistrate, Nicholas Yermolaiyevitch. Tell him to come over—wait, I'll write him a note."

The Inspector posted sentinels around the wing of the house, wrote a letter to the Examining Magistrate, and then went over to the director's for a glass of tea. Ten minutes later he was sitting on a stool, carefully nibbling a lump of sugar, and swallowing the scalding tea.

"There you are," he was saying to Psyekoff; "there you are! A noble by birth, a rich man—a favorite of the gods, you may say, as Pushkin has it, and what did he come to? He drank and dissipated and—there you are—he's murdered."

After a couple of hours the Examining Magistrate drove up. Nicholas Yermolaiyevitch Chubikoff—for that was the Magistrate's name—was a tall fleshy old man of sixty, who had been wrestling with the duties of his office for a quarter of a century. Everybody in the district knew him as an honest man, wise, energetic, and in love with his work. He was accompanied to the scene of the murder by his inveterate companion, fellow worker, and secretary, Dukovski, a tall enterprising young fellow of about twenty-six.

"It is possible, gentlemen?" cried Chubikoff, entering Psyekoff's room, and quickly shaking hands with everyone. "Is it possible? Marcus Ivanovitch? Murdered? No, it is impossible! Im-poss-i-ble!"

"Go in there," sighed the Inspector.

"Lord, have mercy on us! Only last Friday I saw him at the fair in Farabankoff. I had a drink of vodka with him, save the mark!"

"Go in there," again sighed the Inspector.

They sighed, uttered exclamations of horror, drank a glass of tea each, and went to the wing.

"Get back!" the orderly cried to the peasants.

In the wing, the Examining Magistrate began his work by examining the bedroom door. The door proved to be of pine, painted yellow, and was uninjured. Nothing was found which could serve as a clue. They had to break in the door.

"Everyone not here on business is requested to keep away," said the Magistrate, when, after much hammering and shaking, the door yielded to ax and chisel. "I request this, in the interest of the investigation. Orderly, don't let anyone in!"

Chubikoff and his assistant and the Inspector opened the door, and hesitatingly, one after the other, entered the room. Their eyes met the following sight: beside the single window stood the big wooden bed with a huge feather mattress. On the crumpled feather bed lay a tumbled, crumpled quilt. The pillow, in a cotton pillow case, also much crumpled, was dragging on the floor.

On the table beside the bed lay a silver watch and a silver twenty-kopeck piece. Beside them lay some sulphur matches. Beside the bed, the little table, and the single chair, there was no furniture in the room.

Looking under the bed, the Inspector saw a couple of dozen empty bottles, an old straw hat, and a quart of vodka. Under the table lay one top boot, covered with dust.

Casting a glance around the room, the Magistrate frowned and grew red in the face.

"Scoundrels!" he muttered, clenching his fists.

"And where is Marcus Ivanovitch?" asked Dukovski in a low voice.

"Mind your own business," Chubikoff answered roughly. "Be good enough to examine the floor. This is not the first case of the kind I have had to deal with. Eugraph Kuzmitch," he said, turning to the Inspector and lowering his voice, "in 1870 I had another case like this. But you must remember it—the murder of the merchant Portraitoff. It was just the same there. The scoundrels murdered him and dragged the corpse out through the window—"

Chubikoff went up to the window, pulled the curtain to one side, and carefully pushed the window. The window opened.

"It opens, you see! It wasn't fastened. Hm. There are tracks under the window. Look, there is the track of a knee! Somebody got in there. We must examine the window thoroughly."

"There is nothing special to be found on the floor," said Dukovski. "No stains or scratches. The only thing I found was a struck safety match. Here it is. So far as I remember, Marcus Ivanovitch did not smoke. And he always used sulphur matches, never safety matches. Perhaps this safety match may serve as a clue."

"Oh, do shut up," cried the Magistrate deprecatingly. "You go on about your match! I can't abide these dreamers! Instead of chasing matches, you had better examine the bed."

After a thorough examination of the bed, Dukovski reported: "There are no spots, either of blood or of anything else. There are likewise no new torn places. On the pillow there are signs of teeth. The quilt is stained with something which looks like beer and smells like beer. The general aspect of the bed gives grounds for thinking that a struggle took place on it."

"I know there was a struggle, without your telling me! You are not being asked about a struggle. Instead of looking for struggles, you had better—"

"Here is one top boot, but there is no sign of the other."

"Well, and what of that?"

"It proves that they strangled him while he was taking his boots off. He hadn't time to take the second boot off when—"

"There you go!—and how do you know they strangled him?"

"There are marks of teeth on the pillow. The pillow itself is badly crumpled and thrown a couple of yards from the bed."

"Listen to his foolishness! Better come into the garden. You would be better employed examining the garden than digging around here. I can do that without you."

When they reached the garden they began by examining the grass. The grass under the window was crushed and trampled. A bushy burdock growing under the window close to the wall was also trampled. Dukovski succeeded in finding on it some broken twigs and a piece of cotton wool. On the upper branches were found some fine hairs of dark-blue wool.

"What color was his last suit?" Dukovski asked Psyekoff.

"Yellow crash."

"Excellent! You see they wore blue!"

A few twigs of the burdock were cut off and carefully wrapped in paper by the investigators. At this point Police Captain Artsuybasheff Svistakovski and Dr. Tyutyeff arrived. The Captain bade them "Good day," and immediately began to satisfy his curiosity.

The doctor, a tall, very lean man with dull eyes, a long nose, and a pointed chin, without greeting anyone or asking about anything, sat down on a log, sighed, and began: "The Serbians are at war again. What in heaven's name can they want now? Austria, it's all your doing!"

The examination of the window from the outside did not supply any conclusive data. The examination of the grass and the bushes nearest to the window yielded a series of useful clues. For example, Dukovski succeeded in discovering a long dark streak, made up of spots, on the grass, which led some distance into the center of the garden. The streak ended under one of the lilac bushes in a dark brown stain. Under this same lilac bush was found a top boot, which turned out to be the fellow of the boot already found in the bedroom.

"That is a bloodstain made some time ago," said Dukovski.

At the word "blood" the doctor rose, and going over lazily, looked at the stain.

"Yes, it is blood," he muttered.

"That shows he wasn't strangled," said Chubikoff, looking sarcastically at Dukovski.

"They strangled him in the bedroom; and here, fearing he might come round again, they struck him a blow with some sharp-pointed instrument. The stain under the bush proves that he lay there a considerable time, while they were looking about for some way of carrying him out of the garden."

"Well, and how about the boot?"

"The boot confirms completely my idea that they murdered him while he was taking his boots off before going to bed. He had already taken off one boot, and the other, this one here, he had only had time to take half off. The half-off boot came off of itself, while the body was dragged over, and fell—"

"There's a lively imagination for you!" laughed Chubikoff. "He goes on and on like that! When will you learn enough to stop making deductions? Instead of arguing and deducing, it would be much better if you took some of the blood-stained grass for analysis!"

When they had finished their examination and drawn a plan of the locality, the investigators went to the director's office to write their report and have breakfast. While they were breakfasting they went on talking.

"The watch, the money, and so on—all untouched—" Chubikoff began, "show as clearly as two and two are four that the murder was not committed for the purpose of robbery."

"The murder was committed by an educated man," insisted Dukovski.

"What evidence have you of that?"

"The safety match proves that to me, for the peasants hereabouts are not yet acquainted with safety matches. Only the landowners use them, and by no means all of them. And it is evident that there was not one murderer but at least three. Two held him, while one killed him. Klausoff was strong, and the murderers must have known it."

"What would his strength be if asleep?"

"The murderers came on him while he was taking off his boots. That proves that he wasn't asleep."

"Stop inventing deductions! Better eat!"

"In my opinion, your worship," said the gardener Ephraim, setting the samovar on the table, "it was nobody but Nicholas who did this dirty trick."

"Quite possible," said Psyekoff. "Who is Nicholas?"

"The master's valet, your worship," answered Ephraim. "Who else could it be? He's a rascal, your worship. He's a drunkard and a blackguard, the like of which Heaven should not permit. He always took the master his vodka and put the master to bed. Who else could it be? And I also venture to point out to your worship, he once boasted at the inn that he would kill the master! It happened on account of Aquilina, the woman, you know. He was making up to a soldier's widow. She pleased the master; the master made friends with her himself, and Nicholas—naturally, he was mad! He is rolling about drunk in the kitchen now. He is crying, and telling lies, saying he is sorry for the master—"

The Examining Magistrate ordered Nicholas to be brought. Nicholas, a lanky young fellow, with a long freckled nose, narrow-chested, and wearing an old jacket of his master's, entered Psyekoff's room and bowed low before the Magistrate. His face was sleepy and tear-stained. He was tipsy and could hardly keep his feet.

"Where is your master?" Chubikoff asked him.

"Murdered, your worship."

As he said this, Nicholas blinked and began to weep.

"We know he was murdered. But where is his body?"

"They say he was dragged out of the window and buried in the garden, your worship."

"Hm! The results of the investigation are known in the kitchen already— that's bad! Where were you, my good fellow, the night the master was murdered? Saturday night, that is."

Nicholas raised his head, and began to think.

"I don't know, your worship," he said. "I was drunk and don't remember."

"An alibi," whispered Dukovski, smiling and rubbing his hands.

"So-o! And why is there blood under the window?"

Nicholas jerked his head up and considered.

"Hurry up!" said the Captain of Police.

"Right away. That blood doesn't amount to anything, your worship. I was cutting a chicken's throat. I was doing it quite simply, in the usual way, when all of a sudden it broke away and started to run. That is where the blood came from."

Ephraim declared that Nicholas did kill a chicken every evening, and always in some new place, but that nobody ever heard of a half-killed chicken running about the garden, though of course it wasn't impossible.

"An alibi," sneered Dukovski, "and what an asinine alibi!"

"Did you know Aquilina?"

"Yes, your worship, I know her."

"And the master cut you out with her?"

"Not at all. *He* cut me out—Mr. Psyekoff there, Ivan Mikhailovitch; and the master cut Ivan Mikhailovitch out. That is how it was."

Psyekoff grew confused and began to scratch his left eye. Dukovski looked at him attentively, noted his confusion, and started. He noticed that the director had dark-blue trousers, which he had not observed before. The trousers reminded him of the dark-blue threads found on the burdock. Chubikoff in his turn glanced suspiciously at Psyekoff.

"Go," he said to Nicholas. "And now permit me to put a question to you, Mr. Psyekoff. Of course you were here last Saturday evening?"

"Yes, I had supper with Marcus Ivanovitch about ten o'clock."

"And afterward?"

"Afterward—afterward—Really, I do not remember," stammered Psyekoff. "I had a good deal to drink at supper. I don't remember when or where I went to sleep. Why are you all looking at me like that, as if I was the murderer?"

"Where were you when you woke up?"

"I was in the servants' kitchen, lying behind the stove. They can all confirm it. How I got behind the stove I don't know—"

"Do not get agitated. Did you know Aquilina?"

"There's nothing extraordinary about that—"

"She first liked you and then preferred Klausoff?"

"Yes. Ephraim, give us some more mushrooms. Do you want some more tea, Eugraph Kuzmitch?"

A heavy, oppressive silence began and lasted fully five minutes. Dukovski silently kept his piercing eyes fixed on Psyekoff's pale face.

The silence was finally broken by the Examining Magistrate. "We must go to the house and talk with Maria Ivanovna, the sister of the deceased. Perhaps she may be able to supply some clues."

Chubikoff and his assistant expressed their thanks for the breakfast, and went toward the house. They found Klausoff's sister, Maria Ivanovna, an old maid of forty-five, at prayer before the big case of family icons. When she saw the portfolios in her guests' hands, and their official caps, she grew pale.

"Let me begin by apologizing for disturbing, so to speak, your devotions," began the gallant Chubikoff, bowing and scraping. "We have come to you with a request. Of course, you have heard already. There is a suspicion that your dear brother, in some way or other, has been murdered. The will of God, you know. No one can escape death, neither czar nor plow-man. Could you not help us with some clue, some explanation—?"

"Oh, don't ask me!" said Maria Ivanovna, growing still paler, and cover-ing her face with her hands. "I can tell you nothing. Nothing! I beg you! I know nothing—What can I do? Oh, no, no!—not a word about my brother! If I die, I won't say anything!"

Maria Ivanovna began to weep, and left the room. The investigators looked at each other, shrugged, and beat a retreat.

"Confound the woman!" scolded Dukovski, going out of the house. "It is clear she knows something, and is concealing it. And the chambermaid has a queer expression too. Wait, you wretches, we'll ferret it all out!"

In the evening Chubikoff and his deputy, lit on their road by the pale moon, wended their way homeward. They sat in their carriage and thought over the results of the day. Both were tired and kept silent. Chubikoff was always unwilling to talk while traveling, and the talkative Dukovski re-mained silent, to fall in with the elder man's humor. But at the end of their journey the deputy could hold in no longer.

"It is quite certain," he said, "that Nicholas had something to do with the matter. *Non dubitandum!* You can see by his face what sort of case he is. His alibi betrays him, body and bones. But it is also certain that he did not set the thing going. He was only the stupid hired tool. You agree? And the humble Psyekoff was not without some slight share in the matter. His dark-blue breeches, his agitation, his lying behind the stove in terror after the murder, his alibi and—Aquilina—"

" 'Grind away, Emilian; it's your week!' So, according to you, whoever knew Aquilina is the murderer? Hothead! You ought to be sucking a bottle, and not handling affairs. You were one of Aquilina's admirers yourself—does it follow that you are also implicated?"

"Aquilina was cook in your house for a month—I am saying nothing about that. The night before that Saturday I was playing cards with you, and saw you—otherwise I should be after you too. It isn't the woman that matters, old chap—it is the mean, nasty, low spirit of jealousy that matters. The retiring young man was not pleased when they got the better of him. His vanity, don't you see? He wanted revenge. Then, those thick lips of his suggest passion. So there you have it: wounded self-love and passion. That is quite enough motive for a murder. We have two of them in our hands. But who is the third? Nicholas and Psyekoff held him, but who smothered him? Psyekoff is shy, timid, an all-round coward. And Nicholas would not smother with a pillow—his sort use an ax or a club. Some third person did the smothering. But who was it?"

Dukovski crammed his hat down over his eyes and pondered. He remained silent until the carriage rolled up to the Magistrate's door.

"Eureka!" he said, entering the little house and throwing off his overcoat. "Eureka, Nicholas Yermolaiyevitch! The only thing I can't understand is, how it did not occur to me sooner! Do you know who the third person was?"

"Oh, for goodness' sake, shut up! Here is supper."

The Magistrate and Dukovski sat down to supper. Dukovski poured himself a glass of vodka, rose, drew himself up, and said, with sparkling eyes, "Well, the third person, who acted in concert with that scoundrel Psyekoff and did the smothering, was a woman! Yes-s! I mean—the murdered man's sister, Maria Ivanovna!"

Chubikoff choked over his vodka, and fixed his eyes on Dukovski.

"You aren't—what's-it's-name? Your head isn't—what-do-you-call-it? You haven't a pain in it?"

"I am perfectly well! Very well, let us say that I am crazy; but how do you explain her confusion when we appeared? How do you explain her unwillingness to give us any information? Let us admit that these are trifles. Very well. But remember their relations. She detested her brother. She never forgave him for living apart from his wife. She of the Old Faith—in her eyes he is a godless profligate. There is where the germ of her hate was hatched. They say he succeeded in making her believe that he was an angel of Satan. He even went in for spiritualism in her presence."

"Well, what of that?"

"You don't understand? She, as a member of the Old Faith, murdered him through fanaticism. It was not only that she was putting to death a weed, a profligate—she was freeing the world of an Antichrist! Oh, you don't know those old maids of the Old Faith. Read Dostoyevsky! And what does Lyeskoff say about them, or Petcherski? It was she, and nobody else, even if you cut me open. She smothered him! Oh, treacherous woman, wasn't that the reason why she was kneeling before the icons, when we came in, just to take our attention away? 'Let me kneel down and pray,' she said to herself, 'and they will think I am tranquil and did not expect them.' That is the plan of all novices in crime, Nicholas Yermolaiyevitch, old pal. My dear old man, won't you intrust this business to me? Let me personally bring it through. Friend, I began it and I will finish it!"

Chubikoff shook his head and frowned.

"We know how to manage difficult matters ourselves," he said, "and your business is not to push yourself in where you don't belong. Write from dictation when you are dictated to—that is your job!"

Dukovski flared up, banged the door, and disappeared.

"Clever rascal," muttered Chubikoff, glancing after him. "Awfully clever! But too much of a hothead. I must buy him a cigar case at the fair as a present."

The next day, early in the morning, a young man with a big head and a pursed-up mouth, who came from Klausoff's place, was introduced to the Magistrate's office. He said he was the shepherd Daniel, and brought a very interesting piece of information.

"I was a bit drunk," he said. "I was with my pal till midnight. On my way home I went into the river for a bath. I was taking a bath, when I looked up. Two men were walking along the dam, carrying something black. 'Shoo!' I cried at them. They got scared and went off like the wind toward Makareff's cabbage garden. Strike me dead, if they weren't carrying the master!"

That same day, toward evening, Psyekoff and Nicholas were arrested and brought under guard to the district town. In the town they were committed to the cells of the prison.

A fortnight passed. It was morning. Magistrate Nicholas Yermolaiyevitch was sitting in his office before a green table, turning over the papers of the "Klausoff case." Dukovski was striding restlessly up and down like a wolf in a cage.

"You are convinced of the guilt of Nicholas and Psyekoff," he said, nervously plucking at his young beard. "Why will you not believe in the guilt of Maria Ivanovna? Are there not proofs enough for you?"

"I don't say I am not convinced. I am convinced, but somehow I don't believe it! There are no real proofs, but just a kind of philosophizing—fanaticism, this and that—"

"You can't do without an ax and bloodstained sheets. Those jurists! Very well, I'll prove it to you. You will stop sneering at the psychological side of the affair. To Siberia with your Maria Ivanovna! I will prove it! If philosophy is not enough for you, I have something substantial for you. It will show you how correct my philosophy is. Just give me permission—"

"What are you raving about?"

"About the safety match! Have you forgotten it? I haven't! I am going to find out who struck it in the murdered man's room. It was not Nicholas that struck it; it was not Psyekoff, for neither of them had any matches when they were examined. It was the third person, Maria Ivanovna. I will prove it to you. Just give me permission to go through the district to find out."

"That's enough! Sit down. Let us go on with the examination."

Dukovski sat down at a little table and plunged his long nose in a bundle of papers.

"Bring in Nicholas Tetekhoff!" cried the Examining Magistrate.

They brought Nicholas in. He was pale and thin as a rail, and trembling.

"Tetekhoff!" began Chubikoff. "In 1879 you were tried in the Court of the First Division, convicted of theft, and sentenced to imprisonment. In 1882 you were tried a second time for theft and were again imprisoned. We know all—"

Astonishment was depicted on Nicholas' face. The Examining Magistrate's omniscience startled him. But soon his expression of astonishment changed to extreme indignation. He began to cry and requested permission to go and wash his face and quiet down. They led him away.

"Bring in Psyekoff!" ordered the Examining Magistrate.

They brought in Psyekoff. The young man had changed greatly during the last few days. He had grown thin and pale, and looked haggard. His eyes had an apathetic expression.

"Sit down, Psyekoff," said Chubikoff. "I hope that today you are going to be reasonable and will not tell lies, as you did before. All these days you have denied that you had anything to do with the murder of Klausoff, in spite of all the proofs that testify against you. That is foolish. Confession will lighten your guilt. This is the last time I am going to talk to you. If you do not confess today, tomorrow it will be too late. Come tell me all—"

"I know nothing about it. I know nothing about your proofs," answered Psyekoff, almost inaudibly.

"It's no use! Well, let me relate to you how the matter took place. On Saturday evening you were sitting in Klausoff's sleeping room and drinking vodka and beer with him. Nicholas was waiting on you. At one o'clock Marcus Ivanovitch announced his intention of going to bed. He always went to bed at one o'clock.

"When he was taking off his boots, and was giving you directions about details of management, you and Nicholas, at a given signal, seized your drunken master and threw him on the bed. One of you sat on his legs, the other on his head. Then a third person came in from the passage—a woman in a black dress, whom you know well, and who had previously arranged with you as to her share in your criminal deed. She seized a pillow and began to smother him.

"While the struggle was going on, the candle went out. The woman took a box of safety matches from her pocket and lit the candle. Was it not so? I see by your face that I am speaking the truth. But to go on. After you saw that he had ceased breathing, you and Nicholas pulled him out through the window and laid him down near the burdock. Fearing that he might come round again, you struck him with something sharp.

"Then you carried him away and laid him under a lilac bush for a short time. After resting a while and considering, you carried him across the fence. Then you entered the road. After that comes the dam. Near the dam, a peasant frightened you. Well, what is the matter with you?"

"I am suffocating!" replied Psyekoff. "Very well—have it so. Only let me go out, please!"

They led Psyekoff away.

"At last! He has confessed!" cried Chubikoff, stretching himself luxuriously. "He has betrayed himself. And didn't I get round him cleverly!"

"And he doesn't deny the woman in the black dress!" exulted Dukovski. "But all the same, that safety match is tormenting me. I can't stand it any longer. Goodbye. I am off!"

Dukovski put on his cap and drove off. Chubikoff began to examine Aquilina, who declared she knew nothing whatever about it.

At six that evening Dukovski returned. He was more agitated than he had ever been before. His hands trembled so that he could not even unbutton his greatcoat. His cheeks glowed. It was clear that he did not come empty-handed.

*"Veni, vidi, vici!"* he cried, rushing into Chubikoff's room and falling into an armchair. "I swear to you on my honor, I begin to believe that I am a genius. Listen, devil take us all! It is funny and it is sad. We have caught three already—isn't that so? Well, I have found the fourth, and a woman at that. You will never believe who it is! But listen.

"I went to Klausoff's village and began to make a spiral round it. I visited all the little shops on the road, everywhere asking for safety matches. Everywhere they said they hadn't any. I made a whole round. Twenty times I lost faith, and twenty times I got it back again. I knocked about the whole day, and only an hour ago I got on the track. Three versts from here. They gave me a packet of ten boxes. One box was missing.

"Immediately I asked, 'Who bought the other box?' 'Such-a-one—she was pleased with them.' See what a fellow who was expelled from the seminary and who has read Gaboriau can do! From today on I begin to respect myself! Well, come."

"Come where?"

"To her, to number four! We must hurry, otherwise—otherwise I'll burst with impatience! Do you know who she is? You'll never guess! Olga Petrovna, Marcus Ivanovitch's wife—his own wife—that's who it is! She is the person who bought the matchbox."

"You—you are out of your mind!"

"It's quite simple! To begin with, she smokes. Secondly, she was head and ears in love with Klausoff, even after he refused to live in the same house with her, because she was always scolding his head off. Why, they say she used to beat him because she loved him so much. And then he positively refused to stay in the same house. Love turned sour. 'Hell hath no fury like a woman scorned.' But come along. Quick, or it will be dark."

"I am not yet sufficiently crazy to go and disturb a respectable, honorable woman in the middle of the night!"

"Respectable, honorable! Do honorable women murder their husbands? I never ventured to call you names before, but now you compel me to. Rag! Dressing gown! Dear Nicholas Yermolaiyevitch, do come, I beg of you!"

The Magistrate made a deprecating motion.

"I beg of you! I ask, not for myself, but in the interests of justice. I implore you! Do what I ask you to, just this once."

Dukovski went down on his knees. "Be kind! Call me a blackguard, a ne'er-do-well, if I am mistaken about this woman. You see what an affair it is, what a case it is. A romance! A woman murdering her own husband for love! The fame of it will go all over Russia. They will make you investigator in all important cases. Understand, Oh, foolish old man!"

The Magistrate frowned and undecidedly stretched his hand toward his cap.

"Oh, the devil take you!" he said. "Let us go."

It was dark when the Magistrate's carriage rolled up to the porch of the old country house in which Olga Petrovna had taken refuge with her brother.

"What pigs we are," said Chubikoff, taking hold of the bell, "to disturb a poor woman like this!"

"It's all right. Don't get frightened. We can say that we have broken a spring."

Chubikoff and Dukovski were met at the threshold by a tall buxom woman, with pitch-black brows and juicy red lips. It was Olga Petrovna herself, apparently not the least distressed by the recent tragedy.

"Oh, what a pleasant surprise!" she said, smiling broadly. "You are just in time for supper. Kuzma Petrovitch is not at home. He is visiting the priest and has stayed late. But we'll get on without him. Be seated. You have come from the examination?"

"Yes. We broke a spring, you know," began Chubikoff, entering the sitting room and sinking into an armchair.

"Take her unawares—at once!" whispered Dukovski. "Take her unawares!"

"A spring—hm—yes—so we came in."

"Take her unawares, I tell you! She will guess what the matter is if you drag things out like that."

"Well, do it yourself as you want. But let me out of it," muttered Chubikoff, rising and going to the window.

"Yes, a spring," began Dukovski, going close to Olga Petrovna and wrinkling his long nose. "We did not drive over here—to take supper with you or—to see Kuzma Petrovich. We came here to ask you, respected madam, where Marcus Ivanovitch is, whom you murdered!"

"What? Marcus Ivanovitch murdered?" stammered Olga Petrovna, and her face suddenly flushed bright scarlet. "I don't understand!"

"I ask you in the name of the law. Where is the body of Klausoff? We know all!"

"Who told you?" Olga Petrovna asked in a low voice, unable to endure Dukovski's glance.

"Be so good as to show us where your husband is!"

"But how did you find out? Who told you?"

The Examining Magistrate, emboldened by her confusion, came forward and said, "Show us and we will go away. Otherwise, we—"

"What do you want with him?"

"Madam, what is the use of these questions? We ask you to show us! You tremble, you are agitated. Yes, he has been murdered, and, if you must have it, murdered by you! Your accomplices have betrayed you!"

Olga Petrovna grew pale.

"Come!" she said in a low voice, wringing her hands.

"I have him—hidden in the bathhouse. Only for heaven's sake, do not tell Kuzma Petrovitch. I beg and implore you! He will never forgive me!"

Olga Petrovna took down a big key from the wall and led her guests through the kitchen and passage to the courtyard. The courtyard was in darkness. Fine rain was falling. Olga Petrovna walked in advance of them. Chubikoff and Dukovski strode behind her through the long grass.

The courtyard was wide. Soon they felt freshly broken earth under their feet. In the darkness appeared the shadowy outlines of trees, and among the trees a little house with a crooked chimney.

"That is the bathhouse," said Olga Petrovna. "But I implore you, do not tell my brother! If you do, I'll never hear the end of it!"

Going up to the bathhouse, Chubikoff and Dukovski saw a huge padlock on the door.

"Get your candle and matches ready," whispered the Examining Magistrate to his deputy.

Olga Petrovna unfastened the padlock and let her guests into the bathhouse. Dukovski struck a match and lit up the anteroom. In the middle of the anteroom stood a table. On the table, beside a sturdy little samovar, stood a soup tureen with cold cabbage soup and a plate with the remnants of some sauce.

"Forward!"

They went into the next room, where the bath was. There was a table there also. On the table was some ham, a bottle of vodka, plates, knives, forks.

"But where is—where is the murdered man?" asked the Examining Magistrate.

"On the top tier," whispered Olga Petrovna, still pale and trembling.

Dukovski took the candle in his hand and climbed to the top tier of the sweating frame. There he saw a long human body lying motionless on a large feather bed. A slight snore came from the body.

"You are making fun of us, devil take it!" cried Dukovski. "That is not the murdered man! Some live fool is lying here. Here, whoever you are, the devil take you!"

The body drew in a quick breath and stirred. Dukovski stuck his elbow into it. It raised a hand, stretched itself, and lifted its head.

"Who is sneaking in here?" asked a hoarse, heavy bass. "What do you want?"

Dukovski raised the candle to the face of the unknown and cried out. In the red nose, disheveled and unkempt hair, the pitch-black mustaches, one of which was jauntily twisted and pointed insolently toward the ceiling, he recognized the gallant cavalryman Klausoff.

"You—Marcus Ivanovitch? Is it possible?"

The Examining Magistrate glanced sharply up at him and stood spellbound.

"Yes, it is I. That's you, Dukovski? What the devil do you want here? And who's that other mug down there? Great snakes, it is the Examining Magistrate! What fate has brought him here?"

Klausoff rushed down and threw his arms round Chubikoff in a cordial embrace. Olga Petrovna slipped through the door.

"How did you come here? Let's have a drink—tra-ta-ti-to-tum—let us drink! But who brought you here? How did you find out I was here? But it doesn't matter—let's have a drink!"

Klausoff lit the lamp and poured out three glasses of vodka.

"That is—I don't understand you," said the Examining Magistrate. "Is this you or not you?"

"Oh, shut up! You want to preach me a sermon? Don't trouble yourself. Young Dukovski, empty your glass. Friends, let us bring this—what are you looking at? Drink!"

"All the same, I do not understand!" said the Examining Magistrate, mechanically drinking off the vodka. "What are you here for?"

"Why shouldn't I be here, if I am all right here?"

Klausoff drained his glass and took a bite of ham.

"I am in captivity here, as you see. In solitude, in a cavern, like a ghost or a bogey. Drink! She carried me off and locked me up, and—well, I am living here, in the deserted bathhouse, like a hermit. I am fed. Next week I think I'll try to get out. I am getting tired of it here."

"Incomprehensible!" said Dukovski.

"What is incomprehensible about it?"

"Incomprehensible! For heaven's sake, how did your boot get into the garden?"

"What boot?"

"We found one boot in your bedroom and the other in the garden."

"And what do you want to know that for? Why don't you drink, devil take you? If you wakened me, then drink with me! It is an interesting tale, brother, that of the boot. I didn't want to go with Olga. I don't like to be bossed. She came under the window and began to abuse me. She always was a termagant. You know what women are like, all of them. I was a bit drunk, so I took a boot and heaved it at her. Ha-ha-ha! Teach her not to scold another time! But it didn't—not a bit of it! She climbed in at the window, lit the lamp, and began to hammer poor tipsy me. She thrashed me, dragged me over here, and locked me in. She feeds me now—on love, vodka, and ham! But where are you off to, Chubikoff? Where are you going?"

The Examining Magistrate swore and left the bathhouse. Dukovski followed him, crestfallen. They silently took their seats in the carriage and drove off. The road never seemed to them so long and disagreeable.

Both remained silent. Chubikoff trembled with rage all the way. Dukovski hid his nose in the collar of his overcoat, as if he was afraid the darkness and drizzling rain might read the shame in his face.

When they reached home, the Examining Magistrate found Dr. Tyutyeff awaiting him. The doctor was sitting at the table, and, sighing deeply, was turning over the pages of the *Neva*.

"Such goings on there are in the world!" he said, meeting the Examining Magistrate with a sad smile. "Austria is at it again! And Gladstone also to some extent—"

Chubikoff threw his cap under the table and shook himself.

"Devils' skeletons—don't plague me! A thousand times I have told you not to bother me with your politics! And you," said Chubikoff, turning to Dukovski and shaking his fist, "I won't forget this in a thousand years!"

"But the safety match? How could I know?"

"Choke yourself with your safety match! Don't make me mad or the devil only knows what I'll do to you! Don't let me see a trace of you!"

Dukovski sighed, took his hat, and went out.

"I'll get drunk," he decided, going through the door and gloomily wending his way to the inn.

# ASIA

# THE CHING LADY

*By Doug Allyn*

Bradley cunningham has an endless reserve of small talk, a valuable trait in a bureaucrat, I suppose. So far we'd discussed the coming monsoon season, local Taiwanese politics, and even the new Buicks, though I knew he wouldn't buy one from me. Embassy staffers can import their personal cars duty-free.

I wondered when he'd get to it. We weren't friends, and I couldn't see him stopping by my office just to chat. Besides, he seemed a wee bit uneasy, though maybe that was because his tropical worsted was a better fit twenty or thirty pounds ago.

"Those Ming scrolls look authentic, Charlie," he said, with semi-sincere admiration, "business must be good."

"I sell a car now and again," I said. "In fact, I'm running a bit behind with my paperwork, so, was there something . . . ?"

"An odd thing did come up at the embassy this week," he admitted, "the ah, ambassador was approached unofficially by the Taiwanese Minister of the Interior. It seems they have a prisoner they're concerned about, a man named Doherty. They want to come to an . . . arrangement."

"Why are they concerned about him? He a Kennedy nephew, is he?"

"No, he's nobody, but they don't want an American dying of dysentery in one of their jails just now. Bad public relations, you know."

The showroom bell jingled out front. An elderly Taiwanese in a three-piece suit and thong sandals wandered in out of the April heat to check out our stock of new and pre-owned Buicks. I kept an eye on him through my office doorway, hoping he wouldn't need mouth-to-mouth when he saw the sticker prices.

"So why don't they just cut whatsisname loose?" I said, "deport him or something?"

"They can't," Cunningham sighed. "He still has half of a twenty year sentence to serve. For smuggling drugs, I believe it was. His work record is good though, so they're ah, willing to parole him here in Taipei if we can find him some kind of a job."

He paused, waiting for me to volunteer.

I let him wait. When I decided to muster out of the army here back in '78, the American embassy treated me like the amazing invisible leper. If they wanted a favor from me now, they could ask. Politely.

"Well, Charlie," Cunningham said at last, "what do you think?"

"I can ask around," I said doubtfully, "but you know how tough it is for foreigners to find work here."

"Actually, we ah, we were hoping you could take him on."

"Me? To do what, exactly? Besides, even if I wanted to, which I don't, I don't do the hiring for the dealership."

"But you're the manager here—"

"Only because Mr. Liang thinks his customers are more likely to buy American cars from an American. If I ask him to hire some jailbird I may need a new job myself."

Cunningham leaned forward, his pudgy face grim. "Doherty's going to be released from the hospital tomorrow, Charlie. If we don't come up with something, they'll send him back to the work camps at Gaoshung. He won't last six months. The ambassador can't ask you to do it officially, of course, but if you could manage something we'd consider it a favor."

"Okay, okay," I grumbled, "I guess he can sweep up or whatever, but you owe me one, Brad."

"I won't forget it," he said, looking pleased with himself. "I don't mind telling you this thing's been a real headache."

"Most of us take aspirins for a headache," I said, "you guys just delegate yours. What's Doherty like, anyway?"

"He's ah—colorful," Cunningham said blandly, "you'll like him, Charlie. Trust me."

"Mmmmm," I said.

The next afternoon two hard-eyed Taiwanese military cops in a battered jeep dropped a passenger in front of the dealership. I'm not sure what I'd been expecting, a bombed-out flower child I suppose, but what I got looked more like a leprechaun, a wizened, wiry little character in a rumpled secondhand suit. He strolled casually through the dealership, checking it over as though he was thinking of buying the building. I didn't bother to get up.

"Mr. Doherty, I presume?" I said.

"Patrick Aloysius Doherty, at your service," he nodded brusquely, "and you'd be Charlie Marks, the gentleman in difficulty?"

"Difficulty?"

"You needn't be embarrassed, Mr. Marks, I've been in a jam or two myself in my time. Fortunately, as I'm between positions at the moment, I may be able to help you out. Assumin' we can come to an understandin' about wages, of course."

"Right," I said, "look, Mr. Doherty—"

"Don't feel you have to thank me, Mr. Marks; if Americans don't help each other out in this godforsaken country, who will, eh?"

We eyed each other in silence for a moment, across a generation or two and a teakwood desk. "How long were you in the work camp at Gaoshung?" I asked at last.

"Ten years or so," he said evenly, "you lose track of time after a while."

"I suppose a man could work up a thirst in ten years," I said, taking the bottle of Chivas Regal from my file drawer and placing it on the desk. "Can I buy you a drink?"

"No," he sighed. "I'm afraid not. A man oughtn't to accept a drink if he can't stand a round in turn, and I'm just a tad short of funds this week."

"Mr. Doherty," I said, "I think we may just get along."

And we did. In fact, hiring Patrick was the smartest move I'd made in years. He was dependable, affable, and a born salesman who could hustle cars in three different Chinese dialects. Our gross sales rose by a quarter during his first month. Mr. Liang gave me a bonus, Patrick was grateful to be free, and I was feeling thoroughly smug about the situation. Until I took him with me to a Wednesday night poker game at Liang's villa.

Liang's home is north of the city, a mile or so up Yangminshan, Grass Mountain. The house is typical Taiwanese middle class, a rambling, red-brick ranch with a green tile roof, thick, earthquake-resistant walls, and narrow, thief-resistant windows.

Liang's wife greeted us at the door, a stolid, smiling peasant woman from down island, uneducated but a hard worker and as devoted to Liang as an Irish setter. She led us through to the verandah at the rear of the house, a cobblestoned terrace with a fantastic view of the city lights below.

The two men seated at the low mahogany table were similarly dressed, shortsleeved white shirts over dark slacks, but there the resemblance ended. Fred Chen, Liang's brother-in-law, stood six four in his sandals and resembled an outsized stork in horn-rimmed glasses. He taught history at Taipei

University and handled the books for Liang's varied enterprises. Liang himself was nearly a foot shorter, a reserved, gourd-shaped Taiwanese with hair and eyes as black as anthracite and a soul to match.

Liang rose as we came in. "Hello, Charlie," he nodded, "and this must be your Mr. Doherty," he said, offering his hand. "Welcome to my home."

"I'm honored, Liang Syansheng," Patrick said in flawless Mandarin.

"I'm afraid you must content yourself with conversing in English, Mr. Doherty," Liang said. "I need the practice and I prefer that my wife doesn't know how much I lose. Or win," he added slyly. "And this is Mr. Chen."

"Doherty," Fred nodded, without rising, "Liang tells me Charlie hired you out of the Gaoshung prison camp. I hope you weren't there for cheating at cards."

"I've been known to shade a deal or two in my time," Patrick said smoothly, "but never in games with big fellas played on the edge of a cliff."

"A sound philosophy," Fred smiled. "Mr. Doherty, I look forward to taking your money."

"Likewise, Mr. Chen," Patrick said, with a curt bow.

"Shall we get started, gentlemen," Liang said, easing into one of the tower-backed rattan chairs. "The game is spit-in-the-ocean, jacks or better to open."

The evening passed agreeably, cutthroat poker with evenly matched opponents, sipping plum brandy with the lights of Taipei spread out below us like a blanket of stars. Patrick proved to be a ferocious poker player as well as a mighty storyteller, regaling us with tales of the Boston underworld, or smuggling in Hong Kong, while each of us waited for the run of cards that would reduce the others to begging rice in the streets.

It was as fine a night as I can remember until sometime long past midnight, when Patrick told us about Cockeye Hwei and the old lady's grave.

"Cockeye was a crazy little fella," Patrick said, frowning at his cards. "Now, mind you, grave robbers are all crazy anyway, since there's nothin' in the tombs worth stealin' but an occasional trinket, and the graves are deathtraps that'll collapse on you if you look at 'em sideways, which Hwei couldn't help doin' because he was cockeyed. Are you familiar with the tombs I refer to, Charles?"

"Sure," I said, "little brick domes like igloos. They had 'em in Vietnam, too." I didn't bother to add that sometimes we'd stomp holes in the tops because it was easier than digging a latrine trench.

"Igloos," he nodded approvingly. "I've always thought they look more like roadside barbecue ovens. In any case, Hwei got caught when a tomb caved in on him, leaving only his poor head free. Howled like a banshee for three days and nights, which the villagers thought he was. Some soldiers found him eventually. When I met him in Gaoshung he was a certifiable loony. Claustrophobia. Afraid of the dark, couldn't sleep, couldn't even cover himself with a blanket. Many a night I held him just to keep him quiet while he mumbled and shivered. Then we began work on the Tam Sui levee, and the guards made sure Cockeye always worked in the deep trenches. Shoveled like a madman down there, afraid of bein' buried, you see, and gettin' dafter by the day. Then one night he wakes me, perfectly calm. Said he was leavin' and wanted to give me somethin' for my kindness. Told me there was a great lady buried in the Imperial Cemetery at Chunghsin, buried with all of her clan's wealth. Said I should raid the crypt and burn joss for him."

"Why didn't he raid it himself when he got out?" I asked.

"Grave rats don't get out," Patrick said. "Twenty years is the usual sentence. Or life."

"He must have been crazy," Liang said. "There are many thousands of tombs at Chunghsin. It's like a city of the dead."

"What happened to Cockeye?" I asked. "Did he get away?"

"Sort of," Patrick said. "He ran the next day. Came screaming up out of the trench. The guards shot him down."

*"Sz ren buyau dzai dzji sweijyau,"* Liang said, and tapped the rim of his glass with a fingernail for more brandy, which his wife brought at a trot.

"Dead men don't what?" I asked.

"The dead grow lonely in their tombs," Fred translated in his impeccable university English. "It's a folk saying, probably derived from the fact that grave robbers are so often killed when the tombs collapse."

"You'd have to be nuts to risk it," I said, tossing in my cards. Nobody was paying attention to the game anyway. "Besides, it's not a Chinese custom to bury anything really valuable, is it?"

"No," Fred said thoughtfully, "it's not. So I wonder why this Hwei thought . . . Did he know what the lady's name was, Patrick? Or when she died?"

"Shr Dz Hsi. Year of the Dog, 1889."

"So what's in a name?" I asked.

"Probably nothing," Fred shrugged, "but the name is northern Chinese, so perhaps I can throw some light on the mystery."

"Really?" Patrick said, a bit too casually, I thought.

"There are some imperial records in the basement of the university library," Fred said, "deeds, tax records, and so forth."

"Come on, Fred," I said, "she's been dead a hundred years."

"My ancestors were keeping records, Charlie, when yours were still living with wolves and painting themselves blue. If this lady is more than just a fairy tale, there should be some record of her, and looking for it might be interesting, like a difficult crossword puzzle."

Fred was a crossword addict. He should have stuck to them.

* * *

The following Wednesday night, Fred Chen anteed a single sheet of paper, covered with calligraphy. "The great lady's obituary," he said smugly. "She was Ching."

We waited.

"Well for the luvva Jesus, man," Patrick exploded, "what's a Ching?"

Fred stared at him in total disbelief. "The Ching Dynasty ruled Imperial China for three hundred years," he said coolly, "but they were not Chinese. They were Manchurians. Manchu. And the Manchu did sometimes bury things."

"You're saying she was some kind of queen?"

"No, her family was military, but they must have been noble. She was buried with a dozen retainers."

"Retainers?" I said, "you mean they buried her damn servants with her?"

"Not real servants," Fred said, suppressing his irritation, "replicas of them, to serve in the afterworld. It was an old Chinese custom some of the Manchu adopted."

"But what about treasure," Patrick pressed, "gold, or jewels?"

"No mention of anything like that, only family mementoes."

Patrick sagged in his chair. Fred glanced around the table, noting our obvious disappointment. "It's like trying to explain the Buddha to baboons," he sighed, removing his glasses and massaging the bridge of his nose. "Her retainers. It says they were carved in jade. Antiques. From the Sung Dynasty."

"My God," Liang breathed softly. "Northern Sung? Or Pienching?"

"It doesn't say, but it really doesn't matter, does it?"

It didn't. I'm no antiques expert, but if the figurines were Sung Dynasty pieces of the quality that a noblewoman would have possessed, Liang might be able to afford one or two if he sold everything he owned. A dozen? Priceless.

"Does it ah, mention where she's buried?" I asked.

"Of course," Fred said, "on the Hill of Nobles." And he burst out laughing, a choking cackle that sounded like he was being strangled. And he would have been if he hadn't paused for breath and realized how private his little joke was. "The hill has perhaps five or six hundred tombs on it," he gasped, "maybe more. She could be anywhere."

"But aren't the graves marked?" I asked.

"Yes, but she was a woman. Her name would only have been written on red paper pasted above the door when the tomb was sealed."

"You mean there's no carving on the stone to say where she lies?" Patrick asked. "What the hell kind of heathen way is that to mark a grave?"

"Perhaps," Liang said quietly, "they were afraid of thieves."

For a moment something dangerous flickered between them, but then

Patrick slowly shook his head and began to chuckle, and Fred got the giggles again, and we all wound up laughing until the tears came. Easy come, easy go. And that might have been the end of it if Patricia Cargill hadn't dragged me kicking and screaming to the opera.

Patti runs the Air Australia agency across the street from the Buick dealership on Chungshan Road. She has hair that shines like a raven's wing, a smile like sunrise, and the body of a pro football player. But, two out of three ain't bad, as the saying goes, and in the army I learned to appreciate substantial women. And every other kind.

Patti's bright, pert, and good company. Her only flaw is that she's an evangelist for all things Chinese, and our occasional evenings together are usually spent at excruciating cultural events; museums, lectures, or whatever. But afterwards, well . . . she makes it almost worthwhile.

She called me on Saturday and said she'd had the amazing luck to score two tickets to the opera, a Chou Dynasty classic. Amazing luck is right, I thought, smothering a groan, but I said okay. There was always afterwards.

Our tickets were for the second performance. We stood in a line that stretched two and a half blocks, at nine thirty on a Tuesday night. In the rain. To see a twenty-five-hundred-year-old opera that had been playing in Taipei for over a year. The Chinese take opera a lot more seriously than we do. I can't imagine why. The singing's deafening, the music's weird, and the plots make as much sense as ours do. None.

The story was the rough equivalent of Romeo and Juliet in Old Shanghai. Chinese opera does have one refinement ours lacks, cymbals crash at odd moments to keep you awake, which is why I was when Romeo, or whoever he was, bought the farm. Juliet told him she was going to marry his rich rival, so Romeo coughed up a little ketchup, sang for another ten minutes, and dropped dead of a broken heart. They loaded him on a bier with his daddy's sword and stuck him in a tomb, stage right.

That's when it hit me.

I stood up and stumbled across assorted ankles and toes to the aisle, ignoring comments about foreign devils in general, and some specific ones about my mother the turtle.

"Dianhwa?" I asked an usher at the door, "telephone?" But he was in tears like everybody else in the place, and just waved me past. I finally found a pay phone in the deserted lobby and rang Fred Chen. No answer. I reentered the darkened theater just in time for the opera's big finish.

Juliet was dressed in her wedding gown, singing her heart out in front of Romeo's tomb. I'd just blundered back to my seat when there was a flash of lightning onstage. Suddenly Romeo's grave split open. Juliet rushed inside it and then the whole thing collapsed, burying them together for eternity. I couldn't sit down. I just stood in the darkness, staring at the shattered tomb while my insides congealed into ice and the chorus bellowed about true love lasting forever.

Patti glanced up at me, her mascara in streaks. "Charlie," she sniffled, "what's wrong? You look like you've seen a ghost."

When I arrived at Liang's villa the next night, Patrick was already there. The sharp tang of opium smoke hung in the air, and Patrick and Liang watched, glassy-eyed and bemused, as I paced the terrace waiting for Fred. I began grilling him the moment he walked in.

"You told us the old lady's family was military, Fred. What did you mean by that?"

"Her father was a Manchu general."

"Okay, I saw an opera last night where a guy was buried with a sword. Would the old lady have been buried with any weapons?"

"The Manchu were a nomadic warrior people," he said, shaking his head, "they didn't bury weapons with women."

"But if the family was military—"

"She was a spinster," he said, "and her father's weapons and armor would have been buried with him."

"But nothing like that with her? No metal?"

"I doubt it. Only mementoes, dresses perhaps, things like that. Why?"

I sighed and poured myself a glass of brandy. I needed it. "I just had the idea that if she was buried with weapons, we could use a metal detector to find her."

"A metal detector?" Fred echoed blankly.

"Yeah, a minefinder. Like we used in Vietnam."

"The American mind is an amazing thing," Fred smiled, "always seeking answers with technology. A minefinder. I wouldn't have thought of that."

"Yeah, well, it doesn't matter."

"Do you have any idea how many tombs are in the Imperial Cemetery, Charlie?"

"Not really, thousands, I guess."

"Correct, but the Manchu have their own section, the Hill of Nobles, perhaps five or six hundred tombs, some marked only with the family name, many not marked at all. Shr is quite a common Manchu name, you know, there might be twenty or thirty tombs bearing that name."

"So what's your point, Fred?"

"Bear with me," he said smugly, "and perhaps learn something. For instance, in Imperial China, soldiers, even generals, were low-caste, only rarely rising to the nobility. The Ching lady's father is almost certainly the only soldier named Shr on that hill."

"So?"

"And with your metal detector, we could probably locate his tomb."

"But why would we—?" I began, but suddenly I realized why, and we were grinning at each other like complete morons. "She's buried beside him, isn't she?"

"Of course," he giggled, "with no husband, where else?"

Patrick wasn't smiling. He watched us congratulate each other with an odd, hard look in his eyes that had a distinctly sobering effect. "Something eating you?" I asked.

"Nooo," he said coolly, "but before you wear your shoulders out pattin' each other on the back, even if you could find the grave, what makes you think the jade would still be there?"

"The time element," Fred said, irritated. "She was buried in 1889, during the Manchu rule. They worshipped their ancestors so the cemeteries were guarded, and later, when the Japanese occupied the island and sealed it off, no one would have risked death to steal trinkets they couldn't sell."

"Mebbe so," Patrick conceded, "I don't know about history and such, so I'll tell you what I do know about. Prison. Twenty years is the sentence for grave robbin'. Twenty damn years. We've had fun with this thing, but it's not a joke any more, is it? I can see the avarice shinin' in your faces like fire, I—" He broke off, massaging his eyes with his fingertips as though he were suddenly very tired. "I owe you and Liang my life, Charlie," he said quietly, "for gettin' me out of jail. I'd've died there. And you've all been kind to me, treated me like kin when you owed me nothin'. So I just want to remind you that the poor bastard who told me this story died in a ditch with his brains blowed out. There was no luck in it for him. We'd best forget the whole thing. Leave her be."

"Since your risk would be greater than ours," Liang said carefully, "perhaps you would rather not—"

"Hell, you can't do it without me," Patrick flared, "I'm the only professional thief here! In fact, if you're gonna have a go, I figure you owe me an extra ten percent for tellin' you the story in the first place."

"Ten percent?" I said. "Gee, Patrick, what about owing us your life?"

"It's true," he said, nodding vigorously, "the dysentery woulda taken me. I had to count my ribs every mornin' to make sure I hadn't shat one into my pallet durin' the night. But on the other hand, how much is the life of a dyin' man worth? I figure if I gave you twenty bucks apiece you'd owe me change. Besides, stealin' is my trade. I've given this a lot of thought. I've got a plan. A foolproof plan."

"An extra five percent," Liang said, smiling, "for your expertise. Five percent."

Patrick glanced at us and Fred and I nodded, and that was it. It was settled without so much as a handshake. We were about to become grave robbers. And honey-dippers.

* * *

Four days later I was standing in a benjo ditch, ankle deep in sewage, while Patrick and Liang smeared slop on me, on my clothes, and on each other. The stench was terrible, but not as grim as watching Fred fumble in the muck trying to find his glasses, which he'd lost while he was coughing up his lunch. Patrick's plan was clever, but it was a little short on style.

Fred scouted the Imperial Cemetery the day after the meeting. He entered the grounds with a busload of Japanese tourists, and then wandered around with a clipboard. Nobody bothers anybody with a clipboard. He spent the day mapping the place, and noting the tombs with the Shr family name. Thirteen of them.

While Fred was playing tourist, I scrounged a serviceable metal detector from a black market dealer, a British army #4C minefinder. It weighs fourteen kilos, looks like a discus on the end of a stick, and can sense metal within thirty inches. It has a sensitivity gauge and a buzzer loud enough to wake the dead. I disconnected the buzzer.

On Sunday we met at a deserted farmhouse Liang had located, a crumbling brick building with an enclosed courtyard in the rice paddy country north of Chunghsin. When I saw the honey-wagon in the courtyard, I realized how Patrick intended to avoid the patrols, but it was too late to back out.

Since relations between Taiwan and mainland China are tense, there are army patrols all over the place, especially at night, and nobody does much traveling without being stopped. Well, almost nobody. The island may have jet ports and atomic power, but the sewer system is still fairly crude, a network of benjo ditches which carry the raw sewage to the sea. Or they're supposed to. Sometimes the stuff clots, which is where the honey-dippers come in, three or four guys with a barrel-shaped truck which they fill with muck from the ditches, using long-handled scoops. Since the men and the trucks get thoroughly grubby in the process, everybody avoids them, including the patrols, so using a honey-wagon for camouflage was brilliant, except for the part about having to look and smell authentic.

Still, when we drove out of the courtyard in the wagon that night, our skin and clothing smeared with goo and giving off a stench that would gag a graveyard rat, we could have fooled Charlie Chan himself. Except that every now and then Fred would lean out the window to retch on the running boards. Real honey-dippers hardly ever do that.

Blundering down the back roads in a rickety sewer truck was bad enough, but we also had to listen to Patrick's machine gun stream of advice. Our professional thief was as nervous as a nun on her first date.

"Remember, if we're stopped, nobody talks but Liang. On the hill, keep low when you're near the top so you're not skylined, and don't forget to—"

Suddenly Liang cranked the wheel over and we careened off the road, crashing through a wall of vegetation, and lurching to a halt in a bamboo thicket. I didn't know if he'd seen something in the road, or only wanted to stop long enough to strangle Patrick, but it was neither. Through the shattered bamboo branches I could see a dark shape looming over us, blotting out the stars. A monstrous, barren hill, its skeletal ridges covered with hundreds of bulbous shapes which seemed to cling to its sides like feeding leeches. Leeches made of brick. We had arrived.

We sat silently for a moment, awed by the sheer size of the hill and its thousands of graves.

"All right, young virgins," Patrick said quietly, "it's time for the dance. Liang stays with the truck, Fred leads the way. Let's go."

I grabbed the minefinder and stumbled after Fred and Patrick into the dark. It was rough going. The light from the waning moon barely penetrated the tangled bamboo, and we were thoroughly battered and scratched when we finally emerged at the foot of the hill. Fred was all business. He took a moment to orient himself and check his map, and then led us to the nearest of the Shr family tombs.

The tombs aren't large, usually no taller than a man's head, with sealed entrances surrounded by ornate stonework. I motioned the others back and switched on the metal detector, sweeping it over the door as though I were brushing away cobwebs, my eyes riveted on the magnetometer. Nothing. We repeated the process on a second tomb near the base with the same results, and then cautiously made our way up the hill, sweeping four other widely scattered graves as we climbed. Still nothing, and Fred's list was dwindling. We swept the seventh tomb unsuccessfully and were moving across the brow of the hill when I fell.

We'd picked up our pace. The wind was rising, harrying patchy clouds across the face of the moon, and during an interval of darkness I stepped into space. And tumbled twenty feet down an eroded trough. Patrick came scrambling down after me.

"Are ya all right, Charlie?" he hissed.

I wasn't all right. I'd jolted my ribs on a boulder and torn my calf open. Fireworks were dancing in my eyes and my head was pounding and then Patrick was on me, his hand clamping my mouth. The pounding wasn't in my head. It was the sound of heavy footsteps. Running.

In the faint light it took a moment to spot the source. Soldiers. At least a dozen, moving at a trot on the main road. They were in full pack and carrying heavy weapons. Night maneuvers then, not a search patrol, but we stayed glued to the hill all the same as they jogged away from us down the dirty ribbon of highway and disappeared into the dark.

Patrick helped me up and we made our way carefully back up the trough. Fred was sitting on the ground, his arms folded around his knees, rocking slowly, moaning softly to himself.

"Fred?" Patrick touched him gently on the shoulder. He looked up at us blankly, his face empty.

"I couldn't find you," he said. "My eyes are not good. And then I . . . heard footsteps coming. I didn't know what to do."

"It's all right," Patrick said. "Charlie fell, but everything's okay now."

I collected the minefinder while Patrick calmed Fred. My leg was throbbing with a bone-deep ache. We were losing the light more often now as the wind grew stronger, mourning through the tombs. Fred consulted his map and shambled off like a zombie to the next grave. I swept it. The needle flipped over. I switched the amplifier off, shook it, and tried again. No mistake, but I was hurting so badly I hardly cared. I glanced down the slope. Damn!

"Fred, Patrick, I think this is it."

"Are you sure?" Patrick said.

I nodded grimly.

"Then what's wrong?"

"If this is the general's tomb, the old lady should be in an unmarked crypt at the foot of his grave, right? So take a look. There are two of 'em."

Fred examined the domes, carefully running his hands over the lintels. "I don't know," he said, shaking his head, "maybe another daughter, maybe his wife. Neither one is marked. I just don't know."

"All right," Patrick said angrily, "so there's two of 'em. So we bust 'em both, that's all. But we can't do it tonight. The storm'll be on us soon and we can't risk a light up here. We'll have to come back."

We moved out like walking wounded, Fred first, stumbling in a daze, and Patrick occasionally supporting me as I limped behind. The moon was covered most of the time now, and the wind was an enemy, chilling us and tearing at our clothes as we made our way down the face of the hill.

We were almost to the thicket when I heard a voice, a woman's voice, howling above the wind. I froze, then turned back toward the hill. Patrick, following with the minefinder, was staring, too.

The hill was only intermittently visible in the rising storm, but I could see something moving among the tombs at the summit. The howling was growing louder. There was nothing ghostly about it. It sounded like an animal screaming in pain.

Suddenly Patrick whirled on me. "Get moving!" he said.

"But what the hell—?"

"Move, damn you, Charlie, or I'll brain you where you stand!" He was brandishing the detector like a club, his face a mask of fear and rage. I didn't know what was on the hill, but there was a killing fury in Patrick's eyes.

I turned and limped into the bamboo after Fred.

*   *   *

The next day the farmhouse was like a penitentiary under siege. We slept like dead men till past noon, then stayed cooped up inside to avoid being spotted.

Liang was eager to hear about the hunt, but other than telling him we thought we'd found the grave, no one had much to say. Fred sat by a window, dull-eyed and apathetic, staring into the empty courtyard. Patrick's usual good humor had a manic edge to it, and his lips had an unhealthy bluish tinge, a reminder of how recently he'd been ill. I was feverish. The wound in my calf was inflamed, an angry, swollen gash with scarlet tendrils radiating from it. Blood poison. Probably from the muck in the ditch.

Patrick, ever prepared, had a G.I. first aid kit. He did a competent job of cleaning the wound, dusted it with antibiotics, and bandaged it tightly. He maintained a cheery, non-stop banter while he worked, all the while warning me with his eyes to say nothing about whatever we'd seen on that hill.

And he was absolutely right. I'd seen guys like Fred in Vietnam. He was on the edge of the darkness. A wrong word could push him over. The afternoon dragged slowly past. We were four friends, only hours away from mortal risk, and perhaps riches, but we had nothing to say to each other. Fred stared, Patrick paced, and Liang watched the rest of us in gloomy speculation. I dozed, and went back to the opera.

I was in the darkened theater again, making my way through a vast, unseen audience toward a stage covered with tombs. Juliet was wearing a white gown, singing her heart out in front of Romeo's crypt, and I took my place beside her, waiting. The chorus was bellowing about true love eternal, when suddenly Juliet ran away from me. She was flitting back and forth like a moth trapped in a lantern, lost among the tombs. And she wasn't singing any more. She was howling. Like an animal. The sky exploded into light, and the tomb before me split open. I rushed into the blackness and a hand touched my shoulder.

It was Patrick.

"Charlie," he said, shaking me gently, "wake up. It's time to go."

We carefully erased all signs of our stay at the farmhouse, and buried the minefinder in the ditch. The inflammation in my calf had receded a bit, and I felt better. Even Fred seemed more animated as we loaded the tools in the honey-wagon and set off in the dark.

Liang stayed with the truck as before and Patrick and I followed Fred as he moved stiffly up the hill. The moonlight was uncertain in a leaden sky with scattered clouds, but the wind was little more than a breeze. Sounds were much more audible than they'd been the previous night. The Imperial Cemetery was alive with them, rustlings and whispering, the scrabbling of tiny creatures fleeing the crunch of our shoes.

The general's crypt was near the crest of the hill and we were all a bit winded when we reached it. Fred pointed it out and then sat down without a word, folding his long arms around his knees, watching us, his gaze intense, but unreadable.

Patrick knelt and unrolled the dirty rag we'd used to muffle the tools, a leather-covered eight-pound maul, a twenty-inch steel chisel, and two pry bars. He handed me the chisel.

"We'll take the one on the left first," he said quietly.

I eased down on my knees in front of the door of the unmarked tomb, and placed the chisel tip against the brick. Patrick picked up the hammer and set himself, his feet wide apart. Our eyes met and held, and for a moment I thought he was going to say something. But he just nodded and shot me a lopsided grin. And then he swung the hammer.

Stone chips stung my face as the chisel bit into the brick and the tomb echoed with the force of the blow. He swung again, grunting with the effort. The brick shattered, splitting the face of the tomb.

And the sky exploded into light.

A parachute flare, and then another, drifting in the night sky above us, bathing the hill in an unnatural alabaster glare. A distant voice, rendered metallic and inhuman by a bullhorn, was screaming at us not to move, and a warning shot buzzed angrily overhead.

And then Fred ran. Arms flailing, legs pumping in long, ungainly strides, he fled blindly across the hillside, stumbling, his legs continuing to thrust even when he fell, jerking him along like a smashed insect. I reset the chisel on the tomb face, a foot to the right of the split. "Bust it," I said.

Patrick tore his gaze away from the distant ring of policemen scrambling toward us from the base of the hill.

"Bust it!" I yelled. "Swing, dammit, or we'll never know!"

He stared at me blankly for a moment, then he nodded, set himself again, and swung. But he was shaking. He struck a glancing blow that wrenched the chisel out of my hands and sent it spinning down the hillside. The force of the missed swing carried Patrick off his feet, slamming him into a stone marker. He crumpled, his face ashen, sides heaving, unable to rise.

I grabbed the maul, squared off, and swung at the crack, hammering at the door of the grave until it shattered, opening like a gaping mouth, and then I plunged inside, into the dust and the dark.

Bradley Cunningham faced me through the wire mesh of the visitors' cell. His usual air of smug self-assurance was absent. He was sweating, and he seemed nervous and uncertain, a rare thing in a bureaucrat. And a bad omen.

"I've just come from a conference with the government prosecutors," he said. "I'm afraid the outcome of the hearing is a foregone conclusion, but—"

"They were waiting for us," I said. "How did they know?"

"That's not important now," he said, "what matters is—"

"It's important to me. Look, nobody's told me anything since they busted us three days ago. Now how the hell did they know?"

"I understand that Mr. Liang's wife—"

"That's impossible," I said flatly. "She barely speaks Chinese, let alone English. She couldn't have known."

"Mr. Liang told her."

"He told her," I echoed stupidly.

"Your employer is an opium user," Cunningham sighed, "and apparently he talks in his dreams. She followed you out to the cemetery with some notion of protecting her husband. They found her Monday morning carrying a cross with an image of the Buddha on it. She'd been lost all night in the storm. She was raving, terrified. The guards weren't sure what was up, but they knew something was. And so they just waited."

I slowly shook my head. "What will happen to her?"

"I don't know. Perhaps nothing."

"What about Patrick?"

"Mr. Doherty will be returned to the work camp at Gaoshung to serve the remainder of his term. Plus ten more years."

"My God." I felt like I'd been kicked in the belly. It was a death sentence. There was a roaring in my ears and I could feel my chest constrict as I struggled to keep from crying for Patrick, and for myself. Cunningham's voice seemed to be coming from very far away. "I'm sorry," I said, "what did you say?"

"I ah, that is, the embassy, has interceded on your behalf. I feel . . . responsible, to some extent, for your involvement in this. At the trial you'll be sentenced to twenty years, but it will be commuted to time served, and you'll be deported."

"Deported?" I felt a flood of relief, followed instantly by a rush of shame. Cunningham seemed to understand, nodding in sympathy.

"And the others?" I said tightly, not trusting my voice.

"Mr. Liang will receive twenty years as well, although with his financial resources, I doubt that he'll serve much of it. Mr. Chen—" He looked away, avoiding my eyes. "Mr. Chen hanged himself the night you were arrested. I'm sorry."

I took a deep, shuddering breath.

For a moment I could see Fred, grinning at me like an idiot. Then the image swam. And dissolved.

"Thank you for coming," I said, getting to my feet. "I appreciate all you've done."

He stared up at me, making no move to leave, and I knew what he wanted.

"The police, ah," he cleared his throat, "the police told me they found you in a tomb that contained nothing of value. Why, Charlie? Why did you break into an empty tomb?"

There was an intensity in his gaze that seemed very familiar. I'd seen it a lot lately, in the eyes of my friends. And in the mirror. And I couldn't help smiling a little as I considered the possibilities. And how much I was going to tell him.

Apparently, I'd found a new partner.

# THE EVIDENCE I SHALL GIVE

*H. R. F. Keating*

S ERGEANT MOOS was a dashed bore. Inspector Ghote thought he was actually the most boring person he had ever known, a one-hundred-and-one-percent burden and bugbear. The trouble was the man could talk about just only one thing. His job, his kaam. Fingerprints.

Certainly there was no one to touch him in entire Bombay Crime Branch as an expert. For that reason, though he was past the statutory age of retirement, he had somehow stayed on in his little cabin, its filing cabinets crammed with the prints of every miscreant who had ever come to police notice. He was, in fact, one famous fellow. It should have been a great honor even to know him. Except he was altogether unable to speak of anything else than his whorls, his loops, and his arches.

So although from time to time Ghote felt obliged to allow himself to be caught by Moos, who seemed to know by some sort of telepathy if he had gone across for something to eat or was on the point of leaving for home, mostly he went to a good deal of trouble to keep out of his way. He had heard Moos's stories and accounts too often, each and every one of them.

"Ghote bhai, was I ever telling you one trick your clever badmash is sometimes trying? You know what it is such a fellow is attempting? He is presenting his fingers to be printed in wrong order only. Yes, yes, one devilish cunning move. He is thinking that when the said card is coming before me and I am seeing twinned loops and tented arches on third finger of right hand when on my records I have such on fourth finger, I would be altogether deceived."

At that point in this story—each time it was told—a glow of simple pleasure would come into the big soft brown eyes in Moos's moonlike face and the cigarette that seemed to dangle permanently from his loose lips would for a moment burn with a brighter light.

"But what a badmash like that is not at all counting on," he would continue, filling in every possible corner of the picture, "is that I am having a tiptop memory for any shape or form of fingerprint. Yes, tiptop though I am saying it. So every time I am catching out such fellows. Never once failing."

"Shabash, Sergeant, shabash," Ghote would dutifully offer congratulation.

But congratulations never brought to a halt the steady dribble of fingerprint fact and fingerprint theory, the be-all and end-all of Sergeant Moos's existence. He had no other interests. He was not married, and all he did when at last he left his cabin after a day's work was get something to eat and then retire to his quarters, where—Ghote had heard this at least a hundred times—he was collecting information to write the really definitive Indian book on—well, fingerprints.

So when at the end of his own long day Ghote might be heading for home, thinking only of his Protima with his food waiting—or ready, if he was particularly tired, to press his feet—and Moos would appear suddenly at his elbow with "Inspector, what luck I am spotting you," his first reaction would be to put up some excuse. Any excuse.

"Oh, hello, Moos bhai. I am just off to—well, I am in one devil of a hurry."

But then, more often than he could have wished, that excuse would fall away into nothingness. The look of pleading in Moos's big brown eyes would be too sad to ignore.

"But perhaps I can spare some minutes only."

Then, over a cold drink at Moos's expense—he was punctilious about paying for his pleasure—there would come once again the story about how such-and-such a history-sheeter had failed to beat Moos's fabulous memory by presenting his fingers to an inexperienced print taker in the wrong order. Or perhaps it would be some other piece of oft-repeated information.

"Did I ever tell, Inspector—not many people are knowing this—it is between the third and fourth what they are calling foetal month that the fingerprints are formed on the unborn child. And those prints thereafter are remaining for the whole of the said person's life unchanged? Those unique prints. Did you know that?"

And Moos would lean back from the little round table with the two fizzing glasses of Thums Up or Limca on it and a look of sun-effulgent pleasure at the beauty of that fact would spread all over his round face. The wet-tipped cigarette between his lips would perk up till it was pointing straight out in front of him, jauntily.

How then could Ghote say, "Yes, Sergeant, you have told me this already?" But after each such session he would say to himself that he was now entitled to adopt any evasive tactics that came to hand to prevent himself being caught again. For at least two weeks.

So it was with a feeling of entirely justified fury that late one afternoon he looked up from his desk to see Moos come bursting in. Only two days before had he not listened patiently for nearly three-quarters of an hour while he had been told—as if it wasn't something he had known since he had been a probationary sub-inspector at Nasik Police Training School— that a workable method of classifying fingerprints had first been developed in India in 1897 by Mr. Edward Henry, later Sir Edward, Commissioner of Police at Scotland Yard, and that his trusted assistant, Sub-Inspector Azizul Haque, had earned the title Rai Bahadur and an award of rupees 5,000?

"Oh, Ghote, you are here?"

"Yes. Why would I not be in my seat? Unless I was out on a case. As I have been till one hour past, and my report not yet finished."

But the pointed remark went for nothing. Moos simply slouched forward, pulled away one of the chairs in front of the desk, and slumped down onto it.

On his innocent typewriter Ghote took out the rage he felt at this blatant disregard of the unacknowledged agreement that he should be badgered by Moos only when he was not actually at work. He seized the wretched machine and dumped it on the floor beside his narrow desk with a crash that risked yet another key becoming appallingly stuck.

But then, as he looked across at Moos, something in the fellow's wide round face drained all his anger away. He did not look at all well. He looked, in fact, grey with illness, or with perhaps the effect of some catastrophic news. And, for surely the first time ever in Ghote's recollection of him, he was not mangling a cigarette between his lips.

"What is it you are wanting, bhai?" he asked then, fearing what he might hear in reply.

But to his surprise Moos answered with his usual request.

"I was wondering— If—if you have some minutes only to spare, Inspector, can we go for a cold drink?"

For a moment Ghote contemplated saying straight out that they did have an arrangement, however much it had never been spoken of, that Moos would not get more than one chat per fortnight. But the grey look on the fellow's face was still there, undiminished. So, although this happened to be the first evening for a week that Ghote was going to be able to get home at a decent hour, he yielded.

He received another surprise then. Moos, although scrupulous about standing treat, invariably took him to an Irani restaurant some way from Headquarters where the prices were moderate. Now, unexpectedly, he proposed a complete break with tradition.

"It is good of you to find some time, Inspector," he said. "I am well knowing you must be wanting to get back to your wife and child. But— But— Well, shall we go to Badshah Juice Bar? You were once stating you were very much enjoying their Ganga Jamuna."

It was true that the mixture of fresh lemon and orange juice, called in comparison with the confluence of the two holiest of India's rivers a Ganga Jamuna, was something—served deliciously chilled—that Ghote particularly delighted in on the rare occasions he felt he could allow himself to sample the air-conditioned luxury of the Badshah, just over the way from Headquarters. But it was extraordinary that, since there could be no fingerprint link to that indulgence of his, Moos should ever have remembered it.

And why was Moos offering to take him to such a posh place at all?

Evidently he was not going to find the answer in a hurry. Once having secured himself the promise of an audience, Moos lapsed into heavy silence. Ghote rapidly cleared the papers from his desk—acknowledging to himself that he had had little intention of finishing his report that day—called to the office peon that he was leaving, and made his way, with Moos a looming, stonelike presence at his side, out and across the jostling, horn-hooting streams of traffic to the Badshah Juice Bar.

When at last he was seated in front of a tall condensation-pearled glass of Ganga Jamuna, and Moos, opposite, had a simple mosambi juice—which despite the fact that he was still not smoking it looked as if he had little intention of touching—Ghote ventured to put a question.

"Well, Sergeant, what is it you are wanting to chat?"

But Moos did not answer.

Ghote shot him a glance in the cool dimness of the bar's upstairs room. Certainly, he did not look at all well.

"Bhai, are you ill itself? Is it serious?"

Thoughts of cancer—all those cigarettes—of leprosy, even, flashed into Ghote's mind.

"No, no," Moos replied, however, "I am hundred percent fit, Inspector. You are knowing I have never had one day of sick-leave in all my years of service?"

"Yes, yes—I remember you saying it. But, all the same, you look as if you are not keeping well, bhai."

"Well?"

Moos sounded as if this was the first he had ever heard of any suggestion that he might be ill. But, if he was not so, what could be wrong with him?

And this silence! He was hardly reluctant normally to talk, to talk and to talk, whenever he had secured a captive audience. So why was he saying nothing now?

Ghote took a sip of his Ganga Jamuna. It was, as ever, delicious. But somehow he could not quite savor it to the full. He looked across at Moos.

"Inspector," the old fellow said at last, seeming to drag the word syllable by syllable, letter almost by letter, from deep inside himself. "Inspector, there is something I have to tell."

"Yes? But that is what we have come here for, isn't it? For you to chat?"

Moos picked up his glass of mosambi juice, looked at it, and put it down again. "Inspector," he asked, lowering his voice almost to a murmur, "Inspector, you are knowing the Phalnikar case?"

"But, yes, Sergeant, of course. Up in court tomorrow, no? Plenty of kudos for Crime Branch there. Who would ever have thought we would be able to lay hands on the culprit when they were first finding his Honor's body in that flat that day? And your evidence will be the clincher, bhai. No getting past fingerprints."

Sergeant Moos was famous, too, for his demeanor in the witness box. No defense pleader, however wily his tactics, however hectoring, had ever been known to shake Moos's simple certainties.

But instead of the slow smile of satisfaction Ghote had hoped to call up on Moos's face by that tribute to the part he would play next day in bringing a murderer to justice, he replied only with a heaving groan.

"Moos? Moos, bhai, what is it? What has happened?"

"It— It—is this."

But there followed only another groan. From the depths.

"Yes, bhai? What it is?"

"Inspector, I have found—I have found something."

"Found something? What? Surely not that you have misidentified that print from the Phalnikar flat? You were telling a fortnight ago how good it was."

"No, no. It is not that."

"But then what is it, bhai? It is to do with the Phalnikar case? It cannot be anything too bad if it does not affect the evidence you would be giving."

"Inspector, it is worse. Worse. Altogether worse."

"No! What? Tell me, bhai. Tell me."

"Inspector—" Moos's voice had sunk yet lower. A mere sloshy whisper. "Inspector, it is this. I have found—I have found one print that is altogether identical with the one belonging to the culprit in the Phalnikar case."

"Identical?" Ghote repeated, struggling with bafflement. "But—but that cannot be, bhai. So often you are telling, I was learning it at P.T.S. even, no fingerprints are identical."

Wearily, with bowed-under weariness, Moos wagged his head in negative.

"No, Ghote, that is not what I have ever said. It is not what you were
truly taught at training school, either. What I have always stated is that
chances of two prints being one and the same have been calculated from the
number of variable factors to be found on each finger—ridge endings, islands, lakes, spurs, crossovers, and bifurcations—as coming out at one in
one hundred thousand crores. It is because of this that it is always accepted
that prints constitute infallible evidence."

Figures slowly surfaced in Ghote's mind. 1:1,000,000,000,000. It was
an incredibly small chance.

He looked at Moos across the narrow marble table. "And you are telling
that this fantastic chance has actually happened? That you have seen a print
that is cent per cent the same as the Phalnikar murderer's?"

"Yes."

It was a whisper of a whisper.

"You are sure?"

The question was ridiculous, he knew. Moos, when it was anything at all
to do with fingerprints, was always doubly, trebly cast-iron sure.

"Yes, bhai. I am sure." The voice came as a series of small, dull hammer-
strokes.

After a moment, Moos gave another of his beaten and battered groans.
"You are knowing, Inspector," he went on ploddingly after a moment,
"that in different countries they have different standards of comparison for
prints. It is something I must have told one lakh times. We are having
different standards in the different states of India even. In Karnataka it is
twelve points that must agree before identity is accepted. In the U.P. it is six
only. While in France it is as many as seventeen. And in the U.K. it is
sixteen."

"Yes, yes."

It was true, as Moos had said, that he had produced these figures and
others like them time and again in their chats. But never till now had he
admitted by so much as a hint that the substance of their conversations had
often been repeated and repeated.

"Well, Inspector, in these two prints I am telling you about I have
checked, point for point, more than twenty-five agreeing. It was just only
this morning that I was going over my evidence for court tomorrow—I am
liking to have everything clear in my head, you know—and, suddenly, looking at the Phalnikar culprit's print, something became triggered off in my
mind. A similarity, a most close similarity. I thought for a few moments
only, and then I was able to go straight to the file in question. It was that of
one Ram Prasad, just only one conviction for H.B."

"One housebreaking conviction only, and you were remembering that print? Moos bhai, you are altogether a wonder."

But the flattery did nothing for old Moos. He sat, his face still as grey as if he was working up to a dose of high fever, his expression that of a man who has just learned he is going to be hanged or shot.

"But," Ghote said eventually, "this is going to cast doubt upon all fingerprint evidences in each and every court, no? I mean, I can hear defense pleaders one and all referring to this discovery which you are making and stating that someone other than the accused must have committed the crime."

"Yes, yes. But it is worse, much worse. I have been sitting all day since I was checking and double-checking what I had found, and I have been thinking—it is not just only our cases, Inspector. It is worldwide also."

"Worldwide?" Ghote thought. "Yes. Yes, you are right. It would be worldwide. As soon as the news is getting out, everywhere in the world where a case is depending on fingerprint evidence your discovery will be brought in. You will be more famous, Moos bhai, than Rajiv Gandhi himself."

But Moos was as stolidly unimpressed by this as ever he was in the witness box by the bullying tactics of a defense pleader. "Soon there will be no more cases depending on fingerprint evidence," he said. "Before one year is out, the fingerprint departments of every police force in the world will be closed down. All the science that has been accumulated since year 1897 is destined to be doomed. All the energies and efforts of nearly one hundred years will be like dew on the grass before the scorch of the sun itself."

Now it was Ghote's turn to sit in silence. Moos, too, his terrible secret told, was again deprived of speech. His glass of mosambi juice remained untouched in front of him. Ghote's Ganga Jamuna seemed equally to be a mere token allowing him to sit in the dark cool privacy of the almost empty upstairs room of the Badshah Bar. To sit and think.

Everything Moos had said was true. That single discovery of his, made thanks to his phenomenal memory for every detail of his day-in, day-out study, was going to put paid forever to a whole highly important branch of the science of criminal identification. Yes, the name of Moos would be heard on the lips of lawyers from the furthermost west of America to the easternmost parts of Japan. Of Moos, destroyer of Sir Edward Henry, of Sub-Inspector Azizul Haque, of all the scientists and police technicians who had ever worked to create the vast system of fingerprinting.

And then his slow-circling thoughts arrived at a conclusion. He looked up.

"Moos bhai," he said. "There is one thing only for you to do. You must forget what you have seen. You must put back into the files that fingerprint

of Ram Prasad and forget that you were ever even suspecting that it was
identically the same as that one of the Phalnikar culprit's."

"No, Ghote bhai. Do not think I have not asked myself one lakh times if
I should do that—if it was not my bounden duty even. But do it I cannot. It
is there. I have seen it. I cannot persuade myself that I have not."

"But, bhai, you must. You must. You know what would be the terrible
consequences if you do not. You have yourself said it. Criminals by the
thousand, by the lakh, by the crore, will escape justice if what you have
found ever becomes—"

An appalling thought flashed into his mind.

"Moos bhai," he said with frenzied intentness, "have you already told
any other person except myself?"

"No, no, Ghote bhai. You know you are the only man in entire Crime
Branch who will ever listen to me."

Ghote registered that, for the second time, Moos had admitted the inad-
missible. So it was certain that only the two of them, Moos and himself,
knew what had been discovered. Himself. He, too, now knew the world-
shattering secret.

He sat in silence again, examining his conscience. What did he feel was
his course in answer to the dilemma that now faced him and Moos equally?

Before long he found that his mind was made up. There must be some
occasions in life when to lie, or at least to blot out the truth, was the one
and only right thing to do. And this, beyond doubt, was one such occasion.

"Moos bhai," he said with renewed earnestness, "what you have found
out must go no further. Not one inch. Ever."

"But, Ghote, have you thought? I have been thinking and thinking all
day, remember. It is not all so simple. I cannot, I cannot, forget what I have
seen with my own two eyes. I have seen it. And you, you will not be able to
forget, either. Because I will show you the evidence. I must. That much I
am owing you. And, once you have seen, you will have always before you
the temptation to speak."

"No," Ghote jerked out in absolute denial. "No, no, no."

"Yes, my friend, you will. I have thought whether I would have this
temptation, and I know that it would come to me. Perhaps on my deathbed
only I will suddenly crave for that worldwide fame you have spoken of. Or
when I am giving my biannual lecture at Nasik P.T.S., that lecture which
Commissioner sahib himself was insisting I must give, perhaps then, even as
I am explaining about odds of one hundred thousand crores to one, I
would suddenly succumb to this temptation. Or what if I am one day
getting drunk?"

"But, Moos bhai, you are never getting drunk."

"Yes, yes, it is true I have never touched any kinds of wines—I have not dared. But in my remaining life who can say that I will not? And then—"

"But, no, that will not happen. It must not. It will not for me, I am promising. I will never fall to the temptation to speak of this. Never. I have decided. Already my mind is made up. Moos, old friend, I am going to forget we have ever met today."

"Ghote bhai, you would not be able."

"Yes. Yes, I would. It is possible to forget as well as to remember. By one effort of will. From this moment on, I am putting out of my mind each and every word that you have said. And I am telling you to do the same. Forget. Forget. Make yourself to forget."

"No."

"Yes. It can be done. It can. If you are willing. Go back to your cabin now. Take that card with the prints of Ram Prasad on it and burn the same. Take out your lighter or your matchbox and then, better than putting the record of a two-per-paisa criminal back into the files, burn it. Just only burn it."

"But, Ghote, tomorrow itself I am to give evidence. In the High Court. And when I am asked by the State pleader, as they are always asking as a matter of routine only, whether the fingerprint put in as evidence is that of the accused and the accused only, what am I to say?"

Ghote braced himself. "You are going to say," he ordered Moos with all the authority he could bring to bear, "that the print put in as evidence is that of the accused. You know that this is so. Say it."

"But the Phalnikar culprit committed his atrocity in the course of house-breaking, you remember that. And Ram Prasad, whose fingerprint is utterly the same as the one I myself was finding at the scene of the crime, has one conviction for H.B. itself."

"Nevertheless," Ghote answered, leaning forward and directing his full gaze into Moos's face, "you are not going to remember that chance discovery you were making when tomorrow you are in the witness box. You are not."

"Ghote, I am. I will. I cannot help myself. Ghote bhai, fingerprints have been my whole life. Without my belief in the truth of them, where would I be? Ghote, on the matter of fingerprints I cannot lie."

"But, Moos bhai, think. If tomorrow in court you come out with this, then from that moment on the whole of your beloved science of finger-printing will begin to crumble into dust. Into dust of dust."

"I know, Ghote, old friend, I know. But what to do? What to do?"

"Forget, bhai. I have said. Forget, forget, forget. Tell yourself that you have dreamt the whole thing. Tell yourself you were for two–three moments mad. One way or another, forget."

"Well, I have wondered that: whether I had gone mad. But that record card, that fingerprint, it is there, Ghote. It is there." Moos picked up the untouched glass of mosambi juice and banged it so emphatically on the surface of the table that a dollop of the pale lime slopped out over his hand. He failed to notice it. "Listen," he said, "you must see that card also. Come now—come and see with your own eyes."

Ghote wriggled on his bench. "But what use would that be?" he said, the thought of how long he had been delayed in going home suddenly blooming in his mind. "I am not at all a fingerprint expert. I could not tell whether you are right or wrong, bhai."

"No—please to come. Please. I want one more pair of eyes to see what I have seen."

"No. I'm sorry, bhai," Ghote said, sweat springing up between his thighs despite the air-conditioned coolness all around. "I must really be going home. Already I am behind schedule one half hour. But I *will* come. First thing in the morning I will come to your cabin, I am promising."

He drained in one long swallow all the rest of his big glass of Ganga Jamuna. It had lost its chill and tasted only of sour sharpness. "But, listen, bhai," he said, looking across at Moos with all the seriousness he could command. "Think about what I have been saying, yes? Just only forget what you saw. Burn that record card. Or at least put it back into the files. Or, better still, do what they are doing in government offices with inconvenient letters. Misfile same. And then forget. Forget it all."

But Moos's big round face remained sullenly lugubrious.

"It has happened," he said dully. "It has happened, and I cannot forget it. I will remember all my life. In court also tomorrow I will not be able to forget." But he pushed himself to his feet and Ghote knew with a wash of inner relief that he himself was free now to go home, to cast off if he could the image of Moos's woebegone face.

"Well, tomorrow we will see," he said. "Go back to your quarters now and get a good night's sleep. In the morning it will all look very much of rosier."

"Yes, I will go. No. No, I will take one more look at those prints. One final final check. Yes, I must. I must. Goodnight, bhai. And thank you for listening to me."

Moos had never before offered a word of thanks for all the long hours Ghote had spent hearing his talk of radial loops, ulnar loops, twinned loops, and lateral pocket loops, or whatever aspect of his obsession happened to come into his mind at any one time. And Ghote now was sharply conscious of the change. For an instant he wondered whether he ought after all to go back to Headquarters and let Moos show him the wretched, damnable record card, little though he probably would be able to make of it. But the thought of Protima waiting for him—or, more to the point, the thought of a wrathful Protima waiting—deterred him.

"Goodnight then, bhai," he said. "See you first thing in the morning."

In a way, however, Ghote saw Moos much sooner than first thing next morning. He saw him in his head through most of that night. He had been unable, indeed, to rid himself of the thought of Moos and his terrible discovery from the moment he had left him. He had been thoroughly poor company for Protima all the evening, till eventually she said that if she was not going to get one word out of him she might as well go early to bed as she had done every night of the week.

And when, after sitting for half an hour trying to push from his mind every looming remembrance of Moos and his fearful horn-sharp dilemma and not succeeding, he went to bed himself, he found, tired though he felt —bone-tired suddenly—that he still could not chase away the sight of Moos's round face, for once without a dangling wet-tipped cigarette at its center, and the look of battered hopelessness in his eyes.

Wryly, he thought of the advice he had offered with such conviction. To forget. To blot it all out. He had said to Moos he was going to do that himself—and here he was, completely unable so much as to begin.

Was Moos really right in the discovery? Had he actually, point by point, seen incontrovertible evidence that the two fingerprints from the hands of different men were exactly and absolutely the same? Could he, despite his years-long reputation, have been mistaken?

Had he—this was a new, sudden thought—had he somehow *desired* to make his discovery, appalling though it had seemed to him? Had he in his innermost self wanted to make it? That chance of two prints being identical, however mathematically unlikely, might well be something that obscurely would haunt someone as obsessed with fingerprints as Moos. So had he, perhaps driven by that obsession to the point of madness, gone so far as actually to invent what he had most dreaded? It was possible. Possible.

Now, violently, Ghote wished he had after all gone to see those two record cards. He would not have been able to make any expert comparison, but he might have been able to see enough to decide there was a prima facie case. Or not. He might even with a single glance have realized that the prints on the two cards were in no way like each other, and have then sadly to have had to escort a mad Moos to the pagalkhana.

Then, lying in the dark and biting his lower lip in vexation, he told himself that this was the merest wishful thinking. Of course Moos, star witness in hundreds of cases involving fingerprints, never successfully challenged, never found wrong, was bound to be right in what he had seen with his own eyes. Yes, the whole huge edifice of fingerprinting was on the point of tumbling down. Tomorrow in the Bombay High Court when Sergeant

Moos was called to give evidence, a whole new era in criminology would begin. A black era.

At last sleep spread over him.

A sleep plagued with dreams. He saw Moos sitting opposite him in the Badshah Juice Bar and showing him all his fingers and thumbs, each one of them with the same pattern clear to be seen. Whirling, twirling question marks. He saw Moos in the High Court witness box, standing on his head. He saw the judges themselves shrinking and shrinking away into nothingness. He saw his own fingers, and there were no tips to them at all.

He woke early, was as bad-tempered as he had been the evening before, pushed aside the beautifully crisp puris Protima had cooked for his breakfast, stamped out well before his accustomed time, and rode his motorscooter down to Headquarters with unaccustomed recklessness.

He had thought, on arriving, that he might even be too early for Moos. But it seemed not: There was a light on in his cabin, the lines of it bright above and below the door.

Strange, he thought.

But perhaps Moos was taking one more look at that fearful evidence and had given himself the very strongest possible light to check on each and every one of those inescapable points of correspondence.

Ghote turned the knob and opened the door.

The moment he stepped into the little crowded room, where the fan in the ceiling was whirring grindingly, he realized he was seeing something which at the back of his mind he had been expecting all along, for all that he had pushed the thought down.

Old Moos was slumped across his examination bench in a limp heap. Beside him was a small blue-glass bottle with squared-off sides, its stopper out. Ghote, at that moment, was unable to recall the name of the liquid it had contained, though only a month earlier Moos had shown him the bottle and told him at length for what abstruse purpose he used minute quantities of its contents. "I have to keep always under lock and key itself," he had said. "It is a Number One dangerous poison."

On the table almost directly in front of the cabin's door there was a large stiff brown envelope. On it, in staring block capitals, was Ghote's name.

He took a step forward and picked it up. But for a moment he found himself totally incapable of opening it.

What if inside there were, as surely there were bound to be, two fingerprint record cards, each bearing a different name, each with the same absolutely identical print? Had the burden which Moos had found too much for him been transferred to his own shoulders? Was he going to be left with the evidence, incontrovertible evidence, that there could be two totally identical fingerprints? And if he was, would he now be able to do what he had with such easy assurance told Moos he would be able to do? To forget that he had ever known of their existence?

Yet, just possibly, one single glance at the cards might be enough to tell him that poor Moos had been driven by his obsession into the mere delusions of insanity.

With sweaty, trembling fingers he tore away the top of the envelope, turned it upside down, and tipped its contents onto the table in front of him: a small pile of grey ashes.

# THE CHINESE GUILT TRIP

*By Wyc Toole*

THE MAN sitting across from me looked as if he had stepped directly out of a British Airways ad for a two week tour of England . . . tall, lean, bowler hat, furled umbrella, dark suit, snow white shirt with high collar, and a thin, striped regimental tie. His accent was crisp, precise Londonese, and his face long and ruddy, split into two unmatching parts by a sharp, hooked nose. His mouth was tight and austere with no signs of smile lines, and the small attempts at humor I had attempted to inject into our conversation had been totally ignored.

He had introduced himself as Andrew Thorton, a British solicitor, and we had been talking for the better part of an hour about a man I had known in Hong Kong a very long time ago. A man and a place I had managed not to think of for many years. But as soon as Thorton asked me if I knew a Mr. Harpe, good old Robert bounded out of my subconscious along with the vivid memory of anger, copper red hair, and sky blue eyes.

Since I was not sure what Thorton was after, I had cautiously answered his questions as well as I could, considering what had happened and the passage of forty-odd years; yet I still had no better understanding of the reason for his visit than I did when he first marched into my office and inquired if I was indeed Mathew Bolton.

Mr. Thorton had called me "on a matter of the *utmost* urgency" earlier that morning and I had squeezed twenty minutes out of a full schedule for his visit. However, I had gotten lost in the memories of the days he was asking about, and now my secretary had begun peeking nervously into my office as a reminder of the time. I was just starting to tell him I was enjoying our conversation but would have to leave, when I saw his pale grey eyes register a decision.

Before I could speak, he sat back, nodded in agreement with his own thoughts, picked up his briefcase, set the combination lock, snapped it open, and said, "Well now, Mr. Bolton, your credentials and our conversation are more than adequate for my purposes. If you will be good enough to sign this acknowledgment of receipt, I will give you Mr. Harpe's letter."

I read the document he handed me, and it was precisely what he had said it was: an acknowledgment that he had delivered into my hands a sealed letter from Mr. Robert T. Harpe to Mr. Mathew R. Bolton.

As I was signing the paper, he commented, "I'm terribly afraid you may find the date on the letter somewhat disturbing. A year is a long time in transit. However, you were not all that easy to locate, you know. All Mr. Harpe was able to give us was your name and a hotel in Hong Kong that is now an office building. Rather difficult, that."

"He *is* still alive?" I questioned.

"No. Very sad. Robert died about six months ago. We are handling the estate and your letter is one of the loose ends we need to tie up."

"Do you know what's in the letter?" I asked.

"Not really. Mr. Harpe could be most secretive about his private affairs. I suspect you know that already, uh? I am privy to the knowledge that there is to be some sort of accounting for something that happened between you two in those days, and my firm is prepared to honor whatever instructions the letter contains for us. You can reach me here at any time," he offered, handing me a card. He tried to smile, but didn't quite make it. I had never thought about it before, but I guess you have to do anything—even smile—more than once a year to make it seem natural.

My curiosity level was well over the 98.2 mark and the afternoon was shot anyway, so I told my disapproving secretary to cancel the rest of my appointments, hold all calls, not to peek into my office to see if I was alive or anything like that, closed the door firmly, returned to my desk, and sat looking at the unopened envelope and thinking of Hong Kong in 1946. My God! Nineteen forty-six . . . forty-two years ago . . . not possible . . . but when you subtracted the numbers that's how it came out.

So much time and so much change. I see what they say is Hong Kong on television today and all I recognize is a bit of the harbor. Which doesn't bother me, because the Hong Kong I knew was more exciting and I had the world right by the tail then. I was twenty in 1946 . . . big, strong, healthy, and bullet proof. Absolutely nothing could happen to me I couldn't handle . . . nothing. I was in the Merchant Marines and the whole world was a big beautiful park just made for me to play in and I was enjoying every minute of it. And confident . . . it's almost unbelievable to me now what a clear sense I had then of being very lucky and very special, which is sort of how I came to be in Hong Kong in the first place.

My mother died when I was ten and my father didn't take it well. I ended up living with an uncle, who I know now was a pretty fine man to accept the responsibility for an eleven-year-old boy when he was divorced and trying to live like a carefree bachelor. I have no complaints, however. He did well by me and I think of him now more as a brother than a surrogate father. Anyway, I was a big kid and when I was just sixteen he signed papers that hedged on my age a bit and I went off to sea in 1942 on a freighter to see the world and the war.

I didn't enjoy the war as much as the world, but it was a good time for me. I liked the excitement and learned a lot and by the end of the fighting in '45 I was second mate on a tanker. In June of '46, the ship was en route from Singapore to Tsingtao when we hit a leftover mine floating around loose south of Formosa . . . that's Taiwan now. We lost the ship and four of the crew, but I never got a scratch. The lifeboat was dry, the weather good, and I rather enjoyed the two days of fishing before we were picked up by a passing destroyer and taken to Hong Kong.

As I said, Hong Kong was a much different place in '46. Not rich and sleek like it is today, but crowded, dirty, and hungry . . . busy digging its way out from under the destruction and poverty of a long brutal war . . . a little paint slapped here and there . . . a few buildings starting to go up on the hillsides and around the harbor . . . more being torn down . . . a million refugees jamming the streets and squabbling over what little housing there was. It was all noise and confusion, ugliness and beauty, wild smells and excitement, and you could buy anything you could imagine. Quite a place that Hong Kong.

I wanted to stay a while and the company I worked for gave me recuperation leave. Living space was damn hard to come by, but luckily, the company agent located an empty bed for me in a room at the Gloucester Hotel. From what Mr. Thorton said, it's an office building now, but it was a first-rate hotel then. You notice I said a *bed* in a room at the hotel, because only the very rich and very powerful could get a whole room to themselves and I didn't come close to being either one. However, after the ship, what I had seemed luxurious.

It was a big room on the fourth floor that smelled musty. You entered it from a high, wide, dark corridor through a door into a short hallway. Off the hallway, on the left, was a huge, old fashioned, tiled bathroom with ancient plumbing that worked surprisingly well. The hallway then led into the main room, which was enclosed on three sides by high, cracked, dull yellow plaster walls. The fourth side of the room was an ornately carved

Chinese separating screen that stood in front of two vast french doors lead-ing onto a wide, deep balcony. In the main room were two beds, a sofa, a coffee table, three chairs, and a floor lamp. Two large wooden clothes closets stood against the left wall, and a faded, threadbare Chinese carpet covered the tile floor. There was another bed on the balcony.

I had one of the beds in the main room. The other was occupied by Robert Harpe, the man I had been discussing with Andrew Thorton. He told me he owned a rubber plantation in Malaya.

At that time I guess Harpe was in his early to middle thirties. We swapped reasons for being in Hong Kong and his was to arrange for the purchase of some machinery needed to get his operation going again. He laughed and told me that both he and his plantation had had a hard war. His pallor, emaciation, and a deep, livid scar running the length of his left arm supported his contention. What saved him from looking like an escapee from a hospital bed was his thick, bushy, copper red hair and clear blue eyes. His handshake was firm and he smiled easily and often. His heavy bone structure, erect posture, and graceful movements were additional evidence that a lot of sun and good food would take care of any remaining physical problems he might have. I liked Harpe immediately, and he seemed to feel the same about me.

The balcony formed the living quarters of the third member of our group. His room was almost private in that the french doors could be closed and the screen provided additional concealment. However, because of the sticky, humid summer heat, the doors were kept open to allow the big, slow fan turning noisily on the high ceiling of the main room to move the heavy air a little. In addition to a bed, a squat wooden bureau, and two chairs on the balcony, he had a battered old steamer trunk plastered with ancient ship labels pushed into one corner.

The man living on the balcony was an old Irishman named Patrick Fran-cis O'Halloran. The day I moved in he came into the main room and introduced himself with a brogue so thick it flowed off his tongue and so heavy it sounded fake. I never did find out how old Patrick was and it was impossible to tell by looking at him. He claimed to have spent forty-five years in China—five of them in Japanese prison camps—and that will age anyone a lot faster than mere years. If I had to guess, I would say he was in his middle seventies when I met him.

Patrick was a bit taller than I am. Even slightly stooped with age and the weight of prison camps, he was about six feet two inches and weighed over two hundred pounds—none of it fat. He had two tufts of white hair that stuck straight out from the sides of his shiny bald head and the scraggiest white mustache I had ever seen on a man anywhere. He had a big red nose and amber eyes and I remember that the heat didn't seem to bother him. I never saw him dressed in anything other than a heavy dark blue serge suit, a

white shirt with a high collar, dark tie, and black hightop shoes. As soon as
he dressed in the morning he put on a black derby hat and wore it all day as
he sat on the balcony and talked aloud to himself. Patrick didn't seem to
belong in Hong Kong. He was an anachronism, knocked out of his world
by the war and unable to find his way back.

While I was there, I never knew of a time when Patrick left the room.
The room boy brought in all his meals and any other things he needed.
Occasionally, when he was lucid, he talked to us about going back to Ireland where he claimed to have a sister living in Dublin. However, he never
got any mail and he was very seldom lucid. Perhaps it was age or the
pressures of war or the things he had seen and endured; but whatever the
reasons, his mind was muddled and he was often confused about where he
was and the time he was in and he spent most of his days reliving the past.
When he was happy, he sang old Irish ballads.

I know it sounds bizarre, but that was Hong Kong in 1946, and a crazy
old Irishman could live in a hotel room with two strangers and no one
thought much about it or really even cared. Perhaps it was the conditioning
from the lack of privacy that comes with war; but in those days, if you had
the slightest choice, you accepted people as they were, lived with them,
ignored their eccentricities, and didn't worry about it. Although
O'Halloran did scare hell out of me the first night I spent in the room.

I had gone to bed about two in the morning, exhausted from trying to
see all of the city in one night, and was deeply asleep when the sound of a
heated conversation on the balcony dragged me to the surface of wakeful-
ness. It was sometime between three and four o'clock, that weird, grey time
of night that is always confusing when you wake suddenly, and I distinctly
remember a moment of pure panic as I tried to make sense out of my
strange surroundings and the odd noises that jumbled reality.

The street lights reflecting off the glass of the french doors cast a pale,
sinister luminescence over the room, filling it with distorted black shapes
that made no sense in my bewildered mind. I was completely disoriented
and the loud voice coming from the balcony added to my confusion. I
could only hear one side of the angry conversation . . . one audible voice
demanding and accusing and waiting for answers I couldn't hear.

I had been sleeping face down on the pillow and I pushed myself cautiously up on my elbows and looked around. On the bed to my right I
could make out the sleeping shape of Robert Harpe. To my left the balcony
was hazy, as if filled with a fine mist. Randomly, as I lay listening and trying
to bring the scene into focus, I could see what appeared to be the large
form of O'Halloran pacing back and forth on the balcony, pausing often to
point a distorted hand at someone or something I could not see. His words
were harsh and intense and then I made out the shape of a pistol in his black

hand. My skin tightened and I could feel the hair on my arms rise and rub against the stiff sheets.

"Harpe!" I whispered as loud as I dared. "Harpe. Wake up!"

The dark shape on the bed next to mine moaned, stirred, and a black head rose out of the dark mound on the bed. "Yeah? Whatayawant?" it mumbled.

"Not so damn loud," I cautioned. "O'Halloran's out there arguing with somebody and he's got a gun."

The shapeless head fell wearily back into the black mass of the bed and a detached, sleepy voice said casually, "It's awright . . . he does it all the time . . . doan worry about it . . . le's go back asleep, okay?"

"Harpe! You're not listening to me!" I hissed. "He's bloody angry and he's waving that gun around like he means it. We've got to do something!"

"I got all the bullets to his gun . . . please, Matt . . . lemme go back to sleep, okay?"

I couldn't believe what I was hearing. "Are you crazy?" I said, forgetting to lower my voice. "That damned old man is going to shoot somebody and you keep telling me to go back to sleep! Who's out there with him, for God's sake?"

The head came out of the dark bed again. "Nobody's out there. O'Halloran is nuts. He's buggy. He isn't playing with a full deck. He's talking to somebody who isn't there. I've heard this same fight at least four times since I been here. He's yelling at his wife. She ran off with some bloke in Shanghai years ago and he caught 'em. I think he killed 'em, but maybe he didn't. It was a long time ago and I bloody well don't care. I took all the bullets to that damn gun after the first night I went through one of his spells. If Patrick wants to talk to himself, it is perfectly fine with me. At least *he* doesn't wake me up." Harpe dropped back onto his bed with a finality I was unable to ignore. Within seconds I heard the soft sounds of heavy sleep.

I eased back down on my bed and listened. Harpe was right. Patrick was accusing his wife of sleeping with another man. The words made sense once you understood that one side of the conversation existed only in his mind.

For a full hour I listened to O'Halloran and his ethereal wife fighting on the misty balcony. Then, except for the muffled street sounds, the room became quiet.

That night set the pattern. At least twice a week I would be awakened by O'Halloran's conversations or arguments with apparitions from his past. Also, during the day or late in the evening, I would often return to the room to find him having tea with several empty chairs grouped around the table. After two weeks he began to introduce me to his ghostly guests. By then I was so accustomed to his odd ways that I would acknowledge the eerie introductions and even join the weird scene for a few minutes. On other occasions Patrick would be perfectly normal, laughing and talking with Harpe and me, telling fascinating stories of the old China. Once he even tried to sell me a silver mine he claimed to own in Korea. But on the whole he stayed pretty much to himself on the balcony with his memories of the past.

Harpe and I, on the other hand, had to adjust to each other in the matters of practical living. If one of us brought a girl back for the evening or had a party, the other either kept the lights off, joined in, or left as appropriate. It is hard now to remember just how adaptable I was then. It took Robert and me only a few days to establish a friendship that would have taken years before the war. We shared food, drink, fun, and games with equal enthusiasm, and I found him to be a very exuberant person, totally incapable of abiding inactivity. He was full of plans and ambitions and sure of his future fortunes. He drank well, talked intelligently, and smiled a lot as if he knew things no one else did about how life was going to turn out.

Our lives flowed along like this for about three more weeks. Then, early one evening I left Harpe at the Press Club and returned to the hotel to change clothes for a dinner date. As I entered the lobby the manager intercepted me and asked if either Harpe or I had been having any unusual problems with Mr. O'Halloran. He knew Mr. O'Halloran was "a bit addled," as he put it, but since he paid his bills promptly and we had not complained, the hotel had seen no reason to make an issue of his "condition." However, he was now "concerned," since Mr. O'Halloran had attacked the Chinese laundryman returning my wash that afternoon.

It seemed the room boy had let the laundryman enter our room unaccompanied—which the manager admitted never should have been allowed —where he had been confronted by O'Halloran. The laundryman claimed that without any provocation or warning O'Halloran had gone wild, striking him with a heavy cane and throwing him bodily from the room. The hotel was now worried about our safety.

I told the manager that Mr. O'Halloran was a gentleman and had caused us no trouble whatsoever. Further, that I doubted the entire story and trusted there would be no repetition of people being allowed in our room alone. That it appeared to me the hotel was responsible for the misunderstanding and I certainly hoped it would not happen again. I said all of this in a very loud and indignant tone of voice. My adamant defense of Patrick was not expected, and it so flustered the manager he decided it was best to forget the whole matter and I continued up to my room.

When I shut the door behind me, Patrick came off the balcony and proceeded to tell me with great animation that a thief had broken into the room that afternoon. "Beggar was after my jewelry," he shouted. "Rushed in here bold as a brass monkey. But I gave him a good slash with my cane and threw him out. Nothing safe since the bloody war!" he complained.

I don't remember how the conversation went after his initial outburst because I was busy changing clothes and I had no idea the jewelry existed anywhere other than in his mind. However, I eventually asked him—more as conversation than with any real interest—what kind of jewelry he had and where he kept it. Patrick looked at me with half-closed eyes for a few moments before leading me onto the balcony and over to the old steamer trunk. I was still expecting to make the proper noises over his imaginary stones when he pushed open the trunk, pulled out two drawers and pointed to the contents. To say I was shocked and surprised doesn't come close, for on that open balcony in an unlocked steamer trunk O'Halloran had two deep drawers filled with jewelry. I saw unset stones, rings, necklaces, bracelets, and brooches all tossed together in an untidy jumble. I was no expert, but like most people who traveled the world during the war, I had learned a lot about gems because of the bargains in precious stones available from refugees desperate for dollars. There was no doubt in my mind the stones were real and that there was more than a million dollars' worth in O'Halloran's trunk, unprotected and readily available for the taking. They may have been worth even more, but a million in 1946 dollars was all my mind could handle at that age.

"Where did you get these, Patrick?"

"Here and there . . . round and about," he smiled slyly. "I used to have more. Lots more, but they got lost. I hid these in Shanghai. Had a devil of a time getting them out. Real pretty, ain't they?"

"You should put these in a bank vault."

"Don't trust banks. I only keep money in banks and no more of that than I have to."

"How many people know you've got these up here?" I asked nervously.

"Just you. And I can trust you. All my friends like you, you know."

"Patrick," I warned, "don't trust anyone else. You understand what I'm saying?"

He drew himself up and said proudly, "Of course. What do you take me for? Don't worry so. Now come over here and meet my good friends Toby Rake and John Morse. On their way to India. Beastly place, that damned India. Should go to Ceylon. But they won't listen to me. Everybody has to learn for themselves these days."

I followed him to the table, nodded to the two empty chairs, gave my apologies for a previous date, and left the room in a daze.

I can't explain what happened next. I keep blaming things on the war and that may just be an easy way out. I do know, however, that when you take on a man's job and a man's life when you're sixteen, and you live with death and destruction on almost a daily basis, those fine lines between right and wrong can get very wavy and indistinct. In this case they virtually disappeared and from the moment I saw the jewels I began to think of them as mine. The rationalization was not difficult, either. I was young and O'Halloran was old. If he died, as he probably would in the next year or two, the jewels would be taken by the first person who stumbled across them. More likely, however, someone besides me would learn they were in the room and come after them, killing all three of us if they had to. But uppermost in my mind was the fact that a chance like this would never again come along in my lifetime and I could make much better use of all that money than a crazy old man lost in Hong Kong. Once I convinced myself of those things, it seemed only logical to begin planning how to steal them.

I like to think now that I would never have done any more than plan if I hadn't been pushed so hard so soon after seeing the jewels. But fate leaped up and bit me again two days later.

It was Tuesday morning when the shipping line called and said they needed a second mate on a tanker departing Hong Kong for Basra Friday evening. I had already turned down two ships and I didn't want to go, but the offer was made in a way I couldn't refuse. It was either go or quit and I was almost broke.

By Tuesday evening I had decided whatever I was going to do had to be done by Thursday night and my options were limited. I couldn't just take the jewels and walk away. O'Halloran could convince someone I had taken them, and a ship is easy for the authorities to track. So, as much as I disliked the idea, the safest thing all around was for O'Halloran to commit suicide. With him out of the way I could take the jewels and be gone by Friday night. No one would keep me from sailing to attend an inquest, if I did it right. Harpe might wonder where Patrick got the bullets for his gun, but that wouldn't be enough to stop me from leaving.

I also considered the possibility that Harpe might know about the jewels and have his own plans. If that turned out to be true, I'd just have to split with him. Half was better than nothing and it was a problem I would face if and when it occurred.

The plan I came up with was simple. I would drug O'Halloran Thursday afternoon when he was having tea. While the drug was working I would go down to the bar and drink for an hour or two, giving me a chance to tell the bartender how depressed Patrick seemed. After that, I'd go back to the room, take the jewels and hide them in my luggage, stage the suicide, call the hotel manager, and tell him O'Halloran had just killed himself.

I wasn't worried about anyone's finding out O'Halloran had been drugged. There was too much real trouble in Hong Kong for the authorities to perform a complete autopsy on a demented old man who had obviously shot himself. Also, the hotel would want to keep things as quiet as possible, and his attack on the laundryman would provide ample evidence of his unstable mental condition. Harpe posed no problems, either. According to O'Halloran, he knew nothing about the jewels, and he had a new girl. For the past week he had been coming in at two and three in the morning.

The more I thought about it, the more I realized there just wasn't much that could go wrong. So Wednesday morning I bought a strong sleeping potion from a Chinese herb shop and bullets for O'Halloran's gun from a street vendor. I hid them in my clothes closet. After that there was nothing more I could do until Thursday afternoon.

I tried to pass the rest of the day getting ready to leave, but every now and then a stray doubt that I could actually kill O'Halloran would slip into my mind and fight hard to stay there. I had a miserable day and a worse night. I got very little sleep and that punctuated with terrible nightmares.

The next morning when we were having breakfast Harpe asked me why I was so jumpy. I told him I wasn't happy about leaving and he seemed to buy that as a logical explanation. It was too bad I couldn't convince myself also, because the emptiness in my stomach got worse and the rest of the day seemed to last forever. I was into something I had no experience with, and what I would actually do when the time came to put the gun in O'Halloran's hand and pull the trigger seemed to be the only flaw in my plan.

I left the hotel immediately after breakfast and submerged myself in all the sights and smells of the emerging city, fighting my conscience, the rising excitement of potential wealth, and the fear of what could go wrong. By three thirty, the July heat pressed on me like a heavy blanket, and I was physically drained and mentally exhausted. However, it was time to begin. O'Halloran always had afternoon tea at four, and I started pushing my way through the hot, crowded streets towards the hotel.

I let myself into the room about five minutes after four. The high ceilings and dim light made it seem almost cool, but the palms of my hands were slippery with sweat and my breathing slightly faster than normal. Patrick was sitting at the table drinking tea. There was a cup and saucer in front of the empty chair opposite him. He smiled, stood, and greeted me.

"Mathew, my boy. Do come in and join us. Just started." He turned to the side tray, picked up a cup, and began filling it with the hot, strong tea. While he was busy doing this I moved in behind him, took the packet of sleeping powder from my pocket, and emptied it into his cup. He drank his tea strong, heavily sweetened with brown sugar and thick condensed milk. I was not afraid he would detect any difference in taste.

Patrick turned, handed me the cup, and continued loudly, "Let me introduce you to my friend Colonel Gordon Giles." He pointed at the empty chair. "The colonel lives in Canton. Just in for Christmas holidays. Wonderful time of year, Christmas. Sit down. Might even sing a carol or two."

I nodded to the chair, sipped my tea, and said, "Thought you were going home to Ireland for Christmas this year, Patrick."

O'Halloran frowned, thought a minute, then laughed, "Was, you know. But couldn't leave my friends during the holidays." He looked at a spot above the empty chair where a head would have been if someone were sitting there and asked, "Couldn't do that, could I, Gordy? What's that you say?" Patrick listened, nodded and turned to me. "Gordy says you look disturbed, Mathew. Is there anything wrong?"

The question startled me enough to speak to the fictional Gordy. "Nothing other than I'm leaving tomorrow. I'm not too happy about that."

Patrick listened carefully to the imaginary reply and then, as if translating, said to me, "Interesting. Gordy thinks it's more than that. Thinks you've got the 'not enough time' disease, he does. He says the way your face looks makes him believe you're trying to push the future around some. Bad move, that. Young men always worry needlessly about changing the future. When you get older, you'll understand there's really not much you can do. It rolls over you like a big wave, it does, and I never found a way to stop it or change it one little bit.

"Oh, we all believe we can when we fiddle around and get something we think we want. Pretty sure we changed everything, we are, but that's just fate having a little joke, it is, to teach us a lesson.

"Hard to believe at your age, Mathew, but your needs and ideas *will* change . . . quite often, too. What you want now is totally different from what you'll want in another year or two. That's why I believe when fate gets to feeling frisky and lets you have you that very important thing of the moment, more often than not you'll soon find yourself stuck with something that's nothing but a damn burden you'll carry till you're bloody sick to death of it and not one way in hell to put it down. No, Mathew, we don't change anything. Fate just has fun with us sometimes. And if you doubt what I'm saying, take a good look at me."

Patrick paused, smiled wanly, looked at the empty chair, shrugged, and said quietly, "Although you could be right. I'll admit leaving any place or anyone is sad. A bit like dying, it is. After tomorrow, I'll be dead to you and you'll be dead to me. We'll be no more than little fragments of memories to each other, which is what death usually leaves behind." He turned to the empty chair. "Did I get it right, Gordy?"

The conversation was bothering me. It was either my imagination and guilt or Patrick was using his phantom friend to tell me he knew what I was doing. I suddenly had the eerie feeling that Gordon Giles had seen me put the drug in Patrick's tea and had warned him. I knew right then I had to get out of the room while I still had some rationality and a little nerve left.

I stood up. "Thank you for the tea, Patrick, but I really have to go. I've a girl waiting."

O'Halloran looked at me and then the empty chair. "Young people get nervous when the conversation turns serious, uh, Gordy. Well, you run along, Mathew. When you get to be our ages the young ladies have all come and gone. So kiss as many as you can before the years take them away from you." He took a deep swallow of his tea and looked directly into my eyes, "God bless, Mathew, and don't worry. Things sort themselves out eventually."

I left hurriedly and went to the bar. I drank and talked with the bartender just as planned, but an hour and three gins later I finally admitted to myself there was *no* way I could kill Patrick. It might have been the things he had said to me or perhaps I never did have it in me; but, whatever the reason, I couldn't do it. If fate wanted me rich it would have to show me a better way than murder. The best thing to do, I decided, was go back and make sure he was comfortable while he slept.

I was more relaxed when I entered the room this time. I had been carrying a very large load of fear and guilt that I had put down in the bar and walked away from, and it felt good to be rid of it. I closed the door quietly and walked softly towards the balcony. About halfway there I realized the room was too still. When I reached the french doors I saw why. It was O'Halloran. He was lying curled up on his left side, his right hand clutching the material of his shirt over the area of his heart. His derby hat had rolled under his chair, and his cane lay about two feet from his body. The color of his face and his open, sightless eyes completed the picture of death. I muttered a short prayer, which was more for me than him. Apparently his heart had been unable to cope with the strong sleeping potion I had put in his tea and despite all my good intentions of the past hour, I had murdered him.

I stood looking down at O'Halloran's body for a full two minutes before I finally shook my head hard enough to bring back reality. I had very little time and I had wasted too much already. I turned and ran to my clothes closet, took the handbag I had ready, went to the trunk and began to cram the jewels into it. I was so nervous I dropped some and had to crawl frantically around the floor to find them. When I was satisfied I had them all, I moved quickly back to my clothes closet and put the bag on the top shelf. Then I went back to the trunk, took some clothes from the other drawers and put them in the ones I had just emptied. When that was done, I stood back and surveyed the scene to make certain everything was in order before I went for help. It looked fine at first, but just as I was turning away, out of the corner of my eye, I picked up a bright reflection over by O'Halloran's derby. I went back and saw a large diamond I had missed resting against the brim. I picked it up, started back to my closet, and then the door to the room opened.

I spun sharply and saw Harpe standing in the entrance to the hallway. He looked at me strangely and said, "Dear God, man, you're white as death! What's wrong?"

"I just found Patrick lying on the balcony. It looks like he's had a heart attack. I think he's dead." My voice sounded hollow and far away to me.

"Go get help," he told me. "I'll see what I can do here."

The rest of the day was about what you would expect. The doctor came and said O'Halloran had died of a heart attack and they carried his body away. The police took our statements, and the manager rushed around worrying about what to do with Patrick's possessions and trying to keep everything quiet so as not to disturb the other guests.

It was about eight o'clock when everyone finally left Harpe and me alone. We were both depressed and went out to eat and drink. We ended up just drinking and I awoke the next morning with a horrible hangover. Robert was already in the shower, singing happily, when I dragged myself out of bed and sat trying to make sense of the preceding day. It was too much to handle right then, so I settled for cursing at Harpe when he came out of the bathroom laughing at me.

"You young lads just can't handle it, can you?" He grinned.

I tried to throw a pillow at him, but it didn't make it. "No matter," he roared. "I'll take care of you. Your last day and breakfast is on me. A good lot of eggs, bacon, toast, and gin and you'll be in proper form to impress your new captain. But no dawdling, now. It's already past ten and we have to move you out by noon, you know. So perk up, laddie. Forget about O'Halloran. Terrible thing I know, but we all get old. Even me, I'm afraid," he concluded thoughtfully.

I groaned and headed for the bath. In the shower, I got my mind working enough to decide that Harpe had not known about the jewelry. Otherwise, we would have been having totally different conversations last night and this morning. The water eased the pain in my head, and I began to relax. I was rich and there was little that could beat that for a promising future.

After breakfast, Harpe said goodbye to me on the street in front of the hotel. Nothing elaborate; like most partings of those days it was just a quick handshake and good wishes for the future. It was something you did so often you really couldn't afford much emotion, and I was truly surprised at the very strong sense of loss and sadness that gripped me as the rickshaw bounced along the waterfront to my new ship.

It was two hours after I got on board before I had a moment to myself and went to my cabin to unpack. It occurred to me as I locked the door behind me that I had not been alone since I found Patrick's body. Harpe had been in the room when I packed and I only had a chance to check the weight of the bag and glance inside to see that the jewelry was still there. This was the first time I could see and feel my new wealth in comfort. Naturally, I got the handbag first and dumped its contents on the bunk. At first the jewels appeared to be exactly what I had taken from O'Halloran's trunk. Then, as I touched them, the difference became apparent to me. What lay on the white top sheet of the bunk was cheap costume jewelry.

I remember very little about the trip back to the Gloucester. I was too angry with Harpe and myself to pay attention to much around me. Of course, when I got there, I found that Harpe had checked out immediately after I had. He left no forwarding address and there wasn't enough time to do anything other than return to the ship.

One of the most vivid memories I have of Hong Kong is that final sad evening when the tugs cut us loose and we sailed down the channel, the harbor crowded with bum boats and junks, the white broad wake of the ferry crossing to Hong Kong from Kowloon, the evening light fading the day's bright colors to deep blues and greys, lights beginning to show in the hills and around the harbor, the lingering smell of garlic and the sure knowledge that an important part of my life was coming to an end.

As we rounded the point and headed for the open sea, the rolling waters were a smooth slate grey and the skies were just showing the first faint tinges of the brilliant reds and yellows and blues that would soon create a magnificent sunset. I stood quietly on the starboard wing of the bridge, my hand in the right pocket of my khaki pants clutching the diamond I had found by O'Halloran's derby, and took one long last look at a place I would never return to. I didn't understand it all right then, but I did know there were some storms that neither a man nor a ship could survive completely intact and I had just experienced one. It was time to go home.

We never got to Basra on that run. I forget now the exact reason, but there was one of the local wars of political squabbles going on in the Persian Gulf—like there always have been for the past five thousand years or so— and we were diverted to Bahrain. Bahrain is a free port, and I sold O'Halloran's diamond there to an Indian gold dealer working out of a small office on Jufair road. It was a very fine diamond and I got enough money from it to get home and go through four years of college. I owe Patrick O'Halloran a lot.

It was a long mental journey from those strange days in Hong Kong and the deck of that tanker back to the chair in my office, and the residual sadness of the sailing still clung to me like black oil as I picked up Robert Harpe's letter and opened it.

"Dear Matt," it began. "As I write, I do not even know if you are alive. If you are and are reading this, good! If not, I need to get these thoughts on paper for my own peace of mind. So the letter is not an exercise in futility whatever your situation may be.

"The purpose of this letter is to tell you I have always regretted what happened in China. I didn't realize that Patrick had shown you the jewels. He said I was the only one who knew, but he was so flaky and forgetful I felt all along someone else had seen them. I just didn't think it was you. I suppose he told you the same thing and we both got greedy. I have no idea what your reasons may have been for trying to take them, but I needed the money desperately. I was there frantically trying to raise money to reopen my plantation and not having much luck. Investors couldn't see the quick returns from a war ravaged rubber plantation that were so readily available to them in other areas. I had one more month to come up with something or I was going to lose everything left to me. That's the kind of pressure that forces you to do things you ordinarily would abhor. I had already lost my wife and two children to the war and I was damned if I would lose the last thing I had in the world. It was that simple. The jewels were the answer to all my problems, so I took them.

"I am sure you have relived that day hundreds of times in your mind, seeking answers to what really took place. You even may have guessed the truth. But to resolve any questions that may remain, what happened was that as soon as I heard you were leaving I decided it was best to steal the jewels the night before you were to sail, because I did not want to take a chance on who might replace you in the room. You were very young and very naive. You believed what you were told and accepted whatever went on at face value. You appeared to be the perfect witness for Patrick's death, you would be leaving immediately and seemed to be no threat at all to my intentions. I felt I couldn't count on being that lucky again. Obviously, I was mistaken.

"I didn't have an elaborate plan. I merely intended to kill Patrick in a way that would enable you to swear along with me that his death was natural, take the jewels to a place I had ready for them, and get out of Hong Kong as soon as possible. The only clever part—or what I thought was clever—was covering the possibility that someone else had seen the jewels. If Patrick had shown them to anyone else, I was confident they had never been able to examine them carefully. He had stayed too close to them for that. So I purchased a good quantity of excellent paste and costume jewelry to replace them with after I removed the real ones from his trunk. In that way, even if someone else did know about them, the paste jewels would be there and there was very little chance anyone could prove they were not the ones that had been there originally. As it turned out I used them a bit differently to fool you, but the effect was the same.

"The death part wasn't difficult, either. As you remember, you could buy anything in Hong Kong then, and I got my hands on a drug that would simulate a heart attack. I went up to the room at teatime that day and found Patrick visiting with one of his invisible friends. He said you had been there earlier and had left to see a girl, which fitted my program beautifully.

"I know it will be hard for you to believe, but I honestly had strong feelings for Patrick. I could easily picture myself in the same lonely situation someday in the future, and I couldn't stand the thought of watching him die. It just seemed to me that I needed the money more than he did and I had no other choice; or if there was one I couldn't see it. So as soon as I had put the drug in his tea I left the hotel and walked the streets for an hour, waiting for it to kill him.

"Needless to say, I was surprised to find you in the room when I returned and even more surprised to find the jewels gone. It was not hard to locate them after I sent you for help. There were only so many places they could be in the room, and I found them almost immediately. Perhaps I should have shared them with you, but at the time I was terribly angry. I had done all the work and you were trying to take everything. It seemed quite fair at the time to leave you with nothing.

"Although I did not get as much for the jewels as I had hoped, there was plenty to save the plantation and buy more land. I expanded from there into shipping, mining, and newspapers. I am now very rich and very old. I never remarried and probably would remind you a great deal of Patrick. I even have those moments when the past is more clear to me than the present and I find conversations with old friends more real than the ones I have with the living. I rather enjoy the odd expressions on the faces of those I introduce to my absent friends. I like to sing those Irish ballads of his, too.

"I know this sounds weird, but even Colonel Giles has turned up in my memories. Patrick may have introduced you to him. We have tea together almost every day and long conversations about the old China. This causes great consternation to those around me. However, I never go far enough for them to have me declared incompetent. I think I learned to walk that thin line from Patrick.

"It is also interesting to me that I keep wishing Patrick would come one day. There is a lot I would like to explain to him, but I guess I am still carrying too much guilt from China to face him yet. I do need to talk with him, though, because I am now sure he did kill his wife and whoever the man was that took her. I think when you murder someone something happens to you that later lets you spot that same potential intensity in others. This is why I felt so strongly at the end that Patrick knew exactly what I was planning to do.

"I am even more convinced now, for I have two nephews who are looking at me in the same way I looked at Patrick's jewels. They stand to gain a great deal from my death and can barely disguise their impatience for it to happen. I am just afraid they don't have the nerve to take a chance on hurrying it along, but I am sure they are trying to work it out. I can see it in their faces just as I am sure Patrick could see it in mine."

I put down the letter for a moment, rubbed my eyes and said aloud, "And he could see it in mine, too, Robert."

I picked up the letter and began reading again. "If I am dead when you get this, you will know they finally decided it was worth the risk. But I do not want you to do anything about it. If they were smart enough to get what they think they want, let them alone. I am tired and more than ready to pass my guilt on to someone else. I'm not certain they can handle it. However, that will be their problem just as it was mine.

"Another reason for this letter is that I wish you to have something of what I took from you. I have authorized my solicitor, Mr. Thorton, to give you a check for five hundred thousand dollars. It comes late, but it is the least you are due and my nephews should not have what is yours." The letter ended abruptly and was signed simply, "Robert."

I put the letter on my desk and called the number that Thorton had left. He was waiting for my call and returned to my office immediately. Everyone else had left for the day, and we were alone.

"The letter says you are to give me five hundred thousand dollars," I told him when he was seated, "but if I have to return the letter to get the money, let's forget it."

He looked at me with interest. "I realize you are wealthy, Mr. Bolton, but no one is that wealthy. It must be an unusual letter."

"It is, Mr. Thorton. Do I get the money or not?"

He reached into his briefcase and handed me a check. "I have no instructions to get the letter from you, and I believe that completes our business. Good evening, Mr. Bolton," he said, rising from the chair. To my surprise a genuine smile grew on his face. "I had hoped you would satisfy my curiosity. However, I can see you and Robert are from the same tree."

"Not exactly, but close enough." I stood up, walked with him to the door. "How did Robert die?" I asked.

He stopped short, turned and said, "A bad fall. He fell down a steep flight of stairs leading from the second floor hallway to the servants' pantry. Broke his neck."

"Anything unusual about it?"

Thorton started to speak, paused, and then said, "Only that he had never been known to use those stairs before. However, he was becoming more and more erratic . . . talking with people who weren't there . . . doing odd things . . . times and places were getting mixed up in his mind. Who knows what Robert was thinking or doing when he tried to go down those stairs. Is there anything in the letter that would lead you to believe differently? Frankly, I have never been satisfied with the report of the inquest."

"No," I lied. "Thank you, and have a pleasant journey home." Thorton nodded and left.

I went back to my desk, picked up the telephone, and called home. My wife answered and asked, "Where in the world are you, darling?"

"I'm in a bar drinking with a beautiful blonde."

"Don't lie to me, Matt Bolton. You are in that dreary office working late again. You come home right now! We have three of *your* grandchildren spending the night and I need all the moral and physical support I can get."

"*Mine?* Being that bad are they?"

"If they were not so handsome, like my side of the family, I would have called Animal Control an hour ago." She lowered her voice and did her sexy imitation, "And furthermore, I am all the beautiful blonde *you* can handle."

"Indeed you are, pretty girl. Put a scotch on ice and wear a sexy dress. I'm leaving in ten minutes."

"The eternal optimist," she laughed and hung up the phone.

I began gathering papers and stuffing them in my briefcase. Harpe's letter I put carefully in an inside pocket. Tomorrow it would go in my safety deposit box. I slipped the check into my inside coat pocket to show my wife. I had once told her part of the story of my life in Hong Kong and I knew she would be fascinated to hear the ending. Also, I would have to talk with her about whether we should keep the money. Like Harpe, I had always been troubled over what had happened in Hong Kong. I had been so sure I had killed Patrick I never even considered that Harpe might have done it. Time makes it easier, but murder is a pretty heavy thing to carry around most of your life. Harpe's letter had relieved me of that load, and I wasn't certain it would be worthwhile to pick up even a little of it by accepting the money. In any case, there would be some happy charities over the next few years.

I put my desk lamp on low, picked up my briefcase, and started for the door. The room was coated with long deep shadows that varied in colors from inky black to misty grey. Patches of faint yellow light spilled over the edges of the desk, softly illuminating my leather chair. And suddenly, half hidden in the hazy darkness, I was sure I could see Patrick Francis O'Halloran sitting there with his two big hands resting on his cane, his black derby sitting square on his big head with tufts of white hair spilling wildly from under it, and a big smile stretching his big mouth and raising both ends of his thick bushy mustache. I couldn't see his eyes, but I could sense they were smiling, too.

"Thanks for coming, Patrick," I said to the shadows. "It was kind of you to come all that way so I'd know our Chinese guilt trip is finally over."

I closed the door and started walking down the dimly lighted corridor towards the elevators. I know there are always strange echoes in empty buildings at night; but, behind me, in my office, I would swear I could hear two men singing happily.

# THE BLACKMARKET DETAIL

*By Martin Limón*

**A**FULL-LENGTH dress clung to the soft, round parts of her short body like cellophane on a peach.

"Looks like we've found our culprit," Ernie said.

We'd been sitting in the parking lot of the Yongsan Commissary for about thirty minutes, sipping acidic coffee, watching the housewives parade in and out, trying to decide which one to pinch for blackmarket activities.

None of them had been good-looking enough. Until now. She pushed her overflowing shopping cart towards the taxi stand and smiled at the bright spring day. A voluptuous Oriental doll come to life.

"Instant coffee, strawberry jam, a case of oranges, about twenty pounds of bananas. Is she blackmarketing or what?"

"Either that or she's got a pet gorilla."

The bag boy helped load her booty into the trunk of the big PX taxi. The driver closed the door for her as she got in the back seat, ran around, and started the engine.

Ernie tossed his Styrofoam cup onto the pavement and choked the old motor pool Jeep to life. He slammed the gear shift into low, we jerked forward, and I barely managed to keep what was left of my coffee from splashing all over the front of my coat and tie.

Shadowing hardened criminals is never easy.

Ernie slid expertly through the busy afternoon Seoul traffic and stayed within a few yards of the cab. In Itaewon the cabby turned left, ran the big Ford up a steep hill through a walled residential area, and took a quick right. Ernie waited at the base of the hill until he was out of sight and then, the sturdy old engine whining all the way, charged up after him. At the corner he turned off the Jeep and wedged us up against a stone wall.

I got out and peered around the corner. The cab driver was helping her unload the groceries. I went back to the Jeep and waited.

Most Korean wives of GI's will finish their blackmarket activities in the afternoon before their husbands get home from work. They don't want to jeopardize his military career by getting caught selling a few jars of mayonnaise and maraschino cherries for twice what they paid for them in the commissary. Sometimes the husbands are a little squeamish about the whole thing, but most of them like the extra income just as much as their wives do. An extra four or five hundred dollars a month. Easy. And if they get serious, go for the big ticket items—TV's, microwaves, VCR's—they can make as much as fifty thousand dollars during a one year tour.

My name is George Sueño, U.S. Army Criminal Investigation Division. My partner Ernie Bascom and I usually get stuck with the blackmarket detail. Our job is to bust housewives, embarrass their husbands, and cut back on the flow of duty-free goods from the U.S. bases to the Korean economy.

So far we'd managed to keep the deluge down to about a couple million dollars a week. Exactly what it had always been.

The cab driver finished unloading the groceries, accepted his tip with both hands, bowed, and in a few seconds the walled street was empty and quiet.

Ernie and I walked by her front gate. Stopped. Listened. Nothing I could make out.

Down about fifteen yards on the other side of the road was a small neighborhood store, fronted by an ice cream freezer and a couple of rickety metal tables under an awning emblazoned with the Oriental Beer logo. We rummaged around, Ernie bought some gum, and the old woman smiled as she came up with two paper cups to go with the liter of beer we bought. We sat outside, under the awning, and waited.

Spring was becoming summer in Korea and the afternoon was clear and bright but not hot. It reminded me of the endless days of sunshine I'd survived in foster homes throughout East L.A. The sun had been as glaring and unrelenting as the gaze of the adults I'd been forced to live with. I'd cursed my mother for dying and my father for disappearing into the bottomless pit south of the border.

It hadn't all been grim, though. One of my foster parents, Mrs. Aaronson, made sure I brought my schoolbooks home and then took the time to correct my homework. She showed me that arithmetic and spelling and science are all puzzles. Games. The greatest games. And as I lost myself in these games for hours, I looked forward, for the first time in my life, to being praised by the teacher and respected by the other children for something besides my fists.

The first payoff was when I joined the army and my high test scores got me a clerical job—on the other side of the pond. As time went by, the clerks on the left of me and the clerks on the right of me got sent off to Vietnam. With only a year more to go on my enlistment, orders came down for Korea. I couldn't believe my luck. After a quick "Kimchi Orientation" from a couple of old sergeants who'd been there before, I was strapped into my first jet airplane and sent on my way.

I loved the seasons. A short tropical summer and snow-covered frigid winter. In between came the blossoming of spring and the long, slow, red and yellow dying of autumn.

East L.A. had been asphalt and heat and smog. All year long.

After I got my discharge, I went to L.A. City College on the GI Bill, but before the second semester had a chance to get started, I dropped out and reenlisted in the army. But now I was a college boy and after a brief stint in the military police I found myself graduating from the Criminal Investigation School—and on my way back to Korea.

Ernie and I had gravitated together somehow. The two duds of the CID Detachment. The first sergeant kept us together mainly to keep an eye on us. We both had this bad habit of following an investigation through even after the right slots had been filled in the provost marshall's statistical charts. They wanted a body count of GI's caught selling coffee in the village—not a report on how it was a customs violation for a general's wife to ship Korean antiques back to the States at government expense and then sell them at a three hundred percent profit.

There was no briefing chart for that.

By all rights Ernie should have been in Georgetown trying to pass the bar exam or working his way up through the ranks of young stockbrokers on Wall Street. His dad was a big honcho somewhere in the government, and Ernie's younger brothers were busy back home piling one degree upon the other. But for Ernie, Vietnam had interrupted everybody's plans.

After the girls and the madness and the unrelenting adrenaline rush of life in Vietnam, Ernie'd been transferred back to Fort Hood, Texas. He'd spent a couple of months gutting it out but finally couldn't take the humdrum existence and volunteered for another tour in Vietnam.

Most people would blame his choices on the horse. But I knew him better than that. It was the loathing of routine, of predictability, that had caused him to reject a life of seeking riches in the States and caused him to reenlist in the army. And besides he'd put down the heroin now—you couldn't buy it in Korea anyway—and replaced it with the duty-free, shipped-at-taxpayer-expense, happy-hour-priced booze, that gushed from the army warehouses like crude from a grounded oil tanker.

A Korean man wearing sandals, a T-shirt, and loose-fitting gray work pants rode past us on a sturdy old bicycle.

Ernie elbowed me. "Must be the pickup, pal."

The produce displays kept the man from seeing us, and Ernie and I got up, taking our beer with us, and faded deeper into the darkness of the grocery store.

The man parked his bicycle in front of the doll's front gate and rang the bell. In less than a minute the door opened and the man went through, carrying some flattened cardboard boxes and some string.

We sat back down and finished our beer. Ready for action.

A rag dealer pushing a wooden cart on oversized bicycle tires rolled past us. He clanged his big rusty metal shears and wailed something incomprehensible to his prospective customers. A woman down the street, across from the doll's house, came out from behind her big metal gate and bartered with the rag dealer for a while, finally selling him a brown paper bag filled with flattened aluminum cans.

The Koreans have been recycling for centuries.

The rag dealer tried to interest her in some bits of clothing he held up for her but she shook her head and demanded money instead. A few coins changed hands, the woman went back behind her protective walls, and the rag dealer clanged down the road, turned left, and was out of sight.

In the distance his clanging and wailing stopped for a while and I figured he must have found another customer.

The man on the bicycle reappeared carrying two large cardboard boxes wrapped in string. He struggled beneath their weight but managed to hoist them up onto the heavy-duty stand on the back of his bicycle. He secured the boxes with rope, hopped on the bike, and rode off. The gate behind him had long since been closed.

"Let's go, pal." Ernie and I trotted down the hill after him, and then jumped in our Jeep and followed at a safe distance as he crossed the Main Supply Route and went about a half mile farther into the heart of Itaewon.

A steep alley turned up a hill, and the man jumped off his bicycle and pushed it slowly up the incline. Ernie pulled over, and I got out of the Jeep. I followed the man to the top of the hill and down a couple of alleys, and watched as he parked in front of a small house surrounded by a rickety old wooden fence. He unloaded his boxes and entered. Then he took his bicycle in and closed the gate.

On the way back to the Jeep I stopped at a public phone and called the Korean National Police liaison officer.

By the time I got back to where Ernie was waiting, a small blue and white Korean police car was just pulling up. Two uniformed KNP's got out, and the four of us walked up into the catacombs of the Korean working class neighborhood.

They kicked the door in. In about ten seconds the man was face down on the floor of his home, his wrists handcuffed securely behind him. Some of the fruit was smashed and the U.S. made canned goods rolled slowly across the small room. They took him to the Itaewon police box.

Ernie and I popped back to the doll's house and knocked on the door. There was no answer. We waited for a while and then a GI sauntered towards us carrying a briefcase. He was tall and thin, with a pencil-line mustache and the strut of a Southern aristocrat.

The insignia on his neatly pressed khaki uniform identified him as Chief Warrant Officer Three Janson. Medical Corps.

"What do you want?"

I flashed my badge. "To question your wife concerning blackmarket activities."

"No way."

Janson opened the door and told us to wait, but it didn't take long because we barged in when we heard his scream.

The voluptuous Oriental doll lay dead on the floor, blood seeping from a hole in her side where her ribs should have been.

The big red brick building that was the headquarters of the CID detachment seemed to be waiting to swallow us as we approached.

The first sergeant wasn't in his office, but down in the admin section barking into telephones and ripping off teletype reports.

"What the hell happened with you guys?" he said when he noticed us. "I send you on a simple blackmarket detail, and you turn up with a corpse."

Ernie sat down on the edge of Miss Kim's desk and offered her a stick of gum. She smiled and accepted a piece with her long manicured fingernails.

"Bascom! Get down to my office! You too, Sueño!"

The asschewing was royal. You would've thought we killed the girl ourselves, and in a way that's sort of what he said. At least we'd been in the vicinity and had the opportunity—if not the motive. He told us that if she'd been raped we'd probably have been charged and locked up by now.

Shows you the high opinion our leadership has of us.

He'd given the case to Burrows and Slabem, affectionately known around the office as the Boot Hill Brothers, his favorite investigators when it came to burying inconvenient facts. When the dependent of a U.S. serviceman gets murdered, all hell breaks loose up at the Eighth Army Headquarters. Colonel Stoneheart, our provost marshall, was briefing the commanding general right now. The first sergeant felt that only a trustworthy pair of sleuths like Burrows and Slabem could properly handle the case.

"You mean properly cover it up," Ernie said.

The first sergeant freaked, chasing us out of his office and warning us to stay off the case unless Burrows and Slabem had some questions for us that weren't covered in our initial reports.

We wandered down the long hallway.

"What would we do without the first sergeant's hoarse voice echoing down the halls?"

"I wouldn't know how to act."

Ernie winked at Miss Kim on the way out, and we jumped in his Jeep and went directly to the Itaewon police box.

Exactly what the first sergeant had told us not to do.

Burrows and Slabem were there. Burrows, tall and skinny with a pock-marked face, Slabem, short and round with a pimply face. The Korean police wouldn't talk to them. Neither would we. They harrumphed and tried to look officious. Chins met necks. Except in Slabem's case.

I greeted Captain Kim, commander of the Itaewon police box, and spoke to him in his own language.

"Were you told anything by the offender?"

"Yes. He told us everything."

"How did you get his confession so quickly?"

Captain Kim slammed his fist into his cupped hand. "The lie detector."

He ushered us back to the cells and the guy on the bicycle lay on a moist cement floor. I recognized him because of his clothes. His face was a puffed hive of purple welts.

Burrows and Slabem, the Boot Hill Brothers, glared at us as we walked out. Somehow I didn't think they'd keep our little visit a secret from the first sergeant.

We talked to a lot of the folks in the neighborhood, covering much of the same ground the Korean police had already covered. The only thing un-usual anyone had noticed was me and Ernie hanging around. The man on the bicycle had been conducting blackmarket business with the GI wife in the neighborhood for many months, without incident as far as anyone knew.

The whole thing was a mystery to me. Why would a blackmarketeer kill one of his sources of income?

Ernie thought it might have been Janson. Husbands are always a first suspect in a murder case. But we checked the back of the building. The walls were ten feet high, sheer, and studded with shards of glass embedded in cement on the top. When we had seen Janson, his uniform was still neat, with no more wear than one would expect from a hard day's work at the office.

We couldn't interrogate him, though. Burrows and Slabem would be handling that. On compound. In conjunction with the chaplain who was giving him counseling and trying to pull him through this crisis.

"Might as well forget it," Ernie said. "If it wasn't the blackmarket guy, Burrows and Slabem might figure out who it was. And anyway the first sergeant said to stay off the case. We're potential suspects. Nothing we can do about it."

But we both knew what was at stake. The guys who played everything by the regulations considered us a couple of screwoffs anyway. And a young woman, a U.S. army dependent, had been murdered while we were actually staking out her home. We both planned a long career in the army, probably in the CID, and I wasn't going to walk into one assignment after another with the stigma of an unsolved murder, one that happened right under my nose, hanging around my neck.

"We got to find out who killed her," I said.

Ernie shrugged.

We went back to the compound and started making some phone calls. Calling in every favor we had out there. Tracking Janson.

Somehow all our investigations seem to lead us directly to the Itaewon nightclub district.

In this case we found out that Janson was the chief inspector for the Preventive Medicine division. They're the guys who give the mess sergeants and the Officer's Club managers a hard time about the cleanliness of their kitchens, the temperatures of their food storage facilities, stuff like that.

Janson's NCO-in-charge, the guy who actually ran the operation, was Sergeant First Class Billings. Billings was sort of a soft guy; I'd seen him before at the NCO Club. A little out of shape. Never with a woman. Suspect. And he always puffed on his scroags through a cigarette holder.

Word was that he was a real brown-noser. His boss, Chief Janson, or anybody else up the chain of command, could do no wrong as far as he was concerned. The privates who worked for him, though, couldn't do anything right, and he made their lives miserable. Much to the pleasure of Chief Janson, who felt that suffering subordinates meant a well-run ship.

Captain Bligh in khaki.

Sergeant Billings' desire to please his superiors extended beyond the working day, and we had heard from one of his cronies that Billings and Chief Janson regularly ran the village of Itaewon together. The guy had heard Billings mention the Spider Lady Club, a little hole-in-the-wall amongst the bigger, gaudier nightclubs, as their favorite hangout.

Ernie and I had changed into our running the ville outfits: sneakers, blue jeans, and a nylon jacket with a golden dragon embroidered on the back. It was nighttime and we were in the Spider Lady Club, having a welcome cold one and checking out the exceptionally attractive ladies. The music was mellow and the place was lit by red lamps and the flickering blue light from a row of tropical aquariums.

"Janson's got good taste," Ernie said. "First his late wife and now this joint."

"Living his life to the full."

After about twenty minutes, Billings walked in, which didn't surprise us much but what did surprise us was the guy he had in tow. Chief Janson.

We were at a table in a dark corner; my back was to them, and Ernie adjusted his seat so his face couldn't be easily seen from where they sat at the bar.

"Looks like the chaplain's counseling has done wonders for Janson," Ernie said.

I heard their laughter as the excited barmaids brought them their drinks without their having to order. Regulars. Through the smoke-covered mirror on the back wall I made out the smiling woman who leaned over to serve Janson. She was tall, thin, and elegant. Gorgeous, all in all. Black hair billowed around her pale, heart-shaped face. Her eyes slanted up, painted heavily with shadow.

The Spider Lady.

Ernie had checked with one of the girls earlier and gotten her story. She owned the joint, having apparently gotten the initial capital outlay from working as a nurse. Some of the girls claimed it didn't come so much from her salary but from making some extracurricular arrangements with a few of the doctors. On a cash basis.

That would explain her infatuation with the white-coated types who worked in the Preventive Medicine division.

I wondered if she knew that Janson was actually a veterinarian—a horse doctor. But maybe it was just the rubber gloves that turned her on.

Could this be it? Could it be as simple as Janson's wanting to break free from his present old lady to hook up with the Spider Lady? We waited until Janson walked into the latrine and Billings was deep in conversation with one of the Spider Lady's girls and we slipped out of the club.

We walked into the crisp night air of Itaewon, rejected two propositions, and sauntered down the hill towards our favorite beer hall.

"We got the motive," Ernie said. "All we got to do is find the opportunity."

The big beer hall was on the outskirts of Itaewon. We drank draft beer, rubbed elbows with the Korean working men, and bantered with the big rotund Mongolian woman who slammed down frothing mugs in front of us.

All I could think about was the small Oriental doll and how she had looked with that bloody gash beneath her breast.

\* \* \*

In the morning we slipped out of the office as early as we could, supposedly on our way to pump up Colonel Stoneheart's blackmarket arrest statistics but actually on our way to see Captain Kim and get the key to Janson's house. It went smooth. Captain Kim liked the way we didn't try to revamp four thousand years of Korean culture every time we ran into a procedure we didn't approve of. He gave us the key.

The first sergeant would have had a fit if he'd known we were entering the restricted premises of a murder site. But we didn't plan on telling him.

Janson had moved most of his stuff out and was staying in officers' quarters on the base.

White tape in the shape of a small woman surrounded a caked blot of blood. The Korean police usually use tape instead of chalk since it's sort of hard to make a good outline of the victim with chalk on vinyl floors that are heated from below by hot-air ducts. The floor we walked on in our stocking feet was cold now.

We surveyed the entire apartment. It was just a one bedroom job with a small kitchen and a cement-floored bathroom. There was no beer in the refrigerator.

Metal clanged and I heard an old man wailing for his life.

The rag dealer.

We put our shoes back on and hurried out to stop the old man and ask if he'd seen anything unusual yesterday afternoon.

I greeted him in Korean. *"Anyonghaseiyo."*

The old man halted his cart, smiled, and his leathery brown face folded into so many neat rows that I almost thought I heard it crinkle. He kept his mouth open and didn't seem to know what to say. Talking to Americans wasn't exactly an everyday occurrence for him. Folks in the UFO society probably have more conversations with aliens.

"Yesterday," I said, "we were sitting in that store over there when you came by."

The old man nodded. "Yes. I saw you."

"You bought some aluminum cans from this woman in this house here."

"Yes, yes. That's right."

"And then you went around the corner, down the hill."

"Yes."

"Did you notice anything unusual?"

"Unusual?"

"Yes. Did you see any American people in the neighborhood?"

"No. I saw no American people. The Korean police already asked me that. Look, I am an old man and I have to support myself and an old sick wife. Do you want to buy something?"

"No. We don't want to buy anything."

We went back into the house and the old man trundled his cart down the road, clanging his metal shears and wailing his plaintive song.

We searched the grounds, passing through a narrow passageway that ran between the side of the apartment and the big sandstone brick wall that separated the building from the two story house next door. Out back, a small cement-floored courtyard sat behind Janson's apartment and the landlord's apartment next door. It was enclosed by the big ten foot masonry wall topped with the shards of glass.

The entire complex was on a corner, formed by the alley that ran up the steep hill we had originally come up in our Jeep and the street that ran in front of the little store from which we had conducted our surveillance.

The only way for someone to enter this house while we were watching from the store was over the back walls, which seemed unlikely since they faced other people's residences, or over this ten foot stone wall which faced the public street. We had already checked the other side and it was sheer and very difficult to climb. But the inside of the wall was not as high, since the level of the back courtyard was higher than the street by a couple of feet. It also provided a number of footholds, from a clinging vine and from some protruding rocks imbedded in the wall.

The wall had been designed to keep out intruders. From inside it could be easily climbed.

So I climbed it. Ernie stayed on the ground, clicking his gum and telling me—sarcastically, I think—to be careful.

The tricky part about the climb was the handholds on the top of the wall, since you had to be careful to grab a spot between the randomly spaced shards of glass. If you were in a hurry you'd cut yourself for sure.

The jump down into the street would be a little rough also, although not impossible. About twelve or fourteen feet, depending on which part of the rapidly descending pavement you landed on. An airborne trooper, with a good hit and roll, would have no trouble with it.

As I gazed over the wall and out into the street, I noticed something fluttering in the gentle breeze. It was blue and stuck to the base of one of the shards of glass. Fiber. Wool maybe. A clump of it. I reached out and pulled the material off the jagged edge of the glass. It was soft and blue. Baby blue.

It didn't look worn. It looked sort of new, but it would be impossible to tell much about it without a lab analysis and that would be sort of difficult since I wasn't officially on the case. And anyway the lab was in Tokyo. Before a packet could be sent there it had to be approved by the first sergeant.

So much for high technology. I fell back on my meager allotment of common sense.

It looked like threads from a woman's sweater. Maybe a woman climbed this fence and got part of her clothing caught on these jagged shards of glass. It would be easy, of course, with a ladder, but the Korean police had already interviewed everyone in the neighborhood and no one had seen any workmen or anyone setting up any sort of apparatus.

I climbed down and showed the fiber to Ernie.

He thought for a while and then he said, "The problem is how did she get over the wall? It would have to be something that would give her a lift without causing any particular notice from the neighbors. Trashcans maybe?"

That was it. "Or a trash cart."

Ernie and I ran outside and scoured the neighborhood until we found the old rag dealer.

"Yesterday, when you rounded the corner away from the store, you stopped calling and clanging your shears for a while. You had a customer."

"Yes."

"Who was it?"

"A beautiful young lady. Very tall. Very fancy." The old man slashed his fingertips across his eyes and up. "She locked herself out of her house."

"So she had to climb the wall?"

"Yes. I rolled my cart over and tilted it up. She climbed over easily."

"And then what?"

"And then I went about my business." The old man looked at the ground, shaking his head slightly. "But she was a very strange woman. Later, down at the bottom of the hill, I saw her again. She was all out of breath from her climb and she had torn her sweater."

"Her sweater? What color was it?"

The old man reached under some stacks of cardboard. "Here. She sold it to me, cheap, because it had been torn. My wife repaired it, and it looks just fine now. I should be able to sell it for a good price."

The old man held it up to us, and I reached into my pocket for my small wad of Korean bills.

It was soft and fluffy and baby blue.

Since the Spider Lady was a Korean citizen and therefore not under our jurisdiction, we contacted Captain Kim and had him go along with us to make the pinch.

She was behind the bar of the Spider Lady Club, just getting ready for the evening's business, laughing and joking with the other girls.

Ernie and I came in the door first, wearing our coats and ties, and when she saw Captain Kim behind us and the blue sweater in my hand, the exquisite lines of her face sagged and her narrow eyes focused on me, like arrows held taut in a bow. Blood drained from her skin, and she stood stock-still for a moment. Thinking.

Then she reached under the bar and pulled out a long glistening paring knife, and as her girlfriends chattered away she kept her eyes on me and pulled the point of the blade straight down the flesh of her forearm.

She kept pulling and ripping until finally the other girls realized what was going on and by the time we got to her, her arm was a shredded mess.

Her nurse training had come in handy because she knew that stitches weren't likely to close arteries that had been cut lengthwise. We applied a tourniquet, but somehow she managed to let it loose while she was in the ambulance and, turning her back to the attendant, kept her secret long enough to do what she wanted to do: die.

Janson was put on the first flight out of the country by order of the commanding general, his personal effects packed and shipped to him later.

Billings spent a lot of time at the NCO Club, restricted to post. He spun romantic tales about his two friends and what he saw as their self-sacrificing love.

The girls at the Spider Lady Club told us the truth. About how proud the Spider Lady had been to be marrying a doctor.

Through it all, from bar to bar, all I could think about was the doll-like woman with the nice curves.

Whose smile had been filled with life.

# BY THE TERRIBLE MOUNTAIN

*By Ron Butler*

O N A muggy July evening in the Year of the Rat, my old electric fan finally expired. I vowed to determine the cause and set it right.

"But," said Noriko, standing to one side of me on the tatami of our downstairs bedroom, "a new one will cost only a few thousand yen."

I glanced down into the eyes of my beautiful wife. "It's the principle of the thing, love. Save a little here, a little there—it all adds up. Ten to one says your father and I can have it working again in an hour."

Noriko put a finger to her lips and smiled. *"Hai,* husband. If you say so."

I picked up the black telephone nested on a cushion by the bedding closet and dialed Okayama Police Inspector Toshihiko Ueki's home number. "Why not simply buy another fan, Sam?" my father-in-law said after I asked if he'd like to come over and lend a hand.

My thrift message was repeated. Ueki sighed, but he consented.

Within half an hour, his car pulled into the gravel lane by our house. I brought the fan into the family room and set it on the coffee table.

Ueki removed his jacket and sat down next to me on the sofa. We contemplated the defunct fan for several seconds. "Well," I said, "we might as well open the patient up and see what surgery's required."

"Tools," the inspector said. "Do you have the tools for the job, Sam?"

"Sure." I pulled a folding vinyl implement case from my hip pocket.

Ueki took the fan, checked the motor housing, and passed it to me. The back took a slot screwdriver, and the sides needed the variety named for Henry F. Phillips. I loosened the screws, and Ueki pried the metal covering off.

I eyeballed the interior and jabbed at the obvious cause of the problem—one of the wires leading from the switch was dangling loose from its connection. "Almost too simple, right?" I commented as the inspector undertook his own examination.

"I would say so," he concurred. "If you will bring a soldering iron and the other requisites, this will be the work of only a few seconds."

Defeat, so close on the heels of success? "Ah, Toshihiko, that's something I haven't gotten around to buying. What'll we do?"

Inspector Ueki reassembled the housing and put the screws back in place. "Let me think, Sam. It seems to me that Esho Yamaguchi, the man who maintains our police equipment, should have everything we need. I will call his home and ask when he can spare us a moment."

There was no answer, so Ueki tried Police Headquarters on the theory that Yamaguchi might still be in his shop. He was, and after Ueki described the problem, Yamaguchi suggested that we bring the fan in.

"You may not return until after our sons are in bed," Noriko said as I fetched my coat from its perch on the kitchen chair, "so please look in on their bath and bid them good night."

"*Hai*," old Yumiko added, "and do not forget your house keys and money."

"Yumiko-san," I said cheerfully to the outspoken octogenarian who shared our home as resident nanny, "we're only going downtown and back, and my memory's clear as a bell." I dangled my keys and patted the wallet in my breast pocket for emphasis, then turned to the entranceway where Ueki was waiting.

"The boys?" Noriko said with a smile.

I backtracked to the bath and told Kenji and Jotaro I'd be right back.

"The fan?" Yumiko chortled as I started to step down into my street shoes.

I returned for it with strained dignity, avoiding Ueki's eyes.

"Do not feel bad, Sam," the inspector smiled as he started his car. "Men who are deep thinkers often overlook simple things."

"You've got that right," I grinned.

Ueki eased his car across the narrow bridge spanning the small river near our house. After he was on the main thoroughfare, I turned my attention to a determined green mosquito that was buzzing my ears.

Esho Yamaguchi welcomed us to the repair shop with bows and cups of green tea, which he placed in the only empty space on a littered workbench.

"The name of Sam Brent," he said after the ritual first sip, "Is, I imagine, known to almost everyone in Okayama."

I beamed at the man with the jolly round face. "Always gives me a boost to hear that folks know about my computer hardware business."

"Oh," Yamaguchi said politely, "I think you are mostly known for being Inspector Ueki's son-in-law."

"About the fan," I said. "Sure it won't be imposing on you to patch it up?"

Yamaguchi expertly exposed the machine's innards and rectified the broken connection with the deft application of a soldering gun. "Please plug it in, Brent-san, and we will test it."

I turned the switch and the fan came to life, building up speed with its customary clack and rattle. "Perfect, Yamaguchi-san." I knew better than to offend him by offering to pay for his help, but did ask if he would meet Ueki and me for lunch someday.

Yamaguchi accepted as if he were the recipient of some magnificent honor, and Ueki suggested that we be on our way home. As we trod down the corridor leading to the parking lot exit, a cop I recognized emerged from an office, frowning at a report he was holding.

"Is something wrong, Sergeant Onuma?" Ueki said.

The officer looked up and sucked in his breath. "Yes, Inspector Ueki, and I am glad that you are here." He held out the papers in his hand. "Yoshio Suda was released from prison early today, and for some reason, we were not notified until just now."

Ueki grimaced and took the report, hurriedly reading over the rows of Japanese characters. "Assign as many men as necessary for guard duty, Sergeant Onuma, and I will leave for the prison early in the morning for some overdue inquiries."

The inspector turned to me. "Pardon me for a few minutes, Sam. I must call my superiors and make arrangements."

Not long afterward, we were driving past the garishly lit nightclubs of the entertainment district, the now-working fan on the back seat.

"What's the deal with this Suda fellow?" I asked. "How come the cops are so interested in his release?"

Before Inspector Ueki finished his account, I was interested, too. The story he told me concerned a convicted murderer who had been freed that day on the basis of a deathbed statement by his chief accuser.

Yoshio Suda (Ueki recounted) was arrested in Okayama in 1955 for the murder of his wife, following a lengthy investigation by the authorities. During repeated questioning, Suda never varied from his initial claim: he had found his wife strangled with the sash of her kimono when he came home from work late one night.

Suda, who owned a factory that turned out transistor radios, insisted that he had stayed at his office far past the closing hour in order to go over the books. His wife, Suda contended, died at the hands of an unknown assailant, for reasons he could not fathom.

The police could neither prove nor disprove Suda's version of his whereabouts, as all his employees had left at the usual quitting time. All the police had to go on was the autopsy: it established that Mrs. Suda died sometime in the early evening, perhaps five or six hours before Suda telephoned the police at one A.M. And this estimate, the police surgeon said, could be off by several hours one way or the other.

After a period of routine interrogation of friends and neighbors, the police told the prosecutor that there were rumors—no more than vague insinuations, really—of marital infidelity on Mrs. Suda's part. Some people said that her husband devoted most of his time to the factory, and that Mrs. Suda, a vivacious and lovely woman, appeared to be increasingly bored with her lonely existence. Although no one could offer specifics, it was hinted that Mrs. Suda might have had an illicit relationship with another man, as there had been several recent occasions when she was seen leaving home dressed too smartly for mere shopping trips.

Having nothing more substantial than innuendo for motive, the prosecutor was reluctant to take Suda before a judge, and there was no progress in the case until the police called on another of Suda's friends, a business associate named Hisao Nakai. Nakai said that Suda had complained to him often that he suspected his wife of wanton behavior, and that, during a discussion over the telephone on the very afternoon of the slaying, Suda had indicated that he intended to end forever the mockery heaped on him by his wife, rejecting Nakai's plea to remain calm.

"Why, then," a lieutenant of police had asked, "did you not come forward immediately when you learned of Mrs. Suda's death?"

The policeman's report, filed so long ago, recorded that Nakai had hesitated, apparently searching carefully for the right words. "I delayed," Nakai finally said, "because I only *think* that Suda killed his wife. I do not have proof, only his angry words."

The prosecutor at that point felt that Nakai's information, coupled with the time of death, provided adequate grounds for a charge of murder, a feeling that was reinforced by Suda's refusal to speak when he was asked the names of the man—or men—who might have been engaged in an affair with his wife.

"I did no wrong," Suda maintained when brought to trial. "Hisao Nakai lied when he said I made a threat against my wife." During the rest of the trial, Suda sat sullen and silent, disdaining to respond to any of the questions put to him by judge or prosecutor, showing no remorse for his wife's death, and offering no extenuating circumstances that might have mitigated the severity of the outcome.

After he was ordered to spend the remainder of his life in a cell, Suda was overheard to say, as he was led away, that someday, somehow, he would find a way to repay those who had brought him to ruin through what he damned as treachery and stupidity.

Now, as Ueki drove along the treelined boulevard that led past Okayama University, I asked the obvious question: why had Suda's freedom been restored?

Ueki took a pack of cigarettes from the top of the dash and pushed in the electric lighter. "Just before he died a few weeks ago, Nakai recanted his original accusation, confessing that he lied about Suda's threatening to kill his wife. He did so because he was convinced that Suda had cheated him in several business deals."

"Hell of a way to get even for being ripped off," I said, "sending a buddy away for life like that."

"There is more to the deathbed statement," Ueki said. "Nakai swore, in his last hours, that he had been with Suda throughout the day and night of the murder, putting together plans for increased parts purchases and higher productivity levels for the factory. In his confession, Nakai stressed that Suda's home life was exemplary, and that he had never heard Suda speak ill of his wife."

At this point, I was having difficulty trying to dogpaddle through the pounding surf of discrepancies. "Whoa, Toshihiko! Something doesn't jibe here. If Nakai was with Suda at the time of the killing, why the heck didn't Suda say so when he had the chance? Seems like an airtight alibi to me."

Inspector Ueki flicked cigarette ashes out the window. "Sam, I do not believe we possess a fraction of the facts yet. Suda would not defend himself at his trial, and it was Nakai's statement concerning alleged adultery and Suda's supposed intention to end it that ultimately led to the conviction. And now Nakai has provided yet another account—one that caused the court to restore Suda's liberty. The officers who went to Nakai's home, at his request, to take down his admission had read all the material on file and had many questions, including where the two men were that night. Unfortunately, Nakai was already at the point of death, too weak to go beyond saying that they went to a restaurant together and left separately."

"Some mess, huh?" I commented as we turned into Tsushima District. "If Nakai was trying to ease a guilty conscience by coming clean before he died, that leaves me wondering why Suda didn't complain that he'd been framed. Also, if Suda didn't do away with his wife, who did?"

Ueki shifted into low gear to cross the bridge near my house. "I do not know, Sam, but the identity of the murderer is only one of our worries at present. Remember, during the trial Suda claimed that lies had been told, and afterward he spoke of treachery and of avenging himself. Nakai, of course, is gone, but the judge and prosecutor who handled Suda's trial are still living. Until we know more, these people must be protected. Some of the answers, I hope, will be found at the prison among the people who knew Suda all these years."

"You know," I said as Ueki stopped in the lane by the house, "the computer system used at the prison you mentioned was sold by my company, and I think I just might be able to justify popping in to see how everything's going."

Ueki smiled. "Excellent! The monotony of travel is always lessened by the presence of a good friend. If you can manage to arise early enough, we will go together."

"Be up with the birdies," I promised. "By the way, what's Suda look like?"

Inspector Ueki turned on the dome light and handed me a picture taken at the prison. Suda appeared to be in his late fifties, and might have been a heart surgeon, a nuclear physicist, a truck driver, or a candy salesman.

"Mr. Joe Average," I remarked.

"That may be true as far as looks are concerned," Ueki said, "but what we cannot tell from that photograph is what Suda has on his mind."

I nodded, got out of the car, and waved good night, then went inside. "Noriko," I called out. "I'm home, and wait'll you hear where I'm going!"

That night was suffocatingly hot. Noriko prepared a snack of summer noodles, served over ice, and sat beside me at the kitchen table while I reviewed the situation with Yoshio Suda. "Your father," I said, "seems to be afraid that Suda is out to get the judge and prosecutor."

Noriko rested her head on my shoulder. "I always want you and Father to be careful, Sam, and especially at the prison. There must be many dangerous men there."

I bussed her cheek. "We'll be fine, love, and we won't forget to keep an eye out for the bad guys."

Yumiko, who was replacing a bottle of juice in the fridge, turned and humphed. "What you *did* forget, it seems, is that precious fan of yours. Can you remember where it is?"

The fan! How would I get through a stifling night without it? I summoned forth a casual smile. "Left it in Toshihiko's car, Yumiko-san. He was in a hurry to get home, and I didn't want to hold him up."

Yumiko shut the refrigerator door, shook her head, and thumped up the stairs to her room.

"Never mind, husband," Noriko said. "I have opened all the windows, and we will have fresh breezes. You will sleep as well as ever and be refreshed for your journey with Father tomorrow."

Turning off the overhead fluorescent light in our room and snuggling next to Noriko on the lightweight futon, I doubted that I could find dreamland without the comforting whisper of air from the fan, and its familiar and lulling vibrations. Counting sheep never worked for me, so instead I counted and recounted the meager facts in the Suda affair until I yawned mightily with the effort and flopped over on my side. Someone died, someone lied, a man was tried. . . .

. . . and then it was morning.

"All set to go," I announced as I put a loose knot in my tie.

Yumiko inserted a folded handkerchief in my breast pocket. "Have you forgotten anything this time?" she said pleasantly.

I grinned, tapping various other pockets in my coat and trousers. "Money, keys, and alien registration papers. All I need."

"So," Yumiko responded, still amiably. "And did you remember to call your office and tell someone you will not be in today?"

"Ah . . . just getting ready to do that." I went to the telephone. Masahige Goto, my associate director, answered, and I advised him that I was headed out of Okayama with Inspector Ueki.

*"Doko e ikimasuka?"* Goto said.

"Where am I going? Believe it or not, Goto-san, I'm off to prison." When he showed no inclination to terminate the silence, I went on to explain that Ueki was going for an official inquiry and that I was making a courtesy call to see how our computer system was working out. "Of course," I added, "I'd really like to find out something about Japanese prisons. I've seen how the cops operate, and now I'm going to get some of the inside dope on what happens to the guys they collar. Anyway, will you please call the warden and let him know I'll be there?"

"Immediately," Goto said. "When will you return, Bulentu-san?"

"Be in the office bright and early tomorrow. I'm not even taking a toothbrush."

Goto made a noncommittal sound and hung up.

Inspector Ueki pulled up to the house in a crunch of loose gravel and honked twice. I kissed Noriko, hugged the boys, and stepped down from the entranceway into my street shoes.

We arrived at Okayama Station with ample time for a cup of coffee, but Ueki wasn't in the best of moods. "Suda has not been located yet," he said, "and I have to assume he entered Okayama unnoticed. I am troubled about the safety of the judge and prosecutor, Sam, although my best men have been ordered to watch their homes."

"Have you warned them about Suda?"

*"Hai,* but both of them say they have lived too long to begin bowing to unfounded fears."

We got up and I passed over four hundred yen to the coffee shop cashier.

Our eastbound bullet train came in precisely on schedule, and we stood back on the platform as hundreds of passengers disembarked and thronged toward the exits. Was one of them, I wondered, a man with a long-nurtured hatred in his heart?

We were in Tokyo by one P.M., merging with the ever-present swarm of humanity to catch one of the local trains that circle the vast city. From a stop some twenty-four kilometers west of the Imperial Palace, we took a taxi the rest of the way, and soon I was looking at the high concrete walls of the prison.

There was a lone uniformed guard stationed in a glass booth outside the massive iron gate. He came out when we left the cab, scrutinizing us closely, and, although he carried no weapons, the man looked as if he could handle anything that came his way.

My father-in-law took out his identification and displayed it. "I am Inspector Toshihiko Ueki of the Okayama Police Department, and I believe I am expected by the warden."

"Yes," the guard said, eyes on me. "And who is this foreign gentleman with you?"

The guard was taken aback when I answered for myself—in Japanese. "Sam Brent's the name, and I'm expected, too. I want to inspect the computers my company installed."

"That is so," Ueki verified as I tried to convince myself that I hadn't deviated too far from the truth. "Mr. Brent is a friend, and I will vouch for his character."

"*Chotto matte, kudasai,*" the guard said. Please wait a minute. He went to the telephone in the booth and began speaking in the sharp, clipped words of a man addressing a superior, then wrote out entry passes. "You will be escorted," he said, using the telephone again to have us admitted.

As the gates swung inward with a ponderous groaning of metal, we were met by two hard-faced men—men whose bearing reflected rigid training and discipline. Their uniforms were blue, with short-sleeved summer shirts breaking at the elbow, black-belted trousers tucked into black boots, white gloves, and soft-billed caps reminiscent of those worn in the Japanese Imperial Army.

The two men took our passes, about-faced, and marched in step across a broad expanse of sward toward a long, one story concrete building separated from the prison proper. As we followed, we passed four prisoners in ordinary civilian clothing standing at attention before another guard, bowing in turn as their names were called, then lining up to be taken to some work detail. This guard, too, I observed, bore no weapons.

Outside the warden's office, another unarmed sentinel stood, feet slightly apart, hands behind his back. He took the passes from our escorts, knocked on the door after checking them, and, with a nod, opened the door. We entered.

"Warden Takeshi Genba?" Ueki said.

The short, thin man behind the gray metal desk arose, bowing. *"Hai.* I do not intend to be abrupt or impolite, Inspector Ueki, but the Okayama Police Department has just informed me that Yoshio Suda was spotted in one of the city's bus stations several hours ago, and that he is being kept under constant surveillance until your return."

Ueki, with a look of relief, thanked the warden and introduced me. "The real reason Sam is here," he said with a smile, "has less to do with computers than with a large curiosity about our prisons."

Genba pressed his palms flat on the desk top and regarded me at length. "I appreciate your interest. We have no secrets here, and I would even suggest that you talk to some of the inmates for a more complete understanding. While Inspector Ueki reads our files on Suda, I will personally conduct you through our facilities, Brent-san."

The warden showed the way to the documents room. And then he took me into the realm of the condemned.

"Awed," I said in reply to Warden Genba's query as to how I felt about what I'd seen. "Totally awed."

We were seated in Genba's office after the tour, which had included a brief but satisfactory look at the computers. It was a major effort for me to reconcile what I knew about convict life in my own country with the Japanese approach to legal punishment.

Japanese prisoners, I had found, were all treated equally. There were no special privileges, no extra fillips or considerations related to status or wealth, no tennis courts, hot tubs, private rooms with television, and, emphatically, no drugs or alcohol.

Conditions for everyone, regardless of the particular crime, were what I had to call harsh: dank cells unheated in winter and without air conditioning. The staple diet was built around fish, seaweed, and rice, and television cameras mounted on the cell walls followed every move of the inmates. And, with the exception of the aged, the infirm, or the handicapped, everyone worked. Warden Genba told me that each convict spent up to forty-four hours a week producing everything from chopsticks to paper sacks and tea bags.

There were other major differences, too. I was informed that prison guards, who are required to undertake extensive training, are seldom armed, and that most prison officials are university graduates. Escape attempts are relatively rare, and the last prison disturbance occurred in the 1950's. No Japanese guards have been killed by prisoners, and during the past ten years, only one convict has been slain by another.

Maybe—just maybe, I mused—the Japanese perspective on dealing with criminals could be summed up by what I took to be the principal attitude of the people in charge: if you're here, we do not care who you are or how much money you have, only that you are no longer entitled to call yourself a free citizen. Behind these walls, you are criminals, sent to learn the consequences of your actions. You will work and show respect, and if you are intelligent, you will also reflect on what you gave up by breaking our laws.

One of the impressive aspects of the system, I thought as Genba poured more black tea, was that it functioned without physical force: for a Japanese guard to strike a prisoner without the utmost provocation meant a mandatory prison sentence of seven years for the guard.

The two inmates I'd talked to had put their experiences in almost the same words: they weren't mistreated, but one stay was enough.

"What about backsliding?" I asked, stirring my tea.

Warden Genba smiled. "Ah, you refer to recidivism. Well, we do have a few people who seem to learn nothing here, but the police know who they are and watch them closely once their terms are up."

Okay, I concluded, if a system works—it works. I might have mulled it over longer, but Ueki came back to the warden's office then, carrying a thick sheaf of papers under one arm. "Genba-san," the inspector said, "I have all the personnel data on Yoshio Suda, but they are only marginally helpful. Do you have time to give me the benefit of your memory?"

"I am pleased to offer my services," Genba said, "but all I can tell you is that Suda kept his thoughts to himself, seldom speaking to anyone. One man who may be of some assistance, however, is our censor, who has been here almost as long as Suda was. He has spoken to me often of the strange letters Suda received."

"What was the nature of these communications?" Ueki asked.

"Without exception," Warden Genba said, "the letters were from the man who was instrumental in sending Suda here—Hisao Nakai."

"Let us meet with this prison censor without delay," Ueki said. "It is late, and I do not wish to be absent from Okayama any longer than necessary as long as the judge and prosecutor may be in danger."

I glanced out a window and saw leaden masses of thunderheads sweeping down from the north. A summer storm appeared to be in the making.

Inspector Ueki smacked a fist against his thigh. "Of all the inopportune times . . . !"

I couldn't fault his irritation. Aboard the last westbound bullet train of the night, we had traveled without a hitch as far as Nagoya. Then, while Ueki was in the middle of a call to police headquarters in Okayama, the jolt of one of Japan's frequent earthquakes automatically cut power to our train, and we crawled to a stop in an isolated stretch of dark countryside. Tele-

phone service was disrupted at the point of conversation when Ueki learned
that Suda had eluded the men following him.

As a final twist to obstructing fate, the summer storm I had predicted
earlier had turned into a major weather front now drenching a large area of
Honshu: we were notified over the onboard public address system that
there would be additional delays while night emergency crews went over
the tracks looking for damage due to mudslides.

With the restaurant and snack bar closed, all we could do was stay put
and hash over the information provided by the man who checked all incoming and outgoing convict mail. The first few of the letters in question, as the
censor remembered them, were remonstrations by Nakai, reminding Suda
that he had brought his plight upon himself by a murderous deed, reaping a
just sentence that he might have escaped were it not for Nakai's determina-
tion to see justice done.

Through the years, however, there was a radical change in the tone and
content of the letters. Nakai began to side with Suda, gradually leaving
rebukes behind and moving on to sympathy, holding that the blame lay
with Mrs. Suda, not Yoshio. Time and again, the censor said, Nakai elabo-
rated on the theme that no husband should be scourged by the courts for
what happens when an unworthy wife seduces another man with ancient
wiles.

The censor remembered especially one recurring phrase in Nakai's letters
during the last years of Suda's incarceration: "We suffer, all of us, for what
we have done."

Inspector Ueki had asked the censor how Suda replied.

"That," said the censor, "will always puzzle me. Yoshio Suda never once
answered Nakai-san's mail, nor did he write to anyone else all the time he
was confined here."

As the rain beat against the cars of our motionless train, I pondered the
enigma: the simplest explanation was that Hisao Nakai shared with Suda
some of the old traditional values that once went with marriage, one of
them being that a man had the unquestionable authority to inflict extreme
punishment on an adulterous wife.

But . . . that explanation wasn't adequate. If Nakai and Suda both believed that marriage included certain male rights, why had Nakai turned
against his friend and accused him? And why didn't Suda write back?

"Damned odd," I declared, watching a railroad worker outside the window as he walked along in the rain with a flashlight. "The only thing I can
come up with, Toshihiko, is that Nakai's conscience was getting to him. He
was feeling rotten about giving evidence that was so damaging and tried to
make up for it in the letters."

"Guilt," the inspector conceded, "may prove to be the motive for both
Nakai's letters and his dying claim that Suda was innocent—the victim of

Nakai's reprisal for unethical business dealings. Yet I still have the impression that other factors are involved here, ones that are hidden from us."

"Yeah, maybe," I said. "Anyway, think the trip was worth it? All you really got was what the censor had to say."

Ueki stood up and took his jacket from the overhead rack, searching the pockets until he found an unopened pack of cigarettes. "The visit was productive in one sense, Sam," he said. "Suda's unbroken silence indicates a brooding mind, one that might be bent on violent revenge."

"Right. He also shook the guys following him, and that says a lot to me."

Ueki puffed on his cigarette. "That, as far as I can tell, is an accurate analysis. By the very act of avoiding police scrutiny, Suda seems to be preparing for . . . something."

Hours later, while we were making guesses as to what the future might hold, our train started up and Ueki went to the telephone for the third or fourth time, standing by until service was restored. He got through to headquarters and came back to our car with word that Yoshio Suda's whereabouts remained unknown.

After I called Noriko to tell her not to worry about our delay, we reclined the seats and tried to rest, but both of us were awake when we pulled into Okayama Station shortly before daybreak.

Yumiko was standing in front of the house, chatting with the milkman, when Ueki let me out of the car. "You have overlooked the fan again," she said as he drove off.

"I've been up all night, I'm hot, and I've got to get a rush on to make it to the office," I retorted. "The fan can wait."

"He forgets things," she confided to the milkman, who was busily removing bottles from the wire baskets on either side of his bicycle.

The deliveryman, a retired high school math teacher who often came to our home to practice English conversation, refrained from comment but flashed a sympathetic grin in my direction.

Noriko gave me a royal greeting and put on a gangbuster western breakfast while I bathed and shaved. "I wish you and Father could sleep today," she said as I got ready for the drive to work.

That kind of concern always pleases me. "Don't worry, love. I'm fresh as a daisy, and I'm sure Toshihiko's used to going without a full night's shuteye now and then. If I hear anything about Yoshio Suda, I'll let you know right away."

Noriko gazed up at me lovingly. "Thank you, Sam, and please come home early if you can."

I got into our canary yellow car, revved it up, and, for once, made almost all the green lights, showing up at the office seconds after the habitually early Masahige Goto arrived. We spent a few minutes discussing the events related to Suda, then went over the day's agenda. There were a few contracts to be signed later and the monthly sales reports to be put into graph form for comparative purposes—nothing pressing.

Goto left for his own office with a stack of papers, and I stared at the telephone, debating whether I should call Inspector Ueki, find out what steps the cops were taking to locate Suda. No, I decided, rubbing tired eyes. Police work, like everything else, took time. I closed the office door and stretched out on the sofa. Sure as taxes, Ueki would call if anything came up. Meanwhile, forty winks wouldn't hurt anything, wouldn't be noticed, wouldn't. . . .

Some people bounce from sleep to waking with instant alertness, aware and ready. Not Sam Brent. My sensory systems come on line slowly, and then it takes a while longer for everything to link up in a meaningful way. That day of the long snooze was no exception. The first thing that filtered through to the conscious level was that the Venetian blinds were flapping away. But something was missing—other sounds, like the ringing of telephones, the buzzing of intercoms, the normal background of conversation from clerks and secretaries.

I opened my eyes, blinked, and sat up stiffly, realizing with a hot blush that I was all by my lonesome in the office. Goto and the others must have done a lot of tiptoeing and smothering of chuckles to keep Brent-san slumbering in peace, and I could imagine the grins as they stole away silently at the end of work.

Guiltily, I went to the telephone at my desk and told Noriko that I'd be home for dinner as soon as traffic allowed. I was putting my jacket on when Inspector Ueki walked in.

"I am happy that you are still here, Sam. This has been a hectic day, and I regret that I did not have time to stay in touch."

"Way it goes," I said. "The day really sped by me, too. So, what's up with Suda? Got a lead on him yet?"

Ueki plopped down tiredly on the sofa I had just vacated. "Almost as soon as I got to headquarters this morning, the judge and prosecutor came to see me. They thought I would be pleased to hear that they had decided to leave immediately with their wives to spend a few days at a festival, allowing me to release my men for other duties."

That sounded encouraging to me. "Why the long face, Toshihiko? With them out of harm's way, some of the urgency is gone."

The inspector put his feet up on the coffee table. "If anything, Sam, the situation is much more critical. Yoshio Suda is still following them."

"How do you know?"

Ueki explained. Suda, with the instincts developed by longterm convicts, was aware that his steps were being dogged by plainclothesmen. He ditched them by the simple expedient of hopping a crowded trolley, bulling his way to the rear, and getting off at the next stop. It was a move that caught Ueki's men off balance. By the time they got off the trolley and rushed back to the stop, Suda had vanished.

Once he assigned extra men to the search, Ueki said, he began to speculate on what Suda would do for money, as he could not have had more than a few thousand yen in his pockets after his trip from the prison. Ueki started calling on the Okayama banks and discovered that one Yoshio Suda had, in fact, closed out a savings account that had been untouched since his sentence began. The sum in the account was a respectable one, enough to finance whatever plans he had.

Then, in the afternoon after the judge and prosecutor departed with their wives, a ticket clerk at Okayama Station told a detective that, yes, he did recognize the person in the prison photograph. The clerk said he remembered the man because he seemed unfamiliar with the routes covered by the modern system of bullet trains. His final destination was Osorezan, in the center of the Shimokita Peninsula in northeastern Honshu.

"And that," the inspector concluded, rising from the sofa, "is where the judge and prosecutor went for the festival."

Outside the window, the din of early evening traffic was picking up, and my stomach was making demands for sustenance. "How did Suda find out? You said the cops were watching them carefully."

Ueki raised the blinds, looking down into the crush of vehicles as he gave his account. He began with the hypothesis that Suda had to be operating under two assumptions: one, that the police wanted him for questioning because of his oath of vengeance after the trial, and, two, that security measures undoubtedly had been taken.

Accordingly, Suda then made another simple, direct move: he called both homes and was rewarded for his boldness when the prosecutor's elder sister, who lived with him, answered. This sister, who had decided not to take in the festival, said that Suda had seemed almost cheerful about giving his name, and identified himself as one of her brother's old friends. Knowing nothing of police fears concerning Suda's intentions, the sister disclosed where her brother and the judge had gone.

This news, Ueki conjectured, must have pleased Suda. In Okayama, the police restricted his opportunities. But at the festival, distant from major cities, it was doubtful that prefecture officials could adequately cover all of the towns and villages with tourist facilities. The changes wrought by time would mask Suda's face from his quarry, and he could stalk them at his leisure.

Suda had made one comment before breaking the connection: "They can avoid me no longer."

"Not good," I said. "Not good at all. But can't you get word to the cops near Osorezan and have them head off the judge and prosecutor, send them back to Okayama where you can protect them?"

Ueki leaned against a file cabinet. "I have asked them to do so, Sam, but I would feel infinitely better if I were there in person. All the individuals involved are from Okayama, I am familiar with the background, and it may take the authorities around Osorezan many hours simply to learn where our unsuspecting citizens might choose to stay, once they are there. That will delay the warning they need so urgently."

Ueki said that Suda left Okayama several hours behind the judge and prosecutor, and would not be in the Osorezan area until well past midnight. By then, the inspector said, he hoped the judge and prosecutor would be safely out of sight in one of the numerous inns and hotels. "But," he added, "hoping may not be enough."

"What's holding you back?" I asked. "The trains are still running."

"Yes," Ueki said, "but at this hour I would not be able to make all the necessary connections. I thought about driving, Sam, but I am in the grip of fatigue and do not wish to endanger the lives of other motorists. The best I can do is wait until morning and go by airplane."

An alternative requiring a confession presented itself. "Know what I did all day, Toshihiko? I slept, that's what, right here on the sofa. So there's no reason I can't do some night driving as your chauffeur. Goto can run the store while I'm gone."

The fatigue seemed to evaporate from Ueki's face. "This is one favor that I will find it hard to repay you for, Sam. Now, we can allow ourselves a few minutes to stop by our homes, but not too long."

If we drove steadily at the legal speed limit, Ueki said, we would be at the festival site early the next morning and he could work with the prefecture police.

"Consider it done," I said, closing windows and turning off lights. "As long as we're going to be there, you might as well tell me the name of the festival."

*"Osorezan Dai-Matsuri,"* he replied. "Or, in English, the Great Festival of the Terrible Mountain. But there is another name for that place, Sam— one used by many who travel there."

"Yeah?" I tested the lock on the outer door and moved to the elevators. "What's that?"

"The country of the dead."

There was nothing pleasant about Inspector Ueki's smile when he said it.

On the road, and on my own! The inspector was slumped down on the passenger side of my car, head back, snoring lightly, as I ventured forth into my first go at nocturnal driving in Japan. For the most part, I'm nervous about motoring anywhere or anytime in this part of the world: the roads and highways are narrow by home standards, the numerous stretches of mountain passages and tunnels demand more than a little extra alertness for those accustomed to the wide and the straight, and the panorama of Oriental countryside can be dangerously distracting.

On this July night, however, a hundred kilometers out of Okayama, I had the asphalt almost entirely to myself. The inspector had gone over a map in red marker pen, carefully designating the routes, there was a penlight clipped to my pocket, and the gas tank was full. To complete my sense of satisfaction, there was the recent pleasantness of a splendid quick dinner put together by Noriko and my parting remarks to Yumiko.

"Didn't overlook a thing," I had boasted as Ueki and I put our overnighters in the car. "The fan is right there on the back seat. Transferred it from Toshihiko's buggy to mine in case we have to stay at some hot, stuffy inn."

That seemed to satisfy her, and she went as far as allying herself with Noriko in urging us to be careful.

For a while after we left, the inspector chatted about the case. Judge Mimao Kai and the prosecutor, Tadayoshi Kunishio, were retired, he said, but they were among the most highly admired people in Okayama Prefecture.

As Ueki outlined some of the differences between the Japanese and American legal systems, I could appreciate his praise. Japanese who are charged with crimes do not present their stories to a jury: they must answer to a judge and prosecutor, and the final decision rests solely with the judge. Yet as Ueki told it, the Japanese people would rather place judgment of innocence or guilt in the hands of respected and trusted individuals whose reputations for honesty and fairness were known than with fellow citizens who were strangers.

The conclusion I drew from what he said was the same I arrived at after seeing the prison—if a system works, it works.

Now, hours later, twin cones of light picking out the roadway ahead, I fervently hoped I would get Ueki to the Terrible Mountain before Suda had time to ferret out his prey and strike.

The country of the dead, Ueki had called the place.

I cleared my mind of everything but driving.

A yellowish haze hung in the morning air when we arrived at the town of Tanabu, near Osorezan, and the sun was already burning with a white glare minutes after it cleared the mountain peaks. Even at that early hour, tourists and pilgrims were everywhere in evidence, and when we selected a *ryokan* at random, we were gratified to find that there was still room at the inn.

Inspector Ueki suggested that I sleep: he intended to meet with his police counterparts in the prefecture immediately to see whether Suda or the judge and prosecutor had turned up yet. I postponed rest for a physical need that took precedence at the moment—food.

"Very well," Ueki said. "You do not object to my taking your car for a while?"

"Shoot, no," I grinned. "You probably drive almost as well as I do."

The inspector shook his head and stepped out of our room. I upended my travel bag on the tatami, rooted around for razor, shaving cream, and lotion, and squeezed my feet into slippers several sizes too small for the walk to the communal bath. A leisurely soap-ladle-soak, followed by a shave, left me more famished than before, and after changing into clean clothes I sauntered up to the front desk and asked if I could have a breakfast tray sent to my room.

"*Ma . . .*" said the man behind the desk, and the politely imprecise word that can mean "well," "dear me," or "oh!" took on instant precision: I was too late for the morning meal.

Well, if the kitchen was closed here, should I hike down the road, look for an eatery catering to tourists? No, better not. Ueki could be back any minute, and I didn't want to be left in the dark about the Suda case or stranded if he had to journey out to the boondocks. What to do?

"Mr. Brent?" someone said from behind me. "Mr. Sam Brent of Okayama?"

I turned to check out the source. The two men standing at a respectful distance were at least a foot shorter than I am: one sported a maroon beret over a lined, cheerful face, and the other's visage was decorated with white mustaches that curved downward over the corners of his mouth, where they merged with a fall of beard from the chin. "Yep, I'm Sam Brent, but you seem to have the advantage."

"Ha! I told you it was he," Whiskers said to Beret, then bowed to me. "I am Mimao Kai and this is my very good friend, Tadayoshi Kunishio. Like you, we are natives of Okayama City, and I was positive that I recognized you from the many newspaper stories dealing with your business success and your association with Inspector Toshihiko Ueki."

"Kai-san! Kunishio-san! Then . . . you've *got* to be Judge Kai and Prosecutor Kunishio!"

"That is so," Kunishio laughed, "but surely our fame does not equal yours. Now *you* are the one with the advantage. How is it that you know who we are?"

I told them, winding up with the safe bet that Ueki was going to breathe a lot easier now. "I'll bet the police have been looking everywhere for you."

"Oh," said Prosecutor Kunishio, "we have caused much trouble. We spent the night with friends at a nearby town and checked into this inn only thirty minutes ago."

"Well," I said, "everything has worked out okay. Toshihiko's bound to be back soon, and I'll stick with you, if you don't mind, to see that Suda doesn't try anything."

Judge Kai worried his whiskers with thumb and forefinger. "That is so kind of you, Brent-san, but I doubt that Suda would bother with two old men like us. Nevertheless, we would enjoy your company and would like to ask you to be our guest at the breakfast which all of us seem to have missed. There is, I understand, a good restaurant within walking distance."

I smiled acceptance. Getting something to eat and being able to keep an eye on Kunishio and Kai would be a bird in each hand. I left a message for Ueki with the desk clerk, and my two new acquaintances went to see if their spouses were ready to go.

As I stood admiring an early Chinese watercolor on the wall, Kai and Kunishio came running back to me.

"Our wives!" Kai stammered, out of breath. "They are not in our rooms!"

"We do not know where they are!" Kunishio said in tones of desperation. "Could this Suda have abducted them as . . . as hostages?"

Pangs of hunger fled before stabs of apprehension. I urged the two to calm down, to stay where I could watch them while I talked to the clerk. "The ladies are probably just looking around like the other tourists," I said.

Their dubious looks matched my unspoken fear—that Suda really was behind the disappearance.

The clerk was so startled when I asked him to call the police that I had to repeat the request. Then I returned to Kai and Kunishio—to wait.

Mrs. Kai and Mrs. Kunishio apologized with blushes while the *ryokan* lodgers whispered among themselves and gaped at the scene in the lobby: two elderly men, two embarrassed ladies in print kimonos, a red-haired foreigner, six uniformed cops, and one tall police inspector from another city, all trying to talk at once.

"Sam . . ." Ueki's look was almost imploring as he tried to cut into the babble.

"We are so sorry," Mrs. Kai offered, apparently too flustered to notice the interruption, "but we were only sitting in the shade of the garden."

"All's well that ends well," I philosophized secondhand. "Anyone for breakfast?"

"Sam," Ueki said again, a ripple of impatience in his tone, "all is *not* well, and I want my fellow citizens from Okayama to hear this." He waited until he was sure of everyone's attention. "My colleagues here," and he gave the other officers an all-inclusive bow, "have canvassed this area thoroughly and have a definite identification of Yoshio Suda by a shop owner." Ueki paused, lending impact to his next words. "Suda purchased a knife—a very long, thin knife used to fillet fish. In short, he is armed with a weapon, and we do not know where he is."

Judge Kai moved closer to his wife. "I no longer doubt the need for police protection, Inspector Ueki. Is there anything we can do to make your task less arduous?"

Ueki nodded. "From this moment, until we have control over Suda, I do not want you or your wives to be unguarded. Every officer here will do his utmost, but your fullest cooperation is essential."

The judge and prosecutor promised to give it, and Mrs. Kai shyly interjected a question. "Inspector, sir, will we be able to attend the festival?"

"Oh, yes," Mrs. Kunishio said. "It would be such a disappointment not to see it after coming all this way."

Ueki gave his qualified approval, with the consent of the local officers: the Kais and Kunishios could go anywhere they desired as long as they were accompanied by police. I then made arrangements to meet the judge, the prosecutor, and their wives for an early lunch while Ueki and the other cops set out to look for Suda.

When Inspector Ueki got back to the inn that evening, Suda still had not been found.

I wasn't prepared for the sensory shock created by the bleak surroundings of Osorezan, the Terrible Mountain. It was, I gathered, an extinct volcano, standing like a mute giant over a terrain unlike anything I'd ever seen—or imagined. There were crater lakes of deep, still water, and the barren, boulder-strewn ground, the sluggish streams, and the underground springs all gave off the stench of sulphur, an invisible, eye-stinging effluvium that was wafted for kilometers around on a moaning wind.

At Osorezan, I thought, the ancient and the modern met in a clash bewildering to the western mind. Pilgrims came by bus and ferry to make offerings, mingling with throngs of camera-wielding tourists, while Buddhist mendicants wearing umbrella-shaped straw hats accepted alms. Elsewhere, throngs of the hopeful gathered to ask spirit mediums to cross the gulf between the living and the dead.

Mimao Kai and Tadayoshi Kunishio, at dinner the night before, had outlined some of the beliefs concerning the Terrible Mountain. Over a red drum bridge spanning a lifeless lake called the Pond of Blood for its coloration, the souls of the newly deceased were thought to make the crossing to the other world. Many held Osorezan to be the home of the oldest gods of Japan, where spirits and demons also roamed the rugged earth.

Here, too, was Saino-kawara, the Buddhist netherworld for the souls of unfortunate children who die before they thank their parents for giving them life. These forlorn shadows, so tradition goes, must spend all eternity mounding up pebbles, their task always undone by heartless demons who trample their unending labors.

Judge Kai, who had watched my expression carefully during this part of the discussion, told me with a reassuring smile that many Japanese also believed that the spirits of all other departed children were guarded over by a special being named Jizo. During the festival, Kai said, hundreds of pilgrims would offer straw sandals to protect Jizo's feet from the hot, sulphurous grounds while he kept watch over his wards.

I thought at length about what the judge said. On the one hand, there was a tradition about the fate of children who don't show gratitude to their parents, and on the other, there was the legend of an entity who forever keeps the rest from harm. I decided that the story of the hopeless task of mounding pebbles was for the benefit of youngsters, urging them to show respect, and that the other was an indication of the deep love I knew the Japanese have for children.

Now, under the blazing sun of a new morning, I was caught up by mounting interest in the object of our outing—a meeting with the *itako,* or spirit mediums.

Since our early arrival, the mediums, all older women, had been waiting while friends and relatives pitched army surplus tents. With two uniformed policemen standing by to prevent an unwanted appearance by Yoshio Suda, we entered one of them.

The *itako,* seated on a straight-backed chair, was, like many of the other mediums, totally blind, dressed in simple clothing of the countryside and fingering a rosary of wood beads so rapidly they hissed like the wind-blown sands of the desert.

Mrs. Kai approached the *itako* first, addressing her as *O-funi,* which might be translated as Stepping Stone, or, simply, Missive. The *itako,* in a warm, friendly voice, asked for the names of relatives or friends who had died, requesting times, places, and causes of death. Mrs. Kai complied, and the *itako* shut her unseeing eyes and began a singsong chant in a rural dialect I had trouble following.

Soon the messages came, all of them severely practical, far from what I'd expected from the other side of the known. A brother suggested that Mrs. Kai have some dental work done, and a cherished friend sent the opinion that the dwarf plum trees in the Kai garden be pruned more carefully.

Mrs. Kunishio was next, and the spirit medium passed along loving recommendations from a deceased sister to replace the tiles on the Kunishio house and to put in a new gas heater for the bath water.

From what the judge had told us, I knew there was no set fee for the services rendered by the *itako,* but Mrs. Kunishio left three thousand yen and Mrs. Kai presented the medium with a box containing a whole salted salmon.

We left the canvas shelter, and I saw that almost all the people queued up to see the mediums were women. Then, as we turned away to walk toward the Entsuji Temple in the near distance, a man darted from behind the tents and struck Judge Kai across the face with a cylinder of some sort, which he then dropped.

"Yoshio Suda!" Inspector Ueki shouted.

My own immediate concern was with helping the judge, who staggered against me with a groan of pain. As soon as I determined that he wasn't hurt badly, I looked up and made out Ueki and the two uniformed officers trying to find a passage through the center of a group of pilgrims. The man they were chasing was fleeing toward the Pond of Blood.

Even from a distance, it was possible to tell what the man was holding aloft in one hand.

It was a knife, its shiny blade sending back white bursts of reflected sunlight.

I started running.

Yoshio Suda died by his own hand, in a way only the older generation can recall. When Ueki finally managed to get to him, Suda was already slipping away fast, seated by the Pond of Blood, the knife handle jutting from his abdomen in the self-destruction known as *harakiri*.

Suda knew, as did we, that the two policemen would not be able to return with help in time to save him. Inspector Ueki honored Suda's plea to die unassisted, making no move to make him more comfortable.

"Before this hour is out, Suda-san," Ueki said, "you will undertake your last journey—across the bridge of drums on the Pond of Blood. I think the burden your soul carries will be lighter if you make a gift of truth. Who, Suda-san, murdered your wife, why did Hisao Nakai exonerate you, and why did you strike Judge Kai before you chose *harakiri?*"

Suda's body jerked in a spasm of pain, and then he began to speak, eyes on the far side of the Pond of Blood. "I did kill my wife," he said without emotion, "but it was my right to do so, and I have no regrets."

He related how, those many years past, he and his wife had grown apart, how he had long tolerated her gibes and sarcasm directed at his absences from home, how he had endured her complaints about having a husband who neglected her, denying her the love and attention she deserved. Gradually, Suda said, he became suspicious of his wife's fidelity, and he began to discuss his suspicions with Hisao Nakai, who consistently replied that Suda was overworked, was imagining a situation that really did not exist.

Nakai's point of view, Suda went on, appeared reasonable, and one evening when the bulk of paperwork at his office seemed unusually oppressive, he decided after everyone else was gone to go home early and make amends with his wife.

That evening, however, he found her absent. Suda, angry, heated a pitcher of sake and waited. After his wife returned by taxi, teasing him and laughing at his rage, which was soaring out of control, Suda demanded to know whom she had been with. Mrs. Suda, unrelenting and undaunted, had changed from skirt and blouse into a light blue house kimono. She was combing out her long black hair as she taunted Suda, saying that if she did have a lover, it was because of Suda's inattention.

It was then that Suda had ripped the sash from her kimono and strangled her. When his senses returned, he found himself back at his office, still confused and disoriented. He called Nakai and asked him to meet him for drinks and a meal at a restaurant they sometimes used for business negotiations.

Suda's face was drenched with perspiration by now, and Ueki gave him a handkerchief. "Suda-san, did you tell Nakai what you had done, that your wife was dead?"

"No," Suda said, his words slurred. "I was dazed . . . maybe too much sake to drink. Shock, I do not know, but did not comprehend that . . . I had killed her. Not then, when I met Nakai. Not yet. Recall saying I was tired. Very tired. Later, I realized. Left Nakai, went home. Called police, hoped they would believe I discovered . . . body."

"At your trial," Ueki said, "you insisted that you had done no wrong, and we also fail to grasp why Nakai proclaimed your innocence more than two decades after he gave the authorities grounds for the murder charge."

Suda's eyes were glazed, and I knew that the strand of remaining life was stretching thin. "In old Japan . . . a man's right . . . severely punish unfaithful wife. But . . . changes. Evil. New ideas . . . corrupt. Nakai wrote letters saying wife unworthy. Only truth he ever uttered . . . ever. He thought to . . . to placate me. Never . . . never forgive."

"Nakai?" Ueki said. "Why did Nakai set you free?"

Suda shivered violently. "Nakai was . . . weakling. Treacherous, weak. Wanted to kill him, but . . . denied me . . . pleasure. I guessed. Guessed . . . right after accused me, but useless. Ask Mrs. Nakai. She may know . . . may tell."

His face suddenly relaxed, Suda stopped speaking. Ueki sighed heavily, reached down to close the dead man's eyes, and laid the body back on the hard ground. "We are finished here, Sam. Suda murdered and then confused justice with outmoded and one-sided codes of conduct." He turned away from the corpse and looked at a crowd of curious onlookers being kept away by the prefecture police. "Let us go see if Judge Kai can help us understand why Suda's revenge was no more than a blow to the face."

Ueki walked on, but I lingered, wondering what Suda had expected to find by the Pond of Blood, on the other side of the drum bridge that led from life to death. The forgiving soul of an unfaithful murdered wife? The approval of kindred spirits?

The smell of sulphur was overwhelming, and I hurried to catch up with the inspector.

Judge Kai's nose was bandaged when we met for dinner that night, but he said nothing was broken and that the pain was minimal. The bamboo tube he'd been hit with held a rolled-up piece of foolscap on which Suda had written a condemnation of modern values and what he termed the degeneration of all the old, unwritten laws.

"I deliver this," the scroll said, "as a gesture of contempt, thankful that fate decreed more than a simple protest of your ignorance over the telephone and brought me to confront you in this land of our ancient gods. At first, I planned to kill you and that lesser fool, Prosecutor Kunishio, but could not bring myself to soil my hands on ignoble lackeys of feeble and worthless laws. For choking off the life of a wanton woman who defiled her sacred marriage vows, you judged *me* a criminal. My blood is let with pride in a heritage you have forsaken."

Inspector Ueki poured wine vinegar on his salad. "As far as I am concerned, all that matters is the welfare of honest citizens, not the verbiage of fanatics."

Judge Kai accomplished a feat of dexterity with chopsticks, navigating a chunk of melon cleanly past mustaches and beard. "Suda," he said, "failed to recognize that what prevailed in our feudal past is no longer suitable. Without laws that are equally applicable to all, we would not be a democracy."

Prosecutor Kunishio agreed. "I, for one," he said, "will never, never be ashamed of having brought transgressors before our courts. And you, Inspector Ueki, are especially deserving of praise for your dedication to the enforcement of our laws and the prevention of crime."

Ueki mashed out a cigarette. "Thank you, and please enjoy the rest of your vacation. When all of us are back in Okayama, it may be that we will meet again." He turned to me. "As we will be staying at the *ryokan* until morning, Sam, why not bring in the fan? Tonight promises to be one of the the hottest of the summer, and we need a good rest for the long drive back."

"You got it," I said with a grin. "Be back in a jiffy."

I whistled all the way to the car, congratulating myself for leaving the fan there. Our room at the inn wasn't air-conditioned, and now we'd have some much-welcomed relief. I unlocked the door and flinched at the oven-like interior temperature, then leaned in and pulled out . . . the remains.

Unbelieving, I turned what was left of the fan around and around in my hands. The metal motor housing and guard were intact, but the plastic blades had melted, collapsing into shapeless gray blobs.

"It's ruined," I said when I got back to our table, holding the useless appliance out for visible proof.

"Do not worry, Sam," Ueki said sympathetically. "We will rely on another method of keeping ourselves cool."

"Such as?"

He grinned. "Another cold beer before we retire. I hope it will restore your normal good cheer."

It helped, but I kept visualizing Yumiko's face when she learned what happened to the fan I forgot to remove from a hot car.

We returned to Okayama in the middle of the next afternoon, and I drove Ueki directly to Mrs. Nakai's house. The widow, dressed in black, invited us in as soon as the inspector identified himself and introduced me. She carefully laid out the best pairs of house slippers at the entranceway, and bowing, with hands pressed flat against her knees, she begged us to make ourselves comfortable in the front room. She then backed out of the room with more bows and went to the kitchen to fix a platter of cakes and to brew tea.

Ueki waited for an appropriate interval after she served us before telling her the circumstances of Yoshio Suda's death and mentioning all the points that remained unclear. "Suda suggested," Ueki said, "that you might have information I need to close this case."

Mrs. Nakai looked up at a black-bordered photograph of her husband on the wall. "There were many untruths in Hisao Nakai's life that brought me unending sorrow, Ueki-san, but he was my husband and I kept my silence."

"Of course," the inspector said. "I am not here to accuse you of anything or to criticize you, Mrs. Nakai, only to clarify."

She opened the doors of the past for us then with a dignity and composure that, under the circumstances, I regarded as remarkable. Of all the painful memories she unlocked that day, the one that surprised me was put so simply that I can easily recall her thin, strained voice as she brought it forth.

*"My husband, you see, was Mrs. Suda's secret lover."*

Link by link, Mrs. Nakai proceeded from this revelation until the chain of human passions was complete, beginning with loneliness and lust and ending with suicide in a desolate corner of the earth.

It began with a chance meeting: Nakai was invited to dine with Mr. and Mrs. Suda on one of the infrequent occasions that Yoshio Suda took his wife out to dinner. Nakai became infatuated, and Mrs. Suda encouraged him. Rendezvous were arranged, and the relationship was entering its fourth month when Suda murdered his wife.

In the months after the slaying, Hisao Nakai told his wife about the trysts, pleading for compassion, entreating her to tell no one, promising never again to stray from her side. He admitted that he had been so infuriated by the loss of a woman he thought he loved that he fabricated a story of threats—threats Suda had never made.

Mrs. Nakai forgave her husband, but he could not emerge from the torment and confusion he lived with daily. Increasingly, as time passed, Nakai claimed that he was able to see the world through Suda's eyes, to share the dismay that had swept over his friend when Suda began to suspect Mrs. Suda's marital fidelity. The explosion of rage that left Mrs. Suda with a kimono sash knotted tightly around her throat? Nakai convinced himself that it was natural, something any husband could do, an act for which a man should not be punished.

And so, Mrs. Nakai told us, Nakai expressed these feelings in his unanswered letters to Suda, trying to soothe his own guilt but never finding the courage to disclose that he, indirectly, had caused Mrs. Suda's death.

Once Nakai knew that a lingering illness he had contracted was terminal, he devised the stratagem of a dying statement—a statement contending that he had accused Suda of threatening to kill his wife because he felt Suda had cheated him in business.

"Would I be correct," Ueki said, "if I assumed that your husband waited so long because he wanted to be beyond the questioning that might have uncovered his final lie?"

"Yes," the widow said, teardrops forming in her eyes.

"One thing more," Ueki said, standing up, "and we will leave you to your privacy. Did your husband realize that Suda, once out of prison, might try to retaliate against the people who sent him there?"

Mrs. Nakai put her hands to her face. "His last words to me were that he hoped he had caused no more grief to anyone."

"Thank you," the inspector said gently, and we left her to what I knew was a personal hell.

We went to my car and rolled down the windows. "Toshihiko," I said, "this could have been a lot worse. Suda might have killed the judge and prosecutor if he hadn't gotten so wrapped up in noble gestures of contempt. Nakai should have known better than to let him loose, no matter how guilty he felt."

The inspector loosened his tie and unbuttoned his collar. "If everyone 'knew better,' there would be no need for the police. Shall we go now? There are still several working hours ahead of me."

I drove him to headquarters, extended an invitation to dinner, and checked in at the office.

* * *

There is a drink, cool and refreshing, that our family often enjoys in the garden at the end of the day. It is concocted from the juice of lemons, water, sugar, and ice, and most of my Japanese friends call it remonade.

Seated at the circular stone table near the plum trees that night, I was sipping this drink in contented silence with Inspector Ueki while we watched the domestic scene around us: Noriko and Mrs. Ueki in animated conversation with a neighbor lady standing on her verandah, Yumiko laughing as the boys played in front of a lantern, using their hands to cast shadow figures against a wall.

All about us, there was the rustle of breezes stirring through the trees, the chirping of crickets from the shrubs and flowerbeds, and the perfume of roses and sweet alyssum. On the horizon, above the snaggle-toothed outline of mountain peaks, a full moon rose in a glory of golden orange.

Perfection, I thought with a sigh. I craned my neck back to fix my sights on the Big Dipper. How many people, I wondered, knew that the second star in the handle was a double, one bright, the other so dim it took concentration to find it? From there, I slipped into one of my favorite reveries, trying to guess which of the stars I could see had planets, maybe life, and, possibly, people just like us, all seated in their gardens, having the same hopes and problems we do.

"Toshihiko," I said, "have you ever thought . . . ?"

But then, with a start, I saw that Yumiko was coming our way, ankle-length granny skirt flapping with her brisk stride.

"Uh-oh!" I groaned. "Here comes some flak about the fan!"

"Allow me to handle this," the inspector said. "Yumiko-san," he told her, once she was at the table, "Sam did not return the fan. While he was aiding me in the task of protecting innocent lives, there was no time to remove it from his automobile, and the blades melted in the heat."

"I came to ask if you want more lemonade," she said.

Lemonade! And Ueki had to go and bring up that blasted fan!

The inspector smiled but sailed on in the same direction. "I would like for everyone to hear what I have to say." He called out for Noriko, Mrs. Ueki, and the boys, then stood up to address them. "When Sam drove me to Osorezan, he did so at his own expense. Because of that, and because of many other generous acts which have been of benefit to the police, my fellow officers have donated a sum of money, used to replace an item Sam was fond of."

"A new fan!" I said. "You guys actually chipped in to buy one for me?"

Noriko took her father's arm and squeezed it. "That was so kind of you. Sam and I both thank you."

"Indeed," Mrs. Ueki added, "it is not every man who is fortunate enough to have such a son-in-law. Where is this fan, husband? We would like to see you present it now."

For long seconds, Ueki stood like a silent statue, looking at no one. "Ah, yes. The fan."

Yumiko stepped toward him. *"Hai.* The fan."

Ueki picked up his empty glass, looked at the lantern light through it, and put it down again. "Where. You want to know where it is."

I felt like the Big Dipper had just poured cold water on me. "Toshihiko, it could happen to anyone. I mean, all of us can get busy, you know—preoccupied. Me. Take me, for instance. Look, I can come to headquarters tomorrow, pick it up."

With a prolonged chuckle, Inspector Ueki stooped down and pulled a beautifully wrapped carton from under the table. "I put it here while everyone was finishing dinner, Sam. May both of you last forever."

In the midst of all the people who made life so worthwhile, I helped with the gleeful unwrapping and joined in the applause as old Yumiko carried the fan inside for a ceremonial placing on the straw matting.

I stayed behind in the garden by myself for a while. "Thank you," I smiled, looking up at all those twinkling stars once more.

I didn't consider it necessary to say what for.

# AFRICA

# DEATH IN EGYPT

*By Henry T. Parry*

WHICH ONE? Beasley asked himself. Which one thinks he is going to knock me off?

He looked at the tour members gathered in the riverboat's lounge, where they sat talking and drinking like old friends although they had met only the week before. Reaching for the peanuts, he flicked them expertly one by one into his mouth, displaying the blue shield entwined by a snake that was tattooed on his forearm. As he chewed, he smiled in secret amusement at his answer to the nosey types who had tried to find out from him more than he wished to tell them about himself. "I ain't of no interest to anyone," he had insisted, with an aw-shucks, rough-diamond honesty, adding to himself, Except the Internal Revenue Service.

A cruise up the Nile River was not his idea of a vacation—Las Vegas or Acapulco would be more like it—but Agnes had exclaimed over the folders that Seven League Tours had sent her. His knowledge of Egypt was limited to vague memories of pictures in which overseers stood sideways on huge blocks of stone and lashed the backs of slaves who toiled at the drag ropes. He wished he had some pictures like that to take home to the union president to illustrate the kind of contract he'd like to negotiate next time for Beasley Builders. It seemed to him that Agnes, now that they had money stashed away, was trying to wean him from his construction-site habits, just as she was making him dress more like the president of a company.

She had not been able to get him to stop wearing his diamond ring. "It's the only thing I got that ain't been mortgaged sometime or other," he told her, "and that includes you, Aggie." He was not unfamiliar with violence—he had battled his way from operating a manual concrete-mixer to the presidency of his own company—and had taken part in and known about practices he hoped were behind him forever. But the idea that someone in this soft, easy-going group intended to kill him was ridiculous. They were pussy cats and he had run with tigers.

Just the same, there were the threats. The first had come two days ago, their first day on the boat. He had come down from the bar to their state-room to put on the coat that Aggie insisted he wear for dinner, until she found out that he was the only man in the dining room wearing a coat. He found the small red-bordered label pasted to the mirror.

"You will die for the Arena," it read, in the careful lettering of a drafts-man. He had clumsily removed it with a razor blade and was about to throw it away when he changed his mind and placed the crumpled slip among his traveling papers, saying nothing to Aggie. The next threat, at lunch yester-day, was not two feet from his face when he looked up from the menu at the tall, grave-faced waiter who held his tray pressed vertically against his robe, its bottom displaying the same kind of red-margined sticker that read "Remember the Arena."

He took a slug from his glass, captured a handful of peanuts from the bowl, and mentally went down the list of tour members.

"Our tours are limited to twenty persons to give you the best in travel service," Seven League Tours had boasted.

Van Alt, the tour director? Not likely. They had met only three days earlier at the Cairo airport. One thing he had noticed about Van Alt, and Van Alt seemed to know it and to resent him for it, was a lack that should not have been overlooked by an agency that claimed to take care of every detail, and charged accordingly. A complaint could get Van Alt fired, and Beasley had pointed this out to him, more as a casual comment than as a threat.

He was aware too of Van Alt's practice of privately bestowing nicknames on the tour members. His own, of course, was Beastly, and although he regarded it as mild compared with what he had been called over the years, Van Alt's attitude irritated him. Van Alt had referred to Aggie as the Mink Connection, even though she had not brought any of her furs on the trip. Van Alt was smart, but he wasn't smart enough to know that a nickname should not be too accurate. Nor was he smart enough to keep his mouth shut.

But there was no way he could know about the Arena.

Beasley dismissed the women on the tour—twelve, including Aggie. Not even Aggie knew about the Arena; he never discussed matters of this kind with her. He dismissed Aggie too, although he admitted there had been a time when Aggie had had reason for being sore at him. But that was long ago and she wasn't the type to hold a grudge. Anyway, she wouldn't sneak around and paste up little notes. Pick up the nearest thing and fling it at him —that was Aggie's way.

What about that little grey creep—DeWin? Trewin? something like that —sitting by himself with a glass of dry sherry and an even drier-looking book before him? Or that guy Hunter who showed up at breakfast their first day, wearing a jungle shirt and shorts and a white sailor hat turned down all around so that it looked like a sun helmet? Beasley had to admit that Hunter's nickname, Dr. Livingstone, fitted him.

It couldn't be anyone from the four West Coast couples who kept themselves apart from the others as if they were uneasy about associating with anyone who had ever shoveled snow. And certainly it couldn't be that skinny professorlike fellow, Rogers, who was hired by the agency to keep them standing in the sun while he lectured them on the Middle Kingdom and the old gods and the achievements of ancient architects—a profession which he, as a builder, held in impatient contempt.

Beasley rose from the table to go down to see how Aggie was doing with the bug she seemed to have picked up. Dinner would not interest her, he was certain, nor would she be going ashore to tonight's sound-and-light show at the temple. She would sleep like the dead until morning. He helped himself to the remaining peanuts and, tilting the bowl, he uncovered the sticker on its bottom.

It read: "Soon."

The knocking at the door was insistent but controlled, as though under restraint because of the other passengers. Rogers resisted it, rationalizing that it must be a door other than his or that a crewman was pounding pipes in the overhead. When a vigorous shaking rattled the door, he surrendered and got up to answer it.

Van Alt stood in his pajamas. Behind him was an Egyptian who took pleasure in whatever it was that required people to be aroused at dawn.

"I want you to go with me. Hassan has found a body. He thinks it's someone from our tour."

"Yes. Yes. Your tour. Was in my carriage yesterday," the Egyptian said.

"Who's missing?" Rogers asked. "Surely someone would have reported someone missing by now."

"No one's been reported missing and I can't very well get them all up at this hour to see if anyone is missing."

Rogers saw that Van Alt was shaken and, for some reason, frightened. An experienced tour director who faced with equanimity cancelled flights, the usurpation by oil sheiks of rooms reserved months earlier for his tour, and the even more trying complaints of the tour members, Van Alt would not be expected to be so disturbed by the story the carriage driver had brought him. His was not the only tour on the *Cheops,* so the body might not be his responsibility. On the other hand, he could not afford to assume the driver was wrong.

"I'll meet you at the gangway," Rogers said.

He found the two men waiting beside the watchman and followed them ashore, climbing the stairs up the sandy bank into the palm-lined boulevard that skirted the river. The grey light that lay over the quiet river and the empty street was already dissolving under the oblique sunrise. The boulevard smelled of yesterday's carriage horses. The air, Rogers noted, was not cool. Rather there was an absence of heat, as though it had not completely cooled during the night and now was lying at some thermal nadir before beginning the climb to the daily hundred-degree mark. The dawn had a used quality as if, like everything else in this strange land, it was already old.

"Hassan says he was on his way to the stables. He lives somewhere on the other side of the temple area and cuts through there to get to the boulevard. I personally think he goes through the temple area to see what's been dropped at the sound-and-light show the night before. He was walking through the forecourt of the temple and when he came to the steps he saw feet sticking out from the base of the obelisk—" Van Alt looked at Hassan.

"One look. Dead. I come straightly to you," Hassan said as if in response to a minor pleasantry.

They turned off the boulevard and entered the long approach to the forecourt of the temple, an avenue flanked by massive statues of rams-headed sphinxes who looked down with a brutish, snouted indifference. At the steps of the forecourt they turned left into an intersecting avenue and were led by Hassan to the foot of the obelisk.

"Like I say. Dead." Hassan smiled cheerfully and pointed.

The body of a man lay in the recess between the base of the obelisk and a low ruined wall. No signs of violence were visible. Van Alt knelt in the sand and jammed his hand against the neck under the angle of the jaw, feeling for a pulse. After a few moments he fumbled for the wrist, dropped it, and placed his hand against the man's chest. The open, lightless eyes told him the same message as the absent pulse. He slid his hand under the back of the man's head, feeling cautiously, and hastily withdrew it, plunging his palm into the sand as though to scour it.

"He's dead," he said, squatting back on his heels. "Beastly's dead."

Rogers tried to suppress the first thought that came to him: Now he won't be able to stand in the back of the group and conduct an independent conversation while I'm lecturing. The expression on Van Alt's face, a growing realization of some liberating relief, made Rogers wonder if others were not also experiencing untimely and unsuitable thoughts.

* * *

Rogers found Van Alt sitting on the top deck in the lengthening shadow of the wheelhouse, seemingly unaware that Rogers stood behind him. When Rogers slid a deck chair next to him, Van Alt roused himself from his preoccupation.

"How did it go?"

"Uneventful. Nobody seemed to miss you. We got to the temple at Abydos, where I gave them the full treatment. We stopped at that gift shop you hate so much and at Abdul's papyrus shop—or I guess it's his uncle's, isn't it? What about Beasley?"

"The autopsy showed a fractured skull. I took Mrs. Beasley to the airport. One of our people in Cairo will put her on the plane for New York and make the other arrangements. But take a look at this."

Van Alt took out an envelope used for airline tickets, from which he extracted a red-bordered label, a fragment of paper whose curled thinness indicated that it had been peeled from something it had been stuck to. On it, in neat hand-lettering, were the words: "You will die for the Arena."

"We were waiting at the airport when she found this. It was in the envelope where Beasley had kept their airline tickets."

There was a familiarity about the label that Rogers tried to place. It was a common-enough sticker. Possibly they used them in the file room at the museum.

"What did Mrs. Beasley say about it?"

"She doesn't know anything about it. She says Beasley never mentioned it to her."

"If it was among his travel papers, it could have been there before he left home. It may have nothing to do with his death in spite of what it says. You'll turn it over to the police, I suppose?"

"Of course. When we get back downriver. I'll let our people there handle it."

"All we really know is that he was threatened—maybe back home, maybe on the tour. The Arena sounds like sports, and that might involve gambling. Maybe Beasley had a bookie he didn't treat with sufficient respect."

"We may never know. Anyway, it isn't my problem any longer."

"How about us?" Rogers asked. "Can our tour leave when the boat does?"

"Of course. I saw Achmed, the hotel manager here. He saw a friend in the city. I spread some of Seven League's money around and we're free to continue upriver."

Rogers marvelled at Van Alt's ability to guide the tour through the thickets that flourish in the path of foreign travel. He admired his unobtrusive patience, his unfailing memory for names and faces, his store of neutral pleasantries. He felt that Van Alt, in dealing with the tour members, projected a hint of some shared assumption, as though he were saying: "Obviously, you and I are men and women of the world, and you are already quite aware of what I am about to tell you, but if I may—" The tourists always felt flattered. He noted that although Van Alt was attentive to the women on the tour, he carefully avoided any attachments. There were already two previous Mrs. Van Alts and a third about to be. He dressed too youthfully for a man who found it necessary to bleach out the streaks of grey that appeared in his blond hair. Rogers observed too that he had a way of suddenly withdrawing, as if some social barrier had been abruptly lowered. And sometimes he felt sure that Van Alt hated Americans.

It would not have occurred to Rogers that his own task on the tour was equally demanding, with lectures sometimes three times a day, covering four thousand years of art, architecture, religion, and history. When the Seven League Tour Agency had approached his museum in search of a lecturer for their Egyptian tour, the museum director had unhesitatingly suggested Rogers as the leading young man in the field. The recommendation had provided him with a paid vacation in the country that had fascinated him ever since he was sixteen and where for one trying and glorious year when he was in graduate school he had worked on a dig.

"What did you find out," Van Alt asked, "about last night?"

"Not much. Most of the tour went to the sound-and-light performance behind the temple. Except for Mrs. Beasley—she was sick—and the four couples from the West Coast. They stayed on the boat and played bridge. Imagine paying Seven League's prices and then spending the time playing bridge."

"Did anyone see Beastly—Beasley, I mean? Did anyone see him leave the sound-and-light show?"

"Not leave, exactly. Trewin, that gloomy fellow who's always reading, said he sat next to him at the show. When they were leaving, going through the temple area, he said you caught up with them so he went on ahead."

"That's right. Beasley was interested in some construction details of the temple. I pointed out a few things. Then Mrs. Murray asked me something and she and I went on ahead."

"Well, everybody who was at the show had to come through the forecourt and down the steps. That means they passed within thirty feet of where Hassan found the body. Maybe Beasley walked back to the temple later, to see it by moonlight or something," Rogers said.

"Maybe, but not likely. He struck me as being a tough customer who wouldn't be given to looking at temples by moonlight."

"I did talk to the watchman on the gangplank," Rogers said. "He told me that everybody came back from the sound-and-light about ten-thirty. Some tourists left the boat again after that, and so did some crew members. The card players were among those who went ashore."

"When did they get back?" Van Alt asked.

"He said they were gone for thirty or forty minutes, just for a walk along the boulevard. I asked them about it. They said they went to that café across from the entrance to the temple area and had a drink. Then there were some people, four or five, who came in around three o'clock. They had been at a nightclub in the Fayd-Al-Farm district. They weren't members of our tour."

"So Beasley wasn't bashed by anyone from our group."

"It doesn't seem likely that he was," Rogers said. "He obviously wasn't going to be assaulted in full view of the people returning from the sound-and-light. And after everyone else was back on the boat except Beasley, it isn't likely—"

"I think Beasley got behind the crowd; somebody delayed him around the forecourt and bashed him. Whether the guilty person is found or not, I've got to put together a good story for the home office."

"Well, good luck. By the way, when do we sail?"

"In the morning."

"In that case I'll get below and study my notes on the temple at Komombo. With interesting observations on mummified crocodiles."

"This tour is creating its own candidates for mummification," Van Alt said.

At the head of the companionway, Rogers turned and called, "Van Alt!"

There was no response from the tour director. He sat unmoving, looking across the river with a faint smile, a smile that reflected more than his usual self-approval.

"Van Alt!" Rogers called again, this time more loudly.

Again there was no answer. At that moment Rogers realized what lay beneath Van Alt's machismo posture, his efforts to sustain a youthful appearance. He was also aware that added credence had been given to the story he had been told that afternoon concerning the events of the previous night, a story in which Van Alt figured but about which he was now understandably silent.

He went down to the main deck and headed for the gangplank, passing the bar where the tour was preparing for dinner. He climbed the waterfront steps to the boulevard, ignoring the hawking carriage drivers, whose animated faces offered sharp contrast to the despondency of their horses. "Halloa! Halloa! See temple in sunset. Cheap. See temple in moon. Cheap." He walked under the palms of the boulevard to the temple area and entered the long avenue of the rams-headed sphinxes which ended at the forecourt of the temple. The obelisk stood opposite the forecourt steps and a dozen yards to the left, surrounded on three sides by a low ruined wall, its pointed top pink in the setting sun. He seated himself on a sun-heated fragment of the wall and studied the spot where Beasley's body had lain.

The sand had been disturbed by many feet, official and unofficial. He tried to recall the scene as he had observed it that morning, with Van Alt testing futilely for vital signs. He remembered Van Alt's swift gesture, his hand plunging into the sand. Getting down on his knees, he probed the sand, turning it over in furrows, lifting it and letting it sift back between his fingers.

At the end of twenty-five minutes he had dug up and felt through the entire area where Beasley's body had lain, and found nothing except an empty box that had contained camera film. He sat down, resting his back against the obelisk, hoping that he offended none of the mighty whose cartouches were carved into the yellow stone, and examined the churned-up area. An inch of clear colorless wire projected from a furrow like some worm of the age of technology. Rogers carefully lifted it from the sand to find at the end of it a dime-sized, pencil-thick button. Holding it in the palm of his hand, he thought of the years of scientific progress the tiny object represented, and thought too that, in addition to its other capabilities, it would be enough to convict a man of murder.

When Van Alt had asked him about the trip to Abydos that day, Rogers had forgotten to mention that Mrs. Murray had at last begun to unbend.

"I wish my tours consisted only of women like Mrs. Murray," Van Alt had once said to him. "Women who don't get excited when minor setbacks occur, who don't think all foreigners have designs on their bodies or their property, who don't spread gossip, and don't take up early in the tour with people they have to shun for the rest of the tour."

Van Alt was right, Rogers remembered, in another aspect of his analysis of tourist behavior. There were always some tourists who would rather roam through the sleaziest of souvenir stores and subject themselves to the most brazen robbery in the bazaars than see an impressive temple or the most subtle and elegant hieroglyphics. Rogers had watched the tour split into two groups the day when the bus paused in its journey to Abydos. One group went into the roadside souvenir stand that offered the usual pyramids, finger cymbals, beads, and fly whisks. The other had gone into an adjacent shop where Abdul-al-Amraz demonstrated the ancient art of making paper from the papyrus plant and used his product to prepare cartouches to sell to the tourists. These he made to order, working deftly with his brush and drawing ink to write the names of the customers in ancient Egyptian hieroglyphics.

Rogers knew from Van Alt, who prided himself on his extensive knowledge of the people he dealt with, that Abdul was a member of the faculty of the university in Cairo, his field being early Egyptian history. The souvenir shop and the papyrus-making establishment were owned by an uncle who fostered this sideline which employed his nephew's knowledge and also provided him with a much-needed supplement to his academic income. It interested Rogers that so many tourists should be taken with this esoteric communication. True, it was an unusual souvenir, made more unusual in some instances by the words the tourists requested be sketched on their square of papyrus. One of the West Coast people, for example, asked Abdul to draw "California, here I come," a request that caused Abdul to shake his head in good-natured resignation. But mostly they asked for representations of their own or their children's names.

When the bus was preparing to resume the trip to Abydos, Mrs. Murray climbed aboard, holding out a wet sheet of papyrus inscribed with a cartouche.

"That's my name in the cartouche," she said to Rogers as she seated herself beside him. "Or so he says. The thing I like about it is that no one will ever be able to get it into a computer."

Rogers examined the papyrus. Abdul had inked an oblong border within which a short horizontal zigzag line was drawn over what looked like the branch of a tree. This was followed by a flattened oval, resembling a mouth.

"I don't know if it's my name or not," she said, "and I don't think it matters, because when I get it home nobody will be able to prove it's not."

"Well, this is an R," Rogers said, pointing to the picture of the mouth. "Certainly there are enough R's in Murray to make you think Abdul is close."

"My first name is Ruth."

"This zigzag line means 'water' and this other figure, the branch, means 'wood.' Are you sure your name isn't R. Waterwood?"

She laughed. It was apparent that she was becoming more relaxed in her relations with him and some of the others on the tour. For the first several days she had maintained a friendly reserve. She spoke when spoken to, responding politely, but did nothing to sustain conversation. In this he thought he detected a resemblance to the silent Trewin—possibly as a result of their common New England background. If he remembered the tour data correctly, they both came from Massachusetts. In any case, now that the group had been together for a week Mrs. Murray's reserve was diminishing, especially insofar as Trewin was concerned. Twice they had had drinks together and several times Rogers had seen them chatting at the rail while the *Cheops* pushed upriver.

Mrs. Murray asked him a few questions on the nature of hieroglyphics and then led him into an account of how he had gotten into Egyptology. He found himself talking freely, and not for some time did he realize that she was informing herself about his life without revealing the slightest detail of her own. He determined to break the pattern.

"I suppose your husband was prevented from accompanying you?"

"My husband died fifteen years ago in a fall from a horse. We ran a riding school. We bought this horse we knew very little about and—" She fell silent.

"Do you still run the school?"

"No. I tried operating it for two years by myself but I gave it up and opened a shop specializing in riding clothes and riding equipment. I was just thinking how different my place is from that shop we just left."

"I suppose I shouldn't tell you this, but I suspect that Abdul's uncle, who owns the shop, kicks back something to the agency. I don't know the arrangements. I know that Van Alt hates the whole shopping aspect of these trips, but the agency is convinced the customers want it."

"Some do," she agreed. "But not every tour can provide a murder."

"We do our best."

"It sounds harsh, I know," she said, her face turned away toward the desert bordering their route, "but in my opinion, Mr. Beasley's death was a small loss."

"I know who killed Beasley," Hunter said.

He had dropped into the bus seat beside Rogers vacated by Mrs. Murray. His voice was portentous, as if he were awed at finding himself the possessor of such information, and at the same time he appeared eager, as if he were unaccustomed to having his statements regarded seriously and was pleased to be in a situation where his words would receive weight. Rogers observed his khaki shorts and knee-length stockings. A forty-five-year-old boy scout, he thought.

"Who killed him?"

Hunter glanced over his shoulder to check that the seat behind them was empty.

"Last night when we got back to the boat after the sound-and-light performance, I found that I had left my fly whisk behind. I recalled looping it over the back of the chair in front of me, so I went back to the temple and found the row and the chair where I had been sitting, but there was no fly whisk. It's nothing to make a fuss about, I suppose, but I had come to regard it as a good-luck piece."

"What bearing does—" Rogers began.

"I'm coming to that. I was about to go down the steps of the forecourt into that cross street or whatever when the lights went out. They were a sketchy arrangement anyway—naked bulbs at irregular intervals—but when I reached the street in front of the forecourt steps I could see, in the moonlight, two people coming behind me through the temple itself. I stepped back into the shadows until I could see who they were. They stopped on the steps. Van Alt and Beasley.

" 'I don't like the way you're running this tour, Van Alt,' I heard Beasley say. 'You're a lousy tour director.'

" 'I am regarded as the best tour director in Egypt,' Van Alt said.

" 'That's what you say,' Beasley said. 'Why do you give Aggie the brush-off when she asks you questions about when to be ready for the bus and things like that? You don't answer. I invite you for a drink at my table and you pass me by like I'm not there. Maybe the others will put up with stuff like that, but you ain't going to pull it on Aggie and you ain't going to pull it on me. A tour that costs this much dough ought to be run by a person who can hear when somebody talks to him.'

" 'What are you talking about, you stupid Yank?' Van Alt says. 'Of course I can hear.'

" 'Yeah? Well, O.K., then,' Beasley goes on, 'let me tell you what I'm going to do. When I get home I'm going to complain to the Seven League Tour Agency about you. How do they get away charging such high prices and then give us a director who is hard of hearing? The least they'll do is make you take a hearing examination. Then let's see if they renew your contract.' "

Hunter paused, and then continued.

"Beasley said a couple of words I won't repeat and continued down the steps. I think he made the wrong turn because he went toward the obelisk. Van Alt ran after him and they disappeared behind the obelisk. I could hear a scuffle, then Van Alt reappeared, came back toward the steps, and turned into the main avenue. He was almost running."

"But I don't see that—" Rogers began.

"Beasley was found at the base of that obelisk, wasn't he? The place where I heard them struggling? Van Alt must have hit him on the head and killed him."

"Hit him with what?"

"That's what I'm leading up to. My fly whisk originally had an ebony handle, covered with leather braiding. Some time ago I had the wood replaced by an iron bar twelve inches long and the leather rebraided over it. That fly whisk was more dangerous than any blackjack."

"So?"

"When Van Alt came back past my hiding place, he was carrying my fly whisk."

"I know who killed Beasley," Van Alt said, making the statement in the same off-hand confident manner with which he related triumphs over hotels and airlines. Rogers did not ask the obvious question, knowing that Van Alt would proceed.

"The first night going upriver, I came up here on deck, partly to avoid the tour—they always stay inside with the air-conditioning—and partly to watch the river. I saw Hunter sitting where you are now. He saw that I had seen him so I couldn't very well not acknowledge that he was there, and I sat down to chat with him for a few minutes.

" 'This is my last trip to Africa,' he said as if we had been discussing African trips for an hour. I made some noncommittal reply.

" 'I can't afford these trips any more,' he said. 'I've lost all my money.' Then he blurted out, 'I'm going to have to go to work.'

"I was about to offer some tongue-in-cheek condolence—I've been working ever since I was seventeen—but he went on. 'My grandmother left me some money,' he said. 'Enough so I could live on the income. But I've spent most of it on travel. I'm deeply interested in Africa, especially Egypt and the Sudan. This is the second time I have taken this Nile cruise.'

"Eventually he explained the details of the disastrous transaction. He'd met a man at his broker's office, a man he had seen around but didn't know well. This man put him in touch with a newly organized company that was going to construct a gambling casino and hotel somewhere on one of the Caribbean islands. There were three principal stockholders and because they needed additional capital they were willing to take in smaller investors. Hunter's lawyer advised against the idea but Hunter went ahead anyway. He liquidated the assets his grandmother had left him and put everything into the new company—Insulae Unlimited."

"I think I can see what's coming," Rogers said.

"Right. The casino was about half finished when Insulae ran out of money. They had paid everything they had to the construction company, which had run into all sorts of unforeseen obstacles in the course of construction—at least that's what they said. Insulae went into bankruptcy and Hunter got paid off at about five cents on the dollar. The land and the half-built casino were bought by a new company that went ahead and finished the project with the same builders.

"The upshot is that Hunter helped pay for the casino but never got to own any part of it. The three principal stockholders claimed to have suffered just as much as Hunter and the other minor holders, but Hunter's sure they conspired with the building company to swindle him."

"But how do you tie this in with Beasley's murder?"

"I have an old friend. We used to be guides for the same company. He's become some kind of a social director for the hotel that the successor company to Insulae put up. He was planning to leave and wanted to know if I'd be interested in taking over his job. He told me that the construction company involved in the bankruptcy was owned by a man named Beasley."

"But it isn't likely that Hunter would know about Beasley."

"Maybe he didn't. But I think he did know who was behind the swindle. The other day when we were at one of those bus stops on the field trip, Hunter spilled a whole string of credit cards out of his wallet. I helped him pick them up and among them was a business card. The name caught my eye. Beasley Builders—Sam Beasley, President.''

"So here he is on the same tour with the man who defrauded him. It's a big coincidence," Rogers said.

"If it is a coincidence. You have to admit he had a motive."

"But why would he tell you about losing his money because of Beasley if he intended to kill him? It seems to me he wouldn't mention a word about any connection with Beasley."

"He didn't. He never mentioned Beasley's name—nor the name of Insulae, for that matter. I made that connection. I doubt that Beasley knew Hunter had lost money on one of his buildings. And there was no way for Hunter to know that I knew Beasley was the builder for Insulae. Or that I knew anything at all about Insulae. And there is one other thing."

"Well?"

"I described Hunter to the watchman who was on duty at the gangplank that night. With that outfit of his he's conspicuous. I asked him if he had seen anyone dressed like that return to the boat that night, and, if so, when. He said Hunter came back at the same time as the others, then he went ashore again directly and didn't return for thirty or forty minutes. What more do you want? He's got a motive and he's not accounted for during the period the murder occurred. It's got to be Hunter who killed Beasley."

Van Alt, Rogers thought, in addition to proclaiming himself the best tour director in Egypt, was now establishing himself as the best detective.

Or possibly the best liar.

"What are you reading, Mr. Trewin?" Rogers asked as he stopped at the table where Trewin was sitting alone in the bar. "May I sit down?"

"Please do." Trewin cleared his throat as if reluctantly preparing himself for something. "It's Burton's *Anatomy of Melancholy.*"

"Appropriate in view of what happened last night," Rogers said, and thought how appropriate the title was for Trewin as well. His somber suit, dark frayed tie, and black-edged eyeglasses made him a reserved and gloomy figure in contrast to the easy-going, easy-laughing casualness of his countrymen. Once the others became aware of Trewin's demonstrated desire to be let alone, they no longer paid any attention to him, so that he became like some fixture on the tour, a bus driver or a waiter, who is noticed, if at all, only in a cursory fashion. The exception, of course, was Mrs. Murray, who had been seen having drinks with him and chatting with him on deck.

Trewin passed the book to Rogers who, not knowing what to do with it, idly riffled through the pages. He noted that Trewin, or somebody, had underlined many passages. Trewin had fashioned a bookplate which, like so much about him, had a home-made quality and imparted a purse-mouthed, bookkeeperish accountability that may also have been indicative of its owner: "This book is the property of Thomas Trewin."

"Could you shed any light on last night's events?" Rogers asked, passing the book back. The waiter placed a drink before Trewin. Anticipating Trewin's hesitant invitation, he waved the waiter away. Trewin, he noted with interest, was drinking doubles and, judging by the number of glasses on the table, he was now on his fourth. Maybe the reclusive Trewin was not as self-sufficient as it might appear.

"Very little. You are interested, I assume, in my movements. I sat with Beasley at the sound-and-light show. We walked partway out together and then Van Alt overtook us. I left them and walked ahead to the boulevard and had coffee at that little café opposite the entrance to the temple complex. A little later, maybe ten or fifteen minutes, I can't be sure, I saw Van Alt come out of the temple grounds. About five minutes after that, I saw that Dr. Livingstone fellow, the one who always carries that horsetail, come out. I came back to the boat a little after that myself."

His lips twisted bleakly, as though he enjoyed not being able to provide information, but then Rogers was surprised when he added gratuitously, "I know something about the building business. I knew Beasley by reputation. I'm surprised someone didn't do away with him long before this."

A general approximation, Rogers thought, of what Van Alt knew about the man who had poured Hunter's money into his concrete mixers. Insofar as Trewin himself was concerned, Rogers concluded that the most mysterious thing about him was why he was on the cruise at all.

He had nothing solid to go on, Rogers admitted to himself, but this wasn't a court. It was a cruise where people were supposed to enjoy themselves and not end up lying before a monument with a shattered head. He had motives and some evidence perhaps, and also some suggestions that might point the way to the truth, but he could prove nothing. He couldn't even convince himself. Sometimes he was certain it was Van Alt, other times he was sure it was the strangely immature Hunter. And now he was wondering whether the solemn Trewin was involved. While the real assailant could be hundreds of miles down the river, traceless in some teeming bazaar.

He dismissed the thought. Knowing, and not caring too much, that he would lose his job if he accused the wrong person, he was determined to confront Van Alt, Hunter, and Trewin with what he knew. He had asked Van Alt to get them together, which he did without objection—which was not his customary way of treating Rogers' suggestions.

We're meeting in a frivolous place for a deadly serious purpose, Rogers thought as he waited for the others at a table in the ship's lounge. The air-conditioning, the brightly colored awnings, the splashing and laughter from the pool on the other side of the sliding glass doors all made this a place where shipboard friendships were begun, to last until the following Christmas when cards would be exchanged between already barely remembered people.

Van Alt was already present, his face showing strain. He passed an airlines envelope from one hand to the other and finally slapped it down on the table in frustration.

Hunter arrived and seated himself, placing his fly whisk on the table and following it with his white hat, which he deposited with a ceremonial flourish. Trewin came in from the brilliant morning sun, waited until his eyes adjusted to the lounge's dimness, and took his place, regarding the others soberly and looking as though he would prefer to be left in peace to read the book which he laid before him on the table.

"Mr. Van Alt has asked you to meet with us to see if we can't sort out the facts relating to the—" Rogers groped lamely for a way to avoid the blunt harshness of the word "—death of Sam Beasley. You were asked to bring certain items that might be of help. Mr. Van Alt has brought evidence which he will reveal at the proper time. And you, Mr. Trewin, have brought what was requested. Mr. Hunter has brought his fly whisk." (His sixteen ounces of iron pipe, Rogers thought, his lethal, home-handyman blackjack.)

"First of all," he said, "Mr. Hunter. You had a motive. Beasley's construction company used up your investment and left you broke. And you had a weapon." He pointed to the fly whisk, its black horsehair glittering on the table. "A weapon you always carried with you, that you said you left behind at the sound-and-light performance. I see it has been returned."

"I found it hanging from the doorknob of my stateroom door. And I know who put it there," Hunter gestured toward Van Alt. "He did."

"That's right, I did," Van Alt said. "I found it hanging on the back of a chair at the sound-and-light show. You left it behind and I returned it, that's all."

"Not quite all," Rogers said. "Hunter, will you repeat what you told me?"

Hunter related the argument he had overheard on the steps of the forecourt—how he had seen Van Alt follow Beasley toward the obelisk where the body had been found, how he heard the sounds of conflict. "To me it's open and shut," Hunter concluded. "Van Alt hit him with my fly whisk."

"Did you *see* it? Did you see me *hit him?*" Van Alt's face was white with anger.

"No," Hunter replied. "I didn't actually see you. But it's obvious. He was going to cause you to lose your job. You did follow him to the spot where the crime was committed, and you did have a weapon in your hand."

"Van Alt, you do admit, don't you," Rogers asked, "that there was a struggle? Be careful how you answer. Look at this." Rogers set on the table a small beige-colored button to which a short length of colorless plastic-covered wire was attached.

"This is your hearing aid, Van Alt. You don't wear it in the daytime when it can be readily seen. I submit that you and Beasley had a struggle and that this got torn loose. When you examined his body that morning, you found something under Beasley's head, something you pushed down into the sand."

Van Alt did not look at the tiny device, as though refusing to acknowledge its existence.

"O.K. I punched—or I tried to punch—Beasley. He was going to cost me my job. Who wants a tour director who can't hear, even if he is the best tour director in Egypt? But Beasley was a lot more experienced in physical encounters than I am."

"Then you *were* wearing—"

"My hearing aid. Yes. It *was* pulled loose. I *did* feel it under his head. I *did* try to cover it with sand." Van Alt leaped to his feet and swore, bending across the table and shouting into Rogers' face. "You don't laugh at people who have lost their sight, do you? Then is there something amusing about people who can't hear?"

He regained control of himself and sank back into his chair. "I admit that Beasley and I had a brief tussle. But I never hit him with that." He glanced at Hunter's fly whisk. "Nor with anything else. And nobody can prove I did."

"That's right," Rogers said. "Nobody can prove you did. May I have that envelope I asked you to bring?"

Van Alt passed him the airlines envelope from which Rogers withdrew the red-edged label bearing the warning: "You will die for the Arena." Using a paper napkin to avoid smudging the lettering, he smoothed the fragile bit of paper on the table.

"Now may I have your book, Mr. Trewin?"

With a shrug, Trewin passed *The Anatomy of Melancholy* across the table to him. Rogers opened the front cover of the book and laid it beside the warning message.

Pasted inside the front cover was Trewin's bookplate, a red-edged label identical with that which Beasley had scraped from his mirror, and bearing in similar, precise, draftsmanlike lettering the words: "This book is the property of Thomas Trewin."

The three looked at Trewin, expecting him to dismiss the similarity between the warning label and his homemade bookplate by pointing out that red-edged labels were used by the millions, that draftsmen's lettering was so uniform as to be untraceable to an individual. But Trewin only gave a slight twist to his thin lips, and his dour self-effacing gloom changed to a brooding menace.

"Do you want to explain this to us, Mr. Trewin?" Rogers asked.

"So you're the one," Van Alt said. "*You* killed him."

"Beasley was going to die," Trewin said grimly. "I wanted him to know it."

"I'm a product of the Depression," Trewin began. "After high school I couldn't go on to study to be an architect as I'd always hoped. I got a job, after eighteen months of looking—a job driving a tank truck delivering acid to chemical plants. Then the war came and I was in the Army engineers. Specifications, design, and so forth. Anyway, I liked it because I was building something. When I got out, I sold building materials. I was a terrible salesman but there was such a demand I became good enough to open my own business and hire salesmen. It was a successful operation but I didn't really like it. It was as close, however, as I was ever going to get to being an architect, to building.

"My sister's husband died suddenly, leaving her with a ten-year-old daughter, Eve. I had designed and built myself a house, where I lived alone, so I asked my sister and Eve to come and live with me. Eve was like a daughter to me—I loved her dearly."

Trewin stopped and stared out of the dimness of the lounge at the glaring sand on the other side of the river.

"We all got along well together and the time drifted by. In no time, it seemed, Eve had become a lovely young woman, ready to go off to the university. She was an excellent student. When she was completing her sophomore year she told us that she had decided to go to the architectural school. I was extremely pleased and did everything I could, encouraging her, helping with expenses. I never once mentioned how tough I thought it would be for a woman architect in what is still, in my opinion, a hide-bound profession.

"When Eve came home for Christmas during her last year in architectural school, she announced that she had been offered a job with Rock, Gibbings, and Elston, one of the big architectural firms in the city. We were overjoyed and it appeared that my ambitions were being realized through Eve. I think that Christmas was the happiest of our lives. I know it was our last happy one.

"It had snowed all day, then thawed, and after that we had a quick freeze. On top of it there came a long, heavy rain. Eve had been seeing a young man who was home on vacation from college and that night they went to a basketball game in the city. During the game, the roof of the sports arena collapsed and seven people were killed. Eve was one of them.

"I can't describe how shattered our lives were, the sudden pointlessness of everything. I had not realized how much of my old ambition had been transferred to Eve.

"My sister and I went through the motions of daily living, but the light had gone out of our lives. Then, about a year later, my sister received a letter. Here, let me show you."

Trewin took out a much-handled piece of paper, held together at the folds with tape, and handed it to Rogers.

> *Room 404*
> *Valley Hospital*
>
> *Dear Mrs. Strong:*
>  *Would it be possible for you to come to the hospital to see me? I am told that I have only a short time left and there is something on my conscience I must ask your forgiveness for, if forgiveness is possible after what I have done.*
>
> *Very truly yours,*
> *Edward Brennan*

Rogers set the letter on the table and whispered to Van Alt, who looked at him doubtfully, shrugged, and left the lounge.

"Neither of us had heard of this man," Trewin said, "but we decided I should visit him and see what he wanted. . . ."

He had expected, Trewin explained, to find a man on his deathbed. Instead, Brennan was sitting at the window of the dim hospital room in the early winter twilight, his eyes sunken and troubled and his lips purple, waiting.

"There is something I must explain to Mrs. Strong," Brennan said when Trewin explained who he was. "I'm trying to explain it to all of them. I don't have much time left. And there are others on the list. That list. That dreadful list."

"I don't know what you mean," Trewin said. "What list?"

"It was in the papers. I can see it every time I close my eyes. 'Albert Casseres, 19; Donald McFall, 28—' "

"Those are the names of the others who died when the arena roof collapsed," Trewin broke in.

" '—J. Oliver, 26; Arlene Romero, 21—' "

Brennan's voice had dropped to a monotone. His eyes closed.

" '—Brian Smith, 16; Robert Smith, 14; Eve Strong, 23.' "

Brennan opened his eyes, looked briefly and hopelessly at Trewin, and shifted his gaze back to the window as though unable to face his visitor with what he was about to say.

"I killed them. I killed them all." His voice shook and he covered his face with brown-spotted hands.

Trewin waited, sensing that whatever this man's connection with Eve's death had been, there was no doubt that he believed his guilt to be real. Trewin sensed too, within himself, the spark of an idea, a hope that maybe after the months of anguish and loss over Eve's death, there was something —he didn't yet know what—he could do about it.

"I was a building inspector for the city," Brennan said. "My job was to check on the safety of new construction. The Sports Arena was one of my assignments. I want to explain that I wasn't some incompetent hack filling a job the clubhouse had found for him. I'm a trained engineer and when I took the city job I'd had years of experience in designing steel-frame buildings.

"The arena had been designed by a reliable engineering firm I had worked for in my early days. The roof design involved space-frame trusses, a kind of latticework arrangement of steel that would distribute weight in all directions."

"I know something about them," Trewin said.

"When the roof was finished, I knew it wasn't right. I went up there after a heavy rain and I found ponding. If construction isn't carefully done, you get depressed areas in the roof and in a heavy rain the water doesn't drain as it should—it just lies there like a pond and adds a burden of weight to the roof. It was out of the question that I should pass on the building until this condition was corrected. I discussed it at the office and somehow word got out that the arena wasn't going to be approved.

"One day I arrived home to find a car parked in my driveway, a big expensive car. A man got out and walked back to meet me.

" 'I'm Sam Beasley,' he said. 'I'd like to talk to you.'

"He came around to the other side of my car and sat beside me in the front seat. I won't go into everything he said, but the gist of it was that the arena roof had cost nine hundred and eighty thousand dollars to construct, and would cost another hundred and fifty thousand to correct. He laid an envelope on the seat between us and said it had fourteen thousand dollars in it. It was mine if I approved the building as it was."

He stopped, took a pill box from his pocket, shook out two tablets, and washed them down, the water glass shaking in his hand.

"I can't justify what I did. I took the money. I took it because that was what I had always done since I started to work for the city. I had to turn some of it over, but nevertheless I took it. I *could* have insisted that the roof be fixed and nobody would have opposed me, not publicly anyway. But I took the money. And seven young people died. Two thousand dollars each.

"That roof was designed for thirty pounds per square foot of live load. You remember that we had that heavy snow, a brief thaw, then a freeze followed by unusually heavy rain. So we had the snow load plus the weight of the ponded water, creating an unusual stress. The structural members might have held under either stress separately, but they couldn't hold under both and the roof collapsed."

"What is it you want from us?" Trewin asked.

"If the girl's mother could come to see me, if I could try to convince her I didn't mean harm to her daughter. I just went along with the system. I can't die with this terrible guilt."

Trewin thought for several minutes before he said, "No, she won't be coming here. I'll tell her what you told me, but she won't be coming here."

"Please, if you knew what it's like, sitting here facing—"

"Mr. Brennan, there were seven young people killed in the collapse of that roof. Have the families of any of the others answered your letter?"

"No, none. People don't understand the necessity for forgiveness."

Brennan turned away and stared out into the dark which now waited on the other side of the window. Trewin stood and made his way through the hospital corridors toward the elevators, taking with him a new idea of death.

"I hired a detective agency to learn about Beasley's movements," Trewin told Rogers. "They tracked down somebody on Beasley's secretarial staff. That's how I found out about this trip the Beasleys were planning—and, as you see, I managed to get on the same tour."

Van Alt pushed open the sliding door from the deck and followed Mrs. Murray into the lounge. Her reaction on seeing the group was pleasantly curious, as if instead of meeting the garden-club ladies she expected, their husbands had appeared. She sat down and placed before her the square of papyrus bearing the hieroglyphics Abdul had drawn.

"Good morning, gentlemen," she said. "This looks like a summit conference. Although I brought this papyrus, as requested, I refuse to serve as recording secretary."

"Mr. Trewin here has been telling us about his actions on the night of the murder," Rogers began, "and we thought—"

"Has he indeed?"

"We thought you might be able to help us. But let's have Mr. Trewin finish his story."

"I was determined," Trewin went on, "that Beasley should know he was going to die—and why. There would be no justice in Beasley going out and not knowing why. I also felt some justice in threatening him with those labels during the tour, especially when he was supposed to be enjoying himself.

"I had worked out a number of careful plans for killing him. But it was almost impossible to get him alone. I thought an opportunity might occur on our way to the sound-and-light show. I fell in beside him and said that since we were both involved in building we had a lot in common. This interested him and he indicated that I might not be the nonentity he had thought. We sat together during the performance and started to walk back together after it was over. I deliberately hung back so that the crowd would move on ahead of us. We were the last to leave the sound-and-light area and stopped on the forecourt steps to discuss the span lengths the Egyptians were able to get from limestone when we met Van Alt."

Van Alt made a swift movement of his eyebrows, as if to say, "Now listen to this."

"He said he could show us one of the longest still in place—twenty feet, he estimated, from column top to column top. I often wondered what those people could have built if they had had steel. And crooked building inspectors.

"As long as Van Alt was there, I wasn't going to be able to do anything about Beasley, so I excused myself and went on ahead toward the boulevard. I left just in time because as I came out of the boulevard the lights in the temple area went out. I crossed the boulevard and sat in that café where the carriages are and ordered coffee. In about ten or fifteen minutes I saw Van Alt come out of the temple area and head down the boulevard toward the boat landing. He was carrying that." He pointed to Hunter's fly whisk. "It occurred to me that this was the opportunity I had been waiting for. I was about to cross the boulevard and reenter the temple area when I saw you"—he looked at Hunter—"come out of the area. A tourist carriage turned into the avenue of the sphinxes. I waited until it had turned the corner at the forecourt steps and gone out of sight. I was sure the place was now deserted, that nobody but Beasley remained behind, and I went in to find—and to kill—Beasley.

"In the moonlight everything was either brightly lit or in deep shadow. As I walked along the avenue with all those statues looking down at me, I thought of the thousands of moonlit nights that had passed over this place since it had been built. I wondered if others before me had entered the sacred premises with murder in their hearts.

"If you think, after all I've said, that I killed Beasley, you're wrong. When I reached the steps of the forecourt, I saw him. He was lying at the foot of the obelisk, between it and the remains of a wall. Somebody had already done what I came to do."

"Ask Hassan to come in," said Rogers.

Hassan entered, wearing a long white robe and the red Nubian cap, tall, slender, and serious. He saluted the group gravely, according Mrs. Murray an extra flicker of respect. He placed on the table a heavy package wrapped scantily in newspaper, and stood back, looking expectantly at Rogers. Rogers in turn looked at Van Alt, who, with a wave of his hand, indicated that he should proceed.

"Hassan came to us this morning with this story. And although he understands the language well enough, he would rather I tell you what he told us.

"This morning he was cleaning out his carriage when he noticed something about that"—he pointed at the package—"which made him realize he knew more about Beasley's murder than he thought. He hurried to the boat to catch us before we sailed. On the night of the murder Hassan was waiting outside the temple area in front of the café to see if he couldn't pick up some of the people returning from the sound-and-light show and drive them through the temple area and along the boulevard for a view of the river. About half an hour after the sound-and-light was over, a fare got into his carriage and asked to be driven through the temple grounds. Before they moved off, the passenger asked Hassan to go into the café and get cigarettes, and to have a drink of some kind for himself."

Hassan nodded solemnly.

"When he came back, his carriage was gone. One of the other drivers said he had seen it turning into the temple grounds. Hassan was concerned because these carriages are owned by a concessionaire and if any damage was done, he would lose his job. But he waited, and in about fifteen minutes his horse and carriage drove up in front of the café with no harm done, and Hassan was given a big tip—the equivalent of a full week's earnings."

Hassan shrugged, as though dismissing hyperbole.

"This package Hassan brought with him today contains a concrete building block, the kind that has two apertures running through it from top to bottom. It weighs, I should judge, between fifteen and twenty pounds. A five- or six-foot length of rope is tied to the block and the other end is snapped to the horse's bridle. The block is placed on the ground near the horse's forelegs and its weight discourages him from moving very far. The drivers carry them in their carriages and use them when they can't hitch to a tree. In the old days, the hitching block used to be a solid, conical piece of iron, made especially for the purpose. But what attracted Hassan's attention was this."

Rogers carefully unwrapped the newspaper and set the block up on end. One end was smeared with blackened stains.

"Tell them, Hassan."

With patriarchal dignity, his flowing sleeve dropping away from his thin arm, Hassan pointed at Mrs. Murray.

"This lady. She take my carriage."

Trewin looked at her with puzzled amazement, Hunter with startled awe.

"What nonsense! Yes, I took the carriage. But I didn't kill anyone," Mrs. Murray said.

"But what could be a weapon, one with bloodstains on it, was found in the carriage you made off with," Rogers pointed out.

"The explanation is simple," she said. "Except that." She pointed to the concrete block. "I can't explain that. What happened was that when we returned from the sound-and-light, I didn't feel ready to get back on board. It was a lovely night, with a full moon. I wanted to go back into the temple area where I could see it alone. I walked back to that café where the carriages wait and arranged with one of the drivers—it had occurred to me that the driver himself could become a nuisance, so I gave him some money to go into the café and get himself cigarettes and a drink. As soon as he was gone, I climbed up on the driver's seat, picked up the reins, and drove into the temple grounds. But I didn't kill anyone. What reason would I have to kill a man I'd never seen until a few days before in Cairo?"

"May I have that letter?" Rogers asked Trewin. "The one your sister received from the building inspector. And your papyrus, Mrs. Murray."

He placed the letter on the table before him and held the square of papyrus up for all to see, feeling, as he did so, his lecture manner returning.

"This papyrus with the cartouche sketched on it was bought by Mrs. Murray at Abdul's shop the day we went to the temple at Abydos. The first character, this horizontal zigzag line, is the symbol for water. The next character, the one here under the first one which looks like a tree branch, is the symbol for wood. The last character, here on the right, looks like a mouth and has the phonetic value of R. These are phonograms, in this case representing consonants in the ancient language of Egypt. The zigzag line stands for N and the tree branch stands for HT. These hieroglyphics may be translated as N, H, T, R."

Van Alt stirred in his chair. "This is no time to be giving a lecture on the meaning of hieroglyphics," he muttered.

The others said nothing. Mrs. Murray was quietly attentive, Trewin somber and tense. Hunter reached to pick up his fly whisk, changed his mind, and hastily withdrew his hand.

"Mrs. Murray, you said that you asked Abdul to write your name in hieroglyphics."

"Yes, I did."

"Hieroglyphics are generally read from right to left," Rogers explained. "So the cartouche on your papyrus would show 'R' for your first initial. I think you said your first name is Ruth."

Mrs. Murray nodded.

"The consonants N, H, and T formed the word which meant 'strong' in ancient Egyptian. The name you gave to Abdul, from habit, without thinking, was your full name, Ruth Strong—the same Mrs. Strong to whom this letter was addressed. The mother of Eve Strong, who died when Beasley's roof collapsed."

He held up Trewin's worn letter which opened downward on a hinge of tape.

"You and Trewin are sister and brother. The two of you came on this trip to kill Beasley. Trewin has already admitted his intention. I submit that one of you succeeded—you, Mrs. Murray."

The lounge was silent. Outside, the deckhands were casting off the mooring lines. The ship trembled faintly. The loudspeaker warned.

"I succeeded," Mrs. Murray said tersely. "I got tired of waiting for Tom. He was too cautious. Luck is better than careful planning. And I was lucky.

"I had just driven the carriage around the corner into the cross street in front of the forecourt steps. I saw Beasley sitting there alone. I stopped the carriage and asked him if he would like to ride with me through the temple area. At first he seemed hesitant, and then shrugged his shoulders as if surprised that someone was offering to share something with him on an open, friendly basis. As Beasley bent his head looking for the step to climb up beside me, I hit him."

"With what?"

"With what was at hand. That." She pointed at the building block. "It was on the floor under the driver's seat. He fell, but he wasn't dead. I dragged him into that alcovelike place between the obelisk and the wall. I climbed up on the wall and dropped the block on his head from there— about nine feet, I think. Whatever it was, it was enough. There was no question this time. I put the hitching block back into the carriage, continued along the cross street until I was free of the temple area, turned left, and made it back to the boulevard. Hassan was waiting there, very excited, but I tried to convince him the horse had gotten out of control."

"How did you get back on the boat? The watchman didn't mention your coming back."

"The bridge players were just coming back from a walk on the boulevard. I just followed them up the gangplank. The watchman would assume we were all together. Eight people left for a walk. Nine came back."

"Now what do we do?" Van Alt asked. "We've got a confessed murderer on the tour, and her accomplice."

The *Cheops* moved upriver, the palm-fringed boulevard, Hassan, and the waiting carriages six hours behind. The river banks were thin strips of green behind which the immense and pitiless desert waited. The tour had halted briefly in mid-morning to inspect a lonely ruin, with the *Cheops* uneasily nosed against the sandy bank below the tawny temple columns that waited for the desert to cover them once more.

" 'It's the duty of the tour director to see that all tour members who depart on side trips return from them,' " Rogers said. "If that isn't a quote from the Tour Director's Guide, it ought to be. When we stopped two hours ago at the temple ruins, did everybody get back on the boat?"

"I didn't check. They'd better have. There's nothing here but river and desert."

"Mrs. Murray—Ruth Strong—and Thomas Trewin didn't," Rogers said.

"What do you mean?" said Van Alt in alarm. "Why didn't you tell me? I've got to get to the ship's radio!"

"Wait. When we visited the temple ruins at the last stop, I was the last to leave and come down to the boat. The place seemed empty and I was about to start down the bank when I saw Mrs. Murray and Trewin walking away from the temple and the river. They were heading east, into the desert. I called to them and started after them. They indicated I should go back to the boat and kept walking."

"Heading into the desert!" Van Alt exclaimed. "But they won't last—"

"Probably not. But survival wasn't their intention. What was their alternative? You would have turned them in when we got back downriver. The law is the law whether it's one's own country or another's. They were sentencing themselves."

Van Alt thought for a long time. His face cleared and he nodded.

"This tour," he said. "A man murdered. The two people involved in it turn up missing. Yet everything is in order, nothing more needs to be done, and—" his voice rose as if in a bright and happy conclusion suddenly arrived at "—none of it can be blamed on me. I am still the best tour director in Egypt."

Rogers was silent. We must not break another man's ego bowl, he thought.

# THE GRAVE ROBBER

*By James Holding*

IT WASN'T until the afternoon of that hot, sticky, airless day that Henry Carmichael met the grave robber.

Not that Henry had been idle in the morning. Far from it. With the group of American tourists, of which he was a member, he had wandered bemused for three hot hours among the mists of history that hung almost palpably over the ruins of the temples of Karnak and Luxor—built millennia ago to the glory of Amen in what had been the ancient Egyptian capital of Thebes.

During those three hours, their Egyptian tourguide, a Miss Abdullah, told Henry and his fellow sightseers more than they really wanted to know about hypostyle halls, avenues of rams, lotus columns, and long-dead pharaohs. But Henry, who was nothing if not polite, bore patiently with it all while he studied at leisure and at close quarters an Egyptian artifact that interested him far more than temple ruins. Miss Abdullah herself.

Obviously one of the new generation, thought Henry. Liberated, ambitious, dedicated to her job, marinated while in school (and college?) in the compelling liquor of Egypt's ancient history, and now dispensing her garnered wisdom enthusiastically to dull American tourists. With a little kohl outlining her eyes, Henry thought, she'd look a good deal like one of those ancient queens she told them about—Nefertiti, perhaps, or Hatshepsut. On the other hand, thought Henry, with a small *frisson* of homesickness, if she were just a trifle taller and broader in the beam, she'd be almost a dead ringer for Lorene, his favorite waitress in Adele's Inn-Between Bar and Grill at home.

At length Miss Abdullah shepherded her twenty tourists back to the Winter Palace Hotel in Luxor for a hurried but excellent luncheon, the central ingredient of which, according to the tour's funny man from Chicago, was a camelburger.

Immediately after luncheon, the tour members set out lightheartedly enough, their strength restored, to visit with Miss Abdullah the Valley of the Kings across the Nile, where many of Egypt's ancient pharaohs had been entombed in underground chambers carved into the red cliffs of the Theban hills.

They crossed the Nile from the hotel wharf in a small felucca. When they stepped ashore in the waste of sand on the farther bank, they found they had several hundred yards of desert sand to negotiate on foot before reaching the cavalcade of dusty automobiles that waited to taxi them to the Valley of the Kings.

"Come along, please," said Miss Abdullah briskly, "it's just a short walk," and she determinedly began to slog through the sand. The disembarking tourists followed after her in a straggling line.

Henry Carmichael, polite as always, and considerably younger and stronger than most of the tour members, volunteered to stand on the tiny jetty to which the felucca had tied up and help his fellow sightseers climb out of the boat onto the desert's edge. As a result, he brought up the tail end of the procession that ploughed after Miss Abdullah toward the waiting cars.

It was tiresome, sweaty work, and after fifty yards Henry stopped momentarily to mop his face with his handkerchief and catch his breath. He wasn't all that anxious to visit a bunch of underground graves, anyway, so why hurry? He knew the party wouldn't go forward without him, since Miss Abdullah carefully counted noses before embarking on any expedition.

It was then, as he stood in the hot sunlight, looking around at the featureless desert landscape and wishing he'd thought to bring his sunglasses, that he saw approaching from a southerly direction, and gamboling over the hot sand as blithely as though it were cool green grass, four scrawny goats, guarded by an even scrawnier-looking shepherd—or goatherd, Henry supposed was the proper word.

Three of the goats were piebald black-and-white creatures. The fourth was pure white—greyed-down a trifle, to be sure, by desert dust, but unmistakably white. The goatherd wore a ragged brown burnoose, a filthy turban, and a pair of scruffy, sand-colored sandals over dirty bare feet.

As he came closer, Henry saw that his oval face was also exceptionally dirty. He had mud-colored eyes and a straggle of wispy, dirt-colored beard on the point of his receding chin. And he carried a long river reed with which he occasionally reached out to touch a recalcitrant goat.

Henry stared for a moment at this raffish genie of the desert, then resumed his journey toward the waiting cars.

But the goats and their guardian were now upon him. Henry was about to nod a friendly greeting to them when the goatherd, to Henry's surprise, suddenly held his reed staff stiffly across Henry's line of march with a hand from which half the thumb was missing. The stump, Henry noticed, was ridged and rough and untidy, as though the man's goats might have nibbled off the end of his thumb in an absent-minded moment. Maybe they had, Henry thought, amused. People said that goats would eat anything.

His amusement turned to disquiet, however, when the villainous-looking Arab reached his free hand inside his dirty robe.

The gesture was somehow so dramatic, so singularly provocative of curiosity as well as trepidation, that Henry found himself helplessly waiting with inexplicable interest for the goatherd to withdraw his hand from his robe and reveal what he had concealed beneath it. For his manner left no doubt whatever that something *was* concealed there.

Yet when he withdrew his hand and extended it toward Henry, his words were in the blurred whine of Arab salesmen everywhere. "Souvenir of Egypt, sir? Memento of ancient Nilotic civilization? Very rare. From secret tomb." He waved a dirty paw toward the Valley of the Kings.

Henry looked at what he offered: a carved stone head, perhaps three inches high, of an Egyptian queen wearing the royal ancient headdress over slanting aquiline features. The smooth patina of untold centuries seemed to darken the queenly cheeks.

Despite himself, Henry was impressed. He took the carving from the goatherd's hand. "Where'd you say it came from?"

"Pharaoh's tomb," the goatherd repeated solemnly. "Over there." He pointed again with his river reed. One of his goats ducked as though expecting the raised staff to strike it. "Secret tomb. Nobody know but me. I steal at night. Break off wall carving. Nice souvenir of Egypt, sir! You believe?"

Henry, though polite, was not gullible. "Oh, no, pal," he said. "You probably run these things off by the thousand in some little factory in Luxor and sell them to unsuspecting tourists like me. Isn't that right?" He grinned disarmingly, a tall, lanky man with a deceptively mild expression. "But it's pretty damn good for a fake, I'll hand you that." He stroked the carved head with admiring fingers.

The Arab said, "No fake, sir. That head of Hatshepsut. Great queen, Eighteenth Dynasty." He paused, then threw in the clincher. "She marry her brother, Pharaoh Thotmose the Second."

"How much you want for Queen Hatshepsut?" Henry asked.

"Five pounds," the goatherd said. He looked completely uninterested.

Henry laughed. "Sold!" he said. "Dirt cheap for an antiquity thirty-five hundred years old." He handed over five pounds, grinning, and put the queen's head into his jacket pocket.

"Wait, sir," the Arab said. He brought out a second treasure from beneath his grimy burnoose. He held out his hand, palm up, and passed it slowly under Henry's eyes. "Not fake," he said earnestly. "Real."

Henry stared at the pointed circlet that glinted with a dull gold luster against the dirty palm. The circlet had several rough-shaped studs of what looked like carnelian and turquoise set into it. "Hey!" Henry exclaimed. "What's that?"

The Arab showed a trace of animation now. "Pharaoh's fingertip cover, sir. Worn by kings and queens at banquets. Or when buried in tomb. This one from secret tomb, also. But cost more. One hundred and twenty-five pounds." He shot a sharp glance at Henry. "You like?"

Henry's eyes narrowed. "Prices are certainly going up fast," he said. He took the circlet into his own hand and hefted it thoughtfully. It looked like gold, it felt like gold, it weighed heavily in his hand like gold. Or at least, lead. Maybe it *was* gold. If so, with the price of gold currently over four hundred dollars an ounce, the circlet must be worth considerably more than the goatherd was asking for it. And if it wasn't gold, it would make a nice gift for Lorene, his waitress at the Inn-Between. Lorene, bless her heart, wouldn't know the difference between fake and genuine, anyway.

The goatherd stood stolidly, his dirty face expressionless again, keeping the goats in a tight knot about him by occasional taps with his rod.

Henry made up his mind. "Okay," he said. "I like it. I like it a lot. But a hundred and twenty-five pounds! Let's dicker a little, shall we, pal?"

As he caught up with the other tourists a few minutes later, entered the last taxi in the file, and started off for the Valley of the Kings, Henry looked back from his car at the goatherd. The self-confessed grave robber was now placidly watching his goats drink from the river. Soon he was hidden from Henry's view by the cloud of dust raised by the motor cavalcade.

On the short flight back to Cairo the next morning, Henry maneuvered skillfully and successfully to occupy the seat beside Miss Abdullah, the tourguide. He noted with approval that she looked her usual neat, attractive self this morning, clear-eyed and rested despite yesterday's rigors in old temples, sandy deserts, and underground tombs. Yielding the window seat to her with a gallant bow, Henry thought to himself, not for the first time, this kid is quite a girl.

He decided to begin their conversation by telling her so and she was obviously quite pleased with his praise, but denied, with becoming modesty, having any special talent as a tourguide.

Henry said, "I still maintain you're an outstanding representative of your profession, Miss Abdullah. Why, yesterday on that sandy walk through the desert I thought I'd never catch up with you. There you were, miles ahead, floating along through the sand as though on snowshoes, while I was tagging way behind, sweating and panting for breath!" He grinned at her. "So at least physically, you'll admit, you're something special in the way of girl guides."

"The rest of the party didn't find it so difficult to keep up with me." She gave him a curious side glance. "You kept us all waiting for quite a few minutes at the cars, Mr. Carmichael. What delayed you? Were you ill?"

Henry shook his head. "I was winded and hot, all right, but what kept me from joining you sooner was a traveling souvenir salesman, believe it or not."

"In the desert?" Miss Abdullah gave him another curious look.

"Sure. I guess he was really a goatherder, but he also sold souvenirs. A dirty guy with four goats. But I must say his souvenirs were very genuine-looking. He got them from some pharaoh's tomb, he said. He claimed to be a grave robber."

"He spoke English?"

"Enough to give me quite a sales pitch."

"About robbing a king's tomb for his wares?"

"Or a queen's. I forget which."

Miss Abdullah nodded. "That's a claim many of our souvenir salesmen make when tempting gullible Americans like you, Mr. Carmichael," she said, deadpan.

"Ouch!"

"Because," she went on, "it's just a little white lie that makes you prize your souvenirs so much more highly when you get them home and show them to your friends." She was silent for a moment, looking out the plane window beside her. Then she turned back to Henry. "But a goatherd? In the desert? Speaking English? That really is a new one on me, Mr. Carmichael."

"Want to see what he sold me?" asked Henry, reaching for his flight bag in the rack over Miss Abdullah's head.

"I'd love to," she said with undisguised interest.

Henry took the flight bag into his lap, zipped it open, and brought out the lovely little head of Hatshepsut. He handed it to Miss Abdullah. "So what do you think?" he asked hopefully. "That's Hatshepsut, the man said. Broken off a wall carving in a secret tomb. He also said that Hatshepsut married her brother or something scandalous like that. Now, don't you think it looks at least three thousand years old?"

Miss Abdullah hid a smile. "Oh, at least," she said. "I'm sorry, but you can buy one just like this at any bazaar shop in Cairo or Luxor for a pound or two. They're molded by the gross out of marble dust, then aged by smoking them over a slow fire, the way you smoke fish." She handed it back to him. "It's definitely a fake. I hope you didn't pay too much for it."

Henry said, "I'm a sharp bargainer, Miss Abdullah. I got it for five Egyptian pounds. The sales pitch alone was worth five pounds, even if it is a fake."

For the first time, Miss Abdullah laughed aloud, a very musical cascade of sound that made Henry tingle gently with pleasure. "You didn't *really* think it was a genuine antiquity stolen from a tomb, *did* you, Mr. Carmichael?"

Henry replied honestly, "No, I didn't. But I wasn't so sure about this thing." He brought out the golden fingertip circlet from his flight bag and held it out to her. "Maybe this one *did* come from a pharaoh's tomb. It looks good enough to eat, doesn't it?"

Miss Abdullah froze. She became as motionless as the Great Sphinx Henry expected to see in Gizeh that afternoon. Dead silence seemed to descend on the aircraft in spite of the continuing drone of the engines and the chatter of nineteen American tourists.

At length Miss Abdullah spoke in a hushed, reverent tone. "You bought *that* from your goatherd in the desert?"

Henry nodded and handed the circlet to her. "*You* like it, too, don't you?" he said warmly. "I couldn't resist the darn thing. It's a fingertip cover for some pharaoh, right?"

"That's right," said Miss Abdullah absently. She turned the gold fingertip cover this way and that, held it to the light at the window, then announced, "But *this* souvenir, Mr. Carmichael, is *not* a fake. I think it's the genuine article—a three-thousand-year-old miracle of beauty and craftsmanship." She seemed almost awestruck, Henry thought. Her voice had the rich, deep undertone of respect and nostalgia that had suffused it the last two days whenever she lectured to the tour members about ancient Egypt and its rulers.

He grinned at her solemn expression. "Hold it, Miss Abdullah," he said lightly, "let's not get carried away, okay? Suppose it is genuine? It just means that Arab goatherder *did* stumble on a secret tomb and looted it of everything portable. What's the big deal? I got me a bargain, that's all."

Miss Abdullah said, "Don't you realize, Mr. Carmichael, that there have been more than sixty tombs discovered in the Valley of the Kings, but the tombs of Tut-ankh-amen and Semirameb are the only two that weren't plundered by grave robbers *centuries* ago? I can't believe that when all the archeologists in the world have failed to find another undisturbed tomb, an ignorant goatherd could find one. Even if he *can* speak English!"

"I'm sorry," said Henry. "I didn't mean to upset you, Miss Abdullah. You think that my fingertip cover is genuine, then? A real antiquity?"

"I'm not an expert on Middle Kingdom antiquities," she said, "but I'd be willing to wager my dragoman's license that this fingertip cover is genuine." Miss Abdullah straightened in her seat and looked directly into Henry's eyes. It was a pleasant experience for Henry, because her almond-shaped eyes—as large, brown, and beautiful as two matched topazes—had a strange quickening effect on his breathing. "Mr. Carmichael," she said earnestly, "I must ask you to permit me to show this fingertip cover to the curator of the National Museum in Cairo."

Henry shrugged. "Why not?" he said. Then, after a pause for thought, he said, "On the other hand, *why?*"

"Because he will know instantly whether it is fake or genuine. And if it is genuine, he can perhaps, with good luck, trace the goatherd who sold it to you. And find out how the goatherd came into possession of such an antiquity. And prevent him from selling any more national treasures to tourists. Do you see?"

"Not exactly, no. If my fingertip cover is genuine, the Museum confiscates it, right? And I lose a nifty souvenir." Henry's voice was rueful. "That doesn't seem quite fair, does it?"

She said impatiently, "The Museum would certainly reimburse you for whatever you paid the goatherd." She looked at Henry again, eye to eye. "How much *did* you pay the goatherd for it?"

"A hundred and twenty-five pounds," said Henry. "That's what made me suspect I had a bargain—its steep price compared with the Hatshepsut head."

"Aha!" said Miss Abdullah triumphantly. "You see?"

"All I see is I stand to lose a neat souvenir if it's genuine. A souvenir worth a lot more than what I paid for it."

Miss Abdullah frowned at him. "Don't you understand, Mr. Carmichael, that this little gold fingertip cover is part of Egyptian *history?* A rare and precious relic of the greatest civilization the ancient world ever produced?" She was using her impassioned lecture voice again. "To us, it is a possession beyond value, an artifact to be kept triumphantly in its own land, not carried off to America as a cheap tawdry souvenir of a five-day trip to Egypt."

Henry was enchanted with the way her eyes flashed at him, with her almost religious fervor. "Well—" he murmured weakly.

"Furthermore," said Miss Abdullah, pressing her advantage, "Egypt does not look kindly upon foreigners who try to smuggle national treasures out of our country. You could end up in jail, Mr. Carmichael, do you realize that?"

"I suppose I could," agreed Henry, watching with pleasure the emotional rise and fall of her bosom under the neat uniform blouse. "Where I made my mistake, it's clear to me now, was in showing you the darn thing in the first place." He sighed, then said reluctantly, "Okay. You can show it to your Museum guy if you want to. But only on one condition."

She smiled warm approbation. "What's the condition?"

"You've got to promise me that if the fingertip cover proves genuine, you won't put the cops onto my goatherd until after I've left for Greece tomorrow."

"Oh? Why?"

"Because he's a grave robber, that's why—selling stolen goods to tourists. And the minute you lay him by the heels, I become the star witness against him. And it's well known what happens to witnesses in Egypt. You throw 'em into jail until the trial comes up."

"That is a—a canard!" Miss Abdullah gasped indignantly. "It is simply not true!"

"Just kidding," grinned Henry. "But you've got to admit I might be delayed for a few days if I got involved to that extent. So is it a deal? No putting the cops or the Museum on the goatherd till I'm gone?"

"Of course." Her agreement was prompt. "I'm sure the curator of the Museum will understand your problem. Why don't you come with me to see him? Then you can tell him personally about everything."

"When?"

"This morning. As soon as we land in Cairo."

Henry shook his head regretfully. "Our party is scheduled to visit Gizeh this afternoon—the great pyramid, the Sphinx, the House of the Dead. I thought you were going, too."

"No. I guide only a single Luxor tour once a week. You'll have a different guide this afternoon for Gizeh. Why don't you skip Gizeh and come with me to the Museum? You haven't seen it yet, and it's just as interesting, in its way, as Gizeh."

"There's nothing I'd like better. But I've already paid for the Gizeh tour —and we're flying out to Athens first thing in the morning." He paused. "You wouldn't want to see me gypped out of my Gizeh tour as well as my souvenir, would you?"

"Gypped!" Miss Abdullah's eyes flashed angry lightning. "Do you realize the origin of that odious word, Mr. Carmichael? It comes from the word Egypt! And you use it as though all Egyptians were dishonest, deceitful, and larcenous."

She's magnificent, thought Henry. He soothed her. "Now, please, Miss Abdullah. I used the word innocently. Let's forget it. I apologize, okay?"

Stiffly she said, "I shall give you a written receipt for your fingertip cover, Mr. Carmichael. I want that distinctly understood. And I shall return the cover to you at once if the Museum curator says it is not genuine."

"Never mind the receipt, for Pete's sake," said Henry, enjoying the delicate aroma of the spicy perfume she was wearing. Chypre? Musk? Who cared? He said, "Listen, Miss Abdullah, I trust you, I trust you. If that is distinctly understood, I'll tell you what we can do about this conflict of schedules we seem to have. You go to the Museum with my fingertip cover,

I'll go to Gizeh. Then, when you've done your research and I've finished sightseeing, why don't you join me for dinner at the Nile Hilton? Say about nine o'clock tonight? And you can either return my souvenir or reimburse me for it while we dine. How does that sound to you?"

Miss Abdullah gave Henry a radiant, almost flirtatious smile. "You are a very kind and understanding man, Mr. Carmichael," she said quietly. "Thank you. I'll be happy to have dinner with you tonight."

"I'll be waiting for you. Nine o'clock in the Hilton lobby."

"You must tell me in detail about your goatherd, though. So I can pass it on to the curator if it seems called for. Everything you remember, please— so the police can find him if we discover he is selling genuine artifacts to tourists."

"He's an Arab," Henry said. "Medium height. Herding four goats, three of them black-and-white fellows, one a plain white. He had a dirty turban, dirty face, dirty burnoose or whatever you call those robes, dirty feet, dirty sandals. A wisp of a beard. A four-foot river reed for a staff. Half his right thumb is missing." He grinned at Miss Abdullah. "And you know where I met him in the desert. So he must have come from a village or a goat farm or something not far away."

Miss Abdullah nodded thoughtfully. "There is a village near Deir el-Bahri," she ruminated. "Maybe he came from there."

"Near what?"

"You *saw* it yesterday, Mr. Carmichael. Weren't you listening to my lecture?" Her tone was rallying but forgiving. "The Temple of Queen Hat-shepsut."

"Oh," said Henry, "that one. The one that looked like a big wedding cake."

Miss Abdullah gave a ladylike snort of disgust.

Ten hours later, when Miss Abdullah entered the lobby of the Hilton, Henry scarcely recognized her. Her natty uniform was gone, replaced by a jade-green cocktail dress that left her shoulders bare and did sensational things for her figure. Her sensible shoes of yesterday, suitable for trudging through sandy deserts and ruins, had been abandoned in favor of green pumps with four-inch heels that increased her height and lent a regal quality to her carriage. Her hairdo now looked more Parisian soubrette than Egyptian girl-guide. Her makeup had been applied with a light and skillful hand. Henry, smiling his approval of this new Miss Abdullah, went to meet her.

She held out a hand to him and began with a rush, "Oh, Mr. Carmichael, the most wonderful news!"

He took her hand, tucked it under his arm, and turned her toward the hotel dining room. "Hold everything, Miss Abdullah," he said, "you can tell me all about it over dinner."

She drew every male eye in the dining room as they were ushered to a table for two by a window overlooking the Nile. Once seated, she burst out, "Don't you *want* to hear my news, Mr. Carmichael?"

"Sure," said Henry, "although I'd be perfectly happy just sitting here looking at you."

She ignored this puerile sally. "I was right, Mr. Carmichael! Your finger-tip cover *is* genuine! The curator identified it instantly." Her eyes were shining. "And wait until you hear the rest of it! The curator told me that some months ago a number of items were stolen from the Museum's Semirameb Collection—artifacts found in the tomb of Pharaoh Semirameb. The stolen artifacts have never been traced, nor has the thief been apprehended. A man named Achmed Fayed, who used to be a night caretaker at the Museum and who suddenly resigned his job and disappeared, was suspected of the theft."

"Oh-oh," said Henry, "I think I can see what's coming next."

"Yes! Your fingertip cover is one of the stolen antiquities from the Semirameb Collection! The Curator identified it at once!"

"Ah-ha. And my English-speaking goatherd, then, is—"

"Achmed Fayed! Without a doubt. Achmed Fayed had half his right thumb missing. As did your goatherd."

"Your Mr. Achmed Fayed is a pretty smooth operator, I'd say," Henry commented. "Hiding in the desert with his loot from the Museum. Masquerading as a dirty old goatherd until the heat dies down."

"Heat?"

"Never mind. I get the impression on second thought that he isn't too bright, after all. He was safe up there in the Valley of the Kings, but the dummy started selling golden souvenirs to tourists. What did he do that for, do you suppose?"

Miss Abdullah's ivory cheeks were suddenly suffused by a maidenly blush. She shrugged her shapely shoulders. "Maybe he has a girl friend up there—working at the Winter Palace Hotel, perhaps—and he needs money for her."

"Ah," said Henry, "love will find a way." He cast a quick glance at Miss Abdullah, hoping at least for a smile of acknowledgment.

"And the curator thinks it quite likely," she continued seriously, "that when the police capture your goatherd, they will recover most of the artifacts he stole from the Museum—all except those he has sold to tourists. So—" she regarded him warmly "—do you understand what you've done for us, Mr. Carmichael? You have helped Egypt recover part of her history! Part of her inheritance! Isn't that wonderful? Doesn't it make you feel good?"

"Yeah," said Henry.

"The curator," said Miss Abdullah, "requests that I tender you his respects and his thanks—and indeed the thanks of our whole nation for your helpful and unselfish behavior in this matter."

"Well, now, I appreciate that," said Henry. "But did your curator agree not to nail the goatherd until I've left Egypt?"

"Of course. And—" she smiled teasingly "—I'm to give you back the money you paid for the fingertip cover." She took a roll of bills—American —out of her purse and handed it across the table. Henry accepted it gravely. "A hundred and twenty-five pounds," Miss Abdullah said, almost to herself, "for a treasure like that! Fayed must be mad!"

"Or in love," said Henry.

They ate their dinner in companionable silence. Then, when it was time for after-dinner coffee, Henry said, "Well, it's nice to have the thanks of your Museum and your nation, Miss Abdullah, but how about you? Are you grateful, too?"

She beamed at him. "I certainly am! Do you realize that this will be the talk of Cairo within forty-eight hours? That I shall become, as a result, one of the most popular and best paid tourguides in Egypt? That you have enabled me to strike a blow for Egyptian women, who have been second-class citizens in our land for centuries? Of *course* I'm grateful to you, Mr. Carmichael! More grateful than I can say!"

"Then why don't we go upstairs to my room to have our coffee?" Henry suggested.

After a moment of electric silence, Miss Abdullah fixed Henry with a level, appraising look that was so cool it could have been termed frosty without exaggeration. "I'm grateful to you, Mr. Carmichael," she said at length, "but not that grateful."

Henry sighed. "Okay. I understand. And I apologize. But look here, Miss Abdullah, you can't blame me for trying, can you? *You're* the prettiest Egyptian artifact I've seen since I left home, even if you're not part of the Semirameb Collection."

That melted the ice in her eyes. "It's almost eleven o'clock," she said, "and you have an early flight tomorrow. You'll want to be packing." She pushed back her chair, gathered up her purse, and smiled at him warmly once more. "So I'll be saying goodbye now, Mr. Carmichael. And thank you again from my heart for everything."

She stood up, turned, and left the dining room while Henry was still fumbling for the dinner check. . . .

Folding shirts, pairing socks, he whistled softly to himself, reviewing the evening's adventure with Miss Abdullah. He was quite disappointed, actually, that his pass had failed. Still, he told himself, there were compensations. Miss Abdullah had been successfully conned into getting his gold fingertip cover authenticated by no less an authority than the curator of the National Museum, which ought to be enough authentication to satisfy anybody. So now he knew, without the shadow of a doubt, that the fingertip cover was genuine. It was solid gold, it was from King Semirameb's tomb, it was over three thousand years old, and it was what Miss Abdullah quite simply described as "beyond value."

So, he told himself happily, if *that* fingertip cover was all those wonderful things—genuine, old, solid gold, and priceless—then it followed that the *other* four fingertip covers he had purchased from the goatherd yesterday were also probably genuine, old, solid gold, and priceless.

He dug them out of his flight bag and held them under the bedside lamp for a moment to admire their silken golden sheen, their carnelian and turquoise studs, their aura of mysterious antiquity. Then he rolled them up in a pajama top and put them into his suitcase, contemplating the future with some satisfaction.

Although he considered it the better part of wisdom to remain abroad until the heat generated by his most recent bank-float scam at home had cooled off a bit, he would eventually return home. And when he did, he thought to himself, if he couldn't sell his four gold fingertip covers for half a million dollars to some American museum or private collector with no questions asked, he deserved to be buried alive in some desert, somewhere, or have his thumbs chewed off by four scrawny black-and-white goats.

# THE FEVER TREE

*By Ruth Rendell*

WHERE MALARIA is, there grows the fever tree.

It has the feathery fern-like leaves, fresh green and tender, that are common to so many trees in tropical regions. Its shape is graceful with an air of youth, of immaturity, as if every fever tree is still waiting to grow up. But the most distinctive thing about it is the color of its bark, which is the yellow of an unripe lemon. The fever trees stand out from among the rest because of their slender yellow trunks.

Ford knew what the tree was called and he could recognize it but he didn't know what its botanical name was. Nor had he ever heard why it was called the fever tree, whether the tribesmen used its leaves or bark or fruits as a specific against malaria or if it simply took its name from its warning presence wherever the malaria-carrying mosquito was. The sight of it in Ntsukunyane seemed to promote a fever in his blood.

An African in khaki shorts and shirt lifted up the bar for them so that their car could pass through the opening in the wire fence. Inside it looked no different from outside, the same bush, still, silent, unstirred by wind, stretching away on either side. Ford, driving the two miles along the tarmac road to the reception hut, thought of how it would be if he turned his head and saw Marguerite in the passenger seat beside him. It was an illusion he dared not have and was allowed to keep for perhaps a minute. Tricia shattered it. She began to belabor him with schoolgirl questions, uttered in a bright and desperate voice.

Another African, in a fancier, more decorated uniform, took their booking voucher and checked it against a ledger. You had to pay weeks in advance for the privilege of staying here. Ford had booked the day after he had said goodbye to Marguerite and returned, forever, to Tricia.

"My wife wants to know the area of Ntsukunyane," he said.

"Four million acres."

Ford gave the appropriate whistle. "Do we have a chance of seeing leopard?"

The man shrugged, smiled. "Who knows? You may be lucky. You're here a whole week, so you should see lion, elephant, hippo, cheetah maybe. But the leopard is nocturnal and you must be back in camp by six P.M." He looked at his watch. "I advise you to get on now, sir, if you're to make Thaba before they close the gates."

Ford got back into the car. It was nearly four. The sun of Africa, a living presence, a personal god, burned through a net of haze. There was no wind. Tricia, in a pale yellow sun dress with frills, had hung her arm outside the open window and the fair downy skin was glowing red. He told her what the man had said and he told her about the notice pinned inside the hut: It is strictly forbidden to bring firearms into the game reserve, to feed the animals, to exceed the speed limit, to litter.

"And most of all you mustn't get out of the car," said Ford.

"What, not ever?" said Tricia, making her pale blue eyes round and naive and marble-like.

"That's what it says."

She pulled a face. "Silly old rules!"

"They have to have them," he said.

In here as in the outside world. It is strictly forbidden to fall in love, to leave your wife, to try and begin anew. He glanced at Tricia to see if the same thoughts were passing through her mind. Her face wore its arch expression, winsome.

"A prize," she said, "for the first one to see an animal."

"All right." He had agreed to this reconciliation, to bring her on this holiday, this second honeymoon, and now he must try. He must work at it. It wasn't just going to happen as love had sprung between him and Marguerite, unsought and untried for. "Who's going to award it?" he said.

"You are if it's me and I am if it's you. And if it's me I'd like a presy from the camp shop. A very nice pricey presy."

Ford was the winner. He saw a single zebra come out from among the thorn trees on the right-hand side, then a small herd.

"Do I get a present from the shop?" he asked.

He could sense rather than see her shake her head with calculated coyness. "A kiss," she said and pressed warm dry lips against his cheek.

It made him shiver a little. He slowed down for the zebra to cross the road. The thorn bushes had spines on them two inches long. By the roadside grew a species of wild zinnia with tiny flowers, coral red, and these made red drifts among the coarse pale grass. In the bush were red anthills with tall peaks like towers on a castle in a fairy story. It was thirty miles to Thaba.

He drove on just within the speed limit, ignoring Tricia as far as he could whenever she asked him to slow down. They weren't going to see one of the big predators, anyway, not this afternoon, he was certain of that, only impala and zebra and maybe a giraffe. On business trips in the past he'd taken time off to go to Serengeti and Kruger and he knew.

He got the binoculars out for Tricia and adjusted them and hooked them round her neck, for he hadn't forgotten the binoculars and cameras she had dropped and smashed in the past through failing to do that, and her tears afterward. The car wasn't air-conditioned and the heat lay heavy and still between them. Ahead of them, as they drove westward, the sun was sinking in a dull yellow glare. The sweat flowed out of Ford's armpits and between his shoulder blades, soaking his already wet shirt and laying a cold sticky film on his skin.

A stone pyramid with arrows on it, set in the middle of a junction of roads, pointed the way to Thaba, to the main camp at Waka-suthu and to Hippo Bridge over the Suthu River. On top of it a baboon sat with her gray fluffy infant on her knees. Tricia yearned to it, stretching out her arms. She had never had a child. The baboon began picking fleas out of its baby's scalp. Tricia gave a little nervous scream, half disgusted, half joyful. Ford drove down the road to Thaba and in through the entrance to the camp ten minutes before they closed the gates for the night.

The dark comes down fast in Africa. Dusk is of short duration and no sooner have you noticed it than it is gone and night has fallen. In the few moments of dusk pale things glimmer brightly and birds murmur. In the camp at Thaba were a restaurant and a shop, round huts with thatched roofs, and wooden chalets with porches. Ford and Tricia had been assigned a chalet on the northern perimeter, and from their porch, across an expanse of turf and beyond the high wire fence, you could see the Suthu River flowing smoothly and silently between banks of tall reeds.

Dusk had just come as they walked up the wooden steps, Ford carrying their cases. It was then that he saw the fever trees, two of them, their ferny leaves bleached to gray by the twilight but their trunks a sharper, stronger yellow than in the day.

"Just as well we took our anti-malaria pills," said Ford as he pushed open the door. When the light was switched on he could see two mosquitos on the opposite wall. *"Anopheles* is the malaria carrier, but unfortunately they don't announce whether they're *anopheles* or not."

Twin beds, a table, lamps, an air conditioner, a fridge, a door, standing open, to lavatory and shower. Tricia dropped her makeup case, without which she went nowhere, onto the bed by the window. The light wasn't very bright. None of the lights in the camp were because the electricity came from a generator. They were a small colony of humans in a world that belonged to the animals, a reversal of the usual order of things. From the window you could see other chalets, other dim lights, other parked cars. Tricia talked to the two mosquitos.

"Is your name Anna Phyllis? No, darling, you're quite safe. She says she's Mary Jane and her husband's John Henry."

Ford managed to smile. He had accepted and grown used to Tricia's facetiousness until he had encountered Marguerite's wit. He shoved his case, without unpacking it, into the cupboard and went to have a shower.

Tricia stood on the porch, listening to the cicadas, thousands of them. It had gone pitch-dark while she was hanging up her dresses and the sky was punctured all over with bright stars.

She had got Ford back from that woman and now she had to keep him. She had lost some weight and bought a lot of new clothes and had high-lights put in her hair. Men had always made her feel frightened, starting with her father when she was a child. It was then, when a child, that she had purposely begun *playing* the child with its cajolements and its winning little ways. She had noticed that her father was kinder and more forbearing toward little girls than toward her mother. Ford had married a little girl, clinging and winsome, and had liked it well enough till he met a grown woman.

Tricia knew all that, but now she knew no better how to keep him than by the old methods, as weary and stale to her as she guessed they might be to him. Standing there on the porch, she half wished she were alone and didn't have to have a husband, didn't, for the sake of convention and pride, for support and society, have to hold on tight to him. She listened wistfully for a lion to roar out there in the bush beyond the fence, but there was no sound except the cicadas.

Ford came out in a toweling robe.

"What did you do with the mosquito stuff? The spray?"

Frightened at once, she said, "I don't know."

"What d'you mean, you don't know? You must know. I gave you the aerosol at the hotel and said to put it in that makeup case of yours."

She opened the case although she knew the mosquito stuff wasn't there. Of course it wasn't there. She could see it on the bathroom shelf in the hotel, left behind because it was too bulky. She bit her lip, looked sideways at Ford.

"We can get some more at the shop."

"Tricia, the shop closes at seven and it's now ten past."

"We can get some in the morning."

"Mosquitos happen to be most active at night." He rummaged with his hands among the bottles and jars in the case. "Look at all this useless rubbish. 'Skin cleanser,' 'pearlized foundation,' 'moisturizer'—like some young model girl. I suppose it didn't occur to you to bring the anti-mosquito spray and leave the 'pearlized foundation' behind."

Her lip trembled. She could feel herself, almost involuntarily, rounding her eyes, forming her mouth into the shape of lisping. "We did 'member to take our pills."

"That won't stop the damn things biting." He went back into the shower and slammed the door.

Marguerite wouldn't have forgotten to bring that aerosol. Tricia knew he was thinking of Marguerite again, that his head was full of her, that she had entered his thoughts powerfully and insistently on the long drive to Thaba. She began to cry. The tears went on running out of her eyes and wouldn't stop, so she changed her dress while she cried and the tears came through the powder she put on her face.

They had dinner in the restaurant. Tricia, in pink flowered crepe, was the only dressed-up woman there, and while once she would have fancied that the other diners looked at her in admiration, now she thought it must be with derision. She ate her small piece of overcooked hake and her large piece of overcooked, bread-crumbed veal, and watched the red weals from mosquito bites coming up on Ford's arms.

There were no lights on in the camp but those which shone from the windows of the main building and from the chalets. Gradually the lights went out and it became very dark. In spite of his mosquito bites, Ford fell asleep at once but the noise of the air conditioning kept Tricia awake. At eleven she switched it off and opened the window. Then she did sleep but she awoke again at four, lay awake for half an hour, got up, put on her clothes, and went out.

It was still dark but the darkness was lifting as if the thickest veil of it had been withdrawn. A heavy dew lay on the grass. As she passed under the merula tree, laden with small green apricot-shaped fruits, a flock of bats flew out from its branches and circled her head. If Ford had been with her she would have screamed and clung to him but because she was alone she kept silent. The camp and the bush beyond the fence were full of sound. The sounds brought to Tricia's mind the paintings of Hieronymus Bosch, imps and demons and dreadful homunculi which, if they had uttered, might have made noises like these, gruntings and soft whistles and chirps and little thin squeals.

She walked about, waiting for the dawn, expecting it to come with drama. But it was only a gray pallor in the sky, a paleness between parting black clouds, and the feeling of let-down frightened her as if it were a symbol or an omen of something more significant in her life than the coming of morning.

Ford woke up, unable at first to open his eyes for the swelling from mosquito bites. There were mosquitos like threads of thistledown on the walls, all over the walls. He got up and staggered, half blind, out of the bedroom and let the water from the shower run on his eyes. Tricia came and stared at his face, giggling nervously and biting her lip.

The camp gates opened at five thirty and the cars began their exodus. Tricia had never passed a driving test and Ford couldn't see, so they went to the restaurant for breakfast instead. When the shop opened, Ford bought two kinds of mosquito repellent, and impatiently, because he could no longer bear her apologies and her pleading eyes, a necklace of ivory beads for Tricia and a skirt with giraffes printed on it. At nine o'clock, when the swelling round Ford's eyes had subsided a little, they set off in the car, taking the road for Hippo Bridge.

The day was humid and thickly hot. Ford had counted the number of mosquito bites he had had and the total was twenty-four. It was hard to believe that two little tablets of quinine would be proof against twenty-four bites, some of which must certainly have been inflicted by *anopheles*. Hadn't he seen the two fever trees when they arrived last night? Now he drove the car slowly and doggedly, hardly speaking, his swollen eyes concealed behind sunglasses.

By the Suthu River and then by a water hole he stopped and they watched. But they saw nothing come to the water's edge unless you counted the log which at last disappeared, thus proving itself to have been a crocodile. It was too late in the morning to see much apart from the marabout storks which stood one-legged, still and hunched, in a clearing or on the gaunt branch of a tree. Through binoculars Ford stared at the bush which stretched in unbroken, apparently untenanted, sameness to the blue ridge of mountains on the far horizon.

There could be no real fever from the mosquito bites. If malaria were to come it wouldn't be yet. But Ford, sitting in the car beside Tricia, nevertheless felt something like a delirium of fever. It came perhaps from the gross irritation of the whole surface of his body, from the tender burning of his skin and from his inability to move without setting up fresh torment. It affected his mind too, so that each time he looked at Tricia a kind of panic rose in him. Why had he done it? Why had he gone back to her? Was he mad? His eyes and his head throbbed as if his temperature were raised.

Tricia's pink jeans were too tight for her and the frills on her white voile blouse ridiculous. With the aid of the binoculars she had found a family of small gray monkeys in the branches of a peepul tree and she was cooing at them out of the window. Presently she opened the car door, held it just open, and turned to look at him the way a child looks at her father when he has forbidden something she nevertheless longs and means to do.

They hadn't had sight of a big cat or an elephant, they hadn't even seen a jackal. Ford lifted his shoulders.

"Okay. But if a ranger comes along and catches you we'll be in deep trouble."

She got out of the car, leaving the door open. The grass which began at the roadside and covered the bush as far as the eye could see was long and coarse. It came up above Tricia's knees. A lioness or a cheetah lying in it would have been entirely concealed. Ford picked up the binoculars and looked the other way to avoid watching Tricia who had once again forgotten to put the camera strap round her neck. She was making overtures to the monkeys who shrank away from her, embracing each other and burying heads in shoulders, like menaced refugees in a sentimental painting.

Ford moved the glasses slowly. About a hundred yards from where a small herd of buck grazed uneasily, he saw the two cat faces close together, the bodies nestled together, the spotted backs. Cheetah. It came into his mind how he had heard that they were the fastest animals on earth.

He ought to call to Tricia and get her back at once into the car. He didn't call. Through the glasses he watched the big cats that reclined there so gracefully, satiated, at rest, yet with open eyes. Marguerite would have liked them; she loved cats, she had a Burmese, as lithe and slim and poised as one of these wild creatures.

Tricia got back into the car, exclaiming about how sweet the monkeys were. He started the car and drove off without saying anything to her about the cheetahs.

Later, at about five in the afternoon, she wanted to get out of the car again and he didn't stop her. She walked up and down the road, talking to mongooses. In something over an hour it would be dark. Ford imagined starting up the car and driving back to the camp without her. Leopards were nocturnal hunters, waiting till dark.

The swelling around his eyes had almost subsided now but his neck and arms and hands ached from the stiffness of the bites. The mongooses fled into the grass as Tricia approached, whispering to them, hands outstretched. A car with four men in it was coming along from the Hippo Bridge direction. It slowed down and the driver put his head out. His face was brick-red, thick-featured, his hair corrugated blond, and his voice had the squashed vowel accent of the white man born in Africa.

"The lady shouldn't be out on the road like that."

"I know," Ford said. "I've told her."

"Excuse me, d'you know you're doing a very dangerous thing, leaving your car?"

The voice had a hectoring boom. Tricia blushed. She bridled, smiled, bit her lip, though she was in fact very afraid of this man who was looking at her as if he despised her, as if she disgusted him. When he got back to camp, would he betray her?

"Promise you won't tell on me?" she faltered, her head on one side.

The man gave an exclamation of anger and withdrew his head. The car moved forward. Tricia gave a skip and a jump into the passenger seat beside Ford. They had under an hour to get back to Thaba and Ford followed the car with the four men in it.

At dinner they sat at adjoining tables. Tricia wondered how many people they had told, for she fancied that some of the diners looked at her with curiosity or antagonism. The man with fair curly hair they called Eric boasted loudly of what he and his companions had seen that day, a whole pride of lions, two rhinoceros, hyena, and the rare sable antelope.

"You can't expect to see much down that Hippo Bridge road, you know," he said to Ford. "All the game's up at Sotingwe. You take the Sotingwe road first thing tomorrow and I'll guarantee you lions."

He didn't address Tricia, he didn't even look at her. Ten years before men in restaurants had turned their heads to look at her and though she had feared them, she had basked, trembling, in their gaze. Walking across the grass, back to their chalet, she held on to Ford's arm.

"For God's sake, mind my mosquito bites," said Ford.

He lay awake a long while in the single bed a foot away from Tricia's, thinking about the leopard out there beyond the fence that hunted by night. The leopard would move along the branch of a tree and drop upon its prey. Lionesses hunted in the early morning and brought the kill to their mate and the cubs. Ford had seen all that sort of thing on television. How cheetahs hunted he didn't know except that they were very swift. An angry elephant would lean on a car and crush it or smash a windshield with a blow from its foot.

It was too dark for him to see Tricia but he knew she was awake, lying still, sometimes holding her breath. He heard her breath released in an exhalation, a sigh, that was audible above the rattle of the air conditioner.

Years ago he had tried to teach her to drive. They said a husband should never try to teach his wife, he would have no patience with her and make no allowances. Tricia's progress had never been maintained, she had always been liable to do silly reckless things and then he had shouted at her. She took a driving test and failed and said this was because the examiner had bullied her. Tricia seemed to think no one should ever raise his voice to her, and at one glance from her all men should fall slaves at her feet.

He would have liked her to be able to take a turn at driving. There was no doubt you missed a lot when you had to concentrate on the road. But it was no use suggesting it. Theirs was one of the first cars in the line to leave the gates at five thirty, to slip out beyond the fence into the gray dawn, the still bush. At the stone pyramid, on which a family of baboons sat clustered, Ford took the road for Sotingwe.

A couple of miles up they came upon the lions. Eric and his friends were already there, leaning out of the car windows with cameras. The lions, two full-grown lionesses, two lioness cubs and a lion cub with his mane beginning to sprout, were lying on the roadway. Ford stopped and parked the car on the opposite side to Eric.

"Didn't I say you'd be lucky up here?" Eric called to Tricia. "Not got any ideas about getting out and investigating, I hope."

Tricia didn't answer him or look at him. She looked at the lions. The sun was coming up, radiating the sky with a pinkish-orange glow, and a little breeze fluttered all the pale green, fern-like leaves. The larger of the adult lionesses, bored rather than alarmed by Eric's elaborate photographic equipment, got up slowly and strolled into the bush, in among the long dry grass and the red zinnias. The cubs followed her, the other lioness followed her. Through his binoculars Ford watched them stalk with proud lifted heads, walking, even the little ones, in a graceful, measured, controlled way. There were no impala anywhere, no giraffe, no wildebeest. The world here belonged to the lions.

All the game was gathered at Sotingwe, near the water hole. An elephant with ears like punkahs was powdering himself with red earth blown out through his trunk. Tricia got out of the car to photograph the elephant and Ford didn't try to stop her. He scratched his mosquito bites which had passed the burning and entered the itchy stage.

Once more Tricia had neglected to pass the camera strap around her neck. She made her way down to the water's edge and stood at a safe distance—was it a safe distance? Was any distance safe in here?—looking at a crocodile. Ford thought, without really explaining to himself or even fully understanding what he meant, that it was the wrong time of day, it was too early. They went back to Thaba for breakfast.

At breakfast and again at lunch Eric was full of what he had seen. He had taken the dirt road that ran down from Sotingwe to Suthu Bridge and there, up in a tree near the water, had been a leopard. Malcolm had spotted it first, stretched out asleep on a branch, a long way off but quite easy to see through field glasses.

"Massive great fella with your authentic square-type spots," said Eric, smoking a cigar.

Tricia, of course, wanted to go to Suthu Bridge, so Ford took the dirt road after they had had their siesta. Malcolm described exactly where he had seen the leopard which might, for all he knew, still be sleeping on its branch.

"About half a mile up from the bridge. You look over on your left and there's a sort of clearing with one of those trees with yellow trunks in it. This chap was on a branch on the right side of the clearing."

The dirt road was a track of crimson earth between green verges. Ford found the clearing with the single fever tree but the leopard had gone. He drove slowly down to the bridge that spanned the sluggish green river. When he switched off the engine it was silent and utterly still, the air hot and close, nothing moving but the mosquitos that danced in their haphazard yet regular measure above the surface of the water.

Tricia was getting out of the car as a matter of course now. This time she didn't even trouble to give him the coy glance that asked permission. She was wearing a red and white striped sundress with straps that were too narrow and a skirt that was too tight. She ran down to the water's edge, took off a sandal, and dipped in a daring foot. She laughed and twirled her foot, dabbling the dry round stones with water drops. Ford thought how he had loved this sort of thing when he had first met her, and now he was going to have to bear it for the rest of his life. He broke into a sweat as if his temperature had suddenly risen.

She was prancing about on the stones and in the water, holding up her skirt. There were no animals to be seen. All afternoon they had seen nothing but impala, and the sun was moving down now, beginning to color the hazy pastel sky. Tricia, on the opposite bank, broke another Ntsukunyane rule and picked daisies, tucking one behind each ear. With a flower between her teeth like a Spanish dancer, she swayed her hips and smiled.

Ford turned the ignition key and started the car. It would be dark in just over an hour and long before that they would have closed the gates at Thaba. He moved the car forward, reversed, making what Tricia, no doubt, would call a three-point turn. Facing toward Thaba now, he put the shift into drive, his foot on the accelerator, and took a deep breath as the sweat trickled between his shoulder blades. The heat made mirages on the road and out of them a car was coming. Ford stopped and switched off the engine. It wasn't Eric's car but one belonging to a couple of young Americans on holiday. The boy raised his hand in a salute at Ford.

Ford called out to Tricia, "Come on or we'll be late."

She got into the car, dropping her flowers onto the roadway. Ford had been going to leave her there, that was how much he wanted to be rid of her. Her body began to shake and she clasped her hands tightly together so that he shouldn't see. He had been going to drive away and leave her there to the darkness and the lions, the leopard that hunted by night. He had been driving away, only the Americans' car had come along.

She was silent, thinking about it. The American turned back soon after they did and followed them up the dirt road. Impala stood around the solitary fever tree, listening perhaps to inaudible sounds or scenting invisible danger. The sky was smoky yellow with sunset. Tricia thought about what Ford must have intended to do—drive back to camp just before they closed the gates, watch the darkness come down, knowing she was out there, say not a word of her absence to anyone—and who would miss her? Eric? Malcolm? Ford wouldn't have gone to the restaurant and in the morning when they opened the gates he would have driven away. No need even to check out at Ntsukunyane where you paid weeks in advance.

The perfect murder. Who would search for her, not knowing there was need for search? And if her bones were found? One set of bones, human, impala, waterbuck, looks very much like another when the jackals have been at it and the vultures. And when he reached home he would have said he had left her for Marguerite . . .

He was nicer to her that evening, gentler. Because he was afraid she had guessed or might guess the truth of what had happened at Sotingwe?

"We said we'd have champagne one night. How about now? No time like the present."

"If you like," Tricia said.

She felt sick all the time, she had no appetite. Ford toasted them in champagne.

"To us!"

He ordered the whole gamut of the menu, soup, fish, wiener schnitzel, creme brulee. She picked at her food, thinking how he had meant to kill her. She would never be safe now, for having failed once he would try again. Not the same method perhaps but some other. How was she to know he hadn't already tried? Perhaps, for instance, he had substituted aspirin for those quinine tablets, or when they were back at the hotel in Mombasa he might try to drown her. She would never be safe unless she left him.

Which was what he wanted, which would be the next best thing to her death. Lying awake in the night, she thought of what leaving him would mean—going back to live with her mother while he went to Marguerite. He wasn't asleep either. She could hear the sound of his irregular wakeful breathing. She heard the bed creak as he moved in it restlessly, the air conditioner grinding, the whine of a mosquito.

Now, if she hadn't already been killed, she might be wandering out there in the bush, in terror in the dark, afraid to take a step but afraid to remain still, fearful of every sound yet not knowing which sound most to fear. There was no moon. She had taken note of that before she came to bed and had seen in her diary that tomorrow the moon would be new. The sky had been overcast at nightfall and now it was pitch-dark. The leopard could see, perhaps by the light of the stars or with an inner instinctive eye more sure than simple vision, and would drop silently from its branch to sink its teeth into the lifted throat.

The mosquito that had whined stung Ford in several places on his face and neck and on his left foot. He had forgotten to use the repellent the night before. Early in the morning, at dawn, he got up and dressed and went for a walk round the camp. There was no one about but one of the African staff, hosing down a guest's car. Squeaks and shufflings came from the bush beyond the fence.

Had he really meant to rid himself of Tricia by throwing her, as one might say, to the lions? For a mad moment, he supposed, because fever had got into his blood, poison into his veins. She knew, he could tell that. In a way it might be all to the good, her knowing; it would show her how hopeless the marriage was that she was trying to preserve.

The swellings on his foot, though covered by his sock, were making the instep bulge through the sandal. His foot felt stiff and burning and he became aware that he was limping slightly. Supporting himself against the trunk of a fever tree, his skin against its cool, dampish, yellow bark, he took off his sandal and felt his swollen foot tenderly with his fingertips. Mosquitos never touched Tricia; they seemed to shirk contact with her pale dry flesh.

She was up when he hobbled in; she was sitting on her bed, painting her fingernails. How could he live with a woman who painted her fingernails in a game reserve?

They didn't go out till nine. On the road to Waka-suthu, Eric's car met them, coming back.

"There's nothing down there for miles, you're wasting your time."

"Okay," said Ford. "Thanks."

"Sotingwe's the place. Did you see the leopard yesterday?"

Ford shook his head.

"Oh, well, we can't all be lucky."

Elephants were playing in the river at Hippo Bridge, spraying each other with water and nudging heavy shoulders. Ford thought that was going to be the high spot of the morning until they came upon the kill. They didn't actually see it. The kill had taken place some hours before, but the lioness and her cubs were still picking at the carcass, at a blood-blackened rib cage.

They sat in the car and watched. After a while the lions left the carcass and walked away in file through the grass, but the little jackals were already gathered, a pack of them, posted behind trees. Ford came back that way again at four and by then the vultures had moved in, picking the bones.

It was a hot day of merciless sunshine, the sky blue and perfectly clear. Ford's foot was swollen to twice its normal size. He noticed that Tricia hadn't once left the car that day, nor had she spoken girlishly to him or giggled or given him a roguish kiss. She thought he had been trying to kill her, a preposterous notion really. The truth was he had only been giving her a fright, teaching her how stupid it was to flout the rules and leave the car.

Why should he kill her, anyway? He could leave her, he *would* leave her, and once they were back in Mombasa he would tell her so. The thought of it made him turn to her and smile. He had stopped by the clearing where the fever tree stood, yellow of bark, delicate and fern-like of leaf, in the sunshine like a young sapling in springtime.

"Why don't you get out any more?"

She faltered, "There's nothing to see."

"No?"

He had spotted the porcupine with his naked eye but he handed her the binoculars. She looked and she laughed with pleasure. That was the way she used to laugh when she was young, not from amusement but delight. He shut his eyes.

"Oh, the sweetie porky-pine!"

She reached on to the back seat for the camera. And then she hesitated. He could see the fear, the caution, in her eyes. Silently he took the key out of the ignition and held it out to her on the palm of his hand. She flushed. He stared at her, enjoying her discomfiture, indignant that she should suspect him of such baseness.

She hesitated but she took the key. She picked up the camera and opened the car door, holding the key on its fob in her left hand and the camera in her right. He noticed she hadn't passed the strap of the camera, his treasured Pentax, round her neck. For the thousandth time he could have told her but he lacked the heart to speak. His swollen foot throbbed and he thought of the long days at Ntsukunyane that remained to them. Marguerite seemed infinitely far away, farther even than at the other side of the world where she was.

He knew Tricia was going to drop the camera some fifteen seconds before she did so. It was because she had the key in her other hand. If the strap had been round her neck it wouldn't have mattered. He knew how it was when you held something in each hand and lost your grip or your footing. You had no sense then, in that instant, of which of the objects was valuable and mattered and which was not. Tricia held on to the key and dropped the camera. The better to photograph the porcupine, she had mounted on to the twisted roots of a tree, roots that looked as hard as a flight of stone steps.

She gave a little cry. At the sounds of the crash and the cry the porcupine erected its quills. Ford jumped out of the car, wincing when he put his foot to the ground, hobbling through the grass to Tricia who stood as if petrified with fear of him. The camera, the pieces of camera, had fallen among the gnarled, stone-like tree roots. He dropped onto his knees, shouting at her, cursing her.

Tricia began to run. She ran back to the car and pushed the key into the ignition. The car was pointing in the direction of Thaba and the clock on the dashboard shelf said five thirty-five. Ford came limping back, waving his arms at her, his hands full of broken pieces of camera. She looked away and put her foot down hard on the accelerator.

The sky was clear orange with sunset, black bars of the coming night lying on the horizon. She found she could drive when she had to, even though she couldn't pass a test. A mile along the road she met the American couple. The boy put his head out.

"Anything worth going down there for?"

"Not a thing," said Tricia. "You'd be wasting your time."

The boy turned his car round and followed her back. It was two minutes to six when they entered Thaba, the last cars to do so, and the gates were closed behind them.

# ALADDIN'S CURSE

*By Jeffry Scott*

I T AIN'T never oughta have gone down that way," Steve Roback muttered. The darker his mood, the more cheerfully he mangled grammar
—the day after Artie Clinch's murder, mood and syntax were in terrible
shape. The hangover didn't help, either.

"Don't take it so hard," Bob Mallard advised. The young Englishman
was gruffly sympathetic. "You and Clinch were pals, eh?"

Harsh face slick with sweat, Roback squinted in irritation but didn't
waste breath putting the fool right. He'd known Artie Clinch was all. What
it was, Roback *detested* mysteries. Bafflement of any kind—paperback who-
dunits, Rubik cubes, crosswords, cute riddles offended him at the best of
times. This was no such period, not hardly. Unsolved stuff just might kill a
person in the long run and death—his own, anyway—had no place in Steve
Roback's game plan.

He grinned sourly because this wasn't a game. Steve Roback's stock joke,
when asked his trade, was to respond, "Why, I'm a merc, I guess, only I
ain't no car." *Soldier of fortune* struck him as too fancy a label. He and Bob
Mallard and a score more of their kind currently employed in Luambi province were professionals who'd be in a lot of trouble if the world ever ran out
of wars. . . .

Mallard, misunderstanding the stocky man's restlessness, bobbed his
head nervously and murmured, "Hot."

Roback wanted to snarl that Africa tended to be that way. Even a couple of hours after sundown this battered suite on an upper floor of the New Freedom Hotel came on like a halfhearted sauna. Worms of rust from bygone condensation proved that the air conditioning unit had been dead a long while. Like the mummified bugs lost in the grimy shag rugs. Of course Roback wasn't paying for the place. Colonel Julian Mkere had commandeered the New Freedom as barracks for his hired hands, so one couldn't expect finer nuances of service. As a matter of fact, paying guests suffered as well.

Or rather, they didn't, because the diplomats and salesmen and civil servants had been staying away from Gadaville and Luambi province in general. Colonel Mkere's coup was hardly a month old and very prudently they were waiting to discover whether it would stick.

Cracking his knuckles—Bob Mallard started at the minor noise, hand jerking in reflex to pistol butt, they were all jumpy—Steve Roback told himself that was the core of his worries.

The trouble lay in his being (though the very word made him squirm) a warrior. *And this wasn't a war.* With combat a man knew where he stood, sort of. Lay flat on his belly more likely, taking incoming fire, but at least it was simple. You won and picked up the bonus. You lost and grabbed the nearest jeep, or better yet, light plane, in the traditional cause of putting the border behind you.

Colonel Julian Mkere was a soldier who'd won a victory without fighting. In Luambi province he controlled, however briefly, a piece of land about the size of the average state park. He couldn't hold it long, despite owning the local troops while the Gadaville police were run by a friendly member of the same tribe and the ruling (not to mention only) political party's militia happened to be led by his first cousin.

On the other hand, Colonel Mkere didn't need to hold the province for a lifetime, even a Third World rebel's lifetime. Luambi province had a diamond mine. More to the point, the coffee crop's railhead was in Gadaville and coffee was the nation's brown gold, its economic plasma.

Central government could crush him—providing not too many of their forces changed sides or ran away—but Gadaville was bound to be trashed in the process, and the country's trade artery along with it. So Colonel Mkere, suave crook and budding politician (ignorant Roback thought them the same thing), was playing wait-and-see with his recent masters back in the capital, two hundred miles away.

Mkere was ensuring a fat pot whichever way the cards fell, by systematically if quietly plundering the province meanwhile. The snag over that was safeguarding his loot before spiriting it out to Zurich, Lichtenstein, or wherever. "Who shall guard the guardians?" had been an agonizing question centuries before the Romans immortalized it, centuries ago. For Colonel Mkere the answer came down to the likes of Steve Roback.

But not Artie Clinch, any more. Because Clinch had been murdered. Roback growled and shook his head. Mercs didn't get murdered, they got dead, killed in action. Price of the profession, right? Only this wasn't war so Artie Clinch had been . . . yep, murdered.

"He never stood a chance," Bob Mallard agreed, reading the other man's expression. "They were using *pangas,* of course—I hate those blasted machetes. Hell of a way to go."

Roback stared at him, pokerfaced. The Brit was wrong on every count. Dead was dead, there was no good way. And Artie Clinch had stood a chance . . . or should have. He'd been a bragger but he had grit, and he'd never so much as crossed a Gadaville street unarmed. Yet three assassins had gone up against him with cleavers and Clinch hadn't even pulled his sidearm. Weird, spelt fishy.

Mallard broke in with anxious sincerity, "Look, I did my best. If I'd walked out of that bar one minute earlier . . . Lord, it makes you think! But I didn't. Soon as I spotted those thugs attacking one of our fellows, I fired in the air and they ran for their lives."

"It's not that," Roback assured him without explaining further.

He was musing that Artie Clinch had gone to violent death with a Browning 9mm. automatic untouched in his shoulder rig. Fully loaded, thirteen shots. Clinch had no patience with the warning about full loads eventually weakening the magazine feed-spring and causing jams. The piece hadn't jammed, he'd never pulled it. Steve Roback had worked the action and checked the magazine afterwards, in angry disbelief transforming into blind anger. There was nothing amiss with the Browning.

More than a dozen shots waiting for three attackers who couldn't shoot back; and Clinch was good with handguns, could hit what he pointed at. So why had he made no attempt? The enigma was driving Roback crazy. "I'd love to know who put the contract out on him," he thought aloud.

"You're joking," Bob Mallard exclaimed. "They weren't hired by anyone, bet you a hundred quid. They were ragged, starved—just a street gang, the city's infested with them. Old Clinch walked into them, end of story. And him, R.I.P."

Mallard's certainty was impressive. The youngster might be a green merc, but he'd been born and raised on the continent and could read Gadaville's human fine print easily as a Manhattan straphanger scans a tabloid. If Bob Mallard believed that the killing had been random savagery, he was probably correct.

Which deepened the mystery instead of clearing it. Artie Clinch wasn't the man to submit tamely to slaughter by amateurs. Roback frowned, making the mental amendment that it hadn't been wholly tame. Clinch's fighting knife was dropped near the corpse, and Roback felt sure the blood on it came from at least one attacker.

Say they'd had the drop on Artie Clinch, then . . . No, that didn't play, Steve Roback objected. Failing to draw a gun, under threat, yet pitting a single blade against three machetes—that was lunatic, suicidal.

"Contract?" Bob Mallard picked up belatedly. "Why would anyone pay to have hi—" The question ended in a yelp when his shin was kicked.

"Keep your voice down!" Roback yanked the door open. Frantic rustling erupted as light fanned into the corridor. But it was safely empty, clear of eavesdroppers. He'd disturbed only a party of giant cockroaches foraging over a room service trolley that had stood abandoned near the elevator ever since he had been in-country.

Colonel Julian Mkere wasn't a trusting fellow. His so-called Investigation Unit was staffed by scowling men from his home township and what they investigated was disloyalty to their boss.

Slamming the door, Steve Roback explained, "Artie sold his services but he didn't always stay sold—great guy for playing both ends against the middle. Always looking for the big score." He was recalling his final conversation with Artie Clinch, who'd been seething with excitement when he babbled of Aladdin's Cave.

"My hunch," said Roback, "is he ripped off something belonging to Colonel M., and it got him terminated."

Rubbing his leg, Bob Mallard guffawed, "Only a Yank could think *that* up . . . we're a long way from Chicago. Come on, Steve, if Colonel Julian wanted Artie dead, he'd have had him executed."

"Maybe not, kid. We ain't no band of brothers, all for one and so forth, but bump one of us off and the rest get edgy, kinda hostile and disturbed."

Mallard was unconvinced. "They weren't hit men," he pointed out, "they were displaced farm workers, plantation hands, ragged scum. Colonel Mkere would send Investigation Unit thugs—think I couldn't recognize that breed, even on a dark night?" He popped another can of beer. "Anyway, Clinch was well in with Colonel Julian."

"Huh?"

"Artie was drawing special pay for some duty at the airport, hush-hush stuff. Obviously Colonel Julian wants his personal getaway plane all fettled up and ready to go when needed, and *not* to go off with a loud bang at six thousand feet. Can't blame the chap." He chuckled heartlessly.

"Run that by me again," Roback demanded. The headache had worked down to his boots, now. Sustained thought did it every time. But he kept his tone casual.

"Oh, I forgot you've been up-country lately. Yes, Artie Clinch had been a fixture at the airport for days. Didn't he tell you?"

Abstracted, Roback mumbled, "Maybe he did." *Aladdin's Cave.*

Bob Mallard added resentfully, "I should have had that little plum. *I'm* the pilot. Speak no ill of the dead, but Artie didn't know a trim-tab from a cabin ashtray, so how could he do proper checks on Mkere's plane?"

How, Steve Roback wondered almost affectionately, could somebody otherwise bright, be so dumb? Colonel Mkere's personal Lear jet had a team of highly paid and closely watched line mechanics. In Luambi province, locating surprise packages of plastic explosive nestling among the hydraulics or hidden in an engine shell was near the top of their priority list.

Therefore Clinch had been sent to the airport for some other purpose. Snarling at Bob Mallard to be quiet, Roback clasped his head, willing recall of the recent past. Mallard thought that Roback looked uncannily like a hairless ape posing for Rodin's statue of The Thinker but wisely kept the fancy to himself.

Artie Clinch had given Roback a ride back from the airport on the night of his death. Steve Roback assumed that Clinch was there by chance, had been picking up mail or running an errand. Roback had been bone-weary after a day on his feet capped by a couple of hours' bouncing around in an ancient Cessna two-seater.

What the *hell* had Artie said? Roback groaned, teeth gritting. What with fatigue and hanging on while the jeep bounced from rut to pothole on the neglected highway to Gadaville, he hadn't listened closely. Also, Artie Clinch loved running his mouth and sounded crazier than usual, talking in riddles, taunting.

*"Aladdin's Cave, you sorry ol' mud marine! How'd you like to run inventory on that, huh? Heft gold bars like pumpin' iron, trickle diamonds through your fingers like . . . um . . . goddam dried peas."* Well, that was Artie Clinch. He'd been the same from Angola to Central America, forever drooling over fantasies of treasure. With some men it was sex. Roback always dismissed such doodling as childish, pointless. But supposing—his heart flickered, his mouth dried—supposing Clinch's dream had come true?

Tense and subdued, Bob Mallard whined, "I'm not sure this is a terribly good idea, one way and another."

"Don't talk, watch," Steve Roback commanded. They were sharing a thorn bush and fold of the baked ground beside a disused blind-landing beacon at the airport. The cover was hardly enough for a single observer ("We're not even married," Mallard had quipped hours earlier, before jokes dwindled away) and in order to reach it unobserved, they'd been there since long before dawn.

Wretched Bob Mallard didn't agree, but he had to be there. Should they be caught, there was an outside-edge chance of selling guards the story that Mallard had dropped his watch while walking back from his spotter plane the previous day, and was looking for it. Roback had to be there because only he knew what to seek. When he saw it, he'd know.

"I'm dying," Mallard confided. "In fact, I died this morning. This is hell. Curled up on a griddle with your toe in my ribs. Hell is hour upon hour of damn-fool, gratuitous peril in the company of an insane and terminally terse lout. I wonder who that might be?"

Roback didn't rise to the insult. The thorn bush was perhaps half a mile from the terminal block, slightly less from the maintenance and freight sheds. That was another reason for Mallard's presence: Roback couldn't keep tabs on locations in opposite directions—not without constant wrigglings around, and undue movement would invite attention.

"You'll die," he promised, "if you run your mouth and miss something."

Roback was watching the passenger terminal. A lot of internal flights had ceased with Colonel Mkere's coup, so little was happening there. A group of soldiers drowsed in the shadow cast by an armored half-track. On the flat roof above the entrance, a listless merc sat in a beach chair, rifle across his knees, binoculars unused since a token sweep of the terrain when arriving on post. Steve Roback was irked by an illogical urge to double over there and ream the guy out.

Bob Mallard was responsible for the other set of buildings. Partly through being a flier who should spot unusual activity, mainly because Roback guessed the terminal offices with their safes had to be the likeliest place for valuables. He had pumped a few fellow mercs about Artie Clinch's new duty at the airport, but they'd proved vague and uninterested and he dared not persist. One whiff of possible plunder and there'd be a stampede . . .

Mallard's voice altered suddenly. "Head up, Steve!"

Turning laboriously, Roback was ready to clobber him for a hoax. Then he saw a pair of vertical, fat, black hairs rising in the shimmering heat above distant paving.

"Fuel bunker doors," Bob Mallard reported. "Normally they lie flat, trapdoor style."

Big deal, Roback grumbled inwardly.

"Take a bit of interest," the pilot nagged. "Why open the doors, eh? Hell of a sweat, a couple of horny-handed toilers have been cranking away for ten minutes—no power out there these days, has to be done manually and those doors are steel, weight-supporting in case a plane rolls over them when they're flat."

"What is this bunker?"

"Fuel, it's just an underground tank, a chamber." Mallard was thoughtful. "Funny thing is, there's no aircraft waiting for fuel and you don't need those doors for that anyway. I'm pretty sure it's empty for that matter, never been used in my time here."

Roback's skin tingled. An underground space with steel doors—that was another way of saying "vault." And the bunker was out of sight of the terminal building, whose windows were frosted at the back, while it was out to one side and well away from the maintenance facility.

Mallard said, "Come to think of it, trucks have been stopping over there from time to time. Delivering something? What's going on?"

Before Roback could answer, both men flattened at the noise of an approaching convoy: motorcycles, jeep, and plain van, pulling up at the bunker. Delivering a human fence of men in civilian uniforms of baggy linen pants, dark blazers, and two-tone shoes, deploying to surround the gaping doors.

Mallard ducked, groaning, "Bad news, those are Investigation Unit goons!"

Pinning him down with a meaty paw between the shoulderblades, Roback watched figures emerging from underground—two Investigation Unit men, a province militia officer in dandyish tunic and slacks the color of milky coffee, and a mercenary whom he knew only by sight.

The four men were undressing. Investigation Unit arrivals grabbed discarded clothing and pawed through it; others closed in on the naked former wearers. Body-search, Steve Roback told himself.

He was looking at Aladdin's Cave. Colonel Mkere took no chances over his cache. Round the clock guards inside the bunker: here came another jeep and a rusty white Datsun bearing replacements. Classic technique for avoiding conspiracy among hirelings—a mix of rivals and strangers, teaming Investigation Unit, militia, and mercenaries.

Boxes around boxes, guardians guarding guardians, and that was only the start. For when the inside men went off duty, *they* were searched in turn.

Nice play. The chances of Mkere's thugs from the Investigation Unit's joining forces with a militia man were remote. For them to get a merc on their side was even more remote. Too much mutual suspicion, fear of its being a setup or test. And even if the impossible came to pass, the second cordon waited.

Roback swore admiringly. No need to tip the cordon about Colonel Mkere's stash. They'd just be ordered to search for valuables. But supposing they found some—what prevented their keeping the result for themselves? His eyes narrowed: nobody had got out of the Datsun.

His guess was confirmed. The outgoing guards were dressing, their replacements entering the bunker. And an Investigation Unit officer had gone to the white car, reporting that all was well. When the tinted window rolled down, Roback got a swift sighting of Colonel Julian Mkere. Discreet visit, his stretched Mercedes swapped for something anonymous. . . .

Ten minutes later the bunker doors were shut flat once more, the vehicles had gone. Bob Mallard, released, complained, "I love eating dirt."

Roback wasn't listening. "How big is that fuel store?" he demanded. "Big enough for four guys to operate in there, plus, um, equipment? Wouldn't they keel over from heat?"

"How big? Gigundeous. Much larger than your average big-city bachelor flat, for instance. But heat would be a problem. Those bunkers have to be ventilated to prevent fumes building up, but . . ." Mallard's words tailed off. *"That's* it," he finished.

"What is?"

"Listen. That puttering noise. Wondered what it was getting on my nerves. It's a genny, little portable Japanese job. Generator that size couldn't supply enough juice to raise the doors, but it would be okay for running air conditioning in there."

Bob Mallard turned on his side, peering at Roback. "Why would anyone coop themselves up in a fuel bunker?" He answered himself, with a mixture of greed, awe, and plain fear. "Colonel Julian's private bank. Just a hop and a step from his getaway plane. Handy, eh?"

"You could say. Listen, kid, either we're partners on this, or you got a problem with me."

"If you fancy cracking Mkere's safe deposit out there, rotsa ruck and all that. Positively no competition from me. In fact I feel generous, you can keep that caper all to yourself."

Glee was mellowing Steve Roback, he nearly smiled. "We don't have to, Artie Clinch has done it for us."

Bringing Bob Mallard up to speed helped pass the interminable afternoon. "He good as told me, with that Aladdin's Cave crap," Roback concluded. "Clinch found a gimmick for smuggling stuff out."

"You think," Mallard amended.

"Had to be that way. Clinch was out of his gourd with excitement when he gave me the ride. Because he was on the take. Just knowing the loot was there wouldn't do that for him—he'd have been like to slit his throat from frustration. Clinch was on the take, guards or no. He could be a very tricksy dude, ol' Artie."

"Smuggle bullion past that crowd, with Colonel Julian breathing down their necks? Rubbish."

Roback pondered, unseeing as a column of ants used his leg as a bridge to the thorn bush's branches. Euphoria flickered before flaring anew. "Not gold bars. Diamonds. He gabbled about heaps of diamonds."

Mallard was irritated. "Artie was pulling your leg, then. Diamonds don't come out of the mine here all faceted up and polished, they're dirty pebbles. Unless it's an unusually big stone, you would have to steal a sack of them to make the risk worth the candle. Honestly, Steve—think it through. Your dirty pebbles have to be cut, remember."

"Diamonds," Roback insisted. "Artie wasn't joshing, that guy had greed as a religion, it would have been like . . . uh, *blasphemy*. I tell you, he was so high on greed he had to brag. Until he got hold of himself." Struck by a fresh insight, Roback added, "My hunch is he tried out his gimmick and it worked and then he pulled it again with a raft of stuff, that night he gave me the ride."

Roback's teeth were grinding again. "Jeez, the stuff must have been on him, right next to me. Diamonds—and Artie Clinch wasn't talking no dirty pebbles!"

It was long after dark before they could slip away, Bob Mallard bitterly claiming as he hobbled to the jeep, hidden a mile from the airport perimeter fence, that he was a prematurely old man, cramped for life.

Rounding the bend before the New Freedom Hotel's drive, the head-lights scythed out into space, branding a livid path across the sluggish, grey-green water of the Afur river. A dark, contorted, shiny shape—drowned corpse or leafless tree—surfaced momentarily, spinning and submerging.

Just about here Artie Clinch had fallen. His jeep had run out of gas at the foot of the slope, he'd been less than a hundred yards from safety. Left the jeep, strode up the slope and—Roback braked so hard that Mallard hit the windshield.

"Hey! Could those muggers, bandits, whatever, have lifted the dia-monds?"

"Dode be sudge a twid!" Mallard ran tentative, exploratory fingers down the bridge of his nose and turned a teary gaze on Roback. "There weren't any diamonds. And they didn't have time to steal anything—I went out on the verandah, heard a ruckus, saw what was up, and drove them off.

"You were right on my heels, *you* saw the state Artie was in . . . Noth-ing missing, though; doubt whether they touched him." The youngster swallowed. "Except with those machetes. You checked his gun and every-thing, it was all there."

As Roback put the jeep in gear and moved off, Mallard sniggered, "No wonder you can't remember it straight. Well, you did throw a bit of a wobbly, Steve. Bellowing about bushwhacking and lord knows what. Ter-rific histrionics."

Scowling, Steve Roback mumbled, "I was boozed to the gills. But sober enough to know something was skewed about that business." In truth, he had little memory of the aftermath to murder, apart from confused rage.

They pulled into the New Freedom's parking lot. "Super day," Mallard yawned, "we must do it again soon. Call me, eh? Around the year 2020, preferably."

Roback was reproachful. "I tell you Artie was into something rich enough to make his head spin. We ain't hardly started yet. Shower, eats, *one* good beer, then we got to take his room apart inch by inch."

Clinch's hotel room door was locked, but Steve Roback had the key. He kicked it open.

The smell was appalling, a tray of scrambled eggs, preserves, half a melon —you had to guess—sat on the unmade bed, sprouting Technicolor mold and alive with industrious insect life. Dried blood, at first glance, turned out to be spilt coffee on the tangled sheets. Evidently Artie Clinch had hurried off to the airport the day he died, and nobody had disturbed his lair since then.

"Great," Roback cried, "we're the first."

"And last, no doubt." Bob Mallard, distasteful, hooked discarded jockey shorts on the toe of his cowboy boot, flicking them aside. "Really, Steve, it's *quelle* squalid."

"Well," Roback said generously, "Artie was a dogface soldier, never got educated to live right, police his quarters properly. Now we got to be systematic here." He pursed his lips in thought. "Start at the door, go slow and careful, throw everything into the bathroom as we go. We're looking for diamonds, right?"

The pilot sighed heavily. "If you insist."

Four hours later he was whining, "We can't go over it again. *There's nothing here.*"

Artie Clinch's room wasn't a mess any longer. It was wrecked, gutted. Light shades down, bulbs glaring from naked flex, pillows ripped, mattress slit. Clinch's possessions had been minimal, and they'd scrutinized, probed, broken apart each item.

"You checked the shower head and the faucets, the cistern and all in there?" Roback jerked a thumb at the bathroom, now piled with vandalized gear and clothes with all seams gaping.

"Twice," Mallard confirmed. "And that was after you'd been through them." Letting himself slide down the wall, he sprawled in a corner, eyes closed.

"So they're not here," Roback brooded. "Fine, then we'll extend the search area."

"Yes," Bob Mallard agreed, "you will. Include me out. Talk about obsessions, you make Captain Ahab look a dilettante." Steve Roback, unable to place the officer among mercs and regular military encountered in the past decade, dismissed the passing interest.

"What's the matter?" he asked sharply. Mallard, frowning, had lifted his tail and was picking something out of the rug.

"Spent bullet," he said, holding the thing between finger and thumb. "Funny, I can't see gunshot damage here."

Roback pounced on the slug. "Figures—this little sucker's never been fired. See, smooth as a baby's cheek, no discoloration."

Mallard, shrugging, stifled a yawn and said, "I found an empty cartridge case under the bed. Along with debris I'd rather forget. Maybe that bullet came from it."

Snapping his fingers, Roback said an extremely rude word, reverently. "Cartridges, 9mm. stuff, a half-empty carton. Where are they?" Resignedly, joints cracking, Bob Mallard rose and began sifting through oddments in the bathroom.

"I'll be right back," said his partner, "got to get something out of my room."

The cardboard box of ammunition, fuzzy from being hauled around in holdall and kitbag, was the standard honeycomb arrangement of card partitions with ten or so bullets nosing up from their nests. Mallard slapped it into Roback's shovel palm. "Look, if I don't get to bed I'll fall over. Enjoy. . . ."

"And miss the goddam cabaret?" Roback brandished the pliers he'd brought from his gear. "Shame on you." Hooked despite himself, the pilot lingered.

Lacking a vise, Roback pinched a cartridge between the hinge edge of the door and its jamb. He paused with the pliers' jaws just biting the bullet. "Artie was tricksy, like I said. He knew he'd be searched, but somehow he got stuff out." His arm muscles jumped into prominence, he levered and then yanked, the cartridge case stayed in the crack of door while its bullet came away with the pliers, like a tooth.

Dropping it, Roback took the cartridge case, rapping the little brass tube upside down on the bedside table. This produced a minuscule litter of propellant substance, and an empty case.

"Nice," Mallard applauded.

"Shut the hell up, gimme another cartridge." Murphy's Law decreed that only the last one concealed paydirt. Roback rapped, and this time a tissue-wrapped granule fell onto the table.

Pool-cue fingers delicate, he peeled the paper away. Mallard, exhaling as if hit in the belly, craned closer. Roback grinned fondly, a father catching sight of his baby for the first time. "Worth waiting for," he stated smugly.

The glittering thing burned coldly, a giant ice queen's teardrop. "Dirty pebble, huh? Way it worked, Clinch had a cartridge case rigged ready to open while he was guarding the stash. Snitched this baby, hid it in the cartridge, put it in his weapon. Investigation Unit could frisk him, but in the end he'd get his weapon back. Nice."

"I'm the twit," Mallard conceded, kneeling at the table. "This never came from the province's mine, it's a good stone ripped out of the original setting. Makes sense: Colonel Julian shakes down the fat cats, their jewelry's broken up, settings melted into bars, stones set aside. Gold's heavy, bulky— if you have to travel far and fast, diamonds are the most portable wealth on earth, international currency."

Blinking sweat away, young Mallard giggled wildly. "Dad used to be a jeweller. Any idea what this is worth?"

"Surprise me, kid."

"Ten thousand pounds if it's a penny." The pilot cast a wistful look at the disembowelled cartridges on the rug. "What a shame Clinch got bumped off before he could nick a few more like this one!"

"Wrong," Roback purred. "I guess once he test-ran the gimmick and it worked fine, he went for broke." Mallard, nonplussed by his expression, caught on that Steve Roback was beaming foolishly. "Browning self-loading pistol takes thirteen cartridges, count 'em. Say he took diamonds worth no more than this sucker, let's be cautious—that's thirteen times maybe fourteen thousand dollars. Me, I got simple tastes, and even split two ways it'll make me one happy s.o.b."

Bob Mallard was puzzled. Roback winked jovially. "You still don't get it. Clinch filled his piece with diamond bullets—that's why he didn't use it on those muggers. He couldn't. Fourteen-thousand-dollar bullets but not worth a damn when they jumped him."

Mallard's reaction was weird. His eyes bugged, his arms flailed, he might have been imitating an outboard motor as he stammered, "But . . . but . . . but . . ." Oblivious, Roback hugged him.

"Go get Clinch's Browning, let's practice some more painless dentistry." At last he noticed the pilot's distress, and was struck by a terrible doubt. "You collected his billfold and dogtags and such. Didn't you take the Browning as well?"

"No, you drunken moron," Mallard croaked. "*You* took it. You hurtled onto the scene like a damned boozy bull in a china shop and took charge and, and . . ." Beyond words, he fairly gibbered with fury.

Steve Roback experienced total recall, like a mallet on top of his skull. He hadn't really forgotten, just misplaced knowledge of what happened. First the liquor drew a veil and then his subconscious, saving him searing regret, had ordered brief amnesia.

*Now* he remembered.

It wasn't deep in the forest—that was the far side of the river—but something definitely stirred. A safari sound, ideal for TV jungle shows: an incredibly loud, anguished bellow blending berserk rage and wild lamentation.

It was the sound made by Dwight Steven Roback. Seeing himself in the minutes after Artie Clinch's passing. Swearing a blue streak because Clinch hadn't defended himself right. Checking the Browning, working the slide, snapping the full magazine back into its butt . . .

Then hurling the thing far, not just into the night but out of reach for eternity, somewhere in the deep and muddy Afur river, so treacherously, meanly, unfairly close at hand.

# SOUTH
# AMERICA

# Incident In Bogotá

*By James M. Fox*

I MET General Francisco Vargas Urticaria only once, several years ago, and under circumstances of substantial embarrassment to both of us. These had originated on my side one late November evening, with a call from Washington. I caught a flight from London, where I was stationed at the time, to Miami that same night, and walked into Wayne Latimer's hospital room at breakfast time.

He was a former FBI agent, in his late forties, sharper than a stainless steel tack but not in good physical condition. Gelusil and tranquilizers couldn't always keep him going, and his temper would fall off accordingly. "Why you?" he greeted me. "You don't know South America. You've never even been there." When I told him everybody else was busy and that he'd deprived me of a holiday, he managed to control his sympathy. "You do speak Spanish?"

"Let's not worry about me so much," I said. "What's wrong with you?"

He said the medical profession had been trying to make up its mind if he should be cut open to find out. "They wanted to get on with it in Bogotá. I passed, and grabbed a plane. Our customer is on the hospital board down there."

"He's a doctor?"

"So was Che Guevara."

Latimer looked pretty bad. I put a leash on my impatience and said pleasantly enough: "I know that, Wayne, but Jimmy Dexter mentioned that you were supposed to brief me. You can skip the generalities. Colombia has twenty million people. It's about the size of California and Texas put together. It's politically fairly stable, with a president elected for four years, a senate, and a house of representatives. Exports are coffee, emeralds, and cocaine. Havana has been trying for a long time but can't seem to get anything going there. Now tell me why."

"You see?" he scoffed, exasperated with me. "You don't have a clue. Take you three months to line this up, and you won't get three days." He had a spasm, bit it back, and bared his teeth at me. "Okay, I'll give it to you in one hunk. Castro *is* making progress. There's no reason why he should. The country's fairly prosperous. The Indios are a small minority, well-integrated. There's the usual agrarian-reform problem, and politics are elitist, of course. But you can't get away from those in South America. They need agrarian reforms in Cuba, in reverse, and *their* political elite is even more objectionable since it has no manners. In Colombia, they've organized a half dozen guerrilla outfits. Doesn't mean a thing, the army can take care of them. The only question is, who takes care of the army."

"Don't the politicians?"

"Sure they do, if you mean pay and rations. But there are too many first lieutenants crowding forty, and too many majors who'll never get a regiment."

The straw to make the bricks. Even in ancient Rome, if you were discontented with the government, you talked with four or five centurions and promised each of them a legion. "Who's your doctor friend?" I asked.

"Juan Ruiz-Martinez. Home and office in the Bolivar Hotel. A Castro agent, but he's not responsible for the guerrilla picture. That's supposed to be controlled direct, by Cubans in the field. Ruiz-Martinez is a practicing Colombian physician. Almost all his patients are notorious radicals or student activists."

"His nurse sold you the list," I said.

"His janitor, for fifty pesos. Like three bucks. What should be worth a little more than that is which one of them will assassinate General Vargas. Also when and how."

"Who's he?"

"He's not the president," said Latimer, bitterly patient with me. "Or the chief of staff. He has been both, but he retired about ten years ago. To some extent he's the Colombian De Gaulle. You'll never meet him, and you wouldn't like him if you did."

"If he's all that important, they'll have tried before to take him out," I said.

"At least three times, but his protection's pretty good. This time they'll make it, our informant claims."

"The janitor?"
"No, no. The general's wife."

November is a rainy month in Bogotá, the Avianca hostess told me. My arrival late that afternoon, however, featured sunshine, a mild spring breeze, and the longest landing run I could remember suffering through. The city and its airport are at eighty-seven hundred feet.

The desk clerk at the Tequendama came up with a guest card to their country club.

I caught up on my sleep that night. At nine A.M. the golf pro found me waiting at his door. He had a fairly decent bag of clubs, a cart, and a small item of advice for me. "The party just ahead of you, señor. Do not disturb them, please." I said I wouldn't think of it, which was untrue, and parked near the first tee where, from a courteous distance, I watched Isabella Luz de Vargas hit a very creditable drive. She had a caddie but no partner, and no transportation. As she walked off down the fairway, two men in a pickup truck rolled from the service area along a trail that turned into the rough.

I did my warming up and waited until she'd moved almost out of sight, then fired an easy drive to follow her. The cart was a big help to me, of course. She was a walker, but I stayed behind at a respectful distance for six holes, closed in a little on the seventh, moved up on the eighth, and dropped a nice approach shot about ten yards short of where she was already lining up the green, her caddie at the flag. It made a more or less acceptable excuse for overtaking her on wheels.

"Good morning. I've replaced Wayne Latimer. My name is Stephen Harvester."

The pickup truck was coming fast; its driver plowed up quite a strip of turf when he slammed on his brakes. His partner had an automatic rifle on me. *"No se mueva, por favor, señor!"* I kept my hands in view, on the cart's steering wheel, and didn't move, as ordered. They were competent enough, but they'd forgotten that most laborers in overalls will shave, or trim their mustaches, only on weekends. When the driver started to jump out, Lita de Vargas stopped him with a hand wave. *"Está bien, Jacinto. Señor Harvester es un amigo."*

She bestowed her queenly smile on me where he could see it. Both men stared at me, impassively, filing a mental picture of me; then the driver bowed to her and slipped behind the wheel again, and ruined some more turf going into reverse. "I'm glad you managed to convince him," I said cheerfully.

"Why shouldn't he believe me? He has known me since I was a child."

She sounded cool and distant, and the smile had vanished. Latimer had warned me that I would dislike her, too, and he was right. I said: "Let's agree now on where we've met. Before Jacinto thinks of asking us."

"If he presumes to do that, I shall tell him you were at the same Columbus Day reception at your embassy, last month, where Mr. Latimer was introduced to me."

"No good."

"I beg your pardon?"

"He can check my passport. It'll show I was in England and in France last month."

". . . Very well, you were presented to me at a charity affair in August. In Monaco. By Princess Grace herself. We danced."

I thought about that and said: "Better. Were you unescorted?"

"Always when I am in Europe, yes."

"All right, that'll be it. Finish your round and meet me for a cup of coffee on the clubhouse terrace, please."

She merely nodded, and I backed the cart away. She gave her ball a careless swipe that nearly missed the green and strode on after it.

Later, when she came to my table on the terrace, she looked very elegant indeed, as well as freshly showered, in a simple little cotton print that only an Italian couturier could have whipped up for her at say, a thousand dollars. "What has become of Mr. Latimer, please?"

"He has stomach trouble."

"Yes, of course." She put the matter from her mind. "Have you made progress?"

"I came in last night."

"Why did you wish to talk with me?"

I didn't. I detested her, and it was fairly obvious that she reciprocated. "Wayne suggested *you* might have made progress," I said coolly.

She released her breath in a long sigh. "But how? He knows the situation. He must have explained it to you. There is a young student of good family who has been socially acceptable to both my husband and myself, and who became—infatuated with me. It was he who blurted out to me in privacy, last week, that an attempt on us is being planned. If this succeeds, the army and the government are to be taken over by a group of radicals to which the boy himself belongs. He certainly would not have warned me if my life were not in danger, and he has refused to give me any further information."

"But he wants you to get out of Bogotá right now, and show your appreciation to him later. Is that it?"

Her eyes were green, and scornful of me. Latimer had told me all of this, and that she'd come to him with it because she'd sensed he was in a position to take action. She had made him promise that the boy would not be hurt, a promise she could never have extracted from her husband. Latimer, who knew about Dr. Ruiz-Martinez, had agreed to handle it. He had installed two spike mikes in the Bolivar Hotel that broadcast to a tape recorder in his office in the Esso Building, and he'd paid the janitor to keep a name-and-time log of all visitors. He had been getting interesting but not yet conclusive stuff until two days ago, when he'd thrown up a glass of milk that had turned red.

The answer might be waiting for me there. But it was clearly necessary to come to terms with our informant. "Are you sure that this young man . . ."

She cut me short, imperiously. "Quite sure, thank you. Or we should not be sitting here, discussing it. May I know what you plan to do?"

"Did Wayne explain his plans to you?"

He'd told me he had not. She said, too eagerly: "Of course he did." I shook my head and said I'd be in touch, got up and pulled her chair, and walked her to her car. Jacinto and his partner, who'd been loitering at the nearest corner of the clubhouse, were already in the front seat, wearing livery. The car was a Rolls Silver Cloud. I bowed over her hand, disliking her, and strolled away, aware of the green lilac eyes behind me, resting on my back.

Latimer's key opened a door describing him as the *concesionario* of an obscure brand of American refrigerators. His executive suite did not even bother with a secretarial desk. Its front room held two dusty display models and a box of literature several years old; the back room was much like my own on Oxford Street. I found the tape recorder, which was 15/16th, low fidelity, speech-activated, with a timer circuit. There were still a few feet on the current reel. I put a new one on, set up a separate playback deck, and went to work.

By eight o'clock that night I'd run through everything, including Latimer's old tapes and his interpretative notes.

That a conspiracy existed was beyond the slightest doubt. I counted forty-six participants in the available material. They were so fat and happy with their system of communication that it didn't seem to have occurred to them a doctor's office can be bugged as easily as any other place. Ruiz-Martinez sounded curiously indiscreet himself; he even made me wonder if he might be a police provocateur, and if perhaps another tape recorder might be picking up these fascinating conversations at the *jefatura,* seven blocks away. It certainly would be of interest there to find out the name of the new chief, and of his boss, the minister of the interior, and *his* boss, the new president. The army, too, might like to hear about who would be in command of it, and of its more important units. All of this as of November twenty-third. The day after tomorrow.

There were various discussions of the ways and means to bring these things about, of course. Company X would occupy the television station, Squadrons Y and Z the presidential palace. Regiments in Barranquilla, Medellin, and Cali were to deal with this and that. Soldiers will follow orders, even if they don't completely understand why certain officers have suddenly replaced their seniors.

Unless a voice speaks up, a voice of great authority, commanding very much respect.

The name of General Francisco Vargas was not mentioned on the tapes. Almost inevitably the conspirators had started by deciding how he'd be disposed of, and by whom. Wayne Latimer must have plugged into them too late, probably much too late—perhaps a month or more. At this stage there was little need for any more discussion of the matter. All I could dig up was a few cryptic references that might very easily apply to some entirely different and minor aspect of the plot. *We can depend on Major Robles* (nothing in the context specified for what), and, *if Ortega does his job . . .* (Unspecified again. The speaker was the future minister of justice. His remark was interrupted by a mutter of consensus.) There were many more, but I liked these two best. One reason was that neither of these names appeared on the good doctor's list of patients. Or on the log of visitors kept by the janitor.

I locked up the material, and for a while stood by the only window, looking out. I had missed lunch and hardly noticed it. The city, glistening under the night rain of late spring, loomed even larger than I had anticipated. Bogotá has more than two million people, and the notion that so many could be taken over by so few seemed utterly absurd. Yet it was feasible, I knew that very well. It might even prove easy. Just two bullets might turn out to do the trick, and one of these would very nicely keep Señora Isabella Luz de Vargas from perhaps reaching a radio station, or a barracks, or some other place where she'd be talking out of turn. Too many wives of retired generals have caused too many problems all through history.

Tomorrow night would be the night, I thought, and wondered about Julio Guzmán.

He was the one who'd urged her to leave town. I had him on the tape, several times; he sounded very young, and terribly sincere. Apparently he led a delegation of the student activists involved. Jacinto and his partner would have needed about twenty minutes, wringing him out dry.

But there were other methods. This must have occurred to Latimer as well, because he'd made a casual surveillance of the boy. I checked his notes, went back to my hotel room, changed to a dark suit but did not shave. A steak and salad at La Pampa served to fuel me. It was still early for Colombia, around eleven, when my taxi found what I was looking for, the little coffee bar, one of a dozen in the district bordering the university.

He wasn't difficult to spot, although the others at his table were much like him: early twenties, medium-long hair, cheap slacks, expensive sweaters. But they were deferring to him, not unreasonably—the charisma of the budding politician draped him like a flag and strongly underscored his dark good looks. The group was eating *empanadas,* pancakes filled with spiced ground meat, and still the volume of their conversation shook the walls. I leaned my back against the bar, had coffee, and deliberately put the evil eye right on the kid.

It took a little while. He wasn't stupid or insensitive, but he was busy. When he did become aware of me, he stiffened visibly. I jerked my chin in the direction of the back door and walked out that way. The alley was a mud bath hissing with the rain, but there were garbage cans in a small service court under a strip of roof. The ambiance was exactly right.

I'd never been in South America before, as Latimer had pointed out, but I knew Mexico, and knew it well enough to pass, under the circumstances, for a certain type of Mexican. When Julio Guzmán appeared, he found me sitting on a crate, legs crossed, the collar of my trenchcoat up over my ears. "They told me you were faster on your feet than this, señor," I said.

The phrase, in Mexican, sounds fairly crude. He closed the door, reluctantly. *"Qué quiere?"*

"Major Robles sent for me."

*We can depend on Major Robles.* Therefore, if he sent for somebody like me, he had his reasons. Julio Guzmán accepted that, of course. "I see. But to what purpose?"

"It is now considered necessary to provide a jockstrap for tomorrow night, señor," I said, and spat into the alley past his feet.

He understood me very well. What I was telling him was that there had been a decision to employ a Mexican professional to back up the assassin. It was dark, but I could almost taste and smell his consternation. "At Casa Rosaleda?" I ignored that, struck a match, and lit a cigarette, allowing him to see my sneer. "But what . . . why do you come to me with this?"

"You are familiar with the house, señor. You have a car."

That was more like it. He could breathe again, almost too audibly. *"Muy bien.* Where shall I meet you? At what time?"

"The bottom station of the cable car, señor. You name the time. It is your city, and your car."

"I shall be there at three o'clock tomorrow night."

It was pathetically obvious what he had in mind. I grunted at him, tramped off through the alley, reached the street, and found my taxi where I'd left it down the block. By then I'd pretty well decided how to put a handle on the situation. Latimer had given me the number of her private phone. I rang it with the sun over my early breakfast table. "You'll be at the club this morning?"

"Yes, as usual."

"I wanted to make sure. I'll join you, if I may."

"Of course, with pleasure, Mr. Harvester," she told me distantly.

"Thank you for asking me. Goodbye." The phone clicked in my ear and offered me a dial tone. I caught myself just short of slamming it. No woman had come close to irritating me as much as this in many years. I passed up what was left of breakfast, underdressed deliberately, then concluded that Bermuda shorts might give her the idea that I was trying to look younger than my age.

She was ten minutes late, which almost brought me into conflict with the female foursome booked for a nine thirty start. When she arrived, a fashion plate straight out of *Vogue,* they knew her, fawned on her, and held us up some more while I was being introduced and scrutinized. Then she banged out a two hundred yard drive, not even troubling to warm up, and I produced a slice that screamed about three hundred, right over the clubhouse roof. Nobody laughed, not even when my second ball popped up.

We walked to it along the fairway, in dead silence, and she stood by hipshot, like a model, watching me compose myself and fire my normal brassie distance, halfway to the green. She made no comment as we strolled behind our caddies. I said: "Is your house named Casa Rosaleda?"

"Yes, it is. Didn't you know?"

"My dear lady, I just got here, and Wayne's records don't happen to mention it. The name came up last night and seemed to fit. I have exciting news for you. Your husband's murder has been scheduled for tomorrow morning early, probably at two A.M. You were supposed to be included. But when you pretended to ignore your Mr. Guzmán's warning, he apparently decided to work out something for you. My guess would be that he has made a private deal with the assassin. I imagine that between them they'll just lock you up somewhere for a few days. Until their revolution's running in the groove."

She didn't even glance at me. We'd found her ball, and she reached for a three-wood, hacked away, and landed smartly on the green, about six inches from the cup. We walked, and she asked coolly, "Are you certain?"

"No. There's no such thing. I want to check out two more names with you. Ortega?"

"I've met Señora Carmen Torres de Ortega. She's a widow in her eighties, socially important. And I know two tradesmen by that name."

"We've missed on that score. Major Robles?"

"Which one? There must be as many as a dozen in the army. Surely you're aware that Spanish surnames cannot be identified that way. You need the first name and the mother's name as well, and . . ."

"Do you know any Major Robles?"

"Personally? No. There is one in the Ministry of War. He's the assistant bureau chief of personnel assignment, I believe."

That was more like it, but I made no comment. My ball had an easy lay, and I got on the green with it right next to hers. She was two up on me, but not for long. I shot the nine in thirty-seven, beating her by three, enjoying it. Along the service road, Jacinto's pickup truck kept pace, although I never caught him or his partner watching us.

As we approached the locker room she asked me quietly, "May I know what you propose to do?"

"Arrange for an abortion."

"I beg your pardon."

"My dear lady, you don't *want* a revolution in this country, do you? Even a suppressed one? Neither do my people, so let's just not have one."

"Can you stop it?"

"Yes, I think so. Maybe even without inconveniencing your husband."

"I'd appreciate that very much," she carefully assured me. "But I don't quite understand."

I smiled at her, disliking her. There really wasn't much to smile about. I wasn't going to perform card tricks or do anything particularly clever. Latimer had done his job and made it easy for me. "Just in case," I said, "what are your husband's plans tonight? And yours?"

"We expect friends for bridge and a light supper. They'll have left by two." Routine security was fairly good, as she explained when I inquired about it. The estate was walled, and wired against intruders. Visitors and tradesmen at the gate faced a closed-circuit television camera. She had no children, and at night only Jacinto and an adjutant stayed in the house itself; the servants' quarters were some fifty yards away.

I told her that if there were any problems I'd get back in touch, bowed to her, and left her there. With any luck at all I'd make the early morning Pan Am flight back to Miami. I was certainly not interested in her understanding, or her appreciation, or in ever seeing her again. I caught a taxi back to the hotel and changed, walked to the Esso Building, spent about two hours checking out the current tape, and found what I'd expected— nothing much. There had been no more conferences because none was needed. They were set to go.

Dr. Juan Ruiz-Martinez had been seeing a few real patients. He appeared to specialize in what are tactfully defined as male disorders. I got through to him by phone when he returned from lunch, declared myself a tourist at the Tequendama, and in my best broken Spanish started to explain that I'd been with a woman a few days ago, and now there was something I'd like to talk to him about. He interrupted me in passably good English. "Who referred you to me, sir?"

I said that I was very happy he could speak my language. Didn't he know that his name was listed in a confidential travel guide for members of the Lions Club? It seemed he didn't and that he was much amused by it. He gave me an appointment at five thirty. For a while I listened to the tape recorder monitor, but he made no suspicious phone calls; he just rang the desk at the hotel to ask if I was registered. By five o'clock I'd finished at the Esso Building, packaged the material, and typed a resume of it. Then I called Latimer's crunch contact at the embassy and told him where to find it if he didn't hear from me again by seven on the dot.

Political conspiracies, except for some of the wild-eyed Middle East variety, always provide themselves with a fail-safe routine. They can be simple, and they usually work out pretty well when somebody discovers the red light on the control board. Dr. Juan Ruiz-Martinez saw it right away. He had admitted me himself into his empty waiting room, and looked me over, and had been unable to conceal his agitation. I was rather obviously not a member of the Lions Club.

"Excuse me, please. I have another patient."

He retired into his office, tried to close the door, and found me on his heels. He was a bantam weight in a white jacket, pale and intellectual, with the obligatory little black mustache, but in my thirty years of pottering around the edges I'd come up against a few more like him. It was very necessary to bring up a knee under his spine. He bounced off his examination table, tripped over the chair I kicked into his way, and scuttled for his desk. By then I was behind it with the drawer open and his deadly little German Mauser pistol in my pocket.

"Take it easy, doctor. There's no hurry."

"Who are you, sir?"

"You've got my name right here in your appointment book. It's as I told you on the phone, doctor, we have something to talk about." He had recovered his composure. He picked up the toppled chair and used it, gingerly. His stare at me where I was sitting on his desk relayed the obvious message of distrust and disaffection. "Money," I said cheerfully. "A lot of money. Such as twenty thousand pesos every three months. We'll call it a retainer for professional services."

The peso in Colombia is worth about six cents, but he was not a wealthy doctor. He was interested, and confused, and trying to pretend. "Even a life insurance company pays more than that," he slowly pointed out.

"Not ours, doctor. We throw in free life insurance. You're going to need some, by tonight."

That got us down to basics.

"What is it you wish to buy?"

"You, doctor. It's that simple."

There's an elementary technique in counterespionage, known as the turnaround. It wouldn't have worked out with Che Guevara, but this man looked right for it, which was why Latimer had gone for him even before Señora Isabella Luz de Vargas showed up on the screen. Dr. Ruiz-Martinez knew exactly what I had in mind by then. He didn't have to like it, but it was a reasonable proposition. I was offering protection and a fee, of sorts, if he'd agree to work for us.

A double agent has his problems staying healthy. Still, it must have seemed to him he didn't have much choice. He said: "You take a lot for granted, Mr. Harvester."

"You don't believe that, doctor."

"Are you telling me that you are of the CIA, and the police have been informed about tomorrow's—schedule of events?"

"Oh, that," I said. "We've known about that for six weeks. You're going to turn that off, of course. The warning code is *calderón.*"

It shouldn't have surprised him, but he winced and cursed me anyway. His English ripened into weary pathos. "Have you no eyes, no shame? My country suffers. It needs surgery."

"I wouldn't know, doctor. It doesn't need the Russians, or Fidel. It doesn't need a bunch of discontented officers and politicians who haven't made the grade. Shall we get on the phone and save the firing squad a lot of work?"

He asked me slyly whom I wanted him to call. When I produced the list he glanced at it and shuddered. Then he pulled the phone across the desk. I told him not to get involved in explanations, warned him that my Spanish was as good as his, and prodded him along. But it takes time to complete forty-six connections, many of them on long distance, even if you're only trying to identify your party and communicate a single pregnant word to him. You get a lot of busy signals and wrong numbers, and a lot of wives who can't be sure just when their husbands will be home. We were still at it by eleven, long after I'd called the embassy and taken Latimer's man off the hook.

Then it occurred to me, belatedly, that there were two more names. They were, of course, the first two I should have attended to. But all of us are capable of folly, or stupidity, or mental block, as the case may be. "Catch Robles and Ortega while you're at it, doctor, will you please?"

He stared at me, a complicated stare, part stricken, part defiant. He, too, had forgotten, so to speak. He dialed rapidly and listened to the ringing signal, disconnected, tried again, and shook his head. "It is too late."

"What do you mean, too late? Where are they?"

"I don't know, sir. Major Robles carries the responsibility for the elimination of General Vargas *y su señora.* Captain Rafael Ortega is to execute it and report to me. But none of us was made acquainted with their plans."

*We can depend on Major Robles.* "Wrong," I said. "Call Julio Guzmán. He knows." The student activists had been the last ones on my list because they were the least important. My reluctant helper was already dialing and listening, biting his lips. I noticed with considerable irritation that I was perspiring, which was most unusual for me without exercise.

"There is no answer. I am sorry."

"Call the Bar Café Mercedes," I said harshly, throwing him the phone book. He complied, got through, was told that Julio Guzmán had not come in. I took the phone away from him and rang the private number of her ladyship at Casa Rosaleda, let it ring twice, changed my mind, and banged down the receiver. "There's still time, I'll go myself. Complete the list, please, doctor. Then you'll have to get out of the country like the others, until this blows over. Tell 'em you discovered that your office had been bugged, which happens to be true. Report to me by mail at Postbox 400, London West One."

He had that enigmatic stare for me again. "What if my memory should fail me, sir?"

"I'd move to Cuba or to China in that case, if I were you."

He nodded, sadly, as if he could see my point, and started dialing. I walked out of his office, sprinted down two flights of stairs into the lobby of the Bolivar Hotel, and lost ten minutes like so many hours hunting for a taxi in the rain. It was already close to midnight when the driver pulled up at the gate and eyed me in his rear view mirror. "Here it will be necessary for you to descend, señor, and push the button."

This was set in a white metal box under a spotlight mounted on the gate itself. Both wall and gate looked duly formidable; it would take heavy equipment to contend with them. I got out in the rain and pushed the button, activating a whole bank of floodlights and a slide in the white box that bared the lens of the closed-circuit camera. A grille-protected speaker cleared its throat and asked my name. When I supplied it there was a brief silence, then: *"Lo siento mucho, señor,* you are not expected."

That would be the adjutant on duty. "This is urgent business, and highly confidential," I said. "Please check with Doña Isabella. She will authorize you to admit me."

"She is entertaining guests, señor, and cannot be disturbed. You will be good enough to telephone for an appointment in the morning."

With a click the bank of floods dimmed out. I turned back to my driver, paid him off, and sent him on his way. A witness to my further conversation with the adjutant I didn't need.

The situation was a little delicate. A German or a Frenchman, even an Italian, would have listened to me with the possibility in mind of changing his decision. But the Spanish temperament, admirable otherwise, doesn't accommodate itself to flexibility. The adjutant would be inclined not to believe a word I said.

I was still wasting an allotted sixty seconds' mental concentration on the problem when a silver blue Ferrari growled out of the traffic on the avenue and screamed down to a stop beside me with its headlights glaring at the gate. The driver did not even see me. He burst from the car, stabbed at the button, stood under the lights, and showed himself as Julio Guzmán wearing a dinner jacket, getting wet. But he was recognized: the floods clicked off, the electronic gate hummed open. He flung himself back behind the wheel, and had the car in gear and rolling before he became aware of me sitting beside him with the little Mauser pistol in my lap.

He hit the brakes so hard he would have pitched me through the windshield if I hadn't braced myself for that contingency. He even tried to take the gun away from me. I had to force him back against the headrest with a forearm crushing in his Adam's apple. *"Un momento, niño!* I have news for you."  But he continued clawing at me, gasping for breath until the code got through to him. "It's *calderón,* Guzmán! You understand me? *Calderón!* Where is Captain Ortega? We must stop him!"

"You are not Mexican." He actually sounded like a child.

*"Where is Ortega?"*

I'd released him, and he slumped over the wheel, groaning, debilitated by frustration and bewilderment. "He . . . is here. He will not act until I join him. Who has authorized the cancellation code?"

"Ruiz-Martinez, *niño.* Let us find Ortega."

Shakily, he managed to restart his engine and to put the big Ferrari back in gear. The driveway wandered through severely landscaped grounds, then passed the formal rose bower that gave the place its name. Only two other vehicles were in the parking plaza, one of them a Daimler limousine, the other a plain khaki Ford with military markings. Lights blazed on the ground floor through eight huge french windows curtained in damask. The double row of coach lamps on the porch steps lent an almost festive air. I'd slipped the Mauser back into the pocket of my dripping raincoat, following the kid up to the massive wrought-iron and plate glass front door, which he opened with an easy familiarity, leaning his weight on it. A vestibule paved in Carrara marble, decorated with Italian antiques, confronted us. The anteroom immediately to our left must have been large, but it looked inconsiderable by comparison. It had been furnished with austerity and in a regimental manner with crossed swords and standards on the wall, and battle paintings, and with a big table covered in green baize that bore a television monitor and a control panel. Behind this, from a swivel chair, rose a tall man in his late thirties who wore a ceremonial uniform flashing with silver fourragères.

His rank insignia were unfamiliar to me, and there was no time to study them. He recognized me from the monitor, of course; I had anticipated that, and I was ready with my little speech. But it was not the right one. I was tired, and slow, and I had failed to grasp the obvious. Major Robles, she had told me, was a war ministry officer in charge of personnel assignment. He could place disgruntled juniors by the score in staff positions with the power tap conveniently near at hand. He also could replace the trusted ADC to an ex-president, for one night, on some plausible excuse, and keep himself out of the way.

Captain Rafael Ortega took one look at me and at the cheerless and bedraggled youth accompanying me. His reflexes were too fast for his own good; I found out later that he was on the Olympic team, both as a horseman and a fencer. He attempted the impossible, which was to get his hands on the machine pistol racked up under the table out of sight and cover me with it before my own reflexes pulled the trigger in my pocket. *"Calderón, you idiot,"* I said, about a second and a half too late. The insult was intended to apply to both of us.

He stared at me in utter disbelief, and at his own right arm in which my bullet had smashed through the artery and probably through half the motor nerves. He looked like a good man, accustomed to the best in life, and certainly accustomed to his body functioning efficiently, responsive to his bidding. I felt sorry as all hell for him, and for myself. There wasn't one damn thing that I could do for him at this point. If he kept his mouth shut I could save the boy, but that was all.

"Put on a tourniquet," I said.

The kid yanked out a handkerchief, snatched up a ruler from the table. He'd been briefly paralyzed, then jolted into action. Evidently he'd had training in first aid; he got Ortega's pulsing spout of blood under control immediately. His patient leaned against the wall, below the crossed Colombian and presidential flags, and watched him at his work. By then both of them were expressionless, almost detached.

Behind me, in the doorway to the vestibule, someone demanded irritably: "What has happened here, señores?"

I swung around, keeping both hands in view. This proved to be a sound idea, because Jacinto had another machine pistol on me with the trigger slack already taken up, his finger knuckles gleaming white. The man beside him actually looked a little like De Gaulle. But the resemblance was just facial—he was not particularly tall, and was rather stocky. He wore dinner clothes as if he lived in them. His tan had that distinctive healthy glow; he might be seventy, but he was evidently durable.

Behind him in the vestibule Señora Doña Isabella Luz de Vargas, pale as milk, stood with her guests. They were, as far as I could make out at a glance, just two more people: elderly, aristocratic, troubled but composed. "It would be pleasant to assure your excellency that this was an accident," I said.

"No doubt it would, señor. For you." He wasn't the least little bit amused with me. I was a dangerous intruder who'd shot up one of his officers, in gangster style, my coat stinking of scorched wet gabardine. The only thing that had to puzzle him would be the presence of the kid. "What is the purpose of your visit, Julio?" he carelessly inquired.

I said: "Señor Guzmán was kind enough to drive me here, and to secure admission for me at the gate."

That didn't bowl him over, but it sounded true if inexplicable. It meant that there was something more to this. Jacinto's trigger finger had relaxed, I noticed, and his eyes came slightly out of focus in a sidelong glance at his employer's wife. She noticed it, but she was forced to speak up anyway, of course. "This is the gentleman I've mentioned meeting at the club, Francisco," she said formally. "His name, you may recall, is Stephen Harvester. General Vargas, Señor and Señora Escobar."

Her guests murmured polite acknowledgments. Her husband's stare at me changed character, although not necessarily increasing its benevolence, so far as I could tell. "Why did you shoot?" he asked me bluntly.

"General, if I had not, both you and Doña Isabella would have died. Most probably within ten seconds."

"Please explain."

"Captain Ortega has a private grievance," I said carefully. "He planned to have himself assigned here for one night. This afternoon he boasted to a woman of these plans. She happens to be one of our informants."

Silence clogged the room. None of us moved an inch except the boy, and he only to readjust the tourniquet. At last, Vargas inquired: "You are of the United States intelligence, señor?" I just stared back at him, not answering him. "Can you prove this accusation?"

"Yes, your excellency. If I have to."

Vargas took his eyes off me, glanced at the automatic weapon on the floor. "Captain Ortega?"

The big man in bloodstained ceremonials said coldly: "He is right, the Yanqui."

Vargas sighed and held his hand out to me. "Let me have your gun, please, Señor Harvester," he said. He took the little Mauser I'd removed from Dr. Juan Ruiz-Martinez's desk drawer and gave it to Jacinto. Then he nodded at the self-confessed assassin. "Take him out," he ordered wearily.

At the hotel I walked my room for a long time. It was a good-sized room; it gave me eighteen paces straight across. There was a bottle of Black Label on the dresser, with a siphon and an ice bucket from room service to keep it company. As we all know, whisky is a depressant and should be avoided under stress, but somehow you don't think of that. You think of other things, such as the distant crack of a small pistol, and the whimper of distress beside you from the long-haired man-child fumbling with his starter key and suddenly collapsing on the wheel. No, Julio, there is no Santa Claus. The Rafael Ortegas of this world are not allowed to try again. They commit suicide.

If you must be a revolutionary, copy Major Robles. Then you won't need anyone like me to save your skin for you.

That had got through to him. He'd covered the ten miles or so back to the Tequendama in about six minutes. The Ferrari 365GT goes supersonic on you, if you let it. In Colombia, it'll cost your parents about ninety thousand dollars, duty paid.

The phone started to ring when I unlocked the door.

"I must speak with you."

"Sorry. My plane's at nine A.M."

"I mean right now. I'm coming over."

"Have you lost your mind?"

"Expect me, please." She had hung up on me again.

It turned out that her version of right now was something like an hour and a half. I walked my eighteen paces, wearing furrows in the rug, and used up half a bottle of depressant without notable effect. When she came in without so much as bothering to knock I happened to be in the bathroom. She could see and hear me, but she made no comment or excuse; she fixed herself a drink and sat down on the bed with it. She'd changed from dinner dress into gray jersey slacks with matching tunic and rebozo. Her umbrella dangled from the chair back, dripping on my furrowed wall-to-wall.

I watched her from the bathroom doorway for a while. At last I said: "Three guesses. One, he was your lover, and you're here to settle my account."

"Have you been drinking?"

"Yes, of course. Two, you've grown tired of living. Since we hate each other, it occurred to you to take me with you where you're going. Three, you do this all the time. Your husband doesn't care."

She glanced at me over her shoulder. "Do you have a cigarette? I came away without my purse." I found her one and struck a match for her. She took it from my slightly shaky fingers, used it, blew it out, and tossed it in a corner. "My husband knows I'm here. He often has suggested this. He has been impotent for many years."

"He has suggested it? You mean like whisky, for medicinal purposes?"

"That is his thought."

I made a sound that may have been identifiable as laughter. "Considerate of him. Has it been beneficial to you, this medicine?"

"Do you believe I should have taken it?"

By then I had my back to her, making myself another drink. I needed to do something with my hands to keep from hitting her. "Well, haven't you?"

"Of course not."

In the dresser mirror she looked ice-cream cool. "About a week ago," I said, "you heard from Julio Guzmán about this little fracas that was in the works. You came to us instead of to your husband. You demanded our protection of the boy."

"I had more confidence in you than in our own security organization. I was right."

"You told Wayne Latimer a different story."

"Did I?"

"Oh, come on. The Guzmán kid has no experience, but he's a radical, no question about that. Why should you worry about him? They would've packed him off to jail for a few months, or put him in a sanatorium. His family . . ."

"My husband would have had him killed."

"Why?"

"He'd have been convinced, as you are, that there was something between us. That would have been unacceptable to him. Please, let me show you." She extended her left hand; I turned back from the mirror to inspect it. It was small, and beautifully kept, but there were four small scars a fraction of an inch apart, about an inch above the wrist. "Three years ago a young French diplomat paid me a great deal of attention. I was—interested, but of course I knew that nothing could be done about it. I did not encourage him. But he was stubborn, and perhaps a little obvious, and when my husband spoke to him one evening at a small dinner party there was trouble. I'd had one glass of champagne too many and tried foolishly to intervene. I wound up with a fork driven into my hand, as a reminder of whose property I was. *He* had a hunting accident. Within two weeks."

"Fatal?"

"Oh yes. What you don't understand is that I'm not supposed to get *involved.*"

She rose and put her empty glass down on the dresser, facing me. I said contemptuously, "And you've never taken medicine before."

"No, and I never shall."

Green lilac eyes reached up to mine, grew wider, deeper, drawing me into them, drowning me. I came up shuddering for air and realized that we'd been kissing for a long time, clinging to each other, mouths locked hard together and already thoroughly explored, but drinking from each other thirstily. Emotional inversion can be gradual, but when it is explosive it'll blow your mind. I was so much in love with her and wanted her so badly, I felt stupid, clumsy, nauseated, ill, and she herself seemed not much better off. She choked for breath, tearing herself away from me. *"Tell me you love me! Please!"*

"I love you. I don't know what's happened to us, but I. . . ."

"Say 'I love you, Lita.' Call me by my name."

"Lita. I love you, Lita."

"Prove it to me!" She was trying to undress, and sobbing with frustration at a faulty zipper. When it broke she ripped it out and burst out into laughter. "I can't go back like this. You're stuck with me."

I slapped her, spinning her around. She fell across the bed, abandoning herself to me, as I stood over her, biting my tongue in vain—the words forced themselves through somehow. "You *didn't* sleep with Julio Guzmán?"

"No! Please *believe* in me!"

We were so good together it was frightening. She gave me back my youth, and I released in her the tensions that had built up through twelve years of unsuccessful marriage. But there was more, of course: a genuine ardor for each other that exceeded greatly the emotional involvement she had undertaken to deny herself. "Doesn't your husband realize . . . ?"

"No, no, my darling. Can't you see you're perfect, from his point of view? A Yanqui working for a living. Obviously you are unaccomplished and uncultured, and you have no money."

"Sure I do. I'm worth over a hundred thousand dollars. I've got tax problems."

"Please don't be silly. You're in the same category as Colombian peasants and Italian gigolos. I've been encouraged to experiment with both, at one time and another. Which reminds me, I'm supposed to pay you."

"Beautiful! How much?"

"Whatever we negotiate . . . no, not like that. I'm serious, you'll have to take a check and cash it, you can give the money to a home for wayward girls or something but it's terribly important that Francisco never suspects . . . oh! Oh marvelous! Oh utterly supremely marvelous. Tell me again now! Say my name!"

I said her name; she had not yet called me by mine. She left at five A.M., with a rebozo as a belt to hide the broken zipper. From my window I could watch the general's Silver Cloud drive off with her along Carrera Diez.

Her thousand dollar check I cashed that afternoon, at the Miami branch of the Chase National, and put my own check in the mail to the Red Cross. I visited Wayne Latimer, who wasn't very interested; they had done a good deal more repair work on him than he had been looking for. Then I reported to New York by phone and reconfirmed my two weeks' leave.

She called me at the Fountainbleau that evening, as arranged. The next day I flew to Jamaica, found a cottage at the Tower Isle, and met her plane at four. She'd carried off her end of it. Permission for a further course of treatment had been granted. But she'd been assigned a retinue: Jacinto Gomez and his wife. For her protection and for our convenience.

It meant we had to set a constant watch over ourselves. There is a quite considerable difference between the public conversation and behavior of lovers and those of a lady with her chartered fancy man.

Wayne Latimer recovered and was transferred to Manila. Dr. Juan Ruiz-Martinez disappeared from sight. No mail from him came to my London postbox. I was not especially surprised. You play the averages in this game.

# BLIND TRUST

*Gary Alexander*

Y ou," SAID a woman with two cameras. "You're that upside down
guy!"

Luis Balam smiled and said, "He was Maya, I am Maya."

"Doesn't the blood rush to your head?" someone else said.

After the laughter, Luis explained the "upside down guy," a wall stucco
of an ornately-dressed figure who seemed to be standing on his head. "He
is guarding the doorway of his namesake, the Temple of the Descending
God. Or the Bee God or the Diving God, some historians say. Nobody will
be certain until the glyphs are completely translated. This deity is commonly
represented in ruins throughout the Yucatan."

The woman with two cameras snapped Luis's picture. Through her view-
finder she saw a thirty-seven-year-old Yucatec Maya of average height: five
feet three. She saw a round face, prominent cheekbones, an aquiline nose,
and the almond eyes brought across the Bering landbridge millennia ago.
She saw a deceptive musculature, she saw stockiness without fat.

Luis Balam was short but not small. Some had learned that distinction to
their regret while Luis was with the police. Before the trouble, before he
was forced out.

"The hieroglyphics are being translated, aren't they?"

"More every day," Luis said, leading his group to the finale, the largest
structure at Tulum—El Castillo, the castle. "Still, only a fraction is known."

"Do you?"

"I speak Maya," Luis said. "I cannot read it. When the Spaniards came, they destroyed our writings. Only three codices survived. They are in European museums. Many times I have asked these walls to talk to me."

Luis took his tourists up El Castillo's steps. They caught their collective breath while looking out at the Caribbean. The midday sun was lost above puffy clouds but not forgotten. Intense tropical rays cast the sea the hue of blue topaz.

He said, "Tulum is the largest fortified site on Mexico's Quintana Roo coast. Tulum means 'wall' in Maya. The wall behind us that we came through is up to eighteen feet high and twenty feet thick. The cliff El Castillo and we stand on is forty feet high."

"Tulum was a fort?"

"And a trading center."

"The Spaniards came to Tulum, didn't they?"

This was Luis's favorite part. "In 1511 a Spanish ship hit the reef and sank. Most survivors were sacrificed or died of disease. One Spaniard married a Maya woman, fathered three children, and commanded Maya troops who drove off the next Spanish foray in 1517. Hernán Cortez, no fool, sailed north and took on the Aztecs instead."

"Human sacrifice," a man said. "You Mayans still do that?"

This group was pleasant and playful if not generous. With a straight face, Luis said, "Not regularly."

The laughter was hearty and just slightly nervous.

Outside the wall, in a seedy bazaar offering everything from T-shirts to postcards to ice cream, Luis recounted his money. Eight people, seven U.S. one-dollar bills. There was always a deadbeat in a crowd that size.

But Luis was not complaining. It was June, the beginning of summer. North Americans could stay home and lie on their own beaches and burn under their own sun. Many, many did. With the rabid competition amongst guides for those who came to Cancún, he had been fortunate to snag this cluster of eight. He conceded an edge, though, his resemblance to the "upside down guy." Most of the others were mestizo, mixed European and native ancestry. He could think of no other advantage a full-blooded Indian had over a mainstream Mexican.

"Excuse me. You got a minute?" said a jowly, florid man.

He was in his fifties. His wispy, straw-colored hair was slicked straight back. He had been in the group, studiously anonymous, staying in the rear as if shy, smoking cigarette after cigarette. "I have a minute."

The man extended a beefy, freckled hand. "Bud Lamm, Mr. Balam. I've got me one helluva problem, and I've been told you're the best."

Bud Lamm's stomach protruded as if he were concealing a helmet under the chartreuse pullover that complimented tan plaid shorts. The quarry of a Cancún shop catering to golfers, Luis guessed.

"The best at what?"

"Investigating and getting to the bottom of things around here. I also toured Tulum with you day before yesterday. Remember?"

Luis remembered. He was the sort who endured cultural enrichment on his wife's leash. "You were with a woman. She asked intelligent questions."

"Helen. She's my wife. This archaeology, that's her thing. That and birdwatching. Me, I came for the sun and the margaritas and the golf. We're from up by Chicago. We're renting a condo up the coast a ways, which is what I need to see you about. Yesterday, I was checking you out. Making snap decisions got me in this mess."

"Checking me out?"

Bud Lamm cocked his head, requesting privacy. They walked to the parking area. A line of tour buses howled at fast idle, to run air conditioners for absent passengers.

"You used to be a topnotch cop. That's what your lawyer buddy Ricardo Martinez said."

The engines were deafening, the air foul. Luis nodded an impatient yes.

"What I need is for you to find a guy who flimflammed me and get me my money back."

"Did you go to the police?"

Lamm smirked. "I went in that little station in Tulum City. Three cops were sitting around playing with their handcuffs. They didn't speak English. I got the hell out of there."

Probably a wise retreat, Luis thought. "Swindled by whom, when, and for what?"

"Two days ago. This condo we're in, it's a beauty, right on the beach. The whole building's for sale. This salesman was by with a couple who loved it, but they couldn't agree on price. I bought it out from under them, on the spot. I'm close to retirement. I'd been looking to invest. I should of known better. I'm service manager at a car dealership. I ought to know a phony pitch by now."

"How much money?"

"Sixty grand."

Luis had to think a moment. Sixty thousand pesos was only twenty dollars. "Sixty thousand U.S.?"

Bud Lamm looked at his feet, then said, "Yeah, cashed in my pension fund. Thought I'd surprise Helen."

"Does she know?"

"God, no!"

"How did you meet Martinez?"

"I was up in Cancún City, kind of crying in my beer in this bar. His office is up above it. Funny place for a law office. Will you help me?"

"I'll talk to Martinez," Luis said noncommittally.

"I owe you a buck," Bud Lamm said. "For the tour. Didn't mean to stiff you but, well, finances are tight. You can tack it on your bill."

Eight kilometers north on the coastal highway was BLACK CORAL. It shared its generic name with others along Highway 307. This "black coral" was a large tent, a hand-lettered sign, and, inside, tables of hematite, silver, lapis, and, yes, black coral jewelry. Luis Balam was the proprietor.

Business was slow. Tour buses drove the local economy. Luis and fellow merchants bribed drivers to stop. But in the off season buses were scarce. Between his shop and Tulum, Luis was hanging on by his fingernails until winter. Investigative work for Ricky Martinez helped some, although his assignments were often like rainbows, dazzling but ethereal.

Luis's adolescent daughters, Esther and Rosa, were minding the store. They and his parents ran it while Luis was gone. One bus, they reported. Two private cars. A hitchhiking American hippie who wanted to use the telephone and bathroom they didn't have. Three sales altogether.

Luis told them about Bud Lamm.

"How much is sixty thousand dollars?" Esther asked, wide-eyed. She was eighteen, of his first wife who left him when he first went to Cancún to work.

"I can't imagine," said Luis, who could not.

"Then it isn't real," Esther said.

"Mr. Martinez—" Rosa hesitated, searching for a word "—magnifies everything, Father."

"He does," Luis conceded to his sixteen-year-old, child of his second wife, who died of a fever during his second and last Cancún employment. "Should I or shouldn't I?"

"Talk to him as you promised," Esther said. "After you eat."

Strengthened by warm tortillas and a warmer bottle of Leon beer, Luis headed northward in a VW Golf he had bought as surplus from a Cancún Airport rental agency. Its running gear was shell-shocked from potholed roads, its engine malnourished by eighty-one-octane gas. The one hundred fifteen kilometer trip to Cancún City was always problematical, not to mention the eight kilometers of dust and ruts traveled daily between BLACK CORAL and Luis's village. He had managed to keep his car running with bicycle tools and mechanical intuition. Soon he would need magic.

He worried about his girls. Was haggling with tourists over the price of beads their ultimate destiny? Perhaps. They could clean toilets at Cancún hotels. They could stay in the village, marry farmers, and become baby machines. There was much more a Maya could not do than do. Maybe, just maybe, this time he could get his hands around Ricky's rainbow.

He passed the airport and entered Cancún City, old Mexico, circa 1977. When Mexico City began to develop Cancún Island from nothing in the early 1970's as a tourist mecca, the city became its bedroom and market. Luis had as a teenager left his village to work as a construction laborer on both.

Downtown Cancún's broad avenues were named for the Yucatan's grandest ancient cities: Tulum, Coba, Uxmal, Bonampak. Ricardo Martinez Rodriguez's law office was located in a cement building blocks from any reference to glorious history. Low overhead was an advantage, Martinez was given to point out. As was the proximity of doctors willing to validate Ricky's calamitous diagnoses of his injured clients.

Castanets and guitars on the bar's jukebox serenaded. Luis walked upstairs and found Ricky available. His office smelled vaguely of plastic.

"Luis, Bud Lamm saw you, yes?"

A year ago, Luis Balam had seen an old North American television show. It was called *I Love Lucy*. Shave Ricardo Martinez Rodriguez's pencil mustache and he could be the twin of Ricky Ricardo, the Cuban bandleader. Ricardo had been Ricky to Luis ever since, like it or not. "Yes."

Martinez clapped his hands. "Wonderful! Sixty thousand Yankee dollars. Do you know how much money that is, Luis?"

"No."

"Me neither, but we're rich. If we find it. If *you* find it."

"The money belongs to the Lamms," Luis reminded him.

"Yes, yes, I meant a percentage. We'll be rich on a percentage."

"What percentage?"

"To be negotiated. You have to find the money." Martinez gave Luis a sheaf of documents. "Don't bother to read the papers. They appear legal. Boilerplate real estate forms completed very professionally. They're absolutely bogus. Since foreigners have been permitted to own beach property in Mexico through a trust setup, the land and home business has been crazy. What a trust. In Lamm's case, blind trust, I think."

"Did you recognize Lamm's description of the salesman?"

"No. And that's your department."

Luis paused, thinking.

"Please," Martinez said. "Sixty thousand dollars."

"Real estate salesmen are more common these days than peddlers selling junk silver out of valises," Luis said. "The beaches are black with time-share condo sellers. Like locusts."

"Don't be melodramatic, Luis. You can do it."

Music began to waft upward.

" 'La Bamba?' "

"A mariachi trio. The tourists all request 'La Bamba.' I'm so sick of it. The new carpet muffles it some. Please, Luis. You can call me Ricky forever."

The plastic odor, the carpet. "All right, Ricky."

"Good, Luis, good. Locate the scoundrel. Lamm is broke. He can't pay me until you do."

Lamm's condo was halfway between Ricky's office and BLACK CORAL. A dirt road had been cut from the highway to the sea, through half a kilometer of scrub jungle. Houses and multiplexes Luis had never before seen lined this stretch of beach. Before long, he thought sadly, the beach from Cancún to Belize will be a necklace of vacation homes.

There were four units in Lamm's building, two up and two down. It was stucco, painted flamingo, in arched, pillared Colonial Hacienda style. Three to four years old, Luis gauged, and aging fast, subtly crumbling and mildewing, victim of tropical humidity and substandard construction. Staked on the lawn was a Paradise Investment Properties Associates (PIPA) "For Sale" sign.

Lamm was waiting in a doorway, glass in hand. "Mr. Balam. It's cocktail hour. Can I fix you one? Boy, it's swell you're taking the case."

Luis declined a drink and said, "No promises."

Lamm shrugged, said fair enough, and led him through the unit and out the sliders to a tiled verandah facing the Caribbean. "Pretty nice, huh? Except for doors that stick and a ceiling fan about to fall down, it's in perfect shape."

"What happened?"

"Like I said, this salesman came around with a young couple, showing the units. The place is owned by a guy in Mexico City. He's trying to sell, the whole shebang or piecemeal, either way."

"Through Paradise Investment Properties Associates?"

"Yeah. They got an office in Cancún. A legit outfit. The couple were looking around, real excited, and the salesman and me got to talking. He said they wanted it bad and the owner was in a squeeze and wanted to sell bad, but the couple probably couldn't swing it. His name was Ralph Taggert, which was on the Paradise Investment business card he gave me."

"Does Paradise—"

"First thing I checked. They never heard of any Taggert or anybody who looks like him. Anyway, we're talking and he's saying that the owner's asking seventy-five grand for the two lower units, seventy for the uppers. That's two ninety, too rich for my blood. But he says the seller is flexible. The couple comes back and they talk and the salesman takes me aside and says maybe they'll get the money from her parents, but they're trying to lowball the deal. I ask how much. He says two fifty. Before they leave, I say come back if it falls through. Meanwhile, I'm figuring what we can make, living in one and time-sharing the rest. Look."

Lamm handed Luis a bar napkin with numbers scribbled on it. Printed in a corner was a grinning Mexican wearing a sombrero, shaking maracas. The figures made no sense to Luis. He handed the napkin back and asked, "What did Taggert look like?"

"Brown hair, glasses, thirty-five, medium height and weight. An average Joe."

"And his clients?"

"Is that important?"

Luis shrugged.

Lamm lighted a cigarette and said, "They were your typical yuppies. Blond. Tanning parlor tans. The gal, her T-shirt had a toucan on it."

"Taggert returned?"

"An hour later, alone. The yuppie gal called her daddy, but couldn't swing a loan. I offered two hundred and forty thousand. It just sort of came out. Taggert acted like he was in pain, like I was taking advantage of him, but said his seller was desperate and that he was authorized to accept that low a price if I put a hefty chunk down."

"Sixty thousand U.S. dollars," Luis said.

"Twenty-five percent. In cash. Cash was the clincher." Lamm rubbed thumb against fingers. "Money talks. So I thought. Talked me into the biggest jam of my life. We've been to Bermuda, the Bahamas, and Acapulco. The Yucatan beats them hands down. To retire here—"

A short elderly woman entered the verandah, limping on a brass-handled cane. She was festooned with binoculars, canteen, and knapsack. Smelling of bug repellent and sunscreen, Helen Lamm was a sprightly gray and pink elf. Luis Balam was immediately charmed by her.

Lamm gestured to her cane. "One of my old putters. She sprained an ankle yesterday. Helen won't be happy till she's scaled all those pyramids of yours."

Helen touched Bud's cigarette hand with the putter-cane. "This from a man who smokes three packs of coffin nails a day and compares eighteen holes of golf in an electric cart to a marathon. I climbed Coba's biggest today. Twelve stories. On account of the gimpy ankle it took time, but it was worth it."

They were teasing each other, Luis knew, but their words were tart. "I must go."

Helen smiled and shook his hand. Bud walked him to his car. "You used to be a cop, Martinez said. How come you're not now?"

Luis supposed that Lamm was entitled to a summary. "I went to Cancún to work construction. To escape the village and the cornfields. Back and forth I went. I made money, learned Spanish, then English, but had family problems. I later joined the police. A rich man's son was drunk and speeding in a sports car on the highway. He hit a bicycle and kept going. A Maya man, wife, and child were killed. I investigated and arrested the boy. Money changed hands. The report was altered to show a phantom driver, case closed. He was released. I persisted. I had witnesses, signed statements, and pictures of the car. I made too much noise. He was convicted and jailed. I was fired for unrelated infractions that were manufactured."

"An honest Mexican cop," Lamm said. "You were a rarity."

"I wasn't an honest cop," Luis said. "Not by your standards. Police are paid badly. They have to take small gratuities to feed their families. No amount of money can condone killing."

"I don't blame you, you being Indian, too."

"Maya."

"That's what I said."

"You said Indian," Luis said. "That is like me calling you gringo. I am Maya."

"Sorry," Lamm said, raising hands in mock surrender. "A final question before I get in any more trouble. What's Balam mean? It don't sound Spanish."

"Balam is jaguar in Maya."

Bud Lamm gulped his drink, shivered, and said, "Jaguar. I can use one."

Luis returned to Cancún City, reciting a prayer to any saint specializing in the longevity of Volkswagens. On a broad avenue of government buildings was the Quintana Roo State Judicial Police and Inspector Hector Salgado Reyes.

Salgado was dressed like Luis, in slacks, white shirt, and sandals. He eschewed the military uniform favored by his peers. Hector was roly-poly and nearly bald. Epaulets and khaki would have made him resemble a character in an operetta.

Hector was Luis's mentor. During the scandal, he had tried to save his favorite young officer from Mexico City clout and his own zeal. He, of course, could not. Hector's stand was unpopular. He barely saved his own career.

Luis related his story.

Hector was mildly sympathetic. "Poor stupid man. His wife will kill him."

"Not if we recover the sixty thousand dollars."

"Ricky Martinez and his golden clients," Hector said, clucking his tongue. "Ricky would buy a sweepstakes ticket and be thunderously disappointed if he didn't win. Ricky has no grasp on reality."

"I realize Cancún has no shortage of con men, Hector, but have you received other complaints fitting this pattern?"

"Not of this magnitude. Sixty thousand." Hector whistled. "This could be his first and last job, you know. He accepts his wonderful fortune as an omen, a message from God that he retire from crime and spend it. No. Rental deposits hustled by bogus managers, five hundred, a thousand, that is the usual score."

"I wonder if our Ralph Taggert has flown out already."

"I would," Hector said, rocking thoughtfully in his chair. "Then again, I might not. I might worry."

"Why?"

"You fly home. Whichever city you fly to, you submit to U.S.A. Customs. They don't like the shape of your nose, they search your luggage. They discover the sixty thousand. What do they think?"

"Drug money," Luis said.

"Exactly. You have nothing to do with drugs, but you raise suspicions. They hold onto you and make inquiries."

"Taggert waits in hiding or he converts the money."

"Yes," Hector said, raising a stubby finger. "Remember this, Luis. Dollars flow into Cancún. They do not flow out. That is an unnatural act."

Cancún Island, the hotel zone, is a 7-shaped, fourteen-mile strip of luxury hotels, fine restaurants, a lagoon, and beaches with sand that could be mistaken for granulated sugar. In twenty years Cancún has gone from scrub brush to a sun-and-fun mecca that hosts a million visitors annually.

It got me out of the cornfields, Luis thought yet again as he cruised along Kukulkan Boulevard, the narrow island's single street. Good or bad? he debated for the thousandth time, coming to the same nebulous conclusion.

Paradise Investment Properties Associates rented space in a newer hotel toward the southerly, least developed portion of the island. Luis didn't recall seeing it before. They were springing up like weeds. The architecture was familiar, though: a latter-day Maya pyramid of glass and view decks.

Straight through the lobby was a disco boasting the latest electronic glitz, to the right a coffee shop serving tacos made with American cheese and iceberg lettuce, to the left an arcade of shops and realty offices. Luis, guided by a neon *PIPA,* asked a lovely, green-eyed mestiza receptionist to see the boss. She said that he was unavailable indefinitely. Luis sat on a sofa and said, fine, I'll wait indefinitely. The receptionist went behind a partition. Luis heard whispering, including "Indian."

A man of approximately forty came out with the pouting receptionist. He had Luis's muscular build but was six inches taller. Luis surmised that his hairy arms and hands displayed more gold—watch, bracelet, several rings—than every piece at BLACK CORAL combined.

"Chester Cross," he said. "Call me Chet. I'm the branch manager. Hortencia says you were gonna camp out."

The levity was accompanied by a quick smile, but not in Call-Me-Chet's ice-blue eyes.

"I'd like to ask you a few questions."

"I didn't peg you as a prospect. No offense."

"Bud Lamm."

"C'mon back."

At his desk, Cross said, "I didn't know Lamm from Adam until he came in to see a salesman we don't have about a property this office didn't sell him. Needless to say, he came unglued."

"You don't know Ralph Taggert? He has business cards."

"Anybody can have them printed. Where do you fit in?"

Luis disregarded Cross's question and repeated Bud Lamm's description of Taggert.

"Sorry. He could be anybody. Listen, con artists make it tough. Creeps like that reflect on me. PIPA's situated up and down the Pacific Coast along the Mexican Riviera, and in any other resort town where you can walk across the main drag without tripping over a chicken. Also Hawaii and the Virgin Islands. I make good dough honestly. Gimme half a chance and I'll hand this Taggert clown his head."

Chester Call-Me-Chet Cross was too passionately outraged to be believed. Ralph Taggert had made a fortune in a short afternoon of deception. Chet Cross was a salesman, too; he should have been catatonic with envy.

Luis waited across the street, with plans to follow Cross. An hour later, a visibly unhappy Bud Lamm strode into the hotel. He had changed into a shirt the color of his condo. And now his face. Lamm left in ten minutes, no less agitated. Chet Cross departed ten minutes later.

Luis followed him out of Cancún, south along the highway to a resort. It had a marina catering to fishermen seeking marlin and sailfish. Cross went into the bar and sat with Bud Lamm. Luis was willing to observe discreetly, but Lamm began shouting and jabbing a finger at Cross, who took Lamm by the wrist.

Luis entered, took them each by a wrist, and said, smiling, "Smile, gentlemen, like you're having fun. You're attracting attention."

Cross and Lamm smiled, gritting their teeth. Luis wrenched their arms apart and sat down.

"Nice grip," Cross said.

"That son of a bitch," Lamm said. "I want my money!"

"Slow learner," Cross said to Luis, shaking his head. "I've told him fifty times, I don't know any Taggert and would string him up by the thumbs if I did. I invited him here to get him out of the office, he was raising so much hell."

"You ought to know Taggert," Lamm said, then to Luis, "Helen and I had a blowup after you were there. She knew I'd brought the money. She knew it was gone. She packs and unpacks us. Guess I didn't hide it too good. I confessed the whole deal. Needless to say, she's steamed. She's getting up early tomorrow to go visit Xelha. I'm staying out of her hair till she hits the sack."

"Staying out of her hair and threatening me," Cross said.

"Wanna know why?" Lamm asked Luis.

"Oh, yes."

"This slick talker here, Helen ran into him while he was showing the condo, the morning before Taggert clipped me."

Cross spread his hands and raised his eyebrows. "Prospective clients wish to view a property. I show it. Is that a crime?"

"No crime except if you know Taggert, which I think you do. You show up at the condo. Then Taggert drops by."

"What's your point?" Cross asked him.

"My point is, it's a small world, but it ain't that small."

Luis refereed three rounds of beer, compliments of Cross. The men were surprisingly mellow drinkers. Luis encouraged them into their respective cars before they became traffic menaces. He drove to BLACK CORAL. The sun was setting, and Esther and Rosa were closing.

"I smell beer on you, Father," Rosa admonished.

"In the line of duty," Luis said. He explained.

"Do you think Cross was lying?" Esther asked.

"I don't know." Luis unfolded a military cot and slapped dust from the canvas. He slept at the shop during high season, pistol under his pillow, when there was too much merchandise to lug to the village. "I have to be at Xelha early," he explained.

"What can Mrs. Lamm tell you?" Rosa asked.

"I don't know."

"Ask everything that occurs to you, Father," Esther said. "She may be the only person involved who will speak the truth."

The Xelha (shell-HAH) ruins were ideal for tourists who merely wanted to say they had seen a Maya ruin. Located across Highway 307 from the immensely popular Xelha lagoon, the structures were modest, an isolated and easy walk on a jungle path. At the ruins was a small, brushy cenote—a sinkhole well. The Yucatan was a limestone shelf, flat as a tortilla, riverless and possessing few lakes. Cenotes were considered bodies of water and were sacred to Luis's ancestors.

Luis waved to the visitor center's caretakers. They had soft drinks and souvenirs, but no customers. Xelha, lacking towering pyramids, had once been described to Luis as "not very sexy."

Helen Lamm was aiming binoculars into a copse of trees. She heard Luis's footfalls, lowered her glasses, and said, "Mr. Balam, your homeland is a birder's dream. This morning I've already seen a tody-bill, three species of flycatcher, and a bananaquit."

Luis smiled.

"Our genial and knowledgeable Tulum guide, you aren't a coincidence today either, are you?"

Luis shook his head no.

"I sensed Bud had involved you. We had words. He came home last night and cried. He's a big, strong man. I'd never seen him cry in forty years of marriage." Helen limped by Luis toward the entrance, unaided by the putter-cane, and continued, "Bud's a good man and he isn't stupid. He's punched a time clock all his life. He hoped to finally make a special splash for our retirement. I appreciate anything you and your attorney friend can do to recover our money."

"Your husband is convinced that Cross and Taggert are conspiring."

"I couldn't say. I never met Mr. Taggert."

"You met Cross."

"I did. He showed the condominium to some people. Bud was playing golf."

"What did you and Cross discuss?"

"Not a lot," Helen said. "It's funny, you know. I would have sworn he'd make the sale."

"Why?"

"His clients were an attractive young couple who were positively giddy about it. Evidently they didn't smell the mildew. As they scampered through the rooms like children, Mr. Cross remarked to me how he hoped they could qualify financially, they loved it so, and it was such a bargain. Well, in the final analysis, they couldn't swing it. They were *so* disappointed."

"What did the couple look like?"

"The picture of health. They obviously exercised and ate right. Mr. Bud Lamm could learn a lesson from that pair."

"How were they dressed?"

"Normal for Cancún and the Caribbean. Beach casual. Between you and me and the gatepost, Mr. Balam, he was a cutie. He wore a tank top. Nice skin tone. The young lady, a gorgeous toucan was printed on her T-shirt."

"Did you exchange names?"

"No, but when I spotted that toucan, I asked if she liked birds. She loves them. She has parakeets and finches at home, and she was worried whether their housesitter was caring for them properly. Oh my."

Helen was looking above and behind Luis. He turned and saw a flock of black vultures circling.

"What could be enticing them?"

"The jungle," Luis said. "It always has what they want."

Luis picked up Ricky Martinez as persuasion ammunition and went to Hector Salgado.

"Luis, let me understand," Hector said wearily. "I am to don my uniform and we as a threesome are to intimidate Chester Cross?"

"And scare him witless!" Ricky said, shaking a fist.

"I perceive my role," said a glaring Hector, who did not especially like lawyers.

"I don't believe he will reveal the identities of that couple unless he is frightened," Luis said. "The couple can lead us to Taggert."

"Luis, do I have to put on the uniform?"

"Hector," Luis said, "you are a kind and reasonably honest man, but in khaki and epaulets you are a stereotype of corruption, torture, and filthy Mexican jails."

Hector Salgado Reyes rose, smiled, unbuttoned a shirt button, and said, "Yes, I am, aren't I?"

On the drive to Paradise Investment Properties Associates, Ricky proposed that they stop and buy Hector a riding crop, as an added dash of implied cruelty. Luis and Hector in chorus told Ricky not to push it.

Hortencia was respectful and immediately ushered them in to Chet Cross, who provided scant resistance.

"Salting the mine, what's wrong with that? Their excitement is infectious. They get the renters enthused. They're possibly motivated to make the best investment decision of their lives."

"A valuable public service is performed," Hector said, looking at Luis.

"Who are they?" Luis asked Cross.

"Real nice kids named Beth and Corky. I don't know their last names. I met them at a bar in the hotel here. They had long faces. It was their last night. They were broke and had maxed out their credit cards. They didn't want to go home."

"You provided a means to remain in paradise," Luis said.

"Money," Cross said, twirling a finger, "makes the world go around."

"Where are Beth and Corky?" Luis asked.

"I'm not exactly sure. They're scraping by, but they're not flush enough to stay in these digs."

Inspector Hector Salgado Reyes stood and asked. "Where are Beth and Corky?"

"Xcacel," Cross said quickly. "The campground. They bought a tent."

* * *

Xcacel (sha-SELL) was a beach near BLACK CORAL. A sign at the highway advertised "The Wildest Beach Around." This was not true, Luis knew. The waves were not particularly hazardous, and resort accommodations were primitive. Budget travelers with expectations of tranquility were drawn to Xcacel.

Xcacel was out of Hector's jurisdiction, but he went along for fun and procrastination of paperwork at the station. His value to Luis persisted. The caretaker snapped to attention and directed them to Beth and Corky. They were beside their tent, drying off after a swim, lean North Americans in skimpy bathing suits, blond hair sunbleached more white than yellow, skin as brown as Luis's.

"Chester Cross told you where we were, I presume," Corky said, focused on Hector. "I'm an attorney, incidentally. What we're doing isn't illegal."

"I'm an attorney, too," Ricky said. "And this isn't California. Incidentally."

"Why did you mention Cross?" Luis asked. "He isn't your only client."

"He is," Beth said. "Honestly."

"You don't have to answer their questions," Corky told Beth.

"Correct," Hector said. "You have the right to remain silent in jail while we investigate further."

"What did we do?" Corky said defiantly.

"Bud and Helen Lamm," Luis replied.

"Helen," Beth said. "Isn't she that sweet older lady who likes birds?"

Luis nodded. "Wife of Bud, who was cheated out of sixty thousand dollars, sold the flamingo condo on phony papers."

"Fraud is a crime in any land, attorney," Hector said to Corky.

Corky's and Beth's lower jaws dropped and their suntans momentarily faded.

"Now wait a sec," Corky said, "we were hired as cheerleaders. If a deal turns kinky, we can't be held liable."

"Accessories, before and during and after the fact," Ricky pronounced.

"My partner is taking over my clients," Corky said. "We love the Yucatan. We never want to leave, but it's expensive."

"Live in Mexico for ever," Luis said. "On the beach. Or if you continue lying, in prison."

Corky puffed his chest in defense of his mate's honor. "She didn't lie. We do our thing for Chet Cross exclusively."

"Ralph Taggert," Luis said.

"Same difference," Corky said. "Ralph used to sell for Chet. They're still associated somehow."

* * *

Beth and Corky gave them the address of a cement block apartment house in Cancún City. After repeated knocking, Hector rattled the doorknob and said, "Deadbolt."

"We must obtain a search warrant," Ricky advised.

"Article 16 of the constitution of the Mexican United States permits officials to enter private homes for the sole purpose of ascertaining whether health regulations have been complied with," Hector said.

Luis sniffed. "I smell rotten food, too."

"For the record, I am elsewhere," Ricky said.

Hector kicked the door. "Ow!"

Luis grasped the knob with both hands, pulled, then slammed a shoulder into the door. It opened, splintered jamb and all. Luis said, "You loosened it for me, Hector."

Nowhere in the three cramped rooms was spoiled food or Ralph Taggert. Clothing hung in the closet; suitcases were stacked on the shelf above. Travel brochures on Hawaii and the Mexican West Coast were scattered on a rickety dining table. Ralph Taggert's wallet was in a drawer. It contained California and Quintana Roo driver's licenses and a little cash. There was no other money in the apartment, not sixty thousand dollars, not a peso.

"Why would a person walk out without his wallet?" Ricky wondered.

"You're forgetful when you're in a hurry," Luis said.

"He heard our footsteps or he made a recent transaction," Hector said. "It became time to go."

"Either path," Luis said, "leads to the airport."

In excess of a million people per year fly in and out of Cancún Airport. They tend to congregate in clumps, herded by flight schedules and the demands of Immigration and Customs bureaucracies.

The trio concentrated on the outgoing clumps, checking the identification of men who fit Ralph Taggert's appearance. Given Bud Lamm's "average Joe" description and the fact that they had never seen Taggert, it was a despairing task. They were about to send Ricky for Lamm when Luis pointed out a man and woman.

Hector muttered a curse and quickstepped toward them, parting the crowds as if he were a vehicle. They reached Chester Call-Me-Chet Cross and the beauteous Hortencia as they were handing their boarding passes to a Mexicana Airlines flight attendant.

"What gives?" Cross demanded. "My assistant and I are going to a PIPA management seminar at Mazatlán. There'll be hell to pay if we miss our plane."

"Your airplane flies to Mexico City," Hector said.

"We were going to catch a connecting flight at Mexico City."

"From Mexico City you can catch a connecting flight to anywhere in the world," Hector said, taking his arm. "You will talk now, fly later."

They escorted Cross and Hortencia to seats and asked people in adjacent seats to please move. Travelers sensing a real life Mexican drug bust obeyed promptly. At a safe distance they removed cameras from carryon luggage and recorded the drama.

"Talk to us about Ralph Taggert," Hector said.

Cross shrugged, sighed, and said, "That topic's getting old, guys. I'd love to help but—"

"We've talked to Beth and Corky," Luis said. "What did Taggert buy from you with the Lamms' money?"

"Okay, I didn't tell you the complete story. Taggert worked for me. I fired him. He was lazy and dishonest."

"Taggert's dishonesty offends you?" Luis said. "Ironic."

Cross lunged out of his chair. Luis blocked his path. Cross swung. Luis ducked, assumed a crouch, and took a solid blow to a shoulder. He drove a fist into a midsection softer than it looked. Cross made a noise like an airlock in a science fiction movie and slumped into his chair.

Shutters clicked. Film-advance motors whirred.

Cross was momentarily speechless. Hector spoke gently to Hortencia, "Your lover boy is foolish, and you are too lovely to languish in my filthy jail."

"Ask me anything," Hortencia said.

"He bought Hawaii," Luis said.

"How did you know?"

"It is farther from Cancún than any other resort Paradise Investment Properties Associates sells."

"A Maui condo. Taggert was coming by to sign papers today, but he didn't show." She canted her head at the hyperventilating Cross and wrinkled her nose. "My hero. He panicked. He said there would be trouble and that we had to leave. He was right. The old gringo lady, Helen, she worried him."

"Why?"

"She came to the office yesterday. Chet told her the lies he told you. She refused to accept them. She said she would stand outside and sob and complain to everybody that PIPA was crooked. She would carry a sign and picket. She is made of iron. Chet gave her what she was after, and she went away."

"Which was?"

"The truth about Ralph. And his address."

"Do you have the money?"

Hortencia took an envelope from Cross's bag. "Fifty thousand. Chet was going to wire the money to our Maui office when Taggert signed. No Taggert, so we kept the money. Chet said it was a blessing in disguise."

"The other ten thousand?"

"Ralph had problems," Hortencia said. "He snorted cocaine and gambled."

"Expensive problems," Hector said, taking the envelope.

"Very expensive problems," Luis said, taking the envelope from Hector. "I suppose the Lamms should feel fortunate to recover a penny."

"You will have to mail it to them," she said. "They didn't see us, but we saw them an hour ago. They flew out on United, to Chicago."

Hector and Luis looked at each other. Hortencia had been looking at Ricky out of a corner of her eye. Ricky kissed her hand and presented a business card. Hortencia flushed and smiled. Chet Cross threw up on the floor and in his own shoes.

Shutters clicked. Film-advance motors whirred.

Assisted by a bank, Luis Balam sent forty-nine thousand dollars to Bud and Helen Lamm. He split the fiftieth thousand equally with Ricardo Martinez Rodriguez and Hector Salgado Reyes. It came to three million pesos, a million each.

Hector said his share would be devoted to unspecified administrative costs connected with the prosecution of Chester Cross. Hortencia would be his chief witness. Luis bought tires and a tune up for the Golf. Ricky treated Hortencia to a lavish evening of dinner and dancing in the Cancún hotel zone. Hortencia treated Ricky to a night upstairs. His legal fee thus exhausted, Ricky's romance with Hortencia stalled.

Luis in retrospect was not surprised when the body of an unidentified white male was found in the Xelha cenote. It had not yet been ravaged by black vultures beyond recognition. The true surprise was the facial expression, an eternal countenance of amusement and shock. The federal judicial police and the state judicial police investigated. The localized break in the back of the skull, a button-sized fracture that had thrust bone fragments into the brain, was the stated cause of death.

The police interviewed the Xelha caretakers, who did not recall seeing the victim. They did remind the police that the ground surrounding the cenote was treacherous because of moisture and exposed tree roots.

A homicide required blatant clues. Murder was as bad for Yucatan tourism as a hurricane. The death was ruled accidental.

Luis interviewed the Xelha caretakers. Although they answered him, they were ambiguous. An older woman limping on a cane *might* have rendezvoused with a younger man early that morning. But who really notices those things?

Helen pressing Taggert into a private encounter, insisting on a refund. Taggert laughing at a little old lady, turning his back on her—pure speculation, Luis thought. He ruled the death accidental.

In a month a package and letter and photograph came to BLACK CORAL. The photo was of Helen and Bud on a Hawaiian beach. They were grateful for the money and had applied it as a down payment on a marvelous townhouse with an ocean peek-a-view.

Bud had cut back to two packs a day and walked his daily eighteen holes rather than riding a cart, and was the picture of health.

Bud looked to Luis like the same Bud. Helen appeared haggard, as if she had been sleeping badly. The package was a macadamia nut gift assortment. Luis tried one and thought that it was tasty, but a bit waxy. He did not have an opportunity for a second opinion. Esther and Rosa loved them and polished them off before the day was done.

# WHILE THE RAIN FOREST BURNED

*By Clark Howard*

WHEN JORDAN passed through the Immigration barriers into the airport terminal at Porto Velho, he saw a handsome Brazilian about his own age, thirty-three, in khakis, holding a hand-lettered sign with his name on it.

"I'm Jordan," he said, walking up to the man.

"Raymond Mundo, senor," the man introduced himself, nodding his chin an inch. "Welcome to the Mato Grosso. I am the foreman for Senor Alves. I have transportation outside."

Jordan slung his duffel bag and followed Mundo out into a thickly hot, wet, glaringly bright afternoon. A swarm of sidewalk vendors converged on Jordan as soon as they saw his white face, but several sharp commands from Mundo, in four languages, drove them away.

"Why do you tell them in so many languages?" Jordan asked.

"In the Mato Grosso, one never knows which tongue to use," Mundo replied. "Portuguese is the national language, Spanish has seeped in from Brazil's neighbors at every border, English has come from the priests and nuns that the church sent, and the engineers and teachers from the Peace Corps—and the Indians infuse it all with their own dialect, which they stubbornly cling to even in the face of the government's efforts to educate them. So if one wishes to be obeyed here, it is wise to be certain that one is understood." Mundo glanced smugly at him. "I suppose you will require an interpreter while you are here?"

Jordan shook his head. "I speak nine languages—Portuguese and Spanish among them."

"My compliments," Mundo said. But his expression soured a hint.

In the parking lot was an open-sided Jeep with a canvas canopy to keep out the sun. The name ALVES and the face of an angry bull were painted on the spare-tire cover. Jordan tossed his duffel bag into the rear, draped his windbreaker over it, and rolled up the sleeves of his shirt, which was already darkening in places as the oppressive humidity assaulted his body.

Mundo drove off the lot and headed south out of Porto Velho on BR-364, one of the newly paved roads that jutted off the Trans-Amazon Highway toward Bolivia. Even though the road was fairly new, the asphalt was already cracked and pocked in places because it wasn't solid enough to accommodate heavy equipment; local officials who were supposed to control its traffic accepted bribes instead. The road improved some fifty kilometers south of the city—not many heavy trucks had occasion to travel that far.

As the Jeep went farther south, the terrain on both sides of the road became thicker, greener, more formidable, less inviting, perhaps even threatening. At one point, Jordan saw Mundo reach under his driver's seat and pull out a cartridge belt with a holstered revolver attached. He placed it next to his right thigh, patting it silently as if it were a pet. Jordan said nothing.

"It will be a two-hour trip to the village of Jaru," Mundo said early in the drive, speaking now in Portuguese. "The ranch of Senor Alves is only a short distance farther." He smiled proudly. "It is a magnificent place, senor, as you will see. Thirty rooms in the main house. Everything made of the finest wood and tile and marble—you are in for a real treat, senor, believe me."

Jordan merely nodded. The foreman, he sensed, was testing him on his languages. But Jordan didn't intend to play idle games with him. If Mundo wanted to see how well Jordan spoke Portugese, he would have to ask a direct question.

He did that after about an hour. "Tell me, senor, exactly what is it that you do?" he inquired curiously, with exaggerated politeness. "I understand, of course, that you are here to burn a section of the rain forest. But to bring a man all the way from the U.S. just for that makes no sense to me. Even I, a humble foreman, can strike a match and start a fire."

"I'm not here just to start a fire," Jordan replied in precise, textbook Portuguese, "I'm here to *control* a fire. I'm an agnitechnist. A fire expert. 'Agni' is the ancient word for fire."

"I see," said Mundo. He forced a smile. "Thank you for the information, senor. It is always good to learn something new."

Jordan looked out at the passing forest and said nothing further. Some men, he knew, sought to be offended in order to defend what they were, to defend their place, their reason for being. Apparently Mundo was such a man. Jordan hoped he wouldn't have to work too closely with him. That type liked to see other men fail.

As they neared the outskirts of the village of Jaru, Jordan began to see signs of humanity again. Small clearings appeared, on which stood pitifully poor little farmhouses beside meager crops of beans and corn and tomatoes, most of them stunted in the nutrient-poor soil that could support the most fecund rain forest but was stubbornly resistant to agriculture. Along the road, too, could be seen other signatures of man: carelessly tossed bottles and other trash, an occasional blown-out tire, wandering chickens pecking at the ground for a stray seed. The Jeep sped past a dilapidated country store with a single ancient gasoline pump and a rusted Coca-Cola sign over the door. Boys using sticks prodded scrawny goats somewhere to be milked. Two nuns, both white, in traditional habits despite the heat, walked side by side without speaking. Jordan observed everything without comment.

Presently the Jeep overtook a brown woman in a shapeless, colorless dress hurrying along their side of the road, carrying in her arms a small child who had a bloody foot. As the Jeep sped past, she turned pleading eyes toward them.

"Pull over," Jordan said.

"She's only a Nambi," Mundo told him.

"Pull over," Jordan said again, the simple request becoming at once an order. In a single motion, Mundo glanced at him, saw a clear danger in his eyes, and guided the Jeep to a stop at the side of the road.

Jordan got out and the woman ran to him with the child. "My daughter stepped on broken glass," she panted in broken Portuguese. "I cannot stop the bleeding!"

Jordan snatched his windbreaker from the Jeep and lay the girl on it on the ground. She was about four, wimpering and shivering. "Hold the leg like this—" Jordan instructed the woman, elevating the child's bleeding foot. Unzipping his duffel bag, he found a clean pair of thick boot socks and pressed them to a three-inch gash on the instep of the child's foot, which was gushing blood. "Hold this," he said. "Tight—very tight." To everything he said, the anxious woman replied, "Yes, yes—"

Searching in his duffel again, Jordan removed a metal first-aid box and opened it on the Jeep's fender. Across the hood of the vehicle, he saw Mundo get out and buckle on his gunbelt. It didn't bother Jordan: he was too important to Mundo's employer for Mundo to let anything happen to him.

From the first-aid kit, Jordan took a small plastic bottle of iodine and a roll of gauze. Kneeling next to the child, he opened the bottle of iodine and said to the woman, "This will hurt her, but it's necessary."

"Yes—yes—"

"Hold her." Jordan took away the now blood-soaked boot socks and poured iodine into the cut. The little girl screamed and kicked Jordan with her other foot and tried to pull away from her mother. The woman held her firmly and kept up a stream of words meant to be comforting, though they could barely be heard over the child's painful protest. Jordan folded a thick square of gauze and bound it in place over the wound. "Where were you taking her?" he asked.

"In Jaru there is an infirmary—"

Wrapping the girl in his windbreaker, Jordan put her into her mother's arms and said, "Get in the Jeep."

The woman's eyes flicked to the name and the drawing of the bull's face, then to Mundo standing in the road in his gunbelt, and her eyes widened in fear. "No, please, we will walk now. It is not far and the bleeding has almost stopped—"

"No, get in the Jeep," Jordan insisted. Taking her by the shoulders, he guided her into the back seat. Mundo glared at both of them. Jordan got into the passenger seat and glared back at him. After a moment, the Brazilian, tight-lipped, slipped behind the wheel and pulled back onto the road, heading toward the village.

Senor Alves was a stocky, white-haired man. He sat at the head of his extravagantly laid dinner table dressed in an exquisite handmade silk *guayaberra* shirt, holding a silver-stemmed crystal goblet in a hand laden with three solid-gold rings. Raising the goblet, he smiled at Jordan and said, "To your good health, senor, and to the successful completion of your work here."

Jordan nodded and took a sip of wine. At the other end of the table, Raymond Mundo also drank, as did a fourth man seated across from Jordan, a Japanese named Tonada who had been introduced as an "advisor" from a Tokyo trading company. Exactly what kind of advice he provided had not been explained.

"My man Mundo told me of your Good Samaritan act on the road today," Alves said, still smiling. "I commend you, senor. To see a child suffering is a sad thing. Even a Nambi child."

"Nambi?" Jordan inquired. It was the same term Mundo had used.

"For Nambiquara," Alves explained. "They are the Indians who live hereabouts—most of them in the rain forest, thank goodness. But some of them in and around the village also. They're a troublesome lot—they resist progress, resist modernization of the rain forest, resist the government's efforts to educate them. They are much like what I have read of your own American Indians, senor."

"Was the rain forest theirs before it was yours?" Jordan asked. His tone was neutral but the question was not. Tonada, the Japanese, recognized this at once—his thin lips shifted into the barest of smiles, totally without humor.

"I beg your pardon?" Alves asked, frowning.

"In my country," Jordan said, "the land belonged originally to the Indians. It was taken from them by various means: legislation, theft, armed force. Was it the same with your Indians here?"

Something flashed in Alves' eyes: resentment, irritation—and something stronger. "Senor Jordan," he said, pronouncing it Hor*dan*, "my grandfather and his brothers, my grand-uncles, came to the Mato Grosso when there were no roads, no villages, not even any maps. They came because their government, like your government, declared the land open for settlement. They faced many hazards, many obstacles, to claim and settle a part of what was then an unexplored and almost totally unproductive jungle. Only one thing came from the rain forest in the old days: *aguaje*—a palm fruit. The Nambi, what is left of them, still grow and harvest it exclusively today, stubbornly ignoring all other industry. But *my* ancestors, senor, *my* family, opened up this territory to much more than a simple jungle fruit: they opened it to vast mineral deposits—manganese, bauxite, copper, many others—and they opened it to extensive cattle ranching, including our own. And in an area where cattle feed cannot be grown, my family has overcome the lack of grain production by developing, through our friends in other countries—" he gestured toward Tonada "—synthetic and chemical feed for our herds. We brought this rain forest out of the stone age, senor—not by theft or by force, but through legal settlement."

"I didn't mean to suggest otherwise," Jordan stated without apology. "I was merely curious about the history of the rain forest."

Tonada's smile widened without warming. "I think I detect a streak of humanitarianism in your guest, Senor Alves," he said. His calculating eyes challenged Jordan. "Are you a friend of mankind, Mr. Jordan? One of those good people who feels he has to lend a hand to the downtrodden at every opportunity?"

"I've never really given it much thought," Jordan replied. "I do what I feel I must at the time."

"It would be odd if you *did* consider yourself a humanitarian," Tonada suggested, "given the fact that calculated destruction is your profession."

"I prefer to think of it as creative destruction," Jordan corrected, "in order to accomplish something better. For instance, every year I'm hired to burn the sugar-cane fields in Hawaii. It is necessary in order to harvest the crop. And every year I burn out the scrub brush on the Zambian plains to produce grasslands. For Senor Alves—" he gestured toward his host "—I will burn part of the rain forest, and from that destruction will come a larger, greater cattle ranch."

Alves smiled broadly. "Well said, senor! You will do well here." He rose and his guests immediately did likewise. "Come, let us have brandy in my study. We can look at the map and I will show you what needs to be burned."

The map, in relief, covered a full wall of the rancher's richly furnished study. Lighted all the way around, hand-drawn, beautifully lettered, it was a work of art as well as a geographic chart. A length of red twine had been pinned to it in the shape of a square.

"That is the area, senor," said Alves, pointing. "The main house, where we are, is here. The ranch itself extends from here—" his finger swept "—to here. The access roads are here, here, and here."

"I will need to tour the entire area," Jordan said, studying the map.

"My man Mundo is at your service."

"What time is daybreak?" Jordan asked Mundo. "I must see the trees very early to test their moisture content."

"If we leave at four-thirty," Mundo said, "we can be in the area at first light."

Jordan turned to Alves again. "Do you have adequate labor to dig fire-breaks—perhaps a hundred men?"

"There are many unemployed miners in the Grande Carajas, a mining area a few hundred kilometers to the east. We can have them here in two days."

"Where is the nearest chemicals manufacturer?"

"In Manaus," said Alves. "I can have whatever you need flown to Porto Velho in one day."

"How much time do you need to evacuate people living in the area to be burned?" Jordan asked.

Alves shrugged. "That is not a consideration. Only the Nambi live in the rain forest. They will evacuate themselves when they smell the smoke."

"Where will they go?"

"Into another part of the forest."

Jordan fell silent and looked away to cover his uneasiness. He stared at a display of exquisitely hand-tooled shotguns on an adjacent wall. His mind pitched. Burning a place where people still lived was new to him.

"Our agnitechnist is feeling his conscience again," said Tonada, as he worked a cigarette into a pearl-inlaid holder. Lighting it, he held the lighter with its ellipse of flame in front of him and stared at it for a suspended moment. "Perhaps I understand how you feel, Mr. Jordan," he said when he finally extinguished the flame. "As a boy, I endured the firestorms caused by your country's incendiary bombing of Japan. I don't imagine many Americans remember, but before you dropped the atom bomb on us, you had destroyed sixty-five of our cities by fire-bombing. In Tokyo alone, you destroyed seven square miles and killed eighty-four thousand people in one six-hour raid. That is more people than died at Hiroshima. Were you aware of that, Mr. Jordan?"

Jordan shook his head. "Before my time," he said offhandedly.

"Ah," the Japanese nodded. "I thought perhaps you were a student of fires."

"The only ones I study are the ones I start." Jordan turned to his host. "I must excuse myself now, Senor Alves, to see to my instruments and material for the early start tomorrow."

None of the men offered to shake hands with him before he left the room.

For the next few days, Jordan inspected the condemned area of the rain forest, both by Jeep and on foot. Wherever he went, he was accompanied by Mundo, wearing his pistol belt, and escorted, in a second Jeep, by four *rifleros* from the ranch, all carrying fully automatic carbines loaded with oversize magazines.

Mundo watched with unconcealed curiosity as Jordan set up various instruments from a hard plastic case to measure the relative humidity of the air, the atmospheric temperature and wind velocity, the moisture content of the trees, the properties of their wood, and other characteristics of the rain forest.

"To start a fire, all this is necessary?" Mundo asked at one point, without rancor.

"Yes," said Jordan. "All of the information I gather is used to figure what is called a 'fire load' index. The index tells me how fast and how long the fire will burn, how far the wind will carry a burning ember, how wide the firebreaks must be to stop the burning at given points, and how much and the proper mix of the fire retardant we need for final extinguishment. Without all that and more, I wouldn't be able to control the fire. And without control, it could burn for miles; it could destroy the forest all the way to the mountains."

Mundo shook his head in wonder. "I owe you an apology, senor. I did not think what you did was important. I was mistaken."

Jordan paused in his work and turned to the foreman. "I'd like to ask you a question."

Mundo shrugged. "Ask."

Glancing at their armed escort, Jordan saw that they were too far away to overhear, but he lowered his voice a little, anyway. "Will all the Indians have time to get out once the burning starts?"

"Probably," Mundo said. But he averted his eyes when he said it.

"Only probably? Isn't there some way to warn them in advance? Give them more time?"

Mundo sighed with restrained impatience. "Senor, you underestimate the Nambi. There is not an Indian in the forest who does not already know that you are here and what you have come to do. Why do you think we have four men with rifles escorting us? We are being watched right now, at this moment. The Indians could already be moving deeper into the forest—they have plenty of time. But they won't. They won't go until they smell the smoke and see the flames."

"But why?" Jordan asked. His tone was an appeal for understanding. But Mundo would not satisfy him.

"Because they are Indians," was all the Brazilian would say, and once again he shrugged.

The next morning, Jordan sat down with Alves, Tonada, and Mundo to determine where the firebreaks would be dug by the transient laborers Alves was having bused in from the eastern mines, and to make up the list of chemicals and other supplies Jordan would need to keep the fire burning and to extinguish its final stages. Tonada was concerned about possible damage the chemicals might do to the soil.

"We must have enough good soil left to produce at least a ground cover of grass on which Senor Alves' cattle can graze. They do not have to feed off this grass, of course, because our firm will provide their food synthetically. But there must be a sufficient blanket of grazing growth to accommodate them between feedings."

"The ground won't be hurt below two inches of topsoil," Jordan assured him. "Bulldoze off two inches when you're razing the stumps and burnage, and you'll be able to grow anything then that you can grow now."

"That is satisfactory," Tonada said.

After the meeting, as Mundo was about to leave to drive up to the Trans-Amazon Highway to meet the labor buses, Jordan came out and got into the Jeep with him. "Drop me in the village, will you?" he asked casually.

Mundo hesitated. "I am not sure it is wise for you to go to Jaru alone, senor."

"Why not?"

"The Indians are not to be trusted."

"I'm sure I'll be safe," Jordan said. "I just want to look around, maybe buy some local handicrafts." When Mundo still hesitated, Jordan started to get out. "I can always walk."

"I will take you, senor," the foreman relented, "but I cannot be responsible for your safety."

Jordan smiled. "I didn't ask you to."

They drove the several miles to Jaru and Mundo stopped to let Jordan out.

"I will be back through here in about four hours, senor," Mundo said. "I hope you will be waiting here so that Senor Alves does not have to send *rifleros* from the ranch to look for you."

Jordan watched as the Jeep with the angry bull on the spare-tire cover proceeded on past the little village. Then he turned and began to stroll a cobblestone street that led to a small square built around an ornate stone water-fountain. Around the square were small stores and businesses, some of them in wooden structures with corrugated roofs, some in crude A-frames with palm fronds forming thatched roofs and sides, others simply sidewalk stalls with canopies or old beach umbrellas to ward off the tropical sun. Jordan sauntered around, idly browsing. There wasn't much of interest to him. Jaru was not a *turista* town, and most of the wares were practical items of use to farmers and forest Indians. He did buy a wide-brimmed, flat-crowned straw hat with a woven snake band for which he imagined, from the smile on the vendor's face, he paid about ten times too much. But it didn't bother him—the vendor looked like he could use the money.

As Jordan meandered the square, he became aware that he was being followed. A dark-faced man, younger than he, dressed in a dirty white shirt and trousers, barefoot, seemed to be just behind Jordan wherever he went. And as Jordan moved from stall to stall, he noticed that the man was joined by a second, then a third, both of them dressed identically to the first. A fourth soon appeared, then a fifth. They spread out so that they formed a loose circle around Jordan.

Stopping at a stall, Jordan picked up a pair of braided sandals, pretending to examine them as his eyes, shaded by the wide brim of his new hat, quickly surveyed the area around him for the best possible route of escape. Since the forest was nearby in three directions, his options were limited. To go into that quagmire trying to escape Indians would be like leaping into fire to avoid a sunburn. Across the square, he saw a church of some kind, very modest in appearance, but its front door was open.

Before Jordan could make his move, three of the dark men were suddenly next to him and one was gesturing toward a small cantina a few yards away. Holding up both palms and shaking his head, Jordan tried to move away from them. Two of them flanked him and the third drew from the small of his back a black-bladed machete with a shiny half-inch razor edge from haft to point. With the weapon, the dark man pointed again to the cantina. Lowering his hands, Jordan allowed himself to be escorted toward its open doorway.

Inside, the place was all but squalid: a dirt floor on which stood a dozen scarred tables with leaning wooden chairs, a long plank of wood held up by two petroleum barrels which served as a bar, a portable radio on a wall shelf, from which static came Samba music, and a narrow archway leading to a second room emanating a pungent scent of something spicy being cooked. At a table in one corner sat the young woman and four-year-old girl Jordan had helped on the road. She half smiled at him but then quickly looked away at the sound of an authoritative male voice.

"Sit here, senor."

The voice, speaking Portuguese, came from an older man, perhaps the same age as Senor Alves. His complexion was very dark, like the men who had brought Jordan there, and his hair was black-and-white striped, like a zebra's. Something curved and yellow, perhaps three inches long, was embedded all the way through his left earlobe. Jordan sat down across from him, staring curiously at the earlobe.

"It is the prime tooth of a jaguar that I killed with a spear when I was young," the man said. "It is supposed to be a symbol of bravery. Between us—" he lowered his voice "—it is a symbol of foolishness. Spears are for pigs and small deer. If I faced a jaguar today, I would much prefer to have one of your employer's fancy shotguns."

"My employer?" said Jordan.

"Alves. Is he not your employer?"

"He is my client. I was hired by him to perform professional services."

"As you like," the older man conceded. He turned as a very old woman approached the table and set down two wooden mugs frothing over with something that looked like catalyzed acid. "This is a drink, senor, that you will not get in the magnificent hacienda of your, ah, client. This is specially fermented *aguaje* juice. Only the Nambiquara people know how to make it. To your health, senor," he said, and drank.

Jordan took a swallow. "Good God," he said, barely able to keep from choking. It was like drinking ignited kerosene.

"A few swallows and you will be used to it," the dark man promised. "Now then, as you *yanquis* say, let us be down to business. I am Paulo. At least, that is my name here in the village. In the rain forest, among the Nambiquara, of whom I am the hereditary chief, I have other names and many titles, but they are of no consequence between you and me. I speak to you as one man to another. You have created a problem for me, senor."

"How can that be?" Jordan asked. "Five minutes ago, I didn't even know you existed."

"Sometimes, senor, we cast shadows that we cannot see. Before you even arrived here, your death had been ordered by our tribal council. We knew when you were coming, and why. You were to be skinned and hung by your feet from one of the hacienda trees for Alves to see."

Jordan swallowed drily. Paulo nudged his drink closer and Jordan took another fiery sip. As soon as it went down, he was certain the inside of his mouth had been blistered. "Good *God,*" he said again.

"Soon it will not burn," Paulo assured him. "Soon it will be cool."

It'll be too late, Jordan thought. His throat would be incinerated. Glancing over at the woman and child, he saw that she was watching in amusement. Next time I'll let her kid bleed to death, he thought irritably.

"Back to the problem you have caused," Paulo said. "On the day of your arrival, you gave aid to Apuri, the woman in the corner. You helped her injured child. To do so, you had to defy the half snake Mundo. He had a pistol, but you defied him, anyway. Because of what you did, we now cannot skin you and hang you from a tree at the hacienda."

"I wouldn't worry about it," Jordan said. He raised his wooden mug. "I think you've found another way to kill me." Actually, he had already decided that Paulo wasn't going to harm him at all. People who were serious about hurting someone didn't talk about it first. Jordan drank again. It was just as searing.

"Be patient," Paulo counseled.

"Why are you telling me all this?" Jordan asked. "Are you trying to frighten me?"

Paulo shook his head. "You have already demonstrated that you are not one to be frightened. No, I am telling you this to let you know that we still intend to do something about you. We just do not know what." Paulo pursed his lips for a moment. "Would you consider letting our tribe pay you *not* to burn our rain forest?"

Jordan shook his head. "I have made an agreement. Would you make an agreement and not keep it?"

"No," Paulo admitted.

"Anyhow," Jordan reasoned, "Alves would just bring in someone else."

"Ah, but him we could skin and hang in the tree," Paulo pointed out.

Jordan shook his head again. "I have an agreement."

Paulo sighed quietly. "Tell me," he asked presently, "how much time do we have?"

"Five days. Maybe six."

Paulo raised his mug and, as Jordan watched in awe, drained it in several long swallows. "There is much thinking to do," he said, rising. He beckoned to the woman in the corner. "Come, Apuri."

Apuri rose with her child and came across the room as Paulo walked to the door. At the table she paused and Jordan thought she was going to speak to him. Instead she merely looked at him, as if trying to decide something. Jordan stared back at her, seeing her face up close and not in distress or anguish for the first time. She was lighter than Paulo, clay-colored, with hair that was flat black, not shiny, like bituminous coal. Her eyes, which he initially had assumed were simply wide with the ordeal of her child bleeding, were in fact naturally wide, the widest he had ever seen; they were glossy chocolate, and as she looked down at him he could see flecks of jasmine color in them. When he was sure she wasn't going to speak first, he decided to. But before he could, Paulo called her from the door.

"Apuri, come."

In a moment they were gone and Jordan was left alone in the dingy little cantina. His expression was pensive, almost somber. Without thinking, he raised his mug and drank again. Then he grinned and shook his head. The *aguaje* did not burn this time. It went down cool.

For the next few days, Jordan supervised the digging of the firebreaks around the perimeter to be burned. Long lines of sweating brown men with picks and shovels, following a rope line, chopped out a precise, knee-high trench that looked like a surgical incision on a great green body. As usual, where Jordan went he was accompanied by Mundo, and they were escorted by *rifleros* from the ranch. Several times Senor Alves and the Japanese advisor Tonada drove out to visit the work site, and each time Jordan and Mundo were complimented on the progress being made. The praise meant nothing to Jordan, but Mundo seemed to bask in it. Jordan noticed that whenever Alves was around Mundo straightened his posture, firmed up his expression, and in general brought his demeanor to parade-ground attention. Like a schoolboy trying to become teacher's pet, Jordan thought.

"How long have you worked for Alves?" he asked one day as they drew drinking water from a cask in the Jeep.

"All my life," Mundo said. "When I was a boy, I worked in the hacienda, running errands, helping in the kitchen. When I got older, I was put in the barns to learn about the cattle. Then I was given a part of the herd to supervise. On my thirtieth birthday, Senor Alves promoted me to foreman of the entire ranch. It was a very proud day for me."

"I'm sure," Jordan said. After drinking some water, he asked, "Does Alves live here all alone? I never see anyone about except servants."

"His family is away at the present. At their chateau in Switzerland. His three daughters go to school there. The senora stays with them."

"He has no sons?"

Mundo glanced away. "No. No sons."

Always, during the digging of the firebreaks, Jordan had the eerie feeling that they were being watched by many eyes from the fecund growth around them. It was not difficult to imagine Paulo's dark young men, stripped out of their dirty village whites, wearing loincloths and body paint, peering down from some high tree. How easy it would probably be, he thought, for them to let loose enough poisoned arrows to kill him, Mundo, and all the *rifleros* at one time, and send the hired laborers back where they came from. He asked Mundo why the Nambiquara didn't resist more dynamically.

"If they did," Mundo explained, "they might lose the entire rain forest at once. As it is, the government has decreed that only so many square hectares per year can be burned. But if the Indians rose up in force, the Army would probably come in and wipe them out. Then the entire forest would go at once. If they do nothing to upset the government, they will have their forest, although smaller and smaller, for another ten years."

Jordan thought of Apuri's little girl. She would run out of rain forest when she was about fourteen.

Rinsing his mouth, Jordan turned and spat water onto the ground. "If I was a Nambi," he said, "I'd fight now."

Mundo stiffened. "I beg your pardon, senor?"

"You heard me," Jordan told him, and walked away.

In the middle of the night, in his bed in one of the hacienda guest rooms, Jordan felt a hand cover his mouth and a voice whisper in his ear. "Do not call out. It is Apuri."

He was sleeping naked with only a light sheet over him, and he could feel her body on top of his. She was surprisingly light. With her head bent, her lips to his ear, some of her hair spilled over his face and tickled him gently. "How did you get in?" he whispered.

"Through the window."

"No, I mean how did you get into the hacienda compound?" He knew the grounds were patrolled day and night by armed men.

"I go anywhere I want to in the rain forest," she said. "It is mine. I was born here."

She shifted her weight and slipped under the sheet with him. She was as naked as he. "Aren't you going to ask me why I came?"

"I don't care why you came." He put an arm under her neck and she lay her face against his chest. "Why did you?"

"Perhaps to settle my debt for your help. I have no other way to pay."

Jordan said nothing.

"You do not like that answer," she said matter-of-factly.

Still he didn't speak.

"You would rather I say that I came because I desire you."

"Say whatever you must," he told her, with a trace of irritation. She was silent for what seemed to him an uncommonly long time. Then he felt her putting his hands where she wanted them and she whispered, "I came because I desire you. Very much."

Their lovemaking was far too brief, as it always is the first time, hunger overcoming passion. Then they lay in the dark whispering again, resting, waiting for what they both seemed to know would be a longer, slower, more fulfilling union.

"Paulo was almost captured today," she told him. They were side by side on their backs, only their fingers touching, the sweat drying on their bodies.

"Captured by whom?" Jordan asked.

"By Alves' *rifleros,*" she said in the same matter-of-fact tone. "They have been trying to catch him for many months."

"Why? What has he done?"

"He and his band of young men steal cattle from Alves. They butcher the animals and distribute the meat among our people. Paulo says it is payment for that part of the rain forest that Alves has already taken. The more forest he takes, the less *aguaje* fruit there is to harvest, and the more the income of the tribe is reduced. Paulo says Alves' cattle must make up the difference."

"What will Alves do with Paulo if he catches him?"

"Alves says he will have him taken to Brasilia and turned over to the authorities for trial. But everyone knows he will take him into the forest and hang him."

After a while, when he could feel his vigor returning, his ardor growing again, Jordan eased the conversation back to a personal vein. "How is your little girl—what's her name, anyway?"

"Her name is Evora, and she is well, thank you."

"Where is her father?" he asked, and felt her shrug in the darkness.

"I do not even know who her father is. When I was fifteen, I was very wanton. I had many boys. My mother beat me regularly."

"Are you still wanton?" Jordan rolled over toward her.

"No, I am now very chaste." She placed his hands again. "Can't you tell?"

When the firebreaks were completed, most of the transient laborers were bused back to where they came from. Only a few were retained to hoe out the long, shallow incendiary furrows Jordan had designed to crisscross the area to be burned.

"How are these slits used?" Tonada asked on one of the inspection visits he and Alves regularly made.

"They're for the combustible chemicals I use to feed the fire," Jordan explained. "In an area with as much thick growth as this one, we can't depend on the wind. There's more than enough oxygen, but it doesn't move. So I seed the ground with combustibles to keep the fire moving."

"Ingenious," the Japanese muttered to himself. He was, it seemed to Jordan, fascinated by fire. "Could you," Tonada asked, "use this same method to burn a small town?"

"Probably. Why?"

"My firm has for several years been purchasing property in a small town in the state of Tennessee in your country. As soon as we own the entire town, we plan to evict everyone, raze the place, and with our American partners build a vast automobile-manufacturing plant and industrial complex. One of the problems we have been looking at is how to cost-effectively demolish the town. Until now, fire had not been considered." He smiled his humorless smile at Jordan. "Would you have any reservations about undertaking such a project?"

"Not as long as it's legal," Jordan said.

"Oh, it will be very legal," Tonada assured. "As I said, we have American partners—lawyers, bankers, politicians."

Jordan took out his wallet and gave Tonada a business card. On it was only his name and a Los Angeles telephone number. "This is a service which will relay a message to me. I require full payment in advance, deposited to my Cayman Island bank account."

"Of course." Tonada bowed slightly. "Perhaps we can do business in the future, you and I. You burn what is old, I build what is new. Partners in progress."

"I'm not a partner in anything," Jordan declared. "I'm an independent contractor. I come in, do a job, and leave. I don't get involved."

"That is wise," Tonada allowed.

He was smiling again, and this time there was humor in his expression. He doesn't believe me, Jordan thought.

Jordan turned and resumed his work. It didn't matter to him what Tonada thought. Or anyone else.

Jordan went his own way.

When Mundo was getting ready to drive to Porto Velho to pick up the chemicals that had been flown in from Manaus, he said to Jordan, "Would you like to ride into the village again?"

"I thought you didn't want me going into the village," Jordan remarked. It was actually a question.

Mundo shrugged. "You seem to have been safe enough last time. If anything was going to happen to you, it would already have happened. The Nambi are not patient people."

Jordan considered the offer for a moment. He had already planned to walk into the village after Mundo left. Finally he said, "Sure, I'll ride in with you."

When Mundo dropped him off this time, Jordan walked to the square and went directly to the little cantina where he'd been taken to meet Paulo. Three of Paulo's young barefoot men in dirty white trousers and shirts were sitting at a table drinking the fiery fermented *aguaje* juice and listening to samba music on the radio. They didn't look up as Jordan entered and walked over to them.

"Can someone tell me how to find Apuri?" he asked in Portuguese. No one answered, and still they did not look up, merely kept their eyes on their hands around the wooden mugs from which they drank. Jordan repeated the question in Spanish. He got no reply to that language, either. They understood him, he was certain. Even if he had spoken to them in their own dialect, they probably wouldn't have responded.

Moving to another table, Jordan sat down. The same old woman who had served him and Paulo came out of the kitchen and stood next to him. *"Aguaje,"* Jordan ordered. What the hell, he had survived it once.

As he sat drinking a little while later, one of the young men rose and went into the kitchen and didn't come back. Ten minutes later, Apuri came into the cantina through the same kitchen door and walked directly to his table.

"Why are you looking for me?" she asked.

"Because I want to see you."

"Why do you want to see me?"

"I don't know why, I just do. I've been thinking about you."

"What have you been thinking?"

"Everything. How you look, feel, smell, taste—"

Apuri glanced nervously at the street door. "Is that half snake coming back for you?"

"No. He's gone to Porto Velho."

"We cannot talk here," she said. "Come with me."

She led Jordan through the kitchen and out to a dirt alley. She walked briskly down the alley as he hurried to keep up with her. "You and Paulo both called Mundo a half snake," he said as they walked. "Why only a half?"

"One half of him is human," Apuri said, "because he was born of a Nambiquaran mother. The snake part is from his father—Alves."

"Alves is Mundo's *father?*"

"Yes. Mundo's mother was a domestic at the hacienda. Servants there are treated as property. It is not unusual for a female servant to become pregnant by her master. Mundo was born there in the servants' quarters."

"Is his mother still there?"

"No. Several years later, she contracted syphilis from Alves and died when it was left untreated. He got medical attention for himself, of course." Apuri turned into a path that led away from the alley and up a gradual incline. At the top of the path was a shabby wooden house with smoke coming out of a stovepipe chimney.

"In here—" she took his hand and drew him inside. An older woman and another young woman about Apuri's age were cooking at a black iron stove. A naked baby played on the dirt floor with a large wooden spoon. From behind the house came the sound of other children's voices. "We can talk over here," Apuri said, going to the farthest corner away from the stove. As they passed a rear window, Jordan glanced out and saw Paulo sitting on a stool behind the house, talking to a dozen children of various ages who sat in a group before him. On his lap was Apuri's daughter, Evora.

Apuri sat on the floor in the corner and drew her knees up. "We must whisper," she cautioned Jordan, "so my mother and sister will not hear. They are very meddlesome and will try to listen."

"What is Paulo doing?" Jordan asked, sitting beside her, drawing his own knees up.

"Teaching the village children about our tribe," Apuri said. "He is the hereditary chief and it is his duty to be certain that Nambi children who live in the village know what came before them."

"Isn't it dangerous for him to be here?"

"Yes—but he is here, anyway." A trace of impatience sharpened her tone. "Did you come here to talk about Paulo?"

"No, I came to—"

"Whisper!"

"I came to talk about you," he said in his quietest undertone.

"What about me?"

"The other night was very nice."

"I know."

"Very special."

"Yes, for me as well. But it is over."

"Apuri," he said urgently, "why do you stay here?"

"This is my home, where I belong."

"In a few years, that home will be gone. In a few years, the whole rain forest will be gone. Where will your home be then?"

Apuri stared at Jordan but did not reply. It was a question for which she had no answer.

"Listen," he said, moving his face very close to hers, "when I leave here I'm going to Valparaiso in Chile. There's a big oil field there that's having a lot of burnoff problems and they want me to design a new system for them. I'll probably be there for several months. If you wanted to, you could come with me, just to see how you'd like living away from the rain forest."

"Me?" she said. He saw her shoulders stiffen. "What about my child?"

"Her, too, of course. I—"

"You would take us both?"

"Of course. I wouldn't ask you to leave your child." Jordan took her hand. "You could see how you liked living somewhere else."

"And how I liked living with you?"

"Yes."

"We are very different," she warned.

"On the outside. Not on the inside. Not what we feel."

She tilted her head an inch, in that way she had. "Are you doing this so Paulo won't kill you?"

Jordan shook his head. "Paulo won't kill me."

Apuri sighed. "No, you are right."

Jordan squeezed her hand. "Will you try it, Apuri?"

She glanced at her mother and sister, and caught them looking at her. They quickly looked away. This was an impossible place to make such plans. "Let me consider it," she said.

Before Jordan could speak again, they all suddenly heard the sound of heavy footsteps at the front door. Half a dozen men with weapons burst into the room. Jordan recognized them at once as *rifleros* from the Alves ranch.

"We are looking for the cattle thief!" one of them shouted. "Paulo! Where is he?"

"My God!" Apuri's hand went to her throat in fear. Her mother screamed and her sister ran for the baby.

"Out back!" one of the men yelled.

The intruders bullied through the room toward the rear door. One of them tripped over the baby before Apuri's sister could get to it. The man cursed and roughly pushed the infant aside with his boot. Jordan leaped to his feet and grabbed him.

"You bastard!"

The *riflero* butt-stroked Jordan across the face with the weapon stock and Jordan dropped heavily back to the dirt floor.

"Paulo, flee!" Apuri yelled out the window as the men rushed through the little house.

Rolling over, Jordan got to his knees. Just as he did, there was the sound of gunfire behind the house.

"Oh, dear God, the children!" Apuri screamed.

Jordan tried to stand. Blood rushed out of his brain with the effort and he sank back again. The last thing he saw was Apuri staring out the window, her face stricken with horror. Then he lost consciousness.

When he awoke, he was on his bed in the hacienda guest room. Two women of the household staff were putting wet cloths on his forehead and washing a three-inch abrasion on his jawbone where he'd been hit. Standing on the other side of the bed were Alves, Tonada, and Mundo.

"Where is she?" Jordan asked thickly. "Where's Apuri?"

"Deep in the rain forest, I imagine," said Alves. "That's where they usually run to."

"Paulo?"

"Escaped again." Alves' voice was exasperated and angry at the same time. "The man is like a ghost. He seems to evaporate at will."

Jordan remembered the children and the look on Apuri's face. "There was shooting. Was anyone hurt?"

"I'm afraid," Alves said, glancing away, "that two Nambi children were killed."

"Two *children?*" Jordan rose on one elbow and stared at the wealthy rancher. *Was one of them Apuri's child?*

"It was an unfortunate accident," Alves defended himself, regret obvious in his tone. Then his expression became stern. "And I must remind you, senor, that these matters are not your concern. These are community matters and you are a foreigner here. It was foolish of you to involve yourself with these Indians in the first place. You do not understand them."

Jordan turned hard eyes on Mundo. "You set me up," he accused. "You gave me a ride to the village so that I could be followed."

"That is a lie!" Mundo snapped.

"My foreman knew nothing of this," Alves declared. "You were observed by my informants in the village the first time you talked with Paulo. I had you followed today when Mundo let you off."

Jordan pushed away the hand of the woman treating his face and sat up on the side of the bed. "I'm leaving," he said evenly. "Get somebody else to burn the rain forest."

"Oh, no, senor," Alves said firmly. "We have a contract, you and I. My money has already been deposited in your Cayman Island bank."

"You'll get your money back."

Alves shook his head. "No, senor. You contracted to do this job for me and you will not leave here until it is done."

Jordan stood. "If you think you can force me to do it, you're crazy."

"Mr. Jordan," Tonada interrupted, "I implore you to be reasonable. Our host, I am afraid, is running out of patience."

"Too bad he didn't run out of bullets," Jordan said tightly. "Maybe those two kids wouldn't have been shot."

"I regret that as much as you do, senor," Alves told him stiffly. "But I will not be intimidated by an unfortunate fact that I cannot change. You will complete your contract."

"I will not."

"Think for a moment, Mr. Jordan," Tonada said. "You are in a very precarious position. Everything is ready for the burning. All that remains is to place the combustible chemicals and ignite them. That can be done by anyone."

"Hardly. You don't know how much to use."

"Exactly. If we did it without you, we would no doubt use too much. The result would be a more intense fire. Without you to control it, it would probably spread to parts of the rain forest which are still protected by government decree. There is documented proof that you contracted to do this fire. If it burns out of control, it will be you the government blames. That could result in criminal charges. And Brazil, Mr. Jordan, does not have prisons as modern and comfortable as your country."

"You're not scaring me, Tonada."

"Consider this, then," Alves spoke again. "If the fire burns out of control, many more Nambi will be made homeless. Unhindered, a fire we set might burn all the way to the mountains—you said so yourself, to Mundo. The entire Nambi tribe might find itself without a rain forest in mere days instead of years. You seem to have developed a certain, ah, *affinity* toward them. Do you wish to see them burned out entirely? If you do, senor, believe me, I will most certainly accommodate you."

Jordan stared at Alves without speaking. He thought of Apuri, Paulo, the young men, the women, the children. While the rain forest burned, they would lose everything: their past, their present, their future—everything.

Alves had him, Jordan thought. The rancher, with a set expression on his face, knew it. And Tonada knew it. And Mundo, the half snake.

The following day, Jordan seeded the chemicals in the patchwork of incendiary furrows. The mixed chemicals were granulated, in canvas sacks red in color to signify their volatility. Jordan opened each sack and spread the granules by hand. He worked under a heavy guard of *rifleros*, with Mundo constantly at his side, watching his every move. Jordan made no effort to conceal his animosity for the foreman.

"Do you know what the Nambi call you?" he asked as he stirred the combustibles and sprinkled them in the cut earth.

"I have no interest in what uncivilized savages call me," Mundo replied aloofly.

"They call you a half snake."

Mundo swallowed and looked away.

"I asked you once if Alves had any sons," Jordan reminded him. "You said no. I guess down here bastards don't count."

Resting a hand on his pistol, Mundo looked at him. "You are treading on perilous ground, senor."

Jordan paused in his work and smiled. "What will you do, Mundo? Shoot me? Your daddy wouldn't like that. Who would control the fire then?" When Mundo looked away once again, Jordan shook his head in contempt. "How can you remain so loyal to a man who won't even recognize you as his son?"

Later that day when they were eating lunch in a small clearing, Mundo said, "You do not understand our culture in Brazil, senor. Bloodlines are sacred down here. Senor Alves cannot acknowledge a child born out of wedlock without dishonoring his consecrated family. He is bound by centuries of a tradition which both he and I respect. He has done the best he could to give me a place here."

"Did he do his best by your mother?" Jordan asked quietly.

"He would have. My mother died of malaria when I was very young."

"Your mother died of syphilis," Jordan told him. "She caught it from him."

"That is a lie." Mundo's expression turned hard and dangerous. "My mother died of malaria. It states so on her grave marker."

"A grave marker says only what the living want said."

Mundo stood, his eyes flat and deadly. "I warn you, senor. Do not speak to me of personal matters again. If you do, I will wait until after the rain forest has burned and then I will kill you. If you wish to leave the Mato Grosso alive, concern yourself only with the work you must complete. I will not warn you again."

Jordan watched as Mundo took his plate of food and went over to eat with the *rifleros.*

For the rest of the day, Jordan worked in silence. By late afternoon, all the furrows were seeded. There was a nearly full red sack of the combustible granules left, which Jordan closed up and put in the back of Mundo's Jeep. "Bring this with you tomorrow," he told the foreman. "In case it rains in any part of the burn area, we'll need it to reseed."

"It will not rain," Mundo said impassively. "This is not the rainy season."

"Bring it anyway," Jordan ordered.

Mundo's eyes fixed on him. The Brazilian clearly did not like being given orders by Jordan. "As you wish, senor," he said unsmilingly. "You are still in charge. For now."

They drove back to the hacienda, neither speaking. Approaching the broad clearing where the estate house stood, Jordan couldn't help thinking how placid and serene it all looked. The great house, surrounded by its lush green lawn and rows of exotic flower beds, backdropped by the cornucopian rain forest in all its luxuriant natural beauty, was a splendid sight to behold.

On one of the wide verandas, Alves and Tonada were sitting under rotating ceiling fans, sipping cool drinks as native servants stood nearby to anticipate their needs. On the vast lawn, gardeners pushed fertilizer spreaders, distributing Tonada's synthetic mulch. The gardeners, Jordan noticed, moved in a crisscross pattern much like the layout of the incendiary furrows. Simple gardeners, he thought with a trace of bitterness. Even they contribute—they *grow.* I only destroy. It was the first time in his life that he had ever felt any remorse about what he did. Perhaps, he rationalized, it was the two Nambi children who had been shot. If it were not for him, those children would still be alive. And one of them might have been Apuri's little girl.

The thought haunted him.

\* \* \*

At dawn the following morning, Jordan began the burn.

Fires were lighted at two corners of the squared tract, and the cross-sections ignited in a V-pattern to burn toward the opposite two corners where the firebreaks had been dug. The belt of flame moved along the forest floor like a fiery snake and began to enkindle everything in its path. As it moved steadily forward, it left in its wake many pitches of flame that started climbing upward on trees, vines, leaves, whatever foliage it could reach. From it, the heat came: an invisible cloud of it, gushing out like the hot breath of an unseen monster. And the smoke: first a stream, then a spiral, then a great cloud, rolling across the top of the forest as if released from a sluice.

Ash began to sift out of the scorching mass; it settled on the bare, sweaty face and arms of Jordan and Mundo as they drove back and forth in the face of the fire to chart its progress. Now and again on one of the dirt roads, the two men saw nearly naked Indians—men, women, children, old people—hurrying away from the consuming blaze, carrying their pitiful belongings in their arms, their faces set in fear of what was happening to them today, and in dread of tomorrow. Their world had turned into hell.

When Jordan saw the Nambiquara children, he cursed under his breath, damning Alves, damning Mundo, and damning himself because he was part of it, too. We will all pay for this, he told himself. We *must* pay for it.

The fire burned for nine hours, devastating everything it touched, reducing the fecund square of rain forest to an ugly black landscape of ashes, cinder, and burn waste. As fires went, Jordan knew, it was a good fire: never out of control, burning only what it was set to burn, remaining within the periphery established by him; he could not complain about the fire. He had done his job well, as he always did. When the fire stopped where it was supposed to stop, when the flames became embers, when the smoke drifted away on the high air and the heat started to dissipate, Jordan should have felt satisfaction at his accomplishment. But he didn't. He only felt a bleak despondency that, because of the two children, was distressing him to the very pit of his being.

I must shake this, he told himself firmly. I must get hold of my mind. It's up to me to see that what we've done doesn't go unpunished—

"Is it over now?" Mundo asked, intruding on his dismal thoughts. They were in the Jeep, parked just beyond the firebreak at which the burning had stopped. Jordan looked around at the destruction.

"Yes, it's over," he said. Dry words forced through parched lips.

Jordan watched as Mundo poured water from a canteen onto a handkerchief and washed his face and arms of the black ash that had streaked them. Jordan himself didn't bother. He felt dirty, so he might as well look dirty.

Mundo started the Jeep and drove them back to the hacienda. Alves and

Tonada were standing on the broad front lawn, at the outer edges of which the gardeners were completing the synthetic fertilizing they had begun the previous day. Mundo parked in the drive that bordered the lawn. Jordan saw that his duffel bag was packed and waiting on the driveway. Alves and Tonada walked over to the Jeep. At a gesture from Alves, a nearby servant hurried to put the bag in the back of the Jeep, next to the red sack from the previous day's seeding.

"Your work is done here, senor," said Alves. "Mundo will drive you to Porto Velho. There is a commuter plane back to Manaus tonight. Our association is over."

"No," Jordan told him quietly, "it's not over."

Alves stared at him for a grave moment. "Leave, senor," he said softly, "while you still can." He nodded curtly for Mundo to be on his way.

The Jeep moved away from the great house in the rain forest.

As they drove toward the edge of the clearing, Jordan's mind raced to think of some way to make Mundo pull over when they reached the forest. Mundo, as usual, had his gunbelt on, the holstered pistol on the side next to Jordan. If I pretend to turn and reach toward my duffel bag, Jordan thought, maybe I can grab the gun away from him before he can react. It was risky at best, but Jordan saw no other way.

The Jeep left the clearing and in seconds was into the thick forest, out of sight of the hacienda. Jordan was just about to make his move for the gun when he looked ahead of them on the road and saw that he would not have to.

Paulo and a dozen of his men suddenly appeared from the forest and blocked the road.

Mundo stomped on the brake and brought the Jeep skidding sideways to a halt. He drew his gun and cocked it as the men surrounded them. Four of Paulo's men drew back on taut bowstrings and aimed arrows at Mundo. Everything froze—a moment of looming violence suspended, waiting. Paulo and Mundo locked eyes in a fierce stare.

"Are you going to shoot?" Paulo finally asked.

Mundo swallowed and uncocked the pistol. "No."

Paulo stepped over and took the gun from his hand. "Do you know why we have come for you?" he asked.

Mundo wet his lips. "You think I led the *rifleros* to the house. You think I am responsible for the children dying."

"That is the reason," Paulo acknowledged, nodding.

"I did not do it," Mundo said. "I had no part in it."

"That I cannot believe," said the old chief.

Mundo shrugged. "There is no way I can prove it."

"Maybe there is," said Jordan, speaking for the first time. He got out of the Jeep and walked around behind it. From the back he removed the red canvas sack, opened it, and poured its contents onto the ground. What spilled out was not leftover combustible granules from the previous day, but dirt.

"I don't understand," said Mundo, frowning.

"Come with me," Jordan said, walking back toward the edge of the clearing. Mundo hesitated, but at a nod from Paulo he followed Jordan. Paulo and his men fell in step behind them.

Jordan led them to the last stand of trees, where the forest broke and the clearing began and flowed into the manicured lawn of the hacienda. A group of gardeners working nearby paused and looked at them apprehensively.

"The combustible granules are there," Jordan said, waving an arm. "I slipped out of my room in the middle of the night, took them from your Jeep, and mixed them into Tonada's fertilizer. Then I filled the red sack with dirt and replaced it." From his pocket, he took a small box of stick matches and tossed them to Mundo. "You want Paulo to believe you're innocent? Give him a reason to believe it. Get rid of the half of yourself they call snake."

Mundo stared at Jordan in disbelief. "This is insane—"

"No, it's *right,*" Jordan insisted. His jaw clenched. "Do it."

Mundo looked at Paulo, at Paulo's young men with their inscrutable faces, and back at Jordan. "It's insane!"

"Do it for your mother, Mundo," said Jordan.

The foreman's expression tightened. A grimness settled in it, and his black eyes suddenly took on depth, like two dark wells into his mind. "Yes—" he whispered, more to himself than to the men around him "—I'll do it for my mother."

Mundo took a match from the box, struck it, and tossed it onto the lawn. The granules in the grass ignited at once. Everyone except Jordan watched in awe as the fire spread like a lighted fuse. It swept over the blanket of lawn like a wave breaking on a beach. Then urgent shouts rose as the gardeners ran for safety.

Alves hurried onto the front veranda of his great house, a group of servants in his wake. Tonada rushed to his side. The rancher began waving his arms and shouting orders, but no one seemed to be listening to him. When the fire reached the house and began burning the foundation, the servants followed the gardeners to safety. Presently Alves and Tonada fled also.

Jordan and the others watched until the great house was burning smartly. Then Paulo said, "Come, we must go. It will not take Alves long to organize his *rifleros.*"

\* \* \*

In the Nambi camp, Jordan learned with enormous relief that Apuri's child had not been one of those killed. In front of Paulo and Mundo, he renewed his proposal that she leave the forest and go with him to Chile. She refused.

"I cannot abandon my family, my people, my home," she said. "A person cannot run away from what they are."

Jordan felt as if he had been kicked in the chest. His mind roiled desperately not to lose her. Turning to Paulo, he said, "Let me stay with the Nambi. Let me fight with you."

Paulo shook his head. "If you stay, the government will send the Army into the forest after you." His wise old eyes flicked to Mundo. He handed him the pistol he had taken earlier. "You cannot remain, either. Even though you have redeemed yourself as a Nambiquara, for the good of the tribe you must leave. The gardeners saw you start the fire—the Army would come for you also. But if you both leave, our tribe will face only the *rifleros* again. We can deal with them; we cannot deal with the Army."

Mundo laughed softly and started for the Jeep. "Come on," he said over his shoulder to Jordan, "we don't have much time."

Jordan turned hurt eyes to Apuri. "Is there no way at all for us?"

"Not today," she said quietly. "Perhaps a faroff tomorrow."

"If I come back?"

"Yes." She looked away. "If you come back."

Mundo drove the Jeep up next to him. "If you want to keep living, get in."

Apuri was still looking away. Jordan took a deep breath and got in the Jeep. Without a backward glance, Mundo drove out of the camp.

On the road, Jordan asked, "Where are we going?"

"Bolivia," said Mundo. "It's the nearest border."

"Do you think we'll make it?"

"Maybe," Mundo said. "If we're lucky."

The Jeep sped through what was left of the rain forest.

# MR. FOLSOM FEELS FINE

*By Avram Davidson*

S OME PEOPLE can handle foreign travel, whereas others simply can't. Some can go live in a Himalayan satrapy so remote that it is not perceived on maps more than once in a century (and even that once it appears sketchily in some learned journal showing the distribution of its thirty-seven species of venomous earwigs)—can go live in it and do just fine, riding the small fur-bearing ponies as though they'd been hired for twenty minutes at a fun park and eating the roast slugs as though they were Mighty Max Burgers, whereas there are those who get ptomaine or its latest equivalent from a tortilla chip three feet south by southeast from the border of the U.S.A. Who can say why some people can travel by scooter through bandidi-infested crags and never encounter one single bandido and yet other people manage to alienate the usually imperturbable Royal Horsemen of Bothnia by dropping chewing-gum wrappers in front of their royal horses for a fine of seven *boboes*.

Mr. Edgar Folsom, who retained the same faith in the advertisements that he had had in his twenties, had for a long while planned to "Retire on Two Hundred and Twenty Dollars a Month," and had lavished his savings upon the Good Old Days Retirement Company. Often he and Mamie (Mrs. Edgar) had been almost obliged to chuckle when they considered how they—and other subscribers to the GODRC—were going to beat the system, even if nobody else was—except maybe a handful of intractable

Indians in the Wild Rice Country, who could, of course, always live on wild rice. And baskets. Lots and *lots* of edible baskets, woven from succulent shoots.

"Oh, I got to hand it to *you* two," often said unmarried sister (and sister-in-law) Etta Folsom. (Their grandfather had not been originally named Folsom, he had originally been named something harsh and Nordish, a fact which only a distant cousin still claimed to remember. Mamie Folsom had long ago lost this man's address and made little attempt to find it.) *"You* two know what you're doing."

Did Mamie know what she was doing when she passed away, quite suddenly and quite silently, two weeks before his effective (compulsory) retirement date? Perhaps she did. Edgar's slightly delayed letter of notice to the GODRC was answered, eventually, by a firm of attorneys of which Edgar had never heard. It informed him that the Good Old Days Retirement Company (whose ads had not appeared in magazines for quite some time) no longer existed, as, under the laws of a not very well known and distant state, it had wound up its affairs. Its assets now belonged to a giant conglomerate specializing in, among other things, the manufacture of waxes and wines and the management of ski lodges. This organization had somehow, certainly quite legally, acquired the assets of the Good Old Days Retirement Company without acquiring any of its liabilities. Anyway, the letter pointed out, you couldn't retire on two hundred and twenty dollars a month any more. Not their fault, but as a matter of policy, if not benevolence—being a bunch of real good guys who know how it is—the conglomerate was going to make Mr. Folsom (in his own right and as sole heir and legatee of Mamie P. Folsom, Deceased) a lump sum, that's-*it* payment of eleven hundred dollars.

"Well, you were always a very stubborn boy, Edgar, and no one could ever tell you what to do. Now, *these* quilts I am going to take with me, *those* quilts I am letting the Historical Society have, and *this* quilt I am letting you take with you," said Etta.

"Take with me *where?* Where are we *going?"* her brother asked. He was slightly bewildered. If Mamie hadn't always told him what to do, Etta had always told him what to do.

*"I* am going to the Sons and Daughters of Bothnia Residence in Calico Falls. Women are admitted at sixty, men at eighty. In the meanwhile, where *you* are going I'm sure I couldn't say. Don't you have a pension? Hand me that wrap of tissue paper, please."

Mr. Folsom smote his brow. "A *pension!"* he cried. "Of *course!"*

In the Pensions Office of the Civil Functionaries Administration, Mr. Roswell P. Sawell addressed his assistant, Mr. Merton Rush. "Anything new today, Mert?"

"I've just opened a new file," said Mr. Rush. "Application for pension from a Mr.—" he consulted the file "—Edgar Folsom. From Wampanoack."

"Don't matter where from," said his superior. "What's his timeage?"

"Timeage is seventeen years, seven days."

"*He* doesn't qualify for full payment, Rush."

"*I* know that."

"Minimum pension of, hm, let me calculate a second, um, two hundred and twenty dollars a month. Write him. Application denied. Subject named above may appeal. *You* know the routine."

"*I* know the routine."

"Then we'll hold up the appeal for five years, and of course he draws no interest."

"Of *course.*"

But Mr. Merton Rush did not move back into his own office and Ros Sawell asked, in some surprise, "What are you waiting for, then?"

Mert reminded his boss that it was CFA policy to grant three such applications without delay monthly, that so far they had granted only two, and that it was the last day of the month.

"Oh. Um. Yes, so it is. Shoot. Oh, well, *grant* it. He'll soon enough try to collect the pension in a foreign country with a subversively lower cost of living. *Then* we'll jump him."

Mert said, "Oh, *boy,* yes! Estopped. Suspended pending investigation. That's *right!*"

"We got to think of the taxpayers."

Etta had a very nice room with her own foyer facing the granite statue of The Intrepid Bothnian on the lawn. Constant hot tap water for making instant coffee. "Well, have you made up your *mind* yet, Edgar, what you're going to do? Your lease runs out this month and your rent will be raised."

Mr. Folsom straightened his bowtie. (He always had a little trouble with it.) "Well, I certainly hope and trust the President will do something about it."

Etta was very patriotic, *but.* "Why should he do something about it?" she asked, for once a bit surprised.

"Well, I wrote and asked him to."

"Oh, *you*—Edgar. What's that sticking out of your pocket instead of a nice clean hankie? A letter. What would you do if I weren't here to remind you." Deftly, she opened and read. "Well, I never. You are going to get a Civil Functionary Partial Pension of two hundred and twenty dollars a month. Oh, for goodness sake."

Edgar, however, wasn't surprised. Not at all. "There, you *see.* I guess an American citizen can write to his President fee wants results. Guess that

Good Old Days Retirement Company, he fixed their little red wagon sure enough."

For once Etta had not much to say, but she said it. *"You* can't retire on two hundred and twenty dollars a month. Have you *seen* the prices lately? Where do you *shop?"*

"Tut," said Edgar. "I'll go live in some country with a lower cost of living. Few can't lick 'em, join 'em. Huh?"

The young person in the travel agency repeated his question. "Where can you go for eleven hundred dollars? Well, the pitcheresque Republic of La Banana has just been opened for tourism and foreign migration. We got this bunch of *lit*reature in just today. 'The pitcheresque Republic of La Banana, which gave its name to the familiar succulent yellow fruit, contains one hundred and fifty-two species of edible wild slugs, also many colorful parrots.' Here, you can read it while I make out your package."

In the newly opened consulate and travel office of the Republic of La Banana, Bombo Duzbuz Jambatch looked at Mr. Folsom listlessly. "You wish to go to our country? Fine. So go. One moment. Health precaution. Stick out tongue, please. Thirty-seven dollar, you pay *me*. Okay, now I make out your Permission."

Mr. Folsom had never traveled very much. "You're put?" Mamie used to ask. *"Stay* put."

He now inquired, "Permission for *what?"*

Bombo Duzbuz Jambatch looked up, surprised. *"Everything,"* he replied. "Enter. Exit. Transit. Operate steamroller. Even, you may to run for elective office. Save that no more we have elections. *Kay.* All finish. Here."

Mr. Folsom took the large and colorful paper, folded it. "When does it have to be renewed?"

The bombo suddenly seemed bored. "How *I* know? *I* am not prophet. Do not push fates. Perhaps never. You think we are tyranty? Go."

Edgar went.

In the capital hamlet of Gunk Up High, several gorges away from the non-capital hamlet of Gunk Not So High, Mr. Folsom found there was something of a housing shortage. The best he could obtain for himself was an eight-room *poppick* at a rental of one dollar per room per month, the landlord insisting on renting the *poppick* as a single unit. The other natives rolled their eyes at such cupidity and murmured a local proverb loosely translated as, "Foreigners and their welcome money often make the rich richer." It was, of course, far more room than Edgar needed, but he found that the space gradually filled with the picturesque native furniture, artwork, and bric-a-brac which he found it amusing to buy at the Weeny Bazaar (the

Great Big Bazaar dealt mostly in milch-sheep and rhinoceros legs). Sometimes he spent as much as two or three dollars a month on such items.

*Goro-goro luntch-potch,* as they say in the pawkey idiom of La Banana. Meaning, So the time does pass, even so.

"Well, what did I tell you?" said Mr. Roswell Sawell. "Didn't he run true to form? Here's a change of address for his Civil Functionary Partial Pension check, just as I predicted."

"You certainly can pick 'em, Chief."

"Now, theoretically—" Ros pushed the compliment aside "—any American citizen may elect to receive his pension anywhere in the world—Andorra, Oz, Borrioboola-gha, *any*where. But we don't *like* um to! *We* know that nobody can live on that kind of money! Where's the cost of his *car*? Where's his *gas* money? You know what a *TV set* costs in some a these countries with subversively low standards of living? *Dish*washers? As for, say, the price of *beef,* well, you just price it yourself! If *we* can't make it, *they* can't make it! No, Mert: less a fellow's getting a full career pension of, well, say at least two thousand dollars a month, there's no way he can live on his pension. Which means—well, *you* know what it means!"

Merton nodded his birdy head. "Il-lic-it en-ter-prise." He rolled out the syllables with relish. Relish, and unction.

"Absolutely. Smuggling Scotch whisky. Promoting ox-races. And, increasingly, the notorious bush-wax trade."

His assistant agreed with him. "That's terrible stuff, that bushwax."

Terrible? said his superior. Terrible was hardly the word for it. It was diuretic, euphoric, and non-addictive! No wonder the Pensions Office of the Civil Functionaries Administration worked hand in glove with the Illegal Ear Substances Division of the Crack-Down Department. "So let's put a Stop on his pension, and he can swim back, if he likes, and file an appeal. *There's* a good ten years he won't be robbing the taxpayers.—Why are you just *stand*ing there, Mert?"

Merton said because they had already put Stops on eight hundred and thirty-five pensions that month already, which was tops according to policy, and so they'd better wait till next month.

"Don't rock the boat, in other words?"

"You said it, Chief!"

"Well, you may be right. I have a sort of nose for these things. But, *next* month we drop the Himalayan Mountains on him!"

He and his assistant laughed soundlessly.

Mr. Edgar Folsom never drank Scotch whisky, thought the ox-races were smelly, and would have been bored by TV had there been any. (The mountain ranges made it impracticable. As for washing his dishes, he threw them all into the gorge behind his house and got new ones.) He was spending so little money he was obliged to buy quite a number of boxes to store the money he didn't spend. He was by now probably the richest man in Gunk Up High, and the lower caste of natives never came near his house at night lest the gods, who obviously *love* rich men (else why are they rich—answer *that* one, would you?), eat their kidney-fat. They may not know much, those innocent, childlike, very dirty natives, but they know that without kidney-fat you just ain't got it.

One day Mr. Edgar Folsom was strolling along a road (path, the very particular might call it) which had yet to receive the biannual attentions of the steamroller. (The fact is that the dictator was very fond of operating it himself and paid no attention to any of the schedules the Department of Public Works submitted to him—very, very occasionally.) Rather incuriously, he observed someone he rather thought was a foreigner. In fact, this one admitted as much to him, saying, "I am a foreigner."

"What brings you here? Not that it isn't a nice little place."

The man said he was allowing vortices of energy to carry him along as he observed The Way and The Eternal Snows.

"Oh."

The foreigner took him by the arm and slightly turned him. He gestured. "Just cast your gaze through the, like, mists of illusion and tell me if there are three energy-forms in uniform standing at the crossroads."

Mr. Folsom slightly squinted. "Well," he said, "usually there are two policemen standing there, I don't know why—I mean, there's never *that* much traffic—but today I guess there *are* three."

The foreigner said that that which was not an enigma was an illusion. "Just point out your house—I mean the compass-point where the non-real you is dwelling, as it were, man. There? Good. Now, would you do me one big favor? My arm hurts today—a mere illusion to be sure, but would you just let me put this in your case and I'll meet you later. Right now it's my, um, time of withdrawal and meditation."

Of the three at the crossroads, only one spoke sufficient English to be more than merely amusing. This was Bombo Yimyam Hutchkutch. "Ah, Meestair Edgar Folsom, you are out to ramble, as often, eh?"

Mr. Folsom acknowledged it. "I was taking some snapshots with my little old Kodak brownie camera and the people there started yelling, so I stopped and gave 'em some pennies—anyway *I* call 'em pennies. So then they all kissed my coat-lapels and gave me what they said is the stuffed head of a yeti. I put it in my briefcase. No, that's not it. I dunno what *this* is— some other foreigner asked me to take it down the hill for him, I guess because it will help his hurt arm." And he gazed round the mountain-circled universe with his candid eyes.

From the policemen meanwhile had come noises of suspicion, irritation, and something which another might have taken for dismay. Said the bombo, *"We* will take it down the hill for you, Meestair. *We* will take care to find him and alleviate his hurt arm. What, to think he can move about with this stash and pay us *nothing?* Proceed upon your ramble, Meestair Folsom, and may you live in our nation for a hundred thousand eons."

*"Well,* Chief," said Merton, "guess what just came in?"

"Some more appeals against estopment of pensions, I suppose," suggested Mr. Sawell indifferently. The Pacific Ocean and the entirety of the Indoo Sea might have been filled with swimming appellants, much cared *he.*

Nay, not so, Merton told him. "It's the monthly exchange list from the Illegal Ear Substances Division of the Crack-Down Department, and guess what? Folsom, Edgar, in La Banana has been instrumental in catching a cache of illegal bush-wax!"

They gazed at each other with a wild surmise. Then, slowly but with admiration, Mr. Sawell said, "I guess he is one of the IED's men. This pension thing, it's just his cover. Of *course* he doesn't have to live on it. Get the big red rubber stamp and stamp his file NTBTW. Get going, now, Mert." And Merton, bowing his head respectfully, proceeded to affix the indication that Edgar Folsom's pension was Never To Be Tampered With.

A civil functionary has many, many duties. The public scarcely knows.

As for Mr. Edgar Folsom, he has grown tired of hoarding his money. For one thing, he sends contributions to the worthy causes he finds mentioned in the worn, worn copies of *Reader's Digest* that come his distant way as padding in the ox-caravans. And for another, he has bought a choice and select herd of jet-black milch-sheep, plus three dancing bears.

He feels just fine.

# THE ALIBI

*By Isaac Asimov*

EMMANUEL RUBIN was in an uncharacteristically mild mood during the cocktail hour preceding the Black Widowers' banquet. And uncharacteristically thoughtful, too. But characteristically didactic.

He was saying to Geoffrey Avalon (though his voice was loud enough to reach all corners of the room), "I don't know how many mystery stories—or suspense stories, as they tend to call them these days—have been written, but the number is approaching the astronomical and I certainly haven't read them all.

"Of course, the old-fashioned puzzle story is passe, though I like to write one now and then, but even the modern psychological story, in which the crime is merely mentioned in passing but the inner workings of the criminal's tortured soul occupies thousands of tortured words, may have its puzzle aspects.

"What it amounts to is that I'm trying to think up a new kind of alibi that is broken in a new kind of way, and I wonder—what are the odds of my thinking one up that has never been used before? And no matter how ingenious I am, how can I possibly know that someone long ago, in some obscure volume I never read, didn't use precisely the same bit of ingenuity? I envy the early practitioners in the field. Almost anything they made up had never been used before."

Avalon said, "What are the odds, Manny? If *you* haven't read all the suspense stories written, neither has any reader. Just make up something. If it's a repeat of some obscure device that appeared in a novel published fifty-two years ago, who will know?"

Rubin said bitterly, "Somewhere someone will have read that early novel and he'll write to me, very likely sarcastically."

Mario Gonzalo, from the other end of the room, called out, "In your case, it won't matter, Manny—there are so many other things to criticize in your stories that probably no one will bother pointing out that your gimmicks are old hat!"

"There speaks a man," said Rubin, "who in a lifetime of portraiture has produced only caricature."

"Caricature is a difficult art," said Gonzalo, "as you would know if you knew anything about art."

Gonzalo was sketching the evening's guest in order that the sketch might be added to those that marched along the wall of the room at the Milano Restaurant in which the banquets took place.

He had what seemed an easy task this time, for the guest brought in by Avalon, who was host of the evening, had a magnificent mane of white hair, thick and lightly waved, shining like spun silver in the lamplight. His regular features and spontaneous, even-toothed smile made it quite certain that he was one of those men who grew statelier and more handsome with age. His name was Leonard Koenig and Avalon had introduced him merely as "my friend."

Koenig said, "You're making me look something like a superannuated movie star, Mr. Gonzalo."

"You can't fool an artist's eye, Mr. Koenig," said Gonzalo. "Are you one, by any chance?"

"No," said Koenig, without further elaboration, and Rubin laughed.

"Mario's right, Mr. Koenig," said Rubin, "you can't fool an *artist's* eye."

With that the conversation grew more general, breaking off temporarily only when the soft voice of that peerless waiter, Henry, announced, "Please take your seats, gentlemen. Dinner is being served." —And they sat down to their turtle soup, which Roger Halsted, as the club gourmet, sipped carefully before giving it the benediction of a broad smile.

Over the brandy, Thomas Trumbull, whose crisply waved white hair lost caste, somehow, against the brighter, softer hair of the guest, took up the task of grilling.

"Mr. Koenig, how do you justify your existence?" he asked.

Koenig smiled broadly. "In view of Mr. Rubin's problems with the invention of alibis, I suppose I can most easily justify my existence by pointing out that in my time I have been a breaker of alibis."

"Your profession has not been announced by Jeff," said Trumbull. "May I take it, then, that you're on the police force?"

"Not quite. Not on an ordinary police force. I am in counterespionage— or, to put it more accurately, I was. I retired early and moved into the law, which is how I met Jeff Avalon."

Trumbull's eyebrows shot up. "Counterespionage?"

Koenig smiled again. "I read your mind, Mr. Trumbull. I know of your position with the government and you're wondering why you don't know my name. I assure you I was a minor cog, who, except for one case, never did anything notable. Besides, as you know, it's not department policy to publicize its members. We do our work best in obscurity. And, as I said, I retired early. And have been forgotten, in any case."

Gonzalo said eagerly, "That alibi you broke. How did you do that?"

"It's a long story," said Koenig, "and not something I should talk about in detail."

"You can trust us," said Gonzalo. "Nothing that's said at any Black Widowers' meeting is ever mentioned outside. That includes our waiter, Henry, who's himself a member of the club. Tom, tell him."

"Well, it's true," said Trumbull reluctantly. "We're all souls of discretion. Even so, though, I can't urge you to talk about matters that shouldn't be talked of."

Avalon pursed his lips judiciously. "I'm not sure we can take that attitude, Tom. The condition of the banquet is that the guest must answer all questions and rely on our discretion."

Gonzalo said, "Look, Mr. Koenig, you can leave out anything you think is too sensitive to talk about. Just describe the alibi and don't tell us how you broke it—*we'll* break it for you."

James Drake chuckled. "Don't make rash promises, Mario."

"We can try," said Gonzalo.

Koenig said thoughtfully, "Do you mean you want to make a game of this?"

"Why not?" said Gonzalo. "Tom Trumbull can disqualify himself if it turns out he remembers the case."

"I doubt that he will. The whole thing was on a 'need to know' basis and he wasn't part of the same organization I was." Koenig paused to think for a moment. "I suppose it's possible to play the game, but it was almost thirty years ago. I hope I remember all the details." He cleared his throat and began.

"It's interesting," said Koenig, "that Mr. Rubin mentioned the tales that talk about the psychology of the criminal, because in my old business a lot depended on the psychology of the spy. There were people who betrayed their country for money, or for spite, or out of sexual infatuation. These are easy to handle, in a way, because they have no strong underpinning of conviction and, if caught, give way easily."

"Greed is the thing," said Halsted feelingly. "And you don't have to be a spy. The corrupt politician, the tax-finagling businessman, the industrialist who defrauds the armed forces with overcharges and shoddy work can damage the country as badly as any spy."

"Yes," said Rubin, "but these guys will shout patriotism all over the place. They can steal the government and the people blind, but as long as they hang out the flag on Memorial Day and vilify foreigners and anyone to the left of Genghis Khan they're great guys."

"That's why," said Avalon, "Samuel Johnson pointed out that patriotism was the last refuge of the scoundrel."

"Undoubtedly," said Koenig, "but we're veering from the point. I was going to say that there are also spies who do their job out of a strong ideological feeling. They may do so out of admiration for the ideals of another nation, or because they feel they are serving the cause of world peace, or in some other way are behaving nobly in their own eyes. We can't really complain about this—we have people in foreign countries who work for us for similar idealistic reasons, and, in fact, we have more of these than our enemies have. In any case, these ideologues are the really dangerous spies, for they plan more carefully, are willing to take greater risks, and are far more resolute when caught. A man of that sort was Stephen. Notice that I'm using only his first name, and Stephen was not the true first name, either.

"Stephen lived a quiet life—he didn't draw attention to himself. He didn't make the mistake of trying to cover his true purposes by an unrealistic profession of patriotism. It's just that he had available to him, in the way of his work and of circumstances, a great many items we didn't want the enemy to have. Still, there are many people who know matters that had best be confidential, and the vast majority of them are thoroughly dependable, and there was no reason to suppose that Stephen wasn't as dependable as any of them.

"However, there were certain data that the enemy would particularly want to have—data to which Stephen had access. He could easily pass it along to the enemy. If he did, though, circumstances were such that he would surely be suspected. In fact, there would be what would amount to a moral certainty that he was the culprit. Yet such was the importance of the information that he *had* to obtain it.

"Notice, by the way, that I don't tell you anything at all about the nature of the data in question—about the manner in which he had access or the manner in which he would make the transfer. All that is irrelevant to the little game we are playing. Now let me try to put myself into Stephen's mind—

"He knew he had to perform the task, and he knew he would instantly be suspected, strongly suspected. He felt that he had to protect himself somehow. It wasn't so much that he feared imprisonment, for he might be exchanged. Nor, I imagine, did he fear death, since the circumstances of his life were such that he must have known that he lived with the possibility of death, even unpleasant death, every day.

"Nevertheless, as a patriot—I suppose he could be considered that if viewed through his own eyes—he didn't want to be caught because he knew he couldn't easily be replaced. Furthermore, if he could somehow be absolved of suspicion, our department would have to look elsewhere. That would waste our energies and place any number of innocent people under suspicion, all of which would work to our disadvantage.

"But how could he avoid being caught when he was, of necessity, the obvious culprit? Clearly, he would have to be in two places—in the city, where he could carry through his task, and, at the same time, in a faraway place so that it would seem he could not possibly have had anything to do with the task—the only way he could achieve that was to be two people.

"Here is the way he managed it, as we eventually found out. The country Stephen worked for provided a lookalike, whom we might call Stephen Two. I imagine that if Stephen and Stephen Two stood next to each other it would be easy to distinguish between them, but if someone saw Stephen Two and then, a few days later, Stephen himself, it would seem that he had seen the same person.

"It also seems logical to suppose that Stephen Two's resemblance to Stephen was reinforced. He would be given Stephen's hair-styling, would cultivate Stephen's thin moustache, would practice Stephen's voice as given on recordings and his signature as recorded on documents. He would even have learned to make use of some of Stephen's favorite expressions. Naturally, he would have to be someone who spoke English and understood the culture as well as Stephen did.

"All this must have taken considerable time and effort, but it's a measure of the importance of what the enemy country was after that the time and effort was spent.

"We eventually pieced together what it was that Stephen did and are satisfied that the account is essentially correct.

"As the time approached, Stephen let it be known, in as casual a manner as seemed appropriate, that he would be going to Bermuda for a week's vacation by way of a cruise ship. When the time came, he went into hiding and changed his appearance slightly so that he wouldn't readily be recognized while he carried out the theft and transmission of the data as quietly and as obscurely as possible.

"It was Stephen Two, of course, who took the ship to Bermuda. Stephen himself, as it happened, had never been to Bermuda, and that struck him as a useful fact. Having been there but once would account for the fact that he might not know all there was to know about the island. He had, however, to know what he himself had done on the island, and for that purpose he had Stephen Two send him, by way of a simple code and a secure accommodation-address, a condensed but detailed account of what he did and saw in Bermuda. In particular, Stephen Two must do a number of unimportant things that he would have to recount in detail so that Stephen could use them as proof of having been in Bermuda. A casual reference to the unimportant could be made to seem convincing evidence.

"We're quite certain that Stephen ordered Stephen Two to make friends with some reasonably attractive woman on the ship and get along with her well enough so that she would be certain to remember him—yet not so well that she could detect some difference between the two Stephens. In particular, he didn't want Stephen Two to get intimate and start a romance. I imagine that he didn't want to be handed a situation that might make him uncomfortable, and a woman who imagined they had been lovers, when that was something he wouldn't be able to deny without great danger to himself, would certainly represent something uncomfortable.

"The week during which Stephen Two was in Bermuda must have been a period of great suspense for Stephen. He carried through his own task, but what if the cruise ship foundered or Stephen Two had an accident and was hospitalized, crippled, or even killed? Or suppose Stephen Two were fingerprinted for some reason, or turned traitor? Anything like that would have ruined Stephen's alibi and made his jailing certain.

"In actual fact, of course, none of these things took place. Stephen Two sent his letters faithfully, numbering each so that Stephen could be certain that none had been lost. Stephen carefully memorized each letter as well as he might.

"Eventually, Stephen Two returned from Bermuda and with quiet skill faded out and went back to his own country, while Stephen resumed his identity.

"It was two weeks after the end of the Bermuda trip that we had reason to suspect that the data Stephen had been after had been tampered with. A quick investigation proved the case, and the finger of suspicion pointed forcefully and without question at Stephen.

"A group of us descended upon him.

"He was quite admirable in his way. His distress at the loss of the information seemed quite sincere and he admitted ruefully that he was the logical suspect and, indeed, the only one.

" 'But,' he said, 'I was on *The Island Duchess* from the ninth to the sixteenth, and I was in Bermuda between the eleventh and the fourteenth. If the loss took place during that period, I simply couldn't have done it.'

"He gave us full details and, of course, had ample records to the effect that he had bought tickets, embarked, disembarked, paid his bar bill and some other expenses, and so on. All seemed in order. It didn't even seem suspicious that he could produce this all on demand. He said, 'I'm going to claim part of this as business expense, so I'll need records for the I.R.S.'

"There seemed to be a disposition among my confreres to accept this and to wonder if there might be other suspects, after all. I held off. Stephen seemed, for some reason, to be too smooth to me, and I insisted on continuing to question him while others tackled other angles of the case. That was my big achievement as a spy catcher. If I'd had one or two more like that, the department might not have been so willing to let me go when I asked for retirement, but I didn't. This was my one and only.

"In a second interview, I said to him, 'Were you on the ship or in Bermuda every moment from embarkation to disembarkation?'

" 'Yes, of course,' he said, 'I was at the mercy of the ship.'

" 'Not entirely, sir,' I told him.

"He frowned, as though trying to penetrate my meaning, then said, 'Do you mean that I might have flown from the ship to here and then back to the ship, and in that way have been here for the job and there for an alibi?'

" 'Something like that,' I said grimly.

" 'I couldn't get on a plane without identifying myself,' he protested.

" 'There is such a thing as deliberate misidentification.'

" 'I understand that,' he said, 'but I suppose you can check as to whether any helicopter encountered the ship at any time. I suppose you can check every passenger on every plane between here and Bermuda between the eleventh and the fourteenth and see whether any passenger is unaccounted for or anything but a real person distinct from myself.'

"I didn't bother to tell him that such checks were actually under way.

"Our interviews were recorded, of course, with Stephen's permission. We had read him his rights, but he said he was perfectly willing to talk and required no lawyer. He was the very model of an innocent citizen confident in his innocence, and that simply raised my suspicions somehow. He seemed too good to be true, and too confident. It was about then that I began to wonder if he had a twin brother, so that he could seem to be in Bermuda even while he was at home. That was checked out, too, and it was established he was a single birth and an only son. But the idea of a lookalike remained in my mind.

"I said, in a later interview, 'Did you stay on the ship while in Bermuda or at a hotel?'

" 'On the ship.'

" 'Had you ever been to Bermuda before? Are you a well known figure there in any way?'

" 'It was my first trip to Bermuda.'

" 'Is there anyone who can vouch for your presence on the ship each day? Anyone who can vouch that you were in Bermuda at those times you were off the ship?'

"He hesitated. 'I was on the cruise alone. I didn't go with any friends. After all, I had no idea, no faintest notion that I'd have to prove I was on the ship.'

"I half smiled. That seemed a hair too ingenuous. 'You're not going to tell me,' I said, 'that you were a recluse, skulking in corners and speaking to no one.'

" 'No,' he said, looking a little uncomfortable. 'As a matter of fact, I was friendly enough, but I can't guarantee that any of the people I interacted with casually would remember me. Except—'

" 'Go on. What is the exception?'

" 'There was a young woman I grew friendly with at the start of the cruise. She became my steady companion at ship's meals, and for much of the time in Bermuda. There was nothing intimate about the relationship. I'm not a married man, but even so it was just a casual friendship. I think she might remember me. We danced on board ship, and in Bermuda we visited the aquarium, went on the glass-bottom boat together, took tours, ate at the Princess Hotel. She went to the beach alone, though. I tend to avoid the sun.'

" 'Did you see her every day?'

"He thought a moment. 'Yes, every day. Not all day, and not at night. She was never in my room and I was never in hers.'

" 'What was the young woman's name?'

" 'Artemis.'

" 'Artemis?' I said, rather in disbelief.

" 'That's what she told me her name was, and that's what I heard others call her. She was a very pretty woman—in her early thirties, I should judge, with dark-blonde hair and blue eyes. About five feet six in height.'

" 'And her last name?'

"He hesitated. 'I don't remember. She may not even have mentioned it. It was shipboard, you know—very informal. She called me Stephen. I don't think I ever mentioned my own last name.'

" 'Her address?'

" 'I don't know. She spoke as though she were a New Yorker, but I don't know. You can always look at the ship's records for the week. She'd be listed, and I'd say the chances are virtually zero that there would be two Artemises. They'd surely have her last name and her home address.'

"I turned off the recording device at that and warned him that, as had been established, he'd continue to be confined to his apartment for the duration of the questioning, but that anything necessary would be brought to him, and any reasonable errands would be run for him.

"I was determined to prove if I could that whoever had been in Bermuda, it wasn't Stephen—but for that I would clearly need the woman.

"It took three days to find her, and each day was an annoyance. Obviously I couldn't keep Stephen under wraps indefinitely, and once he began to complain loudly enough we'd have to come up with something definite or let him go.

"But he didn't complain. He continued to be a model citizen, and once I had Artemis in tow I arranged to have her see him when he didn't know she was looking at him. She said, 'It certainly looks like Stephen.'

" 'Let's meet him, then,' I said. 'Just act naturally, but please keep your eyes open and let me know if, for any reason, you think it's not the man you met on the ship.'

"I brought her into the room and Stephen looked at her, smiled, and said, 'Hello, Artemis.'

"She said, a little hesitantly, 'Hello, Stephen.'

"She was no actress. She looked at him anxiously, and Stephen would have had to be far less intelligent than he clearly was not to guess that, under instructions, she was trying to tell whether he might not be an imposter.

"Finally she said, 'He certainly looks like Stephen, except Stephen had little tufts of hair on the back of his fingers. I thought that was so virile. I don't see them now.'

"Stephen didn't seem to mind being discussed in the third person or to be offended that the woman was searching for differences. He merely smiled and held up his hands. 'They're there.'

"She said, 'It should be darker.'

"Stephen said, 'Remember the time I tripped over my two left feet while we were dancing and my hand slipped out of yours and you said it was because it was so smooth?'

"Artemis's face lit up. She turned to me and said, 'Yes, that did happen.'

" 'And you remember I apologized for being a clumsy dancer, and you kept saying I was a good dancer, but I knew you were just being sweet and trying to make me feel better. Remember, Artemis?'

"She said, happily, 'Yes, I remember! Hello, Stephen. I'm glad it's you.'

" 'Thanks for recognizing me, Artemis,' he said. 'I'd have been in considerable trouble if you hadn't.'

"I interrupted—a bit irritably, I suppose—'Wait, Miss Cataldo. Don't rush to conclusions.'

"He said, 'Is *that* your last name, Artemis? They asked me, but I didn't know. You'd never told me.'

"I waved him quiet. I said, 'Ask him some questions, Miss Cataldo—little things that he ought to get right.'

"She flushed. 'Did you ever kiss me, Stephen?'

"Stephen looked a little embarrassed. 'I did once—just once. In the taxi, remember?'

"I didn't give her a chance to reply. I said sharply, 'The details, Stephen.'

"He shrugged. 'We were in a taxi being driven to a place called Spittal Pond, a bird refuge that Artemis wanted to see. She teased me because I said how pleasant it was to be with a young woman who wanted to see bird refuges and not nightclubs. She said that by the following week I'd have forgotten her completely and wouldn't even remember her name. I said, "What? Forget Artemis, the chaste huntress?" I reached over her and wrote the name on the car window on the left. It was a humid day and there was a thin film of moisture on it.'

" 'Where does the kiss come in?' I demanded.

" 'I was seated on her right,' said Stephen, 'and I reached across her with my right arm to write her name. My left arm was on the back of the seat.' He showed me how it was, stretching his left arm behind an imaginary Artemis and pushing his right hand across in front so that his arms nearly enclosed her. 'I had just finished writing her name when the taxi lurched for some reason. My elbow nearly collided with the driver's head and I grabbed Artemis's shoulder to steady myself—and there I was embracing her. I found the position so irresistible that I kissed her.' He smiled. 'Only on the cheek, I'm sorry to say.'

"I looked at the woman. Her eyes were shining. She said, 'That's exactly how it happened, Mr. Koenig. This is Stephen, all right. There's no question about it.'

"Stephen smiled with a touch of triumph and I said, 'Very well. You can leave now, Miss Cataldo—thank you for your help.'

"And that's it. . . ."

Koenig stopped talking and looked at the Black Widowers with his eyebrows raised.

Gonzalo said explosively, "That's *it*? I thought you said you cracked his alibi."

"So I did. But you wanted me to tell you about the alibi so that *you* could break it down."

"And you haven't left out anything?"

"Nothing essential," said Koenig.

Avalon cleared his throat and said, "I presume you found Stephen Two. That would break the alibi."

"So it would," said Koenig cheerfully. "But we never found Stephen Two, I'm sorry to say."

Halstead said, "Is it possible that Miss Whatsername was paid off? That she was lying?"

"If she was," said Koenig, "we found no evidence to back it. In any case, the alibi was broken quite apart from anything she said or didn't say. —Have any of you gentlemen visited Bermuda?"

There was a general silence and then Gonzalo said, "I was taken there when I was four years old. I don't remember anything."

Trumbull said, "Are you hinting that Stephen got some of the places in Bermuda wrong? Was it that there was no bird refuge of the kind he mentioned or no Princess Hotel or something like that?"

"No, he got all the places correct. No mistakes that we could find as far as the geography or sights were concerned."

Again there was a silence until Drake finally said, "Henry, is there anything about this that strikes you as making sense?"

Henry, who was just returning from the reference shelf, said, "I can't speak through first-hand knowledge because I, too, have never been in Bermuda, but it's possible that what the man Mr. Koenig calls Stephen said may prove he was never there, either."

Drake said, "Why? What did he say?"

Henry said, "Mr. Koenig ended his tale with the account of the kiss in the taxi, so I thought perhaps something about that account broke the alibi. Bermuda is a British crown colony and it strikes me that it may follow British custom as far as traffic is concerned. I've just checked the *Columbia Encyclopedia* and it says nothing about that, but it is a possibility.

"If in Bermuda traffic is always on the left, as it is in Great Britain, the automobiles must have the steering wheel, and therefore the driver, on the right side of the front seat. If Stephen was sitting to the young woman's right and reached over her to write her name on the left-hand window exactly as he said, he could scarcely have nearly struck the driver's head when the taxi lurched. The driver would have been on the other side.

"I imagine Stephen Two told Stephen about the kissing incident, but neglected to mention the matter of the steering wheel or the driver, taking for granted he would be aware of the difference. Stephen adding the matter of the driver for verisimilitude was his great mistake, for undoubtedly Mr. Koenig saw the point at once."

Koenig sat back in his chair and smiled admiringly. "That's very good, Henry."

"Not at all. The praise is yours, Mr. Koenig," said Henry. "I knew you had broken the alibi, I knew you had done it by reason, and I knew that the reasoning had to be deduced from the facts you gave us. You, in breaking the alibi, didn't have the advantage of that special knowledge."

# ST. ANNE MYSTERY

*By Tonda Barrett*

I TURNED AWAY from the locked bungalow and walked down the slope to the private beach. The pines that clustered around the cottage continued like a landslide all the way down the slope and almost to the brink of the water. The beach itself was rock, not sand. I stepped onto boulders that looked like the cars you see on top of dump sites and wonder how they get there. From the rocks, a quiet inlet stretched out to a distant line of buoys.

I stuffed my hands in my pockets and looked at the dark ocean. I was in no hurry to get home. My client might still show up. Not that I mind being stood up; I'm used to it. I figured it just meant, "Await further instructions." Anyway, that was the sort of person my client had sounded like over the phone: brisk, cool, in charge.

After a while I had had enough and was turning to walk back to the dock when I heard the rhythmic slapping of the waves pause and then break. I turned around. A few meters away, a pale figure was rising from the sea. Except for the sound of the waves, the emergence was noiseless, creepy. I was reminded of Godzilla coming out of the ocean. Then the figure removed its snorkel and turned its face towards me. It became—although no less dreamlike, more prosaic—a woman, without bathing suit.

She didn't see me at first. She walked over the sharp, tumbled rocks without picking her way as if she did it every night. She bent to pick up a towel that had looked to me, the observant detective, like just another rock in the dark. Although she gave no sign that she saw me, she draped the towel around her, tucking the corner in so it would hold. Then she bent forward and picked up something else.

I had cleared my throat and taken a couple of steps forward before I realized that the little black hole I was staring into was the barrel of a gun. A small gun, but I thought it would work.

I sat down where I was and lit a cigarette. It's a sign that I'm nervous. I watched her wet shoulders and thighs glisten with gooseflesh and moonlight. Especially I watched that gun. I blew smoke toward the roof of my mouth and coughed.

"Sarah Wodeson?" I asked. That was the name of my client. "I'm Gil Ovid. A harmless person, really."

"You're early," she snapped. Lowering the gun, she walked past me to the path. I followed, a good distance back.

"You said eight," I called.

"Eight thirty."

She was probably right. But you find out some interesting things by showing up at the wrong time. Like that a woman doesn't bother to wear a swimsuit (not that unusual on the Caribbean island of St. Anne, where brown and white bodies flit around like hairless moths in the sun) but does carry a gun (very unusual).

"Aren't you afraid of sharks?" I asked. There had been some sightings earlier in the season. It was probably a fear born more of the dark than of razor-sharp teeth, but I wouldn't have been eager to swim in that deserted cove at night.

"No," she said.

I hurried along the path to catch up with her. The strong muscles of her thighs and buttocks showed under the towel, flashing moonlight in my face.

When she reached the bungalow, she felt in the eaves for a key and then unlocked the door. I noticed that she took the key inside rather than replacing it. Unusual again—few doors are locked on St. Anne. She didn't bother to switch on a light. Maybe the towel was sliding.

"Excuse me," her cool voice said and she slipped away, presumably through a door I couldn't see.

I stayed where I was until my eyes began to adjust to the dark. Then I walked around, trying not to bark my shins or fell the lamps. The shades were all pulled down, excluding moonlight.

She returned and snapped on a light. She wore a caftan of yellow cotton, short-sleeved. Its hem brushed the tops of her bare feet. Her hair clung to her neck like fine black seaweed.

She sat down in a chair and motioned for me to sit opposite her. I pulled a cashier's check out of my breast pocket and put it down on the rattan table between us.

"Is that the money?"

"That's it."

"How much?" she asked, as if she were afraid to look.

"See for yourself."

She did and blinked. She stared at the check for a long time.

I wanted her attention on me, not the money, so I said stupidly, "That's the same as cash, Ms. Wodeson. You'd better put it in the bank."

She frowned, but she put the check on the table and said, "I will, Mr. Ovid."

"The first name's Gil."

She nodded but didn't correct herself. She stood up, went to a desk, and wrote a personal check, then handed it to me. I took it without getting up from my chair.

"Thanks."

"It's a lot more than I'd expected, so I owe you the thanks. But Mr. Rungren told me you were efficient as well as honest."

"Is that who gave you my name?" I'd assumed she'd found it in the phone book or maybe through the police.

"Yes, he's my lawyer."

I nodded and didn't say anything else. I'd worked for Caspar Rungren once or twice. I was surprised that he'd recommended me.

"Obviously he knows that I hired you, but if he should happen to ask—" She looked directly at me. "Will you keep the nature of the transaction to yourself?"

"Sure," I said easily. "Why?" I'll keep a secret, but I like to know the reason. I was also wondering what she'd told Rungren she'd hired me for.

She huddled up in her caftan, with her bare feet on the chair cushion and her knees under her chin. "The jewelry you sold belonged to my great-aunt. My mother inherited it from her; then, when she died, it came to me. But my great-aunt's will stipulates that it never be sold outside the family. Caspar is the local representative for the executors of both estates. It would put him in an uncomfortable position."

I nodded. I was looking at her forearms hugged tautly around calves that I imagined brown and smooth under her dress. Her face, still resting on her knees, rose and fell as she talked. She looked serious, worried under the cool surface. I wondered why.

"Why do you need all that money, Ms. Wodeson?"

She put her feet down on the floor and spent some time pulling her dress down around her ankles. "Why do you want to know?" When she sat up, her eyes focused on my face.

"I'm curious," I said. Then on impulse, "I'd like to know if it's something that would interfere with falling in love with you."

She took it as a joke and smiled. Then curled up again. "Like dealing heroin?" she suggested.

"Or gun-running," I said. "I don't like guns."

For some reason that erased the smile. Neither of us spoke for a minute, and I wondered if other guys sat in this chair, hopeful, while she was polite and distant. I thought how beautiful the hard planes of her face were, and the taut muscles of her body.

She rose from her chair and asked me if I'd like a beer.

I was surprised. "Sure, thank you."

She disappeared into the kitchen and came back carrying two cans, no glasses. A kindred soul, I thought: why wash glasses? Looking around the bungalow, I thought I saw the same kind of practicality and austerity in the furnishings. They were simple and I was pretty sure they hadn't cost a fortune. Thinking of the jewelry I'd sold for her, I thought that she must have arrived at her way of life by choice, not necessity like me.

The room had what I, in my ignorance, thought of as artistic touches. Combined with the plain furnishings, they looked good. I got up to look at some paintings hanging without frames on the walls. They were great. Imaginative landscapes glowed with suns and feathery trees and were populated by people-sized rabbits, cats, and round-eyed kangaroos. Another painting showed children flying, cities floating. In another a mother tossed an apronfull of babies, spread-limbed and gleeful, high into the air. Three of the pictures, hung apart from the others, showed bizarre and graphic scenes that struck me as familiar—then I realized that I'd seen similar things on book jackets of popular science fiction. The initials S.W. were scratched in forest green on each.

"You're a book illustrator," I said.

She'd been watching me. "Yes. Children's mostly. Except for those, of course." She waved at the last group.

I sat down and thought about it. The paintings weren't what I would have expected from this cool, reserved woman, but I liked them.

I picked up my beer can from the table, forgetting it was empty. Sarah watched me try to drink air, then close one eye as I glared into the can.

"You're welcome to another."

"No, thanks." I limit myself to one drink with a client, but it always goes too fast. I made an effort not to sigh. Then I put the can down. "You never told me why you need the money."

She seemed surprised, but this time she answered. "I need it to finance the completion of St. Anne's maternity and child welfare clinic. Construction has been started, but the funds are gone." She tried to lighten things up. "How does that affect your opinion of me, Mr. Ovid?"

Gil, I thought, dammit. "Adversely," I told her. "You're too good for me."

She smiled, then looked worried again. "This money should be enough. The building's almost done, but there's so much equipment. . . ."

"Why can't you use the Brewingate Hospital for your clinic?" I thought I already knew the answer. The hospital is staffed by Europeans, and it caters to the small, but rich, flow of tourists that come to St. Anne. None of the natives, including myself, would dream of going there, knowing they'd spend the rest of their lives paying off the debt. However, there are several well-trained midwives on the island; one had delivered Kim. I was about to say so, but she was shaking her head vehemently.

"No, no. This clinic is founded on a totally different basis. It will be available to everyone, regardless of ability to pay. And the staff will be local people from the islands, as much as possible."

That sounded all right. "But even the amount of money you have won't pay salaries for long," I objected. For some reason, I wasn't feeling very encouraging. Maybe it was that I didn't see Sarah as the board and committee member type.

"No, of course not. There are grants being applied for and some already approved. That will be the administrator's job, to keep the clinic funded and running. I am just making sure the clinic is built and equipped."

She stood up, looking beautiful and uncertain. Can't decide how to get rid of me, I thought with a pang. I stood up, too.

"Well—" she began. But I didn't let her finish. I have a rule against getting involved with clients. I had broken it last about a decade ago and the results had been pretty disastrous (well, not entirely—I thought of Kim). But it seemed time to break the rule again. I stepped around the table, put my hands on the sleeves that lay on Sarah's shoulders like upended buttercups, felt her shoulders hard and smooth beneath them, and kissed her.

Remarkably, she kissed back. After a while my initial clumsiness passed and I knew her mouth, her tongue, knew what she liked, which was what I liked, too. She pulled away and walked into her bedroom. I followed.

I woke up before Sarah did. Leaving her curled on her side under the covers, I sat up and pulled on my shirt and pants, and went out to the kitchen. I looked around for coffee and found a can in the refrigerator and a drip percolator on the stove. I made two cups and carried them back to the bedroom. She was just coming out of the bathroom, a robe tied loosely around her waist, the inside of her breasts and thighs showing. Her face looked terrible.

"I thought you'd left."

"Without my shoes?" They were still lying beside the bed. My socks were somewhere underneath.

I put the cups on the bedside table and pulled a chair from near the window next to it. I sat on the chair and Sarah sat on the edge of the bed. Our knees almost touched and Sarah's robe still covered only half her body, but she wouldn't look at me. She picked up her coffee and sipped at it.

"What happened last night?" I asked. Detectives are used to asking difficult questions. It doesn't embarrass us. We're good at it. Of course, the problem is that some people don't answer. Like Sarah. She sat there as if she hadn't heard me.

I asked again. My ego was bruised by the way she was shutting me out, had shut me out last night as soon as we'd made love. I felt I'd spent the night on sufferance. I wanted to know what was going on.

She looked up at me as if she were startled, then she shrugged. "My husband died a year ago," she said.

"Oh."

What detectives aren't so good at is making sensitive responses. But I was pretty good at listening.

Sarah's story tumbled out. Her husband had been Richard Kazlowsky, a noted epidemiologist who halfway through his career had decided he'd had enough of pure research. He had begun to establish maternity and child-health clinics; the one on St. Anne would have been his sixth. The other five were now models for public health clinics all over the world. He had been a gifted doctor, but he had also been a genius at convincing others of the value of his work, and at obtaining grants and choosing the right administrators.

I was wondering why the wife of this genius had been forced to sell family heirlooms to complete his work. But Sarah was still talking.

"We were married five years," she said. "Happily. I respected his work and aided him when I could. He respected my work in turn and gave me the privacy I needed for it."

It was then that I realized I hadn't seen a tube of paint or even a sketch pad since I'd entered the cottage. Inadvertently, I looked around. She noticed.

"I can't work now," she said dully. "Ever since Richard died." When I didn't comment, she went on to tell me more—intimate details about her and "Richard" that I really didn't want to hear but she needed to tell. A lot about how happy they'd been, how much she'd enjoyed getting to know the different islands and people through his work. They'd only been on St. Anne a few months when he'd died. She spoke of how withdrawn he'd been at times, abrupt and irascible whenever she or anyone else tried to draw his attention away from his work. But that, she said, was to be expected of a truly great man.

It's often amazed me how "great" men—and their wives—get to be convinced of their importance in the face of a total lack of supporting evidence. But Sarah was convinced, and that was all that mattered now. According to her, he'd been a man with a mission. And she told me, in a hesitant voice, how he hadn't wanted children, feeling he couldn't devote enough time to them. Her face looked pained when she told that part. Finally, she worked up to his death.

"That morning he was fine—*happy*. By afternoon he was dead. He wasn't even late getting home when they came and told me. I was painting here while he was shot, murdered."

She sagged a little. She was done telling her story. Then she noticed that her robe was gaping and pulled it closed. I picked up the cups to take them back to the kitchen. I figured it was time for me to go. Old Gil—he might not be much in bed but he's great to tell your troubles to. I wasn't feeling too happy about that, and I was also angry at the dead Richard Kazlowsky whom Sarah had loved, still loved, and who sounded to me like a prize ass. Maybe, too, I had been left uneasy by a story that was really about an aching loneliness temporarily patched by marriage—only to leave the wound larger when the bandage was ripped away. It sounded too familiar. I stood up, coffee cups in my hands.

"Actually," Sarah said, "Richard is part of why I hired you to sell the jewelry. I wanted to meet you and see if—well, I hoped I might hire you to investigate my husband's death. They never found who shot him. I've tried to find out myself, but everyone knows who I am. They won't say anything that might make me unhappy. Unhappy! God!" She stopped a minute, then said quietly, "I need a professional."

I walked around the room a little, put the cups down on top of her dresser, and turned around.

"I don't take murder investigations."

"Mr. Rungren told me. But he said he thought you might—"

I interrupted. "Did he tell you why?"

"No, he didn't."

"My partner was killed during a murder investigation." He had been shot with a Magnum and he lost his face as well as his life, but I didn't tell her that. "We were both on the case. He was the one who got too close. There are big stakes in murder; it's not just a two year sentence or a fine. Nobody worries about mowing down a private dick to protect their skins. They're less happy about shooting constables. Let the police handle it. I'll stick with insurance investigations and missing relatives."

"And divorces?" she asked. There was scorn, as well as coldness, in her voice. She already thought I was a coward; now she had another label. Opportunist. She was a woman who had never strayed, had known only marital bliss. She wasn't likely to think highly of adultery or of someone (me) who made his living documenting it.

"Sure," I said. "Divorces aren't so bad. Gee, I've even had one myself." I could tell she didn't like that. "Look, it's safe work and it pays the bills. There won't be any bills if I'm dead." I had had enough close calls to make the possibility seem very real, even before Mel's death. "I want to stay alive," I said.

"That's funny," she replied, staring past me out the window. "I don't."

I had a feeling that was supposed to make me feel sorry for her, but all it did was fuel the anger that was swirling around in my chest. Thinking about Mel, the uselessness of his death, hadn't helped. But I was feeling put down and used and manipulated and a few other things besides. I was remembering how surprised I'd been when Sarah had let me kiss her. Now maybe it wasn't so surprising. She had wanted something from me and Rungren had let her know I'd have to be persuaded. She'd offered some bait to get me hooked—herself. Now I wondered if even the apparition of her glistening body rising from the water had been planned. She wouldn't consider it prostitution—it was all in the name of her husband's memory.

I said as much. I said a lot of things. When I ran out of comments and bothered to glance at Sarah's face; I should have noticed that she looked like she'd been slapped, repeatedly. But I didn't, not until I remembered it later.

"You can leave now, Mr. Ovid." Her voice was as quavery and tight as my old man's shaking grip on a rudder. I remembered his white knuckles.

I felt like a heel. "Look, I—"

"I said get out." Her voice was quieter this time. And for the second time in twelve hours I was looking down her gun.

My jaw flapped. "But I'll—"

"There are other detectives. Now *leave*." She pulled down the safety catch and straightened her arm. I grabbed my shoes and ran out of the room with about as much dignity as a scared cat.

My dirty socks stayed behind.

Back in the boat, with my sneakers on, I headed not eastward and home, but to the west. I found an empty berth next to the police boats.

I knew there were no other detectives on St. Anne or the other islands. If Sarah Wodeson didn't know that, she'd soon find out.

I walked into the whitewashed building and sat down across the desk from Julio. The Spanish had left "Santa Anna" two hundred years ago, but almost everyone, black or brown, born on the island, has a Spanish name, or a perversion of one. Spanish names and British accents: that's St. Anne.

Julio was frowning over some messy-looking paperwork. He motioned me to the coffeepot sitting on a hot plate in the corner of the barracks office. I poured two mugfuls and left a coin in the jar.

He shoved the papers to one side and leaned back in his chair, all six and a half feet of him. He's a young looking and earnest man, with mahogany skin. There had been a Spanish great-great-grandfather somewhere. Both of Julio's parents are much darker, his mother beautiful and slender. She still treats me like a son, more like one, anyway, than anyone else ever has.

A lot of times when I look at Julio in his clean, pressed uniform, I get a flashback. I see him twenty-five years ago, undersized and scabby-kneed, following his dad through the barracks (then wooden) and helping carry the trash and mop the floors and clean up the crud left by the last inmate in the lock-up. Sometimes it seems that the memory and the old pervasive smell of piss and cigarette smoke are more real than the present. Chief inspector, we call him, and with eight constables beneath him.

In those same years that Julio had been janitor's helper, I was working with my own father. He navigated and I passed out drinks and canapes and emptied ashtrays and fetched tanning lotion and did everything but kiss the feet of the "guests" we took on tours of the islands.

Both Julio and I had envied each other's jobs. I was impressed by the glory of seeing real police work; he hankered for the relative ease of working on the yacht, and the money, too. Back then it was the only sailboat that gave tours. The guests had liked that; they liked to watch my dad sweat and grunt and yell orders at me.

Eventually we both realized how little glamor there was in either, but it was long after our disillusionment with our own jobs. My dad, though not cruel, was mean—small-hearted and caring only about himself. I'd preferred him drunk to sober and most of the time I got my way. But finally, as a teenager, I'd walked out one day, picking up odd jobs and paying criminally low rent to Julio's mom. I went back to the school that I hadn't attended regularly since I was twelve. I felt backward and dumb, and I was relieved when I finally, with difficulty, graduated. Maybe that's why I read a lot, still trying to catch up.

Anyway, by this time Julio's family had scraped up their savings and sent him to a police training school. He came back while I was bartending, serving the same rich slobs I'd waited on on the boat. He was hired at the barracks, and he too ended up doing much the same as he had originally—stepping and fetching for the British officers. But then St. Anne declared its independence, the last of the islands to get off its butt, and the British cleared out. Julio was left the logical, and excellent, choice for chief inspector.

He had promised to hire me if he could, but I was white and had been born off-island, so that made it an impossibility, especially at a time when

St. Anne was trying to regain control of her own affairs. But I lucked out, too: Mel came along.

Mel was a sixty-year-old man who had been an inspector on one of the other islands. When the British pulled out, he'd retired early and gone back to England, only to find himself cold and bored. So he came back, picking St. Anne as the largest and least developed of the islands, and he had set up the only detective agency in a thousand-mile radius of islands and sea. On Julio's recommendation, he hired me. At first I did the dumb stuff, legwork at best, but eventually he taught me everything he knew. I stopped feeling so backward, got good at my job. We did a pretty good business. The islanders remembered the old corruption and some of them still didn't trust the police, even when the faces got dark and the titles changed. And there were always tourists who trusted only whites and who were unimpressed by the tiny barracks and lock-up. So we kept ourselves fed and Julio, who at first had only four constables, didn't mind the competition. Later, though, he made a good reputation for himself, and our business slacked off. When Mel got killed, I decided to work alone.

Julio put down his mug. During the silence neither of us had been in a hurry to break, I'd finished my coffee, too.

"How is your boy?" he asked. Julio has a beautiful voice, rich with native cadences, careful pronunciation, and an overlay of British accent.

"Just fine. He's too little to be in trouble yet." Kim's seven.

"Don't be so sure of that, my friend," warned Julio, but his eyes twinkled. He's fond of Kim.

"I came over to ask you about the Kazlowsky case. His widow wants me to look into it."

He frowned, remembering. "The widow has a different name, correct? Wood. . . ."

"Wodeson."

"A striking woman. She is still distressed? Well, a year is not so long." He got up and went to a file cabinet, coming back with a thin folder. I could tell from the outside that it wasn't going to tell me much.

I glanced through it quickly and learned the caliber of the bullet, the gun it was likely to have come from (never found), and the fact that Kazlowsky had been found in a rowboat drifting in with the tide. The jargon of the autopsy report slowed me down, but it all boiled down to a lot of side effects from having a bullet pass through his heart. There were also notes from interviews: with Sarah, the housekeeper, the members of the clinic board, and then, very briefly, the Minister of Health. All, again, boiling down to almost nothing. I noticed that no one had been interviewed who hadn't been connected with the clinic or his household. I wondered why and said so.

"Are you thinking of a side of his life we perhaps did not uncover?" Julio asked.

"I hope so," I said.

"His housekeeper did tell us she was certain he had a girlfriend. It is not in the official file because there was no evidence. She told me it was just a feeling. I frankly thought she was being vindictive. She also accused the widow of shooting her husband. The woman had been with Kazlowsky for many years, and I believe she resented it very much when he married. Ms. Wodeson fired her almost immediately following his death."

"Well, that's a start." I flipped through the notes until I found the housekeeper's name and address. "One other thing I've found is more recent. At least I don't see anything about it in here. Did you know that the funds for the clinic have dried up? The wife's trying to fund it out of her own, uh, savings. I figure there might be something behind that."

"Perhaps Dr. Kazlowsky's death itself caused the funds to be withheld. It may have required his signature—or his persuasiveness—for the money to come through. Ms. Wodeson should speak with her lawyer."

Rungren. I wondered if she had.

I stood up. "I'd better get going. If I need to talk to any bigshots, can I say I have your approval?"

"Okay, Gil. But be tactful, please?"

I ignored that. I'm always tactful. I rinsed out the mugs in the bathroom sink and replaced them near the hot plate. When I came back, Julio was on the phone, rolling his eyes to the ceiling. I heard an androgynous squawking coming through the receiver. I lifted my hand in farewell, but Julio held up one finger and then scribbled a note. I looked at it: "Dinner, Sat., 6, bring K?"

I nodded and mouthed, "Thanks." Then I walked out into the yellow St. Anne sunshine.

I spent the rest of the day spinning my wheels. The Minister of Health wouldn't see me for a week. Kazlowsky's housekeeper, a Mrs. Elissa Vietch, was out every time I called. They asked me to stop calling. Somewhere between phone calls I ate lunch. I talked to a couple of the clinic board members and found out nothing more useful than that Mrs. Kazlowsky, as they all insisted on calling Sarah, held all legal and financial documents pertaining to the clinic. Great. I hoped I would spot evidence of embezzlement if it got up and slapped me in the face, but I wasn't sure I was going to get the chance. I wasn't even sure why I was on the case—just so I'd stop feeling like a heel?—and I was even less sure how Sarah would feel about it. Anyway, I thought she'd be able to interpret the records better than I could. Maybe she already had.

By afternoon I was discouraged and I didn't have much time before picking up Kim for the weekend, so I got a beer out of the refrigerator and went down to the sailboat. When my old man had died, I sold the old yacht to buy an outboard and a day sailer, a nineteen-footer, just before I met Marilyn. Then, after the baby was born, I'd changed the name of the boat to *Sunny Boy* because that's what I wanted Kim to be, not little and dour like me, but big and sunny like Julio's family. Kimmie loves it when I sail *Sunny Boy* over to St. Mark to get him, and I hadn't done it for a long time. The wind was good and I had plenty of time. I try not to be late picking him up, ever since one time when I found him sobbing on his bed. He'd been sure I was dead or, worse, had left him for good, like Marilyn.

I made good time and had just slurped the last of my beer and tossed the can in the trash when I thought I saw him walking down the hill to the wharf. He was easy to spot because he was wearing that bright purple dashiki thing that Marilyn had sent from some country in Africa I'd never heard of. It's awful looking and he loves it. As I got closer, I saw he was with a teacher, holding his hand. Kim's old enough to walk to the wharf alone, but the school is careful.

He was jumping up and down and then running ahead of the teacher by the time *Sunny Boy's* hull knocked against the piles.

"You brought *Sunny Boy!*" he shrieked. He made it sound like a dog or something.

"Hi, Punkin." It sounds babyish but he hasn't complained, so I keep calling him that.

We hugged each other and didn't notice when the teacher turned to walk back up the hill, giving up on manfully shaking my hand, which is what they always seem to want to do. I might be ready to send Kim to Siberia by Sunday afternoon, but on Fridays it's a joy to see him.

He loves his school, though. It's a ritzy boarding school. Marilyn pays the tuition. That was part of the custody agreement when we divorced, but she'd do it anyway. Some people seem to think that a mother who leaves her children is a monster. I don't see it that way. Marilyn knew Kim would be better off with me and I know what it cost her to leave him. I see the look on her face when she says goodbye at the end of those month-long vacations she gets every year. That's when she swoops down like some exotic bird out of the sky and spoils the daylights out of him for four weeks. They usually go off together somewhere; the kid's seen more of the world than I have. I miss Kimmie a lot when he's gone, maybe because I don't have an exciting career like Marilyn's—she's an international correspondent for a big U.S. newspaper—to keep my mind off him. I think she knows that, too.

The two of us had a good weekend. We sailed a lot and tramped around a couple of the little unpopulated islands and tried to identify flora and fauna from some books Kim lugs around with him (he has a scientific bent). On

Saturday we went to Julio's mom's house, where he still lives. His girlfriend, a nurse, little and pretty, was there, too, giving me almost as big a kiss as his mother did. We all relaxed and ate a lot and watched Julio trying to teach Kim karate. I know some, too, but the academy taught Julio more, and besides, he's a natural teacher. If he hadn't been practically born a cop, he'd have ended up in a kindergarten.

By Sunday evening, I was back on my own, kicking the outgrown toys that Kim leaves at home as I scuffed from room to room. I didn't have the heart to clean up. I found his magnifying glass, a good one, and thought how he'd miss that in the next few days.

Finally, I put on a loud record and started to work. I picked up the toys and books, swept the floor, washed two days' worth of dishes. I even changed the sheets on both beds. By the time I was done, I felt less like a lost lamb. I was ready to get back on the case.

I decided to see Mrs. Vietch. She should be home on Sunday evening and anyway, I wasn't in a hurry to ask Sarah if I could see those papers. I called a taxi, since where Mrs. Vietch worked now was inland, and rode it to the door. It was a fancy place, a Spanish-style sprawling house with rough stucco walls and one of those roofs that look as if they're made out of bisected red clay drainage pipes. I knocked and asked for the housekeeper. A maid took my card—I had scribbled "Concerning Dr. Kazlowsky" on it. I figured that meant Mrs. Vietch rated pretty high in the household, considering she was just paid help, too. Then the maid came back and I followed her to the back of the house and to a large bedroom with adjoining bath. It was set up with two chairs and a table and a desk. An ornate screen hid the bed from view. Elissa Vietch sat at the desk, half-turned as if she was waiting for me but wanted to look casual. She shook my hand and motioned me to sit down. She was a woman in her forties with salt and pepper hair and a heavy nose. She looked both trim and well-dressed. I was surprised. I had expected a battle-axe.

"The police are doing some checking into the death of Dr. Kazlowsky, Mrs. Vietch. I know it's been nearly a year since you've been interviewed, but no unsolved case is ever entirely closed, as I hope you realize." What a lie. "I was hoping you could help us once more."

"Certainly, I'll try. But the chief inspector, Mr. . . . ."

"Arego. He is currently busy with other matters and asked me to take this over for the time being."

"I see," she said. I thought she might say more, but she didn't.

"I've been reviewing the files, and one thing I found interesting was that only professional associates were interviewed. I know Dr. Kazlowsky lived here only a short time before his death, but I would expect a distinguished man like the doctor to have made many friends on St. Anne." I wasn't sure how that followed myself, but she didn't seem to notice.

"Well . . ." she began. I took out a small notebook and leaned back a little. "Dr. Kazlowsky was an unusual man. Some might have thought a difficult man, but when you knew him as well as I did . . . His work was his life. The other doctors and the members of the board were his friends. I believe he thought of his patients as his family." It sounded like a quote.

"So he had no social life per se."

"I would say that's accurate."

"Of course, you were his longtime and valued companion," I put in. She looked down at her loosely folded hands in her lap. "Yes, I was."

"And he was married."

Annoyance flashed over her face. "Only for the last few years of his life."

"Did Dr. Kazlowsky and his wife have a typical relationship?"

"I'm not sure I know what you mean," she said stiffly.

"You know—affection, loyalty—that sort of thing."

"Oh. Well, I certainly was surprised when he married her."

"Don't you think he loved her?"

"Oh, I believe he thought he did. She followed him around with a stricken schoolgirl look on her face that few men could resist. And her family was wealthy, of course."

"Then you think he married her for her money?"

"Of course not! He was a highly moral man. Subconsciously," she conceded, "it may have been a factor. He was human, after all."

Somehow I'd never doubted it.

"Anything else you could tell me about their relationship would be very helpful," I said intently. "We're looking very carefully at Mrs. Kaz—I mean, Ms. Wodeson."

"Finally? I said as much twelve long months ago to that chief of yours." She made him sound like the head of a tribe. "Now maybe he'll believe me."

"Believe what, Mrs. Vietch?"

"That woman should have been behind bars long ago. I am convinced of her guilt."

"I think you'll understand that we have to be very careful. We do have some evidence that's come to light recently and it strengthens our case. But there's still a problem of motive. We can hardly push indictment without that."

"Her motive was jealousy," she said shrilly. "I told Mr. Arego that a year ago."

"But there was no name of any other woman, no description given. And no one else has mentioned the possibility."

"Do you think he would have made it public knowledge? It's only that I —I knew him well enough to notice certain things."

"Like her name?"

"No." Her hands were shaking. "I don't know her name. But there *was* a woman."

I stood up. "Well, thank you for your time—"

"You don't believe me!" she said. "And that murderess will go free because of it!"

"I'm sorry but—"

"Wait!" She walked quickly around the screen and came back, after a series of shuffling noises, holding out a small photograph. "This was the woman."

I took the picture from her hand. "Where did you find this?"

"In the pocket of one of his suits. I—I didn't want Ms. Wodeson to find it."

I'll bet, I thought. The woman in the photo was smiling and blonde. On the back was a phone number.

"Did you ever see them together?"

"Once," she said unhappily. Then reluctantly, "I think she worked at the Palm and Coconut."

"Oh?" My tone was bland. "Well, I can't thank you enough. I'm sure this will be helpful." I held out my hand.

She ignored it, and said, "I hope none of this will be made public."

"I don't think you have to worry about that, Mrs. Vietch." Who would care, I thought? Certainly not the media.

She shuddered and turned away. I let myself out.

Sunday night wasn't the best time to visit a nightclub, even one that regularly defies the legal limits on serving liquor. I walked home, in no hurry.

Now I knew why Julio had not learned the identity of Kazlowsky's girlfriend before. Elissa Vietch had probably hoped that other evidence would come out against Sarah. She was horrified that the sterling Dr. Kazlowsky had kept such low company and only slightly more horrified that a year had gone by, leaving his murderer still at large.

I woke early the next morning, and since it was still off-hours for the Palm and Coconut, I showered, dressed, and jumped into the outboard to head over to Sarah's. I didn't eat; my stomach felt leaden already. And the lead must have been molten because it churned.

I tied up the boat and walked the quarter mile to the bungalow. Approached in daylight, the cottage reminded me of my own place, the key word being unpretentious. But that's not surprising, considering there are hundreds of little places like that on St. Anne and St. Mark. I remembered how Marilyn had hated our bungalow, although she'd been a good sport about it. Being a good sport wears you down after a few years, I guess, especially if you feel that way about your husband, too.

Having mulled that over, I was now depressed enough that my stomach settled down. I knocked. It was a long time before the door opened.

Sarah stood there, her hair wild and her face puffy. She had purple half-moons under her eyes and wore the same yellow dress I'd seen before. It was hitched up on one shoulder, the hem uneven, as if she'd just pulled it on. I almost reached to straighten it, the habit of several years of getting Kim dressed, but I noticed she held the damned gun again, hanging at the end of her limp arm.

She looked at me with zero recognition as far as I could see, then stepped back for me to come in. The first thing I noticed was an empty whisky bottle and a glass knocked over on the floor with a large wet patch beside it. It smelled like scotch. Then I took in the erected easel and the canvas on it, then the tubes of paint scattered like bright cigarette butts all over the furniture and floor. It looked as if they'd been thrown across the room. There was a streak of paint down the back of one chair and a tube lying on its seat, leaking. On the canvas was an embryonic painting that had been crossed out by a broad X painted in red. I sat down, dazed.

"Welcome to my lovely home. Want some coffee?" She looked as if she needed some.

"Yeah."

She padded out on bare feet.

I kept looking at the mess—books knocked over, a wastebasket on its side, white guts spilling out—and I noticed some scraps of paper on the little rattan table, under another empty bottle. I hoped neither bottle had been full to begin with. I pieced together the scraps and found myself looking at the pencilled words: LEAVE THE ISLAND. OR END UP LIKE YOUR HUSBAND. Succinct.

Sarah came back in and put a tray with two sloshing cups of black coffee on top of the scraps. She didn't ask if I wanted milk or sugar. She picked up her coffee, still too hot to drink, and sat down, holding it in both hands close to her face. She had left the gun in the kitchen.

"I got that last night," she said, looking down at the tray as if she could see right through it. "It's the third I've received in the last couple of months."

I leaned back and accidentally kicked the whisky bottle that lay on the floor. At the dull thunk my sneaker made on the glass, Sarah's gaze shifted to the bottle, then away. She looked a little green.

"You tried to paint?" I asked.

"Tried is right. After you left on Friday, I spent a couple of days—well, deciding to get on with my life. Your refusal to investigate Richard's death triggered it. That and—" She didn't finish, sipped coffee instead. "I guess something had to sooner or later. I got out my paints and had worked for a few hours when a boy brought the note. I thought it might be you—

coming back for your socks." She smiled crookedly. "But then I saw him running and I found the note shoved under the door. So much for my new life," she said, and the smile twisted downward.

I watched my coffee get cold and thought for a minute. "Why didn't you go to the police after the first threat? Or at least tell me about it on Friday?"

"Don't you refuse cases with damsels in distress?"

I was stung. "Look, I have a kid whose welfare I care about a lot more than the opinion of someone who wants me to risk my life so she can keep living in the past." I was tired of being insulted. But she just looked at me as if I'd sprouted wings.

"You have a child?"

"Yeah." I drank my coffee in a gulp. "And, as it turns out, I have been looking into your husband's murder." She opened her mouth, but I interrupted. "I don't *know* why. Maybe because I felt like a heel after Friday morning. Why don't we just assume that's not what you intended and I'll keep my illusion of free will." I heard her suck in her breath and I went on quickly. "Let's just stick to business. I think I've got a lead. I'll keep working on that. All you need to do is report these threats to the police. And explain why you didn't do that in the first place."

"Their progress on the investigation a year ago didn't impress me. I thought they'd just scare away whoever was sending the threats. I don't want that," she said grimly.

"Why? So you can shoot him?"

"That's right." She looked at me as if I might make a good practice target. Now I knew why a woman who wasn't afraid of sharks kept a gun at her side. She wanted revenge, not safety.

"Not exactly a damsel in distress, are you?"

She lifted her chin. "Correct."

I changed the subject. "How long have you known the clinic money was all gone?"

She sagged. "I don't know. I guess it was in July that I first looked at the records and started calling people, trying to get the clinic going again."

July. Three months ago.

"What happened to the money?"

"You tell me. The assets are there in black and white. I even have the bankbook with no withdrawals recorded. But when I went to the bank. . . . It's all gone."

"Who could have taken it?"

"Richard," she said. "It had to be him. He must have been paying out expenses for the clinic. They could have been higher than he'd thought. Maybe he misplaced the bankbook before he made the withdrawals. They must have given him a new one."

That left the question of where the new book was, but I let it go. I was about to ask to see the records when there was a knock at the door.

Sarah got up to answer it. I twisted in my chair to see who it was and felt relieved when Julio walked in. Now that I knew about the threats, Sarah's paranoia was rubbing off on me.

"I thought you might be here," he said. He looked around at the mess. I hoped he didn't think I'd helped make it. Then what he'd said seeped in.

"Kim—!" I stood up, the adrenalin already starting to rush.

"No, no. Nothing like that." But he still looked grim. "I just got a request from the FBI for your arrest, Gil. Passing fake jewels."

"Wha—?" The exclamation died out. I looked at Sarah. She looked white now, instead of green.

"I told them I was sure they'd been passed in good conscience, probably for a client. Is that right?"

"Yeah."

"Me," Sarah croaked. "I'm the client. I can't believe it."

"Do you still have the money from the sale?" Julio asked.

"Yes, thank God." Her voice had the mixture of horror and fear typical of someone who's never been in trouble with the police. "It's in the clinic account at the bank."

"Ask the bank to wire the money back," Julio directed kindly. "I have the name and address." He tore it from his notebook and handed it to her. "The fakes will probably be impounded for a while. You will have to request their return."

"I don't want them," Sarah shuddered.

"They're worth some money," Julio said. I could believe it. I'd had a good look at them when Sarah's bank manager had first handed them over to me. I'm no expert, but they'd looked good then and later, at the sale. They must have been superb fakes.

"They should cancel the request for your arrest, Gil," Julio was saying. "But you'll both have to make a statement."

"Okay," I said.

Julio looked as if he might say more, then decided not to. He was letting me handle it. I remembered the threats Sarah had been getting and showed him the one I'd put together. He asked Sarah a few questions and then carefully tapped the scraps of paper off the table and into an envelope. He told Sarah to keep her doors locked and then left.

"Kazlowsky?" I asked, as soon as he'd gone. I was sick of calling him her husband. He wasn't any more, was he?

"It had to be. It wasn't my great-aunt!" She sounded a little hysterical.

"Yeah."

She looked down at her wrinkled caftan. "I have to get changed and go to the bank. I'll feel like a criminal until I do."

I was waiting for an apology—after all, it was my name the FBI had on file. Just great for business. But she stood there waiting for me to leave and, otherwise, not thinking about me at all.

To punish her, I left without saying goodbye.

I went to town next. My first stop was the bank. I was able to confirm that Kazlowsky had been issued a new bankbook, after reporting the old one lost. But I still didn't know where it was—maybe burned after the money ran out. He'd kept the old book to cover up his withdrawals. I wondered how long he'd thought that would work.

I walked over to the Palm and Coconut. The manager identified the woman in the picture as Lydia Poole, an entertainer who had quit a year earlier. He confirmed the phone number written on the back as the club's. After I fed him a cock-and-bull story about locating her for Mr. Rungren's law firm so she could collect some inheritance, he gave me the address she had asked him to forward her paycheck to. It was on St. Edward.

I shook hands with the dark, pudgy man and only hesitated a few seconds when he said warmly, "—and give my best to Caspar."

Caspar? Oh—yeah. Him.

I caught the boat to St. Edward by the skin of my teeth. It's too far for my little outboard and I wasn't in the mood for a long sail. By three o'clock I was there and had grabbed some lunch (and breakfast) and found the address the manager had given me, a tall modern apartment building.

Lydia Poole's name was posted over a mail slot inside the lobby. I took the elevator up to the second floor—there aren't many on the islands, so I couldn't resist the novelty—and knocked on her door.

She was home, dressed in tight white jeans and a halter top, her hair tied up in a scarf. She was eating what seemed to be her breakfast—sweetrolls, melon, and a pot of tea, steam coming up the spout. My stomach rumbled a little over my hurried lunch.

"Want some tea?" she said, without even asking who I was.

"Thanks, that sounds great."

We sat down and she poured a cup, then offered me a roll. It tasted great. She smiled and told me her name, the real one, not stage. Maybe she wasn't working as an "entertainer" (read "sparsely-clothed dancer") any more. But she obviously still kept late nights.

I decided to tell the truth this time to get the dope I wanted. It was a mistake. At the sound of Kazlowsky's name, her face became as hard as, if broader than, Sarah's. She heard me out and then asked me to leave. I tried a simple question like, "Did you used to work at the Palm and Coconut?" and got "None of your goddamn business" in reply.

"Look," I said, "the police don't have your name, but they're going to

get it if you don't cough up some information. Were you having an affair
with Dr. Kazlowsky?"

"Of course I was," she said crossly, pouring more tea.

"How much money did he give you?"

She put the pot down. "None! What the hell do you think I am? I
support myself, for your information. We liked each other, that's all.
Okay?"

I kept my mouth shut.

"He bought me drinks and dinner sometimes," she added sullenly. "But
he wasn't so flush that I never picked up the tab."

"Yeah?" That surprised me. Would someone of Kazlowsky's generation
let a lady pay unless he was really hard up? I didn't think so.

"Why did you leave St. Anne?"

"I didn't want to get involved with the police. I left when I heard about
Rich's death—they said it was murder."

"Yeah. Any idea who did it?"

"No." She bit into a roll.

"When did you see him last?"

"A week or so before he died, I guess. He said he was going to be busy
for a while. I figured he was just letting me down easy."

"Did you care?"

She shrugged. I thought that meant yes, but she wasn't going to admit it
to a jerk like me.

"Did he mention his wife to you?"

"Sometimes. It sounded like they were pretty happy."

I swallowed hard over that. "Did anyone know he was seeing you? Like
at the club? Or did you ever see anyone there who might have recognized
him?"

"Like who? The place was a dump," she said, with all the fine scorn of
someone who's gone on to better things.

"Kazlowsky went there," I pointed out.

"Just to see me," she said.

I almost didn't catch the implications, then I sat up like a shot. "You'd
known him from before?"

"Sure, we met on another island. Kipaka."

"At a club?"

"Are you crazy? He wasn't the type to hang around in clubs. I met him
at the clinic there. He was my doctor."

"That was a maternity clinic, wasn't it?"

She looked at me, then said with no change of expression, "Yeah. I was
pregnant. I miscarried."

I was silent a moment in deference to the flat tone of pain in her voice,
then I reminded her of the Palm and Coconut. "Who else went there?"

She rattled off a few names. None of them meant anything to me. Except one. Caspar Rungren.

It had been an unusual case. People had been cooperative, even friendly. And it looked as if I was getting close to the end. But walking back from the late boat to my bungalow that night, things got more typical.

I hadn't told Sarah the other reason I avoided investigation of serious crime. Some investigators rely on their brains, some on intuition, the majority on routine. Not me. I get beaten up. In a big case, probably more than once. Sometimes, with my smattering of karate, I hold my own. Usually I don't. Believe it or not, this is how I solve cases. I follow the bloody trail (*my* blood) left behind by thugs who think I'm too smart to risk getting beaten up again. Wrong.

This time it was two guys. The smaller one ran off after I kicked him near his kidney. But the larger one, an albino with one of the ugliest faces I've ever seen, should have been a linebacker. He was big and quick and he knew karate, too. After a while, I collapsed on the pavement and let him kick me a few times. But I could tell his heart wasn't in it. We had met once before, and this time I could still breathe. I waited until he was gone, and then I got up. And gasped. Maybe he hadn't been so half-hearted after all. I limped to a phone outside a drugstore a few blocks away and called a taxi. I knew where I was going, but I wasn't sure why. Maybe I'd been wrong about being close to the end of the case.

I banged on the door of a townhouse on a fancy street not far from the business district. The smaller guy (he's only a few inches taller than me) opened it and looked surprised.

"I want to talk to your boss," I said.

"Just a minute," he mumbled. He looked scared—not of me.

I followed noiselessly behind him down a hallway to a big, comfortable study. I'd seen it before.

A large black man sat behind an antique desk worth more than my income for life. He was about an inch taller than the big albino and had an extra hundred points of IQ. I'd heard he came from Cleveland, but he'd been on St. Anne as long as I had. He saw me standing in the doorway. And remembered who I was. For a while I'd had the idea he was behind Mel's death. I'd been wrong, but it hadn't endeared us to each other.

"Hi, Sid," I said.

The smaller guy whirled. "Hey—!"

"Never mind," said Sid. "Get lost." He did. "Close the door, Ovid. And sit down."

"No, thanks." I went up and took a cigarette from the box on his desk. Getting beaten up a lot makes you do things like that. It's part of the act. Sid played his part and frowned, but I spoke first.

"Why don't you tell me how you're involved in the Kazlowsky murder, Sid? That's why I'm here, right?"

"What makes you think I'm involved?" He passed a big hand over the back of his head. He didn't look too worried.

"Why don't we cut the crap? I know you didn't kill him."

"You're right." He leaned forward and lit my cigarette with his lighter. I took one drag and put it out. I was nervous, but I was dizzy, too, after that beating. Sid watched me. "How'd you figure that out?"

"For one thing, your commandos would've done a better job."

He chuckled, looked gratified. "That's right." He lit a cigarette for himself. "I heard you were asking around about Kazlowsky. Lydia called me. I thought my friends might discourage you, that's all. Or—"

"Or they'd bring me right to your door. You always send unique invitations, Sid."

He chuckled again. I was making a real hit. But I was tired, aching. "Let's just hear what you want to tell me, so I can go to bed."

"What can *you* tell me, Ovid?"

I shrugged—and winced. "I'm in this for the satisfaction of the widow, Sid. The police don't come into it. Okay?"

"That's just fine." He settled back in his chair, his face looking like a dented shovel. Expressionless. "You know that .38 caliber they were looking for last year?"

"Sure."

"Mine."

I felt for a chair, sat down. "How'd Kazlowsky get it?"

"I gave it to him. What d'ya think, he stole it from my safe?"

I ignored the bluster. "Was this just generosity or what?"

The bluster got dangerous. "You want to hear this story or you want your brains kicked in?"

"Hear the story," I muttered like a sullen kid.

"All right. He came here the night before he died, wanting to borrow money. I said forget it, he couldn't afford my rates. I need to get a good return, you know that, Gil."

I shrugged, acknowledging the way of business.

"But then he decides to tell me the story of his life. He was being hit up for the money because of Lydia—somebody knew he was seeing her." He noticed me getting restless. "And I don't know who, so don't ask!" He glared at me.

"All right," I said. "Was the blackmailer threatening to tell his wife?" That's what I'd been figuring.

"Nah, it was the Board of Directors he was worried about. His international reputation. The whole baloney."

With Lydia Poole having once been a patient, the truth could have been pretty damaging. I wondered if the blackmailer had known that part or if it had been blind luck.

"So then this guy asks me for a gun. Said he had a score to settle. He sounded like a bad actor, you know?"

"So you sold it to him."

He spread his hands. "Why not?"

We looked at each other for a minute. I don't know what Sid was thinking and I'd rather not, but I was imagining Kazlowsky buying a gun. A man who'd spent his life saving and improving lives. For the first time, I felt some respect for Kazlowsky. Because he hadn't been able to settle any score but his own.

"Suicide," I said.

"That's what I figured. Okay, Ovid, you have it now. You tell Arego you're finished with the case and keep my name out of it, you hear?"

"Yeah." I stood up. "Why'd he come to you, Sid?"

"How the hell should I know? I'd never seen the guy before."

I nodded. At the door I turned. "Who's your lawyer?" I expected to hear "What's it to you?" But he told me. When I heard the name, I wasn't surprised.

I went home to get cleaned up. I believed Sidney, partly out of instinct (I have a little, besides being a good punching bag) and mostly because I knew it would be easier for him to kill me than lie to me. He wanted his name in the clear. Selling the gun didn't mean anything to Sid; he'd take that rap any day to avoid suspicion of murder.

And the story fit with what I'd already figured out. Kazlowsky had dropped the gun in the water when he fell against the side of the boat. There had been a bruise on his face, but that could have come from anywhere. There had been no other signs of struggle. I suspected the only reason Julio hadn't guessed suicide in the first place was the lack of motive; he'd had everything to live for—the clinic, his devoted wife. As for the lost clinic funds, Julio wouldn't be the first cop to check the bankbook and forget to double-check with the bank. I've made bigger mistakes.

Now I had to decide what to do. I showered and painfully pulled clean clothes over what promised to be impressive-looking bruises.

The phone rang. I glanced at a clock. Midnight, a little after. It was Julio.

"Meet me at the Wodeson house, Gil. Sarah Wodeson has just called in a homicide."

A vision of Sarah as I'd first seen her, skin goosefleshed and glistening in the moonlight, pointing a gun at me, stuck with me after I hung up the phone. Only now the gun smoked. That's half how I expected to find her.

I wasn't far off. She sat on the chair facing the door, wearing a bathrobe pulled tightly around her. She had the little gun in her hands. It wasn't smoking, but it had been used. She stared at the man on the floor as if afraid he might get up.

He wouldn't. It was Caspar Rungren and he was dead.

When Sarah saw us, she stood up, letting the gun fall. I let Julio ask the questions.

"What happened, Ms. Wodeson?"

"He knocked at the door. I said, 'Come in,' and then he shot at me." Her voice was steady. "I shot back. He's dead, isn't he?"

"Yes." He had checked. "Were you holding the gun when he came in?"

"Yes—those threats, you know." I was glad I had showed the torn one to Julio that morning.

We all looked at Rungren's face, undistinguished, flaccid, not particularly dead looking. That would come later. There was a gun by his limp hand.

Julio said, "I think I've found the boy who delivered the last threatening letter to you. He was unable to give a description, but perhaps a photograph will help."

He walked around the place. It had been cleaned up since the morning. Sarah and I watched. He found a bullet hole in the window across from the front door. A wild shot. I thought that Rungren must have panicked when he saw Sarah holding a gun of her own. Julio made one of the constables go outside to look for the bullet.

"Will I be charged, inspector?" Sarah asked.

"You will be questioned at the inquest. Then the jury will decide. But if we can trace the threats you received to the dead man and demonstrate that he fired that gun, I don't believe you will have anything to worry about."

Julio and another constable began to dust for prints and crawl around on the floor, looking for another bullet they thought Rungren's gun had fired. I'd seen it all before and Sarah looked not so much fascinated as stunned.

"Can we get out of here?" I asked.

"All right," Julio said, looking up. "But please be back in an hour."

"Walk down to the beach?" I asked Sarah. She nodded.

We sat on rocks near the water. Sarah said quietly, "I don't understand why Caspar tried to kill me. And why did he murder Richard?"

"He didn't shoot Richard," I said gently, or at least tried.

"Then who did? And if he didn't kill Richard, why shoot at me?" She sounded angry. I had made things complicated.

"Rungren was blackmailing Dr. Kazlowsky. That's why he spent all the clinic funds and sold your family jewels, replacing them with fakes. When he ran out of money and couldn't get any more, he shot himself."

I heard an intake of breath, didn't try to look at her face. It was dark, clouds over the moon.

"What was the blackmail? Did a patient die through his negligence? What could be so awful?"

"He had an affair with a patient. She was a dancer at the Palm and Coconut for a while."

She made a noise like a final utterance of a broken talking doll. I remembered how I'd felt when Marilyn told me she was leaving to marry some guy she'd interviewed a few months earlier. She never had, but I remembered feeling as if I'd been kicked in the chest and would never breathe again. And it hadn't even been a surprise to me the way it was, now, to Sarah. I had always known Marilyn would leave me.

I tried to offer some comfort. "He loved you," I said. "He didn't want you to know."

"Me!" Her voice was full and bitter. "Do you know what the Minister of Health, what *everyone* would have thought of his seducing a patient? No matter how it really was, that's how it would have been construed. It would have ruined him. When did he meet her?" she asked abruptly.

"I don't know. It was on Kipaka."

"We were there the first two years of our marriage." Her voice was flat. "Tell me how you found out."

I did. I told her everything but Sid's name, in case she'd ever mention it to Julio and get my ribs kicked in on the other side. I told her about interviewing Lydia Poole.

She listened in silence, then said, "I still don't understand why Rungren threatened me."

"I think his guilty conscience made him paranoid. He was responsible for Kazlowsky's death. And you were pushing an investigation. Did anyone else know that the clinic funds were gone?"

"He did. I asked his advice. And I asked him not to tell anyone else, to protect the clinic."

"I had wondered why he recommended me to you. He wasn't exactly my biggest fan. He probably thought he was safer with me poking around than the police. He must have intended to make your death look like suicide," I said.

"But he missed."

"Your gun scared him. He expected to shoot you while you offered him tea."

I felt her shudder. Then she seemed to look at my suspiciously erect back in the dark. Or maybe she just sensed that I ached all over. "You should see a doctor," she said. I'd told her about getting worked over.

"Yeah."

Our hour wasn't up, but I stood and walked back to the bungalow with Sarah at my side. Inside the cottage, the body had disappeared. I said, "See you tomorrow," and went home elated because she absently replied, "Fine."

*   *   *

I woke up thinking what a beautiful day it was. Actually, most days on St. Anne are beautiful. The clouds the night before must have broken some kind of record. But I'd slept long after having two ribs taped and I felt great. Well, better.

I dressed and packed sandwiches and fruit in a basket, then on second thought stuck in a book. I stowed the stuff in the outboard, figuring I would switch it to the day sailer if my plans worked out.

At the bungalow, Sarah's voice called for me to come in. I had wondered, walking up the path, if she'd be feeling horror that she'd killed a man or fresh grief for the husband she thought she'd buried but had lost years before. But she was sitting on the floor in a flowered skirt, sketching on a big pad. Horror and grief didn't seem to come into the picture. She looked up at me, her face a little blank as she refocused her attention away from her work. Then she smiled. She had the look of someone who had dedicated herself to another to find in the end that she had the greater strength. And maybe even the loyalty hadn't been wasted if she could respect the integrity that had gone into it. Those were my thoughts. I hoped they were hers.

"I was going to call you," she said. "I owe you your fee."

"I'll send you a bill," I said, then quickly, "Want to come on a picnic?"

She hesitated, looked down at her sketch, then at me, then at the sketchpad again. "Not today—Saturday?"

"Okay," I said. "I'll bring my kid."

She looked pleased. Then her attention swivelled back to the sketch and she began to shade something in, curling up over the pad. "I'll see you on Saturday then." It was a pleasant, muffled dismissal.

"Yeah." I turned to go.

Her voice stopped me, suddenly clear. "Gil—thank you for everything. For the picnic, too."

"Sure." We smiled at each other.

I headed for the dock, and my book, whistling.

# CANADA

# THE CASE OF THE FROZEN DIPLOMAT

*By Tim Heald*

S IMON BOGNOR, Britain's special Board of Trade representative in Canada, buttered another slice of toast and spread a thick layer of Gentleman's Relish on top. The combination of spiced anchovy paste and butter-saturated crust was immensely appealing and he allowed himself an indulgent moment of gratitude to Macpherson. Without Macpherson there would have been no Gentleman's Relish. Toronto had run out of the stuff. The manufacturers were refusing to stick on bilingual labels, so Trudeau's excise men were banning it. Bognor smirked. Macpherson must have bought up every one of the little black-and-white jars in the entire province, perhaps even beyond. When Bognor had opened Macpherson's safe three weeks ago, 79 of them had come tumbling out—Macpherson's last will and testament.

Bognor remembered his predecessor well, for they had shared a taste for food, drink, and thin cigars, and occasionally indulged it in a small Italian restaurant near the office. Bognor did not like to think of Macpherson lying under the snow all winter. He had gone missing during the first blizzard of December. Three weeks ago at the beginning of the thaw, a cross-country skier had fallen over his boot in a conservation area thirty miles north of Toronto. The consul general said he was perfectly preserved, though he had been drinking. In one pocket was a frozen ham sandwich, half eaten; in the other was an unopened jar of Gentleman's Relish. He was, of course, extremely dead.

Bognor sighed, picked up *The Globe and Mail,* and turned to the "daily mistake." The persistent apology was, he had decided, a Canadian characteristic. Ever since his arrival, Canadians had been apologizing: for the unusual weather, for the poor quality of the television, for the Toronto Maple Leafs. But not so often for Macpherson's death. The man from the RCMP had said, in so many words, that Macpherson had asked for it; he had become involved in what should have been left to the RCMP. Bognor had been expecting a man in a red tunic with a cowboy hat. Instead the Mountie had worn a neat Tip Top Tailors three-piece suit. He was called Jay Walewska and he chewed gum.

"Brits here keep a low profile, sir," he said, pseudo-friendly. "Like you shouldn't bust your ass. Have a good trip. Watch the Blue Jays. Find yourself a cottage. Get yourself a girl. No reason to mess around." Bognor, not wishing to give offense, had nodded agreeably and for the past three weeks had sifted through Macpherson's papers and personal effects.

He sighed again, put down the paper, and dug his knife into the Gentleman's Relish, scooping out another gob of the dark-brown paste. The jar was a masterpiece of packaging: heavy white stone with utterly discreet black lettering and the Latin subtitle *patum peperium.* It was the peanut butter of the English upper class. It belonged on the same shelf as the Oxford Marmalade and the Bollinger Champagne. He spread it absentmindedly and realized with a sudden start of irritation that the relish contained a foreign object.

He paused, then scraped with his knife and revealed a paper sachet that looked like a very small teabag. Odd. He set the packet down on top of his desk and contemplated it. He'd never come across such a thing before. A two-inch nail in a take-out chop suey once and a wedding ring in a bowl of cold soup at a private dinner party. Never this.

He picked it up and tore it open, then frowned as a thin stream of white powder poured out into a neat pyramid. He rolled a little between finger and thumb. Finer than salt, rougher than icing sugar. He licked a finger. It tasted of nothing. In London, he would have taken it downstairs for analysis, but the consulate boasted no such facility. He would send it to Ottawa and on to London in the diplomatic bag.

He sighed again. This Canadian assignment was another piece of miscasting in a life that, in its middle years, was turning from light comedy to farce and might yet end in tragedy. He had meant, on leaving Oxford, to enter the civil service. When the interviewer, oily and ingratiating, had leaned forward and said, *sotto voce,* that there was *"another* branch of the civil service," he had nodded eagerly, wishing to appear keen, not knowing what he meant, and had allowed himself to be swept along by the ensuing charade of clandestine meetings and country-house weekends. Now he was stuck: an undercover agent in the Special Operations Department of the Board of Trade, a secret agent of sorts, ill-suited by temperament, inclination, breeding, and education for the world of codes and ciphers and industrial secrets.

He swept the little pile of powder into an envelope and sealed it with a lick. LSD, cocaine, heroin—he tried to remember the details of the dangerous-drugs course he had been sent on four years ago on the Scottish island of Benbecula and failed. No matter. Analysis would tell him soon enough.

It was 12:30. Time for a cheeseburger. He picked up his notebook, the jar of Gentleman's Relish and Macpherson's diary, then crossed the road to the Crazy Cow Dining Lounge for a light lunch and further research. He had been through that diary every lunch since he had arrived, so that it was filthy with fingermarks, cheese stains, and spilled Molson's. Still it had not yet yielded a plausible secret. Indeed, the only clue worthy of the name was that brand-new jar of Gentleman's Relish in Macpherson's left pocket. It was obviously a new purchase.

Bognor had taken a photograph of Macpherson to every high-class grocer and delicatessen in town. Finally, in a suburban cheese "shoppe" he had found what he feared. Yes, the diminutive gourmet behind the counter recognized the photograph. A Saturday morning last December, the day of the storm. The man had had an English accent and had just bought the last jar of Gentleman's Relish when he was confronted by a ferret-faced person with a ginger moustache and a limp. Ferret-face had two friends, and between them they'd bundled the Englishman outside and into a car. There had been a lot of shouting.

Since then, Bognor had kept his eyes peeled for a ferret-faced man with a limp and a ginger moustache. To no avail. He wiped a streak of warm rubbery cheese from his chin and picked up the half empty jar of Gentleman's Relish. It reminded him of home as he turned it slowly in his fingers, savoring its feel and appearance, remembering nursery teas with Nanny: the smell of charred bread against the gas fire; of the carbolic soap that Nanny used. In a changed world, at least Gentleman's Relish was what it had always been. At least—he frowned. Why in God's name had he not noticed it before?

He stared hard at the label, blinked, turned away, stared again, had another swig of beer, took a final peer, and decided that the undersized teabag was not the only peculiarity of this particular jar. There, tiny but distinct, proudly prancing below the middle letters of the label, was a small rampant beaver with a spoon thrust in its mouth. Bognor's eyes glazed. "Interesting," he said, as he got up to pay the bill.

The beaver and the spoon was the personal emblem of Sir Roderick Farquhar, the world-famous millionaire financier who headed "Mammon-

Corp," the Mammon Corporation. Farquhar was so smart that he had kept his name out of Peter Newman's book on the Canadian business elite, allowing such lesser rivals as E.P. Taylor of Argus Corporation and Paul Desmarais of Power Corporation to take the limelight. To those in the know, however, Farquhar of Mammon was the man who controlled Canada; who had half the cabinet in his pocket; who was on Christian-name terms with the Queen; who kept a cruiser-sized yacht in the Mediterranean and apartments in a half dozen countries, as well as a Scottish grouse moor and a private pack of hounds in Dorset.

All this was known to Bognor, who had gone through the Canada files before leaving London. Now a sachet of drugs had turned up in a jar of Gentleman's Relish marked with Farquhar's personal insignia. Bognor's mind struggled inexorably to the obvious conclusion. Farquhar was importing drugs and Macpherson had found out. He had been murdered on Sir Roderick Farquhar's say-so. Bognor's mind boggled.

Bognor was not methodical by nature but he often attempted to remedy the deficiency by drawing up lists on pieces of paper, which he subsequently lost. Now he set about cataloguing the remaining jars of relish. Twelve had already been consumed and discarded, leaving 67. First he examined each one for the distinctive sign of the beaver and was disappointed to find no more. Then he procured a large black garbage bag from Miss Sims and scooped out the contents of each jar in the search for more sachets. Nothing. He could scarcely believe his bad luck. All he had to show for his labors was a garbage bag full of anchovy paste.

"Bloody silly!" he exclaimed, running his fingers through his thinning hair. He decided to telephone and sort the whole affair out personally, man to man. He thumbed through the phonebook clumsily, then dialed and listened to the ringing tone, heard the answering secretary.

"Sir Roderick Farquhar," he said.

"Sir Roderick is in conference. Would you like to speak to Mr. Lewandowski?"

Lewandowski, it transpired, was Farquhar's personal assistant. He sounded antiseptic, capable of unending evasion, a specialist in a politeness so polite it was ruder than insults. Bognor had dealt with his sort before. There was nothing as insufferable as a great man's flunky.

"I wish to speak with Sir Roderick. It's important. It's about the death of a colleague of mine, a Mr. Macpherson from the Board of Trade."

"I am truly sorry, Mr. Bognor, Sir Roderick does not give interviews. He is extremely busy. Perhaps I can help?"

"I want to see him."

"I am afraid that is not possible."

"What if I were to tell you that it was about Gentleman's Relish?" A pause. A long one. Then a click. Lewandowski had hung up. Bognor stared at the receiver blankly, then hung up himself. Something had happened, though he wasn't quite sure what.

Late in the afternoon, just as he was about to go home frustrated and dispirited, the consul general summoned him.

"Sherry?"

"Thank you."

"I gather you're trying to see Farquhar of Mammon over this damned Macpherson business?" A censorious exhalation of blue tobacco smoke.

"Yes."

"May I ask why?" The consul general wrinkled his nose and squinted down it, then, as Bognor hesitated, examined his fingernails, individually, not much liking what he saw.

"I think he may have killed Macpherson," said Bognor. "I found drugs in a pot of his personal Gentleman's Relish."

The consul general gave him a very old-fashioned look. "Come on, old boy." He smiled like a benevolent uncle. "Between you and me, we're involved in some rather tricky negotiations with Farquhar over the new fighter aircraft. Not to mention the James Bay project. Fact of the matter is, I don't want anything screwed up by your banging around annoying the fellow."

Bognor pinked, his throat dry. "Sir, with respect, a man's dead."

"Precisely, Bognor." The consul general screwed the remains of his cigarette viciously into the ashtray. "And nothing you can do will bring him back. We need these contracts, Bognor. Farquhar's an important chap. Personal friend of the Queen, got most of the cabinet in his pocket. I don't want him offended."

"Oh, for God's sake." Bognor had left then, half his sherry undrunk. He had liked Macpherson and was appalled as always by the private cynicism that governed public life. Well, if no one else was going to do his late lamented colleague justice, he at least would. He returned to his office and pushed the buttons that would connect him to Mammon-Corp. The number rang for a full minute, then a male voice answered.

"This is a personal call for Mr. Lewandowski."

"Are you a friend of his?"

"In a manner of speaking. We have—or had—a mutual acquaintance." Bognor relished the bitter accuracy of the words.

"I'll see if he's still here."

Bognor waited minutes, then there was a sequence of whirring and clicking and a new voice, silky smooth, immediately recognizable as Lewandowski's, came on the line.

"Lewandowski?"

"This is he."

"Bognor here, Board of Trade. Now just you listen to me. If you think I'm going to be fobbed off because your precious boss wants to invoke the Old Pals' Act you've got another think coming. Just you tell Sir Roderick bloody Farquhar that I have his number. Got it?" Bognor slammed the phone down and found that he was shaking. In London he would have found a search warrant, perhaps even indulged in a burglary, gone round to Mammon Corporation and impounded all the Gentleman's Relish he could find. Here in Toronto he found himself surrounded by strangeness and hostility and he was afraid. He needed a drink.

That night, in his apartment in a building on Bloor Street, he got drunk on rye. The apartment was owned by the office. It had been Macpherson's before him and he felt his predecessor's presence more keenly the drunker he became. Macpherson, he was certain as he staggered into alcohol-induced slumber, had penetrated the secret of the Gentleman's Relish and had been about to confront Farquhar. Farquhar had got him first. The ferret-faced man with the limp and the whiskers was obviously a Mammon hit man.

In his dreams that night, Bognor imagined what his own fate might be. He visualized the karate chop from behind; the weights tied to his feet; the early-morning drop into Lake Ontario.

He woke at five, sweating, made coffee, and read two chapters of Hardy's *Jude the Obscure*. It did not improve his temper. On the bus, his umbrella struck a fellow passenger. She glared at him so unforgivingly that he glared back. At the office, his coffee was even weaker than at home so that he complained to Miss Sims—nice, helpful Miss Sims, whose parents had come from Glasgow in the Depression. She sulked, not understanding his ill temper, but still gave him the message: "Sir Roderick Farquhar will see you Monday at four. Mammon Centre, one hundred and first floor."

"He what?"

Mouselike, Miss Sims flinched from such unexpected aggression, and Bognor softened. "I'm sorry," he said, "old war wound. Or an ulcer. I don't know. What did you say?"

"Sir Roderick Farquhar will see you on Monday at four," she repeated, wide-eyed and nervous.

"The devil he will," said Bognor, narrowing his eyes and thinking hard. "Did he phone?"

"A man called personally to deliver the message."

"Really?"

"Yes."

"Ginger-haired? Moustache? Walked with a limp? Ferrety sort of face?" Miss Sims' eyes widened. Sometimes Bognor's powers of intuition amazed even himself. "Say no more, Miss Sims," he said, smiling for the first time in days. "All is forgiven." He gave her a light peck on the cheek and went to his desk humming the Grand March from *Aida*.

Not that he was under any illusions. He realized that Mammon meant danger and that once inside its portals he might never come out alive. Therefore he took precautions. He sent a coded cable over the CN-CP wires to Parkinson, his immediate superior for many years and now director general of the SOD(BOT). It set out all that had happened and was about to happen. He could rely on Parkinson. Then he sent a similar wire to London Analysis, telling them to expect a sample soonest, to give it their immediate attention and liaise with Parkinson. Then, to make absolutely certain, he telephoned Monica, the loyal, boring girl friend who had been one of the few fixed points in his life for almost as long as Parkinson.

"Monica, it's me."

"Darling, how nice."

"Yes. I'm in Toronto."

"I know. How is it?"

"Cold. Windy."

"How interesting. But I don't suppose you phoned to talk weather."

"No. This is important. I'm seeing someone called Sir Roderick Farquhar at four o'clock on Monday. He's world famous and madly respectable and rich, but in fact he's a drug pusher and a murderer. He killed Macpherson."

"Goodness. Are you sure?"

"Pretty positive. I'll know for certain by four-thirty. The point is, he's dangerous. There's not much he won't stop at."

"Oh, yes." Monica sounded bored. She had been here before.

"Darling, this is important. I may not get out alive."

"Quite."

"So I want you to phone the office at five. If I'm not back, get hold of Parkinson, tell him to send in the troops. The Mounties, that is."

"Right you are," said Monica. "Darling, are you getting enough sleep? You sound peculiar."

"Yes, I'm fine. Just nervous."

"Of course."

They had exchanged pleasantries and Monica had promised, twice, to do as she was told. His life depended on it. He hoped she realized. He hoped she cared.

It was late now, and Friday night. Somehow he did not like the idea of being alone in his apartment. Instead he drove to a country inn at Niagara-on-the-Lake, where he spent as comfortable a weekend as possible with his old service revolver strapped to his shirt and a sick apprehension inside him. On Sunday he came back, ready to face his epic confrontation.

This time he drank only one stiff whiskey before bed. Sleep did not come until after midnight and was shallow and fitful when it did. Nor was it long-lived. His bedside travelling clock showed 2:15 when he heard the crisp click of his lock, expertly picked—probably with nothing more sophisticated than a credit card. Seconds later, they were in the room. He had a fleeting impression of stocking masks, a man with a limp, then the hospital smell of ether clamped hard to his mouth and nose. A perfunctory struggle, a moment of numb despair and panic, then a slipping away of consciousness into a world of darkness and wild, disturbing dreams.

He came round in a room with the feel and smell of basement. The mean cream paint was peeling off the brick walls. There were pipes everywhere. Two heavy men with prize-fighter faces and black-leather jackets lounged by the door, drinking from plastic cups. On the other side of the bare table sat, as he had rather expected, a man with a ginger moustache.

The man smiled and offered a cigarette. Bognor seldom smoked but he had a sense of occasion so took it in his lips and allowed his captor to light it from a gold Dunhill. His own hands were tied to the back of his chair.

"Who are you?" Bognor's voice sounded frightened. He wished he could control himself better.

The man stood and limped toward him. "How rude of me," he said. "Lewandowski. Jim Lewandowski. Executive assistant to Sir Roderick. We have spoken."

From some untapped source, Bognor dredged up defiance. "Executive assistant," he laughed. "Big name for a crummy little job. Yes sir, no sir, three bags full. All you do is answer the phone and arrange your master's life. Buy him his booze, and—" he paused dramatically "—his Gentleman's Relish."

Lewandowski's ferret face froze. "Fritzy," he said, "give our friend a drink." One of the henchmen went to a cupboard and took out a quart of Wiser's Special Blend. The other heavy pulled Bognor's head back, Lewandowski pried his mouth open, and the third man forced a pint of Wiser's down the protesting gullet.

"We have plans for you," said Lewandowski. "As you may realize, your inquiries have become—" he flicked ash onto the floor "—as tiresome as your predecessor's! Like you, he was fond of his whiskey, so that, most unfortunately, he was too drunk to find his way home from Bruce's Mill. In your case, the coroner will be shocked but unsurprised to discover that you attempted to drive at one hundred miles an hour along Lakeshore Boulevard after drinking almost two bottles of rye." He shook his head and smiled thinly.

Bognor began to feel drunk. "We'll keep you here for the day, and then some time after midnight we'll let you drive home on your own. What could be more civilized?" Again that laugh and its echo from the doorway.

"I don't understand," said Bognor, understanding, he feared, all too well.

"Then let me explain." Lewandowski folded his arms and grinned. "Your friend Mr. Macpherson shared our beloved master's love for this absurd British teatime savory paste called Gentleman's Relish. As you now presumably realize, we have a particular interest in ensuring that our own, rather special not to say individual pots of relish do not find their way onto the public market. Alas—" he spread his hands in a gesture of muted despair "—whether it was a computer fault or human error I can't tell. One of our jars went missing. We found it was on the market. When we checked the local outlets, we discovered that for the previous week a strange fat Englishman had been buying the whole Toronto stock. Finally, we trapped him, but by then it was too late. For all of us. Fritzy here became a little, how shall we say—overenthusiastic."

"And you never found your jar?"

"No. We were unable to penetrate the security of your British consulate. Macpherson would not give up the combination of the safe. He was a brave man." Lewandowski lowered his eyes. "But we have all day. Another drink?"

The procedure was repeated, and Bognor felt himself losing all control. He wondered what time it was. He just hoped the basement was in the Mammon Building. That the Mounties would get to him before dark.

"Why the message?" he asked. "Why did you pretend Sir Roderick would see me at four?"

"No pretense," said Lewandowski. "The message was genuine."

He was drunk, blind drunk, when they found him. His early warning distress signals to London had done the trick. The analysis of the tea bag, confirming Swindow LSD, had helped. A Scotland Yard dawn raid had uncovered a London drug factory plus a hoard of Gentleman's Relish jars and an accomplished art student who had been making money on the side painting tiny beavers with silver spoons in their mouths. Parkinson had flown over at once. He was concerned, as he put it, to "give those damned Mounties a kick up the bum. They're too busy doing a Watergate on Quebec's froggoes to worry about crime." But he had other worries, too.

"May I go home now?" Bognor asked, eventually, still drunk.

Parkinson stared at him with the expression that had withered countless colleagues in every reach of the British civil service.

"May?" he repeated finally, with a devastatingly ironic softness. "May, Bognor?"

Bognor swallowed hard. He was not sober but he was not so far off sobriety that he didn't recognize Parkinson's anger.

"I just thought—" His voice trailed away.

"I know what you thought, Bognor." Parkinson was still talking very softly but he was having trouble keeping his voice down. "You thought you were some sort of a hero. Thought you'd broken a great international drug-smuggling racket, involving the most powerful man in Canada."

"Well, yes, actually."

"You're an imbecile, Bognor. It's true there has been a rather amateur little drug-smuggling operation going on. And it's true that one end of it was organized from within the Mammon organization. But instead of seeing it for the small-time nonsense it is, you have to go right to the top, don't you? You can't accept that it's the embittered male secretary on an inadequate salary who's trying to make a fast buck. Oh, no. For you, only the best. 'Multi-millionaire in drug scandal.' You want your name in lights along with Inspector Maigret and Sherlock Holmes."

Bognor bit his lip. The worst was to come, he knew. This was not the first time.

"Farquhar had nothing to do with it. Nothing whatever. Lewandowski was working a little fiddle all on his own. The RCMP were already onto him. But Farquhar's angry now. Not just with you but with us. You've botched the fighter deal; you've screwed up any chance of collaborating in James Bay. The foreign office is livid with rage. The prime minister wants your head on a plate. The external-affairs chappies in Ottawa say if you're not out in twenty-four hours they'll expel you like they did the Soviets. And yet you still manage to ask, all nice and smug and pleased with yourself: 'May I go home?' God help us."

Bognor flew home that night, badly hungover, vaguely regretting that he had never got to see the Blue Jays play, nor found a cottage, nor a girl. It was the only time he had crossed the Atlantic sober.

"Have a good day!" smiled the pretty Air Canada blonde as he slouched out of the 747 into a thin London drizzle.

"Sure," he said.

# New Zealand

# What's Afoot?

*By Geoffrey Hitchcock*

PERCY PAUSED IN his work of digging up his old strawberry patch and leaned on his spade. An idea for a poem was coming into his mind. "The glory that was Greece gives way to Rome; the glory of the strawberries gives way to lowly spuds"—but before he could develop the theme, his wife came into the garden and at the same time he noticed something.

"Come over here," he said. "I've just noticed that standing here you can see straight down Tauhou Street."

"So you can!"

"There must be fifty houses in that street, and I don't know a single person living in any of them. That's terrible."

But Pauli didn't see anything terrible about it; as far as she could see it was perfectly normal. Why, they hardly knew their next door neighbors in Tihoi Street, so how could they be expected to know people in Tauhou Street, even if they did walk along it nearly every day.

"But don't you see," Percy persisted, "if we can't be interested in our neighbors—find out what they think, what makes them tick—how can we expect nations to understand nations? What hope of peace?"

"Would you like to have smoko now, dear?" said Pauli.

Percy sighed and followed her into the house. A new poem was forming in his mind and he reached for his pencil and paper and wrote it down.

*"Who lives in Number One?*
*Is it Mr. Duncan Dunn?*
*Across the road in Number Two—*
*Hindu? Muslim? Christian? Jew?*
*That big house at Number Three*
*Has room for quite a family.*
*But perhaps there's only Widow Gee*
*Who'll ask me in and give me tea.*
*Who knows, who cares,*
*Indeed who cares one jot*
*Who lives in Number Three?*

*"Who lives in Number Eight?*
*Old Mr. Tate,*
*Leaning, lonely, on his gate,*
*Hoping to pass the time of day*
*With all of those who pass his way?*
*And does Miss Vine*
*In Number Nine*
*Hang out nappies on the line*
*And softly sigh and sadly pine?*
*Who knows—who cares?*

*"Is Mrs. Dean,*
*Who's in Fifteen,*
*Always tidy, neat, and clean?*
*While Mrs. Surtee*
*In Number Thirty*
*Is she (now I'll fool you)—flirty?*
*Do they have fun*
*In Twenty-one*
*And live on stew*
*In Forty-two?*

*"Who knows—who cares?*
*Who dares*
*To knock on Number Twenty-four?*
*Ah me,*
*Could I but see*
*What dangers lurk behind the door*
*Of fearsome Number Twenty-four?"*

Pauli came in with the tea tray.

"Listen to the poem I'm writing," said Percy, and proceeded to read it to her while she poured out. "What do you think?"

"Why do you always rhyme so much?" she complained.

"I can't help it—not when I'm in a good mood."

"You must always be in a good mood."

"I am, mostly—is that bad?"

"I suppose not, but you'll never get a poem in the *Listener*."

"Who knows? Who cares? Who dares to send the *Listener* a rhyme? A poem that makes sense first time? These scones are good."

And with that he addressed himself to the business at hand while his mind went off on its own track and his automatic defense system took over.

Pauli's fault was that she never stopped talking and Percy had remained happy and sane simply by not listening while his own thoughts kept him entertained. His automatic mechanism dropped in an occasional "Yes, dear," or "No, dear," or "Fancy that" about every thirty seconds.

So Pauli chatted away and Percy worked on the problem of the sinister occupant of Number Twenty-four. Perhaps there was a Russian spy sending *Listener* poems to Moscow because he was convinced they were in code.

"Mrs. Jones's cousin's daughter, you know, the one who married the commercial traveler, had twins last week—that's four girls she's got now. More tea?"

"Yes, dear." Or perhaps there was a white slaver who planned to kidnap Mrs. Jones's four daughters and send them to a house of delight in Buenos Aires.

"The Stevensons' holiday bach was broken into and two thousand dollars' worth of jewelry was stolen. Would you believe anybody could leave so much jewelry in a bach? And a television."

"No, dear." It's a hideout for a gang of thieves. Our hero watches from the shadows while masked men carry in stolen jewels and television sets.

"Mrs. Brown says her uncle has invented an electronic dog that growls and barks if burglars break in, but you can pat it if you're a friend."

"Fancy that." There's a mad professor living there. He is making robots in the shape of hideous beasts that roam the streets at night and frighten people to death.

"The Atkinsons are coming to tea this afternoon, but they won't be here until three thirty because they're going to the hospital first to look in on her cousin who's got . . ."

"Yes, dear." The man in Twenty-four strangled his wife because she never stopped talking.

"You haven't been listening to a word I've been saying." She gave him an affectionate pat on the knee. "Have you?"

Percy blinked and surfaced. The situation wasn't all that uncommon.

"Sorry, dear, I was preoccupied with ideas for a story about Number Twenty-four."

"If Number Twenty-four is worrying you so much, why don't you simply go round there and pay the occupants a visit?"

"What a good idea. In fact, why don't I visit all the houses? I'll start this very afternoon!"

"Bully for you," said Pauli, knowing quite well that her dearly beloved was much too timid ever to knock on a stranger's door.

"I'll go straight after my after-lunch nap. I won't take Bonzo—he might not be welcome."

"And mind you wrap up warm."

"I'll take my scarf," said Percy, looking out on the brilliant autumn sunshine.

"And don't be too long. The Atkinsons will be here about half past three."

"Oh, are they coming to tea today? I didn't know."

"At half past three." Pauli knew it was no use getting into strife about it.

Ten past two found Percy starting his walk along Tauhou Street. It was disappointing from the start. The first house was Number Forty-six and there was a name on the letterbox—Johnson, not Quix. Percy sighed and moved along, observing the houses really carefully for perhaps the first time.

Most of the houses didn't have the occupants' names displayed, and when they did, they didn't rhyme with the numbers at all. Mrs. Dean, who had such a wide choice, had elected to live in Thirty-seven! Maddening! Percy gradually came out of his poetic fantasy. He looked at Number Twenty-four with some trepidation, but there wasn't really anything fearsome about its front door at all. It was a stout paneled door, set off center in a green weatherboard house with large, welcoming windows and tiled roof. Two steps led to a porch that sheltered the door. A pleasant if somewhat ordinary house.

The section on which it was built sloped away rather steeply, and Percy guessed that the house would be high off the ground at the back with probably the garage underneath it. Indeed, a driveway led down past the side of the house. The front garden was neat but not excessively so, unlike Number Fifteen where Percy felt he daren't call for fear he'd leave a footprint in the garden.

On then to the end of the road, rapidly losing interest until Number One, which had a small nameplate: B. and M. Gunn. By Jove, thought Percy, Ben Gunn in Number One—if I'd brought some cheese I'd have been sure of a welcome! But the carport was empty and the letterbox was stuffed with circulars.

The whole street's dead, thought Percy. No wonder we don't know anybody here. He turned to walk back, thinking that the idea was silly and he'd just have to brave Pauli's taunts. He hadn't seen a soul in the whole street, but now in Number Twenty-three there was a woman in a sundress and a floppy hat (dress up warm, thought Percy, whose muffler was in his pocket) snipping at her roses.

"Lovely day for gardening," he volunteered.

"Oh, hello, Mr. Bannister, going for a walk? Where's your dog?"

"Do you know old Bonzo, then?"

"Of course. He's always so good about waiting for you outside the shop."

That pressed a key. "Of course—it's Mrs. Lee from the dairy. I didn't recognize you in your sun hat and out of your natural element, so to speak. So I do know somebody in Tauhou Street after all!" He proceeded to tell her the whole tale, and even recited his verse.

She listened with great interest. "Of course being in the dairy I know most of the folk around here, but I think it's a perfectly splendid idea. Where will you begin? At Number One? Oh no—the Gunns are in Australia for the month and the Pughs are both at work."

"Are they really called Pugh in Number Two?"

"Not really—they're Morrisons—I was just joining in the fun. I don't think there are any number-rhyming names in the street apart from the Gunns."

"And yourself," said Percy, warming to her.

"Of course, Mrs. Lee in Twenty-three—she may invite you in to tea! I'd never thought of it before. And right opposite are Mr. and Mrs. Shaw in Twenty-four! Well I never!" She thought for a moment. "But that's all I can think of. Why don't you start there? They're a nice elderly couple about your age, though she's away, I think. But he'll be there, I saw his station wagon drive in just a few minutes ago."

"But that's where the terrors lurk," objected Percy. "What about Twenty-two?"

Mrs. Lee laughed. "I doubt very much you'll find any terrors there, they are really nice people. But as to Twenty-two I'd better warn you that there's a widow living there, and if you make her acquaintance, she'll be forever pestering you. And she's a troublemaker."

"A troublemaker?"

"A gossip. Just now she's spreading a rumor that Mr. Shaw has murdered his wife."

"Did he, do you think?"

"Of course not, but she's sure of it because Mrs. Shaw went away without telling her. My guess is that Margaret went away to get Mrs. Drew off her back for a while."

"Then why don't I call in and find out?"

"Why not indeed," agreed Mrs. Lee. "What a splendid opportunity to put Mrs. Drew in her place."

"Because," said Percy honestly, "I'm not brave enough."

But Mrs. Lee scoffed at the suggestion, and our hero found himself with a big iron knocker in his hand. Almost immediately the sinister door was opened by a big greyhaired man whose usually kind lines were creased into a puzzled frown.

"You don't look like a policeman," he said. That threw Percy, and all he could think of to say was, "Oh! Don't I?"

"No. But I suppose if Dietrich and Wojo are anything to go by, it doesn't mean a thing. Come in anyway."

He ushered Percy into a large, comfortably furnished room, the main feature of which was several mounted sets of antlers overshadowed by a magnificent stag's head.

"Take a pew," said the man, indicating a comfortable armchair. Percy sat and gazed round the room.

"I say," he said, "what a magnificent head . . . you didn't . . . did you?"

"Yes, I did. I'm a deer stalker. Do you hunt?"

"Not me—you need to be a big strong fellow for that. I fish sometimes. Mostly I work in the garden and round the house, but for a hobby I write a bit—not much—just the odd short story and a bit of verse."

"A poet! You seem less and less like a policeman."

"I'm not. I'm Percy Bannister and I live at the end of the road in Tihoi Street."

"Then why the devil didn't you say so?"

"I was going to, but you seemed so obsessed with the police—are you expecting them?"

"Not exactly." The big man dismissed the matter as of no importance. "So what can I do for you, Percy?"

Percy explained. He considered reciting his verse, of which he was rather proud and at which Mrs. Lee had clapped her hands with pleasure, but in time he remembered the line about the door of Twenty-four. "What do you think of the idea?" he concluded.

His host was delighted. "I think that's great. You're quite right—we should be more caring of each other. Glad to know you, Percy. Uncommon name. I'm Dick Shaw, though my wife called me Richard—thought it was more classy."

"Don't you have a wife any more?" asked Percy, pleased with himself for being able to broach the subject so soon.

Dick considered the question before answering. Then he shrugged. "I suppose I have."

"Don't you know?"

"Well, I suppose the answer is yes I have, but we had a flaming row a while back and she left home. Haven't seen her since."

"I am sorry."

"Well," Dick considered, "so am I in a way. On the other hand it's pretty marvelous. Terrible nag she's become lately. Do this—do that—why don't you do the other. All day long, it was beginning to drive me mad. Why couldn't I have a bit of peace now that I'm retired and do what I wanted? I wasn't causing any trouble."

"No. I see what you mean, I can understand how you felt."

"Can you, Percy? Does your wife nag you too?"

"Not much really, but she never stops talking. I don't listen, of course, but there are times when I could cheerfully bash her one."

"I could strangle mine sometimes."

"You didn't. Did you?"

"Don't be ridiculous. What . . . oh, the police thing. There's a stupid woman next door—she was on good nagging terms with Mag and just because Mag went off without telling her—and why should she, for Pete's sake—she's spreading a rumor that I've done the old girl in."

"Ah, so that accounts for the police business." Percy began to feel a wave of sympathy for Dick.

"I've been half expecting her to go to them and report a murder. Not a shred to go on, of course, but I wouldn't put it past the silly old cow. They'd only laugh at her."

"They'd curse her and all you'd do is tell them where your wife is and Mrs. Drew would look a right Charleen."

"Mrs. Drew?"

"From Twenty-two."

"Of course, old poet—sorry, I'm a bit slow on the uptake. Not quite as easy as that, though. I haven't the foggiest where she's gone."

"You mean you don't know where she is?"

"No, and I don't care. She's welcome back any time, but I'm not going chasing after her. She walked out, not me."

"But if she's been gone more than a week, shouldn't you report her missing?"

"If I did that, old boy, they'd be sure to find her. After all, she must have gone somewhere—to some friend or cousin that I don't know about, or to a hotel. Back to England, even."

"Could she really walk out just like that?"

"It wasn't quite so casual. I say, old visitor, I'm being very inhospitable burdening you with my troubles without offering you something. What'll it be? Something alcoholic, or are you a tea and coffee man?"

"Thank you, we generally do have a cup of coffee at this time of the day, but that would be imposing."

"Not at all. Not at all. If you hadn't called, I'd be putting the kettle on anyway."

He led Percy through to a pleasant room with kitchen at one end and dining table at the other and seated him on a high stool at a counter that divided the room while he busied himself with the kettle. From his seat, Percy looked through a wide picture window to an unobstructed view of lake and mountains.

"I like this room best," said Dick.

"It's easy to see why." Percy was enthusiastic. "What a magnificent open view. Mine's restricted by trees."

"Trees are good, too, but I love my mountains and the forest." He put two steaming mugs of coffee and slices of fruit cake on the counter, which was wide enough for him to sit opposite Percy. For a while they were quiet, savoring the view and the coffee.

"You make an excellent cup of coffee and this cake's good. You didn't make it, did you?"

Dick laughed. "No, Mrs. Adams or Mrs. Irvine made the cake. I'm strictly a bush cook, and that doesn't run to fruit cake. Mag was a dab hand at cake, I'll say that for her."

"So you had a barney one evening, and when you woke up next morning she'd gone?" Percy was anxious not to let the subject drop.

"No, no, it wasn't like that. I got up very early and went into the Kaimanawas. I stayed there two days."

"I see," said Percy. It did make sense now. She was fed up with his always going off and leaving her, so she had plenty of time to pack a bag and take off. "And when you came back she was gone. It must have been a shock."

"Percy, my friend, it was, and at the same time, it was wonderful. I'd had two glorious days in the bush—not stalking, just communing with nature as they say. Tane had soothed my shattered nerves. I had walked until I was physically exhausted and was filled with that glow of contentment that only such days can produce. Heaven would be a hot tub and a long, cool beer, but I braced myself for an earbashing."

"Which didn't come."

"No," said Dick, "talk about all this and a Seven too—only I don't smoke, do you?"

"No, gave it up years ago, but I know how you felt. I hate coming home after a day's fishing and being fussed over and put in a hot bath. But it must have been a shock for all that."

"Yes and no. She had always threatened to leave home if I went into the bush alone. But of course she never had—before."

"No. I can understand her being anxious if you do that. Isn't it one of the first rules . . ."

"Aw, come off it, old comrade, don't you start nagging now. I've been tramping in the bush since I was a kid."

"But perhaps she thought you were getting past it."

"Hey, steady on, how old do you think I am?"

"Sixty-five?"

"Well, I'm not, I'm only seventy-two!"

"Oh well, that's different." They had a good laugh over that.

"And I'm still very strong," Dick said.

"I can see that." Everything was quite clear to Percy now. Silly old codger didn't know when it was time to slow down. No mystery now about his wife walking out. It was time to change the subject.

"This coffee is good," he said.

"Bush style," said Dick, topping up their mugs. Percy sniffed the coffee, appreciated the aroma, and then some other not so pleasant odor, crept into his nostrils. He lifted his head away from his mug and sniffed the air. Drains, perhaps?

"I say, Dick, you sure you didn't do for your missus?"

Dick sniffed the air and frowned. He stood up and took a large meat cleaver off the wall, then he came round the counter and, trying hard to conceal his mirth, he suddenly grabbed the startled Percy from his stool and steered him towards the outside door before he could think what was happening.

"You have discovered my secret, so now you are implicated and must help me dispose of the corpse."

And before the now thoroughly disconcerted Percy could gather his wits, he found himself being hustled down a flight of wooden steps that led down the side of the house and round the corner into the back yard where, to his horror, he saw Mag in her nightgown hanging from a beam that protruded from the wall. He let out a strangled cry and felt his knees buckle.

When he recovered, he found he'd been propped up comfortably against the wall. Summoning all his courage he looked at the "body." He at once noticed two things about it: it had no head and a small black hoof was protruding below the hem of the nightie. He felt very foolish. What would his new friend think of him? It was obvious now that it was all a big joke and Dick would have been expecting a roar of laughter—not a swooning nincompoop. After all, what murderer would leave his victim hanging up for all to see?

He had just managed to struggle to his feet when Dick came down the stairs with a glass of whisky.

"Sorry about that," he said. "Here, drink this, it'll put the color back in your cheeks." And while Percy was gagging on the strong drink, he burst into uncontrollable mirth.

"If only you could have seen yourself." Tears were running down his cheeks. "I wish it had been Mrs. Drew. She might have died of heart failure!"

"*I* might have died of heart failure," protested Percy.

"Never, old man, your heart is too big, but I do apologize. I get carried away with my leg-pulling. Perhaps that's why I have so few friends. It's the Irish in me."

He went on to explain that he had hung up a side of venison to "ripen" and had covered it with one of Mag's passion-killers to keep the flies off.

"But why the drama with the meat cleaver?"

"No drama. I was going to cut you a joint. You deserve something nice after listening to all my nonsense."

"Thanks very much," said Percy, imagining how Pauli would react to the undoubtedly "ripe" meat, "but I mustn't deprive you."

"No possibility," said Dick, who proceeded to unlock and open a heavy door. "Look—plenty more where that came from."

Percy saw that the door opened into a sizeable cold store. There was a rail across the room from which deer carcasses were hanging, and on the floor at the back a whole heap more. He was about to inquire why they were on the floor when there were so many spare hooks when his eye caught something that gave him such a jolt that Dick couldn't help noticing it.

"What is it now?"

Percy was in a state of shock. "There's a foot sticking out . . . it's . . . got . . . five toes."

Dick looked into the room. "How the hell did that happen." He locked the door carefully.

Percy just stood there waiting for his legs to regain their function. "I'll go home now. I think I've overstayed my welcome."

"No, don't do that. I don't want you to go away thinking badly of me."

"I won't do that," moaned Percy. "I don't doubt you were driven to it. I'm not feeling very well."

But the big man had other ideas. "Come upstairs and I'll give you a drink . . . and we'll decide where we go from here."

Percy looked around for an escape route, but there didn't seem to be one. "I don't really have much option, do I?"

"Not really," said Dick, and guided the unwilling little man up the stairs. Seated at the counter again, Dick poured two enormous drinks in spite of Percy's protests that he wasn't used to whisky.

"You're in a state of shock," he said, "so knock that back. Cheers."

"Cheers," said Percy, obeying. "Wow—that was strong."

"Put you right—there," filling the glasses again. "You can drink this one more slowly while I tell you exactly what happened."

"Hic! Pardon." The two large whiskies were taking effect already. Percy began to feel a warm glow and a feeling of confidence. Maybe his position wasn't as hopeless as it had seemed while he was being hustled up the stairs. He took a generous sip of his third whisky. He was beginning to get a taste for it. "Right you are then, old soldier, fire away and no lies this time."

"Percy, my old bard, I haven't told you a lie yet. I may have noted some unlikely possibilities and left out a few details. I'll fill them in now."

Percy took another sip. He was beginning to feel well in control of the situation. "Carry on, corporal," he said.

Dick took a deep swig himself. "I'd arranged to go on a short hunting trip with Len Gardner, but at the last minute he phoned to say he couldn't make it—Mag took the message. I said never mind, I'd go on my own, and that started it. All the afternoon—what if this, what if that, what if, what if, what if! Drove me barmy."

"Must say I see her point of view."

"Now, Percy, I thought we'd agreed. . . ."

"Not nagging," said Percy, "see your point of view too, but not safe to go in the bush alone."

"Dammit, man, the bush is no more dangerous to me than walking down the street is to you."

"Funny things happen to me walking down the street," said Percy pointedly. Dick decided to let that one ride.

"Anyway I kept out of her way all evening while I got my gear ready. She went to bed early. The trouble was that she'd got old and frail and couldn't understand that I was still strong as an ox. I sleep in the spare room when I'm going off early so's not to disturb her."

"Thoughtful of you." Percy drained his glass.

"I'm not all bad. I went to kiss her goodnight, and damn me if she didn't start all over again. What would happen to her if . . . I let her rant on for ten minutes; then, when I was beginning to lose my temper, I grabbed her by the shoulders and gave her a good shake. 'That's enough,' I shouted, 'now shut up and go to sleep.' I dropped her on the pillow and stalked out. When I got home two days later, she was still there."

Percy was shocked. He pushed his glass towards Dick, who filled it automatically.

"You told me she'd gone."

"She had gone but she was still there, if you get my drift."

"You sure she was still there—not there again?"

"She didn't seem to have moved. Can't be sure, though. A person in bed one night looks much the same as any other night. I think I must have dislocated her neck—her head was floppy."

"The doctor could have told you."

"I didn't send for the doctor. He'd only have confirmed that I'd killed her."

"The pleesh then—it was only an accident."

"I thought about it, but what would they do? Lock me up. Drag me through the courts. Accuse me of womanslaughter, then lock me up again. I don't have time for all that."

"Right, no time for all that. So what did you do?"

"I didn't do anything. I thought, She's gone now, poor dear, and perhaps not much before her time. And nothing will bring her back. And I don't expect to last much longer. A couple of years, perhaps, then one of the things she worried about will happen. So why not leave it at that?"

"You're quite right—couldn't agree more." The mists that had clouded Percy's thinking were beginning to clear. "But laws, customs, and you had a corpse on your hands."

"Yes," replied Dick, "and a busybody neighbor, so I carried poor Mag down to the cold room and hid her behind the carcasses while I thought things through."

"And have you?"

"Well, no. Up to now it's worked very well as it is. 'Nother drink?"

"Cheers," said Percy, clinking his glass with Dick's. "Whatcha mean— up to now?"

"You don't think anything's changed?"

"Why should it? Just because you showed me a foot? Not my bishness is it what a man dush with hish wife? Own affair."

"You mean you don't intend to phone the police as soon as you get home?" Dick eyed him narrowly.

"Not lesh you want me to."

"Why the devil should I want you to?"

"Why'd you show me that damn foot?"

"I didn't mean to. I don't know how it slipped out. I was trying to allay suspicion, wasn't I? Give the busybodies something to think about."

Percy thought about it for a while and emptied his glass. "I wonder," he said.

Dick's temper was beginning to fray. "What do you mean you wonder," he shouted. "What the hell do you think I was doing? Here, have another drink."

"Yesh," said Percy, "helps me to think clearly. Not sh . . . muddled sh . . . usual."

"Good. Think clearly, then."

"I think . . . I think you were calling for help."

Dick exploded. "Help? Me? From a pipsqueak like you that I've never met until today?"

"Not likely, is it?" acknowledged Percy.

"No."

"No—but the point is . . ." If Percy was sure of one thing now, it was that he wanted to go home. "The point is, no matter what you shay, I'm going to be drawn into this. I know you've got a heavy load, even for your broad shoulders, and I'm shorry. Like to help . . . not going to be drawn in." He started to rise unsteadily to his feet, but the big man reached over and sat him down again.

"You are drawn in, old philosopher, up to your neck."

"Yesh, but I'm drawing out now." He tried to get up again.

"No, sit down till we sort this out," said Dick, pressing him down again.

"No need to push me like that. I'm your friend, aren't I? Tell you now . . . feel shorry for you . . . damn shorry . . . know you didn't mean to do it. Know you were still fond of her, elsh why would you kisher goo'night?"

"It wasn't always bad. Mostly it'd been good."

"So, you had acshident . . . should've gone to pleesh . . . cleared the matter up . . . butcha didn't . . . you thought you'd found freedom that'd last. You began to wish the silly ol' biddy next door would go to pleesh . . . but she didn't." Percy's mind was very clear now. He just wished the room wouldn't float up and down.

"But she didn't," prompted Dick.

"So when I came 'long, you took . . . opportunity to get me involved."

Dick was amazed. "You worked all that out?"

"By myshelf," said Percy proudly.

Dick shook his head—slowly, because the drink was beginning to get to him, too.

"You must be off your rocker. I was just trying to allay suspicion. Now I've got you on my hands."

"I'll get off, then, no trouble. Tell you what I'll do, I think you want help so I'll help you . . . tell you what I'll do . . . is the whisky finished?"

"Never!" Dick filled the glasses, then raised his in a toast. "To Mag."

"Yesh, the nag. Tell you what I'm going to do, I'm going to do nothing, that okay, Dick?"

"That's splendid, Percy, couldn't be better."

Percy struggled to his feet and once more Dick pushed him down again.

"You can't go yet, old soldier, I need a guarantee."

"Don't push me down all the time. What guarantee?"

"That you won't tell that chatterbox wife of yours."

"Tell Pauli? Don't ever tell her anything, old com-pat-riot, be all over the neighborhood if you do."

"That's right, Persh. Thash why need guarantee."

Percy thought hard for a moment. "Crosh my heart and hope to die?"

Dick considered this, then shook his head sadly. "Not good enough."

"How about Shcoutsh honor?" suggested Percy hopefully.

"Sorry, old sergeant . . . been a scout m'self . . . have to lock you in the cold room."

"Can't do that, cap'n, haven't got my jersey on. Only a muffler."

"Only soundproof room in the house," said Dick.

"I (hic) presheate your point, old turnkey, but there'sh a problem. Pauli will come looking for me. That'sh it!" He snapped his fingers in delight. "Lock Pauli in cold room."

"Stop her talking," said Dick doubtfully.

"Stop me talking, too, colonel . . . get in trouble if I do."

"Percy, you old Einstein, you're a genius. How do we get her in?"

"Shimple . . . ring her up . . . tell her put on lotsh warm cloze . . . bring basket . . . gonna give her some fenison. Then shut door."

"Full marks, professor. What's her number?"

"Pauli's number? Cucumber." He giggled. He thought hard. "Don't know her number . . . never ring her up, see . . . I'm already there . . . don't have to phone her."

But when they tried to look up the number in the directory, the small print danced about so it was impossible.

"I'll go and get her," said Percy. "Sh not far."

"Don't be long," said Dick. "Going out early tomorrow."

"You gonna kill another old deer?"

"Now, now, none of that. Jush going deep bush for a few days. Clear up some problems. You go get Pauli."

"Three minutes," said Percy, but in his haste to stagger out he opened the wrong door.

"Tha's a cupboard," said Dick.

"Full of Mags," said Percy.

"Relics of the days she had her boutique. Dress shop to you."

"I know . . . this one's got a foot missing."

Somehow he managed to get home and fall up the front steps without hurting himself. Pauli came running out and helped him in.

"Where have you been? I don't know what the Atkinsons must have thought. Thank goodness they didn't see you like this—you've been drinking."

"Jush one or two . . . lishen, Pauli . . . s'important . . . losh and losh cloze . . . big basket . . . get locked in cold shtore."

"What on earth are you on about?"

"Cloze," said Percy, "locked in Dick's cold store . . . oh, I feel bad."

Everything was going black and the house was on a rollercoaster. . . .

\*   \*   \*

Percy woke in the morning and reached across the bed for Pauli. She wasn't there. A sudden vision of her locked in Dick's cold storeroom sent him racing to the phone. He had already dialed the first two digits when he heard Pauli making tea in the kitchen. "Pauli! Thank God you're here."

"Where did you think I'd be?"

"In the freezer."

"Now you just pop back into bed and I'll bring you a nice cup of tea and some aspirin and when you're feeling better you can tell me all about it."

"Ow, my poor head," he said and obeyed her instructions. He thought a lot about how much he should tell her, and eventually, over breakfast, he told her everything—well, as much as he could remember.

Pauli thought it all very funny. She didn't believe Percy had really seen a foot in the cold room.

"What an afternoon you had, my poor darling! What are you going to do now?"

"Nothing," said Percy, whose aching head took all the fun out of the episode.

"You're probably right," said Pauli. "You drank so much whisky that you couldn't be sure what was going on."

"No, it's all very confused. I just wish I'd never noticed that smell. Do you know, I can still smell it."

Pauli sniffed the air. "So can I, it's coming from outside."

She went to the front door and came back with a carton that had an unmistakeable effluvium about it and a note taped to it.

"Dear Percy (he read), I'm going bush for a few days. Here's the venison I promised you. It's just nicely ripe now so you needn't hang it any longer. Sorry I teased you and got you so drunk. You're a good sport. Dick. P.S. I'll come and see you if I get back."

"He means when he gets back," said Pauli.

"Yes," said Percy.

Percy opened the carton. Inside was a haunch of "nicely ripe" venison and beside it a plastic foot. On the foot was written "A souvenir from Mag."

Pauli saw the funny side of it. "What a character. What a weird sense of humor! My poor old muggins, he certainly had you on a string. He must have had it all lined up for Mrs. Pew or whatever the busybody's name is, only you came along and copped the lot."

Percy found it more difficult. "I was the sucker all right. Never mind, we'll have roast venison for dinner. It'll make a nice change."

"Pooh," said his spouse, "we will not. You go and bury it in the garden."

Percy dug a deep hole in the old strawberry patch, a place he thought fitting, and dropped the venison in it. "In you go, you stinking flesh. Dust to dust. . . . Poor Dick. Are you digging a grave for your old mate some-where out there in the forest? And who will bury you, Dick? Tane will take your spirit and cover your body with leaves. Such a strong old body. Such a waste. . . . In you go, poor foot. Such an elegant pink foot. Not a bit like that old bluey-white one with the big bunion that's punched forever on my memory tapes. But I won't tell Pauli. Not ever." He made a two-fingered salute. "Shcouts' honor."

# AUSTRALIA

# Whatever Happened To Crocodile Jarvis?

*By Justin D'Ath*

I HAD NEVER liked that Jarvis kid.

"Jeez, Robin, do we have to bring him?"

Robin pushed in the clutch and hit the anchors hard. I nearly bumped my head on the windscreen. I knew he had done it on purpose; we were out of sight of both houses, and Robin liked to show off a bit. He wasn't old enough yet to have a license, but our Old Man let him drive the ute around so long as he didn't go anywhere near the main road. A cloud of our own dust caught up with us and turned everything red. I cranked my winder-knob flat-out to get the window closed before too much of the stuff got inside.

"He's got nobody else to knock round with, Marty."

Robin is my big brother. It was all very well for him. He was hardly ever on the station these days. He didn't have to put up with Jarvis hanging round all the time like a bad smell. The only thing Robin cared about was that soppy girlfriend of his. And she just happened to be Jarvis's big sister, didn't she?

"Well, I don't like him." I had to shout to make myself heard above the roar of the motor. Robin had the idle turned up way too high. "He's a silly showoff."

"Hey, keep it down!" Robin said out of one side of his mouth so Jarvis wouldn't hear.

The little runt had caught up with us already. He must have really come belting after us as soon as the ute started to slow down. He was puffing like a steam train.

Robin opened his window a crack.

"Doin' anything this afternoon, Crocky?"

Jarvis shook his head. His real name was Adrian, but he liked to be called Croc. I was not sure why—after Crocodile Dundee, most probably. I had never been interested enough to find out.

Robin said, "Marty and I are going out to knock over a few pigs. Like to come?"

It was a pretty dumb question. Jarvis's eyes went big as twenty-cent pieces. "You bet!"

"Let him in your side, Marty."

"He can go in the back," I said. The rifles and knives and ammunition took up most of the middle of the seat. You can bet your bottom dollar I wasn't going to let that wimp Jarvis sit on my knee.

"All right," Robin grumbled. He didn't like me going against what he said, but he saw it was the best thing. What it meant was he couldn't skid round corners or go over bumps so fast any more. If he did, our passenger would probably get bounced right out of the back. Not that that would have been any great loss to the human race, I thought. But it wouldn't have made Big Brother too popular with that prissy Beverly Jarvis, and that was all Robin was worried about. I hated it how he drove like a maniac, though.

"Hop up in the back, Crocky," Robin said.

It took us nearly half an hour to get out to Watson's Dam. Normally it would have taken only about twenty minutes with Robin playing Alain Prost like he used to. I began to feel less sore at Jarvis for coming along. And every time we pulled up in front of a gate, Jarvis was off the back of the ute in a flash, dragging the thing open for us. Usually that was my job. Robin stopped the ute halfway through the last gate and waved to Jarvis to get back on.

"Don't bother closing this one, Crocky—there isn't a beast for twenty miles."

Only pigs, I thought. I began to get an excited, trembly feeling inside. I grabbed the waterbag off the floor. My mouth was a bit dry already.

We had driven only about a mile into the paddock before Robin poked the ute under the low wattle and switched the engine off. I opened my door and slid out, dragging the .22.

Robin growled. "Hey, careful where you point that thing!"

"It isn't loaded."

"Well," says Robin, "lots of people are dead from guns that weren't loaded." He was beginning to sound like the Old Man.

Jarvis had already jumped off my side of the ute. He pulled a real smart-aleck face when he saw the .22.

"That's only a peashooter."

"So?" I said, taking a bead on an imaginary animal.

"I thought we were after pigs."

"This is all right for pigs. You just have to know the right place to hit them."

"Bet you never even shot one, Adams."

"I've shot plenty," I bragged. I felt like shooting Jarvis.

"Bet you haven't really."

"What would *you* know, Adrian?" I knew he hated being called that. "They don't teach you about guns on *Play School*, do they?"

"Hey, knock it off, you two," Robin said from the other side of the car. I could hear him pushing slugs into the magazine of the .303. "You'll scare all the pigs away."

Jarvis gave me a dirty look, then went round to Robin's side of the ute. I bent in and got the packet of .22 bullets out of the glovebox.

"That's a nice Lee Enfield you've got there," I heard him say to Robin. "I see you've given it a free-floating barrel." Smart little prick!

We set off on foot towards the dam. It was only about a mile. Robin went in front, then me, then Jarvis. I noticed Jarvis was wearing Robin's ammunition belt with the big bowie knife hanging in its sheath at the back. It looked almost as big as him. I remember thinking, I bet that gives you a real thrill, Croc. He probably thought he really was Crocodile Dundee.

Poor little bastard.

It's mostly open country all around Watson's Dam. The scrub starts about a hundred yards out. There is a creek that runs into it—comes all the way from the artesian bore on Mr. Jarvis's property three miles away. Without the water we got from the Jarvises, Dad reckoned we could run only about half the number of cattle we did. We used the creek that day to sneak up on the dam, walking crouched down along the channel. There was no wind. If there were any pigs at the dam, there was no way they were going to smell us or see us coming.

Flies were buzzing about, and Robin's and my boots made a slop-suck in the mud at the edge of the water. Jarvis had sneakers on and was walking higher up on the bank where it was dry. The dam was somewhere up ahead, but I couldn't see it. I couldn't even see the trees.

I kept my head down. It felt good to be carrying a rifle. I had lied to Jarvis; I had never shot a pig. Robin and I had come out after them before, but this was the first time I'd been allowed to bring my own gun. Usually I just tagged along like Jarvis was doing today. I felt a lot older than Jarvis. I was glad he was there to see me hunting pigs.

My palms were sweaty as we stalked up on the dam. There might be pigs there, but they still wouldn't know we were coming for them. *Look out, pigs! You better start saying your prayers, pigs!* It was like going to a war. I couldn't have worked up a spit for all the tea in China.

Jarvis kept just behind me. I didn't really mind having him along any more. We were both thirteen, but sometimes you'd think he was just a kid from the way he acted. Still, what could you expect—him the only boy in a family of seven kids. Must have been rough, though—all those silly, giggly girls. Crocodile Jarvis. I felt a bit mean for teasing him about *Play School* back there.

Robin made a sign for us to stop. We were right up at the trees. He squatted down and beckoned for me and Crocky to come up close.

"We'll circle our way round to the bottom end," he whispered. "If there's any here, they'll be holed up in the thick stuff this time of day."

We followed him out of the creek and in among the trees. The bush was fairly open. We had to creep from tree to tree. At one stage we flushed out a wallaby from a clump of brigalow. It whoofed and thump-thumped off ahead of us, leaving me wondering what was noisiest, the wallaby or my bumping heart. I had nearly fired when the stupid thing broke cover.

"I hope that safety catch is on," Robin nagged.

" 'Course it is," I said.

Crocky flashed me a little smile. The wallaby had given him a fright, too.

We continued on. Robin still led the way, but I walked a little to one side of him now, to get a clear shot if any pigs suddenly jumped up. We were getting down towards the end of the dam, and the trees were becoming quite thick. They were lower, too; we had to bend down to push underneath some of them. I could see a bank of reeds ahead. We crossed a boggy area that had been all ploughed up by rooting pigs. It looked as though a bomb had hit it. Robin pointed to a fresh hoofprint in the mud. He turned to me and nodded. It meant the pigs were there. Crocky kept close to me. I think he was a bit scared. I know I was—and I had a rifle.

Something moved among the reeds. We couldn't see it, only the tops of the reeds jiggling a bit, like when there's a wind. But there wasn't any wind. I aimed my rifle at the place. Nothing came out. I knew better than to fire at something I couldn't see, but I wanted to. If Robin hadn't been there, I'd have fired, all right. Perhaps if I had, everything wouldn't have gone wrong like it did. If I had just fired blindly into the reeds old Crocky might still be alive today. I wish I had, but I didn't. Instead, I crept up beside Robin. He was kneeling in the mud, peering into the reeds. His rifle was half raised. He saw me and shook his head and lifted a couple of fingers off the stock of the .303 as if to say, "Hang on a moment." Crocky slid up next to me. He had the bowie knife out of its sheath.

I didn't even see them come out. One moment nothing was there, and

the next four pigs were trotting straight towards us. There were more behind them. They didn't know we were there.

"Take the brown one," Robin said, and the .303 boomed almost at the
same moment.

The leading pig flopped onto its side, legs kicking madly. I heard Robin
reloading. The brown one, I repeated to myself as my own rifle came up.
They were only about fifteen feet away. The brown one. But I fired at the
first one that appeared in my sights—I don't remember *what* color it was.
Beside me, the .303 boomed again. My ears rang. I fumbled another round
into the breech, raised the .22, and fired again. *Boom* went Robin's rifle.
There were pigs rushing everywhere. Two were down. Another was charging in circles blowing red bubbles out of its mouth. Robin shot a half-
grown boar. My fingers fumbled so badly I dropped two bullets into the
mud before I managed to reload again. Crocky had run forward. He was on
top of the wounded pig, leaning on the handle of the bowie knife; the knife
itself was sticking out of the animal's side like it was growing there. The pig
kicked and squealed underneath him. I saw a retreating ginger and black
pig; without thinking, I lifted the rifle and shot at it. There were pigs lying
everywhere. Some of them were still kicking. We could hear others crashing
away through the undergrowth.

"Come on!" said Robin.

Already he was halfway to the reeds. Crocky leapt up with his knife. His
pig was dead. There was blood all over the front of his jeans. He grinned at
me. We both charged after Robin.

I heard Robin fire. He was somewhere ahead of me in the reeds. Suddenly a pig dashed out of cover not ten feet away. It saw me and slewed
sideways. I shot it. It fell, but then it got up again. I raced after it. The mud
sucked at my feet. I saw a smear of blood on some reeds and then there was
a pig lying on its side looking at me. It was all red down its flank. I flung up
my rifle and pulled the trigger. Click. I had forgotten to reload. Not far
away, the .303 crashed. My pig scrambled to its feet and bounded farther
into the thicket. Somewhere a pig was screaming. I closed the breech of the
.22. A smaller pig crossed in front of me. Flinging the rifle up, I sent a
bullet after it. I reloaded. *Boom* went the .303. My ears were ringing. The
little pig had disappeared. I followed the wounded one. There was quite a
blood trail. Suddenly there it was, standing side on, watching me. I fired
quickly. The pig turned and started stumbling towards me; I couldn't believe it. I began to back away. My fingers searched frantically through my
pocket for another bullet. The pig walked towards me. It wasn't charging,
or even running—it was just walking towards me as if I was another pig or
something. I can't remember if I was frightened or not; I guess I was too
excited to be frightened. I had a bullet halfway into the breech, sort of stuck
there. My fingers wouldn't work properly. The pig came toward me, then it

veered off at the last moment and took several more paces before finally collapsing. I bent over and shot it behind the ear the way I had seen Robin do to finish them off.

There was no more shooting. I looked for more pigs. Nothing moved. The dead pig lay in the mud at my feet. A blowfly buzzed.

"Martin?"

That was Robin.

"Over here," I called. My voice sounded funny.

I heard him come stomping through the mud. Reeds rattled. He appeared, grinning, came over and looked at my pig.

"Nice going, Marty."

It was hard to talk. I worked some spit into my mouth. "How many did you get?"

"Don't know," he said. Then he laughed and clapped me on the back. "Hell, it was like World War III!"

We both laughed. But it felt sort of wrong to be laughing. Blowflies were already beginning to work on the red pig at our feet. It was red from its own blood. A single eye looked up at us from between pink, scaly lids. Poor bloody pig! Five minutes ago you were a healthy wild sow. We had to kill them, though—they ruined the Old Man's crops.

"Where's Crocky?"

"I don't know. Hey, check him out with that knife!"

"Crocky the wild man," Robin said, smiling. "You'd never think it, would you?"

"Crocky!" he called.

He waited. He called again.

"God knows where he's got to," I said. I felt a little uneasy.

"Probably still chasing them." Robin tried to make a joke out of it.

We stood listening to the silence.

"How far could he have gone?"

We both called this time: "Cro-o-ckeeee!"

"Probably just playing a joke on us," I suggested. I really wanted to believe it. Somehow, old Crocky didn't seem the type for jokes, though.

Flies buzzed in the heat.

"Crocky!" I shouted. My throat was dry, and it hurt to have to shout. "Crocky, where the hell are you?"

But he couldn't hear me. I think we both knew he couldn't hear us calling.

"We'd better look for him," said Robin. His voice sounded a bit dry, too. I was beginning to feel scared.

"What if one of those pigs got him?"

"There was only that one big boar," Robin was saying as he led the way back through the reeds, "and I nailed him with my first shot."

He stopped suddenly and I almost bumped into him. I saw him drop the .303.

"Hey, Robin, what—"

It was Crocky. He was lying flat on his face in the mud. Robin bent down and slowly rolled him over.

"Jesus!" he whispered.

Crocky's face was all brown with mud. I saw his teeth through the mud. His eyes were open and there was mud on them, too; that was the most horrible thing—the mud on Crocky's eyes. I felt like I was going to be sick.

"Did a pig get him?" I asked. *Dear Jesus,* I prayed, *please make it be a pig that got him.*

Robin lifted back Crocky's collar. There was mud underneath, but you couldn't miss the hole. It was only a very small hole. A .303 doesn't make a hole that little.

Who knows which of my shots hit him. It had been pretty frantic in there, guns going off all over the show and pigs crashing in and out of the reeds like dodge'em cars. It was every man for himself. If only Crocky had stuck close by me and not gone running off on his own pretending he was Crocodile Dundee.

I said, "I killed him!," only it didn't sound like me. I closed my eyes. I felt dizzy. I think I wanted to wake up and make it all just be a dream. But when I opened my eyes again, there was poor Crocky lying there in the mud. The bowie knife was still in his hand.

Robin was looking up at me. He had a funny look on his face.

"Give me your rifle, Marty."

I handed it to him. I wondered what he was going to do. I thought maybe he was going to throw it away or something. I didn't care. It was only the week before that I had gotten it for my birthday. I wished we were back at my birthday again. Crocky was alive then. If only you could turn time backwards. Even half an hour backwards would have been enough. I could still see a picture of old Crocky grinning at me after that wallaby put the wind up us back there. How long ago was that? Ten minutes, maybe. Only ten minutes ago Crocky was right there beside me, grinning at me. How *could* he be dead now?

"I'll need a bullet." Robin held out his hand.

I gave him one. I wasn't even thinking. I tried not to look at Crocky.

Robin loaded the .22. He cocked it and put the muzzle down against Crocky's shirt above where the heart was. I just watched him do it. The shot made hardly any noise at all. Crocky didn't move; only the hand that held the bowie knife came slowly open.

I turned sideways and was sick in the mud. After that I cried for a long time.

\*　　\*　　\*

Robin had his arm round me. I don't know how long I'd been crying.
We weren't in the reeds any more. I couldn't remember coming out,
though. Crocky lay on the ground with Robin's shirt covering his head like
they do on TV when someone's dead. The two rifles were leaning against a
tree. There was a dead pig with its legs sticking straight out. A heron flew
kraa-kraa-kraaing just above the tops of the trees.

All I could think of was how Robin had placed the barrel of my rifle on
Crocky's chest and—

"What—did—you—do—it—for?" It was hard for me to speak.

"He might have been suffering."

"But—but—" I tried again. "Wasn't he dead?"

"Probably," said Robin. "He was as good as dead, anyway."

I couldn't believe it. My brother had finished Crocky off the same as if he
was just a wounded pig. "But if he was alive, you m-murdered him!"

"No," Robin said very softly, "nobody murdered him. It was an accident."

"They won't believe it. When they see two bullet holes they won't believe it was an accident."

"They aren't going to know. They won't ever find the body, so they
won't know anything about what happened, will they?"

Slowly it dawned on me what he meant. As far as everyone else knew,
Crocky hadn't even come out shooting with us that day. Nobody would
have seen us stop and give him a lift back there on MacCasker's Road. "We
have to take him back, Robin."

He stood away from me a little. He looked very white without his shirt
on. I noticed he was wearing his belt and sheath again. The bowie knife was
back in its sheath.

"We don't have to take him back, Martin. You don't want to go to jail,
do you?"

"They don't put kids in jail."

"They'd stick us in one of those detention places. It's as good as being in
jail."

"But it was an accident!"

"That's right. So why should we be punished for it?" Robin asked.

I didn't know. All I knew was that when someone got shot you had to
report it to the police. That was the law.

"Listen," Robin said, "he's dead. There's nothing we can do about it.
And even if we did get punished for it, that's not going to help old Crocky,
is it?"

Nothing was going to help old Crocky now. Only God could help him
now.

"He should have a funeral."

"Marty, he never went to church in his life."

"I don't care. Everyone should have a funeral."

Robin said, "It'll be our funeral if we take him back."

"Why did you have to shoot him again?"

"You little bastard! Who the hell shot him in the first place?" For a minute I thought he was going to hit me. Then he said more quietly, "It was the only thing to do, Martin. Nobody really liked him anyway."

Did he mean he actually *wanted* Crocky dead? There was a look on his face that made me scared to ask. For a minute I even thought he was going to break down. I couldn't remember Robin's ever crying. He was three years older than me. I had always looked up to him and tried to be like him, except for the way he drove Dad's old ute.

"What are we going to do with him?"

"You know the old stone place . . ."

He didn't have to say any more. I understood straight away how he intended getting rid of Crocky's body.

"It's a long way away . . ."

"So?" Robin said. "We've got the ute, haven't we?"

I had to stay with Crocky while Robin went for the ute. I wanted to go with him, but Robin said someone had to stay and mind the body. I didn't know what I was supposed to be minding it from, though. It hardly seemed likely any pigs would come back. Dingoes, perhaps—or goannas. At any rate, it was spooky waiting there in the bush with only poor dead Crocky for company.

After Robin had gone, I went over to him and lifted the shirt. It didn't look much like Crocky with that mud all over his face. I opened the collar of his shirt. My fingers were shaking. The hole was so tiny. It seemed strange that such a small hole could kill you. There wasn't even any blood to speak of, just a little bit near the hole itself. Why did Robin have to shoot him again? To finish him off? Or was he dead already? *Nobody really liked him anyway.* It sent a shiver down my back.

As I crouched there, a blowfly came and landed on Crocky's nose. I swore at it and swatted it angrily away. Then I started blubbering again. But I was over it by the time I heard the ute pull up at the edge of the trees.

Robin carried him out to the ute. Crocky wasn't heavy. It was strange: he seemed even smaller after he died. I followed behind carrying the rifles. The shirt fell off Crocky's head and I picked it up. Robin kept going. Crocky's mouth was open. His head bumped up and down as Robin walked. I stopped and retched, but I couldn't be sick any more.

It must have taken about an hour to get to the old stone place. We took the back tracks. Robin drove very slowly. When we came to the first gate, it was open the way Crocky had left it. That was enough to start me off crying again. All the other gates were closed. I had to open and close them myself.

I tried not to look in the back of the ute each time Robin drove through a gate and then waited for me to close it behind him. We didn't talk at all during the whole trip.

The old stone place was built by our great-grandfather. It hadn't been lived in for over fifty years. There wasn't much left of it. Nobody went there any more. The well is up the back in the middle of a tangle of blackberries. Only Robin and me, and maybe the Old Man, knew that the shaft was there. Someone—Granddad, probably—had covered it with sleepers and old sheets of corrugated iron, and now the blackberries had grown right over the top of that. It took a bit of work and lots of blackberry scratches to open up one corner of the hole. I pitched an old horseshoe in and heard the faraway, echoey splash.

"I don't think we should put him down there."

"We've got to, Martin."

"He should have a proper funeral."

"They'll hold a memorial service," Robin told me. "That's as good as a funeral."

I didn't really believe him.

We walked back down to where he had parked the ute.

"Will he still go to heaven?"

I saw Robin fighting to keep from crying. " 'Course he will."

"I want to clean his face," I said.

"All right," Robin said. He looked at his watch. "But we better not be too long."

I got the waterbag and wet a corner of Robin's shirt. I cleaned Crocky's face with it. Robin stood behind me, watching.

"It's funny," he whispered, "his face like that: he looks a lot like Beverly."

Then we carried him up to the well and slid him into the hole. It was hard getting him through all those blackberries. I tried not to hear the splash. Robin took his bowie knife from its sheath, looked at it for a moment, then dropped it down after Crocky, handle first. I wanted to put something in, too, but there was nothing I could give. We pulled the sleepers and iron back into place. Some of the iron was so old it broke in our hands. Robin arranged a few blackberry vines across the top. It looked like just a pile of old overgrown rubbish. I wished we could have put a cross up.

We both stood there beside Crocky's grave.

"I'm going to pray for him," I promised, "every night before I go to sleep for the rest of my life."

As we drove away, Robin said, "We'll go back and pick up one of those pigs."

"Why?" I didn't ever want to go near Watson's Dam again.

"Because of the blood in the back. Dad will wonder where it came from otherwise."

Robin thought of everything. Crocky had bled a bit on the drive over. Taking a dead pig home would account for any blood in the back of the ute —and on us, too, for that matter. I wanted to spend about a week under the shower.

We went back to the place and dragged one of the pigs out to the ute. First we started to drag Robin's big boar, but it was too heavy, so we got one of the smaller ones. It was the half-grown boar Crocky had finished off with Robin's knife. We heaved it up onto the ute and got the tailgate closed behind it. Already there was blood coming out of it, covering Crocky's blood in the ute. A lot of its blood was on our clothes too, from lifting it. Robin rubbed his shirt in some of the blood and chucked it in the back with the rifles and the dead pig. I think he would have liked to throw it away, but Mum would ask where it was if he did.

We drove home very slowly. I still hated opening and closing the gates. Each time we stopped, I could see Crocky leaping off the back and doing it before I got a chance to. We should have taken it in turns, really—it wasn't fair that I had let him do them all. Poor old Crocky. He had always been a bit of a pain the way he acted and that, but he was nice enough underneath. I knew *I* would have hated to have six giggling sisters. Well, they wouldn't be giggling tonight.

"For chrissake stop that sniveling before we get home!" Robin growled.

The Old Man was up on the verandah reading the Saturday paper when we drove up to the house.

"Get any?" he called over the rail. He didn't sound suspicious at all. I don't know why I expected him to be suspicious.

"Ran into a mob near Watson's," Robin said. "Brought one home for the dogs."

The Old Man folded his paper and stood up. He came down the stairs in his socks.

"That the best you could do?" he ribbed us.

Robin said, "We got a monster boar, but it was too heavy to drag out to the ute."

Dad smiled like it was just a fisherman's story. He looked at me. "How did the new peashooter perform, Buck?"

Something flipped over inside me. Peashooter. Crocky had called it that.

"Okay," I said. I bent quickly to pat Sam and Rusty. They sniffed at my dirty fingers, their tails going like mad. They could probably smell Crocky's blood on them. I jerked my hands away like a town kid that's scared he's going to get bitten. Jeez, I needed that shower.

"Nice going, boys," Dad said. "But you can't feed pig to the dogs;

thought you knew that, Rob." He scratched Rusty's head. "You'll have to dump it in the offal pit," he said. "I'll keep the dogs tied tonight. And then you can give the ute a good washdown.

"By the way," he added, halfway back up the steps, "you didn't happen to see young Adrian anywhere along the road, did you?"

"No," Robin and I said together.

Dad looked at us. He said, "Beverly was over half an hour ago. Apparently he didn't appear for lunch."

"Maybe he's run away from home," I suggested. Robin and I had been working on a story on the way back.

The Old Man took the bait. "Why do you say that, Buck?"

I shrugged. *"I'd* run away from home if *I* had six sisters."

Dad laughed, but as he went up onto the verandah I could see he was thinking about what I'd said. I felt sort of dirty inside for tricking him.

Robin and I dumped the pig up the back, then we washed the ute. I don't think it had ever been so clean since it was new. After that I went inside and had a shower. I used up all the hot water. Robin was waiting to go in when I came out. I thought he would be really mad at me about the hot water, but he didn't say anything. He must have had a cold shower. When he came into the bedroom to get dressed, his skin was all pink from scrubbing.

Beverly came over later in the afternoon and asked if we had seen Adrian. Robin said we hadn't. After she had gone he went into the toilet and stayed there for a long time. I helped Mum peel some apples for a strudel she was making for tea. Then I vacuumed the lounge.

Mum smiled and said, "I'm going to have to let you go shooting more often, Martin."

I just grinned and kept working. But as soon as I was finished I went outside and got my bike and rode down to see the horses. A horse doesn't mind when you cry.

Teatime was the hardest. I didn't feel like eating at all, and I don't think Robin did, either. Mum had cooked a roast. When Dad carved it, I couldn't help thinking of poor Crocky lying there with mud on his eyes. It almost made me sick to eat. Then there was the strudel. I got through it somehow, and then had a second helping so Mum and Dad wouldn't think anything was wrong. All I wanted to do was run outside and throw up. It was the worst meal of my life.

When Robin and I were doing the dishes, I heard a knock on the door. It was Mr. Jarvis. He and Mum talked for a while at the door, then they went into the lounge and we could hear the Old Man talking, too. We couldn't hear what they were saying, though. Then Dad came into the kitchen and asked us if we knew anything about Adrian running away. I said I didn't. Robin kept washing the dishes.

"Buck, are you sure he's never said anything to you about wanting to run away?" Dad asked me.

I looked down at the plate I had been drying.

"I promised I wouldn't tell." It was what Robin and I had worked out I should say.

Dad said, "Listen, Martin—" he only ever called me Martin when it was serious, or when I was in trouble or something "—sometimes we have to break our promises. If Adrian said anything to you about running away, if he said anything at all about it, I want you to tell me now. It doesn't matter if you promised to keep quiet; this is more important. His parents are very worried about him."

I could see Mr. Jarvis and Mum listening in the background. I fiddled with the tea towel.

"Yesterday on the way home from school he said he was going to run away. He made me promise not to say anything. I didn't really think he was going to, though," I added. It was a good act, but I felt really rotten about it.

"Did he say where he was going?" Mr. Jarvis wanted to know.

I shook my head. I felt sorry for Mr. Jarvis. "He didn't say where. He just said he was going to run away. I didn't think he really would, Mr. Jarvis —I thought it was just showing off."

They all looked very serious. Mr. Jarvis said, "Well, thank you, Martin, for telling the truth. I'm sure Adrian won't hold it against you that you had to break your promise. It's for his own good."

Dad and Mr. Jarvis went back outside. Later, Sergeant Hill from Roma came and I had to tell him my story, too. I knew God was never going to forgive me.

That was nearly two years ago now. In all that time Robin and I haven't breathed a word of what really happened to anyone. Robin left home this year and works for an interstate trucking company; I don't think he sees Beverly any more, or even writes to her. I've kept my promise, though: every night before going to sleep I say a prayer for Crocky.

But what's the use of prayers, I ask myself sometimes. Crocky's dead; he'll never come back.

I guess everyone has gotten to accept that now.

Three months ago the Jarvises sold everything and moved down to the city. It was sad to see them go, but sort of a relief, too. Unfortunately, the relief didn't last very long.

The Jarvises' station is now owned by a Mr. Owen Wakelin. From somewhere down south, Wakelin has oodles of money and big ideas; he plans to expand and turn the property into a cattle stud. He wants to buy us out and amalgamate the two stations. In the first four weeks he was here, our new neighbor made the Old Man three offers for our place, but Dad won't sell.

Now Wakelin is getting rough. He's blocked the channel from his artesian bore so that we no longer get his runoff water. It's midsummer and already Watson's Dam is nearly three-quarters empty. And at this time of year it can go months without raining.

"We'll have to accept," I heard Mum saying to the Old Man a week ago. "After all, his last offer *was* very generous."

"I'm not selling," Dad said, "for any price."

"But the cattle can't go without water," Mum pleaded.

The Old Man just smiled. "I know that," he said mildly.

I could tell from his tone of voice that he had something in mind. But it was only this morning, when a dilapidated old truck turned into our gateway, that I realized what it was. Luckily I was the only one home at the time.

"Your father around someplace, son?" asked the man from the truck with the drilling rig on the back.

"He's gone to town," I told him. "Won't be back till tonight."

The man pushed his Akubra farther back on his head. "Perhaps you can help us, then. Your dad sent for us—wants us to look at an old well."

"Old well?" I said stupidly.

"That's right. We're a water exploration company. Your father contracted us to reopen an old, disused well for him." He frowned. "We *have* come to the right place, haven't we? Your name *is* Adams?"

"No," I lied. "There's no one in the district called Adams."

The man looked puzzled. "Well, that *is* strange."

He turned and walked back to the truck, where he spent several minutes in conference with his companion. Finally he came strolling slowly back.

"Beats me," he shrugged. "Some sort of foul-up back at the office, I guess. Can I use your phone?"

"It's out of order," I lied.

He nodded, and slapped at the flies. "Well," he said finally, "I'm sorry to have troubled you."

He turned to go.

"Excuse me?" I called after him. "Would you be able to give me a lift?"

"Where to?" he asked.

Anywhere, I thought. Wherever Crocky Jarvis was meant to have run off to.

"Just to the bus station in town," I said.

# Antarctica

# ICE CAVE

*By Emmy Lou Schenk*

I SN'T THAT something," Michael said to the third man at the table. "In his whole career, Dad's never solved a murder case."

Police Chief Richard K. Wilbur fought hard not to scowl. Lay off, kid, he thought. You say that once more and I'll start flashing your baby pictures.

Catching Chief Wilbur's look of dismay, Michael smiled encouragingly. You might almost have thought he didn't know he was probing a sore point. Haskins, the third man, obviously had his mind elsewhere.

"Incredible," he said, his voice flat, his gaze wandering the room as if in search of more interesting company.

Haskins was a glaciologist, a darkly tanned, broad-shouldered, chunky young man whose muddy brown eyes seemed as cold as the ice he studied. For some reason, he reminded Chief Wilbur of a cowbird.

"You see, Dad," Michael went on cheerfully, "Avecina and Antarctica have that much in common anyway. No sir, you won't get to solve a murder here either, not on the ice."

The three men were sitting at a small table in the dimly lit Polar Big Eye Club, so called because insomnia is endemic at McMurdo Station. To provide escape from Antarctica's never-ending daylight, the club's walls were painted a restful black, its windows were heavily shuttered.

Chief Wilbur, a grizzled bulldog of a man, tried valiantly to force a smile.

Michael hadn't meant to embarrass him. He was sure of that, except—oh, damn, he thought, suddenly giving in to his true feelings with a sigh. Sixty only, but he felt older than Methuselah. It was being surrounded by these kids, these eager beaver young scientists with their Ph.D.'s and their university jargon. Some treated him with exaggerated respect, as if he were a fragile, but possibly valuable, antique. Others, and this was worse, took no notice of him at all. Cold enough for you, sir, they'd ask, and then, without waiting for an answer, go on to some topic they considered more relevant.

And why in the world did Michael keep telling everyone that he, Chief Wilbur, had been police chief of Avecina, Florida, for twenty-two years, but had yet to close the book on a murder. Maybe Mike didn't mean it that way, but somehow he made it sound—well, as if this deficiency showed a lack of manhood in some way.

He'd like to straighten the kid out right this minute, but of course he couldn't, not with Haskins at the table.

"Okay, you guys, you win," he said, as heartily as possible. "Buy you another round?"

Haskins' restless eyes had found a target. "Thanks, no." He pushed back his chair. "Joe's here now."

Glass in hand, he walked across the room to stand at the bar with the sweet-faced seismologist with the chirrupy voice, the one who reminded Chief Wilbur of a bluebird. Little Joe, Michael had said his name was. Little Joe Guthrie.

"Those poor guys," said Michael. "They really got screwed over this last month."

"Look here, Mike," said Chief Wilbur, deciding to get it over with. "Why do you keep saying that?"

Michael looked up in surprise. "I only said it once. Well, it's like this. They had this experiment designed, doing ice core samples over on the Filchner ice shelf, but the arrangements got bollixed up, and now it's too late in the season for them to go out."

"Too bad," said Chief Wilburn. "But that's not—"

"Of course, maybe it's just as well," Michael broke in. "Those two-man expeditions are the pits. That's why Admiral Byrd insisted on three guys or more—two to fight and the third to keep order."

"Byrd, hey. He was one of my heroes."

"Right, Dad. You never met a bird you didn't like."

Chief Wilbur found he was staring at Joe and Haskins, hunched now in deep discussion over their beers. Little Joe was definitely a bluebird. A bright blue tasselled stocking cap hid his sandy hair, a blue wool shirt opened down the front to reveal a red T-shirt. Bluebirds were an engaging species. Cowbirds, on the other hand, had the unlovely habit of laying their eggs in other birds' nests.

"I don't like cowbirds much," he said.

"Not to worry," said Michael. "No cowbirds on the ice."

"I know. But what I—"

"I'm trying to explain, Dad," Michael broke in once again. "The tents are cone-shaped, you can't stand up in them, so if a blizzard whips up, you can be stuck in your sleeping bag for days at a time."

"Real rough, I'm sure, but—"

There was a burst of laughter from the bar. Someone across the room shouted, "Hey, let us hear, too." At the bar, the laughter grew in volume.

Michael waited for the room to quiet. When it didn't, he bent his head closer. "Rough is right. Little things get to you, like the way the other guy clinks his spoon. Or he can't stand how you chew your food, or burp, or—"

"Mike, for God's sake, we're talking about two different things," rasped Chief Wilbur, then bit his lip. "Sorry, son, I do see why folks would get on each other's nerves, maybe even kill each other off once in a while, so why . . ."

Michael reached out to pat his shoulder. "Oh, that's what ruffled your feathers. I'm sorry but, you see, you won't solve a murder here because there won't be one. Guys who come on the ice, they know what they're getting into. Funny thing, but there's never been a murder in Antarctica."

"Never?"

Haskins and Little Joe were heading out the door.

"Nope. And a good thing, too, because there's no real government here —just the international treaty. The navy personnel are under military law, but nobody has any control at all over us civilians."

"No kidding." Rocking back in his chair, Chief Wilbur considered what Michael had said. It was incredible. The fifth largest continent in the world, and no police force. A million questions came to mind, but all were cut off by a loud groan from Michael.

"Damn it all. Look who just came in."

Chief Wilbur's chair legs thumped to the floor.

"Over there." Mike pointed to a man who stood by the door surveying the room. His green parka marked him as navy personnel. The USARP scientists wore red.

"Who is he?"

"The helo pilot. I hope the trip's not off again."

"Me, too," Chief Wilbur agreed somewhat despondently. More even than solving a murder case, Chief Wilbur wanted to visit the Emperor penguin nesting ground at Cape Crozier on the far side of Ross Island. Every time Mike managed to arrange a flight, however, the weather turned sour.

But not this time. The weather, the pilot reported, was fine. Only the mags were on the fritz.

* * *

Later, as they walked down the icy, rutted road to the dormitory, Chief Wilbur found himself marveling, as he had since his arrival, at man's incredible ability to foul his own nest.

Antarctica was the most beautiful place he'd ever seen; McMurdo Station was the ugliest. Rising from hut point, which jutted out into the ice-flecked purity of McMurdo Sound, Mac Town appeared to have been designed with all the care and precision of an angry child dumping out a box of blocks. Hemmed in by a ring of squat round fuel tanks and spiky antennas, the one hundred or so temporary-looking buildings were linked by a spiderweb of heavily insulated heating pipes. Disorderly dumps of supplies and equipment lay strewn about, seemingly without plan. Over all hung the acrid scent of diesel oil.

I shouldn't have come, he thought, suddenly homesick for the clean warm air of the Everglades. Wondering if his thin Florida blood would ever adapt, Chief Wilbur stared across McMurdo Sound at the ice-covered Transantarctic Mountains. Pink-tinged from the sun, the mountains' glacial skin was always on the move, creeping slowly but inexorably toward the sea. Antarctica was a dead land. Only the ice had life.

No, his blood would not adapt, nor his mind either. Never mind how proud he was that Michael had finally been awarded his Ph.D. in ornithology, not to mention this NSF grant to study penguins. Never mind that the grant permitted Mike to choose his own research assistant.

Truth was, Mike hadn't really chosen him. He was only a fill-in because Mike's first choice had gotten racked up in a car accident one short month before Mike was due to depart. I'm desperate, Dad, Mike had said. I need someone quick, someone reliable.

Reliable maybe, but too old. Good Lord, he was probably the only person over thirty-five on the whole continent.

Hearing laughter, Chief Wilbur turned, then gasped. As if to prove his point, Haskins and Little Joe were jogging toward them. Naked from the waist up, the two men had on only their insulated white bunny boots, their knit caps, and the bottom halves of their thermal underwear. They slowed to a walk as they approached, looking as if they hoped someone would comment on their attire, or lack of it, but Mike didn't oblige.

"Nice night," he said. "Out for a stroll?"

"Right on," puffed Little Joe. "We had this phone patch, see? And then I said, hey, old buddy, we gotta do something, a hero thing maybe. And he said, sure, my thoughts exactly. Hero thing, big stuff, put you right back up on top. Care to join us?"

"Good Lord, no," said Chief Wilbur. Shivering, he pulled back his parka sleeve to look at his watch. Just past ten.

"If you ain't cold, you ain't bold," Haskins whispered loudly behind his hand. He threw his arm over Little Joe's shoulder.

"No fair," said Joe, shrugging it off. The two men careened into an alley between two snow-covered heaps of navy supplies and disappeared.

Chief Wilbur took a deep breath. The frigid air tugged at his nostrils. "Jumping jacksnipes! What are they, drunk or something? They'll freeze."

Mike looked unconcerned. "Not likely. They're old hands around here. Little Joe has wintered over twice."

"And Haskins?"

"He just comes in the summer. This is his second time, I think. Maybe third. They're both at the same University. Joe told me once that they met in graduate school and have been friends ever since."

"Maybe," reflected Chief Wilbur. "But at the moment there's bad blood between them."

"Why do you say that?"

Chief Wilbur cocked a shaggy eyebrow, then shook his head. "Instinct, I guess. I haven't been a cop all these years for nothing, you know."

"Come on, Dad, you're not a cop here."

Lips pursed, Chief Wilbur snuggled deeper into the anonymity of his fur-trimmed hood. Mike was right. He wasn't a cop here. In fact, he wasn't much of anything.

Even so, as they resumed their walk toward the dormitory, he found himself puzzling over his reaction. Bad blood, he'd said. A snap judgment. No reason for it, none at all.

Odd, though. He wasn't usually wrong about such things.

"I figured it out," he told Michael the next morning as they ate breakfast amidst the clanking trays and the smell of bacon in the huge mess hall. "It's because he looks like a cowbird."

"Who looks like a cowbird?"

"Haskins. Do you agree?"

"More of a winter wren," said Mike, responding halfheartedly to the familiar family game. "Damn, the Emperors will be heading out to sea soon. If we don't get to Cape Crozier in the next week or so, you'll miss seeing them for sure."

Chief Wilbur believed heartily in the power of positive thinking. "Relax, Mike. Get your mind off it."

"Yeah, sure, but onto what?" Michael stared dejectedly at his pancakes, then snapped his fingers in the air. "Hey, I know. You haven't seen the ice cave yet. We could take the afternoon off and go there."

Chief Wilbur gulped. He hated caves, any and all kinds of caves, musty places, the walls pushing in on you, the ceilings hung with bats. For that matter, he didn't much care for elevators, he despised small closets, and he could barely imagine why wood ducks and bluebirds were hole nesters. And now an ice cave. Chief Wilbur gulped again.

"Hey, Dad, you aren't scared, are you?"

"Come on, Mike. You know me better than that."

Chief Wilbur's voice was so hearty it sounded phony even to his own ears. Turning from Mike's questioning gaze, he mopped up syrup with his last bit of pancake and choked it down. Maybe if he put enough weight in his stomach, it would stop doing cartwheels.

The cave mouth was an icy tunnel, so narrow and black that Chief Wilbur felt as if he were about to be crammed into a sewer pipe. Think positively, he told himself. Uh-huh!

"Feet first," said Michael. "It's like a kid's slide on a playground. Don't worry. You've got your flash and there's a lantern down there."

"Who's worried. But uh, say, Mike, how deep in do we go?"

"I don't know. Ten or twenty feet. We climb out with the rope there. See, it's tied to an ice anchor."

"It sure enough is," said Chief Wilbur, who was trying to remember when he had last done any rope climbing. In the army probably, but that had been more than thirty years ago.

Then, with a whoosh, he was sliding down, down, into the blackness. He landed at the bottom with a thump, and immediately fumbled for his flash. The frost-encrusted dungeon, clean as a diamond, glittered like a Fourth of July sparkler.

Michael was right behind him. "Hold your flash for me while I light the lantern," he said, looking around. "Hey, that's funny. It's gone. All the survival gear is gone." He shrugged. "Well, it doesn't matter. Hey, Dad, isn't this fantastic?"

"Hoo, boy," Chief Wilbur managed to get out. "This is really something."

"Yeah, it sure is. Slip off your mitt and feel the wall."

Chief Wilbur did as he was told, then drew back his hand in astonishment. The pebbly ice was so cold it seemed almost to sear his skin.

"It's old ice," Michael explained. "Maybe half a million years old. It gets colder as it ages, something to do with pressure. Come on. There's a place farther in that has some real neat ice pillars."

"Wait, Mike. Please. It's beautiful, but, uh, maybe we should come back another time, you know, like when the lantern is here, and we could . . . er . . . see better."

The bats might not have materialized, but Chief Wilbur's claustrophobia was as intense in Antarctica as it was in Florida. Worse, maybe. The ice cave was the remnant of a glacial crevasse. At any moment, the glacier might hiccup forward, enclosing them forever in its icy grasp.

But Michael had already skittered across the icy floor and was standing by a narrow opening on the far side. There was nothing to do but follow.

At the opening, Michael stood aside. "You first, Dad," he said. "I don't want to spoil it for you."

Chief Wilbur's heart was pounding so hard he was sure Michael could hear it, but somehow he managed to shine his flash through the opening. The next cavern burst into jeweled splendor.

"Oh, no," said Chief Wilbur. "Please no."

"What's the matter, Dad?"

"It's—it's—" The words froze in his mouth. Bad blood, he had thought, and he'd been right. Still naked from the waist up, his skin marbled with frostbite, the man lay curled into a ball, his back against a dark pillar of ice.

Last night Haskins had looked like a cowbird. Today he merely looked dead. Very, very dead.

McMurdo Station had a summer population of nearly one thousand. Only Chief Wilbur seemed to think Haskins' death was not an unfortunate accident but murder.

Little Joe was in shock, a garrulous kind of shock at first. I gotta talk it out, he said over and over, in the mess hall, in the Big Eye Club, anywhere where he could find someone willing to listen.

Haskins was his friend, he said. His buddy. Oh, God, if only he'd known where he was. What they'd been talking about was climbing Observation Hill. Stupid, sure. He could see that now. A hero thing. Oh, God.

And the listener would nod, and recall that time half the station went outside and lay in the snow to see who could chicken out first. Or how the Seabees used to welcome newcomers by stripping off their pants, then burying them in snow up to their necks and pouring beer on their heads. That's how it is down here, everyone agreed. Guys have to prove themselves. It wasn't the first time someone had gone too far.

Anyway, as Joe told it, they had walked toward Ob Hill, egging each other on, but then Haskins had said hey let's go in the cave instead, and so they had changed direction. At this point, Joe usually put his head in his hands and started to cry.

"It wasn't my fault," he would say, looking up sadly, wiping his eyes. "There was nothing I could do. Nothing."

For the sun had clouded over. There'd been a whiteout. The two men had gotten separated. Somehow Joe had wandered down toward hut point. Close on to frozen stiff himself, he'd taken refuge in Scott's old hut, found a sleeping bag. Fell asleep.

And all the while, Haskins was—Oh, God, did you see that bump on his head? He must have fallen, knocked himself out. And then just lay there, like Scott, till he died.

"Oh, God," Little Joe said over and over, shaking his head. "If I'd known. If only I'd known."

\* \* \*

"I think he's lying," Chief Wilbur said. "His story stays exactly the same every time he tells it."

"I don't know, Dad. It could have happened that way. Would you hand me that little Adelie we found yesterday."

They were sitting on tall stools in the smelly laboratory where Michael dissected dead penguins, calling out notes for Chief Wilbur to write down for all the world like a medical examiner on TV.

The first penguin had been interesting, but after that Chief Wilbur found himself glad that he was an amateur naturalist who could enjoy the penguins' crazy antics rather than a professional ornithologist who cut them up to find out how they had been affected by pesticides or nuclear pollution.

Turning, he reached into a plastic sack. "But I checked," he said, handing the bird across the table. It was stiff and lifeless, exactly as Haskins had been. "There couldn't have been a whiteout. It didn't snow that night."

"You're talking stateside whiteout, the kind that comes from a blizzard. An antarctic whiteout is, well—" Mike paused to tie a white tag to the penguin's flipper. "It's a kind of mirage. The sky goes white, the ground is already white, and the atmosphere acts like a lens refracting all this whiteness back and forth. It's like walking around in a bottle of milk. You hear a voice, and the speaker won't be three feet away, but you can't see him. You can't even see your own feet." There was another pause while Mike ruffled back the bird's tail feathers. "This is AD-162, a female. You got that?"

"Check." Chief Wilbur blew on his fingers, then noted the information on his chart. "But it doesn't make sense. Haskins must have known about the rope. He wouldn't have left it up at the top."

"What are you saying? That Little Joe murdered Haskins?"

"It's possible. He had the method and the opportunity."

"But no motivation. They were friends."

"So they say, but I have this feeling."

Looking up from the penguin, Michael frowned.

"Okay, okay," said Chief Wilbur. "But shouldn't someone check it out? I mean, like the survival gear? How come that disappeared so conveniently?"

"They say it belonged to a glaciologist who went stateside and took it with him."

"But no one knows for sure, and how about that bump on his head?"

"He slipped on the ice," said Michael, picking up a scalpel. "It could happen."

"Maybe so, Mike, but I'd sure like to ask a few questions. Like, Joe says he holed up in Scott's hut, but how did he get in? We went down there once, and the Kiwis had it locked tight as a drum."

"Maybe he broke a window or something," Michael replied, slitting open the penguin's stomach. "Wow, look at this fish. I've never seen one like it before."

"Yes, but does anyone know for sure?"

"For God's sake, Dad, would you drop it, please? All this talk breaks my concentration."

"Sorry, son. I'll try."

Carefully assuming a look which he hoped showed great interest, Chief Wilbur considered the half digested fish. He supposed he'd have to write that up, too. Professional and amateur, hoo, boy, what a difference.

Suddenly he slapped his hand to his forehead. You dummy, he told himself, you're a professional, too. And if a policeman wanted to investigate a murder, he sure didn't need permission from an ornithologist, even if the ornithologist was his own kid.

Particularly if it was his own kid.

First he'd check on that phone patch, if indeed the two men had really gotten one through. He'd bet a bundle no one else had thought to ask.

The ham shack was warm and cosy, unlike the frigid Jamesway hut where Mike worked. The room was small, with a linoleum floor and stained plywood walls, three of which were hung with maps, the world, New Zealand, a big one of the United States stuck with multicolored pins. On the fourth, there was a battered bank of radios.

The system was simple, yet akin to magic, or at least as far as Chief Wilbur was concerned. Basically, the radioman contacted a ham back in the States who somehow connected his radio to a telephone, then placed a collect call, and the next thing you knew you were talking through thin air to someone twelve thousand miles away. I love you, I miss you, I'm getting pretty horny. The lack of privacy did little to inhibit the conversations.

"Hey, man," the radioman greeted him, his hand over the mike. "What can I do for you?"

He was a dumpy kid, pushing twenty maybe, but not too hard, and he had bright red hair which stuck up through his headset like a cockscomb.

"I'd like to get through to my wife."

"Don't everybody, man. Well, it's pretty early but I'll give it a go."

Wondering what time it was back in Florida, Chief Wilbur gave him the number. It was seven P.M. here, but time zones have no meaning in Antarctica. The longitude lines were so close that the whole continent stuck with Greenwich Mean Time. It was easier that way, not so confusing.

Unless, of course, you were trying to call home. The call was placed easily enough, but the phone merely rang and rang.

"Probably out soaking up some rays," said the kid.

He means sunbathing, thought Chief Wilbur, revising his calculations.

Apparently you didn't add time when you called the States. You subtracted it.

"Yeah, I suppose," he said, then added casually, "Say, you weren't by any chance on duty the night Haskins was ki . . . , I mean, died, were you?"

"Like, wow, talk about your basic tragedy." The kid wiped his forearm across his eyes. "And him talking to his wife only a few hours before."

"So you were here—on duty, I mean."

"Oh, man, was I ever. I thought Little Joe was going to toss his cookies right on the mike. Or was it Haskins? They were both acting kind of funny. Too much beer, I think. His wife is pregnant."

"Pregnant?" Chief Wilbur felt his jaw sag.

"Yeah, and that was the first news he'd had of it. Well, that's how it goes, I guess."

But that isn't usually how it goes, thought Chief Wilbur as he crunched down the ice-covered road to the dormitory. Pregnant! Poor Mrs. Haskins.

A week slid by. Mike's grant gave him two months to collect data, the first two weeks on his own, the next four with the aid of a research assistant, the last two on his own again. As a result, Chief Wilbur's stint of note-taking and preparing slides and keeping track of a million plastic Baggies, each of which contained a pickled sliver of penguin heart or lung or brain, was nearly over.

Research. Chief Wilbur hoped Mike's was going better than his. So far, a big goose egg.

Carding his way into Little Joe's room had been easy, but the search had revealed nothing of importance. Little Joe was obsessively neat. His papers, books, and clothes were arranged with meticulous precision. There were no personal letters. The only things in sight that did not pertain to Joe's work was a new insurance policy, signed and stuck into a stamped envelope. The beneficiary was, naturally enough, his wife. No mystery here. Who wouldn't be concerned with the safety and future of one's loved ones after such a tragic brush with death.

Deciding to take the bull by the horns, he cornered Joe in the mess hall, but their conversation yielded nothing new. After his initial spate of verbal diarrhea, Joe had turned sullen and uncommunicative.

"Drinks a lot, too," said the bartender at the Big Eye Club. "But no wonder. Three and a half months on the ice with nothing to show for it, and then his buddy kicks off that way."

"Three and a half months? But Haskins had only been here a few weeks," said Chief Wilbur. "Didn't they come down together?"

Shaking his head, the bartender swirled a beer stein on a suds-filled brush. "Uh-uh. Little Joe was the setup man. He came in on the first flight in September. Haskins had to teach or something."

"Did Haskins blame Joe for the screw-up in their plans?"

The bartender hung up the clean glass on an overhead rack. "He might have," he said, after a long moment. "He was pretty mad. Kept talking about how everything would go to hell if they didn't get out in the field. He was like the chief honcho. Joe always kowtowed to him."

"Bluebirds are pretty passive," mused Chief Wilbur.

"What?"

"Nothing, just a thought."

The bartender's remarks were interesting, but didn't exactly contradict Little Joe's story. Nothing did. Even the New Zealanders corroborated it. Yes, they said, a window had been broken, the contents of the hut disturbed. Nobody knew exactly what had happened to the missing survival gear. Nobody cared, either.

By the week's end Chief Wilbur had meticulously covered all the bases—all, that is, but one.

Well, he'd gone down in that blasted cave once, hadn't he. It should be easier the second time.

It was worse.

Someone had fixed metal strips across the cave mouth, and plunked a sign alongside. Squinting because his eyes seemed to have gone all funny, Chief Wilbur bent to read the sign.

"Off Limits."

Because of Haskins' death, he wondered? Or had the navy brass decided the cave was unsafe for other reasons?

Trying to ignore his churning stomach, he took a deep breath, sat down on the edge, slung his bag of equipment over his shoulder, then, flashlight at ready, stuck his feet into the hole.

Oh, dear Lord, wait. The rope. He'd forgotten to toss it in. Maybe Haskins had forgotten, too.

No, he thought, remembering Haskins' cold, muddy eyes. Haskins wouldn't forget. He was an old hand down here. Used to danger. Used to thinking ahead.

The slide into the cave was like falling endlessly into eternity, but not to worry. Somehow he'd scrambled out once before, although for the life of him he couldn't remember how.

At the bottom, he stood for a moment. The surprising thing was the silence. With Michael there had been conversation, but now there was silence enough to hear the air bubbles in the ice pop, to hear the glacier groan. Was it preparing to surge? Were the glacial jaws about to snap shut?

No sir, he sure wouldn't have to worry about getting back up that tunnel. The real trick would be to stay down long enough to make a thorough search. Shine the flash, up, down, over. Repeat slowly. Done. The first cave was just as it had been before, clean as a diamond.

On to the second. Get it over with. There'd be nothing there either. He knew that now, knew he was only down here to prove something or other to somebody. But to whom? Mike didn't even know he was here. Nobody knew he was here. In fact, it was dumb to be down here. All at once the desire to turn and run nearly overwhelmed him.

Take it easy, he told himself. Only another minute or two. All he had to do was take a quick look, then he could leave.

Forcing himself forward, each footstep a minor triumph, he ran his flash over the pebbly side walls of the second cave. Up, over a few feet, down. Quick, yes, but thorough, too. A careful search. Nothing. Now, the ceiling. Across, back. Nothing.

Finally, hearing the ice creak all around him, he ran the flashlight beam over to the dark pillar of ice where Haskins had lain. Up, down, repeat. The wall was smooth. The thing, when he saw it, cast a shadow far larger than it should have for its size.

A tassel. Blue. From a stocking cap. Joe's stocking cap.

Quickly he started toward it, too quickly, for the floor here was even more slippery than that of the first cave. My Florida feet aren't up to this, thought Chief Wilbur, and then, as if to prove his point, his feet parted company, his legs took on a life of their own. Frantically he wound his arms in the air, trying to keep his balance, but it was no go. His head hit the side of the cave with a sickening thud.

Well, that explained that anyway. It was the last thought he had for some time.

He awoke to blackness. His head felt flat but inflated, like one of those new-fangled silvery balloons made in the shape of a heart. He was cold, too. Why in the world had Delia Joan turned the air conditioning down so low. And her sound asleep, and not the least bit worried.

For a moment he listened to his wife's soft, measured breathing, then reached out to touch her shoulder. "Too cold, honey," he murmured. "Can't afford it."

But his hand encountered only frigid marble. He was lying face down on a sheet of frigid marble. Not in bed after all. So where was he? Oh, God, the morgue.

Boy, what a messed up job. Who ever heard of putting someone in the morgue face down? Besides, he wasn't even dead. Or was he?

The breathing quickened. Someone was touching him, rolling him over. The blackness changed suddenly to a circle of light, light which pierced his eyes, making sight beyond impossible. Yet someone was there. The breathing went on.

Chief Wilbur stiffened. The light circle moved across the cave floor. The cave!

Suddenly his mind cleared. Not dead. Not in the morgue either. Antarctica, the ice cave, that's where he was. The circle of light was a man holding a flash. The man was heading for the cave entrance. If Chief Wilbur let him go, he would pull up the rope. There'd be no chance for escape, not ever.

Another accident, people would say, and then they'd remember he'd been asking questions about Haskins and Little Joe. They'd figure he came down here. Bumped his head, passed out. Froze solid, just like Haskins.

Easy for the killer. Too easy. He mustn't let it be so easy.

Stand up, he told himself. Clear your head. Think. No, don't think. Thinking was impossible. Everything was too fuzzy, his brain too stiff with cold.

Yet not too far gone to feel the tassel in his hand. Murder had been done once, would be again. He must act now or he'd be here forever. Do something. Anything was better than nothing. Now.

The blackness swirled behind his eyes as he pushed to his feet, then cleared. Quickly he pulled off his mitts.

"Hold it right there," yelled Chief Wilbur, reaching into his parka pocket as if for his gun. "I'm a cop, you know. I've got you covered."

And then his feet betrayed him once again. As slow and inexorable as the glacier itself, they slid forward until he was sitting bolt upright, his back against the wall, his rump anchored to the icy floor.

It was an effort not to laugh. Some cop he was. If he really did have a gun in his pocket, he'd have shot his kneecap all to hell. But at least the man was returning.

Watching the light beam approach, Chief Wilbur ran his tongue over his teeth. The sour taste was gone. His stomach was no longer churning. Now that the danger was real rather than imagined, his claustrophobia had disappeared.

"Put the gun away," said the man. "You can't shoot in here. Too much vibration. The whole cave could fall in. We'd both be killed."

"Right. Either we both get out or we both stay in. You don't think I'd let you just go off and leave me here like you did Haskins."

"Hey, you got it all wrong. I thought you were out cold. I was trying to figure a way to get you up the tunnel."

"Yeah, sure," said Chief Wilbur. "Now hand me that flash." The circle of light stayed put. Wisely deciding not to trust his feet again, he jabbed his pocketed hand toward the light. "I mean now. Otherwise I'll shoot it out."

"Hey, man, take it easy."

The light moved closer. Chief Wilbur grabbed the flash in his left hand, pointed it toward his antagonist, then smiled. It was Little Joe, just as he had thought.

"Now talk," he said. "I want the truth. Not that junk you've been spreading all over Mac Town."

"The truth?" Little Joe looked startled. "What do you mean?"

"About you and Haskins. I think you killed him."

"Come on, man. He was my friend, my partner."

"Yes, but even friends sometimes fight."

"Not us. We never fought. Even back home we got along. Shared everything. Every goddam thing."

Suddenly Little Joe's eyes filled with tears. It was strange to see them well up, then freeze into narrow icicles as they ran down his cheeks.

Chief Wilbur watched for a moment, wondering what had caused the sudden outbreak, then decided to leave the obvious questions till later. For now, it would be better to change to a less emotional subject.

"Tell me about the hut," he said. "You know, Scott's hut. What's it like in there?"

"Haven't you been in?"

"Sure, but I want to know what you saw."

"Just a lot of old junk lying around, all covered with dirt and spiderwebs."

"Spiderwebs? Are you sure?"

Little Joe looked at him blankly. "And cold as a bastard too. But I found an old sleeping bag to cover up."

"You're lying," said Chief Wilbur. "There are no spiders there. There aren't any spiders anywhere around here. It's too cold, too bloody cold."

Little Joe straightened. "I found an old sleeping bag. I told you that."

"Come on, Joe, let's hear it. You were down here together, weren't you? Somehow you knocked him out and then went off and left him to die."

"You're crazy, man. I wasn't in here. I didn't even know where he was."

"You're lying, Joe. Look here." Holding the flash between his knees, Chief Wilbur reached into his pocket. "Look," he repeated, swinging the tassel back and forth like an old-time hypnotist with a shiny watch. "I found this down here. You left him down here to freeze, just like you would have left me, if you'd gotten a chance. Why, Joe? Why?"

Little Joe stared at the swinging tassel. Its shadow moved back and forth across his face. "That's not mine, man." But even as he spoke his fingers were feeling for the tip of his stocking cap. His lips were tensed in a wide line, his mouth slightly open, as if to emit a soundless cry of agony.

"Okay," he whispered after a moment. And then, almost screaming, "Okay, okay, okay."

"So you did leave him in here?"

"Yes. No. I did, but I, well, it's not like you said. I was coming back for him. But there was a whiteout. I couldn't find the cave mouth. I tried. I really did. God knows, I didn't want him dead. Not really." The tears were flowing again, tiny stalactites of ice.

Not really! The two throwaway words were all the proof Chief Wilbur needed.

"It's not easy, is it—knowing what you did, I mean. Is that why you didn't go home for the funeral? Sure. It would be too hard, wouldn't it. Having to face his wife, I mean, particularly with her pregnant."

"His wife?"

Little Joe bent his head. During the long silence that followed, his shoulders narrowed, his whole body seemed to shrink. It was as if he was enveloped in some enormous body wrap of pain.

I'm wrong, thought Chief Wilbur. Right in what had happened perhaps, but wrong even so.

"What is it, Joe," he asked. "What's the matter?"

"Oh, God. You ask so many questions. You talked to everybody all over Mac Town." The words were whispered so softly that the scream which followed took Chief Wilbur completely off guard. "Don't you know? Haskins wasn't married. It's not his wife that's pregnant. It's my wife. Mine."

Chief Wilbur felt his mouth drop open, felt a sudden stab of pain as the cold air hit the filling in his front tooth. Shutting his eyes, he listened in his mind to the bartender's voice. Little Joe was the setup man. He had come in on one of the first flights, way back in September. Haskins had to teach the first semester.

Haskins, the cowbird after all.

"They had it all worked out. We were supposed to go out on trek together, a two-man party, only I wasn't supposed to come back. That's what he told me when we were down here. I wasn't supposed to find out about the baby, you see. It was just that crazy phone patch. She thought it was from him, not me. She didn't know I was right there and could hear everything. My friend. Oh, boy. They even took out an insurance policy for me."

"I saw it."

Fortunately Joe was too intent on his story to notice Chief Wilbur's slip.

"He slipped me a mickey, I think. You see we couldn't get out on trek, so he had to do it here. He had it all planned, only I wasn't supposed to find out about the baby. It didn't occur to me he was the father, not at first, but when we got down here he told me . . . oh, God."

"Told you what, Joe."

"All of it. He told me all of it, how Libby was bored and lonesome with me here on the ice all the time, and how they had decided I might as well stay since I liked it so much. And what I was missing, while he was back there with her. And I got mad, and tried to hit him, but he put up his arm and took a step back, and he slipped—hit his head, I guess, when he fell."

"And you left him."

"He was going to leave me."

Chief Wilbur nodded. "I see."

"He was lying there, and I hated him. I said, 'Die, dammit, I hope you die.' And then, I picked up the flash and climbed out, pulled up the rope, and that was it. I wandered around some, then thought, no, I can't do this. It's wrong. So I started back."

"But then there was the whiteout."

"Yes, and my head was all fuzzy. I couldn't think straight."

"And afterward you wanted to talk about it, but you didn't want anyone to know what really happened."

"My best friend. My wife. Would you have wanted anyone to know?"

"No, Joe, I guess not."

"Will you tell everybody?"

Chief Wilbur bent his head. Mike was right. He had never solved a murder case back home, and he wouldn't get credit for one here either. Not that it mattered. The murderer had already been brought to justice.

"It was an accident, Joe. It's nobody's business but your own."

"Thank you, sir." Little Joe scrubbed his eyes on his sleeve, then sighed. "God, I feel so guilty, like it was all my fault. I shouldn't have left Libby so much. I know that now."

"Maybe you two can still work it out."

"Maybe. I doubt it, though."

Chief Wilbur nodded. He doubted it, too, but there seemed no point in saying so.

Little Joe bit his lip. "Mike sure is lucky to have a dad like you, somebody to talk to, someone who cares. Real lucky. Everybody says so."

"Do they," mused Chief Wilbur. "Do they indeed?"

It was a satisfying thought, one which he would have enjoyed pursuing in a bit more detail. Unfortunately, at that moment, a monstrous groan from the glacier wrote finish to the conversation.

"Trouble," snapped Joe. "We better get our tails out of here."

Seconds later, they were up the rope and standing in the blessed sunshine. The funny thing was, Chief Wilbur couldn't imagine how he'd done it this time either.

On the day before his departure, Chief Wilbur and Mike climbed to the top of Observation Hill.

"You and Joe have gotten mighty friendly lately," said Mike as they climbed. "Is that part of your so-called investigation?"

"No, no," puffed Chief Wilbur. The hill was only eight hundred and fifty feet high, but Chief Wilbur's legs were more accustomed to Florida's flatness. "He just needs someone to talk to. Anyway, I decided you were right. No need to be suspicious."

They climbed in silence for a few minutes. When they reached the summit, the silence continued, each man deep in his own thoughts. The view across that endless expanse of the Ross Ice Shelf was almost more than the mind could bear. Somewhere out there lay the bodies of Scott and his men. Turning, they could see the ice runway of Williams Field, named after a navy Seabee whose bulldozer had crashed through the ice. And Berg Field Center named for a man who died in a helicopter crash over in one of the Dry Valleys.

"So many people have died here," said Michael finally, his hand on the huge cross made of jannah wood which Scott's companions had erected in his memory. "Antarctica is framed in death."

"But not murder," said Chief Wilbur. "You said that yourself."

"Well, sometimes I wonder. There are loose ends, you know, like what happened to the survival gear?"

"It's like you said. It belonged to some glaciologist, and he took it home with him."

"For sure?"

"Oh, yes. I checked it out."

He wished he could remind Mike that Haskins was a glaciologist. He wished he could tell him how Haskins' careful planning to do murder had served only to assure his own death. But he wouldn't. He had promised Little Joe.

"You're a pretty foxy guy," said Mike. "I'm really proud of you."

"Are you, Mike? Are you really?"

"Sure. Don't you believe me?"

"Yes, but—well, if you're so proud, how come you keep apologizing to everybody because I never solved a murder."

"Apologizing! No way, Dad, only when I say you're from Florida, everybody thinks *Miami Vice* or something. So I have to explain that Avecina is just your normal small town where nobody ever kills anyone. I don't mean you couldn't solve a murder case, only that I'm proud you never had to."

Feeling Mike's arm wrap lovingly around his shoulder, Chief Wilbur smiled. The sun had slipped behind a cloud, and the wind was rising. The wind chill factor must have dropped twenty degrees in just a few moments, but even so he felt warm clear down to his toes.

"Yeah, Mike," he said, gruffly. "I suppose I'm kind of proud of that, too."